The Last Summer of Rob

To N Saphaen clan.
Enjoy - may B.

GORDON BRYENTON

TRAFFORD

UK
USA
SPAIN
CANADA
IRELAND

Note for Librarians: a cataloguing record for this book that includes Dewey Decimal Classification and US Library of Congress numbers is available from the Library and Archives of Canada. The complete cataloguing record can be obtained from their online database at:
www.collectionscanada.ca/amicus/index-e.html
ISBN 1-4120-2129-4
Printed in Victoria, BC, Canada

TRAFFORD

Offices in Canada, USA, Ireland, UK and Spain
This book was published on-demand in cooperation with Trafford Publishing. On-demand publishing is a unique process and service of making a book available for retail sale to the public taking advantage of on-demand manufacturing and Internet marketing. On-demand publishing includes promotions, retail sales, manufacturing, order fulfilment, accounting and collecting royalties on behalf of the author.
Book sales for North America and international:
Trafford Publishing, 6E–2333 Government St.,
Victoria, BC v8t 4p4 CANADA
phone 250 383 6864 (toll-free 1 888 232 4444)
fax 250 383 6804; email to orders@trafford.com
Book sales in Europe:
Trafford Publishing (uk) Ltd., Enterprise House, Wistaston Road Business Centre,
Wistaston Road, Crewe, Cheshire cw2 7rp UNITED KINGDOM
phone 01270 251 396 (local rate 0845 230 9601)
facsimile 01270 254 983; orders.uk@trafford.com
Order online at:
www.trafford.com/robots/03-2677.html

10 9 8 7 6 5 4 3

PREFACE

At the University where I was lecturing forty years ago, an unnamed photographer, perhaps a journalism student, climbed onto the roof of the men's dorm and took a candid picture through the skylight of two very young men lying on a bed with their trousers dropped to their ankles and with arms and legs tangled together in a sexual embrace. The picture, without comment or credits, was published on the front page of the student newspaper. The faces of the two young men could not be seen and their names, if known, were never made public. They were, at least, given the courtesy of anonymity, known only to the person who took the picture and perhaps others on the staff of the student newspaper.

There were dozens of questions and comments that raged around the campus about that picture—questions of who, what, where and why regarding the two subjects and the activity in which they were involved, questions of ethics, morality, invasion of privacy and other such matters that are grist for the mills of Philosophy and Psychology. There were those that felt the Administration should exercise its proper authority and bring those responsible to task, and there were others who argued, even away back then, in favour of an absolute freedom of the press. If there were letters to the editor, and there must have been, few, if any as I recall, were ever published. The editors, it appeared, were unyielding in their decision not to fuel any fires by any further reference to the picture. That decision, of course, deflected the temper of the student body to another casually related issue, which, when it had run its course, would settle into the detritus at the bottom of the teacup, remembered only when somebody stirred.

Throughout the years, some event has occasionally stirred my recollection of those two unknown young men. It was the puzzle of their lives that started me writing what follows.

DEDICATION AND THANKS

To Margaret, my wife, with love and gratitude for gentle urging to complete.

and to: Neil Madu, son in law and enthusiastic camera & computer expert, always available

and to: Christopher and Ryan, grandsons who happily posed for the cover and unwittingly gave me clues about adolescent ways and means

and to: my sister, Ernestine and many others for their gentle proddings and confidence in me.

and other friends who supported me even not knowing what I was doing. Thanks guys! Now I know what friends are for!

iv

PROLOGUE

Of the people in this book, which attempts to explore a small segment of the tangled relationships among them, none are real. They are not people that I know or have known, nor have I met any of them, even casually. It is strange that, although I know them to be fictitious because I created them, I have become very fond of some of them but some others have proved to be really quite difficult to like. They are all, then, every one of them, products of my imagination, but as the story of the intertwining of their lives emerged, they took on a novel reality for me, so much so that I could see their city, their homes, cars, places of work and the places where they played. I thought of them as living in British Columbia probably because that is where I live most of the time. I thought of them as having some mountains on the horizons of their lives to seduce the skiers and to inspire the dreamers, a city that is large enough to get lost in but not yet a metropolis with rot in its core, and some sort of shore to walk along where cool winds can clear away those thoughts that, not examined, can rankle and spoil.

The story has no actual locale. I see the characters as being a part of various backdrops I created in my mind's eye, modelled upon some familiar place, visualizing them within this framework so that they could achieve a greater reality for me. I have not detailed any such settings for the reader, leaving it to each reader to place the characters they meet in a setting that is familiar to him or her whether it is Vancouver, as I chose, or Portland, Calgary, Charlottetown, Boulder City or some other. I have also left undescribed the city centre with its noise and frantic pace, where some of the characters are compelled to seek a living, because it has no significant bearing on the story. I offer the reader only the most casual description of the three-bedroom, two-bath, double-garaged, petunia-bordered, no-mowing-on-sundays suburbia where they live. Every reader will know of a city centre and have a collection of remembered suburbia's from which create a personalized setting for the people in this book..

Finally, I feel urged to tell you the way in which this book was written. I started it more than ten years ago and had completed more than 100 pages, until reading it over, I decided that I definitely did not like the characters that were emerging nor the directions their lives were taking. I was vastly disappointed with them. I filed the book away and gave it scarcely a passing thought until a year ago when I pulled it out and reviewed what I had written and was pleased by how much the characters had changed during the intervening years. Each character had assumed a reality that I had not noted before. Each had some of the psychological warts and blemishes that real people have, and for some, strengths had emerged in place of some of the uncertainties and dependencies that had marked their origins.. So I started again and let them live their fictional lives in what follows on these pages. Such a statement says, of course, more about the author than the characters.

CHARACTERS

MARION WILLIAMS: 40 years old, maternal, housewifely, "nice", disenchanted with her marriage and sex and husband, nearing menopause, married young, never worked, generally a very tolerant person, U.U. to Rob

GERRY WILLIAMS: 45 years old, handsome, trim, egotistical, self-centred, can be totally insensitive, sexually active occasionally with males, longstanding affair with secretary Eleanor, partner in insurance business, golfer, belongs to spa, has a butterfly birthmark on his buttock,

CRAIG WILLIAMS: 17, son, blond, chubby, bouncy sensitive to the point of shyness, not a good student, good relationship with mother but not so good with father, fetish with female underwear when very young then switched to doctor play with best friend from childhood, Rob, play still continues, very concerned about his sexuality, inherited his father's birthmark

EDITH (WILLIAMS) ALLEN: 22, daughter, married at 18, twin girls, always sharp, quick, brittle but not with husband, resentful of Craig, thinks he was spoiled, a fast erratic talker, now maturing with marriage.

HARVEY ALLEN: 24, married to Edith, plasterer, a warm and gentle man with limited social background, slow and careful.

IONA and JENNY ALLEN: twins, 3, Iona named after Mar(ion), she is the dominant twin. Jenny has a butterfly birthmark

ROB TURNER: 17, Craig's best friend from childhood, tall and slouchy, dark, wicked sense of humor, everybody likes him but he only likes Craig, talks a lot about making out with girls

GLEN TURNER: Rob's father, operates a small printing business in his home, always involved in some "save the (blank)" society, uptight, volunteer picketer for any cause

CLAUDIA TURNER: Rob's mother, works in the print shop when necessary, also part-time bookkeeping job to augment family income, not as uptight as her husband

BEVERLEY (TURNER) LEWIS: 23, one child, very fond of Rob because she thinks parents neglect him and hard on him, works part-time on-call evenings and weekends in local library

RICHARD LEWIS: 25, math and science teacher in a local high school (not Rob's) working on master's degree, all-around nice guy

LEE CHANG: Craig's girlfriend, lives at home with mother, father, grandmother, and great grandmother, very close family, goes to private school, pert and pretty.

ELEANOR COLMAN: 30, secretary to Gerry W., large woman, sexy, very self-sufficient, long sexual relationship with Gerry, nothing more than physical, frequently bored with Gerry's self- centeredness

DR. STRAWBURN: old family doctor, past retirement, never a big practice, not really a good doctor

MARION (TOM) THOMAS: about 50, works on construction as project manager, married with 2 children, divorced, supports children and his widowed father who is frail and becoming senile; socially and sexually aggressive

MR. THOMAS: Tom's father, gentle man whose main concern is his bowels

FRANK TOMASON: retired new neighbour of Williams at the cottage, very friendly, has telephone and takes calls for other cottagers at Cultus Lake

AUDREY TOMASON: very happy, extroverted woman but almost incapacitated with arthritis

RON TOMASON: their 14 year old grandson

FRANK WILSON: senior partner and chairman of the insurance firm, a stuffed shirt; wife Dorothea

BILL WEBB: another senior partner, a classic manipulator

CYRIL CHESTER: office manager, gay

KEVIN CLAXTON: junior partner, foxy, looking for his chance, always on the alert for one-up-man-ship opportunity

BEN MAHONEY: corporal in local police force, Kevin's cousin

SERGEANT YACOVICH: local policewoman

LOUISE: Eleanor's replacement, frightened mouse

CYNTHIA CONNORS: coordinator for volunteers, very organized, gracious and caring.

CARL CRANSTON: Craig's boss in summer factory job at Cranstons Cartons, good employer; Craig reminds him of his son who drowned last year

MARNY CRANSTON; Carl's wife, has a maternal interest in employees

CELIA: the Madame of a brothel

LILA: female prostitute and

RONNIE: very young male prostitute, both work for Celia

REG, WES & FRANCIS: the police force in a very small upcountry village

CHARLIE: village barman

JIMMIE: hospital maintenance man where Marion volunteers, artificial arm

ELLEN: hospital switchboard operator, confined to a wheelchair

HARRY: hospital orderly, undiagnosed disease causing seizures

BRUNO: the pizza man, known to the boys and their families

SEVEN BRIDGE GIRLS: with Marion equals 8, have played every Thursday for years:

MINNIE: fat and happy

CORA: bids double out of boredom with her lacquered nails

KATE: rides to and from with Marion

DOT: is a gossip

ISABEL: bossy, stops gossip, very tied to her husband

And two others, not named.

THREE GOLFERS:
Chuck English
Carl Zerwithin
Ron Simons

DR SUNDHI: tenant in building where Gerry works, attended Frank Wilson

TIMOTHY T. IRVIN: Titty for short, notary public, Private eye

BRIAN TOBLER & SHEILA CASTLE; "Titty"'s cousins (brother and sister)

VIC CONNETTI: school big shot with a following of wannabees: entices Donna into some drug activity

DICK: student who steps in to help break up a confrontation between Vic and gang vs Rob and Craig

MAX: host of a big party

MR SAONSONG: teacher

JUDGE GERHARDT: small town judge

ALVIN DODD: member of trust company for Gerry's will

BRIAN TOBLER & SHEILA CASTLE: Titty's cousins (brother and sister)

MURRAY ANDREWS: lawyer for the Williams, chiefly Gerry's estate.

DONNA PENSER: Rob's girl friend, comes from a rough home, M is a prostitute and F an alcoholic

WALLY LASSERET & MRS LASSERET: Donna's landlords

BRUNO and PHYLLIS: The Sweet Spot Cafe owners

ANGELA: waitress in the Sweet Spot

STEVE VALDEZ: Angela's boy friend, a cop

ROY COGISON: from the prosecutor's office

MR. ARKISON: Craig's school counsellor

MISS HUTTON: Rob's school counsellor

TRACY CONNISH: substitute in the bridge group

LARRY KOSKI: foreman at the Cranstons Cartons plant

MRS. KOSKI: wife of Larry, Polish, Craig bought her Honda

MR. PENROSE: Rob's boss from the Superstore

MRS. TRENT: one of Rob's little old lady shoppers who adore him

ROGER TODD: new owner of Turner Printing Co., spoiled rich boy, gay, with many gay friends, Ted. Petey, 'bass voice' and others

TOM & THELMA WEBSTER: he is a loud party bore at Marion's New Years party for the Turners, she is mousey but spunky

"JERRY" who turned out to be not the JERRY expected and drove Craig to Whistler

DOROTHY: senior clerk at Cranston's Cartons

TERRY, TINA AND EVAN: party people at the C.C. Xmas office party

HARRY and the GROWLER: police officers arresting Rob on drug charge, better know as:
        POLICE OFFICER WALTON and
        POLICE OFFICER KIRENSKY

REG HAWTHORN: from Murray Andrew's firm; represents Rob

STEVE and ELLA WATHERTON: Donna's aunt and uncle from Sheridan Lake; Donna's only relatives except for M & F

JUDGE ELLEN HARLEY MOORE: judge hearing the case against Rob for possession of narcotics

ALLEN BANDRA SINGH: retired printer hired by Roger until Rob gets out of New Start Institution for Juvenile Offenders. Very competent. Will buy Roger's business.

TOMMY: Gay friend of Roger's

IRENE COHEN: Claudia's neighbour in Prince George

DR. ABBOTT: Donna's doctor

TABLE OF CONTENTS

x

CHAPTER 1

All winter long the skyline of Vancouver had resembled the tumbled crystals of a thunder egg—a chiaroscuro of blue-grey geometric forms against a colourless backdrop. But today, as the washes of fish boats and tugs in Burrard Inlet glistened in the brilliant sun, and as Grouse Mountain set its white cap against a cloudless blue sky and offered its runs and lifts in invitation, the towers of the city were duplicated, multiplied and reversed in mirrored sides of their neighbours. Away from the throat-catching air of the downtown streets, among the aromas of suburbia, if you took a long, slow, careful sniff, you could smell the thick orgasmic green of buds and startled growth. Here, you could sense the palette of spring beginning to mature into the richer colours of summer. Along such streets, sun umbrellas were beginning their mushroom spread and doors and windows were left cautiously ajar, enough to tease and toy with the gentle spring but not too wide in case spring, having come in like a lamb, would roar out like a lion. Only children, in their post-school indolence, were urged to catch and clutch the wind and let its gentle fingers search their faces, toss their hair and poke down the open necks of their shirts. Their parents, pouring over golf magazines and gardening columns, met spring with a slow formality—an introduction through unzipped winter jackets, a glance, a touch, a cautious sharing and finally a love affair, stirring and remembered.

In the suburb of South Cambie, along Talisman Street, off Yukon, a solitary figure moved toward a brown trimmed two storey stucco house. Tied frustratingly to childhood, yet surging to manhood, he walked sometimes with the long broad shouldered, purposeful stride of his potential and sometimes with the pausing erratic bounce of earlier years. He was sixteen, and was looking forward to being seventeen on the last day of May. His name was Craig Williams. His best friend was one week older and his name was Rob Turner.

It was after four, and he had hung around the fringes of the school grounds for a while searching, in the laughing, touching, joking mob, unsuccessfully for Rob. When he failed to find him he decided to come home. He took the steps two at a time, landed with a two footed thud on the back porch and burst open the door. The noisy routine of his arrival had become the habitual signal for his homecoming and it provoked an habitual maternal complaint—but not today.

"Hi!" he shouted. He waited a moment for an answer and then louder, "Hey! Anybody home?" He listened again but the only sound in the house was that of a radio playing in the living room. He walked through the kitchen and dining room expecting to find his mother snoozing on the couch. She was not there but the little radio she liked to listen to when she napped was half-tuned into the station and was growling static and music. He flicked it off then turned it on again and tuned it to a rock station.

"Hey, Mom? Mom?" in a louder voice. A listening pause and then he looked quickly in the downstairs rooms, shouted down the basement stairs, raced quickly upstairs to dump his books and to glance in his mother's room and an equally casual look out her window into the garden. "That's funny," he thought. "That's the second time she's done that. She must have been in a big hurry to get somewhere. And she didn't lock the door or leave a note."

If there had been the beginning of a concern for her whereabouts he dismissed it easily. Back in the kitchen he made himself a quick thick sandwich and ate it in half chewed chunks drinking from the milk carton while standing in front of the open frig searching for something more. Finding nothing of interest, he finished off the milk and left the carton on the counter but took a clean glass and put the few remaining drops of milk in it and left it beside the carton so his mother would not know he had been drinking out of the carton again.

He moved into the living room and flung himself across a chair so he could look out of the front window at the random traffic on Talisman Street only to get up almost immediately to squat, lithe and tight, in front of the TV with his knees tucked into his armpits. He sat idly tapping his genitals while the set warmed up then flicked through the channels without interest: a cartoon, an old movie, a stupid game show, another re-run, a Spanish lesson—nothing. He rolled from his squat onto his hands and knees and crawled with an exaggerated wobble over to the liquor cabinet. Inside he pushed the bottles around until he found the gin and vodka. These he held up at arms length measuring the contents against the afternoon light from the picture window. Then he replaced them and went to the phone in the hall.

The number he dialled was busy. He held the receiver between his thumb and forefinger with his arm extended over the cradle and released it suddenly so that it dropped onto the cradle with a crash and tumbled to the floor. Picking it up, he punched the redial button and again holding at arms length and faking a one-eyed sighting, dropped it again when he heard the busy signal, this time successfully. Turning suddenly, he raced upstairs to the bathroom, stopped in front of the basin to examine his face and his teeth in the mirror. He tried a wide toothy smile then a horror face, squeezed a pimple and then turned to the toilet and urinated as hard as he could force a stream. He stood for a moment straddle-legged in front of the bowl wiggling his hips to shake the drops off until he felt an erection coming. Savouring the tension in his gut for a moment, he stood indecisively for a minute. Then, after making a few jerky coital movements and without tucking himself in, he walked quickly to his parent's room and to his mother's dresser.

Her lingerie was in the middle drawer. He opened it quickly and clutched a handful of panties, bras and belts and flung them on the bed. Then with his gut pulsing he began to fold each article neatly and precisely following some well rehearsed ritual. Replacing them in the drawer, he closed it slowly and carefully. Just as carefully and as slowly he tucked himself into his pants while looking into the full length mirror, pulled the zipper up and walked rigidly from the room.

In the spotty memory of his childhood he could remember that chocolates had been hidden in that drawer. One of his earliest memories was of the excitement of finding chocolates there, hidden under the piles of filmy lingerie—chocolates his father brought to his mother. He had found them first when he was four and during his childhood he had returned stealthily again and again to that drawer that was always full of soft silky collared things hiding the gaily collared box. He never really knew when the boxes of chocolates stopped being there. He never knew when he first felt the strange pulsing in his groin as he searched the drawer and then folded all the panties again so his mother would never know. Later he realized that his mother must have known of his early clumsy stealing but was too unconcerned to have ever mentioned it. He had wondered, too, why she had kept one drawer full of flimsy, lacy, colourful pants—black bikini-like things, sheer ones with frilled edges or wildly flowered, even one with a large cupped hand embroidered over the crotch, none of them worn—and pearly, fluted nighties so short he once thought she had saved them as mementos of her childhood, and another drawer full of thick and sometimes tattered, plain, simple, elasticized nylon or cotton garments, never adorned with lace or print, each well washed and worn. It was to the middle drawer that he went when the house was empty, at first to cram his pockets with chocolate leaving a trail of crushed brown paper cups and a half closed drawer in disarray as evidence of his crime, then later, to steal more cautiously and to leave the drawer as though undisturbed. Still later, even though the boxes of chocolates had long since disappeared, strange urgings impelled him to secretly fondle, sometimes to try on, and refold the flung pile of soft colours. Sometimes when he stood exposed, turning and folding each collared wisp, turmoil overwhelmed him and he had to grab himself and rush to the bathroom to stand by the toilet gritting his teeth in the panic of finishing. Twice the explosion within him had been so sudden that he could only catch himself in the silky thing he was folding and he had to hide the evidence in the rafters of the basement. He remembered both occasions in vivid, guilty detail and since the last time he struggled to restrain himself from any further repetitions.

Downstairs he picked up the phone and dialled again and this time, hearing the ringing signal, he sat straddling the chair back as he waited.

"Hey, Rob! Whatcha doing?"

"Hey, nothing—mucking about."

"I called you a while ago. Who were you talking to?"

"Who says I was talking to anybody?"

"Nobody says. I just wondered who you were talking to. You told me on the way to school this morning that your mom and dad were both picketing some ship at the docks and so I figured it was you on the phone and I wondered who you were talking to. Unless your sister's in town."

"No she isn't. Harry."

"Why Harry?"

"Why not Harry?"

"Well, what were you talking to him about?" Craig's adolescent baritone began to show some tension.

"Oh, nothing," came Rob's dismissive reply. "He just called, that's all. Okay?"

There was a brief silence before the answering "Okay." A vague sense of relief filtered through the monosyllable and then, "So what do you want to do?"

"Why? What do you want to do?"

"C'mon over. There's nobody home." Craig said.

"Yeah?"

"Yeah, and I'll tell you what. I'll buy you a drink."

"Oh, sure! What d'ya mean? You'll buy me a drink."

"I'll buy you a drink—that's what I mean. There's still that half bottle of Vodka that we had last time. Come on! Only hurry up. I don't know where my Mom's gone."

"Okay." And the other phone was hung up.

Craig went quickly to the liquor cabinet and took out the Vodka. Into two kitchen glasses he poured two healthy slugs and refilled the bottle to the same level from the cold water tap. He replaced the liquor bottle and with fast sure motions cracked a tray of ice cubes, loaded the glasses to the brim and filled them with orange juice. After a quick glance around he picked up the glasses and took them in a sedate walk up to his room. Sprawled on the bed, one foot straight up against the wall, he waited.

CHAPTER 2

Mrs. Williams was waiting too. Most of the time while she waited she simply sat, her large hands plumped loosely on the black plastic purse on her lap fiddling with the clasp, oblivious to the regular 'click, click' that punctuated the silence. She fitted the room somehow. She matched it in being, if not nondescript, then without character. The walls were an uninteresting green, neither drab nor olive nor lime—just green. Their bareness was scarcely offset by a bank calendar and a collection of seascapes and sunsets in vividly amateurish oils framed by unvarnished lumber yard moulding. The chairs might have come second-hand from a bankrupt pub—stubbed and worn with wobbly arms and with imitation leather on the backs and seats, the latter now cracked and comfortably molded by years of waiting backsides. A scattering of unmatched scarred end tables held a conglomeration of old magazines, their corners bulked to twice the thickness of their pages, their gloss gone with their covers and the significance of the news they had exclaimed about.

She had picked up a magazine when she first sat down, panting slightly from the stairs, but it was not an action of interest nor was the magazine her fence of protection against the stares of others for she was alone in the room. It was just a waiter's automatic need to do something—even to idly turn unseen pages. But it had been the Atlantic Monthly and there were no daydream pro-voking ads that caught her eye so she had put it down and picked up her purse and sat opening and closing its catch—click, click.

Then she sighed unaware that she had done so—a long, breathy almost rumbling sigh that rose from neither boredom or sadness. It was her response to life and she sighed a dozen times a day without ever knowing she had. This particular sigh had the unexpected result of alerting the doctor's nurse. Her head appeared in the window of the frosted glass divider. "Doctor won't be long, I'm sure, Mrs. Williams," the head said and disappeared. It was said quietly but the words seemed to ricochet around the quiet room long after the blond head disappeared and it took Mrs. Williams a moment to realize she had been addressed. She wanted to say "Thank you" but there was no one to say it to so she said nothing and unknowingly sighed again. At the same time she thought how much the disappearing talking head reminded her of the Punch and Judy shows of her childhood and the memory let a little embarrassing chuckle escape from her. Then the head appeared again and it said "Did you say something, Mrs. Williams?" It was too late to say "Thank you" and she should have said "No" but before she got it sorted out the head had gone away again. She picked up a magazine and fanned herself and sighed. Click, click, and silence again.

In the back of the offices a door opened and voices and footsteps rumbled towards her. The doctor came in not quite leading a thin, old man but certainly escorting him out. The old man continued with a querulous voice, that still had the remnants of an earlier strong bass, to explain his complaints while the doctor stood by the nurse's station, nodding, agreeing and placating the old man's concerns.

"Yes—yes, hm, hm, I know, I know, yes, I see." Then with some finality he said "Well now," interrupting the old fellow's rambling flow of words. "No more mineral oil and cascara and all that roughage you've been eating. You get that prescription filled right away and we'll get you over to the lab for a barium series and some other checks. OK? OK, then. Nurse, see if you can arrange an appointment with the Beckenfield Lab for Mr. Thomas early next week. And Mr. Thomas, nurse will phone you to tell you the time of your appointment at the lab and she'll give you another appointment with me when the lab work is done. OK? Goodbye, then." He gave the old man a gentle pat on the back and was gone.

Mrs. Williams wondered if he had seen her, she wondered if he knew she was there. She could hear the nurse talking on the phone while the old man just stood, waiting, not looking around or fidgeting, just waiting. Finally the nurse reappeared at her window and when she spoke to him her voice was loud, too loud—the kind of voice young people use in kindness and authority with old people.

"Next Tuesday, Mr. Thomas. At half past two. Tuesday, Half past two. You're to go to the Beckenfield Clinic. The Beckenfield Clinic," and her voice was so precise and strong that the old man startled at some of her repetitions.

"But—but he said I had to go to a lab," he finally interrupted.

"Yes, I know," the nurse said with some impatience. "It's the same thing, Mr. Thomas. Sometimes they call it a lab and sometimes they call it a clinic, but it's the same thing, don't you see? Now here's the address right here on their card and I've marked your time on it. See? Two thirty, right there." She reached out of her window and taking the old man's hand put the card in it. "D'you understand, Mr. Thomas? Alright then, Bye bye, Mr. Thomas," and she disappeared behind the partition.

But the old man still stood there and started over again with his list of uncertainties until finally the nurse came out from behind her divider and talking to him, took him gently to the door. "Be careful of the stairs now. Don't lose the prescription. Bye bye," and she closed the door deliberately and just as deliberately walked past Mrs. Williams and disappeared.

Silence again except for 'click,click.'

Suddenly Mrs. Williams felt a rising panic. "They've both gone! They've forgotten me." For a moment she thought of trying the door but she knew that it would be open and that they had not locked up and left. She knew she just had to wait, but even though she knew it, the panic would not disappear.

There was no change in the silence—no footsteps, no telephone bells, no buzz of distant conversation or sounds of outside traffic. Suddenly, quietly the nurse appeared in the hallway leading to the doctor's offices. "Doctor is ready for you now, Mrs. Williams," she said so unexpectedly that Mrs. Williams jumped. "I'm sorry," she continued. "I didn't mean to startle you," and she smiled such a warm and friendly smile that Mrs. Williams rising panic subsided.

"Oh, that's alright," she said. "You didn't startle me. I just wasn't expecting you. I mean I thought maybe you had gone. I don't mean that you had left. It's just that it was so quiet I thought that maybe—." And she came to a flustered halt as she got up awkwardly having to lever herself up with the arms of the chair. Turning to follow the nurse, she realized she still had her coat on and she stopped, trying to remember if she usually went in without her coat or carrying it or wearing it.

"I'll leave my coat here?" The question gave the nurse the responsibility of the decision.

"Alright, Mrs. Williams, that will be fine."

The cloth coat was folded carefully and placed on the chair back. While her hands were free, she resettled her hat and checked on stray strands of hair. Then she smoothed her dress over her thighs, picked up her purse, and followed the nurse down the hall.

Dr. Strawburn was sitting at his desk writing as Mrs. Williams came in. He did not stop immediately and she stood just inside the door until the nurse touched her arm and nodded to a chair. She settled herself and waited, watching the doctor as he wrote. He was a grey lean man wearing a white coat that was so big he had the sleeves folded back and seemed oblivious to her presence as he sat pulling on his lower lip as he read what he had written. Suddenly he swivelled around on his chair so that he was facing her.

"Well, Mrs. Williams." He looked at her without smiling, his old grey eyes hooded by large eyebrows.

"Hello, Dr. Strawburn," and since he made no immediate further response she clicked the snap on her purse and then flushed with embarrassment thinking that he would think she was very nervous.

"I haven't seen you for a while," he said after what seemed to her an eternity.

"About two months, I think," she said. "Yes, it will be just two months next Monday. I was in because of my hand, remember? I burned it on the toaster."

"Oh, yes. Let's see. All better now?" He leaned over and took her hand turning it over briefly and rubbing a faintly lighter area with his thumb and then returned the hand to her in a way that made her feel that it had been momentarily detached and had to be reconnected. "That's just fine. No trouble there at all." He paused and looked more intently at her. "How are you feeling otherwise, Mrs. Williams?"

"Fine, Doctor. Just fine."

"I see. Sleeping well?"

"Yes," she replied, knowing it was not quite the truth but not wanting to say more.

"No more trouble with your headaches?"

"No. Not much."

"I see."

Click, click. Click, click.

Dr. Stawburn slid into a slouch in his chair and watched her clicking the clasp on her purse nervously. She was an old patient whom he saw periodically but only for some minor problems. She was a healthy woman, past forty, superficially placid but bothered occasionally by tension headaches and insomnia. Married, two children, husband (whom he had never seen) in the insurance business, GYN referral two years ago—negative. Mrs. Williams began to show some signs of distress under his gaze.

"You didn't mention to the nurse why you wanted to come in."

"No."

"I see—," and he pulled on his lower lip some more.

Click, click.

"Are you not feeling up to par, Mrs. Williams?" and his voice was gentle but somehow lacking in warmth.

"No—I mean, yes. I'm fine."

"What is it that is wrong, then, Mrs. Williams?"

"I don't know!" And the words streamed out in a falsetto wail that signalled a bursting dam of tears.

Dr Strawburn hesitated. It was late in the day and since he had cut back on his practise he liked to get away early. The last thing he wanted to deal with was a weeping neurotic female who knew there was something wrong but couldn't display any satisfactory symptoms. He glanced at his watch and then it was his turn to sigh.

"I think you do know, Mrs. Williams. Why don't you tell me about it? Then maybe we can do something. We can't do anything if we don't know what's wrong, can we now?"

She looked at him in a pleading helpless way, her gaze fastening on him for, it seemed, an eternity. During that time he saw her neck redden in a kind of turkey mottling, her lips slacken and then tighten again and again and the tears she had been restraining work their way out her nostrils.

"It's not me. There's nothing wrong with me. It's Gerry. It's my husband. It's him. I don't know what's wrong with him. He never comes near me. He hasn't touched me for more than a year—and I can't stand it." The hurt and frustration forced her voice into a high pitched and slightly croaky wail punctuated by jerky sobs and watery sniffs.

CHAPTER 3

In a small comfortable seventh floor office Gerry Williams pushed his chair back from his desk and stretched. He was a tall man with dark hair going to grey and with features that people referred to as handsome. He didn't mind the adjective—it rather pleased him. The stretch he gave pulled up his chest and flattened his stomach and after a half-yawn he brought his arms down and slapped his hands across his stomach, tucked his fingers under his belt and slid into a slouch in his executive style chair. Letting his relaxed middle tighten his fingers against his belt, he toyed with a small roll of fat at his beltline while he looked uncritically at the papers on his desk. Among the assortment, nothing seemed to leap out at him as demanding his immediate attention—it was all routine and ordinary and right now, very dull. Then, sitting back up to his desk again he pushed a buzzer and began to organize the papers into files and piles. The door opened and a dark haired, dark eyed woman with questioning eyebrows stood in the opening. She was tall and big boned and made somewhat tubular by her elastic girding. She appeared to be in her middle thirties.

"Eleanor," Gerry said, "I don't think I'll dictate any of this stuff today. It can all wait until tomorrow. I'll leave it here and we can start it first thing tomorrow. Anything else come in?"

Seeing the slight shake of her head he did not wait for a verbal reply. "Good. That's a relief. I think I'm going to knock off early and go down to the gym for a while. I need a good workout. I'm getting too fat."

Eleanor left her place in the doorway and moved towards the desk with the dignity that seems to come naturally to large women.

"Why don't you go and I'll sort these out?" she said. Her voice was a soft contralto.

"No. Just leave them. I know where everything is and we can start in the morning." But paying no attention to what he had said, she picked up, straightened and organized in spite of his murmured protests and put them neatly into his basket. She knew he was watching and grinning and a slight blush came across her cheeks.

"Well," she said defiantly, "I hate leaving a mess."

"It's not your desk," he teased.

"It is so—at least I'm supposed to look after it. And you."

"And you do that very well, too." But the grin he gave with it was an open comment on something other that her neatness and efficiency, This time the blush was deeper.

Taking his pen from the desk, she capped it and handed it to him with an extended arm flourish. "Your pen, master," she said with heavy sarcasm.

Laughing, he took it from her and got to his feet, clipping the pen into his shirt pocket. He tightened the knot on his tie, tucked his shirt in smoothly and slipped his jacket on, shrugging it into comfort. Eleanor moved toward the door.

"Did Marion call?" he asked.

"No," she answered and accompanied the answer with a shake of her head.

"OK. I wasn't expecting her to. But if she does tell her I've gone to the gym for a while and I might be late. I might stay down for dinner and make some calls."

Eleanor stopped and turned and looked very directly at him, saying nothing verbally but he seemed to get some message.

"Oh, hell," he said. "I might as well call her myself before I go." He moved back to the desk and Eleanor left the room. Without sitting down he picked up the phone, punched the home button and got a busy signal.

CHAPTER 4

Rob Turner and Craig had grown up together. Rob was one week older than Craig and from early childhood they had been inseparable. They lived half a block apart and both sets of parents treated the other child as they treated their own. Their parents were casual friends because the boys were friends but rarely talked together except about matters that concerned the boys. They had romped naked as infants in backyard wading pools, and walked to and from school inseparably until high school. They had shared birthday parties, stolen cigarettes, dirty jokes and homework. Their occasional quarrels were more quickly forgotten than started. But things changed in the first year of high school. Rob had made friends with a group of kids from the "Snob Hill" part of town and, for whatever reasons, it was made clear to Craig that he was not a welcome part of that group. Their individual programs had further separated them when different teachers and different assignments made shared home-work impossible. The rift between them was deep and hurtful and comprehensible to neither. It was only during the last months of that school year when Rob had a harsh falling out with his new friends that he and Craig began to talk cautiously with each other and by the time the summer had faded they were as allied and as thick as they had ever been.

Both were now sixteen. Neither were noticeably athletic, mechanical or academic and any expression of interest in the opposite sex was a private mat-ter between them, although Rob often talked about what he would like to do with a girl—much to Craig's disgust. Their families openly despaired that they would ever amount to anything. Familial urgings to try harder, do better, set some goals and other routine naggings were met with blank puzzlement as to what their parents' problems were. Although both came from two-car families neither of them was permitted to drive—that privilege being withheld from them by mutual consent of four parents until such time as their academic achievements showed that they were making a detectable effort.

Seen together, their physical differences brought smiles from even casual observers. Rob stood in a perpetual lean slouch, his dark eyes and dark straight hair giving him a look of sullen belligerence, but he was neither sullen nor belligerent by nature. He had a quick and teasing wit and an easy laugh that bubbled unexpectedly out of a placid face. Craig was half a head shorter and fleshier without being either muscular or fat. His thick blond hair, longer than most boys wore it, fell untrained over blue eyes that were still wide with childish candour. He had developed a habitual toss of his head to throw the bothersome hank of hair back into place. Walking together, Craig darted, bounced, walked backwards and sideways, juggled books and kicked stones. Rob just walked in longer strides in a no-nonsense straight line. Seen together at a distance they left an impression of a swooping chattering swallow driving an old crow out of its territory.

Rob rarely walked into the William's house without knocking, as he used to when they were small, unless he could see someone in the kitchen. Today, he knocked, opened the door, shouted "Hi!" just to make sure and went quietly up the stairs to Rob's room. His loafers had made no noise on the stairs and stepping through the open door of Craig's room, he saw his friend sprawled on the bed crosswise, feet up on the wall, waving his arms like a conductor to music from the bedside radio. He leaned against the doorjamb and watched unnoticed until in one of Craig's more dramatic head-waving crescendos, Craig saw him standing there with a joker's grin on his face.

"How long have you been there?" Craig demanded.

"You're birdie," was the reply.

"Yeah, I know. But how long have you been standing there?"

"Why, birdie-man? Were you doing something you shouldn't be doing? You know—like what they were talking about in the boy's Social Studies?" and Rob made some jerky movements with a closed fist.

"Now look who's being birdie," Craig said and got to his feet with a quick roll off the bed and lunged at his friend. They wrestled together without effort or malice until Craig stuck a leg behind Rob and tripped him onto the bed.

"The winnah," he announced raising his own arm in victory, turning and bowing until Rob, still on the bed, shot out a long leg and hooked him in the crotch and with a jerk brought him dancing and staggering back to the bed where they wrestled again in a tangle of arms and legs. The struggle ended with Rob sitting straddled on Craig's chest, pinning his shoulders with his knees and holding his wrists in his stronger grasp. Craig stopped struggling and they stayed in that position, looking at each other without any animosity.

"OK, OK," Craig said finally. "Are you going to stay there all day?"

"I might."

"Aw, get off me, Rob!"

"What'll you do if I don't? I like it here and you like me here too, don't you, Craggy?" using what Craig's mother called her sweet-name for him.

"You know what I'll do. I'll bite your bloody cock off!" And Craig lunged with an exaggerated bite towards Rob's crotch who feigned pleasurable agony, let go and fell backwards. The two of them lay on their backs with their legs dangling off the side of the bed.

"So, tough guy," Rob said. "Where's this drink you promised me?"

Craig got up and got the two drinks from the window sill, handing one to Rob, bowing with heels together. "Voila! mon soor. Votre drinky-poo. N'est-ce-pas? A l'ecole. Pas de toot and coup de grace."

Rob sipped his drink. "What is it?" he asked.

"Vodka, I told you. Vodka and orange juice."

"It's called a Bloody Mary," said Rob with authority.

With equal authority Craig responded, "No, it's not. A Bloody Mary's got tomato juice in it."

"Well then, it's a stinger."

"Oh, crap," said Craig. "You don't know what it's called."

Rob tried his drink again. "Are you sure there's vodka in it?"

"Sure I'm sure, dum-dum."

"Well, it doesn't taste like it to me!"

Craig snorted with exaggerated exasperation. "You're not supposed to taste it and you can't smell it either. That's why they make it—so you can drink and nobody knows."

Rob took a great gulp of his drink. "Oh, sure," he said. "And I suppose they make it specially for school kids. Don't they, Craggy?"

"You drink it like that and you'll get drunk," Craig said.

"So what?"

"So nothing! Get drunk then."

Rob finished his drink in two or three swift gulps and laughed. He rolled his eyes in his head, let his tongue hang out and flopped back on the bed. "See! I'm drunk. I'm blotto. I'm pished, that's what I am. I'm pished, pished, p-i-isht."

Craig pulled his knees up on the bed and sat watching his friend, finishing his own drink more slowly. He fished an ice cube out of his glass and sucked on it. "Hey, Rob. What did Harry want?" he asked.

"Oh, nothing," Rob replied offhandedly. "He wanted me to go to a show."

"What show? Are you going?" And there was a hint of tension in Craig's voice.

"Nah," Rob said. "He was feeding me a bunch of bullshit about Joanne wanting to go out with me and he and Phyl and Joanne and me were all supposed to go out to some show."

"So are you going?"

"Yeah. Maybe. I dunno. Why?"

"Nothing." There was a long pause before Craig said "Jim Taylor says that everybody that goes out with Joanne lays her. Are you going to put it to her?"

"Oh, sure! Why not? Probably on the way home with Harry's old man driving the car," came the response with heavy sarcasm.

"Yeah, I bet," Craig persisted. "I bet you're not even going to try. I bet she lays you—more like it. She's a pro. I bet you don't even go!"

"I already said I wasn't, didn't I?

"You said maybe," Craig protested.

"Ah, what the hell do I want to go out with some dumb dame for? They don't do nothing but talk about other guys all the time. She gives me a pain in the ass anyway—so does Harry. He's always BS-ing about the car his dad is going to buy him and what he's going to do with it to soup it up. He's a jerk!" and Rob lapsed into silence without noticing the relief on Craig's face.

Finally Craig said, "Do you feel anything?"

"Sure." Rob replied flippantly. "I got a hard-on."

"Not that! You crazy nut. I mean, do you feel drunk?"

"Sure I feel drunk—I told you I was pished. And furthermore, I know when I'm drunk because when I'm drunk I always get a hard-on and I told you already I got a hard-on."

"I don't believe you," Craig said. "If that's true you must be drunk all the time then."

Rob grinned and said nothing but he made a loose fist with a big knuckle and jabbed Craig in the ribs. Craig's grunt exploded an ice cube out of his mouth and he snatched it off the bed and with a quick darting movement shoved it down the front of Rob's pants.

Rob sprung to a sitting position sucking in his gut as the ice hit his belly and Craig, unmoving, exploded with laughter. Suddenly Rob reached out, grabbed a fistful of blond hair, yanked Craig's head down and locked it hard in the crook of his arm as he flopped back across the bed taking Craig with him. They lay in that position for a minute saying nothing—each waiting for the other to begin. It would be one of many beginnings that had started with their late childhood. "OK, smart-ass," Rob growled in mock fierceness. "Take it out!"

"Make me!" came the muffled response. The arm tightened around Craig's head.

"Awright," he said. "Don't break my neck!" But the pressure did not let up. Craig's hand slid quietly under the other boy's belt, under the band of underwear and down, down into an area he had explored many times before. The ice cube had come to rest in a small tangle of hair but Craig's hand went past it, down, further down, slowly quietly exploring. He felt the ice cube cold on his wrist and he felt Rob's pulsing and throbbing and the tightened stomach muscles against his forearm.

Both boys were quiet. The head lock had been relaxed. The searching hand moved gently, erratically, pulling, squeezing, disturbing. Finally Craig said in a playful voice, "Nothing there. I can't find it." And then, in mock surprise, "Oh! There it is." And he withdrew his hand bringing with it what little was left of the ice cube which he tossed away with a flourish. Both boys remained motionless. Craig's head was still caught up loosely in Rob's arm and the arm relaxed so that Craig's head rested easily on Rob's chest. There was a moment of gentle and embarrassed silence in the room. Rob's free arm went over the side of the bed where he had placed his glass. Quietly he tipped it over and caught a handful of ice. "Hey," he said. "Close your eyes."

"Why?"

"Just close your eyes."

"Why?"

"Oh, for crissake! Close your eyes and I'll give you something." Craig closed his eyes and with a lunge Rob jammed the handful of ice down Craig's pants. Craig doubled over and caught Rob's wrist in the tension of his belt band momentarily until in the ensuing wrestling the hand was released.

"OK," Craig said. "Now you take it out!"

He was laying on his back across the bed with his feet dangling off the side. Rob swung a leg over and straddled Craig's thighs.

"Make me!" Rob said with a laugh.

"Oh, come on," was the petulant reply.

"OK, then, if you insist. But I get to do it my way." He reached out and undid the snap on the jeans and pulled the zipper down. There was no opposition from Craig who half turned his head to one side and lay quietly with half closed eyes. Rob folded back the folds of the fly and slowly worked the shorts down. He sat for a minute across the other boy's legs, pushing, shoving, tumbling Craig in his hands. Then, rising to his knees, he undid his own jeans, dropped his underwear, and slowly, gently spread his dark lean body over his friend. The black hair and the blond tangled together. Uncertain strong arms held each body to the other. Their legs, hampered by the restricting jeans, would not fit into any pattern but between them they explored again the secret, subtle and unspoken bond that tied them to each other in the springtime of their youth. Rob was again the master, the demander, the aggressor and Craig gave back in kind all that his friend demanded of him.

CHAPTER 5

Dr. Strawburn was saying very little—not that he was unsympathetic, but he had never really learned any pat responses to make when a patient broke down in tears in front of him and blubbered on about fears and frustrations. He had learned a technique of busying himself with notes neither looking directly at the patient nor looking deliberately away. He always waited until the first rush of disordered agonies and hurts poured out and the gasping sobs were subdued and replaced by sniffles. That was with women patients. Only one male patient had ever broken down emotionally in his office and Dr. Strawburn had found the experience so upsetting that he felt degraded and he was careful never again to offer any indication to men that he was willing to subject himself to their emotional problems. With Mrs. Williams it seemed to take a long time for her to gain some control and start again.

"We used to be all right, I guess," her voice thin and shaky and the initial outburst under control. "When we were first married it was no good but after

Edith came it was fine. Then when I was pregnant with Craig he never touched me once all the time I was pregnant and not for nearly six months after. I used to think that maybe he was running around but he isn't that kind of man—I don't think. No, he isn't. I know he isn't. He wouldn't do that to me. But I don't know what to do. He never comes near me and if I do something he just puts me off. Maybe there's something wrong with me but I've asked him and he just tells me not to be silly. Maybe I shouldn't need that sort of thing anymore but I'm only forty and I'm not an old woman and I know I'm too fat but I'm not ugly. And I look after the house and I've been a good mother and he just treats me like a housekeeper except he sleeps in the same bed with me. What am I supposed to do?"

The voice that had begun to settle into a less hysterical monotone rose again. Dr. Strawburn, fearing another unproductive and embarrassing weeping session coming to the surface decided he had better take over. He cleared his throat in preparation but before he could get organized to say something, Mrs. Williams had plunged on.

"I can't talk to him about it. He just won't say anything except 'Now, now. You're upset and well talk about it later,' but there's never any later. And if I try anything he makes me feel like a whore. He shouldn't do that to me—it's not right. Somehow he makes me feel the whole thing is dirty and immoral, and now that we've had children we shouldn't do it any more. He used to be so—so—HORNY!" She almost shouted the word and Dr. Strawburn cringed. "What's wrong with him?" she continued. "He used to want it almost every night and I couldn't, then. It was too much when the children were small and I had to get up in the night with them. But now—. How can he just live like that—like a monk—I can't. I just can't. Maybe there's something wrong with me, too. I get so mad or disappointed or frustrated sometimes that I think I'll go out and find another man myself. I did it once before and I could do it again." Dr. Strawburn could hardly conceal a shiver of displeasure. "I mean I think about it, that's all. I wouldn't really," she continued looking directly at him but he could not meet her eye and a panic began to surface within her. "You won't ever tell him I said that, will you? He doesn't know. I've never told him. I've never told anybody. I don't know why I told you. It was a long time ago at a convention and I got a little drunk and got carried away. But it was a long time ago and it isn't important and besides it wasn't any good anyhow. But I don't want Gerry to know. Don't tell him, please, Doctor. You won't, will you." She waited for his answer.

"No, of course not, Mrs. Williams. Not if you don't want me to."

"Thank you, Doctor. I just don't want him to know, that's all. It was a long time ago and it doesn't matter now." Another observer, more sensitive than Dr. Strawburn, might have taken notice of a wistful note in her voice.

The tears had subsided. Mrs. Williams searched in her purse for another tissue and blew hard. She dabbed at her reddened eyes, took a great gulp of air and released it in a long drawn out sigh. It was over now. She had said it all—all she could say and more than she had intended to say—so she waited. She waited for Dr. Strawburn's comfort or wisdom or his miracle.

Looking at him and waiting while he fiddled with his notes, watching him not writing, but drawing careful circles, recalling the intensity of his embarrassment while she was revealing all her private innermost feelings to him, she knew that he had nothing to offer her. She saw him sitting slouched, lean and untidy, in his chair. His socks were wrinkled at the ankle above carelessly polished shoes. The tails of his too-large unbuttoned white smock dragged on the floor beside his chair. He wore an old grey sweater under his smock that had shrunk and pilled from many careless washings. His tie was clumsily tied, his white shirt collar unstarched and, crowning his disarray, a cheap haircut had left a grey wisp of hair sticking out like a rooster's tail from the back of his head.

Suddenly she thought of Gerry and his fastidiousness, of his refusal to wear anything that showed any sign of mending or darning, of his careful attention to his hair, his nails, the press in his pants, the knot in his tie, the starch in his collars. She, for a moment, smelled him, fresh from his shower, with a pungent smell of after shave lotion, trim, handsome—and—impotent.

"Impotent! That's what he is! Impotent!" Her words exploded into the room but Dr. Strawburn, after an initial startle response was grateful for them. He had watched her appraise him. Her eyes had moved critically over every inch of his frame not even missing a penetrating look at his crotch. His mind raced back to her earlier statement: 'I think I'll go out and find another man' and he thought "Good Good! I hope she doesn't think I can help her that way."

"Well, maybe, Mrs. Williams. Maybe," he said in a delayed response to her conclusive outburst. "But that might not be the answer to the problem. I'd like to talk to him though. Would you ask him to come in and see me?" This was his standard safe ploy. He knew from experience that husbands with wives like Mrs. Williams never came in.

Mrs. Williams nodded and sniffed and dabbed while all the time thinking, "He won't come. I know he won't. I won't even ask him. It's useless. It's not him anyway—it's me."

And as if reading her last thought, Dr. Strawburn continued, "But I'm going to give you a prescription. You're pretty unhappy and upset." He slid his chair up to his desk and searched for his prescription pad. "These are very light tranquillizers I want you to take—three a day, after meals, for two weeks. They're very mild but they are all you need at the moment to get rid of some of your tension and depression. Then if you will come and see me in about two weeks time we'll see if you are still upset about the whole situation and if you are, I'll refer you to a friend of mine, Dr. Neale. He's a psychiatrist but don't let that frighten you. He's awfully good at working out these problems. I send a lot of patients to him."

He ripped the sheet off the prescription pad and handed it to her while getting to his feet. "Try not to worry," he said ineffectively. "I'm sure things will work out. You'll see."

Mrs. Williams seemed not to get his message that her time was up. She sat, looking blankly at him, not seeing him. Depressed? she thought. He says I'm depressed. Is that all? Is that what's wrong with me? It _is_ me. It isn't all that other thing at all. It isn't that Gerry hasn't loved me, touched me or paid any attention to me. It isn't that I'm oversexed or something. I'm not, anyway—I know I'm not. I'm a normal woman and I just want a man sometimes—I want my husband. Maybe I am depressed. Who knows? Who cares? I wish somebody cared. I wish Gerry cared. But he doesn't! Damn! Damn! Damn! Damn him! He doesn't care about anybody but himself. And the tears came again.

Dr. Strawburn stood and watched. He saw the face contort and the shaking hands search the purse for another tissue and he controlled a gritted teeth sigh. "Damn it," he said to himself. "If she doesn't pull herself together, I'm going to be late for my tennis game." But aloud he said, "Have a good blow now," as he touched her gently on the shoulder. "And don't feel too badly. Things have a way of working out, You'll see."

He opened the door and stood beside it. Mrs. Williams got to her feet clutching a handful of damp tissues. She looked vaguely around for a waste basket but couldn't see one. She meant to shake the doctor's hand and say thank you, but instead she handed him the bundle of squashed wet tissues. He thought she was going to shake hands and he was startled to find himself with a handful of soggy Kleenex. After he turned away to deposit the tissues in the basket beside his desk, he looked back to see her back moving out the door. The prescription he had written was lying on the floor. He shrugged, picked it up and put it in her file. Uncapping his old pen, he shook it to get the ink flowing and then noted on her file card: Signs of depression; anxiety re no sex with H for 1 yr; tearful and distraught; refer to Dr. Neale? He then added the medical shorthand for the prescription she had been offered and unconsciously rejected.

CHAPTER 6

When he left the office, Gerry Williams got in his car and headed across town to the gym. The car was hot from sitting in the warm May sun. He loved the warmth of the sun but more than the warmth he enjoyed the way his body turned from its winter paleness into a dark healthy looking brown. Naked at a mirror, he would admire the sharp division between the white skin under his trunks and the darkness of the rest of his body. He used to sunbath on the deck at home but two years ago he had joined a health spa on the excuse of needing the physical exercise but mainly for the use of the full length tanning cabinet. If Marion had noticed that he was now brown all year round or that he no longer sunbathed as frequently on the deck she hadn't said anything. But, he thought, she probably just hadn't noticed—she seemed to be very vague these days as if there was something bothering her. Probably she was concerned about Edith, their daughter, whose sharp tongue was constantly upsetting her mother.

Arriving at the gym, he parked and locked his car and, throwing his jacket casually over his shoulder, made his way inside greeting a couple of friends on their way out. He paused to tease the receptionist before picking a phone. Dialling his home number he waited for an answer and after six or seven rings he was about to hang up when he heard his son's gruff "Hullo."

"Craig, for God's sake!" he exploded. "Can't you answer the phone without sounding surly?"

"Hi," was the response.

"You sound like you're mad at the whole world when you say 'Hello' like that," and he made an exaggerated attempt to mimic his son's greeting. "Can't you be civil?" he went on. "You don't know who is calling. It might be one of my clients and it sounds like hell to be greeted on the phone like that.

"Yeah. I guess so." said Craig in a long suffering tone.

Softening his temper, Gerry asked, "Is your mother at home?"

"No."

"No, what?"

"No, she isn't."

"Well, do you know where she is?"

"No."

"No, what?"

"No, I don't"

"Did she leave a note?"

"No."

"Craig!" in parental exasperation. "Getting information from you is like pulling teeth. Listen to me. When your mother gets home tell her I'm going to do some work here, grab a bite of supper and make some calls. But I won't be late. Okay?"

"Yeah. Okay."

"What are you doing?" the father asked feeling a little guilty about his two explosions when he had scarcely talked to his son all week.

"Oh, nothing. Just mucking about and doing some homework."

"Okay, then, Craig. I'll see you later. I won't be late."

Then before he could say goodbye, Craig said. "Hey, Dad, y'know what? Rob thinks maybe his dad is going to get him a car for the summer."

Recognizing the game, the parent replied, "He does,eh? Well good for him. I guess then that his grades are going up, are they?"

"Yeah, maybe a little. But Rob says his dad thinks he might get a good job in the summer if he can drive a car."

"Well, I guess they'll work something out." Then, knowing his son was going to reintroduce the subject of a car of his own, he said with finality, "Craig, I've got to go. See you later. Goodbye."

"Bye," he heard just before he replaced the receiver.

"The little con-artist," he thought. "He'll try every trick in the book to get a car except buckling down and getting the grades."

Moving into the locker room, Gerry stripped, and standing naked carefully hung his clothes in the locker. Only then did he pull his gym strip out and dress for the floor. He fitted on a jockstrap releasing the waist band with a loud snap against his belly, shoved his feet into heavy wool socks and runners and pulled on a thick sweatshirt. The last item of attire was a pair of well-made, tight white shorts that contrasted with the dark tan of his legs. The fact that he was alone in the locker room did not either hasten or alter his pattern of dressing. He had always dressed in a deliberate routine whether the locker room was crowded or empty, taking time to check himself in the full mirror, never hiding his naked- ness nor turning his back to others. There was a time when he was young when he used to be unsure whether or not to turn his back to the other boys. He had a purple collared, butterfly shaped birthmark about the size of two fifty cent pieces together just above the crack of his buttocks. It was the cause of much staring and questioning but when he had grown into adolescence he had be- come so inured to the curious glances that he scarcely noticed them unless they were openly rude. He sometimes wondered how Craig was handling the genetic present he received from him—an identical birthmark—but Craig had never mentioned it not since the boys played naked in their backyard wading pools.

In the gym he started with the exercise bicycle and after ten minutes of vigorous work he was wet with sweat and puffing. The only sounds from the dozen or so men working out, were some huffing and groans and the thumps of the weights and the whir of exercise bikes and treadmills. Most men followed a standard workout but Gerry had set a program for himself targeting his up- per body with a variety of chrome plated barbells, weights and pulleys. He worked his way down the line doing a standard set of exercises detailed for him by the 'coach'—in reality, a keen salesman who fitted each customer with a set of prescribed exercises without any real basis for his variations. Gerry suspected his lack of professionalism but didn't care. His own set pulled at the muscles of his legs, stomach and shoulders. He could feel his back and chest and rump strain and tense as he sweated through a good workout. There were perhaps a dozen other men in the gym, each working and huffing independently and mostly in concentrated silence. There were some days when there was boister- ous laughter and competition but he rarely joined in, preferring his own pace and routines and his aloofness from horseplay and male camaraderie. Today he finished with another short spurt on the bicycle and, then drenched with sweat he returned to the locker room. Tossing his sodden clothes into a hamper to be laundered, and returned to his locker, he picked up a towel and without wrapping it around himself went to the showers. Standing under twin needle showers, he altered the temperature back and forth between scalding hot and icy cold, gasping and rubbing and turning until his skin tingled to the point of hurtfulness. Then, dripping and undraped, he stepped into the sauna.

Whether Gerry Williams knew it consciously or not, the sauna was a basic reason for his decision to take out a membership in the gym. In the sauna room eight other men stood, sat or leaned, nude, flushed, red-eyed and squirting per- spiration. Two of these men Gerry knew casually and he greeted them and they responded with the cautious formality that men demonstrate when they meet naked and unprotected. The room itself was small with three levels. With nine men in it, it was not crowded but each man had to move with care from one level to another to avoid the embarrassing contact of male flesh to male flesh. Gerry found a place on the slotted bench at the highest level where the heat was most intense and waited for it to penetrate and the sweat to start pouring out. And as he waited, he looked around without staring. Around him were thin shanks and bulging bellies, bowed legs and corned feet. There were men whose body hair spread ape-like across their shoulders and down their backs. There were massive and pendulous genitals hanging low and swaying gently, giving their owners the dignity of old bulls, and there were tightly clumped, almost adolescent genitals hidden under protruding stomachs or stuck defiantly against a flat gut ornamented with pelvic bones sticking out like wings. There were the circumcised and the untouched, men who pointed left and men who pointed right. There were some massive breasts that were almost pendulous, and whose ribs and strings of muscles gave them a robot-like tinker toy look. There were displays of scars, straight, curved, jagged or stitched, standing white and purple against mottled skin all of which, Gerry thought, taken together in a creative jumble, would have made an interesting abstract.

Gerry had no need to examine himself in order to make comparisons. He was very much aware of his own straight tanned back and square shoulders, the curl of dark hair on his chest and belly, the long and muscled legs. He could see his own genitals, straight and uniform, neither obscenely bullish nor embarrassingly small. His hands and feet were as tidy and as well groomed as his hair which was only beginning to show the grey signs of maturity. He knew, with no small feeling of pleasure, frequently renewed, that each part of his body matched with the other parts and that the whole showed the narcissistic care he gave it.

Most men sat or stood in silence dripping from every extremity. Others busied themselves with their towels, mopping, rubbing and massaging. Some entered into quiet conversations, managing to convey the impression of a discussion across a board-room table.

Gerry had noticed long ago the ritual for leaving the sauna, and it was one which he deliberately avoided. As each man reached his limit, as he felt purged and dizzy, he would give a snort and announce something like: "Boy, that's enough for me today." then he would proceed to squeegee his arms, stomach and legs with his hands and make his exit puffing and blowing and wiping his face and chest with one end of his towel so that the rest of the towel hung decorously in front. When Gerry had had enough, determined not to follow any ritual, he picked up his towel and left.

From the sauna, he stepped directly into the whirlpool. Clutching his genitals protectively with one hand and holding onto the edge of the pool with the other, he floated on his stomach and let the jet blasts of water pound and pummel him as they twisted and tumbled his relaxed body. Some men preferred to go directly to the massage room Gerry rebelled against the intrusiveness of another man's hands on his body in public.

When he began to feel almost bruised by the water jets returned to the locker room where he put on a pair of tight, low-cut swim trunks, adjusting the waistline carefully to the tan-line and went to the tanning cabinet.

Stepping inside, he set the timer for eight minutes, closed his eyes so as not to bother with the dark goggles, which he disliked using because of the unequal tanning around the eyes, flicked the switch and let the heat from the rings of lamps flood over him. Only then did he permit himself to think of the evening ahead and to let himself grow and tighten against the protective shield of his trunks. Eleanor would be home. The code: "I think I'll knock off early and go down to the gym," had been understood. Had she not wanted him to come she would have made a signal protest, probably about the amount of work he was leaving, but she had not. He was solidly entrenched in the daydream of tonight when the timer bell went off and the lights faded. Back at the locker he waited briefly to get his body urges under control before stripping and heading for a final cold needle shower.

He dressed without haste, left the gym and after buying an evening paper, drove to a quiet restaurant. The onion soup was bubbling in an earthenware bowl. The chicken stew was rich and delicately aromatic and the salad had more garlic in the dressing than he should have permitted himself. He lingered over the paper and some wine, waiting more than reading—waiting for the agreed time to arrive. He was very pleased with himself for having set up the arrangement with Eleanor. She had been assigned to him as a personal secretary three years ago. They had discovered that they both enjoyed sex but most of the time were disinclined to hunt. Before the arrangement with her, he had had to be satisfied with pick-ups and twice he had picked up a young man, but on both occasions he was left with disturbing feelings that he would not recognize as guilt. He rationalized his extramarital affairs by reminding himself that Marion had become so totally passive in her sexual responses that he had long ago ceased to approach her. Just when he had found himself thinking more and more about young men Eleanor had come along and he discovered that her enjoyment of a good sexual romp was enough to help him forget his two homosexual frolics. In his mind, the gym and Eleanor became puzzlingly linked. Sex, for him, had become the finale to the ritual of body care. He never considered what it might mean for her beyond a physical act without emotional strings.

CHAPTER 7

Shortly before Craig's father had called, the two boys disentangled themselves and lying side by side in a tight silence they had continued a sporadic touching until, suddenly, Rob said "Ouch!" elbowed Craig in the ribs and rolled off the bed and got to his feet.

"What did you say 'ouch' for?" Craig asked, not moving from his sprawled position on the bed.

Rob made no answer as he stood grinning down on Craig while he zipped up and tucked his shirt in. Finally he asked with a wicked grin, "Like to try for two?"

"Hah!" derisively was the only response.

"Like to try something different?"

Again "Hah!" with equal derision. Then, quietly, "What?"

"Oh, for God's sake, I'm only joking. But you're kind of interested, aren't you, Craggy-my-lover-boy?"

Craig was still lying bare on his back and Rob sat down beside him and gently pulled his underwear up, giving him a final tuck and ruffle as he did so. "There!" he said. "I've put my toy away."

"Look whose talking about a toy," Craig responded, sitting up. "I'll bet—." and the telephone rang.

He listened to it ring three times then rushed downstairs to answer it, pulling his clothes together as he ran. Coming back upstairs, he found Rob tilted back on a chair with his feet propped on the desk. "That was my dad. He's not coming home for dinner again," he announced. "You know what I told him? I told him you thought your dad would get you a car for the summer so you could get a good job."

"What did you tell him that for?"

"Why not? You can tell your dad the same thing about me," Craig said, oblivious to the fact that their parents still contacted each other as necessary to check on 'the boys.'

"Yeah, fat chance, Rob responded. "My old man will let me have a car when I get a straight B average or when I'm eighteen and I got at least half the cash. And that's what your old man is going to do, too."

Craig shrugged. "I know—but no harm in trying. If there's a spark there, keep blowing on it, it might just burst into flame. Got to give it the old school try. Rah! Rah! Rah! Get out there and fight. If at first you don't succeed, cheat! Et cetera and rah and rah and rah."

"Ah, shut up!" said Rob.

"All right, then. I'll shut up. I'll never say another word. My lips are sealed. The secret will go with me to the grave. Neither storm nor sleet nor darkness of night will tear the secret from me."

"Oh for crissake. You're an idiot. I'm going home," and Rob got to his feet.

"Rob?" Quietly from Craig. "Did we get a little drunk?"

"Not me! On one piddly little drink?"

"Well, it wasn't exactly a little drink. I put a lot in it."

"Well, it wasn't enough to make me drunk. I knew what I was doing all the time."

"Yeah, I guess so. So did I. I could drink ten of those and never feel it," Craig bragged.

"I bet you'd be flat on your ass," Rob said as he walked out of the room and down the stairs with Craig following with a question.

"What are you gonna do tonight? Coming over?"

"I dunno. See ya," Rob said.

"Okay, See ya."

As Craig closed the door the phone rang. Answering it in his usual gruff manner, he heard the high and frantic voice of his sister who plunged into a streak of conversation as soon as the connection was made. Edith had married suddenly and young, and just as suddenly had produced twin girls. She lived in the Fraser Valley on the edge of a sprawling suburb in Abbotsford that was an unsuccessful attempt to resurrect old farm land and bring town and country together on lots large enough that some people kept a horse or two or a few she sheep. Harvey Allen, her husband, was a plasterer-drywaller, lean bodied, slow brained and big hearted. They lived in an old farmhouse that Harvey, on weekends and evenings, continued to renovate. The house, at the moment, was marred by Harvey's amateur carpentry but showed promise. Edith had flung herself out of the family home at 18, momentarily bitter because of a quarrel with her mother, rushed Harvey to a minister and to bed. Three months later she had mended the rift with her mother, and the two of them, now with some miles of freeway between them, were friendly and as close as either wanted to be. They saw each other every about every two weeks, talked on the telephone more frequently and had grown to like each other at a safe distance. But Edith's life was always full of emergencies and last minute panics. The energy from her thin body seemed as endless as it was directionless. Her mother simply found her to be tiring and frustrating except in small doses. Edith rarely bothered with her father except for necessary courtesies when they visited. She knew he was angered easily, with a cold, formal, un-verbalized anger, by untidiness and by babies. She did not know that he had bitterly resented the grandfather label pinned on him, unasked at 43. Still, she watched her husband and her father carefully when they were together on rare occasions, knowing that her father's unsolicited advice would be taken by Harvey as fact and acted on. Harvey could cautiously admire his father-in-law in whom he could see all those signs of success and acceptance that he desired but could not even clumsily grab at. Between Harvey and Craig there was nothing. Harvey had long ago forgotten his own brief adolescence and in spite of his generally open nature, he could not discover in himself any feeling for Craig's uncertainties and vagaries. Between brother and sister there was the unbridgeable gap of six years. To Edith, Craig was simply the resented favoured child. Years of having to give in to him in any squabble, and years of having to look after him during the long summers of her own childhood, were tied together in a bundle of hot resentments. She saw him as her mother's safeguard against any friendship she attempted. "Well," her mother would say, "if you're only going down to the beach with your friend, why can't you take Craig? He'd love to go. Wouldn't you, Craggy?" Furiously, reluctantly, she would drag her young brother along and spend her precious day telling him to go away or come back, finding him when he was lost, hoping that he had been kidnapped or drowned, sending him to the washroom when she was embarrassed by the dark, growing stain on his swimsuit and loathing him or her mother, she was never sure which.

    "Craig? Oh, it's you!" came Edith's shrill voice. "Is Mom there? Well, where is she? When will she be back? Didn't she say where she was going? Well, she probably just went shopping. She said yesterday she had to get some sheets.

Darn her! I wish she had phoned. I wanted her to get me some things too, if she was going shopping. Well, it doesn't matter. What are you doing? Anyway, I wanted to talk to you. What did you get Mom for her birthday? It's today. What do you mean you didn't know? Didn't you get her anything? Do you know what Dad's getting her? Is he taking her out or anything? He's not?! He's not even coming home for dinner? Oh, Craig, that's awful! Poor Mom. Tell her I'll phone her later. Tell her I was going to get her something and bring it in only Harvey needed the car all day and besides the twins are sick. I think they got something. A couple of the kids next door have spots. I was going to take them to the doctor only Harvey had the car all day. Tell Mom 'Happy Birthday' for us and I'll phone her before I put the girls down. I think that's awful—not coming home on her birthday or getting her anything at all. Jenny! Put that down! Right now! I've got to go. Jenny's into the cat food. Jenny! Craig, I've got to go. Don't forget to tell Mom. Wha-a-a-t? Tell her Happy Birthday—what do you think we've been talking about. Honestly, Craig, sometimes I don't know about you. Really! Jenny! Now where's Iona? Craig, goodbye."

Craig hung up the dead phone and wondered idly where his mother was. Then he got an apple, went upstairs and flopped on the bed with his radio blasting.

CHAPTER 8

When Marion Williams came out of the doctor's building she had succeeded in composing herself. The waiting room was empty and the nurse hidden behind her barricade so she had an opportunity to dab her eyes dry and put on some fresh lipstick before putting on her coat and leaving. The May afternoon sun was still bright and warm. She wished she had thought to bring her dark glasses but she hadn't intended to get weepy and red-eyed. She had meant to be very matter-of-fact and enquiring. She wondered what Gerry would say if she told him what she had told the doctor. She knew she wouldn't tell him. She couldn't tell him. They never talked about those things. She wondered if he ever talked about his private life to other men. She had heard that some men did. Two women she knew were hurt and furious because their husbands told other men what they did in bed. Said it publicly, laughing, boasting—all the details of their sex life together. Thank God, Gerry never did that. But then, he never did anything so she couldn't imagine he would ever boast about that publicly.

Feeling a surge of self pity and tears start inside her, she checked her thoughts and busied herself with the problem of getting home. A taxi or a bus. The busses would be getting crowded at this time of day. Maybe a taxi. But taxis were an extravagance and a last resort for her. She wished she had cancelled her appointment until the garage had phoned and told her the parts were in and her car was fixed. But no, that wouldn't have been a good thing to do because if she backed down about going to see the doctor she knew she would never have made another appointment. Not that the whole appointment was much help—she was depressed, that's what he said, go home and forget about it. "Big deal!" she thought. "That's what Craig would say."

Turning towards the bus stop at the other end of the block, she saw Mr. Thomas who had been almost rudely escorted out of the doctor's office earlier by the nurse. As she approached him she noticed how shaky and confused he appeared. "Poor old man," she mused to herself. "Waiting here ever since he left the office. I wonder if he's lost of just waiting." It seemed like a long time and he did look distressed. Going up to him, she asked, "Mr. Thomas? Are you all right?"

The old man gathered himself erect when he realized she was addressing him and, with an old world courtesy, lifted his hat briefly off his grey head in greeting. "How do you do," he said.

"How do you do, Mr. Thomas," she responded with a smile. "I'm Mrs. Williams. I was in Dr. Strawburn's office when you were there and I just wondered if you were all right."

"It's my bowels," the old man started, then seeing her kindly smile continued. "I go for days and nothing happens and then I get cramps—terrible, terrible cramps—all across here," and he touched himself vaguely on a little sagging paunch.

"Oh, that really is too bad," she commiserated. "But what I really meant was can you find your way home. You seemed a little lost. Is someone picking you up?"

"He's not my regular doctor, you know. He's Marion's doctor. My doctor retired and he wasn't as old as I am. I'm 78. And all my life I've had this trouble but my own doctor would always give me some of those little yellow pills and they'd do the trick. But this new doctor won't give me anything." He grumbled on some more, then said, "What did you say the name was?"

"My name is Mrs. Williams," and there was no sign of impatience in her voice.

"No! No!" the old man said and there was a little edge in his voice. "I know that. You told me that already. I mean the Doctor's name. He never introduced himself, you know."

"Oh, I see," she said. "His name is Dr. Strawburn. I suppose he thought you would know his name."

"I did know it. It was on his card. But it's not the same as introducing himself, is it? Like you did. Anyhow, I think I forgot it."

"Well, then. Now you know it. Now, is anyone picking you up, Mr. Thomas? Can you get home by yourself?" she persisted.

"Home," he said. "Yes, home. I'd better get on home." And he looked uncertainly up the street and around.

"Where do you live, Mr. Thomas? Do you remember where you live? Tell me where you live and I'll help you find the right bus."

"Bus?" he said. "I don't need a bus. Marion's picking me up." He reached into his pocket, took out a gold watch, flipped the lid, looked at it intently, and returned it to his pocket.

"When? Mr. Thomas. When was she going to pick you up?" I'll have to take him home, she thought, or to the police station. I can't just leave him just standing here. I'll get a taxi and take him home.

"Pick you up," the old man repeated with a tired sigh, his eyes cloudy with fatigue.

"Your address must be in your wallet," she said. "Show me your wallet, Mr. Thomas. Let me see your wallet and I'll find your address and get a taxi and take you home."

Slowly, he reached into his hip pocket and after a lot of tugging, and she had to restrain herself not to help him, he took out a well-worn thin wallet. She took it from him and opened it. The two thin plastic envelopes were empty. She opened the wallet over its length and tucked in behind a few bills she found a card. Taking it out she was about to read it when a voice beside her said, "C'mon sister. Pick on someone your own age!"

Startled, reddening, she turned to see a tall, thin man in work clothes, hat on the back of his head, grinning at her. He took the wallet from her and slipped it into his own pocket.

"I'm not..." she said. "I wasn't... I mean I was just..."

"She was going to take me home with her," the old man volunteered in a soft, vague voice.

"Mr. Thomas!" she exclaimed in a chastening tone. "Not to my home. To your home. That's why I was trying to find his address so that... Besides, that's an awful thing to say. I wasn't picking on him. I was trying to help him."

The man beside them continued to grin and as she spoke she began to see it, not as a malicious, accusing grin but one that was friendly and teasing and she relaxed a little.

"How did you know his name?"

"I didn't, really. We were in the doctor's office together and..." Again, the grin and this time it was a stag leer. "We were not together," she said firmly. "Will you stop that! You know what I mean and you make me say all the wrong things. I was waiting in the doctor's office and he came out and I heard the nurse talking to him. And then when I came out, after my appointment, he was still here and I thought he might be lost. Besides, he introduced himself to me—charmingly!" Then, suddenly, "Who are you?"

"Tom Thomas."

"Tom Thomas—oh! Then is he—?" and the question trailed off.

"Yes," he said. "He's my father."

"Oh, I see. He did say something about Marion meeting him here," and there seemed to be nothing more to say.

"And who are you?" The question exploded from him with a suddenness, volume and inflection that mimicked her own earlier question.

"I'm Marion Williams," she said, unconsciously extending her hand. "How do you do."

He took the extended hand, holding it firmly and fractionally too long and with the other arm he grasped his hat and lifted it with the same odd courtliness his father had shown earlier.

"I'm Marion Thomas," he said. "How do you do?" and again there was a hint of mimicry.

"Williams, Marion Williams," emphasizing the surname.

"I'm Marion Thomas," he said, again mimicking her.

She wriggled her hand out of his, somewhat puzzled and exasperated. Then suddenly she exclaimed, "Oh, you're the Marion. You're Marion Thomas!"

"Yessiree! You bet! Give the lady a cigar. I'm Marion Thomas."

She giggled. "I'm sorry," she said. "I just thought..."

"Everyone always 'just thinks' the first time they hear it."

"But you said your name was Tom."

"Yes, wouldn't you?"

"Yes," she said. "I guess so," and giggled again and then had to say she was sorry again.

"Thank you, Marion Williams," he said quietly to her, all the teasing inflections gone from his voice. "Thank you for looking out for him. I had a flat and couldn't get here on time. I figured if I was late he would just sit in the waiting room until I got here. But he's getting more and more forgetful. Are you OK, Dad?" This last question to the old man was mouthed precisely but not shouted and accompanied with a searching look. Satisfied with his father's nod, he turned back to her. "He's tired," he said. "He needs a cup of tea to last him until supper time. As a matter of fact I do too." The concern for his father showed on his face as he continued. "Marion, if I can call you that, I'm sorry I put you on. Can I say thank you and make my apologies by asking you to come with us? You could use a cup of tea, too, couldn't you?" He turned and looked up and down the street. "There's a little place over there. We'd both be pleased."

She hesitated, looking at him and thinking what he could mean by that both. Him and his father? Or was he teasing again and suggesting him and her. Then she saw him grinning again.

"We'd be well chaperoned, you know."

She blushed and hesitated, but strangely, she wanted to go with this friendly open man.

"Tell you what," he said when her answer was delayed. "We'll get Dad to buy it. He likes to splurge on ladies. Like father, like son," and he gave a throaty chuckle. "Dad?" and again he addressed his father with carefully spoken words. "Would you like to take Mrs. Williams to tea? To say thank you for talking to you until I got here?"

The old man who had paid little attention to what the conversation had been about now straightened, and looking directly at her, lifted his hat again and said, "My pleasure, madam."

"No, mine, Mr. Thomas," and giving the slightest of little bows hoped her words matched his old world grace. "I'd be delighted!"

In the small, casual cafe they found a booth. Mr. Thomas seated her, hung his hat on the peg and eased himself into the booth beside her. She found herself looking across the table at Tom and she examined him while he was busy looking across the room trying to catch the attention of the waitress. His once fair hair, still curly, was greying slightly and the hairline was beginning to recede. There was a relaxed and comfortable look about him and his brown eyes had crinkles at the corners which she always associated with laughter. The blue work shirt was open at the neck and covered by a good but well-worn tweed jacket. He signalled to the waitress and turned back to face her.

"Three teas, please," he said when the waitress approached. "Unless you would like coffee, perhaps. No?" As Marion shook her head. "Three teas, then. Dad, would you like a bran muffin?"

The old man fish-mouthed his lips to make a reply but Tom didn't wait for it.

"Sure you would," he said. "What the hell! We all would. We'll have a party. It's a long time until supper. Make that three bran muffins, please, Miss. And a little marmalade or jam."

They sat smiling and waiting for the tea until there was the beginning of a silence. She knew she should be gracious and break the silence but somehow she was quite satisfied to sit and enjoy his quiet company. Finally, Tom leaned toward his father and asked, "What did the doctor say, Dad?"

He didn't give me any of those little yellow pills," the old man said. "I told him my own doctor always gave me little yellow pills but he wouldn't give me any."

"Well, maybe he will give you something just as good," Tom said placating. And then to Marion, "He got along great with his old doctor but he retired."

"I know," said Marion. "He told me."

"Did he tell you what was wrong with him, too?" asked Tom with a smile.

Marion nodded and returned a small smile because she saw that the old man eyes had brightened as he became aware that he was the subject of their conversation.

"It's my bowels," he said, as if to make everything absolutely clear. "I get terrible cramps and I can't move my bowels for days at a time."

"Dad!" Tom said in a tone that was only slightly reproving. "Mrs Williams doesn't want to hear about your bowels—not while she's eating."

"Perfectly normal function," the father grumbled. "Besides," and this in a childish aside, "she's not eating."

"We will be in a minute, Dad. Be patient."

They all sat quietly together for a minute.

"Were you in to see the doctor, too?" Tom asked. "What was wrong with you?" Then quickly appalled by his bluntness and openly contrite he exclaimed, "Good lord! I'm sorry. I shouldn't ask that. I just forgot that I've only known you for fifteen minutes. People should know each other at least thirty minutes before they get that personal!" And he grinned again but behind the grin was a fading blush.

"It was nothing. Just routine," she said with a smile trying to assuage his embarrassment and her own for she had felt her heart stop on hearing the question and frantic replies were being sorted out before he made his apology.

"I should go for a routine check myself one of these days. It's a smart thing to do."

The tea and muffins came. Old Mr. Thomas shakily buttered, sugared and stirred and settled into a series of quiet little sips without returning his cup to the table. Tom broke his muffin and popped each buttered half into his mouth helping them on their way with great gulps of tea.

"Does the Mrs. mean you are still married, Marion?" Tom asked.

"Yes," she replied vaguely. "I guess so." Then alerting herself and chastened by her unconscious exposure of her unhappiness she stated with determined precision, "Yes, I mean. Happily married and two children and two grandchildren."

"Grandchildren!" he exclaimed. "You're kidding. You don't look old enough to have grandchildren."

"Well, I am and I do—and I don't mind being a grandparent at all." She had caught herself in time not to say grandmother. Somehow the label grandparent seemed more appropriate at the moment.

"What does your husband do?"

"He's an insurance adjuster."

"Oh, I see. I guess he travels a lot then."

"No, not any more. He used to. Now he just works late." She was surprised again by the unexpected way she had let down her guard and surprised too by the note of bitterness in her own voice. "I mean, he's very busy," she finished lamely.

"I see," said Tom and the tone of understanding was touchingly friendly and she buried her nose in her teacup with her elbows planted domestically on the table.

"You don't want the rest of your muffin. I'll have it," Tom said, more to change the conversation for her sake than for any other reason. He reached across the table, picked up her half-eaten muffin and scraped up her remaining butter with his own knife.

Old Mr. Thomas announced suddenly, in good voice, as if the tea had revived him, "I have to see another doctor."

"What do you mean, Dad? Don't you like Dr. Strawburn?"

"He wouldn't give me any pills. He said I had to see someone else," the old man replied.

"No, I think he means Dr. Strawburn referred him to a clinic," Marion interjected. "Isn't that right, Mr. Thomas? Don't you have to go to a clinic next week some time?" Turning back to Tom she said, "I think they wrote it down for him. They phoned and made an appointment and he is to go to the clinic and then come back and see Dr. Strawburn."

"Good thing you were there," Tom said to her and then to his father, "Where is the piece of paper with the address on it, Dad?"

The old man looked at his son without comprehending for a minute and then began poking in various pockets finally finding a tightly creased paper. Tom reached over and took it from him.

"The Schoenfeld Clinic!" he exploded. "At two-thirty! Great Jesus, that's the other side of town. He'll never get there on his own and it's too early for me to take him." He paused, frowning. "Well, I'll have to phone them and get a later time. That's what I'll have to do."

"It's at two-thirty," said the old man.

"Yes, but I'll have to change it, otherwise I'll lose a whole half-a-day's work."

"The nurse said two-thirty next Tuesday," and there was a hint of obduracy in the old voice.

"Yes, but we'll have to change it so I can drive you. It's too far for you by bus."

The old man leaned back defeated but still muttering, "She <u>said</u> two-thirty."

The talk of time made Marion look at her watch and noting the time she became almost instantly formal. "Thank you for the tea," she said to Tom. "But I'm afraid I really have to go."

"Don't thank me, thank Dad," Tom said with a smile determined not to let things finish on her note of formality. "It's on him. Isn't it, Dad? You're paying this time, aren't you?"

"Yes, yes. You are my guests," said Mr. Thomas leaning over towards Marion and attempting to reach his wallet in his hip pocket. Not finding it, he patted other pockets and said querulously, "I think I've lost my wallet. I had it before... I had it when..." and his thin voice trailed off.

"Are you sure you didn't give it to some strange woman on the street?" Tom teased, with a wide grin at Marion.

"I haven't.... I mean, I must have... Surely I didn't put it in my purse!" and flustered and embarrassed, she clicked open her black purse on her lap and rummaged in it with her head down, reddening as she looked.

A chuckle from Tom made her look up. He was sitting with a huge smile on his face, elbows on the table and dangling the old wallet in front of her. "Oh, you!" she said in exasperation, feeling caught by his teasing again.

Tom's explosion of laughter made her smile and shake her head in spite of herself and even the old man's eyes crinkled in delight. Still laughing, Tom reached across the table and laid his hand on hers, holding it firmly and releasing it with a little shake. "I'm sorry," he said. "It was too good to miss. I can't help teasing people like you."

Uncertain of what to say, Marion said nothing, simply giving another smiling sigh and headshake.

"Pay the bill, Dad," Tom said, handing his father the wallet. "We'd better get on our way."

Together they made their way to the front of the cafe, and the two of them watched the old man work out his little problem of paying and tipping. Outside, Tom said, "May we drive you home, Marion?"

"No, thank you. It's not far," she replied.

"Well, if it's not far, all the easier for us to say thank you."

"It isn't necessary, really, Tom. I can quite easily go by bus."

"Oh, come along," Tom persisted. "We'll drop you wherever you want to go. Won't we, Dad?" The old man nodded agreeably without any real understanding.

Proceeding towards the car, Marion gave him her address and they talked about the easiest route to take. At the car, which was old but not ancient and in need of a wash, Tom settled his father carefully in the back seat and helped him fasten his seat belt, before turning his attention to Marion. It was in the car as they drove off that Marion felt urged to respond to Tom's earlier statement.

"What did you mean—teasing people like me?" she asked.

Sensitive immediately to her inquiry, he replied as though time and other words had not intervened. "Oh, you know. Innocent. Naive. Nice people who like other people and believe everything."

"Is that what you think of me?" she asked.

"I could think a great deal of you," he said, and said nothing more, looking ahead at the traffic, unsmiling.

They travelled in silence for a few minutes. "Turn right at the next light. I think that's the best way," she finally said.

"Right," he responded.

Another minute of silence that was heavy between them was broken again by Marion. "Tom? Are you married? Or should I ask?"

"No, it's okay," he said. "I mean, yes, I'm married and it's okay to ask. I should say I was married but now I'm not." His voice was level and matter of fact.

"I see," she said not wanting to pry further but hoping he would say more, not knowing why she was hoping.

"Well, it was a kind of different reason for breaking up. Not the ordinary sort of thing. My mother died and Dad was alone and I'm his only son—his only child as far as that goes. And he had to have some place to live and there wasn't enough money to place him in an old peoples' home. He had to have someone caring for him so I brought him home. But she wouldn't live with him, she said. So she packed up the kids and left. Simple as that!"

But it wasn't as simple as that and she sensed it from the attempt at flippancy and from the altered timbre in his voice. She did not want to but she felt strangely compelled to know more about him.

"The children?" she asked.

"Yes," he said. "Two. A boy and a girl. But I'm not permitted to see them. It's just a legal argument. She wants three hundred a month for each child. I'd be lucky to dig up half of that. But until I do, the rule is that I can't see them and they can't see me unless she's there and she will never make a time that is possible for me. But there's a lot more to it and it's really too messy to talk about. The fact is the kids are not mine." His face was closed and hard.

"I'm sorry, Tom. That must be awfully hard on you," she said with obvious sympathy.

"I'm sorry for the kids," he said. "She's living with some inski or olski guy and telling the kids that he's their new father. But they're old enough to know better." He drew a somewhat shuddering breath and remained silent. Then he said after a tense silence, "I guess I should have pressed for a divorce long ago, but, I dunno, I always kind of liked the idea of being a father—so I kept on hoping. He shrugged and stared down the street..

"I see," she said and wished she could find something better to say than those two ineffectual words.

They were silent again. Presently she broke the silence, "Half way down the next block on this side," she instructed him. "The white stucco house with the brown shutters."

He coasted to a stop in front and leaned over, touching her shoulder to look past her. "Nice house," he said.

"Thank you. It was good of you to drive me home." Twisting around to talk to Mr. Thomas, she said, "And thank you for the tea, Mr. Thomas. It was just what I needed. I hope you're feeling better soon. Goodbye." And she made uncertain motions looking for the door handle. Tom leaned across, his elbow resting on her thigh and opened the door. There was no unnecessary pressure on her, no lingering pause or fumbling, but suddenly her body responded with something she hadn't felt in years. Hastily, she swung herself out of the car.

"Thank you again," she said, turning about to close the door. But Tom had leaned across the seat she had vacated, his right arm on the back of the seat and his left hand holding the window ledge of the half-open door.

"May I call you sometime?" he asked, very directly.

"Tom! No! The idea! I told you I'm a married woman."

"You told me much more than that."

"I didn't.... I mean, I didn't mean to lead you to think that—well, that I was interested or anything."

"Well you did and I'm not sorry you did. I like talking to you. I'd like to talk to you again and I think I'll call you."

It's gone too far, she thought in panic. It never even started and it's gone too far.

If Tom hadn't grinned at that point she probably would have said something different, but he did and in it she saw something direct and sexual and confronting.

"Mr. Thomas!" she said, addressing the son, not the father. "Thank you for the ride and for tea. I'm glad I could be of some help to your father. As far as anything else goes, there's not nothing else—I mean, there is nothing else," and she turned and walked away. But even as she turned she could see that her bungled attempt at a dignified refusal had not diminished the grin on Tom's face. Walking towards the house, she heard Tom's voice say quietly before the car door closed, "Be seeing you, Mrs. Williams."

She stiffened and blushed and at the base of her neck a little pulse throbbed.

CHAPTER 9

Inside the house, Marion moved quickly. Leaving her coat and purse on a dining room chair, she went immediately to the kitchen and tied on an apron as she stood in front of the open frig surveying the possibilities for a quick cold supper. As she stood looking, but not really seeing because half her mind was elsewhere, she became aware of Craig's radio upstairs. Going to the foot of the stairs she called to her son without succeeding in getting a response. She had a low voice, one that could not transform into a shout and which always forged on her when she tried. When Craig was younger she had called him with a fluty trill an octave higher than her normal voice, but she hadn't used that call for years. Moving to the dining room, she took off a shoe and banged on an air register that was shared with the outlet in Craig's room. Without putting her shoe back on, she stood balanced like a sturdy stork, listening, until she heard the music fade and Craig's feet thump across the floor to his door.

"Hi!" his voice called down.

"You're home, are you? Are you alone?" Then hearing something that she interpreted as an affirmative grunt, she continued, "Get ready for dinner then."

Craig was used to his mother's get-ready-for-dinner urgings which usually started well before the table was laid and continued if she saw him idle and waiting. Normally, he would have stayed in his room or out of the way until a note of frustration in her voice indicated that she was laying the table and nobody was coming. Today, he came down to the kitchen and sat straddled backwards on a kitchen chair. She smiled at him as she bustled around putting a cold meal together.

"Hi," he said again. "Where did you go?"

"Oh, I was at the doctor's and I had to wait. My goodness, he's a slow man," she said.

"You didn't lock the door when you went out," Craig said.

"No, I know that. I went out just before you got home from school and I didn't see the sense."

"You left the radio on."

"What radio?"

"In the living room."

"I didn't, did I? I don't think I had it on today at all. Oh, yes, I did. I remember. Are you sure it was on?"

"Yep!"

"Well," she explained. "I guess I was just in a hurry and I forgot."

"You're getting old, Ma," Craig said teasingly.

"Craig! I am not! And don't call me 'Ma'." And finding nothing else to say, she scolded, "Do go and get ready for supper."

Craig sat unmoving, drumming his fingers on the chair back. "Oh!" he said suddenly. "Dad called. He's going to eat out and make some calls."

His mother stopped and regarded her preparations. "Craig." she said in a remonstrative tone. "Why, didn't you tell me? I've made too much."

"You just got in," he replied simply.

"Well, then, there's just the two of us." and she stopped herself from adding a bitter 'again' in front of her son. "Let's see. Let's have some cold meat and salad and tomatoes, and you get some French fries from the freezer and we'll have those. Or would you rather have hash browns? There's some in the freezer if you want those. And there's a big piece of rhubarb pie for you—unless you ate it after school. Oh, no, you didn't—I see it right there. That was good, wasn't it? Fresh spring rhubarb right from the garden? And there's some ice cream for you, and I'll have a bran muffin." Suddenly she reddened, remembering, and turned her back on her son but he, getting up from his chair would not have seen her blush anyway. "This is my bran muffin day," she said to herself and caught a small chuckle in the back of her throat. In a flash of introspection she was aware that she had been savouring a taste of happiness.

In the quick efficient way that was second nature to her when doing her household routines she put together the simple meal. Seated across from each other at the table, they talked of little friendly things. She was determined to hold on to the mood she was in, and refrained from maternal corrections and adjurations. Craig noted his mother's apparent pleasure with the world and made use of it.

"Rob said his dad was thinking that he should get a car so he can get a good job this summer," he said, throwing out the idea for size.

"Oh, he did, did he," was his mother's response as she watched her son across the table and seeing his ploy plainly in his voice and casual manner. Then because she loved him deeply and warmly, she fed him the response she knew he wanted.

"That doesn't sound like a bad idea, does it?"

Craig was so taken aback by the unexpectedness of her reply that he stumbled with his response. He rattled on about cars and jobs and running errands and taking her to the doctor when her car wasn't working, like today, and how little it really costs.

"I suppose what you are really telling me is that you want one too," she said, almost interrupting him.

He couldn't find the right answer. He didn't want to give her a blunt 'yes' nor a pleading 'please' nor a non-committal 'oh, I don't know' or 'I guess so.'

"I guess you're right," she finally went on, holding back any sign of her amusement at his struggle. "After all, you are sixteen and growing up, too."

Craig could not restrain the happy "Oh, Mom Mom!" that burst from him. And as an added bonus, she had not, this time, subtracted from his age by saying "only sixteen."

She had practically promised.

"You mean I can get one?" and he had to guard his voice against becoming an excited squeal.

"I didn't say that," she protested. "But I will speak to your father. After all, you will need a car if you get a job this summer."

Craig put on a grave face in spite of the churning excitement within him. Then his mother said, "Of course, you really should get a driver's licence first before we start talking about a car. We could probably work something out with my car so you could get some experience, like taking me shopping or out to see Edith. Come to think of it, I suppose your father would think that would be the best idea because we really don't need three cars. I don't use it much any way, Sometimes I don't use it for a whole week."

The mention of Edith made him remember her call. His mother had been talking while she had cleared the plates and cut him his piece of pie. Waiting until she got back to the table and was seated, he said, "Hey, Mom. Close your eyes!"

"Why?"

"Just close your eyes and don't peek," he ordered.

"Whatever for? she persisted but closed them very briefly.

"No, don't peek," he said and, taking her apron off her chair back he draped it over her head. "Now don't take it off until I tell you."

Quickly taking her plate and bran muffin from in front of her, he went on long tiptoe strides to the dining room, pulled open a drawer and took one small red birthday cake candle from a box. Sticking it in the muffin, he lit it and went to the kitchen door.

"Okay, now you can look! Happy birthday to you. Happy birthday to you. Happy birthday, dear mother. Happy birthday to you," he sang as he walked towards her, his voice carefully deep and toneless.

"Oh, Craig! It's my birthday and I forgot. Can you imagine that?"

"I forgot, too." Craig said. "I didn't get you anything, I'm sorry. But I will. Happy birthday, any way," and he leaned over and kissed her awkwardly on the cheek. "Edith phoned and told me. This afternoon. She said to say Happy Birthday for her."

Craig watched his mother out of the corner of his eye as he tackled his pie. Her finger ends were pressed against her lips, her eyes misted over and she was taking tense little sniffs and uncertain swallows.

"Oh, Craig, I am getting old."

"Aw, Mom. I was only teasing."

"But I forgot my own birthday. So did everybody, even your dad."

"Oh, Dad's probably got something. He just couldn't get home." But he said it more to allay his mother's unhappiness than to defend his father's neglect.

She dabbed her eyes with her apron, got up and blew her nose. From across the kitchen she said in a firm voice, "I'm sorry, Craig," and seating herself again at the table, continued "Eat your pie!"

Craig forked a big piece into his mouth and mumbled around it, "Good pie! I like it better cold than hot."

The little candle still burned in front of her. "Shall I make a wish?" she said gaily.

"Sure, and all your dreams will come true," he responded, attempting to match his mother's party mood.

She looked at the tiny muffin and its candle and suddenly blew it out. "No No!" she said. "Better to trust to luck than go around wishing and dreaming."

They ate in silence for a minute.

"How old are you, Mom?"

"Craig!"

"Well, I just wondered. How old are you?" he persisted.

"I'm thirty three, and next year when you ask me I'll be thirty three again. Does that answer you question, Mr. Curiosity?"

"Yep," he said, with a full mouth. "Let's see. Edith is twenty two. That would make you about eleven when she was born. So you were about ten when you got married. A real child bride virgin."

"Craig Williams! That's enough of that smart talk. The idea! What a thing to say to your mother!" She looked fierce, but she laughed, mostly at his scarlet embarrassment for his slip of the tongue. "Save that kind of talk for your friends," she said without any great severity.

They were finished their meal and now sat inactive at the table. "What are you going to do?" she asked.

"Oh, I dunno. Maybe I'll go up the park for a while."

"Have you done your homework?"

"Yes," he lied. "But we didn't have much."

"Well," his mother said, getting up from the table. "Don't be late, then. Be in before dark."

"Oh, Mom! I'm nearly seventeen," he protested.

"My, how the months fly by," she replied, smiling at him. And then, softly to him, "Craig? I really will ask your father about the car. But you have to promise one thing. You have to promise to be careful."

"Thanks, Mom," and his blue eyes were dancing.

"Promise, Craig."

"Sure, Mom. I promise. Really!" And then in a pulpit voice he intoned, "If you can't be good, be careful."

"Oh, you," she said in loving exasperation. "You better be good and careful both!"

"Yes, madam," he replied with mock formality.

She turned, half expecting him to lift an imaginary hat from his head. "Get out of here," she said, happy with the way her day was ending.

CHAPTER 10

Gerry stopped and parked a block away from an apartment building he had entered many times before. The button he pushed with three quick rings was labelled simply 'E. Colman' and he waited without impatience for the unlocking buzzer. When it sounded he entered quickly and walked up the three flights of stairs rather than wait for the old wheezy elevator. The garishly carpeted and dimly lighted halls were stuffily redolent of evening meals and camouflaging spray scents. But if personal odours drifted into the hallways the sounds of living behind the doors he passed did not. The door he sought was slightly ajar by invitation. He tapped without giving the impression of a formal knock and walked in. The room he entered was small but neatly organized with heavy furniture. On the far side, half the width of the room was given over to a small kitchen separated from the living room by a counter in front of which stood broad and solid wicker stools. An open door showed the other half contained the bedroom, and off it, behind the kitchen, the bathroom. In a bulky solid chair, facing an enormous television, Eleanor sat with her feet tucked under her, wrapped in an ancient bathrobe of muted colons and nursing a mug of coffee in both hands.

"Hi," she said over her shoulder, hearing the door latch click behind her.

He walked the two or three steps towards her and stood behind her and by way of greeting grasped the top of her head lightly with spread fingers. Her short dark hair was damp and curly and soft to his touch. She moved her head slightly from his touch and with only a hint of impatience said, "Don't, Gerry, please. I'm in the middle of a show—a roaring good mystery—and it will only take fifteen minutes or so." She turned her head up towards him, smiled briefly and returned to the television.

Without offence at her offhandedness, Gerry went into the bedroom, took off his jacket and tie and hung them carefully on the chair back and crossed through to the kitchen.

"Want a drink?" he asked.

"Not right now," Eleanor responded with a wave of her hand that signalled her desire for silence from him.

"Hey," he interrupted a minute later. "We're nearly out of scotch."

"Put something in the pot, boy," was all she said.

Chuckling, he returned to the bedroom, extracted twenty dollars from his wallet and returned to the kitchen where he opened a cupboard and put the money in a jar that already housed a loose collection of small bills and change.

Pouring himself a drink in a large glass and loading it with ice, he returned to the living room and sprawled at length on the sofa directly across from where she sat. Looking at her, he saw her unadorned face flickering with the brief emotions fed to her from the television. Whatever she did she did with total absorption and with competence. But she was a one thing at a time person— work was work, food was food, drink was drink and sex was sex. He grinned to himself in recollection. Yes, indeed! Sex was indeed sex with her! Tall, solid and heavy in her body but with a small and handsome face, she sat unconcerned under his gaze, her loose robe showing that it was her only garment.

The program finished and before the credits rolled she got to her feet and turned off the set. Stretching, she said, "That was a good grabber. Too bad you don't like mysteries. Now, I think I'd like that drink."

"What would you like?"

"Did you finish the scotch?"

"Nearly."

"Damn," she said, picking up his drink and taking a large swallow. "Phew!"

she continued after making a face. "No wonder we're out of scotch—when did you start drinking it straight?" Then, getting no response except a grin, "How about making me a Martini?"

"Okay," he said, agreeably, knowing her complete disregard for the social niceties of drinking. She drank what she fancied when she had an urge for it. In the kitchen, he mixed her a double Martini, nineteen to one, not bothering with the olive and poured it into a brandy snifter loaded with ice. She hated the delicate shallow cocktail glasses that held so little and had to be handled so carefully. As he mixed her drink, he could see her move through the living room, turning down lights, tidying and selecting records. When he brought the drink to her she had reseated herself comfortably on the sofa. He sat beside her.

"That's good," she said, tasting her drink. "Just the way I like it."

"Good," he replied.

"That was really a good show," she continued. "I really like good mysteries."

He made no response and they sat in comfortable silence listening to the music. Then, out of his unconscious because he had not been thinking of his wife, he suddenly asked, "Did Marion call?" There was no reply and the quality of the silence between them changed subtly.

"Sorry," he said, remembering their rule too late. "It's just that I didn't get her when I called home and...," he finished lamely.

There was a continued silence, broken eventually when Eleanor said quietly and coldly, "No, she didn't."

Gerry picked up his glass and swirled the ice cubes noisily in the glass. Struggling to return to their easy twoness, he asked, "Have you eaten?"

She nodded and said, "Yes." Then, picking up the loosened threads, she asked, "Did you?"

"Yes," he replied quickly, grateful for her effort to get things back to normal. "A good dinner. Chicken stew. What did you have?"

"Oh, a real gourmet's delight," she replied. "Meat pie, nicely charred on the outside and frozen inside, topped with catsup and surrounded by heaps of cottage cheese with mayonnaise."

"Bleagh-gh!" he said, and she laughed.

She finished her drink and put the glass on the floor beside her. Then twisting sideways, without any attempt to curl up beside him, she leaned over and with one hand undid his shirt buttons while the other rested loosely and playfully on the back of his neck. Slipping her hand inside his shirt, she gently rubbed his ribs and ran her fingers over his nipples and the hair on his chest. He permitted her to play briefly before he reached out and put an encircling arm under her robe. Without any enticement from him she began to press towards him. Her free hand now undid his belt, the waistband catch and zipper then moved purposefully down under his underwear.

"Come on, Tiger," she said. "Let's not waste a good thing," and she got up and moved across the room to the bedroom.

If there was any such thing as love in their relationship it was never stated in words. If there was any love play in their relationship it had already taken place. What there was between them was a long and solid understanding of each other's physical needs, and a carefully guarded agreement that there was no future. He needed to reassure himself periodically that his body was under his control, that he could withhold or give whatever the surging passions of his partner. Eleanor gave him a challenge every time he entered her body—a body so lacking in grace and femininity that, in his mind, there could never be a true affair. She challenged him in other ways too, with her blunt, honest mind and her fraternal ways. Without sex they could have been buddies. For her, he was equally remote as a person. What he had, she wanted and the well of passion within her was large and deep and rarely had been plumbed until they met and, by an almost unspoken understanding, recognized each other's needs. Sex between them was a challenge and a journey, each proceeding by a different great circle route to the same distant goal. The violence of her demands and the volcanic fire of her need never failed to erupt within him a mountain of passion. Few men she had known could sustain the demanding turmoil she brought to bed. And if Gerry withheld masterfully until the vesuvius of her need, she little cared if his control was less intended to master her than it was to reassert his domination over his own body. Once, when he had drunk too much, she had carried him in her great arms to her bed and there, leisurely, slowly, climactically she had rolled and played with him like a great mother bear, using him at her will and well and truly raping him. He had been furious and unforgiving, had indeed carried his cold fury into the office, and for their next half dozen meetings had cruelly left her searching for the flood to quench her fire. After that debacle the ground rules for their relationship had been laid and honoured.

Tonight, wrapped and twisted together, long before any abandoned action from her, she paused and asked, "Gerry? are you going to marry me?" The question, the answer to which they long ago found an answer, so unsettled him that he lost control and exploded and finished.

"What did you say?" he demanded, pulling himself out of her arms, his voice almost a squeak.

"I said, are you going to marry me."

"Whatever made you think..." he started to say, sitting up beside her, then paused and looked at her in the dim light. "What in God's name did you ask that for?" in a voice that was gritting and furious.

"You were murmuring sweet nothings in my ear," she said, matter-of-factly.

"I was!?" and now his voice was full of disbelief and amazement. Then, believing her, he simply said, "Sorry."

"Okay," she said, smiling. Then, in a more reproving tone, she added, "Just don't get carried away. The last thing I want is to get involved."

He burst into laughter, slapped her on the bottom and flung himself down beside her, his flare of anger gone.

"You know what I mean," she said.

He made no more reply than a simple "Yeah."

They lay quietly side by side, not touching each other except for the joining of hands between their bodies.

"Sorry I left you in the lurch," he said with a little laugh. "But you had no one to blame but yourself."

"No problem," she replied. "I never would have interrupted the performance if I thought I couldn't get you to go for two."

"Hey, lady," he said with a laugh. "Who do you think is in charge around here?"

She looked at him with a cocked eyebrow and said, "It's a puzzle, isn't it? But while you're trying to figure it out, how about a drink?"

"Good idea," he responded, swinging his legs off the bed.

He went into the bathroom and then out to the kitchen while she stretched out on her elbow watching him. In the dim light his white buttocks with its butterfly gleamed in contrast to the dark tan of the rest of his body.

"Gin?" he called.

"Yes, and tonic, please."

Bringing their drinks to the bed, he lay beside her. Facing each other slightly, each head propped on a folded arm, they lay quietly drinking and talking of small things. Then, finishing their drinks in unison, they moved together.

***

Craig had charged out of the house and bounced and skittered out of the yard and up the street to the Turner's like a lamb in a clover patch. Standing in the kitchen talking congenially with Rob's mother while waiting for Rob to appear, he shone with excitement. When Rob put in his quiet appearance at the door, each donned their adolescent masks of implacability and started the ritual of non-committal.

Craig started. "Hi! Whatcha doin'?"

"Nothing. Just homework."

"Finished?"

"Yeah."

"What d'ya wanna do now?"

"I dunno. What do you wanna do?"

"Want to go up to the park?"

"Yeah, okay," said Rob. And then to his mother as if she had been deaf to their conversation, "I'm going up to the park with Craig."

"Have you finished your homework?" came the automatic maternal response.

And equally automatically came the schoolboy lie, "Yeah, we didn't have nothing anyway."

Craig waited until they were half a block away. He was measuring his steps with Rob's longer stride, his hands plunged deeply into his pockets. As casually as he could force it he said, "My mom said I could get a car this summer."

Rob stopped in his tracks and stared at Craig in disbelief. "You're kidding," he said and his adolescent voice cracked as he continued, "I don't believe you! You're nuts!"

"No, really! Honest to God!" And Craig was now bouncing and bubbling with his news. "She really did!" And he reviewed in precise detail the whole of his conversation with his mother.

"That's different," Rob said when Craig had finished. "She only said she would talk to your dad about it." But in his mind, as in Craig's, the matter was firmly settled—Craig would be getting a car this summer and summer was so close it was almost tomorrow.

At the park they sat on the edge of a ballgame knowing neither the players nor the score. Cadging a couple cigarettes, they smoked neither openly nor furtively and talked.

"What kind of car are you going to get?" Rob asked.

"Oh, I dunno." Craig replied cautiously. "But I hope my dad will let me get a little import sports car—like that Mazda with the radial engine?" he finished on a questioning note.

Rob's response was a laughing snort. "Sure!" he said derisively. "Or maybe a Corvette or a Thunderbird. How about a Porsche? You'd look good in a Porsche! The girls would really go for that." Then seeing his friend's stricken face because of his disloyal lack of enthusiasm he stopped his ridicule and said, "Oh, he'll probably let you have an old Toyota or a Rabbit. I know that's what my dad would do."

"Oh, I dunno," Craig responded uncertainly, knowing that his friend was probably right but hating to have the bubble burst.

"Well, it won't be a sports car anyway," said Rob with finality. "You can bet your ass on that. The insurance would cost too much."

"Well, I could pay the extra insurance if I got a job," Craig persisted.

"That's not the point with parents," was Rob's rejoinder.

Feeling the chill of the May night settling in, they got to their feet and wandered away from the final inning of the ballgame. Taking a ball from a couple of small boys they had a game of catch over the heads of the shrill and leaping owners before throwing the ball far across the field and pretending for the boys that they were going to run after it too. They flung themselves violently around a steel framed merry go round, keeping a half dozen smaller children at bay by the speed, then walked through a skipping game out of the park to the coffee shop on the corner. Seated side by side on stools at the counter, their knees and shoulders pressing against each other casually reinforcing their friendship. The afternoon was part of the receding past. The moment was the car and the coming summer.

Marion Williams had collected and washed the few dishes from their supper and found herself again with the prospects of an evening alone. She went out into the garden with a sweater draped over her shoulders against the cooling evening air and circled the borders, picking the occasional obvious weed, examining the work that needed to be done and making casual plans for it. She hoped Gerry would help her with the heavier work but knew sensibly that any

Saturday or Sunday, now that winter was over, he would argue that his golf schedule was more important, that he needed the exercise after sitting around an office all winter. "Oh, well," she said, startling herself because she had said it aloud, "I'll get old Mr. Wasliyn to help me—he always needs the money." Going back into the house, she leafed through the evening paper finding nothing that demanded her attention. A novel she had started days ago also failed to absorb her. With half an ear cocked for the telephone thinking that Edith might call again on her birthday, she turned on the television and, searching the channels found the beginning of a murder mystery. Halfway through she heard Craig come in and trilled an "Hello, dear," to his shouted "Hi, Mom," as he went directly to the basement. The mystery came to an end and she realized that she had dozed off and she let herself fall into the next program without a critical thought. Then she heard Craig call "Goodnight, Mom," as he headed upstairs. "Don't I get a kiss goodnight?" she called. "Oh, sorry," Craig called from the top of the stairs. "Here, I'll throw you one. Catch it!" She heard his bedroom door closed. "I'll bet he's been smoking again, she said to herself. That's why he wouldn't come down and kiss me goodnight. Oh, I wish he wouldn't smoke. I wonder if Rob's mother knows they are smoking on the sly." Suddenly, it was late and she was tired.

She switched off all the house lights except for one in the living room and the front porch light and, with a tired walk, went to the bedroom. With her shoes and her dress off, she caught sight of herself in the double mirrors of the closet. She stood still for a minute gazing at herself and then, "Happy Birthday to you, Happy Birthday to you," she said, singing tunelessly and unhappily to the short, greying, white-slipped reflection.

Then the tears came.

"The bastard!" she said in a hoarse, shaky voice, shocking herself with her own language but finding it strangely satisfying. "The selfish, thoughtless, miserable—" and she searched for more words—"impotent bastard," finishing in a loud shriek.

She cried into the mirror in the bathroom. She cried into the unseen pages of her book. She wept into her pillow in the darkness of her room until, drained, she dropped into a fitful sleep and dreamed that Tom Thomas sat beside her and hung tightly to her hand as they plunged down the alleys of a screaming roller coaster. She wakened and stirred when Gerry turned his night light on.

"Hello, dear," he said quietly. "I didn't mean to waken you."

"I wasn't really sleeping," she replied in a froggy voice. Then, her domesticity stirring, she added tonelessly, "Did you get some dinner?"

"Yes, I did," he answered. "Didn't Craig tell you? I stopped at the gym for a workout and then had some dinner."

She said "Good," in a voice entirely devoid of feeling.

She watched him as he undressed in an unvarying pattern. He emptied his pockets, brushed his jacket before hanging it in the closet over carefully creased slacks, then placed his shoes on a rack and put his shirt and underwear in the hamper. His tanned, nude and muscular body moved back and forth across her line of vision and against her will she felt warm and loving and forgiving. He went out of the bedroom into the bathroom unselfconscious of his nudity and oblivious to its effect on her. She listened to him performing his nightly bathroom ritual. She heard him click off the bathroom light, saw him return to the bedroom, watched him in the dim light as he put on the bottom half of his pyjamas, felt their bed move as he pulled back the covers and rolled into it and smelled him in the darkness as he turned off the light and turned towards her to kiss her dutifully goodnight.

"You've been drinking," she said without reproach.

"Yes," he admitted openly, not hearing any note of disapproval. "I stopped in at a bar after I made my call and had a couple of drinks and got talking."

She said nothing.

"Goodnight, dear," he said after a silence, and after kissing her lightly again, he rolled over with his back to her.

She lay curled on her side feeling something she could not really comprehend. How could she be angry, hurt, disappointed and still feel like she wanted him? Slowly she extended her leg and finding his shin, she rubbed the sole of her foot against it.

"Don't, Marion," he said immediately, with a note of irritation in his voice and withdrawing his leg. "I'm tired. Go to sleep!"

Whether it was the tone of voice, the jerky withdrawal from her touch, the final rejection, the lateness of the hour, the strangeness of the day or the time of the month, she didn't know. Something in her clicked irrevocably off and she felt an immense relief and sadness and sorrow. Turning quickly away she buried her face in her pillow, trying vainly to stifle the sobs that surged suddenly from her.

"Marion?" he said, reaching over and laying a hand gently on her hip. "I really am sorry, but I am tired," half in honesty and half in defence.

He listened to her sobs. "Marion?" he said again, almost pleadingly. "Marion?"

Then in a shrieking voice, racked by sobs, she blurted, "It was my birthday!" as if by that she could explain everything.

"Jesus Christ," he muttered to himself. Turning to her, he pulled her over to him, forcing her resisting body to face his own, talking to her over her protests, telling her he was sorry and that they would do something special tomorrow. He held her tight in his arms stroking her back and hair, kissing her neck, restraining her struggles and waiting for his own body to react.

"Leave me alone!" she half shrieked. "Just don't touch me!"

He was too intent on inner things to hear the finality in her voice.

"C'mon, body," he said to himself. But there was no response.

CHAPTER 11

Marion put the phone down and sighed. It was always such a task to keep up with Edith on the phone. Any conversation was interrupted by Edith's admonitions to the children and made difficult because Edith really never listened even to herself—she just talked. But Marion called her daughter routinely in part because she realized Edith's need to talk to another adult. Lord only knows she didn't get much satisfaction out of talking to Harvey, an agreeable, gentle man who rarely read anything except bedtime stories to his children and who appeared to enjoy the books as much as they did. She had promised Edith to come out for three days to give her a break from the twins but she was not looking forward to sitting across the table from Harvey if Edith planned on being out for dinner with girl friends. She was amazed that Gerry was so patient with Harvey when ever they came in to town. Maybe to have someone hanging on his every word and asking for his advice on everything except mechanical problems was good for Gerry's ego. Not that his ego needs much boosting, she thought bitterly—that is, if ego is equated with selfishness. Again her mind went back to the night two months ago when everything had seemed to come to a head and she had made a decision. Since then she had not changed her mind and, although she was filled with regret at times, she could not see that the dim uncharted future that lay ahead was less appealing than the thought of continuing in the pattern her life had taken during the past fifteen years.

She found herself out in the garden, having wandered out while troubled thoughts tumbled around in her head. She had involuntarily picked weeds and plucked off dead blossom and found that she had wiped the dirt from her fingers off on the legs of her good pants forgetting that she was not wearing her gardening clothes. "Oh, for goodness sake! What's wrong with me?" she scolded herself. She had already changed into light clothes to drive out to Edith's in the hot August afternoon because her old Buick had no air conditioning. (The thought crossed her mind that Gerry had never had a car that she could remember that didn't have air conditioning—and she tucked the fact away as another indicator of his selfishness.) "Now I'll have to change again." At the same time she realized that she was perspiring from her exertions in the heat of the late morning sun, and feeling a little exasperated with herself she hurried inside to shower, change and repack her travelling bag.

Marion made an easy sandwich for herself which she ate standing by the kitchen window looking out into the garden. Glancing at the clock she saw that it was well past the time that Craig would have come home for lunch if school was in, but now he took a lunch pail to his summer job in the shipping department of a paper company. She missed the lunchtimes they had together. She didn't see much of him these days, but she did frequently recall the wonderful joy she felt when he flung his arms around her and thanked her for arranging for driving lessons for him and for her promise to let him use her car sometimes as soon as he got his license. He'd be disappointed that he couldn't use it for the next three days. Rob and Craig were as thick as thieves again. She occasionally puzzled about what had happened between them last year when they had such a serious falling out. It tore her heart out to see Craig so miserable and lonely. They were even more inseparable now that Rob had his driver's licence. Rob's sister had taken him out for practise driving several times because his father wouldn't. She had tried to get Gerry to take Craig out but he said he "just didn't have time." She took him out once and they drove over to the school parking lot but some of Craig's classmates saw them and razzed Craig about his mother teaching him to drive, so she got Rob to go with Craig for practise driving. Gerry was furious and ranted on and on about liabilities. She had simply said, "If you don't like it, then you stick around and teach your son." Craig had heard some of that exchange between his parents and it seemed to put a damper on some of his enthusiasm. She thought that maybe it served a purpose in the long run, because Craig was being careful and sometimes acted as if he couldn't care less about getting his licence, as if the responsibility was too much for him.

She checked the frig again out of habit to reassure herself that she had left enough that Craig and his father could find something for themselves if they wanted to. She knew that Gerry wouldn't bother to fix anything for himself, he would rather eat out, but if they were home together Gerry would tell Craig to make something for them both. She had made two casseroles for them but she knew that one, if not both casseroles would be still there when she returned. So, because the cooler she was taking was already filled with cookies and jellies and other things for her grandchildren, she took the larger casserole out, wrapped it in several sheets of newspaper and put it by her travelling bag to take with her. Then, collecting her coat and purse and all the other things she was taking to her daughter, she packed the car, closed the house and left.

CHAPTER 12

At noon, Craig joined the group of men who had grabbed their lunchboxes and were now sprawled on a strip of grass beside the plant in the July sun. The talk among the regular employees drifted between complaints about management, drinking parties and women but rarely anything, even sports, to which Craig or two other high school kids who had summer jobs, could contribute. The other boys were sons of employees and they grumbled constantly about having to work under the eagle eyes of both the foreman and their respective fathers. Both were older than Craig and went to a different school and he found them to be sometimes unfriendly and patronizing. The rule, which seemed to be paternally set, was work hard, work fast, keep your nose clean and don't make waves. Craig resented the way in which the two fathers thought they had the responsibility to ride herd on him as well as their sons, but he kept his cool and did his "Yes sirs, no sirs." He was glad he didn't have to work with his father. At home his father was getting to be harder than ever to please. He used to work with Craig in the garden when there was a big job to do but lately he just sat around and was not even playing golf as much as he used to. Craig figured he must be drinking a lot more. One night he came home very late and his mother had gone to bed and his father had fallen asleep in his chair with the television on. When Craig shook his arm to wake him up, his father got angry and jumped to his feet, roaring, "Turn off that damn television and get to bed!"

Without really listening, the three boys tired quickly of the talk of the men and, as they did every noon hour, managed to escape without being noticed. Apart from boredom, the other two were always anxious to get off the lot at noon to have a smoke, neither of them wanting to smoke openly and suffer the lecture about kids these days smoking that was certain to come, if not from a father, from somebody with a hacking cough and nicotine stained fingers. Craig did not smoke at work even when offered a cigarette. He and Rob smoked occasionally in the park but neither of them had bought cigarettes for a long time and Craig was not even sure he liked it. Rob was working in a Supermarket two blocks away from the factory where Craig worked but their hours were different so that they couldn't ride the same bus to work or after. Today Craig wanted to catch Rob at noon to tell him that his mother had taken her car out to see Edith and that she would be away until the weekend so they wouldn't have her car.

"Hey, man! How're ya doin?" Rob said when Craig finally found him stocking some shelves. "You missed a great party last night."

"Yeah, well... I had some things to do," Craig lied. The truth was that Rob hadn't mentioned anything about a party to him, and besides his mother wanted to talk to him about going out to Edith's and the casseroles and stuff she had left for him. "Who was there?" he asked, feigning interest.

"Oh, a couple of guys from the store and their girlfriends. We went to the beach for a while and then up to one of the guy's sister's place. She was away on holidays but this guy had a key and we went and hung out there."

"You mean there were five of you?" Craig said with an unbelieving face.

"No, don't be stupid," Rob said. "And pick up a basket and put something in it like you're shopping, The boss raises hell with us if he thinks our friends are just hanging around. No, I wasn't alone," he continued. "I was with a girl from the store here. Jeez, was she stupid," keeping his voice low. "Pretending that she had the hots...." He broke off as an elderly woman asked him to help her get a flour sack into her cart. Then the assistant manager sent Rob off to get something from the stockroom so Craig walked away and back to work feeling slighted that Rob had new friends that were taking his place. He had forgotten to tell Rob about his mother taking her car out to Edith's or to ask him what he was going to do tonight.

When Craig got home he drank some milk straight out of the carton and searched the shelves for the cookies he had seen her making and then gave up on the search figuring that she had taken them out to Edith's. He clicked through the television channels and found nothing but news and game shows and turned the set off. He was settling down on the sofa to study his Driving Handbook when the telephone rang. "Too early for Rob," he thought. "Maybe it's Mom or Dad."

With that thought he picked up the phone and said, "Hello," with a carefully modulated voice.

"That's better, Craig," came the voice of his father. "That sounds more like you learned some manners somewhere."

"Oh, hi, Dad," was all Craig could think of to say. Then, after a moment he continued, "Mom went out to Edith's, I guess."

"I know that," his father said brusquely. "I called to tell you that I wouldn't be home. You get yourself something or go out to eat if you want to. Your mother will have some housekeeping money in the buffet drawer."

"I've got some money," Craig replied. "I don't need to take hers. Besides," he said, attempting some levity, "she'll give me the third degree if she finds some money gone."

"If she does, you can tell her I said you could take it," came the severe reply. Craig made a grimace and shrugged. "What are you going to do tonight—hang out with Rob?" his father continued.

"Yeah, probably. Maybe we'll go to a show."

"That sounds like a good idea. Maybe we should do that sometime."

"Do what?" said Craig.

"Go to a show. You and me."

"Wha-a-at?" Craig's voice was full of disbelief.

"Well, what's wrong with that? Lots of fathers and sons go to the movies together." The voice was parental and stern.

"I didn't mean... I thought that... You don't usually...," and Craig came to a stumbling halt.

"Yes, I know," said his father. "Have a good time," and hung up abruptly.

Gerry sat for a while in the quiet of his office. He had stayed on the pretext of having work to do after everyone else had left. Eleanor had simply nodded when he said goodnight as she tidied up and prepared to leave. Earlier when he had indicated that he would like to come over he had received the signalled rebuff coldly made. I'm getting it from all quarters, he thought. Something's got Eleanor's back up. I don't know what. Not me, as he shrugged off that responsibility. Craig thinks the idea of going to a show with me is from outer space. Marion is sleeping so far away from me she is due to fall out of her side of the bed. He had approached her in bed twice since the big blow-up about her birthday.

The first time she had said, "Stop it! Just stop it!" and had grabbed a blanket and slept on the sofa. The next time, and it was a very tentative approach, she had literally screamed at him, "Take your god damned dirty fucking hands away from me. If you try anything one more time, I'm moving into Edith's room." He was stunned by the vehemence of her response and by her language. He had never heard her swear before, except for an occasional mild profanity, but never an obscenity, and she usually made a tsk-tsk whenever anyone she knew was vulgar or obscene. But before he could stop himself he had said, "You do and I'm out of here." Immediately he regretted the ultimatum but it was said and there was no way he would retract it. He knew, too, that Marion meant what she said. Eventually, he had shrugged it off. "If that's the way she wants it, then its okay with me. It shouldn't be too hard to do without sex with her."

He closed up his desk and left the office with plans to go to the gym and then to someplace for dinner that had a good bar.

Rob called Craig after he got home from work and they talked for a while trying to make a decision about what show they would see if they were going to see a show. Craig said during a lengthy silence, "Hey, you know what? My dad called, and guess what? He asked if we could go out to a movie—him and me!"

"Wha-a-at?" said Rob and the intonation of the word matched Craig's earlier response to his father exactly. "He didn't!"

"Yes, he did. He was serious."

"Jeez!" came Rob's response. "If my Dad had asked me that, I'da shit."

"Asked you what?" came Rob's mother's voice over the phone.

"Oh, nothing. I was just talking to Craig." Craig heard Rob's mumbled excuses to his mother terminated by the maternal "Watch your language, anyway." Then he heard Rob's final "Hurry up and come over," as he hung up.

CHAPTER 13

"When are you and Dad coming up to the cottage for your holidays?" Edith asked, and continued without waiting for an answer. "When we got here, I thought you and Dad would have been up for a long weekend at least, but nobody's been up since we closed it up when Harvey and I were up last Thanksgiving. Everything was just like we left it. But there sure was a lot of spring cleaning to do. I guess it was really summer cleaning. You should have seen the spider webs. Ach-ch!. I hate spiders. Harv had to go around with a rag tied to the broom before I would even go in. Iona! Don't bother Grandma. Go find your sister and play. Where is that little devil anyway. Oh, there you are! I see you, you little monkey. You two go on outside and play. Go on now!" And the two little girls gave a happy scream and scampered for the door when their mother picked up a fly swatter and stamped her feet in little steps in their direction. "Go find your daddy," she added as the girls slammed the screen door behind them.

At the kitchen table where she sat snapping beans, Marion smiled at the frenetic family interactions that were habitual with Edith. She had arrived the day before, late in the afternoon, to discover Edith nervously awaiting her—anxious for her arrival because she and Harvey were going to a supper dance at the municipal hall. Both were dressed for the dance, and as Marion kissed her grandchildren, she heard that there was a light supper for you and the girls in the frig, the girls didn't need a bath tonight, don't let them tease the dog next door, sorry to rush away when you just got here, I was expecting you for lunch, we won't be late—and they were gone. Marion got her bag and all the things she had put together to surprise Edith and took them into the cottage. "Well," she said to herself, "I said I would come out and let Edith have a break and that's what she's doing, so I better not be disappointed by the reception."

Edith had sent Harvey out early in the morning to the local farmers' market to buy some beans. "If they're cheap," she had said, "get a big bagful. You won't mind green beans two nights in a row, will you, Mom?" And Harvey had indeed brought back a big bag so the two women set about companionably to make dilly beans.

"Were the girls good last night while we were out?" asked Edith as she sat opposite her mother arranging beans vertically in jars.

"Oh, yes. As good as gold," Marion replied. "Iona was trying to be so grown up and independent. She was really playing the little hostess and looking after me. She was so cute. Jenny was a little miffed because I guess I was paying more attention than I should have to Iona. I try not to play favourites but I can't help it sometimes ever since you told me where you got her name—by dropping the "Mar" from my name and adding an "A".

"I knew it would tickle you. It's a cute name, isn't it? And there's no way to shorten it. Not like Jennifer. That's why we named her Jenny on her birth certificate. Did we ever tell you we thought of naming her after Harv's mother? But her name is Agnes and the only thing we could come up with was to do the same thing we did with your name but it came out Nessa and we both laughed so hard we just called her Jenny after nobody." And Edith stopped sorting beans and whooped with laughter at the memory until there were tears in her eyes.

Marion laughed gently with her daughter, happily amazed that Edith seemed so content with her life. She always seemed to be so stretched out and on edge that it was a delight to see a side of her that she hadn't seen since Edith was a child.

Then suddenly the everyday Edith was back on duty. "So how come Dad couldn't take a couple of days off and come out with you?" Edith demanded. "Harv would have really liked to see him, and me too," she added hastily. "And the girls. He might even have got Harvey out on a golf course. I wish he would take up golf or something. You know, he's a really good dancer, Mom. You'd never know it, would you? But once the music starts, he's on his feet rarin' to go."

As usual with Edith, Marion did not know what part of the monologue to respond to but she avoided the serious and simply said "Well, Harvey always moved like he was light on his feet."

"Yes, he is," was the response. "But why didn't Dad want to come?"

"Well, Edith, maybe I didn't tell him he was invited. And to tell the truth you never made it clear that you wanted both of us to come when I offered to come and give you some time to yourself without the children."

"Mom!" Edith said, looking at her mother with that look of puzzlement that on Edith's face was frequently confused with anger.

"Why wouldn't I want Dad to come too?" But it was less a question than a scolding.

"Edith! I didn't even mean to suggest anything like that. It's just that…, well, everybody needs to get away from each other every so often," she stumbled. "I mean, I just didn't tell him he was invited, that's all there's to it. So please, just let the matter drop and don't go snooping around trying to find something when there isn't anything." As soon as she said it she was sorry because she knew Edith would take what she had said and worry it like a dog with a rag.

"There is something wrong, isn't there? Dad's not sick or anything, is he?

It's Craig then, isn't it? What's he done now?" "Edith! Stop it! Right now! I've said all I'm going to say, and further more it really isn't any of your affair if your father and I happen to have a difference of opinion, and if you don't stop I'll pack my bag and go home."

"Oh, Mom, I'm so sorry." Edith moved over to her mother and knelt and put her arms around her. She held her without speaking but Marion could feel the jerky breath that she remembered so clearly as Edith's way of covering up a hurt. Finally, Edith was able to say, "It'll be alright, Mom. Things have a way of getting right again, You'll see." And then, getting quickly to her feet she went out the door trailing her justification for a hurried exit, "I better check on the twins. Harvey lets them run wild."

When Marion looked out the window a few minutes later she watched her daughter talking agitatedly to Harvey and then she saw Harvey reach out and hold her in his arms with quiet tenderness and it touched her deeply. Just as she was trying to hide her distress both grandchildren burst into the house demanding, "Grandma! Grandma! Hurry! Come see!" each insistently tugging a hand. The girls had found a bird's nest fallen from a tree. They could not trust her to replace the nest and they raced away to find Daddy, because he would know how to do it. "Don't touch it, Grandma!" one of them warned.

When Harvey approached he gave no indication that he and Edith had just talked very personally about her. With the utmost gravity he followed the instructions of his daughters as to the exact placement of the nest in the tree. When the job was finished he smiled at Marion as he tousled their hair when they each hugged a leg in gratitude. She felt another quick surge of emotion and turned away quickly, saying, "I need a little exercise, Harvey. Maybe I'll just stay out and help you tidy up."

"Sure, Marion," he said. "I'll get you a better rake. The one I'm using has a slivery handle."

In the pleasant warmth of the afternoon, a time of day that Marion loved, they worked together tidying up a yard that had not been touched since the fall. Harvey's pace was slow and methodical but she soon noticed that if she spoke Harvey stopped to listen and if he spoke to her he had to stay still. She amused herself for a while by saying something just as he readied himself to start raking again and watched his mechanical start-stop action. But soon she became ashamed of her childishness and went steadily to work with him.

After an hour or more, Edith came out with the girls and joined them in the yard. As soon as Marion saw her she said, "Oh, Edith. I'm sorry! I left you to finish all those beans by yourself"

"That's alright, Mother. I like putting up pickles. And the girls and I had a good gossip about what a nice grandmother they have. And look what you two have been doing! But you shouldn't be doing that, Mom," she chided. "Just look at your hands—all scratched from those vines."

"Well, now. Who do you think does the gardening at home?" and could have bitten her tongue as the words came out knowing that Edith would hear them as another indicator of the rift she saw developing between her mother and father.

If Edith had read any hidden meaning to her words, she gave no sign. Instead, in her usual direct way, she said, "The girls and I are going for a walk on the beach before dinner. Won't you come with us?"

"I'd like to do that," Marion replied. "Just let me freshen up a little. I don't want to look like a grub if we run into some of your friends. I'll just be a minute. Okay with you, boss?" she asked Harvey with a smile and he acknowledged the question only with a big grin.

"Are you coming, too, Harv?"

"No," he replied. "I'll stay and put the tools away. It's going to rain."

"Mom," Edith shouted to her mother's retreating back. "Tell the girls to hurry, will you? Harvey says it's going to rain."

And it did rain—sooner than anyone expected. They had been far along the beach when the storm hit with sudden violence. Each taking a child's hand they ran for the cottage with the girls squealing with excitement. Harvey waited at the open door wearing a worried look until he heard their laughter, then he shepherded them into the kitchen and gave them towels. The children stood dripping and shivering as they tried to tell their father everything that happened and begged to go out again. The storm worsened with sharp cracks of thunder and brilliant flashes of lightning. Drying the girls quickly and rushing them into dry clothes and warm jackets, they cuddled together, all five, on the veranda to watch the display. Whatever tension Marion thought she might have created seemed to have melted away. Warmed by the bodies of her daughter and grandchildren, filled, as much as a child, with wonder at the magnificence of the display, she felt more relaxed than she had for weeks.

The storm raged on with the flashes of close lightning giving a second of warning for the ear splitting explosions of thunder overhead not much louder than the excited squeals of the children. Counting the seconds between the far-off flashes and the ensuing thunder, they amused themselves by guessing how far away the strike had been until, following a flash of startling brilliance and a thunderclap that was so loud they could feel it, the lights went out. Such storms were a part of their summer and they busied themselves using up the last rays of the day and settling the children who were halfway between excited and scared. Edith set about planning supper while Harvey lighted the wood stove and Marion helped the girls into their night clothes laughing with them in their delight in having had a shower already so they didn't need a bath. Darkness came and they had supper by candlelight.

Edith and Harvey had planned to go to friends for the evening but their friends drove by to tell them that their roof had leaked and everything was soaked and the party had been cancelled. Harvey was reading another bedtime story by the light of a candle to the delight of the girls and Edith and Marion were trotting out all their "remember when's over a second coffee when their domestic scene was interrupted by a knock on the door.

"I wonder what now," said Edith as she moved to the door and opened it for a neighbour. "Come in, Frank," she said to someone Marion could not see in the darkness.

"No thanks, Edith. I'm wet and muddy but I've got a phone message for Harv. His boss wants him back at work right away."

Hello, Harv," he said as Harvey appeared at the door trailed by the girls. "Hello, Iona. Hello, Jenny," he said to them in a little singsong voice, to which they responded by sneaking even further in behind their father's legs. "It looks like your holidays are over for awhile," he said, speaking again to Harvey. "I've written it all down. I hope I got it right. But anyway he left two numbers for you to call, one for tonight and the other for tomorrow." And he handed Harv a handwritten note.

Harvey looked at the note for a minute but did not read it. "That's really good of you, Frank. You must do a lot of running around with messages for other people. Come in, come in. Our lights are out, I guess yours are too, are they."

"No, I won't come in, thanks. I'll get on home. Yeah, the lights are out all over. I heard it on the car radio."

"Well, just step in for a second. I'd like you to meet my mother-in law," Harvey said, pushing the girls back gently to make room.

Marion had heard the exchange and came to the door. Harvey reached out a hand and placed it gently on her shoulder. "Frank," he said, and there was a note of friendly formality in his voice. "I would like you to meet my mother-in-law, Marion Williams. Marion, this is your new neighbour, Frank Tomason. I know you haven't met before because he just bought the cottage in June."

"I'm pleased to meet you, Mrs. Williams," Frank said, holding out a hand that was taken firmly by Marion.

"Marion, please," she said. "That is if I may call you Frank. Particularly if you are going to act as our telephone messenger service."

"It's no problem, Marion," Frank said. "Sometimes I'm the bearer of exciting good news. My wife, Audrey, has very bad arthritis in both ankles and doesn't get around easily, so she answers the phone and I deliver the messages and get the exercise."

"I better be on my way. Nice to have met you, Marion. If you want to call your boss, Harvey, it'll have to wait until tomorrow—the telephones went out at the same time as the power."

The family waved him on his way and closed the door against the wet, cool night.

"What a nice neighbour to have," Marion said.

"Yes, he is, isn't he? When we got here, he came right over and introduced himself and told us he didn't mind taking messages for us. He apparently said the same thing to everybody in the neighbourhood who doesn't have a telephone and said not to be shy about asking to use their phone instead of making a trip to the payphone at the store. He said his wife likes people to drop in because she doesn't get out much because of her legs," Edith responded. "Harvey? That was sweet of you to remember to introduce Mother. You always do it so nicely."

Harvey ducked his head slightly, saying "Oh...," and blushed. "Well, let's see what this message is all about." He settled himself at the table and puzzled over the note by the light of a candle.

"Well, what does he say?" demanded Edith.

"Just a minute, Edith," Harvey said patiently. And then, leaning back, he continued. "He says they are hounding him to get finished. So he wants me to come back ASAP. What does that mean?"

"It means as soon as possible," Marion interjected, then wished she hadn't intruded.

"Oh, that's what it is! Thanks." Harvey smiled and gave no indication that she had interfered.

"Hurry up, Harv!" Edith exclaimed, her impatience showing.

"Okay. He says that we can work around the clock until we are finished, with time and a half after 4:30 weekdays and double time on weekends. He says to plan on seven days. I don't know, Edith. I'll have to work this out before I phone him in the morning. But that's way better than scale."

"Let me see it, Harvey," Edith said.

Marion corralled the girls and completed the bedtime routines while Edith and Harvey got out pencil and paper and puzzled about the best solution to the problem. She read the girls a story and suggested tucking them in but they needed either a mother or a father for a proper tuck-in in the dark. Harvey was quick to see the beginnings of their distress and left Edith alone with her mother to cart them off to bed. They sat quietly for a few minutes, Edith still working at something with pencil and paper.

"Sorry, Mom, to leave you alone. Harvey thinks it is important to get back to work right away. We're just trying to figure out how to do it."

"I see," said Marion. "Is there anything I can do?"

"No, I don't think so, Mom. But thanks. Harvey would have to take the car back if he is going to work at all hours and that would leave me up here without a car for a week. He says he would worry if I was alone without a car and he thinks I should go back with him, but it means packing everything up, and then unpacking and doing the same thing in a week. I'd rather stay here. I could always walk to the store if I needed anything—I've done it before, but not with kids, of course. It sort of ruins our holiday but we worked it out that with overtime and double time, Harvey could easily make enough to pay for our whole holiday. And like Harvey says, it will put him in good with the boss and there's a lot of other projects coming up."

"It's probably not a good idea to be alone here with two small children, even if you do seem to have a neighbour with a telephone," Marion offered.

Edith shrugged and sighed and said, "Yes, you're probably right."

Harvey returned and sat down beside Edith and took her hand. "Well, what do you think, Edie?" Marion watched them as they sat close together in the flickering light of the candles. Their problem did not appear to show itself in sharp words or argument.

Rather, she heard them listening to each other and sorting out possible solutions. She suddenly felt warmly pleased that Edith could show such maturity.

"Oh, Harv! I just don't know. I hate to leave, but I know you have to and I wish you wouldn't worry about me being alone—just for a week."

"I know—I'm sorry," he said.

The three of them sat in a comfortable silence until Marion said quietly, "I have an idea."

"What, Mom?" queried Edith.

"Well, it might work and it might not. It would be easier if we had a telephone, I suppose." At that point, the lights flickered on and went off again, and there was a disappointing groan from all three. Then the lights went on and they sat quietly, expectantly until it appeared that the power outage was over and they happily blew out the candles and set about putting the house in order again.

"What's your idea, Mom?" Edith asked while she was still tidying up.

"I just thought that you really shouldn't be here without a car, Edith. So if Harvey takes the car he can get away early and perhaps get half a day in tomorrow, that's Friday, and we'll still have my car here. Then I can call your Dad and ask him to come up Saturday and drive me home so that I can leave my car here for you for the rest of your holidays. That's what I meant when I said it would be easier if we had a phone. I think it's too late now," she said, looking at her watch, "to use your neighbour's phone."

The other two had listened to her without interruption and then Harvey was the first to speak. "Marion, you really don't need to do that. I don't have to go back to work. Besides you need your car in town. What would you think of driving me to the highway and I'll catch a bus. Then maybe you could stay another few days if Gerry and Craig don't mind and Edith wouldn't be alone."

"I can't stay longer, really I can't. There are too many things I have to do." She was lying and she saw Edith's sharp look as if she knew her mother was lying.

"Mom, I can't let you do that. It isn't—."

"Now look, you two," Marion interrupted in a firm voice. "That's a perfectly reasonable solution. It just means getting in touch with your dad so that he can come and pick me up. And I don't mind being without a car, really I don't. I don't use it that much and anything I have to do next week I can easily do by bus or by getting one of my friends to drive for a change. Goodness knows I have driven them around enough for the past few years so maybe it's time for a payback. So that's that."

Edith said, "Mom!" in a tone that said, "We can't! You shouldn't!" But Harvey got up, walked across the room, and leaning over, gave Marion a soft kiss on the forehead, then returned to his place beside Edith.

After a minute, Marion said, "Well, I expect you two have got some packing and planning to do. I think I'll just head for bed and catch up on my reading." She got up, kissed her daughter goodnight, then, placing her hands on Harvey's shoulders so that he would not get to his feet, returned his kiss in the same manner. There was no way that she could mistake the look on his face as anything but pleasure.

She tried to read for a while in bed but she found she was turning a page mechanically without knowing what she had read. Her thoughts were in a turmoil. She half suspected that Gerry would try to get out of driving up to get her. But she couldn't see any other way to help her daughter and Harvey.

"He really is a fine young man," she thought. She had never been certain that Edith knew what she was doing when she rushed into marriage. "Perhaps she knew a good thing when she saw it," she mused. "Smarter than me, maybe."

She turned out her reading light and tried to sleep but she could hear them trying to be quiet as they packed and got ready for Harvey's early departure. There was soft knock on her door and Edith entered quietly.

"Are you awake, Mom?" Edith asked softly in the dark.

"Yes, dear. What is it? I just now turned off the light."

"You didn't leave your car keys out, and Harvey would like to get away really early but your car is parked behind ours."

"Oh, of course. That was thoughtless of me. They're in my purse over there on the chair."

The light from the hall was enough for Edith to find the purse and sort the car keys from a larger ring. Then she came back to the bed and sat on the edge looking down at her mother. Suddenly Edith flung her arms around her mother. "Oh, Mom! You really are wonderful, you know. And that's what Harv's been saying for the last half hour, too."

"Oh, sweetheart! I'm just happy I could do something useful. And I was just lying here thinking what a fine young man he is and how lucky you were to find him."

Edith kissed her mother and tucked the blankets around her. She said a soft "Goodnight. Sleep well," and closed the door quietly behind her.

Sleep evaded Marion. The night was still and quiet. Try as she might, she could not help but hear the sounds of passion next door. She covered her head with a pillow and hoped that her daughter's sex life was more fulfilling than her own. Finally she fell asleep only to wake with a start from a vividly explicit sexual dream about Harvey. She was glad she would not have to face him in the morning.

CHAPTER 14

The morning sun was streaming through a crack in the bedroom drapes when Marion finally wakened. She had slept so soundly that for a moment she was fuzzy headed and disoriented. Then she heard the sounds of her two granddaughters playing outside her door, waiting for an invitation to come and crawl into bed with her.

"Who do I hear out there?" she called. "Who's that having such a happy time outside my bedroom door? Who would like to come in and have a morning cuddle with a sleepy old Grandma?"

The two girls came tumbling into the room, still in their nighties with signs of breakfast on their happy faces. They settled a minor problem as to who would sleep on what side of Grandma by agreeing to both be on the outside so they wouldn't push Grandma out of bed and hurt herself. Then after much squirming and rearranging of blankets and pillows they decided, by some miracle of twin communication, to run and ask mummy if Grandma could have her breakfast in bed.

"No, girls! Please!" she called after them. "No breakfast in bed. Tell mummy that Grandma is getting up right now." And she did get quickly out of bed and into the bathroom before the twins returned, their breakfast idea forgotten. Then, after hastily making her bed, she was escorted, in her dressing gown, to the sunroom where Edith sat working on a crossword and waiting for her in the warmth of the brilliant morning.

"Oh, Edith. Good morning, dear. I'm glad you didn't take the children seriously about breakfast in bed."

"Good morning, Mom. Of course I didn't pay any attention to those two. I know you are not the breakfast-in-bed type. I just decided to have another cup of coffee and wait for you to see what you would like for breakfast. I haven't had anything myself. What would you like? How about some orange juice and some waffles? Frozen ones, I mean, of course." She chattered on, getting their breakfast ready and sending the girls off to get dressed. "We could try some of the raspberry jam on the waffles. That sounds interesting, doesn't it?" And she went to the frig and typically, bluntly, with her head in the frig, she asked, "When are you going to phone Dad?"

"I guess I'll go down to the store after breakfast when I'm dressed," Marion responded. "Is there something I can pick up for you while I'm there?" She hoped that Edith wouldn't want to go with her. It was going to be a difficult call and she knew Edith would expect an answer as soon as she hung up and before she could get her thoughts organized.

"You could go next door to the Tomason's, Mother," Edith said over her shoulder as she busied herself at the counter. "It would give you a chance to meet Audrey, too."

"No, Edith. I'll go down to the store and say hello to the people there. I'll make a special visit to see Audrey. I'd rather do it that way. It's better, I think. It would be nice to let her feel that I came to visit her not just to use her phone."

"She wouldn't mind," said Edith, who never had picked up her mother's sensitivities about such things.

"Well, I mind, Edith," came the maternal response with a slight tone of finality. "Is there anything you want me to tell your father?" she added, trying to put an end to any thought of Edith accompanying her.

"Say Hi to him for us and sorry he couldn't come. Ask him if he is going to stay over when he comes to pick you up," Edith said as she brought their waffles to the table. "Do you like that orange juice? I think it's kind of watery, isn't it? Try that raspberry jam. If you like it I'll make some extra this year and give it to you for Xmas. I wonder what those kids are up to. They're awfully quiet. Sh-h-h. Just a minute." She tiptoed quietly out of the room and returned a minute later covering her mouth and brimming with laughter. "They're up in your bed, she whispered. "They got into your lipstick and they have lipstick all over their faces. But they are tucked down and Iona has got your reading glasses on and she is pretending to read your book to Jenny." The laughter burst out of her and again Marion saw a softness in her daughter that was new to her. "Oh, they can be such little devils sometimes. I'm sorry about your lipstick. They shouldn't do that. I'll have to give them a good talking to with the flyswatter in my hand." And again she laughed. Then, picking up their coffee mugs and going back to the stove for refills, she said over her shoulder, "Too bad Dad can't find some time to enjoy them." Marion made no response.

She was not looking forward to phoning her husband to ask him to drive out to pick her up. Gerry resented anything that interfered with his weekend golf games and she was trying to prepare some arguments before she telephoned him. Edith's voice terminated her preoccupation with how Gerry would react.

"Craig told me that he was going to get a driver's licence this summer. Is that true? Are you going to give him driving lessons? He's awfully young yet, isn't he? You wouldn't let me have driving lessons until I was eighteen." Marion could hear an old familiar tone of resentment in her daughter's voice and she steeled herself for what she knew was coming and wondered how long Edith had been harbouring this particular rancour.

"Well, actually, Edith, Craig has already had six driving lessons from the same driving school you went to, but..."

"He hasn't, really, has he? He's not eighteen yet!" Edith shrilled, as if the age that had been established for her should automatically apply to her brother. Again, Marion was puzzled by the variations in her daughter's maturity—one moment a mature, happy and responsible parent and the next reverting to a prickly, petulant adolescent.

"Whose car did he use?" Edith demanded.

"He used mine. He wanted to quit after the sixth lesson and take a driving test. Mr. Asterfer advised him—."

"Asferturn! That's his name. He's a good teacher. So did he quit?"

"Well, yes he did, in a way. He took a driving test and failed it. He just couldn't stand the way Mr. Aster—whatever his name is—nagged at him and kept on telling him that you were such a quick learner. He told Craig he needed at least another ten lessons. Craig said he couldn't stand being in the car with him because he smelled terrible and wouldn't allow Craig to open any windows. Besides, Craig said he thought he was a homo although how he every arrived at that idea is beyond me."

"What did Dad say?" Edith was looking hard at her mother with her head cocked and her knuckled hands on her hips.

"About Mr. Asterf—? The instructor?"

"No, mother. I mean about Craig getting lessons and failing and using your car."

"Oh, I see," replied Marion carefully holding back her growing annoyance at Edith's tone and attitude. "Well, your father was against the idea of Craig driving. (Naturally, she thought. He seems to be against a lot of things these days.)

And he fussed about the insurance. But I insisted because it was my car that I bought with some of the money my father left me, and after Rob got his licence I just thought that Craig should—."

"You mean Robbie has got his licence?" Edith's voice was full of disbelief. "How did he manage that?"

"I really don't know, Edith. Craig told me that Beverley took Rob out in her car for some practice and then he took a driving test and passed. I guess he's just a natural. Some boys are, I guess, but Craig doesn't seem to be one of them."

"Well, I'll be darned." Some of Edith's sharpness seemed to have dissipated and she returned to the table across from her mother. Then after a moment of thought she said, "Well, I guess that's fair, after all. Those two have been as close as buddies can be all their lives, haven't they? What did Rob's mom and dad have to say about it? They are such strange people and they were always so hard on Robbie. I often wondered where he got his sense of humor—certainly not from them! What are they doing now?" Edith had relaxed and appeared to be ready to settle into a good gossip session with all hurts forgotten.

"Edith, I can't say for sure. That man changes jobs and affiliations like other men change their socks. And Rob's mother is just as bad. Craig says that he is the General Secretary of some organization whose name he can't remember but it has something to do with raising funds for some kind of research. He thinks it may have something to do with drugs. We don't see much of them any more. Robbie told me one day that their house was so full of office machines and stacks of pamphlets that he couldn't find a table to eat off and that he hated to go home because they would both be after him to help them stuff envelopes."

"I always sort of liked Robbie," Edith mused. "But I could never could be bothered with Bev much. She was three years younger than me and such a show-off, always acting smart, to get attention I guess. Lord knows she never got any at home with those two parents. I guess maybe Robbie got a lot of attention from you and Dad through Craig. Are those two still as thick as thieves?"

"I think they are even thicker now than ever, but they did have a falling out a while ago—I don't know what that was all about. They seem to be having a good time together now, though. I let them have my car on Friday nights and Saturdays as long as they—"

"You don't!" Edith interrupted in tones of utter disbelief.

"Yes, I do!" her mother replied in a voice that told her daughter that she was not about to brook any criticism of her action. "Robbie has his licence and he takes Craig over to the school parking lot so that Craig can practice. Now, never mind," she said holding up her hand as Edith was about to interrupt. "I know what I'm doing. Your father won't take him out and Craig certainly doesn't want his friends to see him out with his mother, so they both have to tell me that their homework is done and they have to be home before dark and keep an account of the miles they drive. That's so I can charge them for the gas." She chuckled in remembrance. "Craig got so mad at me for charging him for the gas, but I thought it was one way to keep an eye on what they were doing. They tell me they go cruising—whatever that is. I suspect they just go driving around trying to pick up girls but they are both so skittish about girls that it would be a lark to hide in the back seat and watch them." Marion chuckled again and Edith sat in puzzlement trying to remember if her mother had ever been so casual with her when she was growing up.

The twins returned to the kitchen eliciting laughter from the two adults at their lip-stick faces. Edith held Iona up to a mirror, saying "Look, Iona! Look at your face. See how pretty you look," to which the child replied matter-of-factly, "I see Jenny."

"Isn't that funny, Mom? When ever I hold one of them up to the mirror she sees the other one. Iona sees Jenny in the mirror and Jenny sees Iona. Neither of them sees herself and if you hold them both up together and ask either of them to point to herself she will always point to the other one. I think that's because they are identical twins even though the doctor says they aren't just because Jenny has the same butterfly birthmark on her bum that Craig and Dad have and Iona doesn't. Sometimes the way I tell them apart is because Iona tends to be the boss and Jenny follows along but I can always be sure if I take down the panties of one of them and look for the birthmark. Can you tell them apart?"

"Not all the time, Edith. But most of the time I think I can but I'm not about to look at a bottom to make sure."

"Well, if you ever have to know for sure you can always take a peek, can't you?" And Edith laughed and pulled up the nightie of one of the twins and said "Whoops, no butterfly on your botty. You must be Jenny. Jenny, you take your sister and go get dressed. Right now! Hurry up! Grandma's got to get dressed too, because she has to go the store and phone Grandpa." But it was Iona who took Grandma's hand and they went off to the bedrooms together followed happily by Jenny.

A few minutes later Marion returned to the kitchen dressed casually with a colored scarf to be greeted by Edith with "Well don't you look all dressed up to go to the country store! Very nice, Mom."

"Thank you, Edie. I didn't get dressed just for the store. I got one outfit all grubby in the garden yesterday and another got soaking wet when we were try-ing to reach home before the storm last night. I thought I would put on some-thing decent if I was going over to welcome my new neighbour after I got back from the store. You're sure you don't need anything?"

"I can't think of a thing I need, Mom. Particularly with Harv not here be-cause we brought a lot of groceries with us so we wouldn't have to depend on the little store here. Their prices are out of this world and their produce—what there is of it—is certainly not very fresh. Unless you decide that you might stay a little longer or Dad wants to stay then we might have to go for something special but I can't think of anything we need right now." By the time Edith had finished her extended answer, Marion had found her car keys on the hook where Edith had left them and was waiting by the open door.

"All right, then," she said. "I won't be long," and she walked out somehow feeling like she was making an escape. As she walked toward her car, her neighbour, Frank Tomason, was backing out of his driveway and they waved good morning to each other. She watched with a sense of relief as he drove off in the opposite direction she would be going, knowing that she would not meet him at the store while she was telephoning.

When she got to the store she passed some time with the owners who had bought the store at the same time that she and Gerry had bought their cottage. They were open, friendly people who asked after Gerry and Craig with warm concern and she carried on a catching-up conversation with one of them while the other tended to other customers until all three felt the social amenities had been satisfactorily attended to and Marion made her way outside to the telephone booth. She realized suddenly that she was very tense and she hoped that her tension had not been noticed by the store owners and misinterpreted as standoffishness. She found herself wishing that there had been other people waiting to use the phone so she would have a reason for delay but she was alone. She entered the booth, closed the door and dialled her husband's number and her long-distance code.

When the switchboard answered she did not recognize the operator and she asked for Gerry and then had to explain who she was. "Oh! Mrs. Williams, I'm sorry—but this is my first morning on the switchboard and I feel like I'm all fingers and thumbs. Just a minute—I'll put you through." Marion waited briefly and the operator came back on the line, "He doesn't seem to be in his office, Mrs. Williams," she said. "But hang on a minute and I'll see if I can find him...."

"Wait," Marion interrupted. "Why don't you just ask Eleanor? She always knows his schedule."

"Eleanor?" queried the switchboard.

"Yes—his secretary, Eleanor," replied Marion.

"But, Mrs. Williams, my list doesn't show that Mr. Williams has a secretary. I think maybe it is out of date or something. But there is an Eleanor in the secretary pool I can ask.... Oh, just a sec! His light came on so he must be back in his office. I'll connect you." Marion waited for what she felt was at least thirty seconds and then she started counting the seconds off, her irritation increasing with each count. She had reached a count of fifty when Gerry answered with an curt "Hello." Hearing the tone of his voice she thought he might as well have added, "What the hell do you want?"

"Gerry, it's me, Marion," she said, trying to keep the ice out of her voice.

"Yes, I know. The switchboard told me." Just that and nothing more so she let a silence build more because she did not want to start something by responding in kind. Finally he said, "Where are you?" This time the tone was less antagonistic.

"I'm up at the cottage. Remember?" And now there was a note of antagonism in her voice.

"Yes," he answered quickly. "Are you OK?"

"I'm fine," she said relaxing a little on hearing the concern in his voice. "And so are Edith and the twins. But this is why I'm calling." And she told him about

Harvey needing to go back to work and taking their car and her decision to leave her car with Edith just for safety. "So I'm calling," she concluded, "to ask you to come and pick me up tomorrow and Edith will bring my car back in a week or so when Harvey is finished with the special job he's on. Maybe it will be longer—he's not sure how long it will take. But I don't want Edith up here alone with the kids without a car and I don't want to stay any longer than I planned." She realized suddenly that she was rushing on and on, just like Edith but she couldn't seem to stop the flow. "Edith told me to be sure to tell you that she wants you to stay over and she's very disappointed that you haven't seen the twins since she brought them to town to the paediatrician and stayed till you got home from work so you could see them."

"I've got a golf game tomorrow," she heard him say and she had known that he was going to say it and all her plans to be diplomatic went down the drain.

"Jesus Christ, Gerry!" she exploded. "Will the goddam world come to an end if you miss your goddam golf game? It's the same every goddam Saturday. You gotta play golf. You gotta play golf. Can't you find anybody to take your goddam place?" She realized that she was saying 'goddam' too much.

"Marion!" he exclaimed, and she could hear the shock in his voice. "Well, good," she thought. "I'll shock him." Then aloud she said, "Phone up the fucking pro and tell him to get somebody to take your place—it's about time he did something useful instead of rubbing his balls against the girls he's pretending to give lessons to."

"Marion!" he said again.

"So are you coming up to get me or not? Would you rather lend your car to Robbie and Craig and let them come up for me?"

"Are you kidding!" There was a shudder in his voice like people give when they hear nails on a blackboard.

"Well?" she demanded in a voice so loud that two people waiting for the telephone gave her startled looks. She wondered if she had been talking loud enough for them to hear the earlier exchange.

"All right," he said tonelessly and hung up.

She was shaking. She did not think she could make it to her car without her knees buckling. To give herself time to get over the shakes she dialled a random number and when the recorded message came on she mouthed a pretended conversation until she felt she could walk to her car without making a fool of herself. She opened the door of the booth and gave the waiting couple what she hoped was an apologetic smile and made it to the car. She sat for a long time in the heat of the enclosed car trying to understand what had happened to her. Not how she had stood up to him but the way she had stood up to him. "Good gracious," she said to herself in her everyday language. "I've got to stop watching some of those awful late movies."

CHAPTER 15

When the noon hour bell rang Craig headed for the lunch room with the rest of the men and found a place that was away from the gang that usually argued about everything in loud voices saving their most obscene language for those occasions when they were failing to impress others with fact or logic. He rarely got involved in these exchanges, usually pretending to give his attention to some magazine so that none of the men could catch his eye and drag him in. The other two boys had learned a technique of deflecting any overtures designed to bring them into an argument by putting on a dimwit face and saying in a nasal voice, "Duh, gee, lessee. I guess I don't know. Maybe they'll learn us that next year." Craig enjoyed listening in on the few discussions and arguments that were on some topic other than the ongoing bitching about the boss or the working conditions or the union. He had become aware of the limited vocabulary and general knowledge displayed by most of the men, and as the hot summer in the noisy factory wore on, he began to see clearly that unless he got through high school and into some kind of special training his life would be exactly like the lives of these men and the thought scared him.

He was wrestling with these thoughts when one of the men noticed his far-off look and said, "What's up with you, Cookie-monster? Dreaming about how you're going to get your piece of nookie this weekend?" The cookie-monster label was a piece of factory hilarity that came from another noon hour when Craig's lunchbox was mistakenly grabbed by an old hand who opened it to find nothing but a bag of cookies, an orange and a can of juice. He sat with the contents arrayed on the lunch table between his limp palms and said in total puzzlement "Wot de focks dis?" three times before Craig was able to retrieve his lunch and attempt to alleviate the man's bewilderment with his feeble explanation that he had slept in and hadn't time to make a lunch.

"Yeah, I guess so," he replied to the man who had expressed the vulgar interest in his weekend activities and at the same time he was thinking "Good God! That's going to be me in thirty years." He closed up his lunchbox with a bang and made his escape from the lunchroom.

When Craig walked over to see Rob on some of his noon breaks, he usually walked down the five blocks using the main streets. Today, without having any reason to change his pattern, he cut through an alley and came out at the truck loading zone of the supermarket. As he approached he could see Rob up on the loading ramp leaning against the wall and talking to some guy he didn't know. He jumped up onto the ramp and walked over to them. Rob saw him approaching and, giving a casual wave, called "Hi!" But the sound was muffled as Rob choked on the cigarette that had just been passed to him. Craig stood by and waited while Rob coughed and gagged and the guy, whose name tag said "Andy", who had passed the cigarette laughed, almost hysterically, Craig thought. Then Andy picked up the butt where Rob had dropped it and took a long drag followed by a great gulp of air. He tried to pass it back to Rob who was still coughing and gasping so he made a casual motion offering the butt to Craig who stared at it for a moment and squeaked "That's a joint!"

"Jeez!" said Andy, rolling his eyeballs, and he took a final long drag on the butt before dropping it and grinding it out with his shoe. "See ya," he said to Rob as he walked away.

"Yeah," Rob responded in a rasping whisper while wiping his watering eyes with the back of his hand.

"What the hell do you think you're doing?" Craig was almost shrieking. "Are you nuts? That was pot, wasn't it? You were smoking marijuana! Weren't you? You're crazy, you know! You're just plain crazy and stupid too. If your boss had walked out here and found you he would have fired you and called the cops on you."

"Oh, shut up, Craig," was all Rob could manage.

"Don't tell me to shut up, you stupid fucking asshole. You know what happens when you start on drugs—any kind of drugs—and here you are sneaking around back alleys and smoking pot. So, shit-for-brains, what do you say about that?" Craig had never been able to display hostility, he tended to move to tears at the peak of anger, but this time he was nose to nose with Rob and shouting. Rob reached out and took a twisting grip on Craig's shirt. "Watch it!" he threatened as they glared at each other.

"What's going on?" said a voice at the loading door. Turning, Rob saw the Assistant Manager watching them.

"Hi, Mr. Walton. Nothin's going on. My friend and I were just having a friendly difference of opinion, that's all. It's nothing new for us. Eh, Craig?"

"Your lunch break was over ten minutes ago, Rob. Get back to work. And you young man," he said looking severely at Craig. "This ramp is private property. It is not open to the public for social purposes. I suggest you leave."

Craig turned and jumped off the loading ramp without a word.

"Call me!" Rob shouted after him.

"Don't hold your breath!" Craig replied in a voice that was as near to a snarl as he had ever managed.

"Your friend, eh?" said the Assistant Manager as he walked away .

When Craig got home from work he was still mulling over his confrontation with Rob while he zapped a frozen muffin his mother had left for them. He dialled Rob's number but hung up before the phone could be answered. He picked up the mail and the paper and a few other things like his father's glass on top of the television and the ice cube tray he had left out to melt on the counter. He tasted the residue in his father's drink and made a wry face. Satisfied that he wouldn't get criticized for slovenliness when his father got home, he went out to the garage and practised some hoops, leaving the door open so he could hear the telephone if it rang. At six-thirty there had been no call from either his father or Rob. He was puffed out and sweaty and, concluding that his father was not coming home for dinner, he went back into the house, put a casserole into the microwave following his mother's explicit taped instructions and showered and changed. He had just settled himself in front of the television in his father's favourite chair with a plate of dinner in his lap when he heard the back door close and his father call, "Craig? Are you home?"

"Hi, Dad. I'm in here," he replied after muting the television. He got to his feet, plate in hand, to greet his father when he came into the room. "I didn't know whether you were coming home for dinner or not, so I didn't wait. But I put a double casserole in just in case—it's tuna, I think, or maybe it's turkey. Mom didn't label it; she just wrote out instructions on how to cook it. Do you want me to get you some?"

His father had been looking through the mail and had picked up the newspaper and was moving to his chair as he said, "Yes, that would be good. Not too much. I had a big lunch."

Craig put his own dinner on the coffee table and went to the kitchen just as his father called after him, "And a glass of wine would be good, too. There's a half bottle of white in the frig—or there should be, unless you drank it."

"I didn't drink it, Dad. I can't stand the stuff."

"You been trying it out, then, have you?" came the unsmiling response, that was not really a question, from his father who had not looked up from his paper.

Craig put the remainder of the casserole on a plate and zapped it in the microwave for a minute just to make sure it would be hot enough, poured a full glass of wine and, remembering a napkin, took them into the living room.

"I said 'not too much' Craig. There's enough there to put meat on a factory worker's ribs—twice as much as I needed. And Craig, while I'm on the subject— (Craig now witnessed one of his father's favourite expressions of displeasure with him, a long silence followed by a deep sigh)—haven't you watched and noted how I pour wine? Don't you remember me telling you to fill a wine glass only three-quarters full at the very most? And remember why? That is so the person you are serving can breathe the air above the wine in the glass in order to appreciate the bouquet of the wine. Try to remember these things. You might not have to work in a factory all your life."

"But Dad, there was only a little bit left in the bottle, not even an ounce. So I figured I might as well put in the whole thing instead of leaving a little bit."

"So there was a little bit left. That's no excuse for not doing it properly," said his father, busying himself with his dinner and the newspaper and ending the conversation.

After an extended silence during which Craig tried desperately not to fidget, he finally asked, "Would you like some dessert, Dad?"

"What have you got in mind?"

"Oh, there's some ice cream and fruit salad and some cake, too, I think. Or a muffin," Craig said, remembering the birthday muffin he had fixed for his mother. "I could fix that."

After a long pause, the answer came, "No. I'll skip dessert. You get what you want."

Craig took his plate out to the kitchen and spooned some fruit salad onto a mound of ice cream, thinking "Maybe he's forgotten how to say please and thank you."

Back in the living room, his father looked up from his newspaper as Craig chopped the hard ice cream and the fruit together and said, "That sounds good and it looks good."

"It is," Craig said, now feeling defiant because he knew his father was expecting him to leap up and get him some and wouldn't ask because asking might mean saying please.

For a minute the only sounds in the room were Craig's spoon scraping the bowl and the rustle of the newspaper.

"Mind if I turn on the TV?" Craig asked finally.

"Not right now. I want to talk to you," his father said, handing his empty plate to Craig who had to lean over and put it on the coffee table that was closer to his father than it was to him, "after you've cleaned up."

Craig felt a prickle in the hair on the nape of his neck, but he didn't know whether it was anger or fear. Quietly he collected the plate and his father's wine glass and went to the kitchen to 'clean up' as his father put it and he took his time doing it as he pondered what his father wanted to talk to him about this time.

Coming back into the living room he settled quietly into a chair without flopping into it and asked, "So what's up, Dad?"

His father did not answer immediately. He finished reading something in the newspaper that interested him more than his son, and then, shoving the newspaper away and turning his head to look over the top of his glasses at Craig, he said, "Your mother called this morning. She is going to leave her car with Edith because Harvey was called back to an important job of plastering," and his voice had a hard edge on it, "and of course he needed his car. At any rate, she wants me to drive up tomorrow and bring her home. In fact she insisted, I might almost say demanded, that I forgo my golf game to drive up and get her." He turned back to the newspaper. "I guess I'll have to go."

Craig sat wondering if this was what his father wanted to talk to him about. Finally he said, "Is Mom okay?"

"She's fine, I guess. She certainly was in fine fettle this morning."

"What does that mean, Dad?"

"You can figure that out. You learned something in High School last year."

"Well, are Edith and the kids okay?"

"Sure."

There was another long pause. Then Craig asked with a note of uncertainty in his voice, "Is that what you wanted to talk to me about?"

"Craig! I had hoped that when I told you the situation you would offer to go with me. You know, father and son, together on a little trip, getting to know each other better. And then the three of us coming back, like a family, like we used to when you were small and Edith was still at home. I am not going to order you to come with me. So, would you like to come?" He turned away from the newspaper and looked directly at Craig.

Craig had started to tense and hold his breath as soon as the first words were out of his father's mouth. Holy shit! he said to himself. How am I going to get out of this one. How did I ever get into it. I should have seen it coming. I knew there was something going on just by the way he was jerking me around. His mind was spinning, thinking of some way of escape. Finally, and his father had not taken his eyes off him, he said with what he hoped was undeniable sincerity, "Oh, Dad, I wish you had told me. I can't go. I'm scheduled to run a Little League game tomorrow, so I...," and he stumbled to a halt in case he rambled on and got caught in his lie.

"Little league, eh? When did this start?"

"Oh, I've been doing it all summer. All the guys from the ball team at school volunteered and there's a schedule drawn up and people get mad if you don't show up. Rob's doing it too." And he stopped talking again to protect himself against himself.

At that moment there was a familiar rattling knock on the back door followed by Rob's voice, "Are you home, Craig?"

"That'll be Rob," Craig said jumping up and going out of the room to the door. "Hi, Rob," he said loudly with his finger on his lips. "C'mon in. No, don't come in! You got a big chunk of mud on your shoe. I'll give you a knife to scrape it off." He closed the door behind them when they went out and said quietly. "Don't ask any questions. You and me have got a Little League game tomorrow afternoon. And you are gonna..."

"Little League! What the..."

"Shut up and listen. My Dad's in there. I told him we've got a Little League game tomorrow. You're home plate ump and I'm scoring. Got it?"

"Yeah, I guess. If you say so."

Craig opened the door and stamped in saying in a loud voice, "I already swept once because my Mom's due home tomorrow. C'mon and say hello to my Dad."

"Hi, Mr. W.," Rob said as the boys ambled into the living room.

"Oh, hello there, Robbie. I haven't seen you for a while. I hear you're working at the supermarket and I also hear you got your driver's licence. Congratulations."

"Thank you. It's not much of a job but like everybody says it keeps me off the streets and off welfare."

"And the driver's licence gives you a big advantage with the ladies, I suppose." Gerry gave the boy a big wink.

"Oh, yeah. You know me, Mr. W. Always the heart throb of the neighbourhood for any lady from six to sixty."

"I hadn't heard that."

"You haven't?" said Rob with exaggerated amazement. "Well, I'll have to speak to my agent about that."

Gerry laughed and then changed the subject. "Craig was just telling me that you two guys have been doing some volunteer work this summer."

Rob was slow to respond until Craig, out of his father's line of vision, put his fists together and leaned into a batting crouch.

"Oh, you mean Little League," he said. "I never think of it as volunteer work. Anything that's that much fun shouldn't be called work. I really like doing it with the little kids. They're a lot of fun. I was telling Craig the other day that maybe that is what I should aim for in life, to work with kids instead of becoming a space engineer or a billionaire."

"Rob's a really good ump, Dad. All the kids like him. And you know what, he signs their gloves for them like he was some kind of superstar and most of the real little kids think he is."

"Another con-game, eh? You two are always up to some con. Sure you're not charging those kids for your autograph?"

For a heart stopping minute Craig thought his father was onto their scheme. But Rob filled the breach. "Hey, Mr. W. What a great idea! Maybe I'll be able to get that car before the summer's out, after all."

Gerry's capacity for banter with adolescents was always limited and he was now threatened with yawning boredom. Turning back to his newspaper, he asked the same question he always asked of Rob every time he saw him. "How are you mother and dad, Rob? Your Dad still in the printing business?"

"Oh, they're fine," replied Rob never wanting to get into any discussion of the many varied ventures that sprouted and died in the hands of his parents.

"Hey, Rob," said Craig. "If we are going to catch that show we better get out of here."

"Yeah, okay. Nice talking to you Mr. W. Say, maybe you would like to come with us. It's the third picture in the outer space series. You might like it—lots of science stuff and blast-offs."

"Rob," Gerry said. "That's an invitation that is bordering on insolence. You both better get out of here now before you get blasted out of your present space."

"Goodnight, Mr. W."

"See you later, Dad."

The two boys made their exit from the house and it was not until they were well away from the yard that Craig gave a whoop of laughter. "Hey, man. that was great. If you hadn't caught on I would have been in the deep, deep stuff."

"So what the hell was going on?" asked Rob.

Craig filled him in about his mother and her car and his dad having to drive up tomorrow to bring her back. "And do you know what he wanted me to do?" Craig's voice was squeaking again. "He wanted me to drive up with him—like buddies! Father and son stuff, he called it. Get to know each other better and all that crap. I nearly shit! But I had to say something to get out of it so I told him we were both scheduled to manage a Little League game tomorrow, and that we couldn't get out of it because there was a schedule and that all the guys from the ball team at school were doing it. That's what we were talking about when you came. I think he bought it, though. Don't you think he bought it?"

"Well, if you keep out of his way tonight, maybe you're in the clear. But he could haul you out of bed in the morning and catch you in your lie and still make you go, so—like you say," Rob stopped and looked from his greater height down at Craig. "Don't hold your breath."

"What d'ya mean?" asked Craig. Then, suddenly remembering the scene between them at noon, he muttered, "Oh, that!"

"Yeah, that," responded Rob and started walking again. Then mimicking Craig's fury at noon he continued, "You know what happens when you lie—he'll catch you and kick your ass and call the cops."

"That's not the same thing at all," protested Craig.

"Not the same thing at all," Rob repeated, mimicking still.

"Well, it isn't!" Craig voice was full of petulance.

They walked on together in silence until Craig said, "Wanna go see that show?"

"Sure," Rob replied with his grin. "As long as you're still going to be my best buddy, and you pay." He reached over and grabbed Craig's collar at the back and jerked him closer as they walked.

"I paid last time," protested Craig, not struggling to get away from Rob's grasp. They went through a series of did-not, did-so while grinning at each other and knowing that their quarrel was forgotten. Two boys drove by in a car and one of them called "Woo-woo" at them through their open window. Neither of them knew the guys in the car but Rob released his grip on Craig's collar and dropped his arm and Craig moved to make some space between them.

Standing in the foyer of the theatre waiting for the early show to get out, Craig said "You know my mom is coming back with my dad and she is leaving her car at the cottage for Edith? So we won't be able to use her car until Edith brings it back next week."

"Oh, is that what is going on?"

"Yeah."

"Shit!"

"Why?"

"Well I was working on a couple of girls for us from the store but I guess I'll just cool it for a while. No sense making a date and then having nothing to do but sit in the park or walk the mall."

Craig felt a little relieved but said nothing. The doors opened and they shoved through the exiting crowd.

***

After she turned her car in the direction of the cottage, Marion realized she was not ready to face Edith so she turned down a side road and drove around aimlessly trying to settle herself down. When she stopped on the road to permit a car to back out of a driveway she recognized the driver as her new neighbour just as he recognized her. They stopped opposite each other and chatted momentarily through their open windows. Finally Frank said, "Well, I better be on my way, I've still got a few things on my list."

"Is Audrey home?" Marion asked. "Is she busy?"

"Oh, yes. She's home and I don't think she had any great plans for the day."

68 GORDON BRYENTON

"Then this might be a good time to call in on her—do you think that would be alright?"

A car tooted behind him and he called his answer as he started to move, "That would be perfect. She'd enjoy that and I won't have to hurry home." They both drove on.

She drove quickly in the direction of her own cottage, past it and turned into the Tomason's driveway quickly hoping Edith had not seen her. As she got out of the car she saw a woman she thought would be Audrey sitting by the window doing some needlework who waved to her inviting her to come in.

"Come in! Come in!" a voice called as she opened the door. "I'm in here."

Marion followed the voice down the hallway to a sunny room where she saw a woman of about fifty years of age seated in a recliner chair with the foot-rest up. Her knees and ankles were swollen with arthritis and as she put her needlework down Marion noticed that her fingers were also terribly twisted by the disease. "I'm Audrey, I'm sure you know that. And you must be Marion. Excuse me for not getting up—its a bit of a struggle some days. I saw you arrive the other day and I also watched you working in the garden. How I envied you, the way you can work out there in the sunshine. Just hang your jacket out there in the hall and come and sit down." Marion had approached her, smiling and was about to offer her hand but restrained when she realized how much it might hurt those crippled hands. When she hung her coat up she paused by a mirror in the hall and was startled to see that her face was still flushed and her neck turkey-wattle from the emotional reaction to her phone call. She hoped it would not be noticed. But there was no hiding from the observant eyes of the other woman.

"You look like you've been rushing around all morning. Sit down, sit down, and we'll find out all about each other. I had a bit of a chat with your daughter last week, but she's on the go all the time with those little girls. My, they are cute, aren't they? Let's have a cup of coffee before you sit. The mugs are to the left of the sink and the instant coffee—is instant okay?—should be right there too, and the sugar." Marion made her way to the kitchen realizing she hadn't said anything other than "Hello." While she busied herself she called out responses to Audrey who continued talking to her from the sunroom.

"Do you take cream? I don't think there's any left. But there's some two percent. Will that do? I don't take any myself. My doctor told me that all milk products are a no-no for me with my kind of arthritis. It's on Frank's shopping list, I hope, because he won't drink coffee without cream. Oh, thank you," as Marion handed her a mug of coffee. "I was thinking about a cup of coffee earlier but I was too lazy to haul myself out of this chair and stumble out to get one for myself. I hope you don't mind playing hostess to yourself. Now then," after a big noisy sip, "how long are you staying?"

That was the beginning of a companionable hour of chatting in the sunny room about neighbours and summer cottage problems and many other things until Marion had to remind herself that she had been absent for a long time and Edith would be fussing. "This has been lovely, Audrey, but I must go. I hope I can invite myself again." "Anytime, Marion. I really look forward to company not just because I make them get the coffee." She laughed heartily as Marion marvelled at the happy nature of a woman so terribly disabled. "I hope I can meet your Gerry sometime. It is too bad he can't stay longer."

"Yes, it is. Edith would like him to stay, but he's pretty busy right now. Thank you for the coffee and the visit. I'll let myself out. Good-bye, Audrey."

"Good-bye and take care, Marion. Remember that what ever is wrong won't go away by worrying at it."

Why did she say that? How did she know that? Marion said to herself as she closed the door.

When she parked the car in her own driveway and walked towards the cottage, the door opened wide and Edith was standing in the doorway with her head cocked and arms almost akimbo. "Where on earth have you been, Mother?" Her tone bordered on demanding which made Marion guard herself from offering a maternal reproof. "I thought you might have been in an accident. I was getting worried."

"Oh, Edith. I've only been gone an hour and a half or so."

"I know. But it doesn't take that long to make a phone call... and you didn't say you were going any place else." She moved aside to let her mother enter, waited as her mother hung up her jacket and said finally, "Well, where were you?"

Marion stifled a sigh. She knew Edith's question came out of simple curiosity and attempted sociability. Oh, dear Edith, she thought. How did I fail you? Why are your edges always so brittle? "As a matter of fact," she said aloud, "I bumped into Frank Tomason and he said Audrey was home, so I decided it would be a good time to visit her and we had a good chat. My, she is a nice person, isn't she? And, oh, she is so terribly crippled. I don't know how she manages to keep so cheerful. Hello, girls," she called to the twins who were playing with a pile of toys on the floor. "Come and give your Grandma a big hug." The two girls came obediently at her call, hugged her without a word and returned to their play.

"They don't chatter much, do they, Edith. Are you concerned at all about their speech?"

"No, Mom, not at all. I read that twins sometimes have a language all their own and they don't need to speak as much as other children. I think it was Spock. What did Dad say?"

That's my girl, thought Marion. Right to the point. Then she said, struggling to keep a note of grimness out of her voice, "He'll be driving up tomorrow to pick me up."

"Is he staying for a day or two?"

"I don't think he plans to, Edith. You know how hard it is to get him away from that golf course." But she really couldn't remember if she had told him that Edith was anxious for him to stay.

Edith turned away. "Come girls, you must pick up some of these things before your grandmother trips over them. I'll help you. C'mon, now. Let's put the dolly things in one box and the train things in another. There now, I helped you start and now you finish all by yourselves. You're big girls, you know. What would you like for lunch, Mother?"

The girls answered for their grandmother in a duet, "Cheese, please, Mommy."

"Those two would live on cheese if I let them," Edith said with a warm smile for her daughters. "But they are not going to get any today." And she turned to the kitchen to make a lunch that she had already decided on.

After lunch, they put the girls down for a nap and sat quietly looking through the local paper that Marion had picked up. Neither of them mentioned tomorrow. Finally, Marion stifled a yawn and Edith said, "Why don't you stretch out on the sofa with a blanket for a while. I've got a few things to do outside and you must be tired of visiting if you spent the whole morning with Audrey." She bustled away, returning with a blanket and stood with it unfolded waiting for her mother to come and lie down. Marion appeared to have no choice.

"Can't I help you with anything, Edie? Besides you're the one who needs a nap. You were up early to get Harvey off."

"No, Mom. I can't nap in the daytime and I'm just going to do odd jobs. And I will skip over to Marcia's for a minute. I want to get one of her recipes. You just rest and keep one ear on the girls." She tucked the blanket around her mother and kissed her gently on the forehead holding her face in her hands as she would a child.

Edith did walk quickly over to Marcia's cottage, visited for a while and then headed out for a thoughtful walk along the beach. she thought of using Marcia's phone to call her father at work, hoping he might shed some light on her mother's upset but discarded the idea as useless. When she got back after an hour, she came quietly into the house and found her mother awake and looking refreshed.

"I've rested long enough, Edith. What do you say to a game of double solitaire until the girls wake up and then perhaps we could all go for a walk on the beach?"

"Oh, great, Mom," replied Edith with smiling enthusiasm. "I'll get the cards," and she hurried away.

They played together, happily competitive, until Edith's noisy excitement about winning wakened the girls. They each dressed a girl, Iona going first to her grandmother and pushing Jenny sleepily away. Then, dressed for a walk, each with a child in tow and armed with poking sticks, pails and shovels headed out for the beach.

After a long stroll on the beach where talk was impossible because of the exciting finds of two small girls, they turned for home. Edith stopped and looked at her Mother. "Just look at you!" she exclaimed. "All rosy-cheeked and windblown. You look like you left all your worries down there for the tide to wash away."

Now I wonder why she said that, Marion said to herself. Audrey said almost the same thing to me. I wonder if I have been going around looking like a sad sack.

As they arrived back at the cottage, Frank came out of his house and walked over. "Audrey told me you were over to visit and how much she enjoyed it, Marion. Thank you, it always brightens her day to have a bit of company."

"Well, it would have to be a toss-up as to who enjoyed it more. She is such a wonderfully happy, chatty person."

"I think she's pretty wonderful, too," said Frank. And they all had a chuckle until Iona piped up with "I like her too," and the chuckles turned to laughter.

"The reason I came over was because you told Audrey that your husband was coming up tomorrow to drive you back to town. And I just wondered if I could ask a favour. That is if you have room. My grandson has been up visiting a friend and he has to go back so I wondered if he could catch a ride with you. He's fourteen and I don't want..."

"Of course he can! I'd be delighted," Marion responded with such enthusiasm that Edith jumped. "No trouble at all, Frank, and we will have lots of room."

"That's great. Thank you. I'll go over to his friend's place and tell him and go get him in the morning before you leave. I'm much relieved. I really didn't want him riding back alone on the bus. There are too many of those men who are too interested in boys around."

"Well, we'll get him home safely, Frank. Rest assured."

They said their goodbyes, the little girls joining in loudly, and went home, leaving Edith to puzzle for the rest of the evening whether it was the prospect of her father's arrival, the walk on the beach or a conversation with another man that had stirred her mother to come out of her doldrums. In spite of poking and prodding, when she went to bed, she had achieved no good answer to her puzzle.

CHAPTER 16

When Gerry arrived it was after two o'clock and Edith greeted him coldly. She had made lunch and waited for him until the girls were cranky from hunger and ready for their naps. She and her mother fed the girls and put them down and waited in a strained silence. Edith broke one long silence by saying, "He is going to come, isn't he?" And another with the direct question, "You knew he wasn't going to stay, didn't you?" To these questions Marion answered obliquely "I'm never sure sometimes with your father what his plans are." She wanted to add "And right now I don't give a damn," but restrained herself so as not to load her problems on her daughter.

"Well, what took you so long?" was Edith's greeting.

Marion had been using the waiting time by pulling weeds in the garden, so when Gerry arrived she walked over to him holding up her dirty hands and offered a cheek which he barely touched in his greeting and said only, "Hi." He said nothing in response.

"I couldn't get anyone to take my place so I had to play. It was a club match with the Redhills Club," Gerry offered by way of explanation for his lateness.

Neither his daughter or his wife said anything so he broke the silence by saying too heartily, "Well, now that I'm here, where are my granddaughters?"

"It's their naptime." Edith could not hide her disappointment with her father, and her response was abrupt. Then, because she knew she was being rude she asked, "Have you had any lunch?"

"Yes, I ate at the club," he said.

"Well, we waited for as long as the girls could and then we went ahead without you."

"That's too bad. What did I miss—one of your famous Irish stews?" with a large laugh.

Marion gave a small groan and looked at the far horizon. The "joke", and he used it so often that Edith had a right to grow red in anger, was about her first attempt to have her parents for dinner after her marriage and the stew had burned to a revolting mess while her father badgered Harvey for yet another drink. Edith just stood looking at her father, wanting to hurt back but afraid to. The tension that resulted from his joke was broken by the twins appearing sleepy-eyed at the door. "There you are, you little sleepy heads. Come and give your grandpa a big kiss!" But the girls scattered and ran, Iona to Marion and Jenny to her mother, and stood clinging to a leg, fingers in mouth and staring uncertainly at him.

"They're shy," Edith said. "All little girls are shy when they're only three, aren't they Jenny?" ruffling the child's hair.

"Oh, that one's Jenny, is it. I can't tell unless I look at a bum. And then I'll know, won't I Jenny? I can tell because Grandpa gave you a pretty little butterfly on your bum, didn't he?" He reached out to touch the child but she drew back and screamed and her sister made it a sympathetic duet. Marion and Edith each picked up a child. "Let's all go in the house," Edith said.

When they were inside and the children were settled down and dressed, Marion said, "Are you staying the night."

"No, I certainly am not. I've got work to do."

"Well, you certainly are staying for dinner, aren't you? You won't have to eat stew, you know!" Edith interjected. "As a matter of fact, we're having hamburgers, hamburgers and cottage cheese salad."

"Sounds like an epicurean delight." The tone was not light.

"Would it hurt you to try not to be nasty!" Marion exclaimed then added "What time do you want to leave? I promised a ride to the grandson of the people next door and I have to tell them."

"Five o'clock."

"Is that your estimated time of departure?" She couldn't keep the sarcasm out of her voice.

"Nothing estimated about it. Anybody expecting a ride better be in the car with the seatbelt buckled."

Marion got to her feet and went out the door to tell the Tomasons. She could feel her anger boiling inside her and if she saw Audrey she knew her flush would give her away again. But she knew, too, that it would be rude not to say goodbye to her. So, putting on her best face, she knocked on their door to give them the departure time. The door was opened by a young man whose face presented a struggle between acne and beard. She heard Audrey call out, "Is that you, Marion? Bring her in, Ron."

"I'm Ron," the young man said, extending his hand. "Gran said you offered me a ride home."

"And I'm Marion Williams, Ron. You have no idea how pleased I am to have your company for the ride back to town."

They entered the room where Audrey sat in her lounge chair by a sunny window. "I can't stay, Audrey. I couldn't leave without saying goodbye."

"I'm glad you did, Marion. I hope you come up for a longer stay soon. This is a great place to get the knots out of your system." She extended both her twisted hands to Marion who took them gently in her own. "Have a safe trip, and thank you for taking Ron."

"I'm delighted to have him along. Five o'clock, Ron. On the dot! My husband runs a tight ship."

"Yes, ma'am, Mrs. W.," he said, giving a mock salute.

Marion had to smile at the easy informality that reminded her of Robbie.

When she got back to the cottage, she saw Edith in the kitchen looking red-eyed and her husband in the far corner of the family room holding a newspaper like a barrier against the world. The children were playing close by their mother.

"Anything I can help you with, Edith?" she asked.

Edith sniffed and shook her head in answer and did not look up from her work at the counter. She was slicing onions but Marion was sure the reddened eyes and the sniff was caused by more than onions.

"Come girls," she called. "How would you like to help Grandma pack and then we'll go out and look for some more kittypillers. But first let's pick up your toys so Mummy doesn't trip over them." The packing went slowly as Iona supervised everything that Jenny did and repacked it. When it was done the girls insisted on carrying the small suitcase for her but before they got to the door Jenny called "Come help, us, Grandpa." It was the first time either had made an open gesture towards him since his arrival.

He lowered the paper and said, "Just leave it there, I'll take it out later."

From the kitchen came a loud sniff and a sound of exasperation from Edith. "Okay, girls. Let's go look for kittypillers," Marion said, and as the children trooped out Marion picked up her case and carried it out to the car. The girls had rushed first to the kittypillar house they had built in the corner of the yard with cardboard and sticks but yesterday's catch had run away so the search was on to find more. "You get one for Grandpa, Jenny. And if I get one I'll give it to you," Iona said and immediately gave an excited shriek. "I've got one!" Carefully the girls picked it up and stroked it gently, placed it on Jenny's arm and went into the house to show Grandpa. He smiled at them, a very small smile, and said, "You shouldn't bring those things into the house. Better take it out now and get rid of it."

"Bring it here to Mummy," Edith interjected. "Let's put it in this jar and we'll put some leaves in for it to eat. And we'll watch and maybe we will see it turn into a beautiful butterfly. Did you know that? Kittypillers turn into butterflies! They really do! Isn't that interesting?" She gave them both a hug and said, "Now you go get some leaves—just three leaves each, that's all now. I don't want you bringing in a whole armful for just one tiny teeny kittypiller do I?"

The girls raced away and Edith turned to her father. "You used to do that for me when I was their age. Have you forgotten how?" She was not smiling.

"No, I don't suppose I have," he answered. "But it's your chore now."

"Chore!?" Marion said and went outside. Edith returned to the kitchen without a word.

After a silence that was broken only by the children's chatter, Edith said, "Remember, Dad, how we always had hamburger and cottage cheese salad on Sundays? Mom said we didn't need a big dinner on Sundays because you had lunch at the golf course. Then we all watch television together. We'd watch that guy, I can't remember his name," she stopped and frowned in concentration. "Anyway," she went on, "he had a lot of entertainers on, singers and jugglers and people like that. He even had the Beatles on for the first time over here. Now, what was his name? Remember how people made fun of the way he said 'Really Big Shoe'."

"Ed Sullivan."

"That's right, Ed Sullivan. That was such a good show," and Edith chortled at the recall.

The girls came rushing back into the house, followed by Marion. Iona had a two handfuls of leaves while Jenny clutched three and looked big-eyed at her sister.

"Iona!' her mother said. "I told you three each, and that's more than three, isn't it? You can count."

The child stood looking innocently at her without guile as she worked on some complex semantics. "I got three for you, and three for me and three for Grandma and three for Grandpa and Jenny got three for herself. Oh!" she exclaimed. "I forgot three for the kittypiller!" She dropped the leaves and raced to the door with Jenny close behind.

"Iona! Come back! We don't need—." But the door closed on her words and her laughter. "Oh, they are such rascals," she said to her mother. "Did you hear that, Dad? Aren't they little terrors?"

"I guess you will have your hands full for a few years yet," was his response.

The girls returned, Iona with three more leaves and Jenny still clutching hers. "Now, then, this is what we'll do," their mother said. "You both can put your leaves in the jar for the kittypiller and we'll leave all the rest in a pile right here in case he gets hungry. Okay?" And she got down on her knees and gathered the two children into her arms, laughing and with little tears in her eyes. "Just wait til I tell your daddy about this."

Marion had watched and laughed along with her daughter and she had seen Gerry watching by turning his head casually and looking over the top of his glasses. His expression had not changed.

"Well, would you look at the time," Edith exclaimed. "Nearly half-past four. Let's have a cup of tea before the—What did you call it, Mom?—the designated hour?"

"I think the terms is 'estimated time of departure'," Marion said smiling but with her face turned away from her husband.

"I know," Edith mouthed silently and said aloud, "Oh!"

"Would you like a cup of tea, Dad? And maybe a cookie, before your estimated time of departure," Edith called.

"As long as it's not decaffeinated, and pour mine last so that it gets strong enough."

"I'll put two bags in."

"Fine."

"You're welcome," Edith muttered very quietly.

Marion looked at her daughter with a scolding face but Edith only shrugged and Marion wished too late that she had given some indication of support rather than a reproof.

When the tea was ready, Edith carried the tray into the living room area and placed it on a table in front of her mother, saying, "You pour, will you please, Mom. I forgot to get the girls their special tea cookies."

Marion poured two cups of tea, shook the pot, then poured her husband's tea, creamed and sugared it, and carried it over to him. He took it without comment, until just as she returned to her place he muttered, "Sweet!"

"Is it too sweet?" she asked. She had made it as she had been making it for him for years—a half teaspoon of sugar and no more than a teaspoon of cream. How could it suddenly be too sweet?

"Fine," he said, his mouth full of cookie.

Edith returned and settled the girls into their tea party, and the girls amused them with their pretence of being ladies by drinking their milk-tea with their little fingers sticking out and giggling at something no adult could share.

At length, Marion rose, determined to be ready in advance of any remark she felt sure her husband would make should she be late. "My bag is already in the car," she said. "I'll just see if Ron is ready." She opened the door, which started a chorus from her grandchildren. "You didn't kiss me goodbye, Grandma!" Don't go, Grandma."

"I'm not going yet, girls. I wouldn't go without giving you twenty hugs and twenty kisses. Do you know how many that is?"

"Twenty is more than three, isn't it Grandma?" said Iona.

"Oh, yes, much, much more. That's how many your daddy will have for each of you when he comes back. Now you come with me and we'll get Ron while your mummy says goodbye to your grandfather."

When she walked outside she saw Frank and Ron standing talking at the gate, so she walked slowly to the car with the children. In less than a minute she was joined by Edith. "Have you said goodbye to your father," she asked.

"I guess so," her daughter replied enigmatically, controlling her face to show neither anger nor hurt.

"Where is he?"

"He had to go to the bathroom."

They continued walking towards the car and at the same time, Frank and Ron finished their conversation and also walked to the car. Gerry came out of the house looking at his watch. Edith and the children were busily engaged in making sure Grandma gave them each twenty hugs and twenty kisses with Edith counting by fives to hurry the process. The two men introduced themselves while Marion and Ron debated about who should sit where. "You sit in the front, Ron," Marion insisted. "If we want to talk, I won't have to turn my head around to talk to you." The fifteen year old was delighted.

Gerry had started a conversation with Frank and he was leaning casually against the front fender. After fifteen minutes Marion was certain that he was deliberately delaying their departure but she held her fury in check. The girls were fidgety and they amused themselves by climbing from the back seat to the front and they were taking turns pretending to drive with their feet on the steering wheel when one of them pushed the horn. Everyone jumped but the girls were so startled by the horn and the adult reaction that they began to howl. Edith got the children out of the car and her father shook hands with Frank and turned to her and the children. He tried to pick one up but when the child struggled he did not even bother with the other one, then turning to Edith he kissed her casually on the cheek while trying to put an arm around her rigid back. When he turned to get into the car, he saw Ron sitting in the passenger seat. "What are you doing here?" he asked, his tone ungracious. The bewildered fifteen year old tried desperately to find an answer. "I'm Ron," he stuttered. "Mrs. Williams said I could ride to town with you."

"I know that. I asked what are you doing up front?"

Again bewilderment overwhelmed the boy's face. "But Mrs. Williams said that—."

"I told him to sit there," Marion interjected. "Let's be on our way. We are well past our estimated time of departure." The words were varnished with sarcasm.

"All right, stay there," Gerry said and started the car. He drove away without even a "shave and a haircut—six bits" toot.

When they got onto the highway, Ron asked Gerry, as a curious fifteen year old, some routine questions about the car and tried to make what he considered to be polite and socially required conversation. The responses he received in return were factual and in a tone that indicated to him that Gerry was not interested in anything he might have to say. He was relieved when Marion broke the uncomfortable silence with casual questions about his school, sports, teachers and other subjects to which he could easily respond and which permitted him some opportunity to ask questions on his own. When they got to the outskirts of the city Gerry broke into their conversation by asking of Ron, "Where are we going to drop you off?"

The boy started to answer quickly, "Oh, any bus stop will—." But Marion answered almost in the same breath, "We are not going to drop you off. We are going to take you home just as I promised your grandmother. But you have to give us the address again. Your Grandfather told me where it was and I know the area but not the exact address."

"You don't have to do that. I can—," the boy protested.

"Yes, we do!" Marion said emphatically. "I promised your grandmother that I would see you home and that's what we're going to do. Besides it much too late for you to be wandering around on your own."

"But Mrs. Williams, I do it all the time. It's not late, you know. It's just after eight o'clock!"

"Ron, please tell Mr. Williams your address and the best way to get there before we have to turn around and go backwards to get you home."

"Okay," the boy said, "but you don't have to." He proceeded to give good directions, and Marion was thankful that the route did not require anything more than a casual side trip, otherwise, she thought, there would be hell to pay.

They found the address without difficulty and dropped Ron off. Gerry did not turn off the engine while the boy got out and retrieved his jacket and some parcels from the back seat beside Marion. He shook hands with her and did extend his hand over into the front seat but it went unnoticed. He was courteous in thanking them although he directed his thanks to Marion without making further effort to include Gerry. The car moved quickly away the instant he closed the door.

"I would have got into the front seat if you had waited a minute," Marion said, although she was quite content with the present arrangement.

"It will only take us ten minutes," he replied somewhat cryptically. They rode the rest of the way in silence.

When they arrived home Gerry picked up her bag and opened the door for her. "Do you want this upstairs?" he asked.

"Yes, but I can take it up, don't bother."

"I have to go up anyway," he said.

"Thank you," she said to his retreating back, puzzled by the sudden civility when he had been so cold and withdrawn since his arrival at the cottage.

When she heard the sounds of the television coming from the family room downstairs she went to the head of the stairs and called down, "Hello, Craig. I'm home." No answer so she tried again. "Yoo-hoo! Craig!" There was still no answer so she went down the stairs and found Craig and Rob sprawled in chairs with the volume turned up to a decibel level that no adult could tolerate but apparently was comfortable to the two adolescents. Standing in the doorway she tried her "Yoo-hoo" again, this time with instant success. Craig leaped out of his chair and Rob turned the volume down as he also got to his feet.

"Hi, Mom. You're home," said Rob giving his mother a quick kiss.

"Gee, Mrs. W.," Rob put in. "Have you ever noticed how observant your son is?" This was Rob's round-about way of saying hello without saying hello and he would say such things usually looking both open-mouthed and grinning.

"It's probably something he's learned from the company he keeps," she said.

"Do mean to tell me that he knows somebody who deserves to be labelled as company?"

"Robbie! Just say hello to me and stop your nonsense."

"Hello to me and stop your nonsense," he said. He was close enough for her to reach out and slap him on the upper arm. "Oh! Ow!" he cried, hugging his arm and feigning agony. "She hit me! She hurt me! I'm going to tell my mommy." Then, dropping the charade, he said with his usual warm smile, "Welcome back, did you have a good visit with Edith and the twins? And before I forget, thanks for dinner. It was delicious. I should take the recipe home."

Marion responded, fully aware of Rob's mother's total disinterest in cooking anything that couldn't be boiled or fried, "I'll give you the recipe when you get a place of your own."

Craig had been listening in to his mother and Rob, happy, as always, that they seemed to enjoy each other. He knew that, in his own home, Rob could rarely get on such easy terms with his own parents no matter how hard he tried. "Where's Dad?" he asked his mother.

"He took my case upstairs. I guess he's still up there."

"I better go up and say hello," Craig said and turned away to go upstairs.

"Tell him I'm just going to make a cold supper. It will be ready in a few minutes."

"I guess I better not go up with him," Rob said with a wry grin.

Marion laughed. "You're so perceptive," she said. "You're so right, you'd better not. Come on up to the kitchen and talk to me while I make supper. Now tell me, did you two behave yourselves while I was away?"

"We were angels! Just like always! Besides, what could we do? We had no car!"

"Poor darlings! And you won't have a car for another week until Edie brings is back."

"I heard, and when I heard I was wrought with dismay! Or was I fraught with dismay? One or the other—which is right?"

"Just be satisfied with dismayed. In your young life the degree of dismay is incidental." They laughed easily together and the conversation turned to Edith and her family. Rob listened to small incidents about getting caught in a thundershower, about their new neighbours and kittypillers and Marion realized again how much Rob needed something from her that he never got at home. She hoped that he and Craig would always be good friends.

Craig came into the kitchen and reported to his mother, "Dad said he would be down in a few minutes." And then including Rob very specifically he said "And he asked me about the ballgame. I guess I forgot to tell you, Mom, that Rob and I volunteered to look after a Little League game this afternoon. It was a lot of fun, too. Rob was the ump. But that's why I couldn't drive up with Dad to pick you up and see Edith and the kids."

"Well, Edith was disappointed, of course. Particularly since your dad didn't arrive until after two o'clock. But I'm glad you two are doing something useful and responsible. Are you going to do it again? I'd like to watch you in action."

"Little League is all finished in our park, that was the last game until the finals. Then the big shots take over the game. Too bad you missed Robbie in action, though. The little kids think he's great. I'm just the scorekeeper."

"Aw, shucks," said Rob, scraping his foot. "But then maybe that's your lot in life, buddy—always a bridesmaid, never a bride."

"Oh, for God's sake, Rob. Don't be an assho..."

"Just about slipped up, didn't you, dear? said his mother.

"Sorry, Mom. Are we going to play tennis or not," he said to Rob. "Where's your racket?"

"At home. You have two." And they started for the door.

"Sure I have two. But that doesn't mean you can borrow one anytime you want."

"What do you want to do, play two-handed tennis by yourself?"

She interrupted their banter as they opened the door. "Are you sure you don't want some supper?"

Rob stopped Craig at the door and answered for both of them. "Mrs. W.," he said. We wish to thank you for your gracious invitation, but it would be exceedingly discourteous of us to take further advantage of your hospitality. Besides, the ice cream is all gone."

She heard their laughter as they walked away and laughed with them.

"Jesus, can you ever lay it on," Craig said.

"Somebody's got to lay something sometime," Rob answered with a leer.

Oh, zip up your mind," was all Craig could answer as they continued towards the park.

CHAPTER 17

When the boys left, Marion finished her preparations for supper and went to the stairs and called Gerry. There were no answers to several calls, so grudgingly she went upstairs and found him solidly asleep. She wakened him and told him that his supper was ready, but in his groggy state he told her he had had his supper.

"How could you?" she snapped. "You just got back from Edith's an hour ago." He looked at her with annoyance and replied, "Well, then, I don't want any."

"For God's sake, Gerry! If you didn't want anything to eat why didn't you say so. You knew I was fixing supper. You could have told Craig when he came up. Well, it's ready. It's on the table. I'm going to have mine." She left the room saying, "If you change your mind, I'll leave yours on the table."

She was sitting at the table in the nook picking at her plate and not enjoying it when Gerry appeared. The huge knot that was becoming a constant part of her life was aching more than usual and she had the knuckles of her left hand pressed against her lower ribs.

"I changed my mind," he said. "I guess I was so sound asleep I didn't know what was going on. I remember Craig coming up and telling me about his ballgame and that's all. You go ahead and finish yours. I think I'll have a drink first." He went to the liquor cabinet and stirred the bottles to find the scotch, thinking that if Craig was going to sneak his booze he should be smart enough not to misplace the bottles. He took a swig from the vodka bottle and grimaced when he decided it was half water. He poured himself a very large scotch. When he returned to the kitchen to get ice, Marion had pushed her unfinished plate to one side and was staring out the window into the twilight with a frown on her face. "Would you like a drink?" he asked. The question was routine rather than courteous and the answer was the usual negative. Suddenly, she said, "No, I've changed my mind too. I think I'll have a vodka and tonic—a large one!"

He thought of the diluted vodka and knew that although she didn't drink much, she would notice it and probably that would be enough to start something. Taking a bottle of tonic from the frig, he opened it and lied, "The tonic has gone flat and I don't think there is any more. Would you like something else? There's a little white wine here but I think it has been open too long. How about some red?"

"Fine," she said without expression. "Bring me the bottle."

He got a bottle of red wine from the cupboard, opened it and placed it and a glass in front of her without pouring any, wondering all the while what she was up to. She was still sitting with her fist pressed to her stomach. "Have you got a stomach ache?" he asked.

"Would you care if I had a stomach ache?" she responded.

"Well, if it's bothering you, why don't you go see your doctor?"

"I've seen him," she said evenly, pouring the wine into the glass slowly until it was almost to the top while wondering if he was going to lecture her also about pouring wine. Craig had told her about the incident.

"What did he say?"

"He said to send you in."

"Why would he want to see me?"

"You'll have to find out from him when you see him—if you ever do."

"You mean there's something wrong with you and he wants to see me?" he exclaimed with anger showing in his voice. "Get yourself another doctor!" He got up and brought the scotch bottle back to the kitchen and poured another drink.

They sat in the nook, still untidy with the supper dishes, his plate untouched. He swirled the scotch and ice in his glass and stared at the table. She sat twisted in her seat so she could not face him and took great gulps of wine. That's the reason she shouldn't drink, he thought. She treats all alcohol as if it were something to quench a thirst. She thought, I never realized before how cold and distant he can make himself. There was only a faint glow from the late summer evening to light the room. "I'm not going to turn on a light," she said to herself. "I don't want to look at him." Then, as if he had read her thoughts, he got up and switched on the light over the table, perversely she was sure, and poured another drink. She frowned against the light and watched him get some ice. "If he can, then I can," she said to herself, and, feeling the courage of a full glass of wine, she poured herself another. The glass was so full she had to lean over it and take a couple of sips before lifting it and taking a big swallow. Then she leaned back and looked directly at him.

"Why were you so hateful to Edith today? What has she done?" Her tone was demanding.

"What are you talking about? I was not being hateful."

"Nobody could call your attitude pleasant or social, that's for damn sure! You couldn't find a thing to say to her, could you? You sat there reading the newspaper the whole time. You paid no attention to your grandchildren and you were so peevish they were afraid of you. Edith was really looking forward to seeing you and I'll bet it wasn't very long after you got there that she was looking forward to you leaving." Now that she could face him and talk the knot in her stomach disappeared. "I really didn't ask much of you. Once, just once, to give up your golf game and do something for me. But would you? Oh, no! You couldn't give up your precious golf game and drive up and see your own grandchildren. I practically had to beg, didn't I? No wonder the children scream and run away when they see you—you're a stranger, that's what you are." She was running out of breath but not of things she wanted to say.

"Now who's being hateful," he interrupted. "And I wouldn't think for a minute that what you said to me on the telephone could be classed as begging."

"Whatever I said seemed to work. Maybe I should get pissed off and talk like that more often. It's obviously language you understand." She was just taking another big gulp of wine when the back door opened.

"Hi!" said Craig in his cheerful young voice. "You guys having a party? You didn't invite me."

"Yeah, a party," his father said sarcastically. "We're having a roaring time—just the two of us."

Craig saw the untouched plate on table. "Is that mine? I told you I had eaten already. If nobody wants it, it shouldn't go to waste. Okay, Mom?" and he reached across and picked it up.

"I made it for your father. Ask him."

"Go ahead," said his father and his voice was rough and surly. Craig watched him pour himself a drink and saw that his mother looked as if she had been drinking, too. He started to pick at the food with his fingers, and his mother said nothing but picked up a fork and gave it to him. Nothing was being said and he realized he had walked in on an argument between them. He looked at his watch and said with exaggerated aplomb, "Oh, I can just catch the end of the basketball game. I'll take this with me," and he headed, plate in hand towards the living room.

"Don't forget the lawns need doing tomorrow! They should have been done today," his father's voice followed him as he left. "And see if you can straighten up the edges. You made a mess of them last time."

"Okay," came the long drawn-out dispirited response.

"And you'll be out there bright and early to help him, won't you? Like a good responsible father," Marion said with a voice like ice.

"I sure as hell won't be. I taught him how to garden long ago. Now he's on his own. All he has to do is put his back into it and stop daydreaming. And I'll be on the golf course if you care to know."

"And what will be your estimated time of departure, great lord and master?" Her voice was thick but she took another drink.

He looked at her with anger but she saw venom. "You're drunk," he said flatly.

She got awkwardly to her feet, placed her hands flat on the table and, with tears starting to spill, cried, her voice too shrill as she remembered, too late, her son in the next room, "And you are a smug bastard! And furthermore you're impotent!" Then she turned and stumbled blindly away up the stairs to her room.

She heard his voice thunder after her. "What do you mean? I damn well am not impotent! Marion! Come back here!" He waited for a minute as if she would obey, then followed her to their room and closed the door.

Craig had heard most of their conversation by turning the TV volume cautiously down and not chewing. "Phew," he whistled as he heard their door close, "I wonder what that's all about." He quickly finished the food, turned off the TV and some lights and went very quietly up to his room.

He could hear his parent's voices but couldn't make out what they were saying. He could hear his mother's higher voice. She seemed to be struggling to make herself understood. There was a period of quiet and then her voice, clear, almost shrieking, "Don't", I said. "Don't!" There was another brief silence and then he heard his mother in the hall yelling, "Just leave me alone!" He ran to the door and opened it and saw his mother going into Edith's old room clutching a pillow, and heard his father and saw him standing naked at their door. "Marion! I said come back here!" he ordered.

"Mom, are you alright?" Craig called anxiously as her door closed.

"Go to bed!" his father roared and Craig watched him turn and saw the purple butterfly on his white rump between the dark tan of his back and legs.

CHAPTER 18

The day following their blow-up was filled with chills and silences that continued throughout the following days without any signs of letting up. Gerry had got up early and quietly and gone to his Sunday golf game. On the course he was surly and quiet, cursing and rude as his game deteriorated to the level of his mood. To the relief of his playing partners he rejected the suggestion of repairing to the bar and went instead to the driving range where he pounded two buckets of balls without regard for form or accuracy.

Craig had awakened earlier than usual and lay for a while listening for sounds from either parent. Finally he arose and on his way to the bathroom he saw the door to his parent's room open so he stuck his head in cautiously and discovered that the room was empty. Pausing to listen at the door to Edith's room, he heard his mother take a deep breath and sigh. There was no noise coming from downstairs so he concluded that his father was up and gone. When he dressed and came downstairs he again checked the house and, finding his father's car gone, was relieved that he would not be subjected to a long dressing down and a parade of orders and criticisms. He cleaned up the dishes that were left from their supper and the wads of sopping tissues that had been tossed on the nook bench, made some breakfast and, radio under his arm, headed out to do his lawns. "And keep the damned edges straight!" he said to himself.

It was not yet nine o'clock, so he did the edges first so as not to upset the neighbours on a Sunday morning. By the time he had finished the edges and some weeding an hour had passed, so he figured it was safe to mow. He mowed by hand but even so the old man across the street came over and scolded him for making so much noise on Sunday morning. The man was deaf and his voice was twice as loud as the mower, which Craig found amusing and could not help smiling as the old man continued at length about Sunday by-laws with a segue into smart aleck kids these days. Craig mouthed, "Drop dead!" to which the old man shouted "What?"

Craig said loudly, leaning closer to him, "I said 'nice hat'." The old man glared at him and breathed so hard that a fine mist emerged from his nose in the bright morning sun, then turned away and crossed the street to his home. Climbing to the top step, he turned and roared, "You tell your father I want to speak to him!"

Craig turned up his radio a little louder and continued mowing the lawn and attacking the more recognizable weeds.

When he had finished and put the tools away, ("Clean! You won't catch me on that.") he went into the house and heard his mother moving around upstairs. "Hi, Mom!" Are you up?"

"Good morning, Craig. Yes, I'm up."

"Have you had breakfast?"

"Not yet. I really don't want any. I'll get something when I finish."

"What are you doing?"

"Oh, Craig, stop shouting. I have a headache."

He went up the stairs and saw his mother with an armful of clothes going into Edith's room. "What are you doing?" and this time his voice was not one of idle curiosity but of concern.

She laid the clothes on the bed and turned to him. She was without makeup, her face blotchy and her eyes swollen and red. "What does it look like, Craig? I'm moving into Edith's room."

"Why, Mom? What's wrong?" His voice was young and shaky.

She sat down suddenly on the bed. "Oh, Craig! How could I tell you. I can't tell you. I probably don't know myself." Her voice broke and ended with a squeak as she covered her face with her hands and broke into tears.

"Mom, don't cry. It'll be alright. You'll see. You'll see, Mom." He was sitting close beside her on the bed, his arm around her, his head nestled into her neck and his young eyes, struggling to be a man, brimmed with tears and splashed down on her shoulder.

For the rest of the day, Craig hovered protectively around his mother. She kept herself busy rearranging Edith's room to meet her needs but it was a child's room and much of what was in it had to be boxed and stored away. Clearing away the keepsakes from her daughter's childhood relieved her at moments from the anxieties of her present dilemma. Even Craig relinquished his need to hover and they laughed together at some of the souvenirs Edith had stashed away. Finally, Marion realized that it was after two 'clock and that she was starving and ready to quit for a while. She found an easy ally in her adolescent son.

She fixed a quick lunch and they ate together in the nook with Craig chattering about anything not related to what he thought was his parent's problem. Not knowing what went wrong except for one shout that kept surfacing in his thoughts ("I damn well am not impotent") he restricted his conversational gambits to incidents from work. His mother listened with one ear, grateful for her son's efforts to keep her thoughts off track, but when lunch was finished and the dishes done, she wanted to be alone.

"I'm awfully tired, Craig. I need a rest. What are you going to do?"

"Oh, I dunno. I guess I'll stick around, watch TV, shoot some hoops or something."

"Aren't you going over to get Robbie?"

"No, it's his Sunday to work. He won't get off until six. I'll just stay home—with you." His voice cracked a little on the last two words.

She loved him dearly for his concern but was afraid of another open weeping session so she said simply "All right, dear," and went to him where he sat and took his head in her hands and kissed his forehead, but he wrapped his arms around her and clung tightly to her, until at length he let go abruptly and rushed out the door.

She went upstairs and stretched out on Edith's narrow bed. She felt sure the turmoil of her thoughts would never stop, but finally she slept.

***

Neither Marion nor Craig saw Gerry during the following week. He had come in quietly late each night and left quietly early in the morning. Craig was getting increasingly concerned about what was going on in his parent's lives and he stayed home each night after work ostensibly to watch some game on television but actually not wanting to leave his mother alone. He really would have liked to talk to Edith, which he thought was strange because they rarely had much to say to each other, but she was still at the cottage without a phone. Marion thought her daughter might have called to say when she was bringing the car back but she was rather glad Edith hadn't called because, for all her idiosyncrasies, Edith had some kind of sixth sense that made her aware of other people's vulnerabilities and she was not yet ready to face Edith's poking and prodding.

Each night when Gerry had come home he had left his laundry in the hamper and Marion had done his laundry, ironed his shirts and returned them to his closet. She changed the sheets on his bed on Wednesday when she always did the sheets. He had left a suit bundled up on a chair and she phoned the dry cleaner for pick-up. She would have felt mean not to have done these routine tasks. By Friday, her shakes and tension had diminished to the point that she was planning a special dinner for Craig and looking forward to it herself when Gerry phoned.

"It's me, Gerry," he said when she answered the phone.

She had tensed immediately on hearing his voice and hesitated not knowing what to say.

"Hello. Marion? Are you there?"

"Yes. I just wasn't expecting a call from you."

"I called to say that I'm going out of town to a tournament on the weekend. I thought you should know just in case—." His voice trailed off.

"Thank you for letting us know." There wasn't much gratitude in her tone.

"Oh, by the way. I don't know when Edith is bringing your car back, but I can go with someone else if you want to use my car."

Marion wrestled for a moment with the ramifications of the offer and thought the better of accepting it. "I'm sure Edith will be bringing it back this weekend sometime so I don't need yours."

"Well, okay," and the line went dead.

She hung up and realized she was shaking again but these were not tension shakes, these were the consequences of raw anger. "Not how are you doing. No questions about Craig or Edith or the grand-children. Nothing. Not one single thing to show that he's a human being. Well, he did offer me his car. Imagine that! A gracious act—that will probably up his record to two for the year. He might even get the medal for Husband of the Year." She ranted on silently to herself and felt her anger dissipating.

The phone rang again. "That will be him again," she thought. "He forgot to say something nasty." And into the phone somewhat abruptly, said "Hello."

It was Edith. "Hi, Mom. I'm calling from Audrey's. She says to say hello. I'm sure glad we've got her for a neighbour. She adores the girls."

"Hello, dear. I'm very fond of Audrey too, and I've..."

"Just a minute, Mom."

Marion waited thinking that there would never come a time when a conversation or telephone call with Edith wasn't interrupted and still covered twenty subjects at the speed of light.

"It was Jenny. She was into Audrey's sewing basket. Anyway I called to say that I am going to bring your car back on Sunday. Harvey is going to work all day and I'm going to close up and drive in with the girls. But I'm going to ask a favour. Will you look after the girls for an hour while I go see Marilyn and her new baby? Remember Marilyn? We went to school together? She plays the violin? Well, would you believe I ran into her mother and that's how I learned about the baby. It wasn't due for three weeks so she had a section. I thought it would be a good chance to see her. Is that okay with you, Mom?"

"Yes, dear. That will be fine. I'd love to have the girls."

"Oh, thank you, Mom. You're a dear. I knew you would. We'll stay for dinner if we're invited. But not Harvey. He won't finish until about five and then it's more than two hours to drive in. Probably three for Harvey—he's a very careful driver," and she laughed hilariously. "That sounds mean but it isn't. He just won't take chances in anything. But he sure took a chance when he married me, didn't he Mom?" and she laughed again.

"I don't think Harvey's a gambler, Edith. He knew what he was doing when he asked you."

"I'll bet you don't know how much I helped him ask me, do you?" And Edith went off on another gale of laughter.

"Isn't it wonderful," Marion thought to hear such happiness.

"I gotta go, Mom. See you Sunday. Love you. Bye."

"I love you too, dear." She barely got the words out before the phone went dead. She started getting ready for Edith. "I wish I knew what girding my loins meant," she thought. "It sounds like a thing I should do before Edith gets here."

***

Edith did arrive as planned after lunch on Sunday. The twins filled the house with laughter and hugs and kisses. They had brought their grandma pictures they had drawn to put on her frig and their kittypiller in the bottle that hadn't turned into a butterfly yet.

When the excitement of their arrival settled down, Edith sent the girls up to her room to get the rag dolls off her bed. Marion said nothing.

"Well, it's Sunday. So I guess we won't see Dad until he gets home for dinner," Edith said. "Where's Craig?"

"Craig's up at the park, I think. As a matter of fact, he didn't say where he was going. But he knows you were coming, so he'll be along shortly. But your father won't. He decided to go out of town for the weekend for some golf tournament."

"Good Lord!" Edith exploded. "Is that all he thinks of doing on a weekend? I'll bet he hasn't spent half and hour with the girls this year. How do you ever put up with it? All the evening calls, and the business trips and the golf every Saturday and Sunday. And even if it rains so hard that he can't play, or snows, he still goes out to the club and hangs around all day." Edith was on a good run. "He might as well have a mistress!" Edith finished flippantly.

Marion startled. "I never thought of that," she said silently.

The twins came thumping down the stairs calling to their mother for help. "No dollies, gone, not there," came the duet from them to their mother's question of what was wrong.

"Of course they're there. Right on Mummy's bed. You go and look properly now. Scoot."

"No, Mummy! Not there." one of them said.

Marion took a deep breath. The time had come as she knew it would—might as well get it out. "The girls are right, Edith. the dolls are not there."

"What do you mean?" Edith demanded.

"I mean the dolls are not there. I cleaned out your room and moved into it. All your things are packed away and Craig put them in the closet downstairs, I think." Marion began to shake.

"What do you mean, you moved into it?"

"Edith, for heaven's sake. Listen to what I'm saying! Your father and I are sleeping in separate rooms."

"Why? What's wrong? Did you have a fight? How long has this been going on? Was that why Dad was so antisocial when he came up last week?"

"I don't know, Edith. I wish I did. And I don't want to talk about it—not yet, anyway."

"Well, what does Dad say about it?"

"Edith, for the last time—stop asking questions. I don't have any answers."

"Good idea, Edith. Let's let them work it out," said Craig who had just walked in the door and knew immediately from his mother's flushed face what they had been talking about.

"But I want to know!" insisted Edith. "I want to help!"

"Every time people try to help somebody when they don't know what is wrong they just make matters worse," Craig said severely.

"Oh, listen to Mr. Know-it all," came the sisterly retort. "Alright, you two that's enough," said their mother who was now weeping. They ceased their bicker and moved towards her to comfort her. Craig held back because he knew that if he got caught in the middle he, too, would have another weeping session. He sat for a minute holding her hand while Edith hugged her close and said comforting things and then noticed the two girls standing wide-eyed as they watched.

"Hey, Twinkletoes and Tweedledee, come on downstairs and I'll show you where I put all Mummy's toys and dollies and love letters."

Hearing this, Edith was able to put aside her compassion for her mother and she said severely to Craig, "You didn't read my letters, did you? If you touched those letters, I'll—."

"Every one," Craig said as he left with the twins. "Wow! I hope you had fire insurance on them."

"I'm going to get them and take them home," Edith said, jumping up from beside her mother and racing after Craig and the girls. Her mother sighed a gigantic sigh of relief as she dabbed at her eyes. "She'll be back. I guess I better gird my loins for the next bout." she said.

Downstairs, Craig was easily able to find the box with the dolls and another holding a jumble of Edith's banners, pictures, letters and miniatures that she had saved. Holding up the packet of letters she said, "You didn't, did you?"

"Oh, for Chissake, Edith. Don't be stupid!

"Don't swear in front of the children," she said more casually than scolding. And then quietly, "Do you know what's going on?"

"Not really," Craig said. "I have noticed that Dad is not coming home nearly as much and when they do they never talk, you know, like they used to about, I dunno, just anything. And he's been as cranky as hell. I can't do anything to satisfy him, so I stay out of his way as much as I can."

"Poor Mom, she's really upset," Edith said.

"I know," Craig said and his voice was shaky. Edith noticed and reached out and patted him gently on the shoulder.

They sat silently for a while repacking the boxes until Edith said, "I want to go over and see Marilyn and her new baby. Mom was going to look after the girls for me, but maybe you'd help, would you?"

"Sure, I've got nothing to do." He watched her checking the twins and preparing to leave. "I should tell you something but I didn't know how to. Anyway, I came in late and they were sitting in the nook and they were both drinking, and—."

"Mom was drinking too?" Edith asked in astonishment. "You mean, like, having a drink?"

"No, I mean drinking. She was all flushed and talking funny."

Edith looked at him in disbelief.

"Well, anyway, it looked like they were in a big fight" he continued, "so I left and I couldn't really hear much of what they were saying. But when it got louder I heard Mom shout something about impotent and Dad just roared 'I sure as hell am not impotent'. Then later I heard her say, upstairs, 'Don't', 'Don't' and then she screamed 'Just leave me alone' and I saw her go into your room and she's been there ever since."

"Jesus Christ," Edith said, looking at him with her eyes wide and her mouth open.

"Don't swear in front of the children," he said

She said, "Oh, shut up! Look after the girls," and left.

Craig spent the rest of the afternoon with the girls playing noisy rough and tumble games to give his mother a chance for privacy. He did go up and check on her once and found her preparing dinner.

"We'll have to eat without Harvey," she said. "He was planning to work a full day, then drive down to get Edith and the girls so it will be late when he gets here. You seem to be keeping the girls amused."

"They are cute," he said. "And they're playing games on me—pretending to be each other—so I put initials on their foreheads to tell them apart but I didn't know I was using a permanent marker pen. Edith will probably be mad at me."

"She'll get over it. I guess people can learn to get over anything." But she had put an emphasis on 'guess' leaving Craig with the feeling that she doubted her own ability to deal with her present plight. He knew she was still feeling hurt and depressed so very carefully restrained from saying anything that would upset her. He hoped Edith would do the same.

When Edith returned she found her mother setting the table and Craig in the living room watching television with the two girls sprawled over him. They ran to kiss their mother and returned immediately to crawl back up on Craig.

"They miss their daddy," Edith said, going back to the kitchen. "I wonder if there is some secret hormone males secrete that attracts women." (Oh, shut up, Edith! she said to herself and changed the subject.) "Mom, before I forget, thanks for your car. I hope you didn't miss it too much. That was really sweet of you, but you always do sweet things. Not that some people ever notice," she muttered.

"Edith!" her mother said warningly.

"Well, that's true," Edith said but heeded the warning. "I washed it and vacuumed it before I left and it's filled with gas."

"You didn't need to, Edith, but it was thoughtful of you."

"Yes I did! You'd have torn a big strip off me if I had brought somebody else's car back dirty and empty."

"I probably would. I'm a very cranky mother." They both laughed together comfortably. "How was Marilyn?" Marion continued. They talked about Marilyn's new baby and about other babies and other women who had difficult childbirths—a good chat and gossip that lasted until their dinner was ready to be served. At the table the two girls sat so close to Craig that he moved his arms only with difficulty.

They agreed to leave the dishes and go into the living room where they could watch for Harvey's arrival. The twins scrambled down from Craig's lap alternately to run to the window to watch. "Now you two listen to me," Edith told them. "When your daddy comes you stay right here and wait until he comes in. Don't you go running out, now. I want to say hello to Daddy first. Are you listening?" The girls nodded in unison and when they did, Craig nodded too, so they sat there, the three of them, nodding their heads violently and laughing hilariously.

"Oh, you— Craig," Edith said, but she laughed and then she nodded too, and then Marion nodded and everyone was laughing and nodding when a car stopped in front of the house.

"There he is," cried Edith and rushed out to meet him closing the door firmly behind her.

Harvey had scarcely closed the car door when Edith tackled him. Marion and the girls watched from the living room window, the girls calling "Daddy! Daddy! as their parents embraced and kissed and embraced again. They talked holding hands and smiling and then as Harvey released her and turned to the door, Edith held him back. They turned to each other again and Edith began to talk, the smiling ceased and when Edith seemed to have finished, Harvey reached out and encircled her with the gentlest and most loving embrace Marion had ever witnessed, so tender that Marion's eyes filled with tears and she gave a little sob. Craig saw and heard and said, "What's wrong, Mom?"

"Nothing, dear," she replied. "My tear glands seem to be working overtime these days. C'mon girls, it's time to kiss your daddy." She shoved away the tears with the back of her hands and moved toward the door, caressing her son's head as she passed by, loving him for his concern.

Outside the greetings were loud and persistent, Harvey tried to talk to Marion about how grateful he was for leaving her car with his family. Edith drove her mother's car close to her own and began the transfer of the load she brought from the lake. Craig appeared and, after greeting Harvey, helped Edith load and drove his mother's car into the garage.

"How's the driving going, Craig?" Harvey asked when he returned.

Craig shrugged, "So-so," he said and grinned. "I didn't get a chance to practice last week."

"My fault," Harvey said, still with a child clutched to each leg and demanding more attention.. "But I guess that's the penalty you have to pay for having such a generous mother."

"Yeah, so now you owe me, Harv."

Edith interrupted, "I'll tell you something exciting, Mom and Craig. Harv told me his company got a big contract on a five storey apartment building down in the ritzy part of town, and—." She paused and hugged his arm. "He's been made foreman of the whole project, all the plastering, tiles and carpets. How's that?" The congratulations were quickly forthcoming and warmly said. Craig, with a summer of work nearly behind him, was suddenly appreciative of how much this meant to Harvey and to Edith. He felt he could shake Harv's hand and congratulate him meaningfully as one man to another. He was happy for them, pleased about some insight into himself, and sorry for his mother who was behaving as if she had totally forgotten the wretched week behind her.

The goodbyes were accomplished at Edith's speed. She fastened the children into their car seats, escorted her mother and Craig to the car to kiss the kids goodbye, and while she had them there, said her goodbyes to them, telling her mother she would call, and giving her brother a kiss on the cheek and a bony hug, from which, for the first time in years, he did not withdraw. "You call me," she told him in firm tones. Harvey had been on the sidelines of her organization, and as Marion watched, she noted how tired he looked.

But Edith, the caring wife, had obviously seen it also. "I'll drive," she announced and they drove away leaving a resounding silence.

CHAPTER 19

On the Friday before Gerry had gone off for a weekend golf tournament, he had buzzed for Eleanor and when she came in they cleared away some outstanding correspondence and other office business. She had noticed that he was slow in dictation and somewhat distracted, and that for the first time since they had begun working together he was looking tired and drawn and not as crisp as usual. When he had stumbled through a letter to its final paragraph and then asked her who he was writing to, she pointed out to him some confusions in what he had dictated and suggested that it could be put aside until next week along with the rest of the correspondence he was planning.

"Well, then, I think I'll knock off early and go to the gym," he said and, since this was a code phrase between them, he waited for some response from her that would indicate her willingness to meet with him later but she said nothing.

He pushed. "What are you doing tonight?"

She looked at him as if his question infringed on her personal life. "I'm not sure but I'm bored with sitting around the apartment so maybe I'll call a girlfriend and go to a show."

He looked at her in puzzlement. This was the first time he could remember that she had rejected his overtures. She liked sex and usually was quickly agreeable unless, as she said, she had a little visitor. She caught him looking at her and said somewhat coldly, "Is there anything wrong with that? I do have a private life, you know."

"No, no, of course not," he said quickly.

She picked up a pile of files and returned to the main office. He sat at his desk for a while, angry about her rejection and wondering how he would spend the evening. Lately he was finding that a long workout at the gym was becoming boring but he decided he better do it anyway.

On Saturday he got up very early and started on his 150 mile trip to the golf tournament, stopping on the way for some breakfast and a take out coffee. He drove alone, and ate alone, preferring to do so rather than call somebody whose name was listed in the clubhouse as needing a ride. He used to offer rides but so many times he had got stuck with such bores, non-drinkers or come-to-Jesus freaks or men who got angry because he did not allow smoking in his car that he quit offering rides.

When he got to the course and changed, he found that his tee-time was very late which annoyed him because he liked to get off early. He was paired with a member from his own club whom he had never met and with two players from the host club with very low handicaps. After paying his green fees and checking with the starter, he went into the club house and got a Bloody Mary which he nursed at a window seat overlooking the 18th green until his tee-time. The checker had told him that the committee had changed their minds about randomly selected foursomes and instead had paired competitive pairs from each club by handicaps. Good, he thought, it looks like we are going to play serious golf. Fifteen minutes before his foursome was due to tee off he collected his bag and went to the first tee. One man broke away from a group of three and approached him. "Are you Gerry Williams?" he asked, and continued as Gerry nodded, "I thought I recognized you. Come and meet the other guys. I'm Ron Simons," and he offered his hand. As they walked towards the other two one was saying with hardly contained laughter, "Hit the ball, drag Charlie, hit the ball, drag Charlie," and his listener doubled over with laughter. Gerry felt a cold hard spot of loathing in his stomach.

This is the way it always starts, he said to himself. All the superficial sociabil-ity, all the forced jocularity, all the bullshit, all the hackneyed excuses for a poor shot, all the prying personal questions. Nobody just plays the game any more.

"Carl," Ron said to the joke teller, "this is Gerry Williams. Gerry—Carl Zerwithin. And Chuck English."

There were handshakes all around with the usual banter while they were bending and stretching. Chuck and Ron were sharing a power cart. Both were grossly overweight. Carl used a battery operated hand cart: "My doctor says I can play as long as I don't ride a power cart," he explained to the world at large. Gerry carried his bag routinely and had never bothered with a cart. They tossed a tee to establish order of play. Carl went first (or finally, Gerry thought after a theatrical process of lining up, wiggling, lining up again and then holding his stance interminably) and sent the ball slicing viciously 150 yards away onto another fairway. Before it had begun its slice, two people had shouted "Good shot!" Gerry groaned. Carl banged his club on the ground and said, "I shoulda waited 'til ladies day."

The game progressed slowly partly due to lost balls but mostly because of Carl's unrelenting fussing with every shot: he changed clubs, reset his stance, walked away and took another look, took three or four practice swings before every shot and a couple more after, and would line up a three foot putt from four directions and miss it two times out of three. Because the other two were riding, Gerry found himself walking down the fairways with Carl listening to a rationalization of each failed shot which ended only when Carl realized that he was drawing no responses from his walking partner. When Carl then switched to private enquiries, Gerry said, "Look, I came to play golf, not to exchange au-tobiographies," and from then on, a pleasant (to Gerry) silence ensued.

The game ended with casual shakes and thank-you's. Gerry had shot a 78 which satisfied him, Carl had carded 110 but a birdie on the last hole made up for every stub and slice. He would not be on tomorrow's card. The other pair put in scores in the 90's. Gerry changed and hung around the boisterous bar until the schedule for tomorrow was posted. The tee-time was again later than he would have liked and he did not know any of his foursome. On most other tournaments he would have taken the time to search them out or find out who they were but today the idea bored him. He had no interest in sitting around in the bar trying to be sociable. So he got the name of a good motel from the pro shop and booked into it. He ate an indifferent dinner at a nearby restaurant, bought a bottle of scotch, returned to his room and turned on the television. He fell asleep reading the Gideon.

He was awakened late the next morning by a car with a defective muffler whose passengers carried on a full volume conversation over the noise of their vehicle. He felt heavy headed and stiff from the motel's soft bed. The television was still on, he was still dressed and the little bit of scotch left in the bottle was not worth putting into a glass to finish it. When he looked out of the window, the parking lot was wet and the sky heavy with dark threatening clouds. The pro shop reported that play had been suspended due to thunder and lightning and that they were so far behind already that it was doubtful if his foursome could tee off before dark.

He stayed in the motel room reading the local paper until it was time to check out, then drove in a downpour to the golf course dining room where he ordered a healthy breakfast that would also do him for lunch. He was eating alone at a table for four when the hostess asked if he would mind sharing his table with a couple. He looked around and saw the dining room was packed so he could scarcely refuse. In a few minutes she brought a middle-aged couple to the table and seated them. There were no introductions. The couple poured over their menus and spoke to each other in whispers in some language he had not heard before but when the waitress came to take their order they both spoke in perfect unaccented English. He suddenly realized that his immense hangover was not diminishing with the food and coffee and that he couldn't stand the people sharing his table so he got up abruptly and left, paying his bill at the counter.

"Did you enjoy your breakfast, sir?" the waitress asked in an off-handed way with her attention focused on other duties.

"I guess I was hungrier than I thought," he said.

"Thank you," she said counting out his change. "It probably was the rain."

He walked away in the direction of the pro shop wondering what in hell she meant by that remark and shook his head as if that could clear away either his fogginess or hers.

The pro shop was crowded with people most asking if the latest weather report indicated that the rain might stop. The schedule was black with the crossed out names of people who had given up and gone home. He approached the pro and, giving his name and tee-time, asked him to take his name off.

"Yeah, might as well," the young man said. "We're not going to get off again today—the course is a mess. The committee is meeting right now and I'll bet they're ready to post a cancellation any minute. They'll decide to go on yesterday's results, I guess."

Gerry walked quickly away from the clubhouse hunched against another downpour and after a long search found his car. When he unlocked it and got in his mood was black. He slammed the door viciously, angry because he had spent so much time searching in the area he had parked in yesterday before remembering that he had parked on the opposite side of the lot this morning. He sat glowering at the world wondering what in hell he could do now. He was hung over, cold, miserable and depressed and, if he didn't know it himself, he was lonely. He drove out of the parking lot and turned in the direction of home. He was driving so slowly and carefully that a cop-car cruised suspiciously behind him for miles.

Halfway back, he suddenly decided that he would take a chance and go to Eleanor's. "What the hell?" he thought. "I've never done it without making an arrangement before, but she might just enjoy the surprise." The idea lifted his leaden mood and he speeded up hurrying towards his fantasy of her warm greeting and a leisurely chunk of sex. Fifteen miles down the road he passed the cop-car sitting behind an overpass. He had been going well over the speed limit so he slowed to the exact speed limit without touching the brakes hoping the police car was not operating a radar. But in another few miles the police car appeared behind him, followed him closely for a couple of miles and then, with lights flashing and a short siren burst, pulled him over. "Shit, shit, shit," he said.

Gerry watched the policeman through his mirror as he talked on his radio and presumably punched his licence number into the computer. He watched as the policeman got out of his cruiser and walked slowly towards him. As he approached, Gerry rolled down his window. "Good afternoon, Officer," he said politely.

The policeman looked carefully at Gerry, peered into the back seat and finally said, "Your driver's licence, please."

Gerry took out his wallet and extracted the licence, passed it to the officer, saying, "I didn't think I was speeding, Officer." He looked at him closely while his licence was being examined. He was young, maybe 23, with blond hair and a show of darker beard, somewhat less than six feet and so slim, well built and handsome that Gerry paled and held his breath against sudden sexual demands. He put the young man in bed, stripped him, tied his hands above his head...

"Is this your correct address," the Officer asked, and to Gerry's ears the voice was exactly right.

"Yes. Yes, it is—Officer," he managed around a lascivious swallow.

His licence was handed back. "I'm not going to give you a ticket," he said. Gerry was gazing at the young face listening more to the voice than to the words. "You have been driving erratically to the endangerment of other vehicles. Your speed has varied as much as fifty kilometres an hour over a fifteen kilometre stretch of highway. I recommend you keep alert and pay more attention to your driving." He stepped back.

"I was having car trouble," Gerry lied quickly to keep the handsome face in sight. "It was sort of sputtering as I changed speeds —as if the carburettor was acting up. So I was just sort of testing it."

"Better get it fixed," the sexy voice said.

Gerry moved carefully into the traffic, picking up speed and noting that the police car did not move. He was trembling and his hands were shaking. He hadn't experienced such an overwhelming sexual urge for a long time. He wanted to hurry to get to Eleanor's (or somewhere, he decided) but he kept within the speed limit and let the stream of traffic pass him. Another thought flitted into his mind as he drove—"I'll have to remember. If I get another place, I'll have to change the address on my driver's licence."

When he arrived at Eleanor's apartment building, he parked on the side street. At the front door, he rang her buzzer but there was no response from the call box. He tried two more times and waited, then reluctantly gave up. "Damn her," he muttered. "Where in hell is she when I need her!" Then just on chance he buzzed the number of the suite next door to her. The squawk box responded with a feeble "Hello."

"I'm sorry to bother you," he said, "but I'm trying to reach Eleanor Colman who lives next door to you. I thought maybe her buzzer was out of order. Did you happen to see her go out?"

He heard the small voice explaining something to somebody else. Then a man's voice came on gruffly, "Hello, what is it you want?"

Gerry explained again but in the middle of the explanation the man said, "She is not here. We don't know her. And I'll tell you right now that we do not like to be bothered by such enquiries. We don't snoop on our neighbours, you know." The intercom went dead.

"Miserable bastard!" he grumbled. He thought about trying the suite on the other side but then remembered a ruse the B and E people used to get into such buildings. He punched a number on the top floor and when a man's voice answered he said, "Telegram! Do you want me to bring it up?"

"Just a minute," the voice said and then he heard some muffled conversation. Then the voice came on loud and strong, "Since when did they start delivering telegrams. I know that scam you guys use to get into apartment buildings. You better bugger off. I'm calling the police right now!"

Gerry didn't wait around. He walked quickly to his car—not running in case he drew attention to himself—and drove away, cursing. He drove to an address in the industrial district of town and knocked on the door of a very plain building. When a peephole opened, he said, "Tell Celia it's Gerry the undertaker." He had told Celia when he first visited the brothel that he was an undertaker but later had to admit the truth when the girls showed an immense reluctance to go with him. He and Celia still laughed about it. The door opened and he went in. Celia gave him a warm greeting and called him a stranger.

"Two of the girls are off with flu, but I've got a couple of young boys, cute as buttons, if you're interested?" She inflected it like a question.

Gerry tensed and held his breath as the idea swirled within him. Then, almost with a sigh, he said, "No, not tonight, some other time."

"Okay," she answered. "You'll have to wait a bit though. Grab yourself a chair and I'll bring you a drink. Scotch and rocks, isn't it?"

CHAPTER 20

When Gerry finally opened his eyes in the morning, he realized that he had slept in and would be very late getting to work. He shaved and showered quickly but nothing seemed to camouflage a night of carousing. His bloodshot eyes looked sunken in his head from the bags under them. He slapped aftershave on his face hard to return some colour but the bathroom mirror told him he would have difficulty concealing his condition from people in the office. He loathed early morning meetings and he was already late. When he left his room as silently as he could he saw that Craig's door was open and as he went down the stairs he heard him rattling his breakfast dishes. He had not seen or spoken to Craig for days and he knew that he should—but not this morning, he couldn't face that this morning. He went into the kitchen and directly to the back door. "Good morning, Craig," he said, not stopping. "I slept in, I'll be late."

His hand was on the doorknob and as he was opening it Craig said, "Oh, hi dad. I thought you had gone. I looked out and didn't see your car in the garage."

Gerry stopped and felt in his pockets for his keys but could not find them then looked on the key rack beside the back door saying at the same time, "Go upstairs and see if I left my keys on the dresser—quickly!" he commanded. He stepped outside and checked the garage, driveway and front of the house. He saw only Marion's car. He came back into the house just as Craig came downstairs announcing, "They're not up there, Dad," and as a horn sounded outside. "That's my ride," Craig said. "Gotta go, bye, Dad."

"I must have left them in the car and somebody stole it," his father stated disregarding Craig's goodbye, but as Craig opened the door he asked abruptly, "Where are you going?"

"I'm going to work, Dad. My ride is waiting." Impatience was showing in his reply.

"Oh, yes. Well, take me to my office first. I'm late."

It was Craig's turn to be exasperated with a man who was now ordering him around and hadn't spoken to him for a week. "I can't, don't you see.? There's five of us in the car and if we could squeeze you in and take you downtown we'd all be late and get docked. Why don't you call a cab or take Mom's car—Edith brought it back yesterday. I gotta go," and he started out the door.

"I'd rather walk!" Craig heard his father snarl as he hurried off to catch his ride.

Gerry heard a car door slam and a car with a bad muffler drive away. He closed the front door and walked up to the local shopping centre where, after using the phone in a new coffee shop run by a Korean couple who did not know him, he tried to get his stomach to deal with a coffee and doughnut while he waited for the taxi. His hand was shaky and the doughnut was sticky. He paid and left quickly when the taxi arrived, not checking himself in the mirror behind the counter and not noticing the dribble of jelly from the doughnut on his face. When he arrived, he headed directly to his office but was stopped on the way by the senior partner.

"Good morning, Gerry," he said with his super salesman heartiness, "Forget the meeting this morning?"

"No, I remembered it but someone stole my car so I had to take a taxi and I haven't yet had a chance to report it."

Another partner stopped by the twosome as he overheard what Gerry had said. "Your car was stolen? You can forget it. By now it has either been stripped or it's on a boat headed for Mexico. Give me the make, model, year, colour and licence. My cousin is a cop and he's on the stolen car detail. I'll get him going on it, but don't hold your breath." Without thinking about it, Gerry grabbed a piece of paper from a nearby desk, scribbled the information and passed it over.

"Thanks, Kevin," he said.

The senior partner walked away saying, disapprovingly to Gerry, "The minutes of the meeting will be distributed shortly. There are a couple of items I would like to talk to you about."

"Geez, Gerry. What's wrong? You look like something the cat dragged in. You've got jam or something all over your face and your fly's open, if you don't mind me telling you." Kevin said in a quiet voice. He didn't say that he smelled like a brewery.

"Great!" Gerry muttered as he walked away. "This is going to be a great day."

When he got to his office, he sorted through some working files without doing anything constructive. He deliberately did not ring for Eleanor, knowing that she would know immediately that he had been on a bender. The coffee trolley went by and he got a cup and as he sipped it at his desk he had to concentrate on steadying his shaking hand. The intercom phone buzzed and he jumped, spilling some coffee on the file on his desk. He reached for some tissues and the phone and said as he mopped, "Yes?"

"Gerry," came the voice of the senior. "I can see you now."

"But Frank, the minutes haven't been distributed yet."

"Never mind the minutes," came the stern voice "They're not important." The line went dead.

"What the hell does he want now," Gerry muttered as he headed up the hall to the senior's office.

The senior was the only one of the partners who had a private secretary guarding his door. She looked up from her desk, gave him a severe look and wiggled a pointing finger to indicate that he should go directly in without her assistance. Frank was sitting at his desk but immediately got up and waved Gerry to the client's chairs in front of his desk, and took one for himself beside him so that they were not looking directly at each other. Frank cleared his throat loudly, took a deep breath and held it while leaving the impression that he was giving the picture on the opposite wall a close scrutiny.

"Gerry," he started and paused. "This is very difficult for me as you might realize, but, as the senior partner, I have certain duties and responsibilities that are not precisely spelled out in our partnership agreement. I feel it is my duty to the firm to take those actions that might serve to protect the firm from any negative or unpleasant publicity. You must appreciate, Gerry, that in speaking to you in this way, privately, man to man, as it were, I do so to save the embarrassment that would surely ensue should the matter come before the partners in regular meeting," he waved his hand to silence Gerry who had made interrupting noises. "You know, Gerry," he went on, still examining the picture, "the reputation of the firm can be seriously jeopardized by the actions of any member of this firm, partner or employee. I must tell you that your appearance in these offices this morning would have been most damaging to the firm if any client—-"

"What the hell are you talking about?" Gerry interrupted sourly.

Frank twisted in his chair but could not face Gerry so he moved to a chair opposite. "I think you know, and if you don't then you have a serious problem. I am talking about your less than acceptable appearance this morning: not only were you late for the Monday morning meeting, but you were unkempt, your fly was undone, you had breakfast smeared on your face and you smelled like a distillery. Those are harsh words, Gerry, but I will not apologise for them nor retract them. Nor will I entertain any attempt on your part to rationalize this unfortunate situation. If you have personal problems that are affecting your performance, then let me urge you to seek help. If such help necessitates time off, in hours, days or weeks, then please send me a requesting memo and I will authorize it. If you feel your work load is heavier than you can handle, then again, send me a memo and part of your client load will be apportioned among members of the firm. Have I made myself clear, Gerry?" He stood up.

Gerry was so hostile he could only trust himself to answer with a single, almost imperceptible jerk of his head. The frown, the glare and the set of his jaw and shoulders did not register with Frank who was now thinking that he had handled that little situation with consummate skill. Gerry stood up and left without a word, the only indicator that caused Frank to think that maybe he had been a little hard on the man.

When he returned to his office, Gerry sat at his desk in a rage so massive he was white and shaking. He would have gone to the washroom to throw up but that would have meant facing people who, by now, through the office prattle line, would know that he had been called up on the carpet. He checked his in-basket and his work file but he could find nothing in either that distracted him from his mood. His telephone was silent and Eleanor had not come in as she usually did early every day, and for some reason, today of all days, the working noises from the general office did not filter through. Eventually, after staring gloomily out on the panorama of mirror-windowed office towers his shakes disappeared and his foul mood gave way to the need to make some decisions. On the internal line he called Kevin, the young partner whose cousin worked on the stolen car detail.

"Kevin? Gerry. Did you get around to phoning your cousin about my car?"

"Yeah, Gerry, I did. I gave all the details. I looked up numbers and things in the Personnel file where all our cars are listed. He says he gets twenty stolen car reports a day but he rarely gets the kind of information I gave him so he said your chances are much better than average for recovery. Gerry, I've got a client waiting. Here's his number. You can call him." He gave a number and an extension. "Oh, yeah. His name is Ben Mahoney."

"I wonder what else the snoopy little bugger found in my file," he said to himself as he disconnected. "I wonder if there's a little note in there that I like young boys."

He dialled the number and got a garbled "Mahoney here." As he gave his name and explained that someone else in the office, Kevin, had called in for him to give details of his stolen car, adding, "He told me he was your cousin." As he stumbled through the explanation he heard the sounds of chewing and swallowing and then, over a mouthful of food, "Oh, yeah. Good old Kevin. Another mark for his good citizen badge. Just a minute. I'll punch it up."

Gerry waited.

"Okay, then. Gerald R. Williams. Is that your name?" Gerry agreed that it was and also agreed to the address that Ken Mahoney had pulled out of the computer. "You're in luck," Mahoney continued. "A patrol car phoned in five minutes ago to say your car has been found parked, no keys in the ignition, no signs of damage, and it hadn't been hotwired. Did you leave your keys in it?"

"No, I didn't. At least I'm pretty sure I didn't. But I haven't got them so maybe I did. I don't know." A long pause ensued. "Where did you find it?"

"I thought you'd never ask," Mahoney said. "Not a nice part of town so we patrol it every hour. That's why we found it so soon." He gave the street name and the hundred block. "Know it?" he asked. But before the question was out Gerry barely covered a unnerved groan.

"I know it's an industrial area," he lied.

"Yeah, it sure is," Mahoney said. "That is, if whorehouses can be classed as an industry." He guffawed at his own joke and Gerry felt obliged to join in.

Gerry desperately wanted to end this conversation. "Thank you, constable. I'm very much obliged to you and your fellow officers for being so efficient. I'll get my other set of keys and pick it up."

"Whoa, there, Mr. Williams. Not so fast. I'm afraid that we have to impound the car while our boys go over it for prints. You know just in case we find that it was stolen by somebody who has the habit. You can probably have it tomorrow—late. Phone this number before you come and see if it has been released. Okay, Mr. Williams?"

"Yes, okay," came the defeated reply.

"By the way, let me ask you," Mahoney continued. "What other keys did you have on your key ring or case or whatever it was."

"I had several," Gerry admitted. "House key, office key, safety deposit box. You know, the usual assortment. Why?"

"Was it a ring or a case?"

"A case. Why?"

"Was your name and address in the case?"

"Yes," abruptly.

"Then may I suggest to you, since you have given an open invitation to a lot of people we have come to know, that you get all your locks changed immediately. Now do you know why I ask all these nosy questions?" Mahoney's voice dripped with sarcasm and he hung up.

Gerry sat back in his chair and let out a long dispirited sigh. "I don't need this, goddammit!" he muttered and he thumped the desk with his fist. "I know exactly what's going to happen now. That smug cop is going to phone his nosy cousin and say, 'Hey, I thought you'd like to be the first to know. We found your partner's car. You know where? In front of a whorehouse!' and then he's going to laugh that stupid laugh." He put his forehead on the desk and stayed like that for a long time.

His thoughts had been in a turmoil but he decided he had to do something and get his head cleared. He dug out his address book and found Celia's unlisted number coded under "undertaker". She answered with a hoarse voice on the second ring.

"It's Gerry, the undertaker," he said.

"Hi! I was expecting a call from you. I've got your keys, remember?"

"How come? What happened?"

"You at the office? You wouldn't want to hear what happened over your office line, would you? With the switchboard listening in? You are listening, aren't you, dearie?" There was a clicking sound of a disconnect. "Little bitch! Come and get your keys and I'll tell you then. Ring two shorts and a long—I don't answer the door in the daytime." She hung up.

"I've got to get out of here," he thought in a panic. "I wonder if Eleanor has heard the latest extension to Gerry Williams' night out." He buzzed for Eleanor and while he waited he searched in his files for a local active case where a call would justify his absence. Eleanor was slow in coming. He buzzed again and waited impatiently. His office door opened and an older woman stood holding the door apparently uncertain about coming in.

"Did you need something, Mr. Williams?" She asked in a small voice.

"I rang for Eleanor." His tone was rude.

"I know. But I'm filling in for her while she's away."

"What do you mean—she's away?" His voice was much louder than he meant it to be and the woman paled and clutching her note pad to her chest backed uncertainly away. At that moment, the Office Manager, Cyril Chester, appeared beside her saying, "It's alright, Louise. You go back to your desk. I'll deal with this."

She turned obediently away and the Office Manager closed the door and came in uninvited. He stood somewhat formally, his long fingers entwined daintily in front of him, while he addressed Gerry. He cleared his throat importantly. "Now what the hell?" Gerry thought and waited.

"Mr. Williams, there are occasions when the ladies in our secretarial pool need some time off for personal reasons and we do our best to accommodate them by adjusting such time off against their earned vacation days."

"Yes, Cyril, I know the policy. Where's Eleanor? That's what I asked."

"Well, Mr. Williams, that's what I'm trying to tell you. Miss Colman came to me on Friday and requested, that for health reasons, she would require a week off. She said that she was reluctant to approach you with the request and I thought that was strange, in that you appeared to have a remarkably compatible working relationship." He cleared his throat again, looked out the window and gave a small sniff. "However, and I'm sure you know, such matters must be cleared at my desk so she acted quite properly. I recommended to her that, because of her age, she might be well advised to consider a two weeks period of borrowed time off. It has been my experience that the younger women on staff are able to get through this, um, what shall I say, this medical procedure more quickly than women of Miss Colman's age. I, of course, on behalf of the firm offered her my assistance in finding, ah, well, in finding, shall we say, appropriate accommodation but she was adamant in making her own arrangements."

"So what the hell are you telling me, Cyril, in your round-about snot-nosed way.?"

The man stiffened and replied with formality, "I am informing you, Mr. Williams, that your secretary, Miss Colman, requested and was granted a two week period of absence for personal reasons, and that, during that period, Louise will do her best to tend to your secretarial requirements." He turned to the door and as he opened it said, "Louise is a very sensitive person. I hope you will take that into consideration." As he walked back to his cubicle he was heard to mutter, "And I don't have to take any shit from you!" Somebody giggled in the background.

"Of course, Cyril dear, I certainly shall," Gerry said in a dragging voice as the door closed. "Now what in hell was the old flower-child trying to tell me? Eleanor is pregnant? She's off to get an abortion? He thinks I'm responsible? Is that the local gossip? Is that why Frank was so uptight this morning?" His head ached and he felt physically exhausted. "I've got to get out of here and pick up those keys and go to the gym and sweat it out." He stared at his office door. "If I don't go now and run the goddamned gantlet, I'll be here all night. So here goes." He put on his jacket, picked up his small briefcase and opened his door. As he stalked through the office, he was sure that the ordinary office sounds diminished with his progress until he reached the corridor in what he thought was a dead silence. Outside he grabbed a cab, gave Celia's address and sat back trying to relax.

When they arrived he had the driver go slowly down the block and not seeing his car on the street he assumed that it had been towed by the police for examination for prints and would be released tomorrow. Telling the driver to wait, he walked up the short sidewalk to the door and gave two shorts and a long on the buzzer and waited. "That was right, wasn't it?" he asked himself. "Two shorts and a long. Or was it two longs and a short. Shit! What was it?" He was about to try again when the peephole opened, closed and the door was unlocked and opened slightly and he saw Celia in a bathrobe with her hair in a net. "Come in," she said, and she closed the door after him. "You look a mess. I'll get your keys."

"How did you get my keys?" he asked as she was rummaging in a drawer in the hall.

"I took them. I wasn't going to let you drive in that state."

"Oh God!" he said. "I guess I got loaded, did I?"

"Loaded! she said laughing. "You could have put a 21 gun salute to shame. You three had a party all right." She handed him his keys. "I see your car's gone. They must have towed it. That's too bad."

He didn't bother to tell her about the car. "What do you mean 'you three'?"

"You and Lila and Ronnie," she said flatly.

"Who's Ronnie?" he asked with a terrifying sinking feeling.

"Don't you remember?" she asked. "One of the cute boys you saw when you came in. You said you didn't want anything to do with him until he came over and talked to you and you changed your mind in a hurry. He sure put you through your paces and then Lila got into the act. You sure had yourself a party."

"What do you mean? What did I do? Did I...?" he stuttered.

"What did you do?" she said, laughing. "It would be easier to tell you what you didn't do. But I'll tell you one thing, I've got a couple of tired workers on my hands today."

There was a chair in the hall and he sank into it, burying his head in his hands. She watched him for a moment, then thinking he was about to break into tears, she slapped him hard across the back of his head, knocking him out of the chair.

"What did you do that for?" he said with anger.

"Because you needed it! Now get up and get out!"

He crawled to his feet. "You drugged me. That's what happened! You drugged me, you bitch, didn't you?"

She had the door unlocked and when he got up, she pulled him by the arm and shoved him out, saying before she slammed the door, "Sometimes the kids play little games."

He staggered to the taxi and crawled in. His heart was pounding, his whole body ached and his thoughts were a meaningless kaleidoscope of possibilities and consequences. The driver was watching him in the mirror. "That was quite a quickie," he said. The snarled answer was "Shut up!" and the address of the gym.

The gym was practically empty. He recognized two people aside from the people on staff and cut them off from any conversation by a curt nod. His routine workout was painful and difficult but he persisted with it as though it were punishment for his sins. He stayed too long in the sauna sweating out the alcohol and, he hoped, whatever else they had forced on him last night. Thinking of last night again, he shuddered in the intense heat of the gym not noticing curious eyes on him. When he got up to leave the sauna he staggered and was helped out by another occupant to whom he offered no word of thanks for the assistance. A punishing cold shower pounded the cobwebs and confusion out of his brain and he began to think lucidly for the first time in the long, demanding day.

In spite of a fatigue that was draining him to the point of the shakes, he was determined not to go home until he could go safely to bed without facing Marion. He bought a paper and found a small cafe where he ate and spent some time circling some ads for bachelor suites. Finally, he gave up, called a cab and went home.

Marion was still up watching television. He realized he had not even seen her face to face for days and he knew he could not now avoid her. He just hoped it would not turn into some kind of confrontation—he knew he couldn't stand that, not tonight, not after this day's chaos.

"Hello," he said without going into the living room. "I should have phoned when I got back from the golf tournament to see if you needed anything."

"I didn't know you were away," she replied. "Neither did Craig, but I heard you coming in last night. Probably the whole neighbourhood heard you."

"Here it comes," he thought. "I'm not going to get into it."

There was a silence broken by Marion. "Corporal Mahoney of the city police wants you to call when you get in. If he's not in you can speak to Sergeant—somebody, I've forgotten his name. I wrote it down on the telephone pad."

"Probably about the car," he said. "Did Craig tell you?"

"Yes."

He turned to the telephone in the hall. "What in hell do they want?" he thought. "They're not going to phone me at night to say they have finished dusting the car." He dialled the number. "Corporal Mahoney, please," and then to save time he added, "If he is off duty, then Sergeant Yacovich."

"Yacovich," the operator corrected him by accenting the second syllable. "One minute."

A female voice came on the line. "Yacovich," it said.

"Oh, I wasn't expecting...," he started, then thought the better of it. "Corporal Mahoney asked me to call him or you." Then he gave her his name and a quick explanation of the problem.

"Hold on a minute," she said, and he could hear paper rustling and the sound of computer keys being punched. "Mr. Williams, Corporal Mahoney instructed you to leave your car until we could send a tow to pick it up. Is that correct?"

"Yes," he answered, puzzled.

"Did you go with another set of keys and take it away."

"No, I didn't," he said. "Don't you have it?"

"No, we don't," she replied. "The tow truck operator reported that when he got to the address he was given there was no car answering the description given."

"Well, I thought you had picked it up." He stopped in time: he was about to say that when he got there the car was gone.

"Well, then it would appear that it was stolen before we could pick it up. You didn't make a formal report when it was stolen last night or early this morning, did you?"

"No, I didn't. It was found so soon that I didn't think it was necessary."

"I'm afraid it is. As a matter of fact, we will require two reports of auto theft from you—one for each occasion."

"Surely, Sergeant, you should report the second theft, since my car was in your custody as it were when it was stolen again."

"Let's not get litigious in these matters, Mr. Williams. We can clear the paperwork if you see Corporal Mahoney tomorrow—early!" She hung up.

He sat on the small chair beside the telephone table in the hall thinking that there could be absolutely nothing else to go wrong in this unendurable day. There was no way he could face Marion with explanations. He got slowly to his feet and dragged himself upstairs to bed.

Marion sat with the television on but not seeing or hearing it. Craig came tramping in the back door and called, "Hi, Mom," before checking the frig. "What are you watching?" he asked.

"I wasn't really watching anything. I was just sitting here."

"Is Dad home?"

She nodded.

"Did he find his car?"

"As far as I can make out, the police found it and then it was stolen again."

"What do you mean, Mom?"

"I don't know, Craig! You'll have to ask him." Her tone told him that she did not want to discuss it.

After a silence, Craig said," Whose been circling the ads for bachelor apartments?"

"What do you mean?"

"In the paper, here." He showed it to her. "It was in the hall."

She read the marked ads. "Progress," she muttered, "finally."

CHAPTER 21

Marion was awake and reading in bed when she heard Craig get up, go to the bathroom and run downstairs. She had made his lunch for him last night but she left him on his own to find something for breakfast. As for Gerry, he had not been home for a meal for so long she was now buying for two habitually and she had decided that it was stupid to keep in mind his food likes and dislikes when she shopped. She turned on her bedside radio, otherwise she would have found herself listening for his morning noises and getting upset by the sounds of his presence. She drifted in and out of a light sleep and when she roused herself, feeling more rested than she had for a long time, it was almost ten o'clock. Guiltily, she started out of bed and then sat on the edge pondering what she was going to do to fill her day. She could, of course, work in the garden but she had done that yesterday and it wasn't ready for a big fall cleanup yet. She remembered that Craig had a jacket with a separated seam on the shoulder that he would want when school started again—his last year, he would be graduating—and then what? She wondered what he would want to do after graduation, certainly not go back to the kind of work he was doing this summer. And she remembered that she always intended to alter that off-mauve skirt and blouse that she shouldn't have bought in the first place—it just wasn't her colour. Maybe she should take it in and give it to Edith, Edith liked odd colors. Then, still sitting on the edge of the bed, she listed the chores: washing, ironing, mending, cleaning, gardening, shopping, cooking, and probably half a dozen other-ings she couldn't think of at the moment, and none of them jobs that she looked forward to much. "I've got to do something," she said to herself and started her day.

She was standing at the window with a cup of coffee watching some people help the old man across the street get into a wheel chair taxi. "I didn't know he was using a wheel chair," she thought. "He must have been okay when he stormed across the street and scolded Craig for mowing on Sunday."

"I know," she said suddenly. "Volunteer work! I wonder if I can do some volunteer work." She went directly to the phone, and after five minutes of searching found what she thought was an appropriate number and, holding her breath, dialled. After a short pleasant discussion, she found herself with an appointment at two o'clock this afternoon. "Of course we can use you," the woman had said. "It doesn't matter that you haven't volunteered before—we'll find something that you'll just love doing. I'll still be here at two, so ask for me, ask for Cynthia Connors."

Craig had bought a pop from the machine and taken it outside into the warm August sun for the morning break. The manager stopped on his way to the parking lot and asked "How're you doing Craig?"

"Okay, Mr. Cranston," Craig answered with a smile. "No problems."

"Enjoying your job?" the manager continued.

"Oh, sure," Craig answered with a laugh. "But I don't want to do it for the rest of my life."

"I know all about that. Going back to school in September?"

"Yes—August 29 will be my last day here."

"Well, check with me next year. You've done a good job here and we could probably find a spot for you."

"Thank you, Mr. Cranston. That's great. I will."

"May I give you a word of advice, Craig?"

"Sure," Craig agreed, wondering what was coming.

"If you haven't got your school program settled, think about taking a computer course or even adding it as an extra. I don't know a damn thing about computers except that we better get started using a computer for inventory, billing, pay sheets and everything else. Maybe we could take you out of the shipping office and upstairs—we'll see. Think about it, Craig. I've got to go. And you got to go, too. There's Harry waiting to give you his favourite lecture about long coffee breaks." He laughed and walked away. Craig got the lecture even if he had been seen talking to the manager. He would walk over to the supermarket at noon and tell Rob the news.

When Gerry got to the office, he called Frank immediately to make an appointment to see him and was asked to come over in five minutes. When he arrived, he got straight to the point and filled Frank in with the second theft of his car, his need to go to the police station and fill out two stolen car reports, then to pick up a rental car until his own was recovered, and if it were never recovered, then he would make a claim against the insurance policy.

"It was found in a slum part of town, I hear. One would wonder how it got there," Frank said. He had listened without changing expression to Gerry's explanations and had made no earlier comment.

"Just as I expected," Gerry thought, his emotional explosiveness of yesterday now under control, "Mahoney to Kevin to Frank and probably by now into the gabble line." Aloud he said, in a mind-your-own-business voice, "One might better wonder how it got out of my garage. Which brings me to the matter I needed to talk to you about. My keys are missing. It is possible that I neglected to take them out of the car when I came home. At any rate, there was no sign of forced entry nor was the car hot wired."

"It's possible that your son or one of his friends took the car for a joyride, isn't it?" Frank interrupted.

"Don't be an asshole!" Gerry's earlier control was slipping quickly away. "Of course it's not possible and I resent your snide remarks that impugn my son's character. That's no more possible than if your wife slipped out of her lover's bed and came over to my house and stole it."

Frank was on his feet, spluttering. "What do you mean by that? Just what do you mean? That's—that's slander! I'll sue you, you...."

Gerry got to his feet, his temper under control, and looked across the desk at a white-faced, shaking, drooling man, and didn't give a damn about anything. "Look, you pompous son of a bitch," he said. "Wipe the dribble off your chin and listen. My car keys are gone. They were in a case with my name on it. One of the keys was the key to the main office. Therefore, the security of the office has been jeopardized. I came to tell you this so that you could initiate arrangements to have the locks changed. Is that clear?"

There was no answer from the glaring, trembling man. Gerry turned to the door, but before opening it said, "About your wife, Frank. She's a good lay. I know!" He looked around the room, "That's funny. No witness." He stepped out and closed the door behind him.

He went back to his office, looked up the addresses of a couple of car rental firms and left the building. He hailed a taxi and directed the driver to the nearest address where he made arrangements for a rental car. He selected a large size expensive model with all the extras—after all, the insurance company was going to pay for it, and he was in the insurance business and he knew they would—or else.

He left the lot and drove straight home. As he arrived, Marion was just backing out of the garage. Seeing an unfamiliar car pull up, she stopped and waited. He got out and went over to her. "I had to get a rental car," he explained through her window.

"Oh, I wondered who it was," she said. "It looks like you picked a good one."

"Why not? It's the insurance company's problem. I've got to get a couple of things." He turned away and entered the house. The door was unlocked.

Marion closed the car window, backed out and muttered, "Have a nice day."

He went directly to the key rack and picked up the extra keys for his car and the house and stopped for a minute to reflect on how he had got in the house the other night. "Thank God for Marion's carelessness about locking up," he thought. "Otherwise I'd have had a big, big problem."

He left the house and at the first mailbox with a pullout drawer he dropped in his own key case after checking that it had a Veteran's Lost Key Service tag.

At the police station, he asked for Mahoney, or Yacovich but neither were in and nobody knew when they would return.

"What is it that you want?" asked the clerk behind the counter.

"I have to fill in two stolen car reports," he said, knowing that there would be more questions to explain that.

"You've had two cars stolen?" the clerk asked.

"No. Just one. But it was stolen twice."

"Twice? What do you mean?" the clerk asked with a look that said 'Don't play games with me.'

"Yes—twice! Once from my house and I reported it verbally and then after you found it and before you could tow it away it was stolen again."

The baffled clerk looked at him and said, "Did you tell the sergeant about this."

"I spoke to her on the phone."

"I don't know what the hell is going on but I guess you better fill out two forms. Let me have your driver's licence." He took the licence and copied the number and the name on two forms. "Is this your present address?" he asked. Gerry nodded and the clerk grinned. "You'd be surprised how many we catch this way—people who haven't bothered to change their address," he said as he filled in the address on both forms. "Fill these in. When you're finished put them in this basket." He walked away and as Gerry was completing the forms, he saw the clerk talking to another clerk and listened to them laughing.

It was well past noon when he left the police station. He stopped at a fast food place and got a burger, fries and coffee and took them to a nearby park. He sat in the car reviewing the events of the past two days while he tried to eat the greasy and unpalatable food. It didn't matter how he searched his memory, there was a great big ugly blank in there somewhere. Celia had tried to fill it in but he couldn't believe her. It couldn't be true. I'll have to go and ask her exactly what happened. Or ask Ron. No, not Ron, if I see him again I'll probably go off the deep end—and I don't even remember what he looks like. Or, what's her name? Lila, Celia told me. I'll bet it all started with that young cop who stopped me on the highway. Jesus! I'd bet anything that's the way it works. He got me all worked up just by looking at him. I should have been with him, instead of Ron. At least was old enough. I can't go back to Celia's. I can't trust her—not if she was in on whatever drugs they gave me. As he sat thinking, it was the image of the handsome young cop that kept surfacing, and creating a tightness in his gut. Suddenly, he got out of the car and threw the remains of his lunch in a nearby trash can and drove to the office.

At the office he parked in his reserved space, left his card on the dash with a note 'Rental Car' and told the doorman who looked after the carlot. He did not want to get into another stolen car scene.

As he passed through the general office on his way to his own office, he could feel the eyes of the clerical staff watching his progress. He deliberately looked casually around the working area and every person, whose eyes he met, lowered their eyes or looking quickly away. He saw Louise as she also dropped her gaze and said to her, loud enough for the others to hear, "Louise, I'll have some dictation for you shortly. Will you bring in my correspondence first?" Louise nodded and blushed.

She entered his office with an armful of files before he had his jacket off and his tie loosened. She left the door carefully open. "That looks like a lot of work, Louise. Just one day?"

"No, Mr. Williams," she replied. "That's yesterday's as well. Cyril was helping me get started and I didn't get around to dealing with yesterday's mail before you...." And she came to an embarrassed stop.

"Close the door, Louise. No, no," he said as she was about to go out and close the door behind her. "I mean, come in and close the door." She did so but stayed close to the door. "I just wanted to get a couple of things clear before we start to work. Eleanor and I have worked together for a long time and she is quite used to my way of doing things. Now, do you prefer to type from a tape or take dictation?"

"I'm sorry, I don't know how to work the tape machine and my shorthand is dreadful, but I'll try," she said, and then added, "I wasn't hired as a secretary. I was hired as a general typist. But I'll certainly try to do my best."

He looked at her, thinking, I can see the limp little hand of Cyril here, the snot-nosed homo! Sending me someone who is learning to type. He had looked at her so long without speaking that she blushed with nervousness. "Well, then," he said aloud, "We'll just have to take it slow and easy till you get the hang of it. And if you make mistakes, well,—-mistakes can be corrected. Okay?"

"God! I wish that were true," he said to himself.

"Okay, Mr. Williams. I'll really try."

"One more thing, Louise. I imagine there is quite a bit of chatter in the office about what happened between Frank Albert and me in his office this morning. If anybody asks if you know anything about it you may say that it was a personal matter and had nothing to do with the firm. I'll buzz you when I'm ready."

"Alright, Mr. Williams." She turned to go and then hesitated. "Maybe you didn't know, because you were out of the office, but after you left, Mr. Albert took suddenly ill and Cyril called one of the doctors in the building and somebody said he was taken to the hospital in an ambulance."

"Thank you for sharing that with me, Louise," he said in a thin, dry monotone. "I'll buzz."

She gave a little, convulsive shiver and left, closing the door carefully.

CHAPTER 22

Marion was flushed with excitement when she arrived home from her appointment with Cynthia Connors, who was, she discovered, a much younger woman than she had anticipated. They talked together for an hour during which Cynthia had spread out all the possible choices Marion could have if she was sincere in wanting to do volunteer work.

"Don't do it if the only reason is boredom," Cynthia advised. "Most women get a little bored when the children grow to the point of not needing Mom as much as they used to. Housework day after day can be boring. But sometimes volunteer work can be boring too. But it rarely gets boring if you are sincerely interested in people and willing to accept their uncertainties, their hesitance in making decisions, their need for someone to steer them. If you really enjoy people, Marion, you'll enjoy volunteer work, even if boredom was one of the motives that brought you here."

Marion had come with the idea in her mind that volunteers worked in hospitals. She had no idea of the variety of places where volunteers could be placed. Many of them appeared exciting, some required physical effort, others seemed to consist mainly of monotony, but in Marion's mind a volunteer worked in a hospital and helped people. So in the end Cynthia found Marion a place in a gift shop in a hospital across town. Marion had thought that an afternoon a week would satisfy her, but she discovered that, as in all work arrangements, preferred times and locations are allocated by seniority. Her schedule would be 9AM-1PM on Thu, Sat & Mon.

Now it was Marion's turn to be uncertain: Monday was washday, but she could switch that, Saturday was not a problem, except that was the day she saved for Edith, Thursday was her bridge day but she was sure she could get the rest of the women to start at 2:30 instead of 2:00. Cynthia watched her sitting across from her, her lips pursed, and a frown of concentration as she worked her way to a decision. "That's quite a busy time at Western, you know, being a maternity hospital too, and the babies going home..." she said. She saw Marion's face light up like a morning sky. "A maternity hospital! Oh! Wouldn't that be wonderful!" And Cynthia knew she had another volunteer for life.

Marion arrived home with a clutch of pamphlets that Cynthia suggested she read before a training session that was scheduled for Friday. She tried to read but she felt too excited. She phoned Edith to tell her and Edith was responsive for a little while but she soon got back on her usual theme these days, a kind of nagging about her parent's problem that Marion found depressing. This time she was a little more broad-minded. "Maybe she's just practising her own peculiar brand of volunteer work," she thought, smiling.

Then she decided that she might as well get started on the chore of telling the women in the bridge club. "I won't phone them all," she decided. "I'll just phone Dot. She's the moccasin telegraph in the club."

Dot was home and probably sitting by the phone as usual because she answered in the middle of the first ring.

"I think that's marvellous, Marion. I don't mind starting half an hour late, but I'll tell you who will—Isabel! She told me that if she was even five minutes late with her husband's supper he raised holy hell and she's scared of him. Isn't that stupid? I told her..." and she went on at length using up an alarming chunk of Marion's patience.

Marion was soon satisfied that she had made the right decision. Within a half hour Minny was on the phone saying that Cora had phoned after Dot called her and, after twenty minutes, the residual of Marion's patience was depleted. "Minny, Minny!" she said. "I'm sorry to cut you off, but remember my problem! I've got a weak bladder, dear. I've got to go." She hung up and laughed. "That will give them something else to call each other about," she said to herself. And she mimicked a catty voice," I didn't know Marion had a weak bladder, did you?" She rushed upstairs, changed into gardening clothes and got outside before the phone rang again.

Rob was on a late shift this week so Craig hadn't had a chance yesterday to talk to him about Mr. Cranston's offer to give him a job next summer and his idea that Craig should take a computer course even as an extra. But today was Rob's day off and he had been down at the beach with a girl he had been out with before and had come home early because she had to go to work. Now he was over in the William's back garden with Craig's mother helping her weed by walking around and trying to find something that matched the weed she had handed him. They chatted amicably together and Marion told him about the volunteer work she was going to do. Some small part of his parent's political attitudes had brushed off on him and he told her he didn't think anybody should have to work for nothing.

"But I will enjoy doing it, Robbie. And it will get me up and out of the house at least three times a week."

"Yeah, but," came the natural adolescent rebuttal, "you have to be there on time, and there's a boss of some kind, and you have to wear a uniform and that sounds like work to me. You don't get paid and it looks to me like somebody is taking advantage of a worker."

"Oh, Robbie! You are your father's son, that's for sure. Now listen! Are you working for me, right now, pulling weeds?"

"No, not really."

"Aren't there people who earn a living by pulling weeds?"

"Yeah, I guess." Cautiously.

"Then pulling weeds for me could be called work, couldn't it?

"But I don't have to do it. I like doing it."

"You like pulling weeds!?"

"No, I don't mean that. I mean I like pulling weeds with you."

"Why?"

"Because I like you! Now I know what you're going to say. You're going to tell me that you can work as a volunteer because you like people so therefore it isn't work. Right? And I'm going to say why do adults have to win all the arguments. It's got to be my turn sometime."

"Your turn will come soon enough—-like when I'm senile."

They were laughing together like old friends when Craig came into the garden. Marion saw him and called, "Know what, Craig? Robbie says he likes me."

"Gee, Mom, that must really make your day," as he walked over to give her a peck on the cheek.

Robbie was quick to move in and peck the other side, then turned to Craig and said "But I would like you to understand, my son," in his deepest possible voice, "we have agreed, in the public interest, not to go courting—yet."

Marion laughed and turned away to her gardening, and the boys moved away into the house and raided the frig.

"What did you do all day," Craig asked.

"Went to the beach with Lex Wilson."

"Who's Lex? I never heard of him."

"Not him, stupid! Her! Alexandra."

"Oh, I thought she was called Alley for alley cat."

"Well, they say she's an alley cat, but ask me if it's true."

"So did you expect to score on a crowded beach in the middle of the afternoon," Craig said scornfully.

"No, but I got something going."

They moved to the living room and turned on the television and didn't bother to either watch or listen.

"I gotta tell you, Rob. Something good. The manager, you know, Mr Cranston, well he stopped me and asked me how things were going and all that shit, you know. Then he told me to be sure and come back next year and he'd hold a job for me. And he said why didn't I think of taking a computer course because they have to get one and he doesn't know beans about computers. And maybe he could move me up to the office out of shipping. How's that, eh?"

"How come? Are you blackmailing him? Or maybe..." Rob poked the finger of one hand through a hole in the fingers of the other.

Craig threw a cushion at him and said, "You lousy..." but he didn't complete it in case his mother had come into the kitchen.

"No, that's great, Craig, you lucked out on that job. I wish I could have got one with you. You know what my manager would say if I asked him about next year? He'd say 'Get lost, kid'."

"Yeah, he sure likes ordering people around, doesn't he? And to think, only yesterday he was a bagboy just like you." The pillow was returned with more force.

"Are you going to hang around?" Craig asked. "I've got to have a shower and get dressed."

"Why? Where are you going?"

"I've got a date."

"You got a date? You? All by yourself? Without checking with me? Some pal! Who? Come on, I've got a right to know."

"You got a right to know balls," Craig replied, happy with Rob's enthusiasm. "Her name is Lee, but you don't know her. She doesn't go to our school—she goes to a private school."

"A private school! Well, fauncy thet! Lah-de-bloody-dah. How did you get to know her?"

"We catch the same bus home from work sometimes and we got to talking, and she's kinda cute and pretty cool, and so-o-o I asked her for a date and she said yes and so we're going out tonight."

"What did you say?" Rob asked.

"What d'ya mean?"

"I mean what actual words did you say when you asked her?"

"I said 'Can I have a date with you?' and she said 'Yes'."

"Oh, Jesus Christ!" Rob groaned and rolled off the chair onto the floor. "You can't say that! Haven't you been listening to me? You need some more instructions."

"Well, it worked, so what's the matter with that?"

"Everything," said the man of the world. "Everything. What's her name, by the way?"

"I was afraid you'd ask."

"Why?"

"Because her name is Lee Chang—really it's Chang Lee. I just knew if I told you, you'd make that dirty joke about Chinese girls."

"Why would I do that?" Rob exclaimed looking dramatically hurt. "Okay. Go have your shower. Or would you like me to come," he grinned wickedly, "and wash your, uh, private parts? Wink! Wink!"

"Wouldn't you just love to! Go home!"

Rob left, saying, "Full report tomorrow—-typed and double spaced."

Before Craig went to get ready for his date he looked for his mother in the garden and told her what happened at work and she reacted with the kind of controlled support and enthusiasm he could cope with. Then he told her about his date and as much about Lee as he knew and, although her delight was obvious and her pleasure great, she satisfied herself with a tear and a gentle kiss on his forehead. He went back into the house, relieved that she had not cried out, "Oh, my darling baby boy is growing up." He had read somewhere that all mothers did that.

Before he could get upstairs the phone rang. It was Rob. "Hey," he said. "I got a great idea. Ask your mother if we can have her car and then I can go with you, and, you know, sort of chaperon you?"

The answer was "Get lost!" and a dead line.

***

When Gerry got to the office the next morning, there were several little knots of clerical staff buzzing about something. He received a cold, if not a hostile look, from some of them as he passed through to his office. He had had a tortured sleep until a vivid nightmare catapulted him into full consciousness, accompanied with a screaming "No!" He had sat bolt upright, sweating, listening, wondering if he had screamed or dreamed he'd screamed. There was no sound from the house, but he went to the bedroom door and listened and heard nothing except Craig's fluttering snore. Relieved, he searched in the medicine cabinet and found some of Marion's sleeping pills and took one, restraining himself from taking two or more. Back in bed he wrestled with residual fragments of the dream until finally the drug took over and when he came slowly awake in the early morning he had only a dim memory of the ugliness of the nightmare.

He had been at his desk less than a half hour when Cyril knocked and opened his door. "Excuse the interruption, Mr. Williams," he said, with his eyes focusing somewhere between the top of Gerry's head and the wall beyond, "Mr. Webb has asked me to inform all partners that there will be a special partners meeting at 10 o'clock this morning in the boardroom. He asked me to tell everyone that this meeting must take first priority." He looked at his watch and wrote something on a pad he was carrying, presumably the time against Gerry's name, and left quickly.

"I guess the gabble groups already know the agenda," he mused.

At ten o'clock he was seated in the board room with ten other members, all men except one. Normally the room was filled with easy talk and laughter as the members waited for the meeting to begin. Today whispered conversations had taken the place of loud talk and laughter. Gerry asked the man next to him what it was all about and the whispered response was that it must be about Frank's condition. Bill Webb entered the room followed immediately by Cyril and went to the place at the top of the table, pushing the chair aside. Cyril stood beside him and counted those present then spoke privately to him and left the room.

"Gentlemen and lady," he began, continuing to stand. "Thank you for coming. It seems that all partners are present with the exception of Donald McCarty." He paused and looked around.

"Don was subpoenaed to appear in court today," a voice said.

"Thank you. And, of course, as you all know, Frank Wilson cannot be here to take his usual place at the head of this table. We are all very concerned about his progress. But first, I must bring to your attention the agreements covering the general management of our partnership. Without going into detail, the agreement states that, in the event of the incapacitation (there are certain other conditions specified which do not apply at the moment) of the chairman of the board, the next senior partner will assume the chairmanship of the firm. I am the next senior partner and that is why I called this meeting. Is there any discussion regarding the propriety of this action?"

There was a silence as the chairman looked around the oval table at the serious faces confronting him.

"Very well. Let me then bring you up to date on Frank's condition and at the same time try to dispel some of the inaccuracies that have been circulating. I have been in touch constantly with the hospital staff, including the two specialists that were called in for consultation, his own doctor and, of course, Dorothea, his wife. It seems that nobody outside the family was aware that Frank has had a long-time serious medical problem related to high blood pressure and his inability to cope with stress. His doctor had recommended certain medications and stress counselling, all of which were refused by Frank. There is no doubt that he was in a stressful position as Chairman and Senior Partner of this firm, and it seems that there were certain other excessively stressful situations in his personal life about which we need not concern ourselves. On

Monday, in his office, Frank became suddenly and seriously ill. He was attended by Dr. Sundhi and one other doctor who are tenants in our building and who, after an examination, called an ambulance, accompanied him to the General Hospital and facilitated his admission. Dr. Sundhi and his colleague should be made personally aware, by those of us who know him, of our gratitude for the competent and quick attention given to our Chairman. As much as is known at the moment, and you must realize that the medical investigation is far from complete, Frank suffered a massive stroke on the left side of his brain. The result is an impairment of his speech and also some other neurological damage that has affected motor activity on his right side. He is conscious, rather heavily medicated because of the pain but the doctors say he is putting up a good fight and that is important."

He stopped and pulled his lower lip in thought. "The only thing I can report to you regarding his recovery is this, and I'm sorry that it is depressing news: it is the consensus of medical opinion that the possibilities of full recovery are minimal." He paused, unsettled by hearing his own words, and continued. "I have, of course, on your behalf, offered Dorothea and the family our sympathy and our full support." He stopped again and looked down at the table in front of him, apparently deep in thought. Then he said, "I think that is all I want to say. I have been completely absorbed in this situation for the last two days, and I don't think I am prepared today to deal with routine matters. Since I have covered all of the details of Frank's illness, at least those of which I have been made aware, I would appreciate not having to deal with questions from you for which I have no answers." He stopped again and looked around the table. "Is that all, then?"

One arm went up.

"Yes, Keith."

"Mr. Webb, I know that..."

"Bill. Please. Let's continue with the informality that Frank insisted on."

"Thank you, Bill. I was about to say that I know that this is a special meeting but it may be important to our clients to see on record that this meeting was unanimous in approving Mr. Bill Webb as Acting Chairman."

There was a general thumping of the table which the chairman took as approval. "Thank you, all," he said. "I will keep you informed daily by memo of Frank's progress and Cyril will keep the staff informed. Shall we adjourn then?"

The chairs were rolled back and people left in twos and threes, talking in low tones.

Bill Webb sat down and stayed, seeking no conversational cues. He wondered if he should talk to Gerry Williams. Cyril had told him that Gerry had a meeting with Frank just before his collapse and had added enigmatically, 'It is not my position to say more.'

CHAPTER 23

On Thursday, Bill Webb stopped by Gerry's office and, upon being invited in, sat down on a chair beside the desk. He preferred this position rather than across the desk, and often advised junior members of the firm to follow his example unless they were in a situation which required them to challenge the client. As Gerry watched him casually as they talked, he could see that Bill was uncomfortable and appeared to be evaluating him which put him on his guard. Finally, Bill got down to the business he had come about.

"Gerry, Frank's appointment book shows that he had an appointment with you just before he had his attack. I was just wondering if you noticed anything odd in his behavior—anything that might suggest that he was, well, that he was acting not in his usual way?"

"There was nothing too unusual about him," Gerry said. "Except that I had missed the Monday morning meeting because my car had been stolen during the night and Frank thought it was his duty as Chairman, I suppose, to offer me a reproof." Gerry chuckled. "At least I guess it was a reproof. Frank was never very good at that sort of thing."

"No, he wasn't, was he? He hated doing it. But you wouldn't think a thing like that would be enough to bring on an attack, would you?"

"No, that hardly seems likely, but one never knows. What do they call these people—walking time bombs? Something like that."

"Yes," Bill said mechanically, and gave a small shudder. "Dreadful term! Well, nothing you can think of that might throw a little light on what went on?"

"Afraid not, Bill. Sorry!"

"And he seemed alright when you left him?"

"Pretty much his usual self, I suppose."

"I have to admit, Gerry, that I'm asking other partners the same sort of question, in part, for somewhat selfish reasons. I would like to know if there are hidden stresses in the Chairman's position of which the rest of us have not been aware. I think you can understand that."

"Of course, Bill. Very reasonable. And if you should happen upon something, I would think it would be of interest to other men in similar positions to yours."

Bill brightened noticeably. "Of course! You're quite right." He stood up. "Thank you, Gerry. Everything going well?"

"Like a well-oiled machine!"

"Good! Any problems, let me know. My office door is open."

"Hm-m," Gerry pondered as the door closed. "If there are hidden stresses, I wonder if there are hidden agendas, too." He was searching through his file cards when Louise entered with the mail. "I'm sorry I'm late," she said. "There was a lot of junk mail this morning and it's still a bit difficult for me to know what is junk mail and what is business mail when it's all personally addressed.

But I'm speeding up, I think."

"Fine," he said not bothering to look up.

"And, oh, I must tell you. The girls had a card from Eleanor. It wasn't much more than, you know, 'Having a good time. Wish you were here.'" She put on a little worried frown. "I do hope everything went alright. Sometimes these..." She flushed and covered her mouth. "Oh! I mean I hope she—she has a good trip home," she finished lamely.

Gerry had stopped looking in his file cards and turned to her. "I'm sure she will," he said. "Where was the card from?"

"I don't remember the actual place," she replied. "But it's up north and there's a picture of the motel on the front."

"I'll bet she went to her uncle's place. Was it the Hanford Motel?" To prod, he had made up an uncle and the Hanford Motel.

"No, that isn't it. Just a minute. I'll look." She went out and was back in a minute. "There! I had to write it down. It's such a crazy name."

He took the slip of paper from her. "Yes," he said, "that is an odd name," He put the slip on his desk and returned to his file cards.

When the door closed behind her, he looked up the number of the Hotel and Motel Association and dialled. The phone was answered by a young female voice.

"Good morning," he said in his brisk business voice and introduced himself and his firm. "We are trying to find the address and telephone number of a motel upcountry someplace. I wonder if you can help. It's an odd name—I'll spell it for you." He spelled the name out slowly and distinctly.

"Certainly, sir, It will just take a minute. Will you wait?"

"Yes, if it doesn't take long. Otherwise, I'll call back."

She was back quickly. "Just as I expected," she said. "It's named after the town. It's about 300 miles from here. You take Number 1 to Hope and cut off towards Penticton but go past Osoyoos and it's in the Kettle Valley area. It's got a very good rating, a restaurant, swimming pool, etc. Anything else, sir?"

"I only wanted the address and telephone number."

"Oh, that's right! I'm sorry. Here it is," and she gave him the information slowly and carefully. She thought he might have said 'thank you' before he hung up.

"What in hell is she doing there," he mused. "She wouldn't go away out in the boondocks to get an abortion."

He sat puzzling about it for a while, wondering why, if she really was pregnant, she hadn't told him. "What the hell is she up to?" he wondered. "Well, there's one way to find out."

He pressed the call buzzer. "Louise," he said when she came in with her notebook poised, "I'm suddenly feeling lousy. It seems like it's more than flu—it was so sudden. If anybody asks, I'm quitting for the day and maybe tomorrow if I'm not better."

He put on his jacket and walked out in the middle of her polite commiserations.

He had decided on the way home that if Marion had gone out he would leave a note. "Getting soft, aren't you?" he said to himself.

She was busy in the kitchen when he walked in. "I'm going on a trip. A couple of days," he said after a cold greeting.

As he turned to go upstairs she said, "Just a minute!" He stopped, surprised at her tone of voice. "I see in the newspaper that Frank Tomason is in hospital, and that he had a stroke."

"That's right," he said.

"Is he going to be alright?"

He shrugged, "Who knows?"

"Is Dorothea holding up?"

"The daily bulletin hadn't arrived before I left, so I don't know. I guess so. Is that all?"

"No, that is not all!" her anger rising. "May I take just another two minutes for our weekly chat. You left a newspaper with some ads marked in the Bachelor Apartments. Are you looking for one for yourself?"

"Yes."

"And?"

"Anything local is too damned expensive and you are bloody well not going to drive me out to some miserable basement room in the suburbs somewhere."

"So what is your decision?" She was pleased with the control she had over her emotions.

"I haven't made a decision." He left the room and went upstairs and packed. In ten minutes she heard the front door close and a car door slam.

"There are too goddamned many people on my back," he muttered as he drove away.

On the outskirts of the city, he stopped at a truck stop and had lunch before settling into the long drive before him.

When the door slammed Marion did not move from where she had been standing, leaning against the kitchen counter and looking out into the garden. She knew that last week a slammed door would have started the tear ducts working and a torrent of confused emotions sweeping through her. Today she said to hell with him and thought the lawn needed mowing—she would have to remind Craig. She wondered how his date went last night and started looking forward to the day when Craig would bring her home for dinner. She thought about what she might serve—perhaps leg of lamb, or did she eat only Chinese food. She'd have to ask. She came out of her reverie with a start remembering she hadn't given a thought to what she would wear to bridge today. It was at Minny's this week, and Minny would be wearing the same old thing, a kind of multi-collared tent that was supposed to hide her weight, and slippers. She pondered about what the others would be wearing and decided everyone except Cora would be wearing one of their same old things, so she went up and rummaged around in her closet until she found one of her same old things that she could dress up with a scarf. She examined herself in the mirror and concluded,

"Not bad! I still got a little figure. Oh, yes. I better remember about my weak bladder!" And she laughed.

She called Kate half an hour before she was due to pick her up and asked her if she was ready. "Good heavens! Is it that time already? I haven't thought about what I'm going to wear. What are you wearing?" Kate could make a recording for use on Thursdays.

"Oh," Marion said casually. "I'm wearing green designer jeans and a pink blouse with hockey pucks all over it, my bolero hat and cowboy boots."

"Hm-m," Kate said blandly as if she hadn't heard a word "Oh, I just haven't got time. I'll have to wear the same old thing! It's so depressing!"

"Hurry up, Kate. I'll be over in fifteen minutes."

When she arrived, Kate came down the steps and did a knock-kneed model walk to the car, swinging a huge purse and wearing a short, shimmering dress and a cocky hat. "I thought if you were going to get dressed up, I would too!" And she tittered like an old-time movie star. "So next time you try to put me on, smarty, remember that a bolero is a jacket not a hat."

They arrived, laughing—the last of the group who had been playing together since their children were babies. Kate, of course, took the floor and held it like an old pro, detailing what she would wear the next time Marion tried to trick her. Then they started to play bridge, most of them quite seriously, each relieved when they had finished playing with Cora, who generally paid more attention to her long, lacquered fingernails than to her bridge hand and who thought that "Double!" was the best response ever invented.

They played their own brand of social bridge, seriously but not intently. There was always some social talk before they started playing and today several had heard various versions of Frank Wilson's hospitalization so Marion was asked several questions for most of which she had no answers. The women tactfully avoided sliding into questions about the split between Marion and Gerry. Marion had Isabel to thank for that. Dot had heard it first and spread it immediately to the others who had phoned Marion with commiserations and advice. Then there were more phone calls between themselves until Isabel became so angry with the gossip that she phoned them all and read the riot act to them and actually made them feel guilty enough to stop making Marion the subject of their idle talk.

Minnie, as usual had provided a lunch break that was loaded with cholesterol and calories—croissants stuffed with lobster and dripping with mayonnaise, a salad of shredded coconut, mandarin orange wedges and chopped walnuts, and a chocolate fudge cake made with dark, light and white chocolate chunks. "Eat, please," she pleaded. "Don't leave me to eat all this by myself."

During their lunch and talk break, Marion said, "Now then, you've all heard, so what do you think about changing the time for our meetings to two-thirty so that I can do some volunteer work?"

There was an immediate chorus of responses.

"I think it's so important to do something like that. I wish I had the time."

"I couldn't work in a hospital...it would be too depressing." "I wish I could but my feet kill me if I'm on them for even an hour."

"Maybe we could start at two thirty and play straight through and just have coffee instead of taking a break to gobble up all this wonderful, delicious, fattening food."

"I've got to get home to get Harry's dinner. I don't know that I would have time if we started late."

"Why don't you just tell the old fart that his dinner will be half an hour late on Thursdays."

In the end it was agreed to start late to accommodate Marion for which Marion thanked them. "I think it's going to be fun," she said. "And good for me. It will help me keep my mind off Gerry."

"How are things between you?" Cora asked bluntly. It was a question they had all wanted to ask.

"Well, he's moving out," Marion said. "If he ever gets around to it. And after that who knows."

"I don't think it's a great surprise to any of us—certainly not to me," someone said.

But it was Isabel, the faithful dinner provider for a cranky man, who said, "Get yourself a tough lawyer. Now let's get on with the game."

Craig waited for Lee at the bus stop when they finished work and they rode to her stop together. Craig got off with her and they walked slowly to her home talking happily together. He would have to walk twelve blocks further to get home. He was happy she lived so close. Lee's home was one of the new monster houses that were rapidly appearing throughout the city. It had stone lions on the gate posts and an ornate front entrance. They stopped at the gate and Lee gave no indication that he was invited further. They had talked about their schools and families last night on the way to the show during which the extent of their intimacy was to lean toward each other, wrap, arms together and hold hands.

"Which is your room?" Craig asked.

"Why?" She wanted to know.

"I might wander by at midnight with my guitar and sing you a serenade," he replied.

She threw her head back and laughed. "That would be fun to see," she said. "And do you know what my father would do? He'd unleash these lions and they would chase you all the way home."

"That's okay. I can handle a couple of toothless old lions. As long as he doesn't come out with his shotgun to protect his daughter I'll be okay."

"My father with a shotgun!" she exclaimed, laughing. "My father is old fashioned. He wouldn't protect me with a shotgun. He would at least attack you with a ceremonial sword, probably wearing a quilted kimono. Oh, I've seen those movies, too."

The car gates beside them swung slowly open and in a moment a large Mercedes drove through and the gates closed. The garage doors rose, but the car stopped outside. A slim, elegantly dressed man got out and walked across the lawn towards them.

"Hi, Pops!" Lee called out.

Her father waved and smiled but did not say anything until he came near. "Hello, my dear," he then said, smiling as he kissed her on the cheek. "And I suppose this is Craig, is it?" turning to look at Craig. "Craig Williams?" He extended his hand.

"Glad to meet you, sir," Craig said, not knowing whether he was called Mr. Chang or Mr. Lee.

"I know a lot about you, Craig. It seems to me that I had you for dinner last night and again this morning for breakfast. Now that I've met you, it appears to be an acceptable diet."

"Daddy, I did not!" Lee protested.

"Oh, yes you did. But I didn't mind. I like to see you happy. Are you coming in now?"

"In a minute. I'll be right there."

"And we'll see you again, Craig?" he asked.

"Yes, I think so," Craig answered uncertainly. "I was hoping to pick Lee up after dinner?" He made it a question.

"You mean you haven't asked her yet? I'd better leave you alone so you can carry on." He smiled and turned away.

They watched him enter the house, touched hands and agreed on a time before they parted.

"Well, you're late," his mother said as Craig thumped up the stairs and entered noisily.

"Hi, Mom. What's for dinner?" He started out of the room.

"Hey, wait for the answer!" she said. "And where have you been?"

"I asked first."

"Okay. I'm getting some shake-and-bake chicken ready and some fries. How's that? Now then!"

"I walked Lee home."

"Is that all you're going to tell me?" she asked laughing. "I know I'm not going to get the same details as Robbie will get, but haven't you got something for your poor old mother to keep her heart beating in hope?"

"Oh, Mom, I really like her. She's pretty, and she's fun to be with, and she's smart and I'm pretty sure she likes me—and we're going out again tonight."

"Well, I guess that just about covers everything. Then I'd better hurry with dinner if you've got another heavy date." She turned back to her meal preparations as he hurried upstairs, her eyes moist with happiness.

The evening was still warm and they took their plates out to the sunroom to eat.

"Your father's off on a trip for the weekend," she said during a period of silence between them.

He said, "Oh," and there wasn't anything more he wanted to say.

After another small silence she said "The lawn needs mowing. How about tomorrow?"

"Okay," he said around a mouthful.

"And try to do the edges properly," she said in a growly voice, knowing he would know who she was mimicking.

He said, "A-argh," showing all his teeth and a mouth full of food. He finished his dinner and sat politely waiting for her.

"Don't wait for me," she told him. "There's a bowl of raspberries in the frig and ice cream in the freezer. Help yourself and don't get any for me. It was my bridge day and I had too many goodies." He left to get his dessert. "By the way," she said loudly so he could hear in the kitchen, "I'm going to start doing some volunteer work."

"What do you mean, Mom?" he asked, standing in the door and eating ice cream straight from the carton.

"I'm going to be helping out at Memorial Hospital three mornings a week— Thursdays, Saturdays and Mondays," she told him.

"You mean you're going to be doing bedpans and all that stuff?" he said aghast.

"No, nothing like that. I won't have any physical contact like that with patients. I'll be working in the gift shop, I think. I'll know more tomorrow. I've got a training session tomorrow."

"Why, Mom?" Still standing in the doorway spooning ice cream.

"Why what, Craig? Oh, I see what you mean. I just need something to do...to keep my mind off things, I guess." She paused and looked away from him out into the garden. "I should tell you, I suppose. Your father is looking for a bachelor apartment."

His face lost its gleam. "Is he moving out?"

"I guess so."

"When?"

She shrugged and said nothing. He went over to her and kneeling beside her, put his arms around her. She could feel his deep uncertain breaths, Finally he got up, kissed her cheek and left. She watched him go, wishing she had not told him, hoping she had not taken all the sparkle out of his evening.

Lee answered the door when he rang and was ready to go. They walked slowly deciding where they would go. Easily they agreed that, because tomorrow was a working day, they would make it a short evening. Tonight they would go to the park and see what was going on, and Saturday they would spend the day at the mall—"after I finish the lawns," he said.

"Would you like some help?" she asked.

"Would you?" he asked eagerly, stopping to look at her.

"Sure," she replied. "What time?"

"Whenever you get there. It can't be too soon for me."

As they continued their walk to the park they found each others hands naturally and comfortably. When the ballgame was over they wandered slowly back to her home. At the gate they said goodnight to each other and she reached up and kissed him on the cheek. Neither of the lions blinked and he flew all the way home.

About the time his wife and son were contemplating his hopefully imminent move out of the house that had been the family home since Edith was
born, Gerry arrived at the unfamiliar town he had been heading for. It was,
as he had expected, a small town with one main street and two or three other
streets that were struggling to change from commercial to residential. It was
on one of these streets that he found the motel, an old style arrangement of
small one-room cottages spread erratically among sturdy trees with a small
pool casually centred. There were small signs pointing the way to the office but
in the direction they pointed he could see no other building that differed from
the cottages. If he could find Eleanor without enquiring at the office he would
prefer it—no sense in advertising in a small town that a single lady had a man
looking for her. As he drove slowly through the complex, he spotted her car and
stopped well away from where it was parked. Now that he was here, he was suddenly not sure of his next move. He had not bothered to analyze the situation
on the drive up. He had taken for granted that he would find the place, knock
on her door and go to bed with her. He had erased from his memory, consciously or unconsciously, the fact that Eleanor had asked for and had been given
time off without once saying anything to him. And there were all these stupid
innuendos from prissy-pants and some of the women that she was pregnant.
She wouldn't be so witless as to get herself pregnant, and even if she did what
in God's name was she doing up in this miserable cow town—she would need a
doctor, not a veterinarian, unless the bitch was having puppies. And he smiled
coldly at his own joke. He sat watching, careful not to attract attention, with
lust and anger and indecision tearing at his insides—-then he saw her come out
of the cottage dressed in her old robe and go to the car. She rummaged in the
trunk and then returned to the cottage carrying some clothes over her arm. He
was out of his car and walking toward the cottage as soon as her door closed.
There was no bell. He knocked hard. The door opened slightly and he saw her
there looking exactly like she used to when he saw her through the partly open
door of her apartment when they first began their arrangement. He was smiling
a wide smile and the need for her was surging inside him.

"What in hell are you doing here?" she said, and her voice was cold, hard and
resentful.

"I got your card and I...."

"I didn't send you a card." Almost a snarl.

"I know, but I thought that we...."

She opened the door wider and stepped out and he was forced to move back
out of her way. The open door gave him an almost full view of the interior
of the cabin. Inside he saw a man standing in jockey shorts in front of a mirror shaving with a noisy electric shaver. When he caught sight of the man, he
stopped suddenly and Eleanor, on her way out bumped into him and then gave
him a shove backwards so that he caught a foot and nearly fell. Physical contact
with her was certainly on his mind but not that way and anger flared in him at
her shove.

"Who's that?" he demanded.

"None of your god damned business!" she enunciated precisely through bared teeth. "I asked you before what you are doing here. What do you think you're doing, spying on me?"

"Well, tell me then, so I don't have to spy. Who is that?"

"I'll tell you this much—he's a hell of a lot more fun than you, you cheap son of a bitch."

"I'll find out," he threatened and tried to move around her to get at the door.

"Get out of here!" she screamed, struggling against him.

They had already attracted the attention of some other residents who stopped at a distance to watch cautiously without getting involved. The door opened and the man from inside stood in the doorway in his shorts. He was tall and brawny and he was not smiling. He took Eleanor by the arm and eased her to one side.

"I've heard enough, mister. Don't you get the message? She wants you to get out of here," he said in an even voice.

Then came the adolescent response from the grown man, "Yeah? Make me!" and he took one step back. "That's my woman and I want to know what you are doing with her."

The man looked at Gerry and gave a short laugh. "Your woman! What planet are you from? Now then, if you want to know something I'll tell you this." He stopped, reached inside and picked up a pair of jeans and stood putting them on. "I'll give you until I zip up my fly to get lost. If you're not gone by then, and I'm giving you fair warning in front of all these witnesses," and he waved his arm at the watchers, "I'm going to beat the living shit out of you. Got that, my man?" and the last words scorched out of his mouth.

Gerry could be accused of many things but not of stupidity. He backed away muttering and threatening innocuous things like, "We'll see about this." "You'll get yours, you...." and the words that followed made some of the watchers wince. They watched him get into his car and drive away spitting gravel. Eleanor and the man went inside and the watchers dispersed.

He headed out of town, driving fast and shaking with anger. Ten miles down the road he stopped and spun the big car 180 degrees like a racing car, tramped hard on the throttle and raced back. "The rotten two-timing bitch!" he roared, pounding his fists on the steering wheel. "She can't do that to me and get away with it!" He drove past the motel slowly and saw that her car was still there. He didn't know what he wanted to do but he knew that the man she was with was bigger and younger, and he was not ready to call his bluff. He drove away from the motel and found a bar on the main street.

The bar was empty except for two men at a table who were pouring over some documents while having a beer. He sat well away from them and ordered a double scotch before the barman got off his stool. When the drink arrived the barman stayed around wiping the counter and rearranging bottles and glasses. "Just passing through?" he tried and got a snarled "No!" "Great day for driving," he tried again. "I'd sure like to be out there, maybe drive up to the bridge and drop a hook in."

"Well, go! For crissake," was what he got in reply to his friendly overtures. "Don't hang around crying on my shoulder. I got enough troubles of my own." The barman gave him a long hard look and turned away. "Bring me another before you get settled on your fat ass."

The barman reached under the counter and pulled out a small bat and walked over to him. "Watch your lips, mister, or I'll make the side of your head look like hamburger."

"Trouble, Charlie?" came a voice from one of the men at the table.

"No, not yet, Reg. But I got a stranger here who doesn't like our town." He continued looking hard at Gerry. "Sure you want that drink?"

"Yes! And another one after that."

The barman brought the drink and put it down.

"Now bring the next one."

"You driving, mister?"

"What makes you suddenly interested in my business. The only interest I have in your business is seeing how fast you can bring me another drink." And he downed the drink in front of him.

The barman brought another drink and carried the bat with him. He put the drink down and rapped the edge of the bar with the bat. "Your last drink in this place, mister—tonight or ever. When you finish that, get the hell out. That's twelve bucks—now!"

Gerry finished the drink, slammed some money down, threw the glass over his shoulder and walked out. One of the men at the table got quickly to his feet and watched the car as it drove away. "Let me use your phone, Charlie," he said and the phone was handed to him. He dialled and said, "Hello, Wes? This is Reg. I'm over at Charlie's. There's a guy just left here, boozed up pretty good and looking for trouble. I'm not on duty and I haven't got my car or I'd tail the miserable-son-of-a-bitch and get him out of town." They talked a little longer and Reg put the phone down and said to Charlie and the other man. "Seems that somebody phoned in a complaint about this guy earlier, blue Olds with rental plates. Seems he was kicking up a ruckus at the Motel and threatening some woman who's staying there. Wes is going to keep an eye out for him."

"Think we should lend a hand?" the other man said.

"Naw. Wes'll handle it. If he needs us he'll turn on the siren. Let's get this stuff out of the way." They turned back to their paperwork.

Gerry didn't go straight to the motel. He drove around looking for another bar but couldn't find one. Three doubles on an empty stomach were working their way through his system. His frustration took him on a round-about way to the motel not noticing the police car that turned into the lot behind him. Wes, the on-duty police officer, had come to check with the manager about the earlier disturbance. Gerry parked behind Eleanor's car blocking it from getting out, walked over to it and kicked the driver's door several times, then walked to the motel door and pounded on it. Wes was out of his police car fast, shouting, "Hold it! Police!" Gerry turned, saw the uniform and slumped, looking at the door and then at the officer.

"What's going on?" he demanded. "Move away from that door! Keep your hands in sight!"

The door opened cautiously and Eleanor's head showed.

"Get back inside, lady," the officer shouted. The door closed quickly and the window curtain was pulled aside.

"That's her! That's the bitch!" Gerry shouted, and made a dash for the door, only to find himself flat on his stomach on the ground with a heavy knee on his back and his arms being jerked back and held until he heard the click of handcuffs.

"Are you related to that woman?" the officer asked.

"Hell, I wouldn't marry that whore." His voice was muffled by the grass in his face.

"Get up!" he heard and he was assisted roughly to his feet and jerked toward the police car. "Get in!" and he was again assisted by a shove. He found himself inside the police car sprawled awkwardly around his handcuffed arms. He watched the officer talking to Eleanor and the man she was with, someone who came from the office, and two other people who emerged from nearby cottages.

"Well, we'll have a field day with you," the officer said when he came back to the car. "Let's see: creating a disturbance, damaged to property, threatening another person, another disturbance at Charlie's bar—you didn't know there were two police officers watching your performance there, did you? Probably some other things we can find. Oh, yes. DWI. That will be easy.

Well, let's get you down to the station and get you registered and tucked away. We haven't had visitors for a long time and the keeper of the keys, his name is Francis, will be delighted to have something to do. Yeah, he'll enjoy your company. We keep him on staff because he likes doing the body searches—he's very thorough, insists he can't do one in less than an hour. Of course we leave him alone, he doesn't like to be watched, you know. Sort of a prima donna, you might say. Well, here we are. Let me give you a hand out, sir. Whoops! Did you trip. Oh, my that must have hurt. I'll bet you skinned your knees. Well, that's too bad. Now let's go in and you can do a blowjob on the breathalyser, and we'll do some bookwork and then I'll let you meet Francis."

Gerry could only groan.

CHAPTER 24

The next three days went racing by for everybody except Gerry. He had appeared before the local judge on Friday, the day following his arrest. He was unkempt and hung over, not so much from drinking because he had frequently had much more to drink without a hangover penalty, but from an excess of anger, hunger, and a miserable night in a jail cell following his session with Francis. The bailiff read out such a long list of charges against him that the judge called the prosecutor to the bench and suggested to him in strong language that he was being overzealous and that he could have fifteen minutes to consult with his colleagues and reduce the charges to something that was adequate to convict and throw out those charges that would be argued interminably and result only in a waste of the court's time.

A young lawyer was present in court waiting for his case to come up, and had approached Gerry with an offer of legal assistance that was quickly accepted. After a short discussion with the prosecutor, the charges were reduced to DWI, creating a disturbance and threatening a police officer. However, in order to arrange bail the young lawyer had to impress the court with Gerry's position in the community, the status of his firm and several other factors he had been able to drag out of Gerry in the fifteen minute hiatus. The trial date was set for two weeks from the day. A local reporter was freelancing in court and from his extensive notes and quickly arranged interviews with some local citizens, sent off a news item to Gerry's home town news service, carefully noting the original list of charges.

Following his release, Gerry foolishly returned to the only motel in town with the hopes of getting cleaned up and spending the night. The manager phoned the police as soon as Gerry opened the office door and five minutes later a siren announced the arrival of Wes who made it loudly known that Gerald Williams was persona non grata in this office, in this motel, on this street and in this town—and, unless he was really anxious to meet Francis again, he'd better seriously consider the idea of making a lot of dust after driving carefully to the town limits, starting—now! And he banged the counter with his nightstick to make his point.

At the next town Gerry booked into a chain motel and, after cleaning up, had a quick meal in a corner of the dining room. He was still in a cold fury because of Eleanor and that whole messy situation she had gotten him into. "Two-timing bitch," he muttered just as the waitress approached his table. Her shocked face escaped his notice. Between thoughts of Eleanor and the man she had hooked up with, the police and that rotten sadist Francis, he kept himself so worked up that his food sat in acid lumps in his stomach so that by nightfall sleep was impossible. He wished he had had the foresight to get a bottle of scotch, which was the only criticism of his own behavior he could make. He had given no thought that the news of his arrest in a small town 300 miles away might reach his home town before him.

On Friday, while Gerry was facing a judge in a small town, Marion had met Cynthia Connors for a training session. There hadn't been much training to do. She had been taken on a walking tour of the whole hospital, into areas that were closed to the public, but were now open to her because of her 'uniform'—a loose, floral, cotton coat that designated her as a volunteer. Her basic job would be in the gift shop, but, she was soon to learn, people expected her to know where every ward was and where a patient with a whispered problem might be found. The gift shop was small and pleasant and, to her immense relief, had only a small drawer for money. She had been terrified that she would have to learn to operate one of those computer things. She was left alone while Cynthia and the duty volunteer went off for coffee and while they were away she helped a woman select a bonnet and bootees for her first grandchild—her first sale! She told the other two all about it when they returned and in the telling remembered that she hadn't made out a sales slip or entered the sale in the daily record, and so was forced to make a blushing confession of her failure.

Cynthia only laughed and asked her if she could start on Monday.

When she got home she was excited and exhausted. She made herself a pot of tea and took it to the telephone to talk to somebody about her day. She phoned Edith first and received from her the measured enthusiasm that Edith meted out for any event not directly related to her children or her husband.

"Oh, Mom, that's wonderful," Edith burbled. "You'll enjoy that. Now don't work too hard. Sometimes those people take advantage of old people, I mean, take advantage of other people—well, you know what I mean. Did I tell you that as soon as Harvey's finished with this job, they've got another one all lined up for him and it's three times as big as the one he's on now, so he'll have a crew of six or seven full-time. The men were so pleased they all went out for a drink. Harvey only had one. He isn't much of a drinker. Isn't that great? He's really all pumped up about it. How's Craig?"

Marion volunteered the skeleton details of Craig's emerging romance which they then built up in their fantasies until Edith asked the girl's name. "Cheng?" she said. "Lee Cheng? That's Chinese, isn't it?"

"Yes, Edith, it is. And don't say it in that tone of voice. Craig told me her family has been over here for four generations and that her father studied at Oxford."

"In Oxford ! That's in England! What was he doing there?"

"I don't know, Edith. Studying, I assume."

"Well, it certainly sounds odd to me. Tell Craig hello for me. I'll call you next week." And Edith said goodbye and hung up having unwittingly pricked her mother's brief bubble of enthusiasm. Marion had noticed that she had not asked after her father. She wakened on Saturday to such a beautiful sparkling day that she thought nothing would ever get her down again. She had slept in until the late morning sun was so bright that it demanded her arousal. She had picked up her book, intent on getting a good read before the shopping and phone calls but the noise of the lawn mower and the happy chatter outside distracted her. She looked out the window and saw Craig and a very pretty dark-haired girl sitting in the middle of the lawn apparently playing she-loves-me-she-loves-me-not with dandelions and laughter. Ordinarily, she would have spent some time in the garden on a good Saturday, but she decided against it and dressed in shopping clothes instead before taking a cup of coffee out to meet the girl.

"Craig is an enigma, Mrs. Williams," Lee said bubbling with laughter after the introductions. "He wants to use dandelions because they have so many petals and it lasts a long time—but then he starts pulling them out two or three at a time to make it go faster, and I tell him it will never come out right if he does that."

"And I tell her that the best way to play is with a flower with just one petal so you have the right answer immediately." Craig picked up a small handful of discarded dandelion petals and sprinkled them on her hair and as she smiled at him she made no move to shake them loose. "Come on, slave!" he ordered. "If we don't hurry up we'll never get down to the mall."

Lee had stood formally with her hands clasped in front of her and made a stiff bow, saying, "Yes, Master," dropping some dandelion petals as she did so.

Craig had moved close to her and was gently picking other leaves from her hair while he said, "I'd like to see you do that to me for the rest of my life."

"Do what?" she asked. "This?" She made another formal bow and he nodded with pleasure.

"Then, Master," Lee replied, standing with theatrical coyness and eyes down cast, "You must present my father with the head of a red dragon slain by your own hand and, for me, two tickets to today's matinee, just as you promised."

They laughed and went back to their gardening. Marion had watched them with such pleasure that her eyes were moist and she was reluctant to leave but knew she should.

"I have to go shopping," she called to them. "Is there anything you would like for lunch?"

"I'd like hamburgers and hot dogs and huckleberry pie, please," Craig shouted.

"You'll probably get a tuna fish sandwich," his mother responded. "Lee? What would you like, dear?"

Lee put down her rake and walked toward her. "Thank you, Mrs. Williams, but I really should go home for lunch."

"I'd be delighted if you could stay, Lee. We could lock the door and keep Craig out in the garden and maybe we could talk."

"Would you invite me some other time, Mrs. Williams? I really do have to go home and look after my great grandmother. She's 102 and very frail and shaky and she likes someone to help her with her food so she doesn't spill. So I try to do it when ever I can so that my mother and grandmother get a little break."

"What a wonderful family!" Marion exclaimed. Your parents, your grandparents and great grandparents all living together."

"It is not quite like that, Mrs. Williams. My great grandfather died many years ago and my grandfather was killed in France during the war. My father is their only son and I have two sisters and no brothers. So my father is the only man around—so it's not quite the ordinary family."

"Just the same, you seem to be a person who comes from a very happy home. You're so sweet and charming. I certainly will invite you some other time, Lee, and not for tuna fish sandwiches."

"Oh, good grief!" Craig interrupted. "Is that what you're feeding me for lunch again?"

"You won't starve," said his mother over her shoulder as she walked to the garage.

When it was time for Lee to go Craig walked her home and got home in time to finish the gardening before his mother returned from shopping. "It looks great, Craig. You've done a good job. Your father...." She had been about to say 'Your father couldn't complain about that' but she stopped realizing she should not spoil the day by opening up their family frictions again.

"Where is Dad?" Craig asked suddenly, blocking her intent.

"I don't know. He didn't say. He just packed a bag, said he was going on a business trip and left."

He took some grocery bags from her and together they went inside.

"Is he really going to move out?" Craig's young face was twisted with concern.

"Craig," his mother turned to face him. "I know you don't want to hear this, but I hope he is. And I hope he is because he doesn't love me any more and now I'm beginning to think he never has. And Craig, that hurts! It hurts more than I could make you believe. All those years...." Her eyes filled with tears and she shook her head sadly and repeated, "All those years. What a fool! And Craig, I don't love him any more either. I've never hated anybody in my whole life. I don't think I know what hate is, but I think I hate him, Craig. I'm sorry because he's your father and I hate him and I can't help it."

"He's a dirty, rotten, selfish bastard," Craig exploded and turned to go.

"Oh, Craig dear. I'm sorry you heard me yell that at him. I shouldn't have...." But Craig had already reached his room and was face down on his bed holding his breath as he did when he was a child until somebody came to make it better. Nobody came this time.

A half hour passed and during that time Craig grew up a little more. He got up and washed his face and found his mother sitting in the sun room, quiet and calm, looking out into the garden.

"I'm sorry, Mom," he said. "I'm not sorry for what I said about him. He is selfish, damned selfish. But then when I was up in my room I thought I was being just as selfish as him. I walked out on you and ran away like a spoiled selfish kid—and I'm sorry for that."

She reached out and took his hand and pulled him gently into the seat beside her. "Thank you, dear, but let's not talk about it any more. If you let yourself dwell on these things it can ruin a beautiful day." They sat together for a while, not talking, until she said. "Didn't I hear talk about you and Lee spending the day at the Mall as soon as you finished the garden chores?"

"Yes, but...."

"Don't 'yesbut' me, Craig Williams. I'll bet you Lee is waiting and wondering what happened to you. Probably thinking the worst—like you dumped her or something."

Craig was on his feet before she finished. "I wouldn't do that!" he protested, looking anxiously at her.

"Then you better get out of here."

He needed no other urging and she watched him go with his usual noisy bounce and banging.

The screen door had scarcely closed behind him when she returned to her earlier thoughts. If he does move out, he is not likely to keep on supporting me in this house. He will sell it, I'm sure of that. I wonder if it is registered in both names. No, it won't be. Oh, to think of losing my lovely garden. I don't think I would ever get over that. One of these days I'll have to draw up a plan of my garden so that whoever buys the house will know where everything is and won't dig in all the wrong places. The thought of it was too much and she found herself deep in self-pity, until, angry with herself for sinking into such a mood, she got out the vacuum and the cleaning box and set to work, cleaning and polishing, until she had worked off her fret and was hot enough to warrant a shower and an afternoon nap.

When Craig arrived at Lee's home, she answered the door almost before the musical bells had stopped ringing. Her face had an anxious look to which Craig responded immediately. "What's wrong?" he asked.

"I thought you weren't coming," she replied in a shaky voice.

"Oh, Lee. I didn't mean to make you worry. I'm sorry. I just got talking to my mother about, well, about my father." He stopped for a moment. "I'll have to tell you about my father but not right now, Lee. He's the kind of man that can spoil your day just thinking about him."

They were walking and she stopped and faced him. "Craig! What a terrible thing to say about your father!" Her face had lost all its liveliness.

"See!" Craig exclaimed, looking at her changed face. "See what he has done to you and you don't even know him."

"It's not that. It's what you said. In a Chinese family no-one would ever say such a terrible thing about the father. And when you said it, I just forgot for a minute.... Let's not talk about it just now. Maybe later you can tell me."

They walked on silently for a while until her hand sneaked out into his and then they moved closer so their bodies touched as they walked rhythmically together, and the rhythm reminded them of a song. So they sang and hummed it together, and tried to harmonize and laughed at their failures and watched the light return to each other's face.

The Mall was crowded. They met some groups and some couples that she knew or he knew and they exchanged greetings and names for a few minutes and walked on. They stopped agreeably to examine whatever had caught the attention of the other, and they bought each other little silly gifts, stuffed themselves with junk food and decided that, someday, they would walk through every corridor in the mall and they would start early in the morning and they would stop at every store that had less than seven letters in its name and they wouldn't eat anything until one of them fainted from hunger. All this was decided while they were sitting close on a bench outside a music shop, listening with one ear to the music and sharing a bag of popcorn.

When they continued walking they came to a grocery stall with vegetables displayed in front. "Oh, look, Craig. Here are my father's vegetables," Lee exclaimed.

"Your father's vegetables? What do you mean?"

She picked up a bag of carrots and said, "See here," pointing to the print on the plastic bag. "It says 'Cheng Lee Produce'. That's my father's."

"Your father's a vegetable farmer?" he asked unbelievingly.

"No, no. He doesn't grow vegetables, he sells them."

"Where? Here?" asked Craig, peering inside the shop, still puzzled.

Lee was doubled up laughing at his confusion. "No, Craig. He buys tons of everything from big growers, oranges, grapefruit, nuts, carrots—see here, it says 'Grown in the Salinas Valley'—everything! And he has five huge packaging plants where all the things he buys are washed and sorted and packaged and shipped all over North America."

"Oh!" Craig exclaimed weakly. "I thought when you said he sold vegetables he had a store someplace and sold vegetables."

"Wait 'til I tell my father," Lee said, laughing.

"No, please don't tell him," pleaded Craig.

"Yes, I will," she teased. "And I'll get him to talk to you in his vegetable man's voice."

"What do you mean, Lee?"

"Well, my father likes to play jokes on people. I told you he lived in England and studied at Oxford, didn't I? When he left England he had a very strong English accent and he still does but it has toned down considerably in the last few years. My grandmother is always scolding him for speaking Chinese to her with an English accent. He tries to speak English without any accent, like a North American but sometimes he forgets. Then, sometimes when he is doing business on the telephone, people won't believe he is Cheng Lee because of his English accent, so he puts on this terrible Chinese grocer's accent and they're happy."

Craig had watched her and had been captivated by her story about her father.

"I wish I could talk about my father the same way you talk about yours," he said wistfully.

They walked on in silence until Lee saw a clock. "Craig!" she exclaimed. "Look at the time. I promised I'd be home half an hour ago. Let's hurry."

They walked quickly without much chance for talking, until Craig slowed her down a little and asked, "What would you like to do tomorrow?"

"I don't know, Craig. I have to go to church with my family in the morning. Then, I don't know. What would you like to do?"

They had reached her gate and the lions were still looking off into the distance. "I know," he said, after she had given him a light kiss on the cheek. "I'll take you fishing. Have you got a bike?"

"Fishing?" she said in astonishment as she reached the front door. "Fishing?" as she disappeared inside.

Craig walked home by way of Rob's house. He knocked on the back door and opened it a crack as he had done since childhood. "Hi!" he called. "Anybody home?" He heard no answer as he listened but he did hear Rob's father shouting and Rob replying in monosyllables. Discreetly he closed the door and went out to the garage to search for Rob's fishing rod. When he found it and stopped to see if it needed any repairs before he borrowed it, Rob's sister Beverley appeared at the garage door. Suddenly aware of him when she wasn't expecting anybody, she let out a little startled scream that made Craig jump too.

"You scared me," she said. "I didn't know anybody was out here."

"Hi, Bev," Craig said. "You scared me, too. I called in the back door but there was no answer but I heard Rob catching it. What did he do now?"

"He didn't do anything, he says. Five of them got fired and the other three got raises and nobody can figure out how the manager made the decisions. It's a shitty way of doing business, if you ask me. Of course, Dad's in there ripping Rob up and down because he thinks Rob must have done something to get fired or didn't do enough to be kept on. You can't win with my Dad sometimes."

"Yeah, I know that scene."

Beverley chuckled. "You getting it, too?"

"Not really now, not any more. But I sure used to. My Dad's never home any more and I guess he's going to move out permanently."

"Oh, Craig, I'm sorry. What happened?"

"I don't know, Bev. I don't think my mother knows for sure. But as far as she's concerned it's the end—period."

"Well, they still might work something out."

"Yeah," he replied with a total lack of enthusiasm.

Rob came out the back door and into the garage and saw Craig.

"Hi," he said.

"Hi."

"What are you doing with my rod?"

"Borrowing it."

"Why?"

"Lee and I are going fishing tomorrow."

"Want me to come?"

"No, I've only got two rods."

"I could borrow one," Rob said.

There was a small silence until Bev said, "Three's a crowd, Rob." He looked at her as if she had dropped in from Mars.

"I heard you got fired," Craig said.

"Yeah. That was the easy part. I just got finished the hard part in there—well, part of the hard part. The telephone rang and I escaped but there's more to come. So I guess I couldn't go fishing with you after all, old buddy." He grinned devilishly.

"What are you doing out here?" He asked turning to his sister.

"I'm glad you asked that question," she replied, talking nasally out of the side of her mouth and flicking the ashes off an imaginary cigar.

"And I'll be glad to get your answer," Rob answered in the same way.

Craig picked up the theme and said, flicking his cigar, "And I'll be glad to pick up my rod and go home for dinner."

"Okay, you guys, just a minute," Bev said in her own voice. "I came out to borrow some car wax—Dad's got cans of it he has never used. So what I just figured out is this: I'm going to get some evening time in the library as soon as school starts, and you guys are probably going to be hounding me to borrow the car while I'm working, and you wouldn't be caught dead trying to pick up girls with a dusty, rusty, dull old car that really does need a good wash and polish right now." She paused. "You guys catching my drift?"

Rob looked at Craig. "Has this lady got us by the short hairs or has she got us by the short hairs?" he said.

"I think she's got us by the short hairs," Craig said. "I'm off to get my dinner and I'll be back in my car washing clothes."

"What a clever lad," Beverley said. "And you, are you ready to go back into the lion's den again? I'll come and run interference."

"Bless you, my child," Rob said. And they went arm and arm into the house.

Craig was late getting home and his mother had already started dinner. "You might have phoned," she scolded when she heard he had been over at Rob's.

He didn't respond except to say, "Rob got fired today."

"Oh, that's too bad. He was trying to save for a car, too. Wasn't he?" She paused. "Speaking of cars, are you going back to Mr. Whats-his-name and get some more driving lessons?"

"I don't know, Mom. I don't want to go back to him, I know that. I told you he smells."

"Well, do you want to ask around and see who some of the other kids went to and find a good instructor that way?"

"Maybe later, Mom. Not right away." He got up to leave the room. "How soon will dinner be ready?"

"Fifteen minutes, or so."

"Good. I've got time to phone Lee. We're going fishing tomorrow."

"Fishing!" she said, and he laughed because she had said it in exactly the same tone of voice Lee had used.

They talked on the phone briefly, Craig explaining that he had to help Rob polish his sister's car, and Lee telling him that neither her grandmother nor great-grandmother would understand a young man taking a girl out to catch fish. They talked some more about the fun day they had and the presents they gave each other, set a time for tomorrow and spent a long time saying goodnight.

"Are you really taking Lee fishing?" his mother asked when he returned to the kitchen.

"Sure!" he said laughing. "What's wrong with that?"

"Nothing, I guess. How come nobody ever asked me to go fishing?"

"I guess you're just not the type, Ma."

"Don't call me 'Ma'. Do you want me to make a picnic for you? Some sandwiches, brownies, apples—something like that?

"I never even thought of that. That would be great! Thanks, Ma. I'm going out to dig some worms before dinner."

"Craig! Your dinner is ready right now. And don't call me 'Ma'."

"Okay, then I'll go up to the park when it's dark and get some night crawlers—they're better anyway."

"U-u-gh!" his mother said.

Around noon the next day, Craig called Lee, hoping she would be home from church. She answered and said she would be ready to go as soon as she finished lunch.

"No, No!" he protested. "Don't have any lunch. My mother made us a picnic."

"Craig," she started to whisper. "I have to eat lunch at home. My grandmother makes a special lunch for us while we are in church and if I don't eat it she will be hurt."

"Well, just eat a little bit and hurry or we won't catch any fish."

"Okay. I'll be ready in thirty minutes. Don't ring—I'll come out. Bye."

When she came out, he was waiting at her gate with two breakdown rods strapped to his back and fishing gear, picnic basket and a can of worms tied onto the carrier of his bike.

"Where's your bike?" he asked after they had greeted each other.

"I think it's in the garage. I haven't ridden it for years. I hope it works." They walked across the lawn and opened the garage doors, but among the three cars, lawnmowers, tools, garden furniture, they could find no bike.

"Just a minute," she said, and disappeared into the house. She was back in a minute with a stricken face. "My mother gave it away last year. She thought I was finished with it. What will we do now?" Her face showed such disappointment he thought she might break into tears. They closed the garage doors and walked slowly back across the lawn to Craig's bike.

"I know!" Craig exclaimed. "Can you ride side-saddle?"

"Yes," she answered dubiously.

"Okay. C'mon, hop on! I'll ride you over to Robbie's and we'll get his bike."

They arrived at Rob's after a wobbling and hilarious ride, during which, much to Craig's delight, there necessarily had been a lot of close body contact. There had also been, for Craig, an enticing girl smell wafting into his nostrils when his nose was only two inches from her neck as he leaned forward to pedal hard. And, leaning forward, without taking his eyes off the road too long, he could see, down the partly open neck of her shirt, the rounded uncovered shape of her left breast. She had felt something hard bumping against her right thigh as he pedalled, something that was not there when they started out. They got off the bike, both flushed or blushing, and avoiding, for the moment, each other's eyes.

Craig left Lee holding the bike at the curb while he ran to the back door, opened it a crack and shouted, "Hi! Is Rob home?"

"No, and I don't know where he is," came a response in a deep male voice.

"I wanted to ask him if I could borrow his bike," Craig shouted. "Think that would be okay?"

Glen Turner, a tall, lean man with an untidy beard, appeared at the door. "What the hell's going on?" he said with pretended gruffness. "Since when did you two guys start asking if you could borrow something from each other."

"I just thought...," Craig started.

"It's probably in the garage. Or if it's broken, it might be down in the work-room. How's your Dad?" The question was asked as he turned away.

The routine question was awarded the routine response as the door closed. "He's okay, I guess. He's off on a trip." He heard through the closed door a shout, "Say hello to your mother," just before the racket of an old printer started.

They found the bike in the garage and a wrench to lower the seat that had accommodated Rob's long legs, and after a couple of erratic starts they ped-alled together out of the city, through the Endowment Lands to a beach where a small stream met the shore. Lee did not flinch when Craig offered her the can of worms. She dug into the can and pulled out a long, very wriggly worm and then said, "You'll have to show me how to tie it on, Craig. I've never done this before."

Craig had watched her in amazement. Girls were supposed to drop worms, cover their mouths, shriek and stand back until the boy handed her the rod all rigged to fish. She had put the rod together, threaded the leader and line through the guides and tied a hook on with a satisfactory knot.

"How did you learn to do that. Yesterday you didn't seem to know anything about fishing," Craig said.

"My father taught me last night. He said if I had agreed to go fishing I should know what to do. He made me hold the worm but he didn't show me how to tie it on."

The black and blond heads were close together as the final preparations of weights and floats were completed. Lee had continued to hold the squirming worm waiting for Craig to tie it on and when he held out his hand to take it from him and she saw the hook poised in his other hand she shrieked "No!" and snatched the worm away. "You're supposed to tie it on," she declared. There then followed a long patient explanation about the difference between fishing with worms and fly fishing until Craig managed to put the worm on the hook, the line in the water and the rod in her hands, and she stood on the shore, her face set in a mixture of determination and uncertainty. She was fishing.

Craig returned to completing his own set-up and put his line in the water and his rod in a rod-holder. He was busy clearing off a piece of beach where they could sit when she called him. "Something's wrong, Craig. The worm's trying to get away or something!"

He rushed over to her and watched the rod. "You caught a fish," he shouted. "Easy now, keep your tip up, reel him in slowly, if he wants to run—let him. Good girl! Gently, gently, now. If you pull too hard you might pull the hook right out. Now then," he was standing behind her with his arms around her helping her with her rod. "Okay, when you've reeled him in close, we're going to pull him in with a long pull, not a jerk. Ready? Now!"

They made a long sweeping pull in unison and a fish lay flopping in the sand.

"I caught a fish, Craig! I caught a fish! Look at him, look at him. How big is he, Craig? Oh, look at him wiggle. Put him back, Craig. Put him back. I don't want him. Oh, the poor thing! Craig, please put him back." And she stood, not wanting to look as Craig unhooked the fish and let it slide back into the water.

"Want to catch another one?" Craig asked as he got her line untangled and set up to go again. She shook her head violently in reply and turned away and sat down on the sandy place he had cleared with her back against a log and her arms folded tightly in front as though she were cold. He checked his own line, threw it out and put the rod in a holder.

"What's wrong?" he asked gently, as he came over and settled himself beside her against the log.

"I don't know, Craig. It was fun. I liked it—until I saw the poor thing dying on the beach and then it wasn't fun anymore, and it seemed—wrong, somehow. I don't know." She snuggled against him and it was easy for him to lift an arm and encircle her. He laid his lips against her hair and said, "I know. I felt exactly the same way when I caught my first fish. My father laughed and said 'Don't be such a baby.'"

They sat together quietly for a while. "Would you like to see what my mother made for a picnic?" he said, hoping she would say no so he would not have to relinquish her from his arm. She shook her head. Again he could look into the slightly open neck of her shirt and see the swelling of her breast. He kissed her on the hair on her forehead and said, quietly and tentatively, "Lee?"

"Can I do something?"

"What, Craig?"

"This," he said in a husky voice and he reached over, undid one more button on her shirt, reached in and cupped a breast gently in his hand. The only movement she made was a slight change of position ton to accommodate his hand. They stayed like that for a while, both tense and breathing cautiously. Then she said, "Can I do something, too?" He did not trust his voice, so he nodded his acquiescence against her head. She reached down, and cupping her hand against the bulge in his pants, squeezed him as gently as he had fondled her breast. He had been aware of his erection earlier and had tried to keep it under control, but suddenly, under her caresses, he became so large and hard that it was on the edge of pain.

"Craig!" she exclaimed. "It got so big and hard! Can you make it do that anytime?"

"No," he said between clenched teeth. "But you can make it do that anytime."

She laughed and took her hand away, twisted her body so that her face tilted towards his and her breast moved from his hand. Then she kissed him full on lips, the first time she had done so, and the pain suddenly burst from his groin.

"That was like fishing," she said. "I like it. It's exciting, but it seems wrong. We better see what's in the picnic basket." She moved away and he suppressed a finishing groan.

If there had been a fish interested in the worm on Craig's line, neither of them noticed it. They picnicked and talked, avoiding any subject that might lead them to talk about what had happened earlier. Somehow they had unconsciously agreed that talking about it would somehow spoil the magic of what was almost a first time for each of them.

They pedalled home in the late afternoon with Craig trying to figure out some scheme so that he could ride her side-saddle again. When they reached her gate, they talked quietly and briefly holding hands. Then she drew him over behind the stone gate post and kissed him again lingeringly on the lips, then turned quickly and ran into the house. The lions continued to stare off into the distance.

He walked both bikes home, not bothering to return Rob's.

"Did you have a nice picnic? Catch any fish?" his mother asked, and then, not seeing any fish on the counter, was amused by his blushing affirmative.

"I think I'll go up and read for a while," Craig said, turning toward the stairs.

"Your father came home a little while ago." She said it in a matter of fact voice, not warningly.

He turned on his heel and reversed direction. "I think I'll go down and read for a while."

CHAPTER 25

Marion opened her eyes to a brilliant morning. After a foggy moment she remembered that it was Monday and she had to be at work by nine. She got quickly out of bed and checked Craig's room to make sure he hadn't slept in—it was empty. The door to the master bedroom was slightly open. That, she knew, was not a subtle invitation, it was just a message. "I should get him a card that reads 'Maid Service' to hang on his door," she thought resentfully, and then gave herself a mental shake and tried to get the day going on a happier note. She was going to work today! That was going to be something new for her—she had never had to go to work before in her life.

Downstairs she cleared up Craig's breakfast dishes (He must have slept in, she thought) and, because she was excited, forced herself to sit down and eat some toast and take time with her coffee. She checked herself in the hall mirror and decided she was ready for work. She had even remembered to wear good shoes because she would be on her feet until one o'clock. She locked the door and went to the garage. A note on her steering wheel in Craig's round hand said, "Have a nice day, Volunteer. XXOO". She drove away smiling.

At half past eight, she parked in the visitor's lot, paid an outrageous fee, and wondered if the hospital gave volunteers a sticker for parking. When she arrived at the Gift Shop, the door was locked and dark and there was an untied pile of morning papers outside with a handful of money scattered on top. She hadn't been told about keys and opening up. She felt herself getting flustered so she said firmly to herself, "Smarten up, Marion Williams. Don't just stand here. Do something!"

She walked over to an inside window behind which a switchboard operator was working. "Good morning," she said when the operator had a moment's break. "I'm Marion Williams. I'm a volunteer at the Gift Shop."

"Oh, you're early!" the operator said in a broad Scottish accent. "Just a minute, dear and I'll call Jimmy to let you in."

She spoke rapidly into the mouthpiece, answered a demanding light on her board, and turned again to Marion. "Here's your cash. Open it and count it and sign the book here. And here are your keys; one's for the storeroom and the other is for the cash drawer." She turned back to her switchboard.

Marion counted the money, signed where the operator had indicated in the book.

"Better put the amount, dearie. So everybody will know. You're new, aren't you?" Marion nodded. "If you get into difficulties just give me a hoot. I used to volunteer there too, before this job opened up. They told me they liked my personality but they weren't sure about my accent. Now, there's a laugh for ye, ain't it?. There's Jimmy, opening up for you. Have a guid day."

Jimmy wore a neatly fitting, tan collared overall with the word 'Maintenance' stitched across the chest under his name. He had opened the door, turned on the light, collected the loose money which was now laying on the counter, stacked the papers into the dispensing box and placed it outside the door.

"You must be the volunteer," he said as she approached. "I usually open up for the ladies just before nine." He also had a broad accent. "But you were a little early."

"Yes, I was. I'm new and I didn't want to be late. I'm Marion Williams," she said, holding out her hand.

"I saw you the other day when Cynthia was walking you through. My name is Jimmy, as you can see," he said, offering his left hand. His other hand was a steel claw. "Welcome to the Hospital, Marion. Call me if you need anything," and he smiled and walked away with a dragging limp.

She opened the small storeroom behind the shop. She found a pile of smocks and a box of name tags underneath a posted sign giving instructions in language that was couched in suggestions rather than orders. She could see Cynthia's competent organizing personality showing through. Dressed and labelled, she went out into the shop, put the cash away, checked the sales book and waited for the rush of customers.

By ten, one man had stopped to buy a newspaper. It took longer than normal because neither knew the price.

At half past ten, the girl from the switchboard, whose name she now found out to be Ellen, wheeled up to the shop in an electric wheelchair, stopped and asked if she could bring some coffee back for her. "Yes, please," Marion said after hesitating, thinking she should be the one to fetch the coffee. "But first, can you stay while I go to the bathroom? Where is it?"

"Of course, dearie," Ellen replied. "But next time you're caught short, put a wee note on the door 'Back in five minutes.'

Cream and sugar?" she called as Marion rushed away.

When she got back, Ellen said, "I sent Harry off to get some coffee for us. I thought I'd stay around and chat a bit. I could see from my window that you hadn't had many customers so you might be wanting a little gab. Here's Harry now."

A young man approached in a white orderly's jacket and slacks carrying two big styrofoam cups of coffee and a handful of plastic milk and sugars. "I scrounged them," he said. "I told them it was for two transplanted doctors in surgery."

"Oh, you're naughty!" Ellen said, laughing. "God'll get for that, y'know."

"I'm Harry," the young man said, looking at Marion's name tag and offering his hand. "And you must be Marion. Excuse my clothes, won't you? I'm really a world famous brain surgeon but I do so dislike the pretension of wearing a stethoscope, you know," he chattered in an affected accent as Ellen laughed.

"And yesterday you claimed you were a proctologist. He's something different every day," she said to Marion.

"Tomorrow I think I'll go into ObGyn. Much more interesting than the other side of things. Ta-ta, dahlings." And he was off before Marion could say hello.

"He's such fun," Ellen said watching him walk away. "And he is so good with patients—especially old people, kind and gentle. Everybody feels better when Harry's around. He's got some disease with a name as long as your arm—some kind of epilepsy, they tell me—anyway you'd never know it from him unless the medications they're trying don't work. Then he might drop like a coconut right in the middle of a sentence. Well, here's a customer for you. I'm back to the chain gang. See you later." And she wheeled away quickly without seeming to be abrupt.

***

When Gerry walked into the general office, he noticed small groups of employees having the usual Monday morning talkfest to compare their weekends of duty or pleasure. Eleanor was a part of one cluster but her back was to him so and he could make no signal to her. He noticed that the group quietened as he walked in—he hoped that Eleanor had the common sense not to go spreading the details of the weekend—either hers (whatever she had been up to) or his.

As he passed Bill Webb's office, he glanced in and saw him busy at his desk and stopped.

"Good morning, Bill. Did you get my message on Thursday that I had come down with some kind of flu bug?" he asked.

Bill raised his eyes from the paper, said "Yes" and went on reading.

"Whew!" Gerry said to himself. "That was frosty." He continued to his office and closed the door. At his desk, he picked up a pile of files from his in-basket but didn't open any as he tried to sort out what possibly might be on everybody's private agenda this morning. Something was going on, he knew that. Finally, he rang for Eleanor. Nothing happened for at least five minutes, so he buzzed again.

The door opened cautiously and Louise came in leaving the door open. "I rang for Eleanor," he said. "She's back, isn't she?"

"Yes, Mr. Williams, but...."

"Send her in, will you, Louise."

"But Cyril said...."

"Never mind what Cyril said. Just tell Eleanor I want to see her here, now."

Louise left, closing the door quietly and carefully behind her, and to anybody's eyes but Gerry's, more upset than when she came in.

In less than a minute, there was a sharp knock on the door and it was opened before any invitation was issued. Cyril Chester came in, closed the door behind him and stood, frowning, lips pursed and ready to do battle.

"Mr. Williams," he said before Gerry had a chance to speak. "There have been some changes in the secretarial pool and a memo is being prepared and will be circulated shortly. In regards to your office, Eleanor has placed a personal request to me to be relieved of all secretarial duties for you. It was not within the purview of my supervisory duties to enquire the reason for the request. Louise has agreed to carry on with you for the time being. If you find her work not to your liking, you may expect any one of the general secretaries who is not busy at the moment to answer your buzzer. Mr. Webb has been informed and has approved of all the changes I have presented." He stopped and turned to go.

"Just a minute, you snivelling excuse for a pimp! Who the hell do you think you are? If I want changes in MY office, I will dictate those change—not some prissy no-balled excuse for a man."

Cyril seemed to swell with outrage. "Mr. Williams! I shouldn't have to remind you that had there been a witness to the remarks you just made, I could close this office completely with one call to the Union. And that, I think, along with this morning's newspaper report of your weekend activity would do immeasurable damage to the firm."

Gerry's rage was so complete that he was white and shaking, and he had drooled down his shirtfront. "Get out of here before I kick you out!" he tried to roar but all the words came out in a squeak so that when Cyril emerged from Gerry's office the women in the secretarial pool saw he was smiling.

Gerry sat in his office for a long time. The work on his desk was untouched. No secretary had come in with messages. His telephone was silent. His thoughts raced in erratic directions. Rarely did they include evaluations of his behavior (If only I hadn't....). Rather they dwelt on the faults of others (If those bastards hadn't been so anxious to pick a fight...). He had a tight feeling in his gut and he noticed that his hands were shaking and his mouth tasted of bile. Then he said to himself, "To hell with them all. I don't give a shit. Let them do their damnedest. I can handle them—all of them. Nobody is going to push Gerry Williams around! Nobody! Then he sat back in his chair waiting for the phone call or the knock on his door."

It was a phone call. "Gerry? Bill Webb. I want to see you in my office." He had managed to sound like a high school principal talking to a freshman.

When he entered Bill's office, there was no invitation to sit down but he sat down regardless. "Okay," he thought. "This will be what he calls a confrontation."

"What is it, Bill? I'm rather busy." (Might as well take the initiative.)

It didn't work. Bill did not raise his head from the newspaper he was reading; he simply gave Gerry a long sideways look over the top of his glasses and took a deep breath and expelled it slowly. Finally he said without bothering to address Gerry by name, "You are familiar with the newspaper report concerning your arrest on Friday." It was neither a question nor a statement—it was just a flat string of words that started the adrenalin pouring into Gerry's system.

"No," he said, holding out his hand to take the paper. It was not extended to him so he pulled it away from Bill's unresisting hand.

There it was, in the local morning paper, already outlined in ink. It started with the name of the town and the date. It detailed his name and address, the name of the firm, the name of the motel, the name of the bar, the name of the arresting officer, the name of the judge, the list of original charges, the reduced charges and the accounts of witnesses of his actions at the bar and at the motel. It stated that the woman he was harassing did not wish her name to be published at this time. It ended with the trial date. He knew it would be repeated in garish detail in the evening paper.

He handed the paper back across the desk but it was not taken from his hand.

There was a long silence.

Finally Bill Webb, now Chairman of the Board, said, as if he were reading from notes, "I would like you to take two weeks vacation, perhaps longer depending on the outcome of the trial, starting right now. I would recommend to you that you seek both legal and psychiatric help. I want you to initiate no, repeat no, contact with this firm until we come to an agreement about the terms of your return. Kevin Claxton will take over your accounts. An agreement between you and the firm regarding these matters is being drawn up by the firm's lawyers which you will be expected to sign. Miss Coleman has indicated that she may take private action against you."

"So the bitch has blown the whole thing," he said to himself. Aloud, looking cold and hard at the man across from him, "Go to hell."

There was a pause as the two men searched for a way out of the impasse, but it had already been anticipated.

"I was afraid you might take that attitude," Bill said. "In the event you did so, I have assembled the Board in the Board Room. If you refuse the offer I, as Chairman of the Board, have made to you, then you may present your position to the Board, right now. They are waiting. Should you refuse that offer, then the Board is prepared to take legal action to remove you from the premises and your name from the firm."

"So you have judged me to be guilty, have you? Without a trial." Gerry was on his feet, ready to leave.

"Miss Coleman's account was sufficient for me to call the matter to the attention of the Board."

"You miserable kiss-assing piece of shit. You came from the same slime pit as Frank Wilson." He had opened the door to go but he heard Bill Webb's final shot.

"By the way, Frank's speech is improving."

The door slammed shut.

***

Craig was on his coffee break sitting by himself on a pile of boxes with a doughnut and coffee and busy daydreaming. "One more week," he was thinking. "Just one more week and then back to school. And then one more year. And then what. I guess I won't be seeing Lee as much if she goes off to private school."

Mr. Cranston walked by and said "How're you doing, Craig?"

"Great, Mr. Cranston. Just one more week and then back to the books."

"Good for you. Have you been thinking about that computer idea I talked to you about?"

"Sure have. I phoned a counselor at the school and he said there wouldn't be any problem and he put my name on the list so I would be sure to get in."

"That's the way to do it. Good luck." He turned to go on his way, then stopped. "By the way, what insurance outfit is your dad with?"

Craig gave him the name. "Why?" he asked.

"Oh, nothing, really. I was just curious. There was a thing in the morning paper about a Gerry Williams—somebody with the same name, I guess."

"He didn't win the 6/49, did he?"

"Not quite," the boss laughed and walked on and Craig went back to work.

Edith had seen the item in the morning paper and phoned her mother immediately. She must be in the shower, she thought when there was no answer. She waited a few minutes and tried again without success. "Where is she when I want her." she fumed. One more try after fifteen long minutes and still no answer—and then she remembered that this was the morning her mother was starting her volunteer work at a hospital. What hospital? She couldn't remember.

"Well, I might as well get it from the horse's mouth," she said to the girls and dialled her father's number. "Good morning," she said when the connection was made. "May I speak to Mr. Gerry Williams, please. This is his daughter calling."

"One moment, please." Then, after a long delay during which Edith's always limited patience almost snapped, "I'm sorry. Mr. Williams in not available."

"Is he out of the office."

Long pause. "I do not have that information."

"Could I speak to his secretary, please."

Long pause. "One moment, please."

Another long pause, and then an arty-articulated man's voice said, "This is Cyril Chester, the Office Manager. How may I be of assistance to you?"

Edith explained impatiently that she was simply trying to make a phone call to her father, and added, snappily that it shouldn't require the intervention of an office manager.

"Miss.... Uh-m. I didn't get your name, sorry."

"Mrs. Allen. Edith Allen."

"Mrs. Allen, the only information this office will give out is that Mr. Gerry Williams has accepted voluntary holidays for a period as yet to be determined."

"What does that mean?" Edith's voice was loud and demanding.

"It means he is not here, Mrs. Allen. Will that be all?"

The voice was so snotty Edith hung up without a word. But there were words said aloud at home in front of the girls who fortunately didn't understand any of them.

Marion was beginning to think that volunteer work was very dull. It was nearly noon and thus far she had sold several papers, a baby bootee set, a book (she had thought the man was going to read the whole book while standing in the shop) and a get-well card. She was stifling a yawn when Cynthia walked in.

"It does get a little boring in the mornings, doesn't it?" Cynthia said, smiling, while Marion smothered an "Excuse me!" with her hand. "But after one o'clock, right through to eight, that's visiting hours, it really does get very busy." She had been looking at Marion critically, almost examining her. She took off her coat and walked into the storeroom, saying, "I thought I'd drop by and give you a hand for an hour on your first day."

"Well, I certainly haven't been busy with customers. But I've met some of the staff and looked at the stock and the prices so that I'm beginning to feel I know what I am doing."

Cynthia had continued to watch her closely, then suddenly said, "Marion have you seen this morning's paper?"

"Yes," came the puzzled response. "Do you mean have I read it?"

Cynthia picked up a paper from the box, opened it to the second section, pointed and said, "Did you read this?"

Marion took the paper from her and started to read. "Oh, my God!" she cried out as she read. "Oh, no! Oh, no!"

"It is your husband, isn't it?" Cynthia asked.

Marion nodded numbly. She was white and her eyes had filled with tears that were spilling unnoticed.

"I thought it might be," Cynthia said. "That's why I came down as soon as I read it. But I knew by your face when I came in that you didn't know about it."

"Whatever was he doing?" Marion said huskily. "He said he was on a business trip. Oh, my! Drunk and disturbing the peace and harassing some woman, and what else does it say?" She reached for the newspaper.

"Never mind now, never mind," Cynthia was saying as she led Marion into the storeroom and sat her down. Then, quickly she picked a notice from the wall "Back in five minutes" and taped it to the closed door.

"It's alright, Marion. Have a good cry. Let it all out." She paused until Marion was ready to listen. "It's just a newspaper story, you know. It could be a mistake. It might not even be your husband."

"Oh, it's him, I know that," she said between sobs and blows. "It's just like him. It's just the kind of rotten thing he could do. Oh, I wish I could dig a big hole and bury myself in it." She buried her face in her hands and continued to cry. Cynthia stood by with a hand on her shoulder and said nothing. Finally, Marion raised her head and took in a deep breath, held it as long as she could and expelled it forcibly. "There!" she said, and stood up. "That's finished!" Cynthia had the feeling she was talking about something other than her crying jag.

"You go home, Marion. I'll finish for you," Cynthia said.

"No, no, I'll do it," Marion protested.

Cynthia smiled and said, "Look at your face in the mirror and then tell me you want to meet customers."

"Oh, my God! What a mess!" she cried as she looked at her blotchy face and swollen red eyes. "I should go home. Thank you. I should see if my children... Oh, I hope.... I must go, Cynthia, I've got to talk to the children." She was trying to put her coat on over her smock, and Cynthia came to her rescue, helped her into her coat, gave her her purse, found out where she had parked and walked her slowly, very slowly, arm in arm, to her car to make sure she didn't drive away in a blind panic.

***

Craig usually walked over to the supermarket once or twice a week to see Rob but now that he had been fired, there was not much sense in going over there. He wondered if maybe Rob had got into some kind of trouble and couldn't tell him yet. He hoped he hadn't got too chummy with the guy he met on the loading dock the day he caught them smoking pot. He had been wandering down a street he didn't usually go on and he found a small bookstore and, browsing casually, found a book titled 'You and Your Computer'. He read a few pages and thought he might get a headstart on the computer course if he studied it. When he was paying for it, he realized he had never bought a book before for himself or for anyone else. He folded it up and put it in his lunch box before anyone could see it. "Imagine me buying a book—a school book!" he said to himself. "I better not tell Rob."

After work, he waited at the bus stop for Lee but two busses went by and he didn't see her waving to him on either so he caught the next one and went home to phone her.

He arrived home with a thump and a bang and shouted "Hi! I'm home!"

There was a weak response from his mother in the living room. "I'm in here, Craig."

He went into the living room and found his mother lying on the sofa with a blanket tucked around her and a cloth on her forehead. "Hi, Mom," he said. "Got a headache?"

She took the cloth off her forehead and struggled to a sitting position. He saw that she had been crying.

"Oh, you don't know. You don't know, do you?" she gasped with relief in her voice. "Thank God nobody told you. I've been lying here thinking—thinking somebody might have told you—and you— you would be all alone."

"Told me what, Mom? What's wrong? Mom! Tell me!" He was still standing in the middle of the room where he had stopped when she said 'You don't know, do you?'. The puzzled look now changed to one of anxiety.

"Come here, Craig," his mother said holding out her arms. He went to her but as he went to sit beside her she took him in her arms and held him to her breast. Her sobs moved him to tears, but he could only plead, in a small, cracked voice, "What is it, Mom? Tell me! Please tell me!"

Finally she released him. "There—on the table, in the paper. I can't—I can't tell you. You'll—you'll have to read it."

He reached out for the paper.

"There," she said, pointing.

Craig started to read and blanched, and as he continued the sobs came. When he finished he turned to his mother with a stricken face but as he looked at her his thoughts turned to rage. He got to his feet and stamped around the room. "The bastard!" he shouted. "The rotten bastard! The.... The.... I'll kill him him him! I'll kill him!" He was shrieking.

In time, they each settled the other down to the point where reality rather than raw emotion began to dictate.

"Does Edie know?" he asked.

She nodded. "I've been on the phone to her all afternoon. She was all alone, poor dear." She sighed. "But she's strong, you know, Craig. Very strong. You know what she did? We had several phone calls back and forth, you know how she is. And finally, she phoned and asked me for a recipe. Then I knew she was alright."

The idea of a recipe triggered a maternal response in Marion. She looked at the clock on the mantle that had been ticking quietly during their periods of silence and started to her feet. "You must be starving," she said. "I haven't even thought about anything for dinner. What would you like, Craig?"

"I'm not really hungry, Mom"

"No, neither am I. But we should eat something, you know."

"I'll tell you what. I'll hop on my bike and go to Bruno's and get a pizza and you can make a salad. How's that?"

He was on his feet, too, and walked over to her and put his arms around her. Their tears were finished and they held each other in silence for a moment. She suddenly realized that she was no longer comforting a child and that she was drawing strength from him.

He rode down to the neighbourhood pizza parlour and walked in. There were no customers waiting.

"Hi, kid," Bruno said. "You gonna eat pizza tonight?"

"Yeah, Bruno. I'm hungry for one of your Number 2 Specials. A medium. And no anchovies—it's for my mother, too. I'll be back."

"OK, big boy. You gotta twenty minutes,—max."

"My name's not Max, it's Craig."

"Yeah, okay. I alla time get mixed up." They grinned at each other over their old joke. "Your modder liksa pepperoni, eh? Its a hot!"

"Okay then, Bruno. Just put it on one side."

Craig rode over to Rob's, opened the back door halfway and shouted. From inside the house, over the sound of the television he heard Rob's father shout, "Rob! Craig!" and then Rob's father appeared at the door.

"That was your dad in the paper, wasn't it?"

Craig nodded.

"Jesus, Craig," he said, shaking his head. "I don't know the whole story or what was going on, but it must be ripping your mother apart. And you, too, Craig, I wish there was something I could do. Tell your father that if he needs a character witness or any kind of support like that, to give me a call."

"Thanks, Mr. T. I'll tell him." And as Craig said it, Rob's father turned and yelled, "Rob! Where the hell are you?" Rob appeared as he yelled, but he still received a "You sure take your time, Speedy," snarl.

Rob came out and they sat side by side on the steps.

"Things are the shits, eh?" Rob said.

"Yeah." There was a long silence that did not need to be filled.

"Maybe it wasn't him. Maybe it was somebody else with the same name."

"No. It was him."

Another silence.

"What's gonna happen now?"

"Dunno." Craig shrugged. "Well, I gotta pick up a pizza."

Rob pushed his elbow against his friend's arm and held it there. "Okay, buddie," he said softly.

When Craig picked up the pizza, Bruno shook his head and refused any payment. "Tell your modder, its present from Bruno. Tell her maybe things not so bad tomorrow."

Craig could only trust himself to say, "Thanks, Bruno," before he left quickly.

Marion had washed her face in cold water and brushed her hair so that when Craig came back with the pizza she would not continue to worry him by her woebegone look and manner.

"What a nice man!" she exclaimed when Craig told her about Bruno. "I've only been in his store twice, but I know his wife. She has that little knitting store across the street. I've got five or six of her beautiful Italian-knit sweaters." She continued to talk on about many casual things trying to keep their conversation away from the depressing events of the day. In the back of her mind, helping to raise her spirits, was the idea that if Bruno and his wife knew and could show sympathy, the other people in the neighbourhood would know and perhaps, as Bruno had said, things would not be so bad tomorrow.

After dinner, Craig said to his mother, "I'm going to walk over to Lee's. Are you okay, Mom?"

"I'm fine now, dear, thanks to you. Go on, go see Lee and give her my love. Maybe you'd better phone first," she suggested carefully.

Craig took his mother's advice and called Lee and the warm spontaneous reception he received speeded him on his way. They walked and talked, talked some more over a soda, had a furious contest on an old pinball machine, and, although Craig knew he should tell her about his father, he could not bring himself to wipe the light of her happy face. They walked very slowly back to her home and lingered by the lions for a long time before Lee kissed him and said goodnight.

The last of the daylight had just disappeared when he got home and thumped up the back stairs. There were no lights on and the house was silent. "Mom?" he called into the basement. "Are you down there?"

"I'm in here, Craig," she called from the living room.

"Hi," he said, after going into the room and finding her sitting in the semi-darkness. "Want a light on?"

"Oh, yes. I didn't even notice how dark it was getting. Summer's nearly over, I guess."

When he turned a light on, he saw that she had been upset again and she knew she couldn't hide it from him.

"Your father was here." Her voice was toneless.

"Is he still here," Craig asked angrily.

"No. He came to get come clothes and some tools."

"Tools? What does he want tools for?"

"He said he's taking some time off from the office and that he is going down to the boat and do some work on it." She gave a great sigh. "He told me he wouldn't be back unless he needed something."

"Where's he going to stay? Has he got another place?" Marion listened to her son and could not make out whether he was just curious or concerned.

"I don't know. I didn't ask. Probably on the boat," she replied.

They sat silently together for a long time.

Finally Craig asked, "Did he say anything about me?"

"No," his mother replied in a flat voice.

"Did he ask about Edith? Or the twins?"

"No," in the same flat, disinterested voice.

"I think I'll phone Edith," Craig said. "I should have done it earlier, anyway." He went over to his mother and sat on the arm of her chair and kissed the top of her head. "Why don't you go to bed, Mom? You've had a rough day."

"I think I will, dear. It has been rather long and wearying."

She pulled herself out of the chair and began walking slowly out of the room. "Oh!" she said, and turned around. "How could I forget?" She waved him to her, and when he came she wrapped her arms around him. "Thank you, dear, for being here and letting me lean on you. I would never have got through this day without you.

"Goodnight. You should go to bed, too."

He watched as she climbed the stairs with leaden feet. She suddenly looked old to him.

When he heard his mother's door close, he went to the phone and called his sister, knowing that by now the twins would be in bed and their conversation would not be interrupted by her admonitions to her children. After the first barrage of questions (How's Mom? Have you talked to Dad? Was there anything more in the late edition of the paper?) they settled down to a quiet talk about the whole family situation.

"I think this is the first time that you and I have ever had a serious talk, Craig. I don't know why we haven't talked before. I guess I thought you were still a kid," she said and laughed.

"Yeah, well.... I guess you've been pretty busy with the girls," he said. "Maybe it takes something like this to bring people closer."

"Good God! I hope not!" Edith exploded. "There must be better ways than having your father accused of drunk and disorderly and harassment and resisting arrest and whatever else they said."

"Maybe he's not guilty, Ede," and whatever else he might have intended to say was cut off by Edith's sharp interruption.

"Of course he's guilty, damn guilty. I know that. I know that for a fact. I'll tell you something about him sometime but I'm not ready to tell you yet. I haven't told anybody—not even Harvey, and I should."

"What about?" he asked.

"I'm not going to tell you—not yet. Now don't tell Mom what we talked about or she'll pry it out of me somehow."

"Okay," he said uncertainly and they finished the telephone call on more mundane matters.

"I wonder what she meant by that," he said to himself as he went about the house closing it up for the night.

CHAPTER 26

The next morning Craig was up at his usual time and, after grabbing some breakfast, waited at the front window for his ride to appear. When it stopped in front, he went out quickly, said "Hi" to the two riders and spoke directly to the driver. "I'm not going in to work today," he said. "In fact yesterday was my last day. I've got a lot of things to do before I go back to school."

"Okay, kid," said the driver. "See you around."

"I'll pay my share of the rides when I pick up my pay check on Friday," Craig said. "And thanks for including me."

"Forget it, Craig. Have a good year. Straight A's, eh?" as he put the car into gear.

"Yeah, sure! I wouldn't want to spoil my record," he said, and as the car started to pull away, he waved goodbye.

"Did you guys see that thing in the paper last night about Craig's father?" the driver asked after they had gone a few blocks. "What thing?" from the back seat.

"Well, some guy by the name of Gerry Williams from some insurance outfit got picked up for drunk driving, bothering some woman and a bunch of other shit. Sure sounded like Craig's dad but it could be somebody else. I was just thinking he didn't want to come to work and take a lot of crap from us about his dad."

"Aw, maybe it was some other guy," from the back seat, followed by a mumble of "Yeah"s and "Probably"s.

"Yeah," the driver agreed and they continued on their way to work in their usual silence.

As the car drove away, Craig went back into the house and picked up the phone. Although he had worked at the plant for the whole summer he could not remember the telephone number and he had to look it up in the book. "Geez! I must be stupid," he chided himself. "I bet I handle a hundred shipping orders a day and that telephone number is printed right there on the order and I can't remember it. Straight A's? Hah!"

"Mr. Cranston?" he enquired when the phone was answered.

"Speaking."

"Oh, Mr. Cranston. This is Craig Williams—you know, I work for you."

"Of course I know you, Craig. What's up?"

"Well, Mr. Cranston, I thought I should phone you to tell you I won't be in for the rest of the week. Something's come up—I mean, I think I'm going to need the time to get ready for school. I know you thought I was going to stay on until Friday, so I hope it's okay with you if I don't. It won't upset your schedule, will it?"

Mr. Cranston listened to the adolescent voice making a confused but polite apology for quitting and now was certain that yesterday's news item had indeed been about Craig's father as he had suspected. "Thanks for alerting me, Craig. That's alright. I'll just move Harry Jenkins up to shipping and it will work out. I'm sorry you're leaving, Craig. Keep in touch, eh?"

"Yes, I will, Mr. Cranston. And thank you for the idea about that computer course. I think I'll be taking that."

"Good for you, Craig. Drop by on Friday afternoon and pick up your pay. I think what I'll do is I'll book you in for the full week. So, on Friday, you can expect a week's pay."

"Gee, Mr. Cranston you don't need to do that!"

"I know I don't need to, Craig, but I want to. You have been a very responsible employee and responsibility should be rewarded."

"Thanks, Mr. Cranston. That's great!"

"Okay, Craig. Drop around and see me sometime. Take care of your mother, and let me know if I can help. Good bye."

When Craig put down the phone he was puzzling about the remark about taking care of your mother. Then, suddenly, he knew why Mr. Cranston had asked him about his father yesterday. He decided he would phone Rob later and needle him by comparing their bosses.

He went into the living room and watched some morning show with the usual giggling weather man until his mother came down. He turned off the television, shouted a good morning to her and went out to the kitchen.

"Oh! Craig! Why aren't you at work? I heard the TV but I thought you must have left it on from last night."

"I didn't want to go to work, Mom. So I phoned the boss and told him I wouldn't be in—but I said I had a lot to do to get ready for school."

"He didn't mind you quitting without any notice?" she asked.

"No, he didn't. And he said he would book me in for the rest of the week so I could get a full week's pay on Friday."

"Why did he do that?"

Craig shrugged. "He said I was a responsible employee and deserved a re-ward."

"Well, for goodness sakes. Isn't that nice."

"Yeah," Craig said. "It kinda makes you feel good when people say things like that about you. I'm going to rub it into Rob today—he got fired, you know."

"Craig! Don't be mean!"

"That's not being mean, Mom. Rob's my friend."

During their conversation, he had noticed that his mother had apparently got over the worst of her upset. Although she wasn't her usual self, she was a far cry from the slumped, swollen-eyed woman who had stumbled, heavy footed, up to bed last night. He decided he would say nothing about Mr. Cranston's advice to take care of his mother in case it would trigger another upset.

"I think I'll phone Rob now and see what he is going to do today," he said. "What are you going to do, Mom?"

"This isn't my day to go to the hospital, but Cynthia phoned last night just before your father came home and asked me if I could possibly substitute for someone who can't do her shift in the morning. I really didn't want to, but I thought I should so I said I would and then your father arrived." She let out a long sigh that had a note of frustration in it. "Now I don't want to phone and say I'm not coming in either." Another big sigh. "But I guess I better—I prom-ised." She got up, leaving her morning coffee, and went to the phone. Craig went outside and did some weeding in his mother's garden, but he could hear most of her conversation drifting out through the screen door.

"Cynthia? Marion Williams again. Sorry to bother you, but just after I talked to you and promised to go in to the shop at the hospital today, my husband walked in." A long silence. "No, it wasn't a big fight or anything like that but it was difficult, I'll tell you that. I'm still shaking a bit." Another pause. "Well, not really, that's why I'm calling. I was hoping you could find someone else. No, Cynthia, I wouldn't want you to do it, That wouldn't be fair. You've got too much to do." There was some quieter talk that Craig couldn't hear. "No, I haven't heard the whole story from him and I don't know that I want to. I just feel that everybody in town knows about it and if I came into the hospital I'd be embarrassed all day long if people.... Yes, I know most people are decent. No, I know they wouldn't put any shame on me. I don't know, Cynthia. I don't think I could. Do you think so? Well, what if I started crying right there, right in the shop—I've been blubbering for days, it seems." There was a long pause. "Alright, Cynthia. If you think it's the best thing for me to do. Okay." And she listened. "Okay." She listened and nodded agreement. "Thank you, Cynthia. I feel a lot better. I'll go get dressed and I'll be there by nine o'clock. Bye."

Craig came to the door when she had finished the call. "What's up, Mom?" he asked.

"I just talked to Cynthia. She's a dear. She convinced me to go to work and look the whole world straight in the eye. After all, I haven't done anything wrong. I've got nothing to be ashamed of—neither have you. If I'd been thinking as clearly as Cynthia, I would have persuaded you to go to work, too. Is it too late for you to go now?"

He didn't bother with a reply because the question was thrown over her shoulder as she rushed away upstairs to get dressed for work. "Hey! Right on, Cynthia. Good for you!" he said to himself.

His mother came downstairs in a fluster of excitement. she stood in the middle of the kitchen putting her earrings on. "Have you had breakfast? There's a new cereal on the second shelf I thought you'd like. Have you seen my car keys? Where on earth could I have put—oh, here they are. I'll be home by one-thirty and make some lunch. Oh, no I won't. I'll have to shop. I haven't got a thing in the house. I know! You heat up the rest of the pizza—"

"Goodbye, Mom," he interrupted. "Have a nice day."

The chatter stopped and she smiled fondly at him, blew him a kiss and left.

Craig decided it was still too early to phone Rob, so he rummaged around looking for the new box of cereal and finally located it in the frig. He thought it would probably taste better cold than warm but rejected it and put it away on the cereal shelf. He imagined the phoney sweetness of the cereal if he ate it at room temperature and said "Blea-agh!" He said it three more times on his way to the garage to get his bike. He remembered on the way to Rob's that he had forgotten to lock the door, but he shrugged off the idea of returning.

At Rob's, he opened the door as usual and shouted, "Hello? Is Rob up?" Then he heard Rob's father's usual shout at full volume, "Rob! Craig!" so he closed the door and sat on the steps to wait. Rob's mother opened the door and looked out. "Hello, Craig," she said, standing in the open door. "I haven't seen you for a long time. I suppose you're getting all excited about going back to school, aren't you? Wink-wink," and she twisted her face into a comedian's big wink.

"Oh, Mrs. T. I tell you, I'm all a-twitter," Craig said smiling up at her familiar, friendly face.

"Really? Dear boy, I would never have imagined it," she said in an outrageous mimic of a English accent. Then, in her normal voice, "How's your mother coping, Craig? I've been meaning to phone her and then I got to thinking I'd better drop in on her instead. Is she home, now?"

"No, she went to work this morning," Craig replied.

"Work?" she said. "What do you mean, work?"

So Craig told her about his mother working in the gift shop at the hospital and how excited she was about having a job even if she was only a volunteer and wasn't getting paid.

"Well, isn't she a gutsy lady! Good for her!"

Rob appeared behind his mother at the door. "Who's a gutsy lady?" he asked, putting both arms around her and resting his chin on the top of her head.

"Craig's mom," she answered over her shoulder. "She's doing volunteer work at the hospital."

"Like I always said, Ma. Gutsy son and gutsy mother. Same as me and you," Rob said, rocking her gently.

"Watch your grammar, oaf!" his mother said, jerking her elbow back as if to jab him in the ribs.

"What! You'd call your only son, your dearly beloved, your devoted, et cetera, et cetera, son—an oaf?" He put on an expression of extreme personal hurt, then said, "Hey! Great names for a race horse—Gutsy Son or Gutsy Mother. I better remember that when I get to be a millionaire."

"Claudie," came the voice of Rob's father as he came to the door and interrupted the smiling threesome. "Where's that order we got a couple of days ago from that animal rights group. I can't find it."

"What do you mean, you can't find it? Have you been messing around on my desk?" and she turned to go. As she released herself from Rob's embrace she growled softly to him, "Get out of here!" just as Rob's father shouted from inside the house, "Rob, I've got a job for you!"

Rob said, "Shit!" Then he opened the door and shouted over his father's continuing instructions, "I've got to go down to the plumber's with Craig and get some stuff and help him fix the leak in his basement before the house floats away and he doesn't know beans about plumbing and I won't be long," and he closed the door. "C'mon!" he ordered Craig. "Let's get outa here."

Over the outrageous lie, Craig had heard Rob's father shouting, "Rob? Didn't you hear me? Will you get in here—now!" But the two of them raced away on their bikes laughing, with Rob in the lead and Craig struggling to keep up. They didn't stop until Craig was half a block behind and out of breath. Rob propped his bike against a low stone wall in the front of a church and sprawled on the grass and waited for Craig to catch up. Craig had been pedalling slower and slower and when he reached Rob he just fell over onto the grass beside Rob without getting off his bike.

"You gotta get yourself a new bike," Rob said laconically.

Craig lay on his back on the grass puffing and said nothing. "Maybe you're just out of shape. Too much sex will do that to you," Rob continued, and that remark aroused a bared teeth snarl. "Oh, it's alive. Look, everybody, Craig's alive." Rob shouted.

"Shut up, Rob!" Craig said, sitting up and looking nervously around, but there was no-one to be seen on the quiet street.

Rob paid no attention to his friend's immediate concerns. He was lying on his side with an elbow supporting his upper body while he looked at Craig. There had never been any need for either of them to be tactful with the other, so Rob said, straight out, "What's up with your old man?"

"Damned if I know. He moved out, I think."

"Yeah? What about that stuff in the paper? Is that true? Geez, they sure threw the book at him. Everything but littering."

Craig shrugged, "I don't know what it's all about. He hasn't said anything about it. And—what's your famous line—'Frankly, my dear, I don't give a damn!'"

"If you're going to use that line, you've got to cock an eyebrow like this," and he said the line with his eyebrow cocked up to his hairline.

Craig tried but could not make his eyebrows work independently and succeeded in looking either startled or stupid, Rob was not sure which. Laughing, Rob sat up and leaned over to Craig. Taking his face in both hands, he held an eyebrow still with one thumb and shoved the other eyebrow up with his other thumb. "There!" he said triumphantly. "Now say your goddamned line."

Obediently, Craig mouthed, "The rains in Spain stay mainly in the plains."

"Asshole!" said Rob, pushing Craig's head away so hard he fell over backwards and then he reached out with a long leg and gave him another shove.

"What's going on here, fellows?" said a voice from the other side of the low stone wall.

They looked up and saw a man with a garden tool in his hand watching them.

"Hello, father," Rob said. "We're just rehearsing for our play."

"I'm not a priest. What play is that."

"School play. Shakespeare. Henry the fourth. If you're not a priest, are you a brother? If you don't mind me asking." Rob said.

"That didn't sound like Shakespeare to me." The man looked hard at the two boys. "And, no, I'm not a brother. Read the sign. This is an Anglican Church. I'm the gardener."

"Oh, thank God, you're not the rectum. I can't stand those assholes."

The man gave a deep sigh and turned away. When he had gone a few steps he turned back and said, "Look here. Why don't you find another place, instead of a church, to do whatever you're doing?"

Craig stepped in before Rob could say anything more. "Perhaps we should, sir. Sorry if we bothered you, C'mon Rob, let's go."

Rob got slowly to his feet and they walked away, pushing their bikes. "Geez! What a suck!" he said. "Sorry-if-we-bothered-you-sir."

"What's the big chip on your shoulder today?' Craig asked.

"What d'ya mean?"

"Back there. You acted like you were trying to pick a fight with that guy."

"Oh, that! I dunno, buddy. Sometimes I just get tired of old people jerking me around. Like getting fired for no reason. Like cops staring at you just because you're a teenager, or the way your dad has been piling it on you and your mom, or my dad on my back all the time, and next week we have to go back to school and the teachers and the principal join in and they start pounding us."

Rob stopped suddenly and looked at Craig, his face a puzzle.

"You're not working—I mean, aren't you supposed to be at work?"

Craig had been waiting for Rob to ask. "I phoned up and quit this morning," he said, grinning.

"You're kidding. You quit? How come?"

"I dunno. I guess all that newspaper stuff about my dad. I just thought I was going to get a lot of questions and stuff, so I quit."

"What did your boss say when you quit like that?" Rob asked.

Craig's grin reappeared. "You'll get a kick out of this," he said. "He told me I was a responsible employee and he's going to keep me on the payroll for the rest of the week. And," he said, "he wants me back—anytime."

"You lucky bugger! I get fired and you get a bonus. Are you sure you're not just joking me?"

"Hell, no! I wouldn't do that." They started walking again. "He read that stuff about my dad," Craig said.

"Maybe he just wants to get you into bed. You're kinda cute, you know." He ducked just in time to get out of the way of Craig's swing.

Craig walked on ahead, muttering. Rob caught up and said, "Hey! Do you know who the broad was that your dad was bugging at that motel?"

They stopped. "No," Craig said. "The only thing the newspaper said was...."

"Yeah, I know. But I heard my dad and mom talking at break-fast, and my dad heard it from one of your dad's golf cronies that he's doing some printing for. It was his secretary."

"You mean Eleanor? Eleanor Coleman?" Craig said dumbfounded.

"I dunno her name. That's all I heard, except the guy told my dad that he had been screwing her regularly for years."

"Who?"

"Who what?"

"Who had been screwing her for years?"

"Your dad," Rob answered bluntly. Then seeing the stricken look on Craig's face. "Aw, you know how those guys make up stories on each other. Maybe it's just gossip stuff."

Craig stood looking at his friend. "I know one person who wouldn't think it was gossip," he said.

"Who? Your mother?"

"No," Craig answered, then said, "Well, maybe. But I was thinking of Edie."

At that moment, Rob's father's car came to a sudden stop across the street from them. The window was rolled down and they heard his familiar voice, "Rob! Where the hell have you been. I want to get that job out today. Will you get off your ass and get to work."

"Yeah, okay, Dad. Right away," Rob shouted across the street.

"We had to go down to the plumber and borrow some tools and we just took them back. It was a big dirty job but we got it done."

"Well, hurry up!" and the car roared away.

Craig stood looking at Rob. "You know," he said, "When I hear you BS-ing your dad like that, I think maybe you were making up all that crap about my old man."

"Naw, I wouldn't do that. I just lie to my old man. I'm practising up to be a cons—cons-something liar."

"Consummate," Craig suggested.

"Yeah, that's it," Rob said, as he mounted his bike and pedalled away. "Sounds good, eh? See ya."

Marion's mind was not on her driving. She did not want to be late and at the same time she did not want to go. Because of her turmoil she turned left on a red light and provoked immediate obscene responses from several drivers and flashing red lights from a police car.

"In a bit of a hurry, lady? Driver's licence, please."

"I was just hurrying,—I mean I have to get to the hospital," she said feebly as she stirred in her handbag looking for her wallet. "Here it is, officer."

The officer glanced at the licence and handed it back. "Are you on the medical staff?" he asked.

"Oh, no!" she exclaimed. "I'm a volunteer."

"I see," the officer said, smiling. "The hospital is just three blocks straight ahead. I want to watch you drive slowly and carefully to your volunteer job. Try to do that, Marion Williams, for the greater safety of others." He stepped away from her car.

"May I go?" she asked uncertainly.

"Please do, slowly and carefully," he replied with a wave of his hand as he returned to his police car.

She did as she was instructed and turned into the parking lot with a sigh of relief and another pleasant feeling. "He really was very nice," she said to herself. "He could have given me a ticket, but he didn't. Cynthia was right. People are basically decent."

She arrived just as Jimmie was picking up the papers and the loose change that had been placed on top of the pile. "There, what more could I ask for?" she asked herself. "People just pick up a paper and leave the money. People are honest and decent."

"Good morning, Jimmy, and thank you," she said.

"Morning, Marion," he replied. "I didn't count the cash or the papers. I'll leave that for you. It usually balances out except sometimes somebody forgets to pay. I have to hurry up to the third floor. There's a spill up there. See you later." And he touched her gently on the arm.

She got into her smock and walked across to the switchboard to pick up her cash. Ellen was busy with a call, but seeing her waiting, handed over the cash envelope and the receipt list with a small smile and a mouthed "Good morning." Marion counted the cash and was signing when Ellen turned from the switchboard and said, "Hi, Marion. That was the third floor. Harry had another big seizure and knocked over some food trays. Poor guy—that's the second big one on that medication. I wonder what they'll try now. Have a good weekend?" she asked with an intent look.

"I've had better, but I'm surviving," Marion responded. "I'm sorry about Jimmie. He's such a nice, happy person." She frowned in sympathy. "But something really nice happened on my way to work." And she told Ellen quickly about nearly getting a ticket.

"Was he good-looking? How old was he? Was he married? Did you get his name?" Ellen spilled out the questions. "I have to know these things to put on my list of possibles."

"Next time I'll bump into his car and faint and he'll bring me in and you can get all the dirt yourself," Marion said, laughing as she turned back to her shop.

To her relief, the morning went quickly. She was nervous helping her first few customers but then began to enjoy it, and in between, she found herself thinking of the pleasant brush with the law, about Jimmie, Ellen, Harry and Cynthia. Her own troubles barely surfaced. Just after noon, when she was daydreaming behind the counter in the shop, a man walked briskly by, looking over his shoulder at her on his way to the elevators. "I know him," she thought, but no name would surface. She went through the alphabet hoping to trigger a name, and worried at it like a cat with a mouse. "Oh, leave it alone, Marion," she told herself. And then it all clicked. "Marion!" she said. "That's it! Marion—something—something. Marion Thomas! Tom Thomas. That's who that was! I wonder what he's doing here."

In less than half an hour, Tom Thomas emerged from the elevator, smiling broadly as he approached her. "As soon as the door closed, I remembered," he said without any greeting. "Marion Williams, isn't it?" holding out his hand. "How are you?"

"Fine, thank you," she replied. "And I remembered yours about the same time, I guess—Tom Thomas, am I right?" He nodded, smiling. "Let me see," she continued. "That was in the spring, and I met your father at the doctor's and he took us to tea. How is your father?"

"That's why I'm here. He's up on the third floor. Nothing much wrong with him, except he had another stroke and lost some use of his right arm, and his memory is getting worse all the time. I've got to find a rest home for him. I hate leaving him home alone, but God! I can't afford the prices these homes charge."

"Yes, I've heard," she said sympathetically. "Some of my friends have been through it."

"Yeah, the thing is, there are some cheap ones but I wouldn't put my father in those dumps. And then the expensive ones are so ritzy, he'd feel out of place even if he hasn't much memory left. Thank God he's not incontinent. Didn't he get into a discussion of his bowels with you over tea? Him and his bloody bowels!" He clucked and shook his head.

Marion laughed and said, "Yes, he did. But I didn't mind. Your father is such a gentleman. I liked him."

"Well, back to the slave shop," he said. "Do you work here all the time? I haven't seen you here before."

"No, just three mornings a week. I'm a volunteer," she said with a touch of pride in her voice. "But a thought just stuck me. I play bridge every Thursday with some friends and some of them have gone through with their parents what you are going through with your father. I thought I could ask them if they kept any lists of places they looked at or any kind of notes about what they thought of them. Would that be of any help to you?"

"Would it!" he exclaimed. "That would be great if you could do that! Honestly! I'd really appreciate it."

"I'll try, then. But I can't promise anything."

"I know," he said. "Shall I phone you at home?"

She hesitated, then said, "No, I'd better phone you. Yes, that would be better."

He saw her hesitation and momentary fluster. Taking a small ring notebook from his shirt pocket, he wrote down his number. "Thanks again, Marion. You're a doll. I could kiss you. Gotta run." She hoped nobody would notice that she was blushing as she watched him go—a trim, tidy man, in clean working clothes and a big laughing smile.

When Rob left for home, Craig went home too and watched some television until he was bored and went upstairs to sort out clothes for school. Looking at the assortment of clothes he had flung onto the bed, he realized that unless he went shopping on his own, his mother would do it for him or insist on going with him again like she did last year. "What a drag," he thought. "No way am I going through that again."

He went downstairs and phoned the Turners, but Rob's father answered with "Turner Print shop."

"Mr. T.?" Craig said. "I didn't know you had a business phone."

"We don't. It just sounds better. Rob's working. If you want to talk to him, come on over. That way you don't plug up the line." He hung up.

Craig walked over to the Turners, opened the back door and shouted before he walked in. He saw Rob in the corner of what used to be the dining room placing piles of paper into the collator. "Hi," he said over the noise of the printer. "I gotta go shopping for some school clothes. Want to come?"

"Make sure you get those pages in the right order," came a shout from Rob's father. "And don't let Craig near that machine."

Craig had fouled up a complete work order a long time ago and now lived happily with Mr. T.'s opinion of him as a total mechanical failure.

"Yeah, sure. I know how," Rob responded. Aside to Craig he said, "He's got me on a really short leash today. Mom's upstairs with the flu or something and he's watching me like a hawk. Sorry, buddy." Then he grinned and said, "Hey! How come you're going shopping without your Mummy?"

"Ah, shut up!" was Craig's friendly reply as he left.

At the mall he found several groups and pairs of people he knew from school, just hanging out and stuffing their pimples with junk food. Most were looking but not buying until they found out what everybody else was wearing this year. He was escorted around to several shops by three guys from his class last year who were intent on showing him the in-thing in jeans, shoes, sweatshirts and caps. Some other guys were with their girl friends which gave him the idea to wait for Lee to get off work and then they could shop together. With a little diplomacy, he escaped from the doubtful good intentions of his friends and walked toward home by way of the tennis courts. The only people on the courts were a threesome he knew and they shouted at him to join them. One of them had an extra racquet and he got involved in a long, sweaty dual until, suddenly aware of the time, he stopped in the middle of a game and ran for home.

"Hi, Mom," he said passing her on his way upstairs. "Did you have a good day? I've got to have a shower before I pick up Lee and then we're going shopping."

"What are you shopping for?" she called after him.

"School clothes," came the distant reply.

"School clothes?" she repeated. "Craig, are you serious?" There was no reply so she gave a "Well, I never!" sort of huff and waited for him to come down.

He came down in a rush. "I gotta hurry. I want to catch Lee before she gets on her bus."

"But Craig! Have you made a list? Do you know what you are looking for?" she protested.

"It's okay, Mom. Lee will help me and I got a lot of ideas from guys over at the mall today."

"Well, I don't know. I've always gone with you. Well..." and she paused in frustration. "Well, make sure you try everything on. And don't buy anything that's made of 100% polyester or rayon, look for a mix, like 60% cotton and 40% synthetic fibres, that's good. And watch your colors. And remember we always go to MacKenzies for shoes."

"Mom! I gotta go!"

"Are you buying underwear and socks? There's a special school sale on..."

He had walked over to her and put his hand over her mouth muffling any further reply. "Good bye," he said. "I've go to run. We'll eat at the Mall. You can have my piece of pizza," and he grinned at her, kissed her on the forehead and ran.

He arrived in front of the office building where Lee worked with fifteen minutes to spare and waited at the curb so that he could see both the door and the bus stop. At ten minutes past five, he was sure he had missed her and at quarter past, he was certain and disappointed. About to give up, he turned toward the bus stop but stopped when he saw Lee's father coming out of the building, hesitate and walk toward him. He was not yet at an age where he could master the art of greeting adults without prior warning.

"Hello, there," Mr. Lee called out.

"Hello, Mr. Lee," Craig replied. Then, helpfully, "Craig, Craig Williams."

Lee's father laughed. "Whatever made you think that anybody in my family would not know and remember your name. It's Craig this, and Craig that all day long. Even the people in the office know who Craig Williams is. Would you like to go up and meet them? Lee is still there." And he laughed again at the consternation in the young man's face. "Room 707," he said as he turned to go. "I'm sure we'll see you again."

"I think I'd better wait for her here," Craig called.

He waited for an eternity but it was less than ten minutes before Lee came out of the building, and he watched her happily as, obviously intent on something, she walked passed him without seeing him. He stepped a pace behind her and watched her jet-black hair swing as they walked in unison in line. She sensed or heard something behind her and threw a quick glance over her shoulder, just enough to recognize Craig's smiling face, and stopped so suddenly that he bumped into her which provided the right opportunity for a public hug.

"Craig!" she cried, her pretty face so alive with delight he thought his heart might stop. He said nothing until the hug was mutually terminated and they walked hand in hand to join the line at the bus stop, unaware of the pleasure they had given to the waiting passengers.

"I saw your dad," he said. "I was just about to give up on you when your dad came out and saw me and told me you were still inside. He told me to go up to room 707 and get you, but I didn't want to, so I stayed here and watched for you."

"Why didn't you want to?"

"Oh, I dunno, just didn't."

"That's too bad," she said. "I wanted to introduce you to some of the people I've been working with."

"I guess maybe that's the reason," he said enigmatically as the bus pulled up, and could say nothing more as the crowd pushed impatiently to get on.

"What do you mean?" she asked when they were seated.

"I can't tell you here," he whispered, taking her hand.

"All right," she whispered back trustingly.

They said nothing more for several stops and the crowd on the bus was thinning out. "The reason I came down to get you was that I wanted you to help me do my shopping," he told her with a big grin.

"What do you have to shop for?" she asked with a puzzled face.

"School clothes and stuff like that."

"Oh, that will be fun, Craig. I've never shopped for boy's clothes before. Men's clothes, I should say," hugging his arm, oblivious to his blush. "But I'll have to phone home and get my mother to let my great grandmother know so she won't fuss. Now," she said, in a take charge voice, "Where's your list?"

"List?" he answered. "I don't have a list."

"You don't? How do you know what to get?"

"I just walk around and look at things and I see things that I know I need and so I buy them," he said in an offhand manner.

She tried to look at him severely, but he thought it only made her look prettier. "Are we going to eat before we shop?" she asked.

"Sure, if you want to. Are you hungry?"

"I'm always hungry. Don't we get off here?" and they hurried to get off before the bus started again.

"Now, I'll tell you what let's do," she said, taking his arm possessively. "Let's find a nice place to eat, and we'll order and after that, I'll go phone home and while you're waiting you can make out a list."

"Are you always so bossy?" he asked with a grin that denied any malice.

"I'm not bossy. I'm just getting you organized."

"You are, too!"

"Am not. Here's a good place to eat. Let's eat here."

"See you did it again," he said, as they went arm in arm into a small cafe and seated themselves across from each other at a table so small their knees were touching.

"Did not," she said, here face glowing with happiness. "Oh, isn't this fun, Craig? We're just like an old married couple having our first fight."

They held hands, pressed their knees together and looked into each other's eyes until a waitress appeared and asked, "Do you two old married people need a menu or do you want to order?"

They pulled their hands apart and sat up straight, looking embarrassed. Then they said, in unison, "We'll order," and broke out laughing.

They ordered and Lee rushed off to find a telephone while Craig struggled with a list. When she returned, she reported, "My mother thinks that going shopping with a boy is the funniest thing she ever heard of. She said why don't you go to a show or a ballgame?"

"Would you rather do that?" he asked, hoping she would not.

"Unh-unh," was the answer through a mouthful of hamburger, then when she had tucked it into a big pouch in her cheek, she asked, looking like a perky squirrel, "Do you know why this is fun?"

It was his turn to be caught with a mouth so full he couldn't answer and too full to laugh, but they managed finally to look away from each other, chew, swallow and sit back, happy with their happiness. "Why?" he asked, remembering her question.

"Because I never get to do it. At my school, everybody wears a uniform—same shoes, socks, skirts, blouses, sweaters, hats, coats, everything. It's a girls school, you know," seeing his puzzled face. "There are no boys."

"I'm glad," he said.

She reached over and slapped his hand lightly. "Anyway," she continued, "it never changes and I just go to the same store every year and give them my list with my sizes and the name of the school and they package it and send it home. Then my mother calls in a dressmaker and she does all the alterations to make things fit. That takes two days at least with me trying things on that are full of pins. And there's nothing pretty in the whole pile!" she finished with a face of vexation. "That's why this is fun!"

"Don't you ever just, you know, shop?"

"Oh, sure for things for the summer. But this year is the first year I haven't gone away for most of the summer to girl's camp."

"Are you sure you're not in the army?" he teased.

"It hasn't been like that," she laughed. But, suddenly serious, she added, "But maybe my new school will be different."

"New school? What new school?" he asked with alarm.

Her face closed up under a veil of concern. Her eyes brimmed with tears. "I didn't know how to tell you," she said in a shaky, small voice.

"Tell me what, Lee?"

"My parents decided it was time for me to go to a school where I can get courses in Chinese history and art. And I have to leave on Saturday." She was crying.

"Leave? What do you mean, leave? Isn't it in town?"

"No, Craig, it isn't, And I asked them not to send me away. But my parents, and my grandmother and even great-grandmother said I should go. I told them I loved you, Craig, and I didn't want to go. Maybe I shouldn't have. Maybe that's why they are sending me away. They said I was too young to be in love. But I am, Craig. You're my first boyfriend and I never knew it could be so exciting just to be with a boy."

"Oh, Lee," he said. "Oh, Lee!" His voice was so husky she could scarcely hear him.

The waitress approached their table. "Anything else, kids?" Then, as Craig shook his head, she saw two very troubled teen-agers. "We've got a bit of a line-up," she said. "But I'll tell you what I'll do. I'll bring you something on the house while you get yourselves settled. Okay?" She smiled at them. "That's just to cover me with the boss."

Her interruption dissipated some of their upset and tears so when she returned with small ice cream floats, they had their emotions under some control. "There you are, guys," she said. "the treat's on me."

They finished quickly and Craig paid their bill at the cashier's counter. He looked around for the waitress who had served them, saw her across the room and walked over to her. "Thank you," he said and shook her hand and she knew it wasn't for the ice cream.

"Nice kids," she said to the people at the table.

Craig and Lee walked through the mall without either of them thinking about shopping. They met several people that Craig knew but didn't stop long enough with any of them to bother with introductions. At one casual encounter, one of the boys made a snide racist remark that so enraged the usually docile Craig that he grabbed the guy by the shirt front, pushed him to the wall and promised him nasty consequences if he didn't watch his tongue.

"Let's get out of here," Craig said to Lee, and together they pushed their way through the evening crowd and reached the street. It was dusk and the sudden cool of the late summer evening made Lee shiver. "Here," he said to her, "take my jacket."

"No," she protested. "I'm not cold."

"Yes, you are," he insisted. "C'mon, put your arms in."

She slipped into it easily and pulled it around her. "Oh, you got it nice and warm. And it smells good too—just like you. It's a kind of a man smell."

He smiled at her and suddenly the melancholy mood that had overtaken them lifted and they were close and happy together again.

"Well now I will have to go shopping for a jacket. How about it? Are you still game to help me?"

"Sure," she replied, already pulling toward another Mall entrance. "Let's go!"

Inside they found a men's shop and worked their way through racks of jackets. She found one that was colourful, he found one that was drab. He tried hers on and looked in the mirror. "I look like a peacock," he declared. He put the drab one on. "You look like a mud turtle," mimicking his tone. In the end, they bought the peacock. They had no trouble over socks—only to make sure there was something mixed with the cotton yarn as his mother had warned him. They bought T-shirts and sweatshirts in all colons and patterns and she insisted that he should try on every sweatshirt so that she could see and approve.

He had made no list and he thought that by now he had everything he needed. They passed by the underwear section and Lee stopped him and said, "Don't you need some of those?"

"I'll get them later," he told her, blushing.

"Oh, come on, Craig. I won't make you try them on," she said, laughing at his embarrassment and pulling him into the section.

They were sorting through piles of jockey shorts when Lee asked him quietly, trying to cover an impish grin, "When they size these things, do they measure the waistband or what goes in the little pouch down there?"

"Lee!" Craig exclaimed in shock.

"It's a waistband measure," said a salesgirl who had come up behind them and overheard. "I think the other measure would be more fun," she said to Lee, smiling. "Don't you?"

"Oh, yes," she replied. "But, then men would probably cheat like women do."

"They do anyway," the salesgirl said to Lee with her hand beside her mouth. And the two girls laughed hilariously.

"Sorry, sir," the salesgirl said smiling. "I came over to help you. I saw you looking at the wrong sizes. You are a very definite 28—not a 30 or 32 where you were looking. Most men don't know their size," she said to Lee.

"You have a fascinating job," Lee said.

"Yeah!" with enthusiasm came the reply. "Call me if you need me."

They finally settled on six pairs of shorts, five of them in wildly collared stripes and one plain white. Craig had resisted totally her efforts to get him to include patterned ones or one she liked that was not much more than a collared jockstrap. "Lee!" he had protested. "I've got to get undressed in front of the guys for PhysEd. I can't wear those." So she acquiesced, smiling, and they gathered their purchases together and took them to a cashier, and watched while she folded each one carefully, almost lovingly, without comment.

Out of the store, they were overloaded with packages but still managed to hook arms while they walked and laughed about their shopping trip. It wasn't a long way to Lee's house and probably took less time than waiting for a bus. Partway home, Lee grew serious. "Craig?" she asked. "When you didn't want to go up and meet some of the people I work with, was it because you thought they would all be Chinese?" Her voice was very quiet and shaky.

He was so startled by her question, he let go of her arms and they dropped some of their packages. "No, Lee! No! That wasn't it! That had nothing to do with it."

"Oh, good! I didn't think so, particularly after the way you tackled that guy in the mall."

"But how could you think that I...?"

"I'm so sorry, Craig. I didn't mean to hurt you. Forgive me, please, Craig. It's just that Asian people are so aware of prejudice that sometimes we are almost paranoid. I shouldn't have asked you that."

She was so sincerely contrite that he put down some more packages and took her in his arms. "Oh, Lee! Lee! I love you," was all he could say and all he had wanted to say for a long time.

They finally sorted out the confusion of packages and walked along.

"Remember I said I had to tell you something but not right then and that I would tell you later?"

"Yes," she replied with some reluctance because by the serious tone in his voice she thought it was not going to be a happy thing.

"Well," he said, determined to tell her everything and equally determined to keep his voice and emotions under control, "it's about my father." So he told her how cold and distant his father was, how he was rarely home, that he drank too much and all about what was in the newspapers and what other people had been saying. He told her that he had been so hurt by his father's behaviour that he had quit his job because he didn't want to get razzed by the people at work. He said that he was afraid that, when he was introduced, people would ask 'Say, are you related to that guy in the newspaper?' and he would have to admit it. He talked all the way to her home and they continued talking under the lions who still stared broodingly into the distance.

They held each other close but not happily for each of them felt that fate, or something malicious, was somehow determined to interfere in their lives.

He said, "I love you, Lee," again and it felt so good that he said it again and she kissed him with such passion that he felt it in his groin. She pressed her body to him without reserve and reached down and touched him but it was too much for him and he trembled with completion.

Reluctantly she said, "I've got to go, Craig." So they kissed each other, this time with more tenderness than passion and parted. She ran to her door, stopped and ran back and he thought she wanted to kiss him again and she did, but she also took off his jacket and returned it to him before disappearing into the house. He stood for a long time looking for a light in her window. Then, taking off his new jacket, and putting on the old one, with her smell still lingering in it, he turned for home.

CHAPTER 27

Craig walked home with his mind in turmoil. As soon as he had turned away from Lee's gate he began thinking about Lee leaving for school. He didn't even know the name of the school of its address except that it was in Ontario. They would have to write when he got her address—it was too far to think of weekends. His mind raced around the rapids of the disappointments of the day and floated through the smooth waters of his happiness.

There were no welcoming outside lights on when he arrived home and the house was dark except for the lights in the living room and the blue light from the TV.

"Hello, Mom," he called when he opened the door. "Are you in there?"

"In here," she trilled. "Come and show me what you bought."

He went into the living room and dropped his all parcels in the middle of the floor and kissed his mother lightly on the forehead noticing her perfume and remembering that Lee didn't wear perfume but always smelled, he thought, like fresh air on a ski slope. Some sixth sense message passed between them and she asked, "Didn't you have a shower before you went out?"

"Sure," he said. "Why?"

"It must be that jacket," his mother answered enigmatically. "It probably needs dry cleaning. You've been wearing it all summer. Show me what you bought."

Craig stirred among his parcels wondering how his mother could have smelled Lee on his jacket or if she had smelled the load he was carrying in his shorts. He pulled out his new jacket and modelled it for her, displayed the T-shirts and sweatshirts but tossed the package of underwear casually aside.

"What are those?" she asked.

"Just some underwear shorts," he said casually.

"Let's see them," he ordered, and he obediently tossed her the package gritting his teeth while waiting for her comments.

"Well! You can certainly see a feminine hand in this underwear," she said smiling at him. "Who picked this one?" holding up the only white pair of jockey shorts.

"I picked those out," he said defensively.

She was busy looking at the labels in all the clothes. Finally she said, "You certainly made some good choices. And nobody will think your mother took you shopping this year. I like your jacket! Who picked that out?"

"Lee did. I picked one out but she said I looked like a mud turtle and made me buy this one. It looks great, doesn't it?" he said, trying it on again and parading around the room. Then, picking up all his purchases, he said, "I better put these away. I'll be down in a minute."

Upstairs he hung up his new jacket and shoved some other stuff aside to make a separate place for his new clothes on the floor. Then he went to the bathroom and washed himself off and put on clean underwear, noting as he did so that he smelled noticeably raunchy and concluded that it wasn't Lee his mother had smelled.

Downstairs again she told him about her day and particularly about meeting Tom Thomas again although she had to tell him again about her earlier meeting with Tom and his father. She told him that during the afternoon she had called some of her bridge friends because she knew that if one of them had seen the paper they would all know, and she promised to tell them everything when they met for bridge on Thursday. And she asked some of them to try and remember the rest homes they had investigated, and seeing Craig's puzzled look she had to tell him why.

He told her about Robbie making up a big story for his father about having to come over and help him with some plumbing. "So," he said, "If Mrs. T calls, and she said she should and would, then please don't let on." She was used to their games and promised she would avoid any plumbing discussion.

Then he told her about Lee's parents deciding to send Lee away to a private school in Ontario, and how upset Lee was, and how he was wondering whether they were doing it to break them up. She listened and heard the perplexity and hurt in his voice but, not knowing for certain and having only surmised the extent of their relationship, she could only offer casual comfort and solace. Wisely she said nothing about growing up, other girls or other loves as she watched him, sad-eyed with a face closed by bewilderment and hurt.

The late news that neither of them had watched nor heard came to an end. They touched softly and briefly as they said their goodnights, and she went upstairs first when she heard the new man of the house say, "I'll lock up, Mom."

Neither had slept well. Craig had torn his bed apart as he tossed in stormy dreams of Lee dressed in striped jockey shorts lying in the grass of a church yard beside Rob. But he got up and dressed and tried to put the dream away. Marion had dreamt she was locked in the cabin of the boat and Gerry was on deck steering and pounding on the deck above her head. The pounding seemed to persist and it was so loud she jerked into wakefulness to discover that it was Craig knocking gently on her door.

"Would you like a cup of coffee—I made some?" he asked when she had gathered her wits and answered his knocking. He had brought her a mug of coffee, lukewarm now, appallingly sweet and strong, and he sat on the edge of her bed while she tried to drink it.

"Is it strong enough?" he asked solicitously. "I tried a cup and I thought it was strong enough for me but maybe you like it a little stronger."

"Its fine," she lied. "Maybe a little strong for first thing in the morning. I like it not so strong in the morning but good and hearty, like this, for dinner."

"Oh, that's the way you do it," he said. "I'll remember that for next time."

"Now look here, Craig Williams," she said with pretended severity, I'm not the kind of woman who likes to be pampered with coffee in bed. Besides, I always spill it and then I've got an extra washing to do," and she softened it with a smile.

"You don't like coffee in bed? I thought..."

"No, I really don't, dear. But it was sweet of you."

"I thought all women liked coffee in bed. I'm sure I read that someplace."

"Not this woman," she said, laughing at his naiveté so hard she spilled her coffee. "See!" she continued, "just like I said."

"Can I get you some more?" he asked without guile.

She laughed harder. "Oh, Craig! Get out of here before I ruin the blankets as well."

He went downstairs and drank some orange juice, ate a bowlful of 'Blea-agh' and noticed that it was 8:15—too early to call Lee, he decided. He had been so used to getting up early all summer, seeing the clock but not the time, that he had not realized how early it was when he made coffee for his mother. He went quietly upstairs and peeked in Edie's bedroom and saw his mother fast asleep. He noticed that she was sleeping much later than she used to; he thought maybe that it was her way of trying to forget the problems she was having with his father.

In his room, he closed the door and surveyed the mess. His mother had long ago refused to enter his room to collect dirty clothes or sheets—either he put them in the laundry hamper or they wouldn't get done. On top of his discarded work clothes, he had dumped the clothes taken out of the closet and drawers yesterday when he had made a feeble attempt to sort them out. Some of these, moved earlier from the bed to the floor, had been kicked aside to make a place for his new clothes. He looked at the room in dismay as if seeing it for the first time. He had harboured thoughts of enticing Lee up to his room some day when his mother was at the hospital or playing bridge, and then he thought of Lee's reaction if she had ever walked into this room. For the first time in his life, he understood why his mother demanded that his bedroom door should be kept closed at all times.

He set to work trying to create order out of the clutter all over the room. Sheets, pillowcases, work clothes, dirty socks, underwear, shirts, sweaters, pyjamas, jeans, sweatshirts were all piled in a heap at the door without examination, although some clothes were rescued from the pile because they were still folded, which was his only criterion for sorting. The huge pile he lugged down to the basement and dumped beside the washing machine. On his way up he grabbed sheets and pillowcases from the linen closet, returned to his room and made the bed, tucking the blankets in so tight the bed could have passed a Marine inspection. He put his new clothes away, even pausing to put them into appropriate drawers.

He surveyed his fifteen minutes of labour with a feeling of completion, not seeing on his desk the jumble of books and papers from last year mixed with assorted indefinable objects sports magazines, chocolate bar wrappers, a sports cap, a bicycle sprocket and three dirty glasses, perhaps more. Nor did he notice the overflowing waste paper basket or the dustballs under the bed hiding coyly among last year's gym shoes, some underwear, a dressing gown and something that had mould on it. "Well, that's done!" he said and looked at his watch. It was still too early to phone Lee.

Downstairs he fried some bacon and made some toast and the aroma floated up the stairs and aroused Marion. Thinking of her son making coffee for her and now making his own breakfast stirred maternal guilt feelings. She went to the top of the stairs and trilled, "Craig? Craggy dear?" and when his head appeared at the bottom of the stairs, she said, "It smells so good. Put a couple of slices on for me, will you, please? I'll be right down."

The morning looked bright and clear and the cloudless sky gave promise of a good day in the garden. She hurried through her morning routines and donned some utilitarian gardening clothes. When she got downstairs, Craig was already halfway through his second breakfast, watching her toast and bacon. Making a cup of instant coffee, she settled into the nook with him.

"What have you been up to?" she asked. "I heard you moving around, up and down."

"I was cleaning up my room," he replied, as he put her bacon and toast on a plate and brought it to the table.

"You were?" she asked with some cynicism but mostly hope, and added, "Thank you."

"Did you finish the marmalade?" she asked. And he nodded his head and tried to say "Yes" with his mouth full.

She got up from the table, saying, "I'll go downstairs and get some. I like marmalade with toast and bacon."

"I'll get it," Craig offered, jumping up, his mouthful now organized in his cheek so he could speak.

"You'd never find it," she called as she left.

He sat back down and got on with the business of fuelling himself with more toast and peanut butter.

"Craig!" came a screaming shout from the basement so loud it made him jump. It was not a distress cry, not a cry for help, it was one of those maternal screams that arise from utter frustration and pure rage. There were no additional instructions such as "Get down here!" nor were there any stated consequences if obedience was not instantaneous. It was an all-inclusive one-word order. He went quickly but cautiously down to the lion's den.

She was standing in the laundry room, hands on her hips, her face tight with anger. "What is this?" and she spit out every word like a Gestapo Oberlieutenant.

"That's my laundry," he said carefully." I was cleaning up my room and there wasn't room in the hamper so I..."

"There wasn't room in your room for all this—this—stuff!" she shouted. "This is laundry!" and she picked up a sheet and flung is aside. "And this!" and she threw aside some dirty work jeans. "But what do you call this? This is a shirt that is still folded that I washed last week! And this! A T-shirt that you haven't worn!"—throwing it at him. "Look at this pile! Half of it you haven't had on."

She stood glaring at him in unadulterated fury.

"Sorry, Mom. I didn't mean..." realizing his mistake and starting an apology.

"Sorry" she roared. "Don't stand there telling me you're sorry. I'll show you what sorry is!" She took a kick at the pile of clothes and continued her tirade, no where near having finished. "How would you like to do your own laundry and see what it is like. The washing, the ironing, the folding, the mending, the sewing on buttons, the trips to the drycleaner? Do you think that's all mothers are good for? That, and cleaning up after you, and making your meals, and shopping, and..." She was running out of breath but catching her second wind. "Now, you get busy and do that whole pile, even the clean ones. And don't ask me how to do it! If you don't know how to do it, then phone 911 or somebody who can help you. Phone Lee—maybe she knows. Now come with me!"

She turned and marched up the stairs to the second floor with Craig following nervously behind like a small boy due for a spanking. She stopped in front of his bedroom door. "Open it!" she commanded. He did and stepped quickly out of her way.

"Hm-mph," she said. "Open that closet door!"

She did not step foot into the room and he scooted around her, opened the closet door and stood back. She bent over from her place in the door way and said, "Bring me a rake!"

"M-o-om," the little boy said. "What do you want a rake for?"

"Just—bring—me—a—rake! Now!" The anger was not diminishing.

He edged around her and went down the stairs in three leaps. She could hear the back door slam, the garage door opened followed by his racing steps up the stairs before the back door snapped shut. He handed her a rake without saying a word. Just as quietly, she stepped into the room and raked everything off the closet floor into the room. She turned and raked under the bed bringing out things she did not want to look at. Then she walked over to his desk whose surface could not be seen and raked everything off it onto the floor. "Now then, get the vacuum and a trash bag and clean up!" she commanded and turned to go downstairs.

"Some of that was good stuff," he called after her, standing by the heap from his desk.

She stopped and glared at him. "If you find anything worth saving in that pile, such as a crayon picture from kindergarten, then put it away and burn the rest." She proceeded down the stairs. At the bottom, she turned again and said, "One piece of helpful advice: one cup of detergent is enough for a load, and don't mix the light clothes with the dark clothes. You have about five loads and all day to do it."

She sat down to her breakfast, but it was cold and tasteless. So, after making herself a fresh cup of instant coffee, she went into the sunroom and sat in the warm sun while she waited for the adrenalin to wear off and the shakes to subside. After a while, she was able to say to herself, "Poor kid. I gave him a terrible hard time." And then the rationalization, "But he deserved it. He had it coming." Finally, a ray of insight, "I think maybe I was shouting mostly at his father."

She got up and started outside to work in her garden. As she passed through the kitchen she heard the vacuum upstairs and the washer in the basement. Then breathing a small sigh of relief, she picked up her cold toast and bacon and munched as she went.

When Craig had sorted through the stuff his mother had raked into the middle of the floor he had a small trash bag full of stuff he didn't know he had and didn't want. He took it downstairs and on his way to the garage passed by his mother busy digging in her flower beds.

"Hi!" she called pleasantly. "Nearly finished?"

"Not yet. I've got another load of washing to do and then I guess I've got to iron a lot of it."

"Good for you. Don't forget it's a steam iron. Keep a little water in it."

"Mom? Do I have to iron jeans?"

"It's up to you Craig. You're the one that has to wear them."

He was about to ask her if she had always ironed his jeans but he thought he better let the subject drop. He was returning to the house when his mother called out, "Craig? I hope you're not washing wool sweaters or good slacks with the rest of your clothes."

"I don't think so but I'll check," he called back.

She groaned and returned to her weeding.

When he went back upstairs he went directly to the master bedroom and took the phone with its long cord over to the window so he could keep an eye on his mother in the garden. He dialled Lee's number and her mother answered, telling him pleasantly that Lee was very busy getting her school clothes fitted but "Just a minute, Craig. I'll see if she can come to the phone." While he waited, he looked around the room at the unmade bed, the pile of fresh laundry his mother had placed on the chair inside the door, and two suits in their plastic bags hanging from the top of the door closet door. For her, an unusual disarray.

"Craig?" the phone said.

"Hi, Lee What are you doing?" He happened to be facing a mirror but he did not see the smile breaking out over his face.

"Oh, the dressmaker's here and she has been sticking pins in me all morning."

"How come?" remembering vaguely what she had told him the night before.

"Craig, it's all happening so fast, I'm dizzy."

"What's happening?" There was a silence broken by the sound of a stifled sob and sniffing. "Lee?" He waited. "Lee, I'm coming over."

"No, Craig, don't!" she said quickly. "Meet me around the corner from my house about four o'clock before my father gets home. Craig, they don't want me to see you any more. I've got to go. They're all calling me. Bye." Before she hung up Craig heard another shuddering sob.

He looked out of the window but could not now see his mother where she had been working a few minutes ago. Very quickly, he put the phone back, tiptoed out and closed the door quietly. He didn't know quite why he was being so secretive but he remembered the feeling he used to have when he was a little boy who had been playing with his mother's lingerie.

"Hi!" said Rob loudly, as Craig came back into his room.

Craig jumped. "Don't do that!" he said. "You scared me."

CHAPTER 28

Craig had not noticed his father's car in the driveway and he had automatically uttered the words, 'Hello Dad' when he saw him sitting across from his mother in the living room. The polite involuntary greeting was met with chilling hostility. There was no response. If they had been talking, there was now a brittle silence. He made a feeble excuse for an exit and got out of the house fast, angry with himself for leaving his mother alone with him. "Maybe they want to talk," he said to himself, "they wouldn't want me there. But maybe I should have stayed."

He saw Rob walking half a block away and whistled. Rob turned around and called, "You okay?" to which Craig yelled, "Sure!" and Rob turned and continued toward home. Then Craig began to feel hostile to Rob, too, for not coming back when he needed him and all the anger and disappointment of the day spilled out into a tantrum and he picked up a sod of grass that his mother had dug up and flung it against the windshield of his father's car without breaking it. He picked up the spade she had been using and ran to the car with it but halted himself in time before he used it on the car. Dropping the spade, he got his bike out of the garage and rode furiously in the opposite direction that Rob had been going, racing as fast as he could, oblivious to the traffic or the route, until he had blown the fury out of his system. Finally, exhausted, he turned around and pedalled slowly in the direction of home.

When he arrived back, his father's car was gone and the light was still on in the kitchen. He entered quietly and called "Mom?" softly. When there was no answer he called louder, and when there was no immediate response, he felt a terrible sense of panic and he shouted, "Mom! Mom! Where are you? Are you all right?" She finally answered, "I'm in here, Craig."

When she had heard the ugliness of her husband's words, and watched his contorted face, the face of a stranger, spewing hate and spittle at her, she looked inside herself and saw a will that was not breaking or bending. She heard the words, as awful, she thought, as any husband could say to a wife and she walked out of the room to get away from them. "I will not cry. I will not shout back. I will not let myself care." She repeated these things over and over, like a Hail Mary, until she heard the door close behind him. But the words kept ringing: "It was always wrong, right from the 'I do's'. Right from the time I got into your cold, proper, oh, so god damned proper bed" She wiped her face as if the saliva he had sprayed in his fury had drenched her, but her face was dry and there were no tears. She covered her ears tightly, pressing hard with her hands, but the harsh words and the hoarse, terrible voice continued on and on until another voice, frantic with concern, called, "Are you alright?" Then she knew she was.

Craig came into the living room as she turned on a light. "I had to come in here, in the dark," she said. "I just couldn't look at him."

"I was afraid he might hurt you—he looked so angry," Craig said, going to her and sitting on the arm of her chair with an arm across her shoulders. "I should have stayed to protect you."

"No, Craig. I don't think he would ever get physical in his anger. He is too good with words—he doesn't need to use physical violence. Words are his weapons"

"What did he say?"

"Nothing that you need to know, should know, or will ever know."

There was a long silence between them. "Did you talk, about—well, about what he was going to do, or anything like that?" he asked and then he blurted, "Oh God! I wish he was dead!"

"Oh Craig, don't say things like that!" She stopped and touched him. "No, dear, we didn't talk. And we never will talk in the sense of the word you're thinking."

"So are you getting a divorce or...?" He was not certain in his young mind what other alternatives there were.

"I said we didn't talk. If he wants a divorce, he'll try to get one—on what grounds, I don't know. Me—I couldn't care less. I can't waste my time and energy trying to legally end a marriage that is finally, totally, irrevocably over anyway."

Again there was a silence until she said, "You know, Craig, this has been a long day, a very long day. Not that there weren't some good moments in it, I won't forget those. But it's been a long, hard day for you, too. What do you say we close up and go to bed?"

"Okay, good idea," he agreed. He turned on the hall light for her and went out to the kitchen to lock the door. On the table he saw the paper and pencils they had used to make their list. Beside it was a check book. He looked at it and saw that it was for his parent's joint account.

Going to the stairs he said to his mother who was halfway up, "Dad left his check book on the kitchen table."

She stopped. "May I see it?" she asked.

He took it to her and she examined it. "I wonder why he did that?" she said almost inaudibly. I'll put it away." She continued up the stairs. "Are you coming, too?" she called from the top of the stairs.

"No, I think I'll work on my list for our hike," he replied.

She smiled, said "Goodnight, then," and blew him a kiss.

The sun wakened her in the morning and she looked out on a clear August sky that gave promise of a warm day. Thinking of the boys and their hike, she hoped the weather would hold for the weekend. It was early enough that she would not have to hurry to get to the hospital by nine. Before she went down-stairs, she looked in on Craig and found him still sleeping. He had on only the bottom of his pyjamas, as usual, and also as usual, his bed was torn apart. She closed the door quietly, remembering how, even as an infant, he had thrashed around in his bed all night. She smiled as she thought of the poor woman he would marry and what she would have to get used to in her marital bed. Then, the thought of her own marital bed came darting into her mind. "Damn," she said, and turned the kitchen radio up loud and tried to sing to the music. Upstairs Craig stirred in his sleep, searched in the wreckage of his bed and found a pillow to put over his head. In thirty seconds, he was dreaming again. In an hour, he came wide enough awake to hear the silence of the house, and the plans for the day stirred him into activity. There was a note from his mother on the kitchen table, "Phone Richard before you go to make sure he will be home, XO."

When he phoned, Richard told him he would be home all day and when he got a minute, he would find the tent and camping gear for him. "Who are you going with?" he asked socially, when Craig told him, he said, "Oh, great! Two old buddies off on a weekend hike. I envy you. And the weather is going to be fabulous."

He had some more 'Blea-agh' and a muffin and juice his mother had left out for him, and after locking up the house, headed for Rob's.

At the hospital, Marion found Ellen and the others in a sombre mood. Harry, the orderly who was everyone's friend and favourite, had died the day before, after a night and a morning of almost continuous seizures. No diagno-sis had yet been made and an autopsy was probably in progress. She thought of the affable, happy man she had met only twice, picturing him now on a slab in the morgue, his body and brain being searched for a cause of his death, and she shuddered. She remembered what Craig had said in his anger last night about wishing his father were dead, and she thought, I know how he feels—but not like Harry's death. Not that—even for him! The morning dragged slowly on. No report from the morgue came by noon.

Just after noon, Tom Thomas came striding through the doors and headed for Marion's gift shop with a big smile breaking out as soon as he saw her. "Hi," he said cheerily. "I'm off to see my father and feed him lunch if he needs me and then, how about I buy you lunch—but I'm warning you, I'm late and I'll have to gobble it. Okay?"

He was off and into the elevator while she was saying, "That would be nice but I can't close the shop for too long." As the door closed, she smiled and shook her head, "That man has only one gear," she said to herself. Then she thought of the line-up in the cafeteria and the crowded tables and the need to share a table with strangers and had a better idea. She closed the shop and put her note 'Back in five minutes' on the door and headed for the cafeteria. The line was not too long. The quiet talk among most people was about Harry and the impatient wait for information. She picked up two wrapped and ready ham and cheese sandwiches, two coffees and little creams and sugars and was back in the shop before Tom came down from his visit.

"Ready?" he asked as he got to the door.

"No, I had a better idea," she said. "Come inn." And she led him through the little shop and into the back room where she had set out the sandwiches and coffee on a shelf and found a stool to add to the only chair she had. "See, a picnic! she said. "No line-up, no waiting, no ants and no crowded tables with strangers."

"Hey, this is great!" he enthused. "I'm impressed! This is so—so intimate," giving a little head twist and grin.

They sat down together, Tom on the chair while she, nearer to the door to watch the shop, perched on the stool. "Cream and sugar right there," she said pointing and speaking with her mouth full.

"Good," he said, "you're right, no ants, no crowds, no stirrers, no napkins."

"I was in a hurry," she laughed, not at all embarrassed by his teasing. She went into the shop and came back with a pencil and two grabs of Kleenex. "Here," she said, handing a Kleenex and the pencil to him, "we'll have to share the pencil."

"But not the Kleenex?" he asked, smiling.

"Not this time," she replied and got up to deal with a customer who only wanted a paper, and thought "What did I say that for? What will he think I meant?"

She returned and they munched in silence for a minute. "Dr. Strawburn was in with Dad when I got up there," Tom said.

"I forgot to ask—how is he?"

"No change, but I've got to get him out of here and into some kind of home. Even Dr. Strawburn was pushing a little and that's not like him."

"No, it isn't," she agreed.

"By the way, we were talking about you," Tom said abruptly.

"You were!" she responded, so startled that she dribbled some coffee she had sipped as she spoke. He reached out with his Kleenex and dabbed the front of her smock.

"See," he said, smiling and holding up the Kleenex, "we shared. These things happen sooner than you think."

"How come you were talking about me?" she asked, puzzled.

"Oh, I happened to mention that I had bumped into you and that I knew he took care of your family. He said that was true but he had never seen your husband. I was making small talk with him. He's kind of a shy man."

"Oh," she said, relieved. "Is that all."

"Well, not quite all. I didn't ask him—he volunteered the information. He said he had heard that you and your husband had split."

"He didn't!" she protested. "He had no right! He's a doctor. He should not go around gossiping about his patients like that."

"If it's not true," Tom said quietly, "then it's gossip. If it is true, then it's a fact." He paused. "Is it true?" he asked looking directly at her.

She hesitated, then met his eyes. "Yes," she said, it's true. But he has no right to…"

"Good!" he said, interrupting her.

She looked at him in surprise. "Why, good?" she asked.

"Because the last time we met, I told you I would like to see you again and you got all flustered and told me you were a married woman but even so, I had the feeling you were interested. Now I can say it again. I would like to see you again. What do you say?"

She blew a long held breath slowly out, shook her head and said, uncertainly, "I don't know."

"We've got to hurry up, Marion," he urged.

"What do you mean?" she asked.

"First, I mean we're both past forty and second, I've got to get back to work. How about dinner tonight?" His whole face was smiling.

"I can't—tonight," she said. He heard the modifier and was alerted to continue, but let her finish. "I've got bridge this afternoon and then I've got to get home to get my son off on a big hike tomorrow. And I was going to phone you if any of the women came up with ideas about rest homes."

"Right!" he enthused. "Then tomorrow for dinner will be perfect. I'll pick you up a seven. Is that okay?"

She nodded.

"Any place you would like to go?"

She shook her head.

"Okay, then. We'll find a nice quiet place and talk about rest homes." He got to his feet and put out his hand. "I'd really like to do more than shake hands," he said, "But this is a public place." Again, she saw his wide smile. "Thank you for lunch. It was delicious but the company was better. See you tomorrow." And he was gone.

She sat watching him stride out the door with an almost 'What happened?' feeling. She saw a woman come into the shop and stand at the counter, but still she did not move.

"Hello?" the woman called tentatively.

"Oh, sorry!" Marion said jumping to her feet. "I was daydreaming."

"It must have been a beautiful dream—you had a lovely smile on your face."

Marion knew her face was scarlet.

***

When Craig reached Rob's house, he opened the door a crack as usual and shouted, "Hey, Rob! You up?"

Rob's mother called from inside, "Come in, Craig. You can go up and haul him out of bed."

Craig followed the voice out to the kitchen. "Hi, Mrs. T. Mr. T. still in bed, too?"

"Not bloody likely," she answered in a broad Cockney accent. "He's t'town workin' up some troops t'meet some bigwig about boosting the jug-time for possession."

"What do you mean?" Craig had to ask, the accent having puzzled him.

"He's got a group together and they are going to picket a meeting of Health Department officials to try to get them to increase the penalty for possession of drugs, you know, like pot, hashish, crack and all the rest."

"Why?" Craig asked.

"I don't know all the reasons," she said. "I think some of it has to do with having watched his brother slowly kill himself with any kind of drug he could put his hands on."

"I didn't know he had a brother."

"I'm not surprised. He hasn't mentioned him for years. He feels strongly that if they had locked him up and thrown away the key, in a manner of speaking, his brother would still be alive. Instead they just slapped his hands and put him back on the street."

Craig was silent only because he didn't know what to say.

She watched him struggling to work something out, and finally said, "What are you guys up to today?"

"We're going out to Bev and Richard's to get some camping equipment from them. We're going to hike into Lake Lovely Water tomorrow and spend two nights there."

"That sounds great," she said. "Isn't that where they hiked, oh, six or seven years ago?"

"Yeah! It sounds neat! I better go get him up or we'll never get started."

"Have fun," she said.

It was not fun trying to rouse Rob, who resisted every attempt to wake him. Finally, Craig gave up and went to the bathroom and came back with a glass of water. Rob was sitting on the edge of the bed wide awake and waiting, naked except for a corner of a sheet pulled across his legs.

"Go ahead! Try it!" he warned. "One drop, one teensy weensy little drop, and you're a dead Williams. Probably with two broken arms before the grisly end." He tried to glare ferociously but he was laughing. "Hey, wanna see me do my morning pushups?"

"Pushups? You?" Craig said.

"Watch, then," said Rob. He threw back the sheet and sat showing an erection. "Ta-da!" he continued, "watch!"

Craig looked and saw a heavier black thatch on Rob's groin than he had seen before. Rob threw himself on the floor with his arms by his sides, and moved his buttocks up and down a few times. "Damn!" he said. "It's not working. Usually it pushes me up at least twelve inches."

Craig dumped the glass of water on him and ran. On his way out the door, he called to Rob's mother, "He's up. Tell him to come over to my house."

At home, Craig checked his tires and the chain. He remembered riding Lee sidesaddle over to Rob's and wondered if he should try to phone her but decided against it. He knew she wouldn't be permitted to answer the phone or even come to the phone to speak to him.

Rob arrived suddenly and Craig backed cautiously away from him. "Come on," Rob said. "We've got to get going," as if Craig had been holding things up. "I'm not going to get you for that miserable trick. I've got a whole weekend to plan your punishment. And it'll come when you least expect it. It will come on the shores of a cold, lovely mountain lake in the dead of night. Aha-hah-hah-hah," he finished in a terrible monster imitation. "Let's go!" and he jumped on his bike and raced away shouting, "Try to keep up this time." He stopped half a block away and as Craig approached he said, "Or would you like to ride side saddle with me?" and he put on a magnificent leer, hopped on this bike again and was almost a block ahead before Craig had worked up any speed.

It took them more than thirty minutes to reach Bev and Richard's small house in the suburbs. Bev was out grocery shopping and would be back anytime, Richard said, looking happy to see them and to take a break. "How's it going?" Rob asked his brother-in-law.

"Slow—and boring by now," Richard replied. "I've got the bibliography to tidy up and I've got to rewrite the introduction. Like an idiot I wrote it first instead of leaving it until the last—but that won't take long. Then I'm finished, thank God! Another degree, more money."

"What's it about?" Craig asked innocently.

"Don't make me tell you. Please!" Richard said. "Don't you guys want to look at the stuff I've pulled out for you?"

"Sure, where is it?" Rob said, briskly.

"Around here on the back porch," Richard said. "There's quite a lot of it. You don't need to take it all."

They looked at the pile and groaned.

"Don't despair," Richard laughed. "This is the stuff we take in the car with the baby. You pick out what's useful."

The two neophytes stood looking puzzled not knowing where to start, so Richard took over.

"You've got sleeping bags of your own, haven't you?" They both nodded. "Here's a marvellous little tent. It sleeps two and a baby, and it weighs about four pounds. Take it. The instructions are inside in a plastic bag. Here's a frying pan and a pot, that's all you need and that's all you'll want to carry. This bag is a bunch of dried food, soup, fruit powder, mixed dried veggies to put in your stew if you remember to take some jerky." He continued on through the large pile, sorting it out for them and giving them hiking tips as he went along.

"Take this piece of nylon rope. I throw it over a branch and put all the food supplies in a bag and pull it up out of reach of bears."

"Bears! I forgot about bears!" Craig said, his city-boy eyes wide.

"Yeah, bears. So don't forget to talk loud and make noises when you're in the woods so you don't happen to bump into the backside of a big, old black bear who really would have appreciated a warning that you were coming so he could get out of the way. And if you happen to see a couple of cute little cubs romping in the woods, don't stand around watching them. Look for the mama bear and when you see her or hear her, don't, repeat don't, walk between her and her cubs."

There was more wide-eyed nodding from both boys.

"Don't take your fishing rods," Richard continued. "They probably don't break down enough. Take mine," and he handed them two small bundles about sixteen inches long. "These won't catch on branches on the trail and they're probably longer than the average rod. Don't clean your fish in camp. Clean them where you catch them and bury the guts,—and your poop—here's a break down shovel. And here's a good hatchet. It's sharp and I lost the guard on it, so be careful." He paused and looked at them and laughed at their expression. "Don't look so panicky," he chided. "There isn't going to be a test when I'm finished. The only test is survival." His laughter did nothing to change their expression.

He went on. "Take some toilet paper—you don't need a whole roll, it's too bulky. Take some salt, pepper is a nuisance. And take some matches, more than you need, and keep them dry—in a plastic bag in your knapsack. And a whistle each, in case you get separated or lost. Remember, I told you, how the trail was marked? With the lids of tin cans and pie plates nailed about eight or nine feet up in trees. You should be able to see them about 100 yards away. Don't wander off the trail. Keep your eye on a pie plate and you won't get lost." He paused and looked at them like a good teacher. "Any questions?"

They looked at one another and shrugged.

Richard asked, "Have you both got a good knife?"

"I've got a Swiss Army Knife," Craig offered.

"Forget it, Craig. You both should have a good hunting knife like this." His hand flicked under his loose shirt tail and appeared holding a hunting knife. "One like this. Never mind switch blades and all that kind of junk." His hand flicked under his shirt tail again and came back empty. He gave them a long look again and asked "OK?" Suddenly they were full of enthusiasm and thanks, itching to get started.

"I've got to run, guys," Richard said. "Help yourself to what ever else you think you'll need. Remember, whatever you start out with will weigh five times as much half-way up the trail. Do me a favour and put the rest in a box in the garage. Looks like a great weekend for a hike. I wish I could go along. Have fun. And oh, by the way, bring your trash out with you like good citizens. See you when you get back," and he disappeared into the house.

They sorted through the rest of Richard's camping equipment and found some more things they thought would be useful, including a three quarter size blow up mattress that Rob insisted they would need. They stored the rest in the garage. They hadn't thought to bring their packsacks with them so they tied two boxes filled with camping gear on the racks of their bikes and headed for home.

On the grass in Craig's back yard, they dumped the boxes and sat for a long time debating about what else they needed and who would carry what. Rob talked of pork and beans and Craig raged, "And I suppose you're going to carry all that canned stuff and cans of pop and your mattress and the hatchet and probably your teddy bear!" He ducked as something flew past his head and said, "Let's go see what Mom left for lunch."

In the kitchen they made themselves thick sandwiches and gulped a quart of milk. "Hey," Rob said suddenly through a mouthful of sandwich, "what do we do about milk and bread? Is there a store up there?"

"Jeez! Rob! Weren't you listening. We have to carry up everything we need."

"Well, how the hell do you pack bread up? Or milk? It would be sour before we got there!"

"I dunno," Craig said. There was a long silence until Craig said, "You're going to have to phone Richard and ask him."

Rob sat staring at Craig as if by magic or serendipity, some answer would spring forth. It didn't. "Phone Richard," Craig said. Rob groaned and went to the phone. Craig heard him talking and went outside where he sat looking at the stuff spread on the lawn.

"He wasn't home," Rob announced when he came out, "so I talked to Bev. She says we don't take bread, we take a plastic bag of biscuit mix and cook it in the frying pan or make stiff dough and wrap it around the end of a stick and hold it up over the fire. And she says to take a plastic bag of milk powder. And she says the Sports Shop on 25th Street has everything anybody would ever need for camping and hiking, peanut butter and jam in tubes and everything. She says we'll know what we'll need as soon as we look around the store."

"Well, come on! Let's go!" Craig jumped up full of enthusiasm.

"She said two more things, I think. One was, take lots of money."

"To the lake?" unbelieving.

"No, meathead—to the store, where else?"

"Shit!" said Craig. "What's the other one?"

"She made me promise to take care of dear, little Craggy. I said I would just love him to death all weekend."

"Oh, go to hell! She did not," Craig blustered. "C'mon, let's go. Have you got your wallet?"

"No, but you've got yours. That's enough."

"We'll stop at your place on the way."

"What a cheap, stingy, miserable excuse for a best friend you turned out to be," Rob said, as they rode away laughing.

**

Marion got away from the hospital on time and drove to Isabel's whose turn it was to have the game this week. She had checked with Ellen before leaving to see if there was any further news about Harry but she had heard none. The only thing she knew was that a memorial service was being planned in the church chapel as soon as the body was officially released from the morgue. She had had an enjoyable morning but the thought of morgues and autopsies gave her a little shiver and a slight depression dampened her spirits and lasted until she opened the door at Isabel's and faced a chattering happy group of old friends.

It was strange, she thought, as she settled into her place at a bridge table, how much there was to talk about from one week to another. They never talked politics, unless someone had heard a mean political joke, or sports, or religion, or even, except occasionally, their lives in the kitchens of their homes. They bragged about their children and grandchildren and sometimes about their husbands, filled each other in on the progress of a favourite soap, sounded a general alert about special sales, and they gossiped.

"So what's the news about you and Gerry?" Dot asked bluntly during a brief lull.

"Dot!" Minnie scolded. "That's none of our business!"

"Well, it certainly is," Dot disagreed. "How else can you defend a friend when other people gossip unless you know the truth?"

"Dot's right," put in Cora. "Don't you think so, Marion? You know we've all been talking about you but we haven't been gossiping about you. But we're friends and we want to protect you against people who are just dirty, mean gossips and we like to know what's going on. But we don't need to know all the gory details."

They nodded, laughed and waited expectantly.

"Unless you really want to include the gory details," called Isabel from the kitchen.

Marion looked around the group. Some, she knew, were waiting for something juicy that they could indeed use, not necessarily maliciously, but in way that continues conversations and at the same time indicates one-up-man-ship in the social game. So she told them straight out. She told them about Gerry's hostility, but not his actual ugly words, his deteriorating appearance, his drinking. She told them of his apparent intention of moving out, and she said she would not be sorry to see him go.

"Are you going to divorce him," one of them asked.

"I don't know. I really don't care," she answered.

"Well, is he supporting you?" Kate said. "That's important, you know. Maybe you should get something in writing."

"Yeah, Marion," Isabel called from the kitchen. "I told you before—get a good, tough lawyer."

"I don't need a lawyer," Marion asserted.

"You will!" "Better late than never!" "It would be a smart thing to do," came a chorus of advice.

"When's his court case?" someone asked

"Next Friday, I think," Marion answered. "A week from tomorrow."

"Are you going to be there?" Cora asked.

"Good God! No!" Marion declared with such force that a short silence followed.

Then from the kitchen, came Isabel's voice. "Let's get started, girls. I don't want to be late with Harry's dinner."

They shuffled and dealt and bid and played, some with greater enthusiasm and intent than others. Marion found her mind wandering away from the game occasionally and discovered Cora's useful ploy of bidding double when she had been caught daydreaming over her lacquered nails. When they broke briefly for lunch, she found she had little interest in food but nibbled away at something to please Isabel. They started play again, and she sat up straight in her chair trying to concentrate on the game, but again her thoughts drifted back to her lunch with Tom and forward to dinner with him tomorrow.

In mid-afternoon Gerry went to the office. He walked in and stood at the counter in the main office and listened to the gradual cessation of talk and business machines. Two people had been talking on the telephone, and as the other routine office sounds diminished their voices also decreased in volume. He intercepted many nervous side-long glances in his direction. Finally, Louise approached him hesitantly and said pleasantly, "Hello, Mr. Williams. It's nice to see you again."

"Is anyone using my office?" he asked, not bothering with a response to her greeting. "There are personal files in there that I want to collect."

"Just a minute," she said, her face red from his rudeness. "I'll get an authorization from Cyril." She scurried away towards a cubicle in the back and stood in the doorway while she talked. As she was returning to the counter, he saw Cyril emerge from the cubicle and disappear down the hall.

"Well?" he said to her loudly before she reached the counter.

"Mr. Chester will bring your effects from the dead files," she told him.

"What in hell are they doing in the dead files?" he asked loudly.

"I don't know, Mr. Williams," she replied, backing away and returning to her desk.

He stood waiting and the general office noise returned to normal only to stop suddenly when Bill Webb appeared beside him at the front counter.

"I understand you are here to pick up your personal effects from, um, your office," he said without any preliminaries. "Cyril and Eleanor went through the files together since you had worked so closely with Eleanor. Here they are now," as Cyril approached the desk carrying a file folder box, that was tied with string.

"There it is, Mr. Webb," he said, placing the box in front of him. "Will that be all?"

"Thank you, Cyril," Bill Webb replied, and with a finger and thumb shoved the box over to Gerry.

"Why was it filed in the dead files?" Gerry asked.

"It was Eleanor's idea."

Gerry stood for a minute searching the faces of the office staff.

"She's taking dictation. She'll be a while," came the final word from Bill Webb as he walked away.

"I was sure you would want me to sign for it in triplicate," Gerry called after him. Webb wiggled a casual hand without turning around and Gerry turned and left through the main office double doors, both of which opened both ways so that his attempt to slam one behind him was futile.

He found a small restaurant down a side street where he knew nobody from the office would lunch and, going to a booth in the back, opened the box. A waitress hurried over, order book in hand, and before she could say anything, he said, "A coffee, now, and then a bacon and tomato toasted on brown, with another coffee. Okay?"

"Yes, sir, would you...," she began.

"I've got a little paper work to do. You don't mind if we don't chat, do you?" as he pulled some files out of the box.

"Oh, no sir! That's alright. I was just going to ask if you wanted salad or fries."

"Whatever." He was already thumbing through one of the files but was not so absorbed that he did not watch her walking away. "Nice ass," he said to himself.

He went through the files slowly and methodically, making notes as he progressed. Leaning back with his fingers tucked into his belt pressing against his gut muscles, he read the notes he had made. Then he put his files back into the box, paid his bill and went back to the office building.

Inside he climbed to the second floor and walked down a hallway to a door whose glass window showed the faded message: Timothy T. Irwin, Notary Public, Private Investigations. He knocked on the door and walked in, just as a grossly fat man dropped a bottle into a drawer with one hand and wiped the back of the other hand across his mouth.

"Hi, Titty," Gerry said.

"You!" was the response as the hand went back into the drawer for the bottle. "What d'ya want?"

Timothy T. Irwin, since childhood was T.T. to his face and Titty behind his back, until from excesses in food and booze he became so obese, with ponderous breasts that interfered with his golf swing, he became Titty openly to everyone in the club. His favourite hangouts now were the bar and the late night buffet. He had passed out so frequently in the bar, that the stewards, unable to push his bulk into a taxi whose driver often speeded away during their attempts, would load him onto a three wheeled dolly, take him to an empty games room and cover him with tablecloths. The story is routinely told of how the Pro suffered from coitus interruptus on the billiard table when a piggish snort from a pile of table-cloths startled the wife of the club President. Titty had done some investigation work for Gerry's firm, but when his dependability decreased with his booze increase, he was no longer employed by the firm. He blamed Gerry openly and vociferously.

"Well?" he snarled, as Gerry pulled up a chair to the desk and opened his box of files.

"I've got a job for you," Gerry said. "Put that god-damned bottle down and listen."

Titty glared at him and raised the bottle to his lips. Gerry reached across the desk and knocked the bottle to the floor.

"Listen, you fat son of a bitch! I've given you enough work over the years for you to buy your own distillery. You'd still be getting more work than you could handle if you weren't such a disreputable drunk. I've got a couple of jobs for you and the only reason I picked you is because you owe me, Titty. You owe me a god damn pile! And because you have worked with a couple of sleazy lawyers before, I need something done that will look squeaky clean. Got it?"

Timothy T. Irwin rumbled something incomprehensible. Gerry continued. "Here's what you're going to do for me—you and any one of the back street lawyers you work with. Now, listen up good!"

Fifteen minutes later when Gerry left the small, messy office, Titty reached down to salvage what was left in the bottle. He looked again at the file containing the names and addresses of the two people Gerry had given him, their sample signatures and the name of his boat and the marina where he could be reached.

"What a contemptible piece of shit," he said. "Setting up his own wife and his mistress! To make it look like Coleman forged a codicil to his will so she gets everything and his wife and family get nothing and they fight the thing out in court forever." He looked at the file with complete distaste. "Who needs this crap," he said, tossing it onto a pile of letters, clippings, files and other miscellany spilling out of a box in the corner.

***

When Marion got home she found the two depressed boys sitting in the back yard surrounded by gear and equipment. They both greeted her with minimal enthusiasm.

"What is this stuff?" she asked picking among the unorganized pile.

"Dried food—soup, veggies, powdered milk, stuff like that," Craig explained.

"Oh," she said. "Then what's the problem?"

"It won't fit in," Rob said. "We've got to leave some stuff out and we can't decide."

"Do you want an arbiter?"

One said "How big is it?" and the other said "What is it?" both looking a little wary.

"It's what parents do for their children when they can't do it themselves." She stopped and looked at them. "They decide for them."

They continued to look at her but the wariness disappeared. Then they made a "What the hell" shrug, grinned and said "Okay" in unison.

"Give me a minute to get into my gardening clothes," she said. "I don't want to crawl around in the grass in these clothes."

When she came back they were back to a normal happy mood and ready to take her advice. "Okay, guys. How many nights and how many meals?"

"Two nights," Craig said, while Rob was still counting the meals. "Six or seven or maybe eight," he finally said.

She was sorting through the pile of stuff they had bought. "Get your pack-sacks and sleeping bags, and Rob, you sit here and Craig, sit there but first get me a cardboard box from the garage." When he returned she said, "Okay, you get the axe, and you get the shovel. What's this?"

"It's an air mattress. I wanted it," Rob declared.

"You got it," she said tossing it to him.

"You get the milk," she said to Craig, tossing him two packages of milk powder. "One package makes a quart. Neither of you will like it, so two is enough." She put the other eight packages in the box. "You get the juices, Rob. Six packs will do you. Two each of orange, grape and raspberry." She dumped the remaining six packs in the box. She divided the dried fruit, mixed vegetables, raisins, egg powder and other dried packages between them and tossed the remainder in the box.

"Here," she said, giving Craig a box of pancake mix and Rob a box of biscuit mix. "They're both practically the same but you might as well take both. Take them into the house and put exactly eight tablespoons of each into plastic bags and close them tight. And label them," she called after them. "And oh, Craig, put two big cupfuls of that cereal in, too, and label it."

Inside the house, following her instructions, Rob said, "Geez! She's a general, isn't she?"

"You should have heard her yesterday," Craig said, laughing.

Outside, Marion distributed some more items and packed the rest in the already full box. The boys came out with their packages, one labelled, she noticed, Blea-agh!

"Okay," she ordered. "Start packing!"

They packed and stood back in amazement with their bags only three-quarters full. "Amazing, isn't it?" she chided them, "what a little organization can do."

"What else?" she said as she sat back, thinking and waiting for them to do some thinking, too. But they were waiting for her. Finally she said, "Toilet paper, socks, underwear, shorts, tooth-brush. small bar of soap—you might decide to wash your hands—pack of playing cards." She paused and Craig was up and running into the house.

"Bring some for me," Rob shouted.

"Okay but get your own toothbrush," came the answer.

"Picky-picky," he said to Marion with a grin.

She smiled back at him loving him as if he were her own, and they waited for Craig to return. "What's the rope for?" she asked.

"You're supposed to put all your food in a bag and hang it up in a tree away from the bears," Rob told her.

"Bears!" she said, and shuddered at the thought of the two innocents in the wilderness facing bears. Rob was wearing a long face also.

When Craig came back, she said, "Can you think of anything else? Oh, I know! There's a small first aid kit in the glove box of my car."

"I'll get it," Rob volunteered, leaping to his feet.

"Well done!" Marion said when Rob returned. "You've got enough room left for your teddy bears and jammies."

"Jammies!" they said in unison.

When they unpacked at Lake Lovely Water the next day, each would find in his packsack a two inch teddy bear that Marion had borrowed from Edith's collection.

CHAPTER 29

On Saturday, Craig was up early and rattling around in the kitchen so noisily that he wakened his mother who came down in her dressing gown.

"What's all the racket," she asked

"Sorry, Mom. Did I wake you? I was checking my pack and had half of it on the table and it all slipped off and I had to repack it."

"Is Rob here?" she asked.

"No, not yet. He said he was going to get up early and have breakfast here."

She looked outside at the bright morning sky. "It looks like a marvellous day for a hike," she said. "There's not a cloud in the sky. I hope it stays like that all weekend for you. Did you put any rain gear in?" She started making breakfast.

"No. Do you think I should?"

"I know that if I was going to be outside for two days in this country at this time of year I would pack some kind of raingear," she said, refusing to make any more decisions for him.

"Yeah," he said and sat puzzling about it. "I know! I'll put in a trash bag and if it rains I can cut a hole in the bottom for my head. I read that someplace. Where are they?" He was rummaging around in the kitchen cupboard. "Here they are. I've got them. I better put one in for Rob in case he doesn't think of it."

He continued to fuss with his pack until breakfast was ready. "Didn't you make any for Rob?" he asked.

"Craig! I'm not going to make breakfast for someone who isn't here and let it go to waste," she scolded.

"I would have eaten it," he argued with his mouth full of bacon and eggs.

"You don't need four eggs and six pieces of bacon. You're not a logger, you know," she said, touched as always by the boys' unwavering concern for each other.

"What are you going to do today," he asked.

"I've got quite a bit of phoning to do," but in her mind was the dinner date she had made.

"Say hello to Edie for me," he said taking it for granted that Edith would be on her list of people to phone. "We should go pretty soon, shouldn't we?"

"Yes, but what about Rob?"

"I'll go get him while you get dressed. It's too early to phone."

She was dressed and ready and making last minute sandwiches for them when Craig got back. "His mother says she'll throw some water on him. She's making some sandwiches for us but he has to get his own breakfast if he missed ours. What are you doing?" seeing her at the counter wrapping sandwiches.

"Didn't you know that there is a fundamental law in nature that all mothers should make sandwiches for their children when they are going into the wilderness?"

"Good law!" he said picking up some crumbs. "I wonder what Mrs. T. is making. Well, I'm ready. My pack, jacket, hat and lunch. Let's go get him!"

"Okay, Tiger. Let's go get him! Want to drive?"

"Uh-uh," he answered, shaking his head. "You drive."

When they drove around the corner to the Turner's, Craig was out of the car before it stopped. Marion followed more slowly and was met at the door by Claudia.

"How long has it been since we've seen each other?" Marion asked rhetorically after the old-friends touching-cheeks greetings.

"I know, Marion. Isn't it awful! Glen just seems to get more and more work and every new print job he gets seems to be from some organization or society and then he gets involved in it, too. But you know, Marion, it's rather fun—going out to meetings and listening to people getting excited about something."

"Craig told me you were walking a picket line last week or so. Did you? Or was he making that up?" Marion asked.

"That's right. It was an environmental group trying to clear up that mess out in the valley where the battery plant was dumping into the creek that runs through some dairy farms—you probably read about it. It was a nice day. I just went out for a change. I don't get excited about these things like Glen, but I thought those guys were wrong to be so blatantly careless."

They were standing in what used to be the living room that was now used as a print shop. "Looks like you got crowded out," Marion observed.

"Kind of an odd set-up," Claudia agreed. "But it's easier this way. People wanting to talk with Glen or making deliveries would have to track right through the house to the basement. So we said, what the hell, we'll make the basement our living room and turn the living room into the plant." She shrugged and laughed. "It works," she said.

She paused, and then speaking from the basis of an old and stable friendship, only occasionally renewed, she said, "Let me change the subject. I think we have been friends too long for me to sidle into this topic, so here goes: I hear that you and Gerry are pretty close to breaking up, Marion. If that's true, is there anything we can do?"

"No, Claudia, I don't think so. If the word is out that our marriage is on the rocks, it isn't gossip, it's a fact. And Claudia, it's funny—but I don't care." Claudia, watching, saw a woman who showed no sign of emotion. Years ago, she thought, when we were closer, she could get upset over a burned apple crisp.

"But you know Gerry," Marion said, flatly. "He has always been a cold, self-centred, demanding son of a bitch. I've put up with it for years, thinking it was me that was in the wrong. But no more. I've had it." She took a long deep breath and expelled it slowly, not as a sigh. "I wonder what those boy are up to," she said. "We should get going."

"If I know them, they are probably eating one of our lunches so they won't have to carry it," Claudia laughed.

They found the boys on the steps outside, fitting backpacks onto each other's back and adjusting them into comfort.

"Let's go!" Marion urged. "You won't get up there before dark if you don't hurry up."

"We've been ready for hours and hours," Rob protested. "OK, everybody line up for goodbyes. That means you, Ma. Do you want an Eskimo nose rub or a Ubangi kiss?" He pursed his lips and pushed them out as far as they would go and approached her standing as tall as he could, which made him tower over her. She stood on tip-toes but could only reach high enough to kiss him just below the ear. "Ooh! That tickles!" he said, then hugged her warmly and said, "Goodbye, Mom. Keep out of the cookies," and pinched a piece of fat at her waistline. Smiling, she slapped his retreating back and he made his way to the car, limping and groaning. "Say goodbye to Dad for me, he's still snoring," he called. "She's a mean, mean woman," he said, tumbling into the back seat and waving as they drove away.

They got lost, of course. They had meant to ask Richard for a map or for directions but they had forgotten. Marion had no plans for the day so she saw no reason to fuss and left it to them to ask directions, lose their way, and ask again. When they got hopelessly lost the third time they were lucky. A local man, filling his farm truck at a gas station, concluding by their behavior that they were lost, asked, and was quickly told, by two young, interrupting voices, what they were looking for—the start of the trail to Lake Lovely Water.

"It's hard to find," he advised them, "If you don't know exactly what you're looking for, you'd never find it. Wait until I fill up and follow me. I'll stop and show you."

They followed the truck about two miles down the highway until it stopped.

"There are two good signs," he said, getting out of the truck and talking to Marion through her window. "if you intend to come back here again sometime and I'll lay odds you do. See here, where the power line crosses the road—that's the first sign. And over there where the rail fence begins—that's the next thing you look for. The trail starts right there and it goes on, oh, I'd say about a good five iron to the river." He smiled and touched a golf course parking sticker on her windshield with a hand that was missing three fingers. "That's a great course," he said, by way of explaining his estimate of distance. "I played it a couple of times, way back. Before this," and he gave his disabled hand a casual wave. "I take it you're not going up with the boys."

"No, I certainly am not," she laughed. "From all I've heard it's for young, strong legs."

"Yes, I suppose," he replied, nodding his head. "But even old geezers like me can still make it if it hasn't been raining. Then the trail is so greasy you can't get a footing. But when you get there, it's worth it. By God, it's worth it." He stopped and gazed off looking wistful.

The boys had been busy shrugging into their backpacks and settling them comfortably.

"Have a good hike, boys," he said. Then he called to them, "Look! Up there. There's that old eagle coming in to her nest. See her? Right up there," and he pointed again. "And look! She's carrying a fish this time. Better a fish than another one of my chickens. Isn't she lovely! Look at the spread of those wings. I'd give anything to fly like that," he said without embarrassment.

They were all watching with him, mirroring the sense of awe the stranger displayed. The eagle landed on the ragtag nest, paused a moment, and flew off without the fish.

"I'll bet she's feeding her young," Craig cried gleefully. "Did you see that, Mom?" He looked up at the nest again. "Wow!"

She smiled and nodded.

"Thank you for your help," Marion said to the man, getting out of the car and offering her hand. "We'd have looked a long time if we hadn't found you."

"Yes," said Craig, followed immediately by Rob in picking up her cue, "Thank you, sir." Both offered their hands and received a strong, bony hand in response.

"Glad I happened along," he said. "Have a good climb." He got into his truck, gave them all a wistful look and drove away.

"So!" the mother in Marion said. "Hadn't you better get started?"

"Yeah, you bet! We're on our way. So!" Craig said mimicking her. "Good bye, Mom. See you Sunday."

"Good bye, my lovely one," said Rob, dramatically. "This parting makes heavy the heart within me. Say! That's a good line. I'll have to remember it." And he kissed her on the forehead.

"And two days without you will seem like—," and she paused miming his drama, "—like heaven," she breathed.

"Darn," he said. "You were supposed to say 'an eternity'."

She watched them cross the road and enter the woods, Rob still waving and throwing kisses in all directions. She turned the car around and drove slowly home, thinking some of the time about the boys out in the wilderness and some of the time about getting some rest home information from the women in her bridge group as she had promised. It would give them something to talk about over dinner. She also wondered what Claudia had made the boys for lunch. "I'll bet she made egg salad sandwiches," she thought. For as long as they had known each other, Claudia had brought egg salad sandwiches to any outing. "I hope the boys eat them soon," she thought. She need not have worried.

The boys set out along a dusty narrow path that wound its way through the woods and arrived suddenly at a well trampled area by the river bank. They shucked off their backpacks and began a search in the underbrush for a boat. After half an hour of searching the underbrush on either side of the path without success, they returned to the spot where they had dumped their packs and sat down.

"Now what in hell do we do?" Rob said. "Richard said there would be a boat here." He dug out his mother's bag of sandwiches and started eating as a routine preliminary to solving a problem.

Craig reached over to help him. "Egg salad," he said without enthusiasm. "Your mother always makes egg salad sandwiches.",

Rob felt no need to respond. Craig was right. His mother did always make egg salad sandwiches. So they sat and finished the lunch, each of them saying, "Oh, shit," periodically with their mouths full.

"Hey! Here comes a boat," Rob yelled suddenly, jumping to his feet. They watched a weather beaten rowboat approaching with one person in it, towing another equally old boat.

"You guys waiting for the boat?" the man in the boat called as he approached the bank while Craig caught the line he threw.

"Yeah, we were wondering about it," Craig said.

"Well, you're in luck this time," he said. "If there's just the two of you and you haven't got much stuff, we can all make it in one trip." The man's voice was a deep bass that seemed to rumble in his chest.

"We could take one boat and you could take the other," Craig suggested, wishing his own voice didn't sound like a child's.

"Then you'd have to bring the other boat back," the man said. They stood looking at him with puzzled faces.

"Hey! Didn't you check with the hiking club about using their boats? They're their boats, you know." His voice was only curious, not antagonistic. "I guess you didn't, because you don't know the rules and they would have told you."

He looked at their stricken faces and laughed. "What the hell," he said. "I've been a member long enough to give you permission. Let's go. Haul this other boat up and tie it to that tree trunk that's painted white." He watched them work quickly and easily together. "Tie the oars to the seats and turn the boat over," he ordered.

"Okay," he said, climbing out of the boat in his bare feet with pantlegs rolled up. "Bring your stuff and climb in. I'll push off. No need all of us having wet feet." He waited while they climbed aboard, holding the boat steady, then pushed off and jumped aboard. The boat drifted out into the river. "Well, kid," he said smiling at Rob. "You chose the driver's seat, so I guess you get to row."

"Oh! Yeah," Rob said blushing with embarrassment. Then, as he struggled with the oars and oarlocks, he returned quickly to his usual role, "Okay, you barnacles," he said. "I'm the captain, see? And if I say heave to and throw up, you gotta heave and throw, right?"

"Right!" said Craig.

"And if you want one of us to shout 'Land Ho', then you'd better head that way," the man said, pointing away to the right, "because we want to arrive there," and he pointed away to the left.

Rob groaned and said to Craig as he began rowing in the direction indicated, "We've caught ourselves a real live sailor, lad. He likes to travel the great circle route."

The other two laughed and Rob bent his back and rowed hard and rhythmically without any more comments.

"Excuse me," Craig said finally. "But why did you bring both boats back?"

"Because I wanted to go back and climb with my friends," was the reply.

"But...," Craig started to say. "Oh, I get it. If you hadn't we'd still be standing there like dummies."

"Yeah, but I would have been the dummy. The first rule of the club is: always leave one boat on each side. Pull a little harder upstream, Captain. The current is fast here." Then to Craig, "Get ready to throw that line."

Craig twisted in his seat and saw a man standing at the water's edge ready to take the line. He coiled it and threw like an expert the first time. It was caught and they were pulled up onto the beach. There were two women waiting behind the man.

"That's what took you so long, Paul. You were picking up hitchhikers," one of the women called.

"Yeah, but look what it got me—a free ride. The man rows like an Olympic champion." He was now sitting on the beach and putting socks and hiking boots on. "Can I leave it to you guys to tie up the boat? Over there," waving in the direction of a painted tree stump.

"Sure," Craig said. "Thanks for the ride."

"OK. You know the route? You are going to Lake Lovely Water, aren't you?"

"Yeah," Craig said, in answer to the last question at least.

"That's the start, over there, where my friends are heading. The other trail is just a saunter along a beach—no fun at all," he said as he put his arms into the harness of a huge backpack. "About a mile up the trail forks. Take the right fork. The left one is not marked and it's a long, hard, brutal climb—for masochists, I guess. You'll know immediately if you've missed the fork in the trail. My advice is to go back until you find it. Are you tenting or staying at the cabin?"

"Tenting," Rob said. He was still standing quietly, trying not to puff from his hard rowing, and wanting to blow on his hands and rub them together.

"We'll be up there before you. The women are tough hikers and we let them travel light, so they are fast. Give us a whistle at the cabin as you go by and I'll know you didn't get lost. Have a good time," he said and quickly disappeared up the trail.

Rob took the opportunity to blow on his hands and rub them together. "I didn't know you could row like that," Craig said. "And what did he say, 'like an Olympic champion'?"

"That's what he said alright. And that's a man that knows. You can tell," Rob said, making the most of the compliment.

They hauled the boat out of the water, secured it as asked, and, making sure their packs were settled on comfortably, they headed for the trail. After the first few yards, the trail narrowed to single file walking. It was well packed from use and the brush along the side had been cut away. They had moved from brilliant sunshine into the dappled light of the forest as the trail wound around thick groves of alder with its dark and shabby bark and stands of elegant poplars whose bark reminded them of the coat of a dalmatian. Beneath the trees, were the remains of mushrooms that had pushed their way through the mulch after the last good rain and lasted a day or two until they hosted a banquet for worms. Further along the trail began a gentle climb and the twisted arbutus with its shedding bark began to disappear. The forest was as quiet as a cathedral and as cool. Earlier they had heard the chattering of squirrels and the calls of many birds, but in the dark, heavily bushed area they were walking through, there was a heavy silence.

"Hey buddy," Rob, who was in the lead yelled back to Craig who was only five or six paces behind, "aren't we supposed to be making some noise as we go?" And as he said it, a deer, beautifully camouflaged in the chequered light, raised its head a stone's throw in front of them, looked, turned and leaped into the brush, leaving only a quick glimpse of a white tail.

"Did you see that?" Rob asked.

"Yeah, I wonder what kind it was. Pretty, wasn't it?"

"You wouldn't have called it pretty if we had startled a bear," Rob said. "We better start making some noise as we go."

They continued on the trail, trying to talk or to make some noise as they proceeded. The trail turned into a forest of huge trees and became so shaded and dark in places that it could almost have been night. It snaked its way around the giants but the walking was easy because there was little underbrush. The markers had become more numerous as game trails through the forest increased. Suddenly the trail started to rise and the walk turned into a climb, each step requiring a decision, until after about five hundred vertical yards and three times as many zigzagged sweaty climbing yards, they emerged onto a plateau that was covered with rocks and small bushes. They threw off their packs and sprawled on the ground to catch their breath.

After a couple of minutes of heavy puffing, Rob, lying flat on his back staring at a cloudless sky, said, "Geez! That was some climb, eh?"

The only response he heard was a kind of grunt-hack, like someone trying to cough up a fish bone, but it was further away than Craig should have been. He sat up and saw Craig sitting up close by, trying to make a sound and pointing off to a patch of blueberry bushes where a black bear with a blue muzzle was oblivious to their presence. Neither of them thought of making a noise. They both saw that the trail they were following lead in the opposite direction to the blueberry patch and they were a long way along that trail before they stopped to put on their packs.

Further along up the gently sloping plateau, they came to a rock outcropping with a trickling stream running out. They filled their water bottles, climbed onto a large boulder that gave them a full circle view and pulled out their second lunch.

"I don't remember taking that right fork in the trail that the guy told us about. Do you?" Craig asked.

"Unh-unh," Rob replied, with his mouth full. Then chewing and parking it in his cheek he said, "We must have taken it and not noticed because he said the other fork was a dull walk along the beach or something like that."

"No, that was a trail along the beach that he said was dull. He said the other trail at the fork was too tough and not to take it," Craig said. "Besides he said the other trail wasn't marked and we've been following pie plates all the way. So this must be right."

"Okay, then, where's the next one? Let's get going," Rob urged.

Craig groaned and grumbled, "Who promoted you to leader?"

Rob was already on his feet and heading up the trial.

"Hey, wait! I'm not ready," Craig called.

Rob answered, "Hurry up. I want to catch a fish for supper."

They did try to hurry but the trail got steeper and more difficult. After a half hour of hard climbing, they came to a place where the trail lead straight up what appeared to be a vertical wall.

They stood for a while, panting and looking around in disbelief.

"This has got to be it," Rob said. "Look, you can see where other people have gone up." He looked at Craig. "We've got to go straight up that son of a bitch, somehow.. Look! There's a pie plate right there—at the top," he said, pointing.

"Holy shit!" Craig said, shaking his head.

They took five minutes to catch their breath, firm up their pack harnesses, and retie shoelaces. Then, by an unspoken signal they approached the cliff. It took them half an hour, using toe-holds and knees, grabbing onto roots and rocks, and pressing belly-tight to the cliff, to reach the top, where they flung themselves on the flat ground and looked down on what they had climbed.

"We made it!" exulted Rob, whacking Craig on his pack.

"I'm going to stay here forever, cause I'm sure as hell not going back down there," Craig said.

They stayed for a while feeling immensely pleased with themselves, then standing up to search for the trail, they saw through the trees, below them and not far away, a small oval shaped lake, its brilliant blue water mirroring mountains with traces of snow on their peaks and covered with the dark green of huge and ancient cedars and pines trees, speckled here and there with the lighter green and gold of aspens. Nowhere within their vision was there a road or the scar of a powerline or pipeline cut or the unnatural balding of a mountain by clear-cut logging. The only evidence of man's intrusion into the scene below them, was a log cabin, with smoke curling out of its chimney, on a small spit of land jabbing into the icy blue water. Nearby, off to one side, a pie plate marked the start of the trail down.

"We're here! We made it! There it is!" they shouted to each other, pounding shoulders and hugging around the clumsy packs.

"Holy!" Craig said, almost reverently. "Isn't that beautiful!" And his eyes were moist.

Rob did not answer immediately. He turned slightly aside and cleared his throat. Then he said, "You know what? We didn't think to bring a camera, did we? Damn!"

They tried a few 'Ya-hoo' shrieks, some yodels and other calls and heard the clear answering echoes. They stood looking out over the lake for a long time trying to decide on a good place to make camp. They came to easy agreement to pitch camp on the west side so that they could catch the morning sun. Elated by their arrival, they started down the easy trail, taking giant strides and digging their heels hard into the well-used path.

A man standing on the edge of the promontory watching the top of the trail heard the yodels and echoes. He turned and went back to the cabin and joined the other three, and, in his rumbling bass voice said, "Well, I guess the boys made it up okay."

They crossed a small promontory below which the cabin stood. They could hear the laughter of the occupants and the sound of wood being chopped so they stopped and blew a couple of shrieks on their whistle. The chopping stopped and a man come around the corner of the cabin, waved a greeting and shouted "Where are you camping?" They waved toward the west shore and shouted "Over there some place."

"Good choice!" he called back and turned away.

They walked on along the edge of the lake until they found a stretch of beach beside a narrow outlet from the lake. Across the lake was a small waterfall that appeared to start at the top of the mountain near the remnants of the snow line, disappeared into a crevasse and leaped out again a distance away to fall slashing onto an outcrop of rock below creating a perpetual rainbow whenever the sun hit it and then trickled down across a gravel bed to join the lake. The lake was calm, the wind still, the fish made rings in the water and the sun was still warm.

Twenty feet back from the beach they found of ring of fire stones in front of a small clearing where other people had pitched camp. They dumped their packs on the ground and, leaning against them, sat looking out at the panorama in front of them, listening to the wailing cry of a loon and the scolding of a squirrel who had scared himself by coming too close before seeing them and was now on a branch above their heads. Further along the shoreline, they could see a beaver house. They watched a muskrat swim by and a kingfisher plunge from a branch into the clear water and fly away with a fish. An eagle circled overhead and Craig was sure it was the same one the farmer had pointed out to them and could understand the farmer's envy of the eagle's easy flight.

"Wow!" Craig said eventually, and it was enough for both of them.

"I want to catch a fish," Rob said. "So let's get off our butts and do things. You get some wood for the fire—lots of it because it's gonna be a cold night—and I'll put up the tent."

When Craig got back with a first load of wood, Rob was still struggling with the tent, muttering and swearing as he tried various combinations of parts.

"Did you read the instructions?" Craig asked, more to heckle than to help.

"You do it, if you're so damned smart," Rob growled.

"Do it yourself, I'm getting the wood," Craig said, disappearing into the bush.

When he got back, dragging another load of dead branches, the tent was up and Rob was blowing up an air mattress he had brought. It was a double size mattress and would take up most of the floor of the tent. Craig, who had intended to sleep on a bed of pine boughs like the camping book said, "That will take up the whole tent, Rob! Where am I going to sleep?"

"You'll see," Rob replied. "I'm in charge of the sleeping arrangements. You get to work on the fire—and dinner! I'm getting hungry."

Craig opened his pack and pulled out his fishing rod. Wrapped up with the rod were two plastic envelopes, one containing a coiled line and leader, the other an assortment of flies. "There's no reel," he shouted to Rob.

"I know," came Rob's answer from inside the tent. "Remember what Richard told us? Just lay your line on the water in a loose coil and be sure to tie the other end to your belt or something. I'll show you when I finish this."

"What are you doing?"

"Making our bed."

Craig puzzled for a minute about what Rob meant, then stuck his head through the tent flap and saw that Rob had zipped their two sleeping bags together and was spreading them out on the mattress.

"What the hell are you doing?" he squeaked.

"There!" said Rob, backing out of the tent that measured about three feet of headroom. When he emerged, grinning wickedly, he looked at Craig who was still sitting with a 'What the hell are you doing' look on his face.

"You didn't think I was going to sleep alone on a cold night up here in the mountains with bears and God knows what else when I've got a nice warm body to curl up to, did you?" And he said it with a grin so that Craig knew he had planned it from the start.

"Oh, Jesus! Rob," Craig said. And then after a moment, "Okay, but no funny stuff. Right?"

"R-i-ght!" Rob said, dragging out his agreement with a leer on his face. "Let's go fishing for our dinner, then, Craggy."

Craig stomped off toward the shoreline, muttering.

Before Rob had assembled his rod and line, Craig shouted, "I've got one. Hey, Rob! Look, I've got one," and he worked his line in by hand and then ran, dragging a pan size trout onto the beach. "Hurry up! They're biting," he shouted to Rob.

Rob came charging down the beach. "Show me what you got on," he said. "If that's what they're biting on, I want the same thing."

They fished along the shore line, catching four more lively small fighting rainbows that were freezer hard from living in the glacier water.

"One more, and we'll have three each for dinner," they agreed.

They fished back toward their camp without success, and as they approached they saw the muskrat run off with the first of their catch.

"Oh, well," Rob said imperturbably, "two apiece is enough for each of us and one's enough for him, so everything works out okay."

By the time they had the fire going and had ransacked through their packs to find the other things they wanted to eat, the sun was beginning to approach the western rim of the encircling mountains. The dinner they created would have been labelled almost edible by polite people with discriminating taste, but was delicious in their judgment. When they had washed their pot and pan in the cold stream, buried the fish remains, and hung all their edibles in a bag over a branch, the sun had long since disappeared, but its rays still gave brilliance to the low clouds in the west until gradually a sunset emerged, so spectacular that even teenagers, pretending sophistication, had to be impressed. They had been sitting on opposite sides of their fire but Rob moved over to Craig's log where they sat, shoulder to shoulder watching night arrive. The loons called each other across the lake in long mournful cracked notes. They heard a coyote or a wolf howling off in the distance, again and again, with no response, until, disappointingly, it suddenly stopped. In the stillness of the night, they heard the occasional burst of laughter from the cabin and watched the lights of a jet escaping from its own detached drone, a horizon behind, in the dark sky.

The fire crackled and threw sparks so high they mingled with the stars. Lying on their backs beside the dying fire, they searched the skies for the North Star and the Milky Way and the Big Dipper which were the only three names they could remember, agreeing only on one, a new location for the North Star, just above where the sun went down—a location that would remain a secret to scientists forever.

They argued about many things, moving easily from one unresolved dispute to another; they reminisced through hilarious 'remember when's', their roars of laughter echoing across the dark lake, and gossiped about classmates of both sexes. Craig talked wistfully about Lee and told Rob again, because he asked in a way that made Craig think he was envious, about the intimacies that had happened in the summer. When the lights of any airplane moved slowly among the profusion of stars in the dark night sky, they wondered together if Lee might be on it.

After a long silence, Rob said in a voice of enthusiasm, "Hey! Have I got a surprise for you. And for me, too."

Craig looked at him in the light of the fire and saw him smiling his 'up to something' smile. "Yeah, what?" he asked cautiously.

"Remember the guy I was with when the manager nearly caught us smoking pot that day on the ramp? His name was Andy?"

"Yeah," still cautious.

"Well, I went back to the market yesterday and bought a couple of joints from him," Rob said smugly.

"What for?" Craig said, both in disbelief and concern.

"What for! For us, you donkey. What d'ya think?"

"Yeah, I know. But..."

"But what? Here we are alone in the wilderness and not a cop for miles. Why not? Everybody's trying it. I tried it just that once and I want to try it again so I know what everybody is raving about. So, are you game?"

Craig took a deep breath and expelled it slowly. "I dunno, Rob," he said, shaking his head. "What if one of those guys up there is a cop and he smells the smoke and comes down here and..."

"Oh, for Crissake, Craig! Don't be such an asshole! How could anybody smell anything that far away." He sat silently fuming at his friend. "They're probably up there higher'n we'd ever get if we smoked one each."

"You mean we don't have to smoke one each?" he asked, looking for a way around his friend's anger.

"No," Rob said, patiently. "One's for tonight and one for tomorrow night. We're buddies—we're supposed to share."

"Oh, well," Craig said, "In that case..."

"Okay!" Rob shouted, his face alight even in the flickering darkness. He reached into his jacket pocket, pulled out a flat can and took out a somewhat thin joint.

"It's pretty skinny, isn't it? I thought they were supposed to be fat."

"Oh, Mr. Know-it-all is suddenly the expert, is he?" Rob said sarcastically.

"No, but that's what they showed us last year in Socials."

"Do you want to go first?"

Craig shook his head. "No, you light it. You've done it before."

"Only that once—and I coughed my guts out because I did it wrong."

"What do you mean? Is there a special way to do it?" Craig asked, beginning to have second thoughts about the whole thing.

"Not exactly, but I don't think you inhale like you do a cigarette. You take a drag and hold it in your mouth and then you kind of swallow it. You ready?"

"Yeah, I guess."

Rob leaned over and stuck a dry twig in the fire and brought the flame to the end of the joint and let the twisted paper burn, then put it between his lips and dragged on it unsuccessfully. "It's not working," he said.

"You've got the other end too tight," Craig said.

Rob gave him a snarly look, untwisted the end a little, lighted the twig and tried again. This time Craig saw the lighted end glow in the dark as Rob took a long drag. In the light of the campfire, he saw Rob's cheeks puffed out and his eyes somewhat bugged as he waved the joint signalling him to take it. He watched Rob go through a series of gags as he tried to get rid of the mouthful of smoke, finally succeeding. He steeled himself, took the joint from Rob and took a little drag which he immediately expelled, making a face and handing the joint back to Rob.

"Not like that," Rob said, in thick whispery voice. "Take a big one."

Craig did, held smoke in his mouth, and then started to cough. He coughed and coughed and his eyes ran and his nose ran. Rob had taken the toke and was again trying to swallow or inhale the smoke in little amounts. He held it out to Craig again, who wiped his nose on his sleeve and tried again, this time with greater success.

Rob applauded.

It hadn't been a very big joint to begin with, and it was soon smoked down to its lip-burning end and tossed into the fire.

"Do you feel anything?" Rob asked.

Craig puzzled for a minute before answering. "I thought I was going to throw up and that's all," he said thoughtfully and slowly. "But right now I think I'm talking too fast." He giggled and reach out and patted the sky. "It's away down here tonight," he said without explanation or introduction.

"Maybe you're away up there," Rob said with perfect understanding and burst into loud laughter that went on and on until Craig had to join in.

They sat watching the fire and the occasional falling star and listening to the night noises, until by unspoken agreement they loaded the fire for the night and checked the security of their supplies. Warming their backs in front of the last embers of the fire before dousing it carefully, they crawled into the tent. through the tent flap, they faced the darkness and watched a million fireflies creating a final spectacle for their day.

They took off their jackets and jeans and rolled them together for pillows. Craig squirmed into the bed first and lay down facing the short wall of the tent. Rob followed and curled up around his back.

"C'mon, Rob," Craig said, not moving away. "No funny stuff. You promised."

"I know," came the answer as he pulled the unresisting body of his friend into a better cuddle. Then after a few minutes of quiet, "Hey, Craig? You didn't ever, you know, screw her, did you?"

The answer he received was a sharp elbow in the ribs and "I told you 'No' already," and he went happily to sleep.

***

Marion had driven slowly back to town thinking sometimes about the boys and wondering how far along they were in their hike. She was pleased with herself that she was just wondering about them, not worrying about them. She was both in a hurry to get home and reluctant as well. Reluctant because she faced a load of laundry that she had put off, not wanting to interrupt Craig's massive assault on his room and she laughed at the recall of his wide-eyed surrender in the face of her maternal storm. And there was the vacuuming and dusting, and she had to do some shopping, even though Craig would not be home and she was going out for dinner. That was the other side of the coin—hurrying to get home, to sort out what she was going to wear and what she was going to wear with it, to wash her hair and soak in the tub because lately she had become too lazy to soak and had hopped into the shower instead.

In town, she went to the supermarket and wandered up and down the aisles, emerging with one small bag of groceries that should have taken her five minutes instead of the forty-five minutes she had spent. "What on earth am I doing?" she scolded herself coming out of the store and continued to chastise herself all the way home. When she got there, before she took off her jacket, she took the vacuum out of the cupboard and left it in the middle of the kitchen to trip over, put on a load of washing, and then attacked the house like a tornado.

By noon, she had finished the vacuuming, polishing and picking up without having paused for morning coffee. The laundry had gone quickly now that she did not have Gerry's clothes to do, and as she worked she struggled with a strong surge of resentment at the hours she had spent ironing his shirts and slacks to the perfection he had demanded. She had worked so hard and fast there were beads of sweat on her upper lip and she was sticky from exertion. Deciding it was time for a break, she turned the heat on under the morning coffee and while she waited for it, she went out to the garden and picked a bouquet of sweet peas and arranged them for the dining room table. Then she settled into the nook with her coffee and the morning paper. In the space of twenty minutes she discovered that she had turned the pages of the newspaper from front to back without having absorbed anything in it and that she had had one or two sips of coffee and the remainder was cold.

She sat for a while puzzling about her frenetic activity of the morning and wondering what had gotten into her. Something was pushing her, driving her to activity to keep her busy. Why? It wasn't guilt, she decided, about having neglected her housekeeping for so long—she'd done that before. It was something else. It must be something about having a date, she thought. She was excited about it, in a way, but somehow it felt wrong to be looking forward to it so much. "Why can't I be sensible about it. It's only a simple dinner date. There's nothing wrong with that," she told herself. "But I'm certainly not going to tell Edith."

She phoned Edith after lunch when she knew the twins would be having a nap and the phone call would have fewer interruptions. When Edith heard that Craig had gone off with Rob for a two day hike, she said, "Well, why didn't you come out and spend the night for a visit. You don't have to wait to be invited, you know. Harvey and the girls always look forward to a visit from you. The girls are always talking about the time when we...oh, my lord! Was it only last month that you were out to the cottage and we got caught in the rain at the beach and the lights went out? It seems like it was a year ago. Have you seen Dad lately?" Edith asked, making one of her fast conversational switches.

"Well, not lately, Edith. I think I told you about the last time. It wasn't very pleasant and we didn't have much to say to one another."

"What are you going to do, Mom?"

"About what, Edith," her mother asked with a hint of impatience. "About counselling? About permanent separation? About divorce?"

"No, Mother. I was certainly not thinking about counselling," Edith said pointedly. "I mean, is he supporting you, looking after the bills, giving you money, things like that. Do you need any...you know, help? Harvey said I should ask you."

"Oh, Edith! Please! Please don't concern yourself with things like that. And tell Harvey, too. But I am touched, dear. Really I am." She felt herself tearing.

"Well, I just felt it doesn't hurt to ask. Sometimes people hold all their problems..."

"Edith, now listen to me. I suppose I should have told you this before, so you wouldn't worry. So I'm going to tell you now. You don't remember, maybe, and certainly Craig won't, but my mother left me quite a lot of money when she died, and I bought a car and a few things for the house and put the rest away for your education and for Craig's. But you decided to get married, and who knows about Craig. Anyway that money is not locked away—I can use it if I need it."

"I'd forgotten about that, Mom. I'm glad you're alright. I mean, you're not worried about money things."

"And another thing, dear. When my father died his whole estate, except for some money he gave to the church and to his lodge, and I think some to the Salvation Army, too, was divided between my brother, that's your Uncle Paul, and me. So I paid off the mortgage on the house and invested the rest and it's still there in good bonds and things like that. And I get a little income from it every month."

"I didn't know any of that, Mom. I'm glad you told me."

"There is one more thing, Edie. When I paid off the mortgage on the house, I insisted that it should be registered in both names. Your father said he wouldn't. It was registered in his name only and he wanted to keep it that way. He said it was necessary for business reasons. And he insisted that he should manage the rest of the money for me because he said I didn't have a head for business. But I dug my heels in and I'm glad I did. Whatever happens, I still have half a house and he would have a hard time getting that away from me."

"Jesus! Am I ever glad you did. I wouldn't trust him right now further than... I don't know. I just don't trust him. He'd probably kick you out of the house and bring in some whore."

"Edith!"

"Well, he would, Mother. That's just what he would do, and you know it."

"Now, Edith! How come you are so violently hostile to him all of a sudden? He is your father, after all."

"My father? Yeah, I suppose he is. But I've got a couple of other labels for him. And there's nothing sudden about it. I'll have to talk about it later. The girls are screaming their heads off. Bye, Mom," and she hung up.

Her mother was left shaking her head, mostly in frustration but in anger too. I shouldn't let you do this to me, Edith, she said to herself. Passing through the dining room on her way upstairs she noticed two of the sweet pea flowers had toppled sideways out of the arrangement and tried, unsuccessfully, to correct it. Then, in a terrible flashback, she recalled Edith who, as a child, had asked politely to pick some 'sweepees' and had pulled up a dozen plants by the roots and dragged the armful into the house as a present for Mommy. She remembered her fury and the harsh scolding the child had received, and she remembered, too, the awful feelings of guilt that overwhelmed her the rest of the summer every time she looked at the barren flower bed. She was in the early stages of her pregnancy with Craig at the time, and the emotional upset she had created for herself was so great she thought she might lose the child so she had gone to bed for the rest of the day with the drapes drawn. Suddenly, she slapped at the flowers, as she had slapped at the child, sending the vase and flowers skittering across the table onto the floor. Then she went upstairs to Edith's room and lay down with the drapes pulled until it was time to dress for her date with Tom.

After her bath, her shakes subsided, and her mood improved—particularly when the clothes she had chosen proved to be too large for her. She had not noticed that she had lost weight but the bathroom scale further elevated her spirits. She found an older outfit that she had put aside when it became too small, a scarf to dress it up, and, for perhaps unconscious reasons, some lingerie from the other drawer that was not too indecent. (After Edith was married, Marion had given some of the cruder panties to her, and Edith had reacted with shock and asked, "Where did you get these, Mom." When she told her daughter that they had come from her father, Edith said flatly "Oh," and put them in a box in the back of her closet.) In the master bedroom, she examined herself from many angles, front, back and sides, in the long mirrors, two of which, at Gerry's insistence had been made so they could be swung out to achieve any view. Today, she was pleased with what she saw and went happily downstairs to wait for Tom, but she double checked in the hall mirror.

Tom arrived on time, looking polished and trim and dressed informally in an old but well-cut tweed jacket and slacks. "Hi Hi," he said, when she answered his ring. "Don't you look smashing! That's a good colour on you. It makes you look, pardon me if I say so, but it makes you look... well, sexy." He smiled as he said it in a way that was not quite lecherous but so close to it she blushed. "Are you ready to go?"

"Yes, I'm ready. But would you like to come in and have a drink before we start?"

He hesitated, peering over her shoulder, so she said, "It's quite alright, Tom. There's no-one here. But I would like to give a couple of nosy neighbours something to gossip about by inviting you in."

"I don't like to drink and drive but I'll tell you what let's do. Stand a little closer and I'll give you a nice, brotherly kiss right here on the front steps and then I'll escort you to the car with my arm around your waist. How's that? Will that get them away from the TV?"

"Away from the TV and onto the telephones," she answered, laughing.

So he kissed her gently on the forehead with his hands on her arms and said "U-m-mm" as he did so, as if he had just tasted a luscious dessert. She picked up her purse from the hall table, set the lock on the door and closed it and together they walked to his car with his arm around her waist.

"Any curtains twitching?" he asked.

"We may not see them but they're twitching, for sure," she replied laughing and feeling more impulsive than she had for twenty years.

Tom helped her into the car and walked around to the driver's side where he stopped and made two theatrical bows to the neighbours in general and got in. They drove away laughing like school kids.

"Where would you like to go for dinner?" he asked as they drove away.

"It doesn't matter," she said. "Except I'd like to go someplace I haven't been

before. That won't be hard. I haven't been out much for a long time, except with
the bridge club, and then half the husbands won't come, including mine." She
failed to notice a bit of a frown on his face at the mention of the word 'husband'
but she was aware of the slip and told herself silently to be more careful.

"I have an idea," he said after a slight silence. "Pick a number between twenty
and forty."

"Why?"

"Just pick!"

"Okay. Thirty seven."

"Now pick two directions: north, west, south or east—but they can't be opposite each other."

She leaned sideways and looked at him warily.

"Just pick," he said.

"North and east," she said obediently.

"Fine! It's too early for dinner, so here's what we're going to do. After we get
out of the tunnel, we're going to drive thirty seven kilometres down the freeway
and then we'll take the first turn north for eighteen and a half kilometres, that's
half of thirty seven, then we'll drive—what did you say, east?"

"Yes," she replied, wondering what he was up to. "North and east."

"Then we'll drive east for another eighteen and a half K's, and we'll start
looking for the first nice place to eat we can find."

"Oh, Tom, that's weird," she exclaimed, but she was obviously enjoying the
game as she continued, "Let's go, then! Drive north into the unknown."

"Okay, partner," Tom said with a laugh as he turned the trip meter back to
zero.

They drove in silence for a while, until Marion said, "Tom? I'm sorry about
mentioning my husband back there. That was clumsy of me."

"No problem, Marion. Look, we can't go tippy-toeing around this husband
and wife thing. What do you say that we take a few minutes while we drive and
each say what we want to say and get it out of the way?"

"Alright," Marion replied, but there was some uncertainty in her voice.

"Fine, let's do it, then. I'll go first since it was my idea." He took a deep
breath and pushed his shoulders back against the seat and started. "I told you
a little bit about my marriage and the woman I am still married to, in name
only I might add quickly, and my kids. It hurts what she is doing to me but
it hurts more to think what she is doing to the kids." He went on into details
of her negligence of the children and her deficiencies as a wife. It was a marriage demanded by her pregnancy, so he thought, only to discover he had been
tricked into it. And then she did get pregnant and he felt trapped. The child was
born, a girl, and she was black and he felt more trapped—because he would not
consider leaving the child with her even if it wasn't his. Then she got pregnant
again and it was impossible that he was the father." He was quiet for a moment.
"I left—I couldn't hack it."

"She went to the Social Service and laid on the tears and a big act," he said,
"and convinced everybody and now I pay support for the kids. Which I don't

mind," he continued after a tense pause, "I'm glad to. But I sure as hell get mad when I think of how much child support money she spends on herself and the guy she's living with—who incidentally is probably the father of her second child. A boy this time, and a cute kid, too. And also," he continued, "she hates my father, who is the kindest, gentlest man you would ever meet. Well, you know. You've met him. I think the reason is that she never had a father, she doesn't know who her father was, so she doesn't know how to respond to a father."

He took a big breath and stopped. After a short silence, he said with a somewhat shaky voice and a tense smile. "Thanks for listening, Marion. Now it's your turn...but only if you want to. I never thought it would be so hard when I brought up the idea."

"Yes, I want to, Tom," she said. "But give me a minute until I sort it out a bit." She blew her nose harder than she meant to and looked out the window getting her thoughts in order.

"Give me another number," he said. "I wasn't paying attention and I passed eighteen and a half without noticing. So this time give me something between, let's say thirty and sixty."

She laughed at the silly game and said, "Fifty."

"Oh, I wish I had paid more attention to math when I was in school. I can't do that in my head. Let's see, we were supposed to go eighteen and a half K's, but now we've gone thirty one. So what do we do? Well, I guess we add half of fifty on to thirty one, that's fifty six, so then we turn east for eighteen and a half K's and we're there—where ever we are. Okay?"

She leaned back and laughed at him. "I'm glad you're not an airline pilot," she said.

They drove on in silence for a while until Tom said quietly, "When we first met, you told me you were a happily married woman." It was just a statement with no hint of questioning in the tone.

She stared out the window for a long time before saying anything. "I think I lied," she said softly, "but I didn't know I lied. I never really looked at my marriage critically. I had a husband, two children, two grandchildren, a house and my garden and I just took it for granted that I was happily married. He supported me and I had a bit of money of my own and we didn't quarrel. He was out of town a lot and he had a lot of evening appointments, so he said, and he spent every weekend at the golf course and we just never seemed to do anything together any more like we used to when we were first married. Something happened—I don't know what—but I opened my eyes one day and realized that I had been married to a cold, unloving, selfish, uncaring man who didn't even like me, let alone love me, and he had no feelings for his children or his grandchildren, or as far as I know, for anybody—except himself. And now there's this police thing. You probably read about it in the paper but maybe you didn't recognize the name. And he's been running around with another woman, and drinking and getting into trouble at his firm so that, well, I guess he got fired, if that's the term. I don't know how they could when he's a partner. But, anyhow, he's not working and he's living on his boat and when he has to come home for something it's like a cold front from the arctic sweeps through the house."

She stopped and Tom intuitively knew she was not finished and said nothing, but reached out and touched her knee gently and waited for her to continue. She was, she realized, in perfect control of her emotions. There were no tears, no anger, nor any desire for retaliation. There was not even a sense of sadness. "You know, Tom," she said, almost conversationally, except now her voice had become husky, "I just don't care. And I don't care that I don't care. That might make me sound like a cold, hard person, but I'm not. He just is not important to me any more. I don't hate him. Hate is too self-destructive. So, as far as I'm concerned, he's gone from my life...as if he were dead. And, you know, I've found myself wishing it." She took a big, deep breath and expelled it slowly. "Now then," she said with finality. "That's all I'm going to say about him. And now you know what a cold-hearted person you are taking out to dinner."

"I can't think that word could ever apply to you," Tom said.

"Oh, you don't think so? Well, listen to this!" and she told him about the rampage she went on with Craig about his room and laundry and how she took a garden rake to clear out his closet. "Now do you still think I'm a gentle, sweet tempered woman?" she asked him, laughing at the memory of Craig's bewildered face as she attacked the mess and of the wary way he reacted for the rest of the day. He was laughing too, because she was a good story teller and he could imagine her quick anger and her immediate remorse.

He stopped the car.

"What's wrong?" Marion asked.

"We're here. Where we are going to have dinner."

"Here?" she said, looking around and seeing nothing but farm houses, fields and milking sheds.

"That's what we agreed," he said laughing at her puzzlement. "Look at the mileage."

She leaned over to look at the dash panel and he could feel her leaning against him and smelled her hair. "Nice!" he said, and leaned toward her and kissed her hair softly. "What shall we do now?"

She did not move quickly away from his touch but she did move back to her side of the car, but not all the way. She waved her hand regally and said, "Drive on, captain! Let's not let storm, or rain or sleet or all those other things keep you from finding the dinner you promised me. I'm famished."

"Aye, aye," he said and they drove on, happy in each other's company.

After a few miles, driven in quiet, easy conversation, they found a motel-restaurant that looked clean and inviting. Inside, the aroma from the small kitchen drifted into the dining room, giving promise of something delicious, and making them both suddenly hungry. The hostess led them to a table by the window casually apart from the only other three other couples in the dining room and gave them menus, saying, "I'll just find out if the special is still on." She turned to go, "Oh, I should ask. Would you like the wine menu?"

"Yes, please," Tom said to her, and to Marion, "Would you like a drink,

Marion?"

"Yes, that would be nice. I'm kind of thirsty. So...what will I have? Let's see..." and she made a thinking face trying to remember what people drank on such occasions.

"How about a gin and tonic?" Tom suggested. "That's always good on a warm evening when you're thirsty."

"That's the one. That's what I was trying to think of," Marion said. "How did you know?"

"He's a mind reader," the waitress said, smiling at them. "Two?" Tom nodded. "I'll bring the wine menu when I check on the special."

"Nice place," Marion said conversationally.

"Yes, it is," he agreed. "And I'll bet the food is as good as it smells, too."

"I wonder where we are?" Marion said. "We were driving all over the place. It was fun! Do you suppose we are lost?"

"Maybe we are. But don't tell anybody and nobody will come looking for us and this will be our desert island."

They chatted small talk until the waitress brought their drinks and the wine list and the information that the special was breaded veal cutlets.

"Cheers!" Marion said, picking up her glass.

"Skoal!" he responded, "And 'Halen Gore'."

"What's that?" she asked.

"It's something a Swedish friend of mine says when we have a drink. I think it means something like 'Bottoms Up'. Only I seem to remember you're supposed to shout it."

"Well, then, 'Halen Gore' to you, too. But I won't."

"Won't what?"

"You know—the whole glass."

"No, nor me," he said, touching her glass as their eyes met. "That's good!" she said with satisfaction, after half emptying her glass.

She picked up the menu and started reading it. "Should we have the special?" she asked. "Truthfully, I'm not very fond of veal—not that it isn't good, it's just the idea of eating something young, like a baby."

He sat smiling at her as she read through the menu, making casual comments as she read.

"What about you? What are you going to have?" she asked.

"I don't know. I was waiting for you to make up your mind and maybe I'd have the same just so I don't have to read the menu."

"Oh! Alright then. I think I'll have the swordfish."

"Tilt!" he said. "No swordfish for me. I guess I'll stick to steak."

"You don't like swordfish?" she asked as she finished her drink.

"I don't know. I've never had it—I don't think. Ready for another?" he asked, pointing to her glass.

"Yes, thank you. I enjoyed that." Then, folding up the menu and putting it aside, she said, "I know! I'll give you a piece of my swordfish and you give me a piece of your steak—as long as it's not too rare."

"That sounds like a good bargain," he replied, enjoying her easy familiarity and lack of pretentiousness.

The waitress approached the table and asked, "Are you ready to order, folks?"

"I think so," Tom said. "The lady will have the swordfish and I'll have the eight-ounce steak—medium. Baked potato, Marion?" She nodded and he went on. "Two baked potatoes, then. And shall we split a Caesar salad?" he asked her and again she nodded. "Can you do that?" he asked the waitress.

"Certainly, sir. Would you like another drink or would you like to order some wine?"

"I think I'd like another drink first. How about you, Marion? How about a Martini?"

"I was going to settle for another gin and tonic, but maybe I'll try a Martini. It's been years since I had one."

"Two, then?" asked the waitress.

Tom nodded. "Very dry, please."

When the Martinis came, he watched her as she tasted it, making a wry face. "Too strong?" he asked.

"Well, it's strong, that's for sure. But it's supposed to be, isn't it?" She took another tiny sip and said, "But I could get used to it, I think." And another little sip and nodded, "Yes, I think I could."

The waitress came with the table settings and a basket of crusty rolls. Marion took a roll and, while chattering on, had soon scattered crumbs around her place on the table, which she cleaned up by licking a finger and picking up crumbs while she talked. She told him about the women she played bridge with and what good friends they were. She said that sometimes they tried to shock each other by telling dirty jokes.

"Do you know any dirty jokes?" she asked him.

"Well, sure," he replied.

"C'mon then, tell me one," she demanded, helping herself to another roll.

"Okay," Tom said, "here's one I remember." And he told her an old farmer's daughter joke.

When he finished, he watched her as she laughed delightfully, with her mouth full of crusty bun and her eyes twinkling, and was again struck by what an open person she was.

"Okay," she said, "here's one I heard at bridge but I don't think I get it." She leaned across the table and in a very quiet voice, looking around to make sure nobody else heard, she told her joke and sat back.

"Marion!" he exclaimed, trying not to laugh. "Do you know what you said? You mean you don't get it?"

"No," she answered. "I can't see anything funny. What's funny about it?"

He was laughing heartily as he beckoned to her to lean closer. Then in a quiet voice, interrupted by chuckles, he gave her an explanation of some of the terms she had used. When he finished she sat back quickly.

"Oh, migod!" she said, covering her reddening cheeks with her hands. "Oh, that's awful!" She was laughing at her naiveté and looking at him with wide eyes. "You're teasing me. Aren't you?"

He shook his head and laughed with her, enjoying her company more than he had enjoyed the company of any other woman for a long, lonely time. She had used her napkin to wipe her eyes and now searched in her purse for a tissue and, after giving her nose a good, loud blow, she looked around in embarrassment to see if anyone else had noticed.

"Oh, dear," she said, still with a laugh just below the surface and shaking her head in recollection. She took another good sip of her Martini, this time without making a face. "It's rather good, isn't it? Quite tasty!"

"I read the other day that the Queen Mother enjoys a Martini. She thinks they are quite tasty, too," he said with a sly smile.

Again, the smile on his face made her uncertain whether he was teasing her or not, but before she could make up her mind, the waitress came with the salad. It had not been divided in the kitchen so she busied herself serving it and the talk ceased momentarily.

"You'll want white wine with your fish," he said. "Any preferences?"

"No, no," she exclaimed. "You'll want red with your steak and, as a matter of fact, I prefer red wine with anything. I never fuss about white wine with chicken and seafood." She picked up her Martini and finished it and started on her salad.

He called the waitress and enquired about the house wine and ordered it without fuss. She could not help comparing his quick decision to Gerry's demand to see the bottle, ensure that it was properly opened to breathe before dinner, and squeeze and smell the cork until the fun of the wine was dulled. But wisely she said nothing.

They were just finishing their salads when one waitress appeared with the wine followed by another with their dinner and a busboy close behind with a tray full of goodies for their potatoes.

"Thank you," he said to the waitress. "You people are fast. Now the only thing we're lacking is a pepperboy. Who's going to grind my pepper for me?"

"The pepperboy has gone fishing in the Bahamas," the waitress said with a big grin. "The boss's son, you know. But Tim, here, is learning the pepper grinding business. He'd be delighted to grind your pepper. Wouldn't you, Tim?"

"Any time, sir," the busboy said as he held the tray for them to dress their potatoes. "Just say the word."

Finally they were left alone to start their dinner. "What a happy place! We must come back again sometime," Marion said and stopped suddenly.

"Yes, it really is," Tom replied, looking up from his plate where he had been busy pushing some broccoli to one side, to see her with pursed lips and her hands folded on her lap as if she were saying grace.

"Sometimes when I dig a hole so I can fall into it," she said with a hard voice, "I think I should pull it in after me."

"What's wrong?" he said.

"Didn't you hear what I said?"

"What? Oh, you mean about coming here again. Oh! I see what you're upset about." And he reached across the table for her hand which she reluctantly took off her lap and gave to him. "I thought that was the most open, the nicest thing I've heard from anybody in a long, long time. And it so touched me that I was busy trying to think when we could come back again."

"Really?" she said, brightening.

"Yes, really!"

"You're some rare guy, Marion Thomas," she said, raising her glass. "'Halen Gore' or whatever your Danish friend says."

"And you're some rare lady, Marion Williams," he replied, raising his glass. "Incidentally, 'Halen Gore' is only what he says to toast men. You should hear the one he uses for ladies."

"What is it."

"Eat your dinner, and don't forget you promised me some of your sword-fish."

They were both hearty eaters and casual about table manners so that occasionally they talked around a full mouth or waved a forkful of food to help make a point. The two steaks, one beef and one swordfish, were divided, tasted and pronounced delicious or interesting. Tom added a rider, saying, "I might try it again sometime—but don't tell any of my friends."

"Are we going to have dessert?" Tom asked when they had finished.

"Not for me, thank you," she replied. "But you have some and I'll just have a bite of yours."

"Oh, you will, will you?" he answered, grinning. "Maybe I won't share it with you. What will you do then?"

"Oh, I'll probably get in a big huff and make a scene and then sweep out like I was going off-stage. Then I'd walk home!" She waved her arm dramatically and knocked over her water glass. "Oh, my God!" she said. "Walk home? I'm getting tiddly. I don't think I can even walk to the bathroom, but excuse me, I've got to go."

She left, walking rather stiffly, if not regally away, after making profuse apologies to the waitress who had arrived to tidy up the spill. Tom sat for a moment, deep in thought, then left the table after asking the waitress to tell Marion that he would be back shortly. He walked out of the restaurant to the front office where he booked a double room for the night. When he returned, she was sitting at their table looking worried and then suddenly brightening when she saw him approaching.

"I thought you might have deserted me," she said, her tone a mixture of relief and pleasure.

"Didn't the waitress give you my message?" he asked just as the waitress rushed to their table.

"I'm sorry," she said to Marion. "Your husband asked me to tell you he would be right back, but I got tied up on the other side of the room and didn't see you return."

"But we're not..." Marion started to say.

"No problem," Tom interrupted smoothly. "But while you're here, maybe we'll have a nightcap. What do you say, dear?"

"Oh, I don't know," she flustered. "I've probably had too much already. You decide, Tom. You're the one that has to drive."

"Okay, let me see. I know! How about a Kalhua with a little cream floated on top? You'd like that," he added for the benefit of the waitress. "Can you manage that?" he said to the waitress. "I can't remember what it's called."

"Certainly, sir," the waitress responded. "And for you, sir? The same?"

"No, thanks. I'll stick to Scotch on the rocks."

"Be right back," she said walking quickly towards the bar.

"She thinks we're married!" Marion said, trying to smother a giggle.

"I know. The people at the desk think so too."

"What do you mean?"

"I mean that when you went to the washroom I went to the front desk and registered us as man and wife for the night."

"Tom! You shouldn't have! Why did you do that?" She was becoming flustered and blushing brightly.

"I could say that the only reason I did it was because, like I said before when you offered me a drink, I don't drink and drive. So I guess we're stuck. I didn't mean to trick you but you were so happy and you made me happy." He reached over and took her hand. "I really want to make love to you. I have ever since I first saw you trying to help my father that day when he was sort of lost. I don't know—there was something so open and honest and genuine about you, I couldn't get you out of my mind. You could never guess what happened to me when I saw you again in the hospital. It was like I got a whole new lease on life. Marion, I really mean it. Look, the room has twin beds. We could sleep apart just like old married people. I don't want to, but if you insist, then okay."

She had listened to him with her mind whirling. She wanted to believe him and she did—mostly. But there was another part of her that trying to protect herself from herself and she felt a little scared and didn't quite know what to do. Oh, she knew she wanted to go to bed with him, but she didn't know how. She had never done it before except that once at the convention and now she couldn't remember. Do people undress each other? With the lights on? Or do they undress privately in the bathroom and then make a dash for the bed when they are naked. She knew what they did in the movies but that was all pretend and they weren't real people anyway. She had unconsciously reached out with her other hand and put it in his. It seemed that they sat hand in hand for an eternity until she heard herself saying, "Yes, I think so."

"You think what, Marion?"

"I think I want to. Not sleep apart like old married people like you said, but together, the two of us in one bed, together."

Their drinks arrived and they had to separate their hands so the waitress could clear the table and serve the drinks, saying, as she worked, "Now, will there be anything else?"

He shook his head and smiled at her, "No, thank you. If you bring the bill,

I'll put it on our room tab. It was a delicious dinner. I think I could get to like swordfish."

"Maybe that's the way to try exotic foods—sharing it with someone. Not that swordfish is very exotic, or steak either, is it, Ma'am?" She was smiling at Marion who was blushing at Tom's easy mention of their room but managed to return the smile. "Have a nice night," she said and turned to go. "Oh! the bill. I'll bring it right over."

"Do you think everyone here knows what we're doing?" Marion whispered nervously.

"Do you think anyone here cares?" Tom answered casually and then continued, "It's too bad they don't have a little music and we could dance. Do you like to dance?"

"I haven't for years. But I did when I was going to school. I never felt I was a very good dancer, though. But I enjoyed it."

"I'm not much of a dancer. either. I guess I know two dances: the one where you do three steps, feet together, another three steps and keep going like that, but I never learned to turn so I had to wait till I got to a wall and then I could push off again, like doing laps in a pool."

"Good heavens, what could that be?" and she was jiggling with silent laughter at the picture he drew. Then, after a moment she was able to say, "What was the other one?"

"I don't know what it was called but there was quite a bit of hopping in it. I was okay with frontward hopping but I was very backward with backward hopping and I usually tripped either me or my partner. I wasn't eagerly sought after by the girls as a dancing partner. In fact, they used to call me Dread Astaire."

During their conversation, the waitress had brought the bill to the table and left it quietly smiling at Marion's attempts to control her laughter. Tom picked up the bill and signed it.

"Ready, Ginger?" he said. "Let's dance our way to heaven."

"Ready, Dread," she agreed. "But if it's okay with you, I'd prefer to walk. There's a rumour around that you have a tendency to dance into walls."

"I wonder who started that awful canard," he said in a shocked voice as she took his arm. "I should sue them."

"I thought a canard was a dog," she said.

"No, you're mixing it up with Cunard, the shipping line."

The waitress watched them leave and said to the barman, "What a darling couple. They're having such fun together."

Tom had picked up the room key when he registered. When he unlocked the door, the lamp between the beds had been switched on and one of the beds had been turned down.

"Well, look at that!" Tom exclaimed. "Either they read my mind or they listened in on our conversation when you decided that we weren't going to sleep separately like old married people."

"They wouldn't! Would they?" Marion said, aghast that they might have been overheard.

"No, no!" he said soothingly, and turned to her, taking her in his arms. "I've been wanting to do this all evening."

She responded with warmth but without excessive eagerness. "There's a lot of mind reading going on," she said, her voice muffled with her face tucked into his neck. "So have I."

They stood, holding each other for a while, he kissing the top of her head and she responding with small kisses under his ear.

"I could order a drink sent up," he said tentatively.

"No! Don't! I don't need a drink. I just need a minute. If I had a drink, I'd pass out."

They stood together for a long minute. Finally, on some unconscious signal they released each other from the embrace. Marion took a deep breath and let it out through puffed cheeks, and sat down.

"Well, Tom Thomas, my Friday night Lothario, what do we do now? You'll have to tell me—I don't think I ever knew the rules."

Tom laughed at her while he was taking off his jacket and tie. "I don't know any rules either. But let's play it by ear—and other organs," he said with a lewd grin. "Maybe you'd like to use the bathroom first. I'll undress out here."

"Alright," she said, getting up from the end of the bed and moving almost obediently past him to the bathroom, closing the door firmly behind her. In less than ten seconds, the door burst open and she emerged in a panic. "What am I doing?" she cried. "I can't do this. I've got to be at the hospital at nine o'clock in the morning."

He had slipped off his shoes and was unbuttoning his shirt when she faced him with her dilemma. "It's okay, Marion. We've got lots of time. Let's just forget about tomorrow for a while and I promise you'll be at work by nine." He moved toward her and held her in his arms again.

"Promise?" she said.

"Have I ever lied to you?"

"There's always a first time," she said, unbuttoning the rest of his shirt and kissing him on each breast. "I'll just be a minute." She collected her purse and returned to the bathroom.

When she came out, dressed in her sexy panties and a bra, she had washed and dabbed on some perfume.

He gave her a raised eyebrow face with a grin and said, "Wow! Are those just your average everyday panties or are they special?"

"They're special and I don't know why I put them on this morning. Some good fairy whispered in my ear, I guess, and told me that something nice was going to happen." She crawled into the bed and patted the place beside her.

"In a minute," he said and disappeared into the bathroom emerged in a couple of minutes washed and naked. "Shall I turn off this light?" he asked. reaching for the light between the beds. She looked at him before answering—slim, lean, face and hands tanned from working in the sun, slightly bald, chest hair beginning to grey and an anxious erection. It was the suntan on his face and hands that moved her. Gerry's perfect tan lines delineating his white buttocks from his tanned legs and upper body at the hip line were always so prissily precise that she recognized them years ago as the mark of a narcissist in love with his own body. She was so long in answering that Tom, standing waiting to turn out the light asked again, "Marion?"

"Oh, yes! Let's turn it out. I was just looking at you. You looked so—so ready."

He laughed and crawled in beside her and she put out her arms to accept him. They moved together, touching and exploring. Their kisses, although gentle rather than abandoned, spoke to each other of wells of passion. There was no clumsiness in their lovemaking, and nothing that hinted of routine or practice. When they came together, a mutuality of understanding, an open awareness of the needs of the other directed their actions, until Marion, climbing to a peak she had never approached before gave an exulting groan as she plunged over, only to find Tom waiting for her to lead her to another peak, and another and yet another, until, exhausted she stayed behind helping and urging him to the culmination of his own needs.

Finally they released each other and moved to a lighter embrace. Marion was panting as she wiped her face and brow with her hands. "Holy Jesus!" she exclaimed. "Is that what it's supposed to be like? It's never happened to me before! I hear other people raving on and on about climaxing and I wonder what in hell they are talking about. I've had climaxes before, but they were little things, like little burps inside, not this demanding urge for an explosion—and I wanted to go on. Inside I was screaming to go on." She pulled back the sheets and exposed him. "Is this what did it?" she said, picking up his flaccid penis and kissing it. "Do you think he could be persuaded to do it again?"

"Oh, I'm sure of it," Tom said. "Just give him a minute to get ready. He's not as young as he used to be."

"Okay," she said and reached down to help.

"You seem to have a lot of catching up to do," Tom said. "I hope you're expecting me to help."

"Expecting? I'm counting on you!" And she rolled over and climbed on top.

This time the interjections in the long luxuriating pattern of their lovemaking were marked by small excited squeals of expectation rather than the little moans of surprise. Finally, exhausted, they slept, naked, twisted together and content.

CHAPTER 30

Tom wakened automatically at five-thirty. He twisted on to his elbow and watched her sleeping, sprawled partly covered, with her mouth slightly open making a tiny fluttering snore. He eased himself off the bed, showered, dressed and walked to the office for the free continental breakfast. She stirred without coming awake when he opened the door and brought in the coffee and icing buns. "Wakey, wakey," he called softly. "Time to wake up!" But it was the aroma of the coffee that opened her eyes.

"Oh, coffee! How did you manage that? And you're dressed. Are we late?" She rummaged in the bedclothes looking for her underwear, and not finding it, wrapped a sheet, sarong-like around her and sat down with him to her coffee.

"How do you feel this morning," he asked.

"You couldn't guess how unbelievably wonderful I feel," she answered around a mouthful of bun. "I can't believe that was me last night. I never knew it could be like that. I wonder if it can happen again. Oh, God! I hope so."

"Would you like to try?" he asked, smiling at her.

"Oh, yes, I would! But we shouldn't. You're all dressed and spruced up and I'm a mess. Let me find my clothes and have a shower first." She stirred among the sheets and found her underwear and hurried to the bathroom, leaving the door ajar. "Do you know where we are, Tom?" she called out to him.

"Yes," he answered. "There's a little map on the motel brochure here. It looks like we're about fifteen miles or so to the freeway and then maybe thirty or forty miles into town."

"So we should leave pretty soon?"

"There's the morning traffic, you know. I think we have to, just to be on the safe side if you want to go home before you go to work."

"Damn!"

"What did you say?"

She emerged from the bathroom, saying, "Nothing. I was just cussing at myself for being such a sleepyhead."

She finished dressing and stood looking at him. "Boy-oh-boy-oh-boy!" she exclaimed. "What a night! What a man!"

He got up and put his arms around her. "What a darling you are and what a lucky man I am." They stood in each other's embrace for a minute until he said, "We better get going before I get ideas."

They drove along the townline road and turned onto the freeway. Because it was Saturday morning, there was little commuter traffic, which they both noticed, and she said regretfully, "I'll bet we could have waited another half hour and still made it,"

He grinned at her and patted her knee.

When they got off the freeway and onto the city streets, she said, "I've got a brilliant idea. How about coming to my place for dinner tonight? Craig's away camping, so there will be just the two of us."

He hesitated, frowning slightly, the idea of invading another man's house making him reluctant, then replied, "Sure! I never refuse an offer of a home cooked meal. What time?"

"Oh, any time," she replied. "Six will be fine and I'll plan time for a drink and dinner around seven."

"Great!"

They turned the corner of her street and he was looking carefully around for the house, and coasted to a stop when Marion pointed it out to him. "I should be able to find it tonight by myself without help," he said. "Shall I escort you to the door for the sake of courtesy or to titillate your neighbours? Or maybe we should just engage in a long lingering goodbye kiss if you think that will arouse them."

"No, a long lingering kiss will arouse me more than it will them and I might never get to work. Goodbye, my dear Tom. Thank you for a fantastic time. I mean that more than you might know. I'll see you tonight." She leaned over and kissed him, got out and waved goodbye as he drove away. Both had forgotten that he always visited his father on Saturdays and she would probably see him at the hospital.

***

In defiance of their plans, the sun took a long time to crawl over the mountain and touch the western beach where the boys had camped. It had been a cold night but neither had been willing to get up and set the fire again. They had dug more clothes out of their packs and crept back into the sleeping bags depending on exchanging body heat to keep warm. Rob argued that because he was skinny, then Craig should let him sleep close again so he could share his body heat. "Okay, close is okay," Craig said, "but not on top, for God's sake. You were around me like an octopus all night."

"Yeah, I know. You were cuddly and warm and I was cold."

"Tonight let's heat up some rocks and put them in the bed before we get in. That will keep it warmer. Hey!" he said, butting his friend, "are you going to get up and put the fire on?"

"You do it."

"I'll do it tomorrow."

"Same old story from you," Craig said with as much of a snarl as is possible between solid friends. "You should set it to music." And he sang in a boyish bass, "Tomorrow, tomorrow, I promise to do it tomorrow, I'll get Craig to do it tomorrow." He unzipped a side of the sleeping bag, rolled roughly over Rob taking as much of the covers as possible and crawled out of the tent.

"Hurry up!" Rob called. "I'm freezing. What are you fixing for breakfast?" But all he heard in reply was a mutter and grumble as he rolled himself back up into both bags and assorted clothes and went back to sleep.

Craig made a roaring fire and sorted through the food supply.

He found some bacon, pancake mix, milk powder and plastic packages of syrup. The bacon was cooked until it was beyond crispy and the pancakes were deep-fried in the bacon fat and the extra butter Craig felt would improve them. Then with the whole thing swimming in syrup he went down to some rocks nearer the water's edge to eat in the company of an inquisitive, scolding squirrel, a couple of running, bobbing peeps feeding at the water line and the warming sun.

He thought about the summer and about Lee and wondered if Lee had been more important to him than Rob. He was reluctant to think that that could ever happen but he knew it probably would. He would find another girl and spend more time with her and less with Rob but he knew that he and Rob would be best friends all their lives. He thought probably Rob would do the same and one of them might even move away, but at that point he refused to carry on with that thought—the idea of a life without Rob always near by. For a while he daydreamed about sex and love, and the idea of loving Lee, but then the feelings he had for Rob entered in and he couldn't differentiate between the feelings he had for Rob and what he felt for Lee, except that one was more sexy than the other, and you could talk about one but the other was secret and unspoken. He wondered if he and Rob were homos. He got teased about it by other guys sometimes and so did Rob but when he talked to Rob about it, he just said 'Screw them'. He wished he could be as offhand as Rob was about these things, but he couldn't. He sighed a long deep sigh that sent the nosy squirrel chithering away from the leftover pancakes he had put out for him and went to the tent and shouted as he shook it, "Get up! You lazy piece of dog turd or I'll go fishing without you."

A mumble sounded like, "Shut up and go away!"

He knelt down and stuck his head inside and shouted, "Hurry up and get up!" Reaching into the tangle of sleeping bags and clothes intending to grab Rob's foot and pull him out of the tent Rob's face emerged, tousled and grinning.

"Aha!" it shouted. "He's not content to mess about with me all night, he comes asking for more before I've had my beauty sleep." He lunged at Craig and caught him and pulled him struggling into the tent. "All right then, Craggy lover-boy of mine! What's it going to be this time—a little ball-to-bally or some dicky-licky or maybe Craigy's got some other ideas, have you, Craggy?" He was holding Craig in a tight wrestling hold from which Craig made only sporadic feeble attempts to escape. Their two heads were close together and Rob blew into Craig's ear. "Is that sexy?" he asked. Then he licked the ear and said, "How about that? It's supposed to be really sexy? Is it? Did you do it to Lee?"

Craig shouted, "Rob! For Christ sake, cut it out!" and then went suddenly limp only to explode into a small fury of arms, elbows, knees and feet and escape. Scrabbling to get outside with Rob hanging futilely onto his pantleg, he shouted, "Hah! Gotcha that time, sucker!"

"Come back, come back," Rob wailed. "I miss you already." He stuck his head outside the tent flap and said, "Okay. If you're not coming back, make my breakfast."

Craig picked up a rock and threw it in the general direction of the tent and Rob ducked inside. Then, grabbing the hatchet he went back into the woods to collect more firewood. The area where they camped had been well used during the summer and he had to go deep into the woods to collect a good supply. While he worked, he wondered if his mother had remembered to lock up the house last night before going to bed. Sometimes she forgot. He could not know, of course, that at that moment his mother was getting out of a stranger's car after an all-night sexual romp. The pile of wood he had been collecting was now too big for one trip so he gathered a big armful and staggered back to camp. Rob was up, tousled and unkempt, but in a happy mood, making his own breakfast and offering to make more for Craig.

"What is it?" Craig asked, looking at a revolting mess in the frying pan.

"Beans on one side and scrambled eggs on the other but they got mixed up. Looks like dog puke, doesn't it? But it's good—want some?" Craig shook his head. "Then tie some bacon on the end of a stick," Rob continued, "and hold it over the fire for me while I eat this and try not to burn it. I saw what you did to yours—even the squirrel wouldn't touch it."

Craig got busy wrapping a half a dozen strips of bacon around a stick and tying them on, then sat beside the fire holding and turning the stick as the bacon sizzled and filled the morning air with its aroma. "This is making me hungry," he called to Rob. "Save me some of that stuff."

"Too late! You'll have to scrape the pan. What are we going to do today."

"We have to go back and get some more firewood and find the axe. I lost it."

"You better find it. Richard will eat your ass if you lose his good hatchet. Then what are we going to do?"

"I dunno. What do you want to do?"

"I dunno."

Craig brought the bacon over and unrolled it from the stick, dropping it into the frying pan Rob had used as utensil and plate, and they squatted together eating it, hot and dripping.

"Don't wash it," Rob said. "Save it for the fish."

"Okay."

The sun was warming up and they sat around for a while, taking off a layer of clothes now and then until they were down to standard dress of jeans and t-shirts.

"Let's fish over around there," Craig said, waving to an area that was more heavily treed without much indication of beach, "up to where that waterfall feeds into the lake. That should be good fishing."

"Okay," Rob said agreeably.

"We should get the wood first, and find the axe."

"Okay."

"Well, c'mon!"

"Okay."

"Oh, for Christ sake, Rob. Get off your ass and let's get going," Craig yelled, as he gathered up his extra clothes and headed for the tent. He opened the tent flap and stuck his head inside and shouted, "Who did this?"

"I thought you'd never notice," Rob answered. "Now don't mess it up!"

Inside the tent, the bed was made and smoothed carefully with the two packs set out for pillows. He had undone the straps of their packs and laid one strap of each pack across the other pack. Craig backed out of the tent and saw Rob already heading towards the place where they had gathered firewood yesterday.

"Don't they look cute and friendly?" Rob shouted back.

Craig started out after Rob but his eye caught something on the trunk of a tree facing the beach. It was two sets of initials: CW and RT carved deeply into the bark and enclosed in a clumsy square, the top of which had been cut into a Vee like a valentine heart.

Craig ran to catch up and tackled him from behind and they went down together in a friendly wrestle, until, as these competitions usually ended, Craig yelled, "Uncle, Uncle."

They got up off the ground and brushed themselves off. "When did you do that?" Craig asked.

"When you weren't around," Rob answered casually, turning away to continue on to the woodpile.

Craig caught up to him and they walked shoulder to shoulder when they could. "Hey, Rob! That's great! Really! It will be there for hundreds of years, I bet. Won't it?"

Rob's only answer was a tight grin and a shoulder and bum bump as they walked.

They found the axe and cut armloads of firewood to carry back to their camp. When they were finished, it was not yet noon, but they were hungry and made a meal out of a large can of dehydrated stew and something that was supposed to be buns when it was cooked. Then they went fishing far down the shore where the waterfall cascades down the craggy face of a mountain under a rainbow and trickles noisily over the rocks into the lake.

***

When Marion arrived at work, Ellen waved to her from the switchboard window and unplugging her mike called over, "Don't you look sparkling this morning. How come you look like you've had a wonderful weekend when it hasn't decently started?"

"I guess I must have lucked out and had a good sleep for a change," Marion answered blushing.

"Aren't you lucky. I sleep like a log and I never get up looking like a spring garden." Ellen laughed and turned back to her demanding switchboard.

After opening the little shop, doing some general housekeeping and rearranging some shelves, she had a chance to examine herself in the small mirror on the wall of the stockroom. She had to agree with Ellen—she did look fresh and maybe even a little younger. If I had known that a roll in the hay would do that, I would have been a farmer's wife, she said to herself and laughed aloud.

A voice from the shop called out "Hello?" and Marion went out quickly to find one of the girls from the office waiting for her. "Sorry to interrupt," she said, "but Ellen said she forgot to tell you that Cynthia wants you to call." Marion thanked her and hoped the girl thought there was somebody in the stockroom with her when she laughed aloud. She thought the call would wait until her coffee break, but it happened that there were so many customers there was no free time for a coffee break. Then just before noon, Tom came striding through the door. Seeing her busy with two customers in the shop, he smiled and waved and walked on. She couldn't believe how disappointed she was. It was if she had been expecting him to rush over and embrace her in front of everybody. The customers left and the shop was empty. Suddenly, she saw Tom getting off the elevator and walking toward her. Oh, good, she thought. I can close up and we can have coffee together. But when he came close she saw that his face was drawn and colourless and the thought struck her that that he was angry about something. He came close to her and said, tonelessly, "Marion, my father died last night."

"Oh, Tom!" she cried, tears springing immediately to her eyes as she put out a hand to touch his arm in comfort. "I'm so sorry."

"They tried to call me several times, but of course..." His voice trailed off. He shrugged as if to get rid of any guilt feelings he might be harbouring. "I have some things to do, Marion. Will you be home this afternoon if I call you?"

"Yes, Tom. Please call. Tell me if there is anything I can do."

"Thank you, I can't think it all through right now, but I will call you if there is anything... thoughtful of you... sorry to put a damper on your morning."

She wanted to move closer to him and find some way to give him understanding and comfort but his closed face presented no invitation. Suddenly he said, "I don't know your number. On the way down, I was afraid you'd be gone and I couldn't phone you." His voice was like that of a small child who had been lost and was found again.

"Here, Tom," she said, writing her number on a card and giving it to him.

"Thank you," he said to her in a husky voice and she knew it was meant for more than the card she gave him. "I'll call." He turned to go then looked back at her, "I have to go down to the morgue and identify him," he said and gave a small shudder.

She closed the door behind him, put up her 'Back in 5 Min' sign and went into the store room to dry her eyes and try to cover some of the blotchiness of her face. That done, she went across to the reception desk to make the call to Cynthia.

Cynthia was as usual, charming and efficient, business-like while being sociable. She asked if Marion could possible come in for the evening shift to cover for some one who was sick.

"I'd like to help out, Cynthia, but I just found out that the father of a friend of mine died last night, and I promised to be home if he needed me," Marion explained honestly, at the same time regretful that she couldn't help Cynthia.

"Was your friend's father in the hospital?" Cynthia asked.

"Yes, he was." Puzzled by the question.

"That wouldn't be Mr. Thomas, would it?" Cynthia asked, so surprising Marion by the breadth of information Cynthia always seemed to have at hand that she asked, "Yes, but how did you know?"

Cynthia gave a small chuckle, "I was over late last night checking the inventory and the word went around. He was a wonderfully gentle man, wasn't he?" She paused for a moment and continued with her original problem. "I'm glad you're there to help out the family, Marion. I better get on with finding someone for tonight, or I'll have to do double duty again. Bye, bye."

Marion returned to the shop and waited for Tom to come back from the morgue. Her replacement arrived and she turned over the cash box to her and stayed around chatting, but Tom didn't return and she went discontentedly home.

She made some plans for a dinner that could be made quickly at any time, and went out to work in her garden with the telephone sitting by an open window. By three o'clock she was beginning to feel disappointed and in another hour she had convinced herself that he wouldn't phone and realized she didn't know his home phone number. Perspiring and dirty, she stopped to make herself a cup of tea and sitting in the quiet of her kitchen she considered calling Ellen at the switchboard and asking her to get one of her friends to get his number from the patient files, but changed her mind and was headed back out to the garden when the phone rang. I hope that's not Edith, she thought, I hate to have to cut her off if I'm waiting for a call.

"Hello," she said tentatively.

"Hello, is this the Williams?" Tom's voice asked.

"Yes. Is that you, Tom?"

"Marion! Oh, good. It is the right number. I wasn't sure because your nines and sevens look the same. I'm sorry I was so long calling but there seemed to be a lot to do. I know you invited me for dinner but I'm not going to be very good company, so I thought that, maybe..."

"Yes, I imagine there's a lot to do. But I think you need some company right now just to talk about things and if you haven't any other plans in mind, why don't you come whenever you are ready. We'll just have a simple dinner and make it an early quiet evening."

"Are you sure that's okay?"

"Tom, I'd be delighted if you came. I think you know that."

"Yes, I do. But I can't give you a time."

"That's okay. You just come when you're ready."

"Alright, Marion. You're something special." He hung up.

Before Tom's sudden reappearance after having gone up to visit his father, Marion had periodically fantasized about what their evening together might be like. In her fantasies, she and Tom had made love on the floor of the living room, in the master bedroom and in Edith's room. But things had not gone well in the master bedroom, and Edith's stuffed toys looked down on them in dismay, so she settled for a romantic evening on the couch and floor of the living room. Now, in reality, she looked at the living room and realized that there would be no lovemaking tonight. Sighing with a preliminary disappointment, she got herself and the house ready for a guest. She discarded the idea of a pantsuit and chose a long, flowing skirt instead with a low-cut blouse: sexier, she thought, even if nothing came of it. There was still a water stain on the rug that resisted her cleaning efforts, the stain created by the spill made when she had slapped the vase of 'sweepeas' off the table. She set the dining room table for two, end and side, and did the preparations for a dinner that required only minimum last minute attention in the kitchen. It was nearly six o'clock and she settled into a chair in the living room that permitted her to watch the news and the street in front. She waited and dozed.

The sound of the back door latch clicking closed wakened her. There was a moment of panic because she knew Tom would not enter without invitation and Craig was not due back until tomorrow. She turned and saw Gerry standing in the living room door.

"Gerry! I wasn't expecting <u>you</u>," she exclaimed, looking at him closely.

He seemed to have lost a lot of weight, his cheeks were sunken and he had not shaved for days. She barely recognized the jacket and slacks he was wearing, the fine wool and expert tailoring he had always demanded now concealed by stains and lack of care. He had the same scuffed slip-on boat shoes he had been wearing the last time he appeared and a wool workshirt she had never seen before.

"But you were obviously expecting somebody," he said, looking into the dining room. "Surely you and Craig don't dine in such style every night."

She refused to rise to the bait. "Craig has gone hiking for the weekend," she said.

"So when the kid's away, the nanny goat plays," he said in a nasty tone. "I need some things." He turned abruptly away.

"I thought your court case was yesterday," she called out.

He stopped and said over his shoulder, "The judge was sick and it was put off for two weeks." He stood still and glared at her. "Is there anything else of my private affairs that you would like to know? Am I eating properly? Am I sleeping well? Am I getting any fucking? I'm sure you care—deeply and sincerely." He turned away and went upstairs. The tone of his voice had been so mean and vicious that she was shaking with either fright or anger. She heard him moving around upstairs and then she heard the shower running. My god, I'm going to be in a mess if Tom arrives now, she thought. She rushed to the closet grabbed her coat and purse and stood by the front window planning to rush out and persuade Tom to drive away with her. She listened carefully for more sounds from upstairs, hoping he hadn't now decided to go to bed. He would do something like that, she thought. She heard him coming down the stairs but she did not turn to look, keeping her back to him. He went directly to the basement and she held her breath listening. She heard him doing something in the work room and go out the basement door. Rushing to the kitchen window, she watched him throw some tools in the trunk of the car and drive away. She went shakily back to the living room and sank into a chair, her head whirling with the thoughts of what might have happened if Tom had arrived before him. After a few minutes getting rid of the shakes, she put away her coat and purse and went upstairs to check the bedroom and bath. His old clothes were piled on a chair in the bedroom, so he had dressed in other clothes but she could not remember from the single glance she saw of him when he went to the car what he had been wearing. After throwing all his soiled clothes in a laundry bag and cleaning the bathroom, she poked around in his closet and drawers for no reason she could understand except a compulsive need to know what he was wearing. Finally, she decided that he had put on a pair of brown cords, maybe a black turtle neck and a black and dark green rainproof jacket he had scarcely ever worn. If he was going to go around looking like a bum, she thought in a moment of concern which she did not understand, he might as well look like a well dressed bum. The doorbell rang and she closed the drawers and closet in the master bedroom and hurried down to open the door for Tom.

He was looking drawn and tired but he smiled as he entered and gave her a small hug and a kiss on the cheek.

"How did things go?" she asked, leading him into the living room. "But maybe you'd like a drink first, would you? A Scotch?"

"Yes, please Marion. I really would."

She got the bottle from the liquor cabinet and went to the kitchen, saying as she left, "Sit over here, Tom. It's a lounger and you can put your feet up."

When she came back with his drink he was sitting in the lounger but not stretched out, and he got to his feet when she came back in. "You're not having one?" he asked.

"Not yet. Are you hungry? Did you remember to eat today?"

"I'm fine," he said, smiling at her maternal concern. "I grabbed a burger during the afternoon sometime."

"You enjoy your drink and excuse me for a couple of minutes while I do a couple of things about dinner. Just relax—you must have had a hard day."

She came back in with a glass of wine for herself and settled in a companion chair next to him. He took another sip of scotch and said, "No, it wasn't a hard day, Marion, in terms of work or things to do. It was hard just getting it through my head that my dad was dead." He took a long snuffly breath through his nose and added, "Even though I have been expecting it for a long time."

He paused and she said nothing.

"I had to identify the body—and that was hard. But after that it was fairly straight forward. We joined a Memorial Society years ago and they have all the details on record. So I contacted them and they got hold of their undertaker, and he picked up the body. I went over and signed the necessary documents, after the undertaker completed the paper work at the hospital. He wanted to be cremated and he will be. He was adamant that there should be no fancy coffin, no viewing, no flowers, no funeral, and not even a Memorial Service. All that kind of thing was written out years ago in the contract with the Memorial Society—so it was relatively easy. They took care of everything, even the notice for the papers. He asked that his ashes be scattered at sea, that's all. He always told me that if I wanted to do that myself, it would be okay, and if I wanted to say a few words when I dumped him into the sea, then keep it short and keep it silent. Of course, that was a few years ago when he could thump the table and argue."

"I've never heard of anything as sensible as that. I always heard the Memorial Societies put a lot of pressure on the family to buy plots and fancy coffins."

"No, not the Vancouver Memorial Society—it's the biggest in North

America, maybe in the world. They keep your records and all you have to do is call them. They do everything. They contract with undertakers who will do exactly what you say you want done when you die, and no hard selling because the costs are fixed."

"It's kind of hard for some people to understand, though. I phoned my brother down east. He said he couldn't come out for the funeral and when I told him there wasn't going to be a funeral, that Dad was going to be cremated, he hung up on me. Then he phoned me back and asked me to take a picture of Dad in the coffin and I hung up on him. Thank God I've only got one brother and no sisters. I also had to phone several of his old friends from army days that he keeps in touch with. One of them wanted to get the rest of them together and be pall bearers. He was very disappointed. Some of these old boys love a parade. He told me that when he went out, he wanted bugles and drums the whole shebang."

Tom laughed in recall and held out his glass. "Could I have another, Marion?"

"Of course," she said. "I got involved listening. I'll check the dinner at the same time."

"Don't get me another if dinner's ready," Tom called.

"It won't be for at least thirty minutes."

She returned with another scotch on the rocks and they sat together in a comfortable silence for a couple of minutes until Tom said, "I had to phone my wife, you know."

She nodded, "Yes, of course. How did she take the news?"

"You wouldn't believe it. She said, 'What are you telling me for?'."

"No, really?"

"Yeah, really. That's the kind of person she is. I told her I only called so that she could tell his grandchildren. And she laughed and said that they didn't even know him. That's true, of course. But it isn't that he didn't try to get to know them."

"That's a shame. He seemed like the kind of man that would enjoy grand-children. But you never know, do you. No, I don't mean it like that. I mean, if the kids never get to see him then it doesn't mean much. I mean, having a grandfather doesn't mean much to them." She stumbled to a halt, thinking of Gerry and his granddaughters and his selfish indifference to them.

There were some moments of quiet between them and Marion said I'll just check on the dinner—I'm afraid it isn't much, but it should be ready in about five minutes. Would you like to get the last of the news and sports?" she asked, getting up and going to the television. "Any particular station you like?"

"I never get around to turning it off the local station. It's good and I always say if you find a good thing, don't let go." He stopped to watch her tune it in and caught her eye. "We had a good thing last night, didn't we? We were both tuned in to the same station." He smiled with a look of pleasant recall and caught her eye. She felt some of the heaviness disappear.

He watched the news while she went to the kitchen and shortly she called him to the dining room and gave him a bottle of wine to open. She served their dinner in the kitchen, a chicken casserole chequered with chopped red peppers and green peas, and carried in with it a cold Caesar salad and a basket of buns hot from the oven.

They ate, sometimes in comfortable silence, sometimes filling the space with small talk. After what seemed an especially long silence, Tom laid down his fork and said, "Marion, I have to tell you. I could have been here half an hour earlier tonight, but when I first drove up, a car was parked in the driveway and a man was doing something in the trunk. I didn't want to intrude, but I thought it might be your husband, so I drove down to the Mall and had a coffee and wondered whether I should phone you and make up some story to say I couldn't come. But I decided to drive by again and the car was gone. I felt kind of juvenile about it but I was in no mood for any socialization other than with you or a confrontation if it happened to be your husband."

"It was Gerry. He needed a change of clothes. He said his court case had been put off for a month. Other than that, nothing —except hostility."

"Does he drop in without warning like that?"

"Yes."

"I see," and he went back to his dinner with a puzzled look on his face.

For the rest of the dinner, and for the hour they sat in the living room with coffee their conversation was strained. Tom finally said, "I'm sorry I'm such poor company, but my mind is cluttered with other things."

"I know," she commiserated. "These things are always hard."

"The other thing is," and he grinned at her with his face lighting up like it had last night, "I'm not very comfortable in another man's house with that man's wife. I see shotguns hiding in hall closets and half-open basement doors and all kinds of Grade B movie junk like that. Not really," he laughed. "But you know..."

"You talk like you had already met my husband," she replied. "But I do know what you mean." There was a long pause. "We could always go back to our motel," she suggested, smiling.

"Or my place," he responded. "It would be cheaper. That is, if I ever get my father's lifetime collection of newspaper clippings picked up, and his clothes off to the Sally Ann. I should just get a great huge vacuum cleaner and suck the whole place out and start fresh."

"Sounds like you need a woman's hand," she said.

"Are you offering?"

"Yes, why not?.. I really haven't any commitments other than three mornings at the hospital and my Thursday bridge."

"You really are special," he said, getting up to tip back her head in his hands and give her a lingering kiss, something she had been wanting him to do all evening. Then, still cuddling her head, he added. "I've got to go and I hate to go, but I know you understand. If you hadn't invited me tonight I'm positive I would have been out at some pub, drinking myself stupid."

"I'm glad I was around," she said, pulling his head down and kissing him gently without passion. Then she got to her feet and moved to the door. Understanding his need for privacy and rest, she kissed him good night as he thanked her again, and closed the door behind him.

***

Craig and Rob had fished the lake without luck up to the point where the small creek from the waterfall met the lake. They stripped to their shorts to wade out to get beyond the ripples, but the water was so cold they could tolerate it for only short periods before getting numb. The mist from the waterfall had drifted down and eventually soaked their shirts but the sun was warm and they took off their shirts and hung them on branches in the sun to dry. It wasn't long before Rob, after bringing in a wildly flopping trout that had soaked his shorts, was fishing naked, and soon, for the same reasons, Craig joined him.

And shortly after that, four people across the lake in a cabin camouflaged by the shadows, sat on the porch sharing binoculars as they watched two white trolls carrying fishing rods race into the water up to their navels, cast a line and wait, and dash out again, sometimes with a fish but more usually to stamp around a small fire and shiver in self hugs to get warm before the next rush into the icy water. The people on the porch had lunch and watched off and on with amused interest. They saw the trolls eventually tire of fishing and find a windless spot on the rocks where they baked in the hot sun, which diminished the interest of the watchers. When they looked again the trolls had turned into boys, dressed and booted, busy kicking sand on the remnants of their fire before standing together and pissing on it like true woodsmen. They watched them gather a string of fish from the beach and wander back along the beach in the direction of their camp.

When the boys got back to their camp, they were still damp and cold and starving. While the fire caught, they wolfed down some sardines and hardtack and admired seven fish they laid out for their dinner and stood alternating their faces and backs to the fire with the steam rising off their clothes. Craig remembered the rocks for their bed and placed four close to the fire to get hot. Rob rummaged in the food supply with a plan in mind to keep their load light on the way down and eventually sorted out what had to be eaten for dinner, for breakfast and for lunch on the way back. Craig looked at the piles and groaned, not only because of the amounts, but because Rob's combination of food was something less than gourmet even to Craig's naive palate.

"I'll get the dinner and you can get breakfast—you like getting up early," Rob announced. And I'm going to need a little assistance from you. It's going to be a fantastic meal, one that you'll remember for the rest of your life." He kissed his grimy fingers like a French chef.

"I'm going to get some dry clothes from my pack," Craig said, heading for the tent. "These are still wet and stinky."

"Don't mess the bed," Rob shouted. And a minute later, "Where's the frying pan?"

"You said to leave it with the bacon fat to fry the fish!"

Rob grumbled around as he searched the beach for the frying pan and found it licked clean by the muskrat, or birds or ants.

"Come and clean the fish," he shouted to Craig.

"Clean them yourself!"

"I can't. I'm getting dinner."

Craig came out of the tent and looked at Rob's preparations. "What's that?" he said with a grimace.

Rob was dumping dried apricots and peaches, into the pot in which rice and beans were already soaking. "Hurry up with the fish." He looked up and saw Craig's face. "What's the matter? You don't like the way I'm making dinner? They all have to soak, you know." He took off his hat and jammed it on his head upside down like a chef's hat. "So dey soak, alla naice an friendly together justa like you'n me, an the chief cookie, thatsa me, hese go get on his dry cookin' clothes. Den I tella you what I'm agonna do. I'ma gonna take desa fruits out dis pot an I gonna wrap him good in dissa piece foil and I put him here nice close to the fire and he's gonna be hot and sweet for dessert. Hokay? Now den, you see dese beeg potatoes all wrap purty in foil? Dey sitting in the hot coal cookin up naice an hot. And purty soon they almost done, and den onto the fire goes the beans an rice an cookem up slow with salt and pep and a lotsa butter. And now, I'ma gonna make de hot biscuit to wrap aron a stick and cook over de fire while we tella de dirty story. And you know what dese nice lovely liddle good tings to eat keep say to me? Dey say 'When that Craig asshole gonna clean dose fish?'"

Craig laughed and picked up the string of fish and went down to the beach.

There are people with fastidious taste who would criticize the dinner presentation that evening as being somewhat deficient in meeting the criteria required to deserve the accolade of 5-star dining, but the potatoes broke open soft and perfect with skins hard baked and chewy and made more delicious by slathers of butter. To the mixture of beans and rice, Rob had added a package of something he called 'Oregano' that spiced the night air and gave an unusual dish a unique taste. The seven small fish lay head to tail, crisply cooked, in the frying pan, their blank eyes staring into space, their soft pink flesh falling away from the skeleton at a touch. The bread had more crust than body and an interesting flavour picked up from the green stick it was cooked around, but served its primary purposes of filler, pusher and supper. And the fruit, oh, the fruit, hot and as succulent as if it had just fallen, sun-baked, from the tree.

In the language of adolescent campers, expressions of appreciation for a meal differ from those used by adults dining out in more cultured settings. Here, under a billion stars, listening to the varied cries of loons answering each other across the lake and waiting for those conversations to be interrupted sporadically by the call of a faroff coyote, appreciation is best expressed in terms of "Hoo-boy! Was that ever good!" accompanied by two hands patting an extended belly, and loud burps and farts, if possible.

The dishes and pots were cleaned off with sand, sloshed in the lake and packed out of harms way. The remaining food supply was bagged and tied over a branch. They yawned at each other over the embers of the fire, talking in low tones about their day. Finally, Rob said, without much enthusiasm, "Hey, I've still got that joint left. How about it?"

Craig shrugged in the dark. "Sure, I guess so. Why not?"

From some hiding place in his pack Rob pulled out a thinly rolled joint and lit it with a burning twig. They passed it back and forth between them, this time managing the smoke without choking or sputtering, until fingers were burned in the passing. Neither one was certain that a real high was achieved, except that Rob insisted he had got a hard on, but Craig argued that there was nothing very special about that for Rob. As for himself, Craig reported that the blinking of the stars had speeded up and the cries of the loons were louder and closer, probably just down there by the beach, but he didn't want to go down to see in case he scared them away. Rob nodded in perfect understanding. They competed in mimicking the varied cries of the loons lurking by the beach, until the loons, apparently dismayed but unchallenged by their attempted duplication, returned to the far end of the lake.

The fire died to a glowing bank of coals. They warmed fronts and backs, yawning and recalling the day. Then, with the fire sanded down and pissed on, they crawled into the tent, folded their jeans and jackets for pillows and settled in the twisted arrangement of legs and arms demanded by Rob by jerks and pushes, and quickly settled into sleep.

But not before the quiet night heard a complaining "Ro-o-ob!"

And the answer, "Oh, shut up and go to sleep!"

CHAPTER 31

They had slept soundly throughout the night unaware of a sudden rain and hail storm that had raced through the mountains soaking the ground, including, they would discover later, the trail down, and pounding the early fall leaves off the birches and poplars. When they roused from their hibernation, the smell of rain and the damp chill in the air did not stir them to rush out and greet the day. The tent had been tightly closed and they were for the moment warm and dry with no urge to alter the atmosphere of cozy, sleepy contentment until nature demanded it. Sleep would not return to Craig but Rob drifted away periodically as Craig talked about getting ready for the trip down, school, the money he had saved during the summer, Lee and other subjects some of which shifted Rob out of a doze while others required a sharp jab in the ribs to get a response. When the full rays of the morning sun finally bathed the tent in light and warmth, something derived more from animal instinct than intelligence prompted them to rise, scratch, dress, build a fire and eat. Breakfast consisted of anything in their food supply that could be quickly and easily made ready to eat. Underlying the activities of the morning meal was the unspoken understanding that the more they ate the less there would be to pack and carry. That done, they set about with the speed of sloths to gather together all the scattered equipment they had carried in. Neither felt any need for order or organization. Whatever was found was packed in whatever pack was closer. Only the tent, now aired and dried by the sun, demanded their studied concern. The floor was wiped out with a pair of socks, the whole tent was hoisted and the leaves and sand wiped off before it was carefully folded in the air and packed away in its bag without touching the ground again. The aluminium poles and supports were dismantled, wiped, tied together and packed in the bag with the tent. Craig casually placed it beside Rob's pack and just as casually tied the bag to the pack and wandered away.

"Do you want to catch some fish before we go?" Rob called from their latrine hole on the edge of the woods.

"We haven't got anything to carry them in," Craig shouted back as he walked over toward the tree where Rob had carved their initials.

"We could just stick them in our old socks and tie them to the outside of your pack."

"Why my pack?" Craig answered disinterestedly, standing in front of the tree wishing again that they had thought to bring a camera.

"Because, my surreptitious friend," Rob said, coming out of the bushes. "I saw you tying that tent to my pack."

"Well, I carried it up. Besides, it's surreptitious, not strep—whatever you said," returning to the campsite

"Whatever, just watch it, smart ass!" and he started stalking Craig, menacingly, stretched tall with hunched shoulders, herding him toward the shoreline. But laughter diluted the threat and Craig stopped retreating and was dragged unresisting back to the campsite. "Wasn't that just the greatest two days?" Rob continued, his usually sombre face sparkling with happiness. "Let's unpack and stay here forever. We could catch fish, and find berries, and grow some pot. It'd be..., It would be SUPER!" he shouted across the lake.

"SUPER!" Craig shouted in agreement.

They tried a few more shouts then stopped in disappointment when the warm noon air inhibited an echo.

"I guess we better get going," Craig said.

"Yeah," Rob replied without enthusiasm.

They checked the campsite for anything they might have forgotten, wet down the black coals of the fire, struggled into their packs and headed down the trail, passing the tree with their initials, where they stopped to pat the tree and grin at each other.

"Goodbye, lake," Rob called, continuing on the trail.

"Goodbye, fish," added Craig.

"Goodbye, loons."

"Goodbye, campsite."

They called goodbye to anything they could think of as they plodded along the trail, past the now deserted cabin on the spit, and stopping only when the climb up the slope to the top of the ridge demanded better use of their breath.

At the top they stopped and looked back at the lake, still, sparkling and blue, with its ribbon of a waterfall and the cabin on the spit. "Why didn't you remember your camera?" Rob complained without malice, his face glowing with inner feelings he rarely showed.

"You know why, bean brain! Because yours is broken and you took mine and now you don't know what you did with it."

Rob was quiet for a long moment as he continued to look out over the lake. "We gotta come back, Craig. We gotta come back soon. Just you and me. What d'ya say, eh, old buddy?"

"Yeah," Craig replied quietly. "Maybe next spring. It'll be different in the spring." He waited for Rob to come out of his reverie, and finally turned and walked away, calling over his shoulder, "C'mon, Robbie! Let's go."

The path down was freshly marked by the four people from the cabin who had left earlier. The night rain had made the path slippery and at first they picked their way carefully down the slope and then discovered from examining the tracks of the other people that they had gone down by taking giant strides and digging in with their heels through the wet surface to drier and more solid ground underneath. Robbie, with his longer legs and generally greater daring, followed the leaping strides the previous campers had made and was soon so far ahead of Craig that Craig became alarmed at being lost. He had been picking his way down, looking for secure footholds, but was slipping and falling and getting muddy. "Rob!" he shouted periodically. "Wait for me!" But Rob was far ahead leaping like a mountain goat down the steep path, too caught up in the challenge of the slope to answer. Craig tried the giant strides that had taken Rob so quickly out of sight, but his caution made his stride only half as long as the tracks made by others and he reverted to a safer, slower descent. He finally arrived at the point where the trail flattened out and turned. He found Rob sprawled on the ground with his pack off, eating crackers.

"I could have got lost, you know," he fumed at Rob.

"I would have found you."

"Or I might have broken my leg."

"But you didn't, did you? Want a cracker?"

"No! I don't want any of your god damn crackers!" He turned and stomped away along the now flat trail.

"Craig! Craig!" Rob shouted after him. "Don't leave me! I might get lost! A bear might eat me!" But he got to his feet, shrugged into his pack and followed Craig. He caught up to him within a hundred yards and began walking close behind him, matching steps, then holding the sides of Craig's pack and steering him along the path.

"Cut it out, Rob!" Craig shouted. "Grow up!"

But Rob had found a tuneless child's song that matched the rhythm of their walk. "One little, two little, three little Indians," he sang as they walked, changing the cadence as Craig struggled to alter the speed and length of his steps to try to confuse him. Then they were laughing and singing together, and, as always in their long friendship, the flash of Craig's earlier petulant anger, was never openly acknowledged by Rob.

They reached the river bank and found the boat and after considerable discussion figured out how to get two bodies and two packs to the other side and leave one boat on each shore. That pseudo-military exercise accomplished, they stood on the side of the road, thumbs out, hitching. Neither of them had the wit to realize that nobody in that torrent of Sunday afternoon traffic, unless they were the embodiment of the ancient Samaritan, would stop to offer assistance to two unkempt, muddy, perhaps even dangerous strangers. So they walked the two miles to town, found the bus station and after a thirty minute wait, filled contentedly by two Mars bars and a Coke each, boarded an intercity bus and were directed to the back seat by the driver, where they slept soundly for the hour trip to the city.

At the terminal they struggled off the bus with their packs and headed for a city bus stop. Craig had bought the bars and cokes and had only a handful of change left, not enough for two tickets.

"What are we going to do now?" Rob said, not terribly concerned.

"Whadya mean?" Craig demanded.

"I mean you haven't got enough money and I didn't bring any."

"Didn't you bring any at all?"

"No! I forgot. Well, I didn't exactly forget. I just didn't bring any. There's a difference, you know, between just not doing something and forgetting to do something."

"Oh, shut up. Who wants to listen to that crap. I can wait until I get to school tomorrow for that. Phone Bev and see if she will pick us up. She's closer than my Mom."

Rob sauntered over to a bank of phones and stopped on the way to have a long, laughing chat with a guy and a girl Craig did not recognize. When he finally came back, he reported, "No answer."

"Who were you talking to?" Craig asked.

"Nobody—there was no answer, I said."

"I mean who was that guy and the girl you talked to."

"Oh, somebody from the store. I don't remember their names."

"Why don't you borrow a couple of bucks from them."

"Hey! Good idea. I never thought of it."

They looked around the waiting room and in the line-ups for the buses but the couple had disappeared. Reluctantly, because in the back of his mind he wanted to arrive home and surprise her, Craig phoned his mother who seemed happy to come and pick them up. "Put an old blanket on the back seat, Mom," Craig said. "we're kinda dirty."

It seemed to Marion that Craig had been away a week, not just two nights. And what two nights they had been for her. She felt herself flushing as she thought of the night she had spent in the motel with Tom. But what pleased her most was that she could not find any feelings of guilt for what she had done and what she would do again, given an opportunity. I should feel guilty, she told herself. I wonder why I don't. Probably because I have known for years that

Gerry was whoring around and I wouldn't admit it to myself.

Earlier in the day she had been waiting, somewhat anxiously, for a call from Tom when the phone rang and she heard the syrupy voice of the pro at the golf club asking for Gerry, because, he said, "The office told me that Gerry was on extended holidays. Could I speak to him?"

"He's not in, sorry." He was one of her least favourite people and she was not about to change her opinion.

"Would you mind giving him a message?"

"Certainly not—or maybe he should call you?"

"Yes, that would be better."

"I think so."

"He's feeling okay, is he?"

"He hasn't said he was not feeling okay—why do you ask?"

"Well, he hasn't been around and he has missed a couple of scheduled games and he doesn't usually miss without calling in to tell me to get a fill-in if he has to go out of town."

"Maybe he called and somebody else took the message and forgot to tell you."

"Yeah, maybe that's what happened."

"Well, then, goodbye."

"Goodbye, Mrs.—ah—Marion, isn't it?"

She had hung up without answering.

When they were disconnected, one of them said "Cold bitch! If I ever got you on a pool table, I'd warm you up."

The other one said, "Try to figure that out for your gossip sessions, you fat-ass fornicator. As if you didn't know exactly what's going on."

She had not heard from Tom by noon so she put away her anxiety and settled down after lunch to make some phone calls. She called Dot first because she knew that anything she had to say would be passed on immediately to the other women in the bridge club.

"How are things between you and Gerry?" Dot asked straight out after the brief social preliminaries.

"No change," Marion answered. "And I'm not looking for one. He's still a rotten SOB in my books."

"So you're not going to do anything about it?" Dot asked.

"You mean like counseling or starting divorce proceedings?"

"Yes, I suppose. It seems to me that when something like this happens, people usually DO something. Like the woman across the street from me: she suspected her husband of running around and she got this detective and he got pictures and everything. And then she went to this divorce lawyer, I can't think of his name but he's in the celebrity party news all the time, you know the gossip column in the second section of the paper. Anyways, he told her to sue him for everything he's got and she started to but her husband came back crying and promising to be good so she stopped everything and they're back together again but now they're fighting because they have to pay both the detective and the lawyer." She stopped and laughed. "I guess that's the way it goes sometimes."

"Yes, I guess it is," Marion agreed, not really knowing what it was she was agreeing to. They chatted for a while about routine things until Marion was satisfied that Dot was not going to question her further and probably wanted to start passing on whatever little information Marion had given her. So she said, "Well, Dot, I've got to run. We play at your place this week, don't we?" After she heard Dot's affirmation, she quickly cut in. "See you then, Dot. Bye now."

Well, that's that, she said to herself. If Dot doesn't know about me being out all night, then I guess nobody knows. It should be safe to call Edith, then.

Her call was answered by one of the twins and before she could say anything to the garbled greeting she could hear Edith in the background, "Who is it, Iona? Tell Mummmy who it is."

"It's Grandma, Iona. How are you, dear."

"It's Grandma, Mummy!" Iona shrieked excitedly into the telephone, making Marion jump, and said nothing more.

"How are you, dear? And how is Jenny?" Marion asked.

"Granny?"

"Yes, dear."

"We just got back. And Jenny went, too. Mummy said we were good. Didn't you, Mummy?" she shouted. Then, again directly into the mouthpiece, "Jenny! You have to come and talk to Grandma on the telephone."

Marion waited a moment and then said, "Where did you go when you went out, Iona?"

There was no response. Marion heard, "Not now, Jenny! I'm talking to Grandma." Then there were sounds of a children's squabble, the crash of the receiver on the floor and a wail for "Mummy!"

Edith came on the line: "Hi, Mom. Just a minute until I settle this pair down." Her muffled voice continued, "Now stop that crying right now, Jenny. And Iona, say you're sorry. You are not supposed to hit, remember. Now you both go out and tell Daddy that Grandma's on the phone. Sorry, Mom. They're a little hyper right now. We took them to church this morning and they were as good as gold. It was a special family day and you wouldn't believe how many people were there. And the kids! Crying and running all over the place—not my two, they were so-o good. You would have been proud of them. Then we took them out for lunch and it was so funny. They have never been in a real restaurant before and they ooh-ed and ah-ed and people kept smiling and talking to them when they were walking past. They had a great time. Harv and I just sat and laughed about it when we got home." She laughed again giving Marion a chance to interrupt.

"What church did you go to, Edith?" Puzzled that she would even think of taking the children to church when church and Sunday School had never been a part of her life.

"Oh, it's the one just a few blocks from us. We were going to walk but it looked a little cloudy, so we took the car. It's a good thing we did because we would have had to walk another five or six blocks to the restaurant, then home. They would have been pooped. Well, they are, anyway. It's the Unit-something church. That sprawly white one a little bit further on from where you turn down our street. Unit-something."

"United? Unity? Unitarian?" Marion suggested.

"Unitarian! That's the one. I kind of like it. They didn't do a lot of kneeling and praying. Suited me and Harv, too. We just went to see if maybe we should get involved in a church, you know, for the kids' education. How's Craig?" It was another of her conversational vaults.

"He left Friday on a hike. He'll be back today—I hope. Because the first day of school is tomorrow."

"Where'd he go?" The response was so minimal and so unlike Edith that Marion could see her leaning around the corner as far as the telephone cord could reach to check on the girls.

"A little lake up in the mountains called Lake Lovely Water. I drove them up to the place where the trail starts."

"Oh, really! Wasn't that the lake that Bev and Richard hiked into a couple of years ago? No," she corrected herself. "It was longer ago than that. I remember, because I was pregnant with the twins. Oh, yes. And they came back raving about it! And they had hundreds of beautiful pictures. He went with Rob, I bet, didn't he?" It was more of a statement than a question, and taking it as fact, she plunged on. "They're such good buddies. Probably will be all the rest of their lives. They're lucky, Harv says. He says he never had a buddy because they lived so far out in the country. He says his best buddy was a dog, and I asked him a little while ago if he would like another dog and he said that he had one once and he didn't think he could bear to have another one die on him. And they do you know, Mom. Dogs don't live very long. Any how," she began to wind down, "he's sure lucky. Craig, I mean. Probably lucky to be a boy with Dad around."

"What? What do you mean, Edith?"

But Edith had suddenly backed away from conversation and her voice took on a cold and bitter tone. "Oh, I don't know, Mom. I don't know what I meant. I guess I meant Craig was lucky to have a father like Dad to take him on hikes, and go fishing and things like that."

"Your father? Taking Craig on hikes and going fishing with him? Why, I can't remember him doing anything like that. Where did you get that idea."

"Oh, I don't know, Mom. I guess I was thinking of something else. He probably never did anything to Craig—I mean with Craig."

"Edith, is something wrong. Did I say something?"

"No, no, Mom! It isn't you. It's just—well, I don't want to talk about it. I will some day but not right now. Harv says I should and I think he's right but I'm not ready."

"What on earth are you talking about, Edith. Can't you give me some kind of clue?"

"No, Mom, I don't want to. It's not your problem—it's mine. And the minister said something this morning about throwing away your feelings of guilt instead of living with them. I don't know how you do that." She gave a short laugh that had no humor in it. "Anyhow it just got me thinking. You know how it is."

"No, I don't, dear! And I wish you'd tell me."

"I will, Mom. But not right now. I'm not going to put a worry load on your shoulders. It's bad enough that I dumped it on Harvey. Mom, listen, I really have to go. I'll call you. OK?"

"Alright, Edie. But I'm not very happy leaving it like this."

"I'm sorry, Mom," Edith said shakily. "I'll call you."

Marion put down the phone and her hand was as shaky as Edith's voice. I hope nothing is wrong between them in their marriage, she thought. No, it was something else. What on earth is going on? She moved away from the phone and into the comfort of the kitchen with its sunshine. She had planned to do more calls to other friends today, but the social urge had gone out of her.

She was dozing in front of the muted television with a book in her hand when the telephone rang. "That's Tom!" she exclaimed with a pleasant feeling of excitement warming her as she rushed to answer it.

"Hi, Mom!" came Craig's happy voice.

"Craig! Where are you? I was half expecting you to call."

"We just got down from the lake and we were going to catch a bus home but we ran out of money and so I was wondering if...."

"I know! You want me to come and pick you up, don't you?" I might as well, she thought. No sense sitting here waiting for a call that may not come. "Where are you?"

"We're at the bus depot downtown. Do you think you could drop down and pick us up? We did have enough money for the intercity bus but now we're broke."

"I think I can do that. How come you ran out of money? What on earth is there up in the mountains to spend money on?"

"We didn't spend it on anything much. I guess we didn't bring enough." There was no thought in his mind of blaming Rob for not remembering to bring any.

"Sounds like poor planning to me," she said, laughing. "Now, listen! I'm not quite ready to dash out of the house so it will take me about three quarters of an hour to get there. Don't leave the depot! Do you hear me? Stay right there. I don't want to drive all the way out there and find you've hitched a ride with one of your friends. You got it? Now repeat what I just said." One of his mother's all-time favourite tactics.

Craig repeated the essence of what she had said in a sing-song mother-nagging voice and they laughed together and hung up but not before Craig added, "Oh yeah, Mom. Throw an old blanket over the back seat—we're kinda muddy."

Rob was sprawled on a bench with his feet propped on his pack, dozing with his mouth open. "Whad'she say?" Rob asked when Craig kicked his pack to waken him.

Craig mimicked the last response from his mother.

"Okay," Rob said and closed his eyes.

Marion found them in the depot and her first reaction was to drive away and disown them. They were slouched down on a bench, dirty, unkempt and asleep. She stood in front of them and sighed. Blanket indeed! she thought, they need a hosing down. She kicked the nearest pack and Rob opened an eye and was on his feet. His movement stirred Craig.

"UU!" Rob cried, leaping to his feet and throwing his long arms around her. "You're here! I've brought your little boy back to you. He's been very good. Didn't wet the bed or anything." All this in a loud voice that had Craig blushing. "C'mon Craig, get up and say hello to your mother."

Craig came closer but Rob flung out an arm and pushed him away. "Not yet! I'm not finished." He held Marion a little longer saying "Yum-yum-yum" into the top of her head. Then he released her and said, "Craig, you may kiss your mother."

It was not a dutiful peck Craig gave his mother. During the two days away, he had had twinges of worry about her living alone, and worried that his father might cause trouble. His greeting was warm and satisfying to them both.

"Why did you take his chains off?" Marion said in a voice as loud as Rob's had been.

"He chewed them off," Craig replied.

"The zoo-keeper will be very angry," she said, turning away towards the door. "Well, let's get going and give him back."

The two boys picked up their packs and followed her, Rob walking in a foot-dragging pigeon-toed slouch with a goofy look on his face to satisfy the curiosity of a few onlookers, with Craig trotting along in the rear.

On the way home, she was regaled with all the events of their two days. She heard most of it, the traffic noises coming in the window she had opened for fresh air masking some of their narrative but none of their enthusiasm.

Marion stopped in front of the Turner's first to let Rob off. There were no lights on, and suddenly she felt she should take him home with her rather than let him face the anticlimax of an empty house but thought better of it. Maybe they're downstairs, she thought. Rob untangled himself and got out. "Thanks for the buggy ride, UU. You're a life saver. I could never have dragged him all the way home," he said, and when his usual humor faltered she realized how tired he was. He opened the back door of the car and shook hands with Craig, something they had never done before, creating a moment of electricity between them.

"See ya," one said.

"Yeah."

"Did you have a good weekend, Mom?" Craig asked from the back seat as they drove around the corner to home.

"Yes, I did, Craig. It was a little lonely without you around, but I managed." They were now stopped in their driveway. She turned around in the front seat.

"I want you to take your pack into the basement and dump it—just dump it on the floor of the laundry room. Then strip, right down to your bare scuddy, and run upstairs and have a good hot scrub. I don't think you two have any idea how bad you smell. By that time, I'll have dinner ready."

He sniffed down his open shirt front. "I don't think I smell that bad," he said. "Maybe it was Rob."

He came downstairs almost an hour later, dressed and shining and, she noted, he had shaved. He wasn't bristly yet but he did have a heavy facial down that blonds develop before a real beard. "I thought you'd put on your PJ's and robe," she said.

"No, I wanted to get dressed," he said. "I was checking these out to see if their okay for school tomorrow. Everybody gets all dressed up for the first day and then after that you can relax."

"They look very nice," his mother said. "Did Lee help you pick them out?"

"Yes, she did, but she had a couple of others she thought were great but they were too wild for me—oranges and apples and stuff like that—, so we settled on this and one other, sort of like this one." He turned away as if he no longer wanted to dwell on the subject of Lee.

"Do you want to eat in front of the TV or do you want to sit out here and tell me all about your hike?"

"Oh, out here!" and he sat down in the nook and started in from the time they had waved good-bye to her, leaving out only the little bits like fishing in the nude, sleeping together and some things like that. His excitement in the telling was such that he only poked at his dinner instead of shovelling, and his mother then knew how wonderful the weekend must have been. He told about the way Rob had baked bread around a stick, how Rob had carved their initials in a tree, the loons, the coyote or maybe a wolf, the bear in the blueberry patch, the stars, the cold water, the waterfall, the beautiful little rainbow trout, and he was prepared to go on until his mother said, smiling at him, "Save some for another telling, Craig, and finish your dinner."

Craig pushed some food around his plate and picked at bits of it and she sat quietly watching him for a while realizing that he was even too tired to eat but couldn't give in.

"Go to bed, Craig," she told him. "You need a good sleep or you'll be too dopey to go to school tomorrow. Besides," she lied, getting up from the table, "there's a program about breast cancer that I really want to watch. It's coming on in a few minutes and I've got to do the dishes."

"Oh, sure," he said. "Hey, Mom. I can't eat all this. You gave me too much."

"That's a first for you," she answered. "Just leave it."

"I better phone Rob and see how he's doing," he said, heading for the hall telephone. He was back in a minute. "No answer. He must have gone to bed."

She was standing at the sink with her hands in the water, not doing the dishes but quietly marvelling at the depth and the strength and the longevity of the friendship between the two boys. It was a bond that the term 'friendship' could not quite describe.

"By the way," she said, "Edie sends her love and she was remarking on how lucky you and Rob are to have a good buddy and that it will probably last all your lives. She said that Harvey was envious of you two because he never had a close friend when he was growing up."

"Yeah, it's pretty nice alright."

"Was there one day during the whole summer that you and Rob did not see each other?" she asked.

"Oh, maybe," he said, reflecting, "but I don't think so."

"Remember the summer Edie got married?" she suddenly asked him.

"Well, yes, sort of," he replied hesitantly. "I remember them getting married."

"Well, you wouldn't remember it as well as I do. The whole summer was taken up with Edie and her wedding and the dresses and finding a bridesmaid, because Edie never did have a life-long good friend. Oh, and everything else and then, of course, after a whole summer of shopping and planning and getting ready, she ran off and got married. I always think of that summer as the summer of Edie." She smiled at him and continued. "And for entirely different reasons," she said, "I think I'll remember this summer as the summer of Rob."

"Yeah!" he responded. "I see what you mean. The summer of Rob." He chuckled over some private memories while he stood mulling over what the words meant to him as a slow smile enveloped his whole face.

"Better go to bed, dear," she suggested finally.

"Yeah, I should," he said and he kissed her and went upstairs smiling, and fastening the words down in the private places of his mind.

CHAPTER 32

After the exhilaration of Lake Lovely Water, Craig felt that the days and later on even the weeks were dropping slowly around him like autumn leaves. On the first day of school, there was an overlay of excitement as people found old friends and talked happily about the summer. Craig found himself saying "Rob and I" frequently but he avoided any mention of Lee although when asked, was forced to say that she had gone to a private school whose name he did not know.

"Oh, Craig! That's too bad," was the usual response from the girls. "She was so cute."

He had called at Rob's on the way to school, but Rob's mother had said, "Better not wait for him, Craig. I'm still trying to haul him out of bed. How come you look so chipper after your big hike? Rob looks like something the cat dragged in." When Craig finally saw Rob at school at the end of the hall, looking baggy-eyed and weary, the assembly bell rang and they went different directions to their last term's home room, but not before Rob made a gun out of a finger and thumb and shot a greeting at Craig with a big grin. It took a long time for teachers to get the term schedules sorted out and students settled down after another bell announced the beginning of class. Students in Craig's room were told that because of the increase in the registration, the school was moving to a completely different scheduling system, also that school hours had been lengthened and when they received their individual timetables they might be lucky and find an early start and an early finish, or they might get an early start and a late finish. There were groans when it was announced that some sports programs had been reduced to make room for academic programs. Some shouting and chanting was heard outside the building and later students learned that a student named Vic had tried to organize a walk-out that fizzled and had been escorted off the school property by the police and the new principal who was six foot two with a voice like a bull and a temper to match. Finally they were told that because some students had given prior indication of their intent to register and had not appeared today, there would be some openings in some classes. Students wishing to change their computerized timetables could do so by going to the counselling office, or they might seek out the teachers involved in the change and get permission through that route. That started a mass exodus in the direction of the counselling office. Some classes had been told to pick up their textbooks right away because there was a shortage, others, that all books would be available at their first class. The period bell rang and pandemonium broke out. The corridors were filled with lineups of unhappy and angry students and dozens of small groups of students who were trying to make private exchanges.

"How'd you do, buddy?" Rob said coming up behind Craig in the hall and draping an arm over his shoulder.

"Great!" Craig exclaimed happily. "I don't start until 9:15 and I'm all through by three. I even got the computer programming course I asked for. How'd you do?"

"I dunno," Rob said with a shrug. "I got some crazy courses."

"Let's see," Craig said, grabbing Rob's timetable. "French and French History! What are you taking those for? And what the hell's this? Intro to Ballet? Oh, for God's sake—this is not your timetable. It's Robin Turner's! That tall skinny girl, the one that wears braces."

"I know," Rob said laconically.

"Well, what are you going to do?"

"Oh, I figure I'll just go along with that timetable and someone will start thinking I don't belong and they'll straighten it out. That's a hell of a lot better than lining up for three hours to see a counsellor. Let's get out of here."

"Where you going?"

"I dunno. I just want to get out of this rat race."

"I can't. I gotta get my books."

"Okay. See ya!" And Rob wandered off.

When Rob finally got his timetable sorted out a week later by locating Robin and exchanging schedules, Craig was dismayed to discover that Rob had one early class and the rest late in the day. "We haven't got one single class together," he complained. "And when I'm free, you've got classes and it's the same for you. Why didn't you go and complain and get some decent courses and times."

"Ah! What's the use? They'd just jerk me around like they always do. Why don't you go and change a couple of your courses so that we've got something that's the same."

"Hell, Rob! I've got good courses and good times. The counselor would think I was nuts if I traded for crap courses and crazy times."

"Well, I guess we're stuck."

Craig walked away morosely wondering why Rob was acting like he didn't care about anything, even him.

Another week went by and Craig saw Rob only periodically but he began to hear a lot of gossip about the new crowd of friends Rob was hanging out with—a gang that was known for drinking and dealing in pot. A guy by the name of Vic was the big man in the gang. He was the son of a rich family with his own car and a big allowance who had been kicked out of school again last week, this time for having liquor and condoms in his locker. Craig didn't know him except by reputation. On those evenings when Craig and Rob got together, Rob talked so constantly of Vic that Craig's jealousy turned into a burning hatred of Vic. Craig made the mistake of venting his hate by mouthing off too much in the hallways. On a Friday when he was leaving school, Craig was stopped outside the school grounds by Vic and a backup of two guys Craig knew only vaguely.

"So big mouth, I hear you don't like me much. That so?" Vic said as he moved closer to Craig, followed by the other two, both grinning at the prospects of a fight.

"Where'd you hear that?" Craig replied, looking around for an escape route.

"Around," Vic said with a hard smile.

"Couldn't have been me," said Craig in a voice that was so close to a squeak it embarrassed him. "I haven't been around."

"And a smart-ass, too," Vic growled in a voice as low as he could make it in contrast to Craig's falsetto. At the same time, he grabbed the neck of Craig's shirt and yanked down, tearing off some buttons and ripping the shirt.

"What'd you do that for?," Craig shouted, with anger overtaking fear.

Rob suddenly appeared and stepped between Vic and Craig. "Yeah! What did you do that for?" he said menacingly.

"Watch it, Turner," Vic snarled and his two cohorts moved in closer, not smiling now.

"Back off, you pricks," Rob said to the other two while staring hard-eyed at Vic and towering over him.

"Who's gonna make us?" one of them said belligerently.

Rob said nothing but he put his fingers in his mouth and whistled at the same time waving his arm in a 'Come here!' gesture to a group of five guys behind Vic who happened to be walking by. Vic and the other two turned to see who he was signalling to and, at the same time, the five guys stopped, looked over, consulted a moment, then moved towards them. Vic might not have been smart, but he wasn't stupid. He could figure the odds—seven to three—and he didn't like them. He pushed quickly past Rob and Craig, saying to Rob as he went by, "I've had it with you, shit-face. Don't come sucking around me again."

One of the other two was so busy glaring at Rob and Craig that he stumbled as he went by. Rob faked a jump in his direction and the guy took off, leaving a string of obscenities behind him.

"You boys hold hands now, so you don't get lost on the way to your tea party," Rob called after them.

"Hi, Rob," one of the five guys said when they got near. Rob knew him but not the other four.

"Hi, Dick," Rob replied. "For a minute there, I thought we were going to need a little back-up, but we managed to scare them off."

"That was that Vic character, wasn't it?" one of the others asked rhetorically. "I wouldn't mess with him if I was you."

"Oh, I dunno! Maybe he just learned that he shouldn't mess with Turner and Williams. Eh, Craig?"

"Yeah!" Craig managed with a firm nod.

"Thanks for dropping by, guys," Rob said.

"Anytime," Dick said over his shoulder as they left.

There was silence between Rob and Craig for a moment. Then Rob said in a cold, angry tone, "Just what in the name of Jesus did you think you were doing?"

"What? I wasn't doing..."

"Shut up, stupid. You were yakking your big mouth off all over the school about what a jerk Vic is. Don't you think he's got spies. And the word was out that he was going to get you today. Didn't anybody tell you?"

"No!" Craig said with real alarm in his voice even though the situation had been diffused. "You mean they were going to beat me up?"

"They sure as hell weren't looking for you to invite you to a birthday party. I've been tailing you since you got out of your last class."

"Jeez, Rob! I didn't know!"

"Well, now you do. Let's get out of here."

They had started walking toward home when Craig stopped and said, "Aren't you supposed to have a class right now?"

"Yeah. To hell with it!"

They walked on. Craig finally broke a silence by saying, "I guess you won't be seeing much of Vic's crowd now."

"Who needs them? Who needs a bunch of kiss-asses when he's got a real, I mean a really real, good buddy." He gave Craig a hip-bump that nearly knocked him off the sidewalk and erased all the hurts and anxieties that he had been harbouring.

"Hey, Bev's working at the library tonight, and she says I can have the car between six and nine. Let's go out on the town. What d'ya say?"

Craig was so ecstatic to have his whole world back together again that he could only say falteringly, "I'll have to change my shirt."

*＊＊

On a Friday morning, Marion had settled herself in the nook with a cup of coffee, the superstore ads and her check book. She intended to spend the morning paying the monthly household bills and making a big shopping list. For too long, she thought, I have been buying things as I ran out instead of shopping properly and having a good stock on hand. She had settled into her pattern of three mornings a week at the hospital and enjoyed the routine. She was now beginning to recognize and talk to an increasing number of people on the staff so that even in the slack times there was always someone to chat with. Many incidents in the hospital, emergencies, dramatic surgical procedures or even the nursing station gossip about the private lives of some of the top specialists were worth remembering to entertain her friends in the bridge club at their weekly sessions. They always seemed to look forward to a couple of stories from her. But Craig was never very impressed by her hospital stories and his eyes began to glaze over now whenever she started 'Oh, I should tell you what happened at the hospital today.' So she stopped those attempts at conversation with him and stopped asking questions about school to which there were inevitably only monosyllabic answers. She moved a small television out to the kitchen and now they filled the dinner silence with news and game show noise. Craig was moody and unresponsive and she knew that something was wrong between him and Rob but she didn't want to pry. Craig had told her only that he and Rob had got entirely opposite schedules and that they would be lucky if they ever saw each other for the rest of the term. Maybe that was what was wrong with him and would explain his moodiness and the way he was hanging around home all the time. Maybe he missed having his father around, she thought, but before the thought was fully formed she discarded it as being totally preposterous. It did make her remember, however, that the last time Gerry came home he said his court case had been postponed for a month, she thought he said a month, so it must be anytime now.

The phone rang. "Tom!" she exclaimed when she had answered it. "How nice to hear from you."

They talked for a while about how much time it took, and how hard it was, to tidy up the lifetime affairs of someone you love. "But I think I'm pretty well through it now," he said.

"I was going to come over and give you a hand in doing that," she reminded him.

"Yes, I know and thank you, but I decided I'd better do it myself. Dad was pretty confused at the end and he was somewhat incontinent, and to complicate things more he got mixed up between laundry and clean clothes. So when I started to clean house, I found some very strange things tucked away in strange places." He laughed. "It's a good thing you weren't here."

"I wouldn't have minded," she said.

"Thanks anyway, Marion. But that's not the reason I called. I have to go to Seattle on the first weekend in October. There's a piece of equipment being demonstrated there that we're interested in, so the boss told me to go because it's in my line, sort of, and besides he said it was time for me to take a break. I thought that was good of him. He's a nice guy. Anyway, before I phone down for a reservation I got to wondering whether I should make it a single or a double." He paused.

She was slow in answering. "What do you mean?" she asked and at the same time she realized what he had said. "Oh!" she said. "Oh! I don't think I could. There's Craig and I have to be at the hospital on Saturdays and…"

"Anything that can't be postponed or changed, Marion?" he asked.

"No, not really." And she began to think more coherently. "Craig can certainly look after himself for a weekend and there's plenty of time for me to arrange an exchange with one of the other volunteers. Why can't I, Tom?"

"Why can't you what, Marion?"

"Why can't I say I want to go when I want to go?"

"So you'll go?"

"Yes, I sure will," she said emphatically.

"Okay," he said with equal emphasis and laughed. "I'm calling from the office right now, but I'll call you tonight. Is that OK?"

"I'll be here," she said and hung up feeling very excited.

Gerry was living on his boat and now that the weather was promising to get wetter and colder he was trying to force himself to start looking around for drier and warmer accommodation. Some time last night in a brief moment of coherent thought, he had made a decision to spend today searching for a room. But this morning, like most others mornings, when he threw back a tangle of covers and crawled out of the bunk, fully dressed with his shoes still on, he had only a vague recall of the previous night. Again this morning his head was a roaring battleground of misery. Not only the dull generalized hangover ache, although there was that too, but the other harsh, cold, deep pain, penetrating behind and above his left ear. It wasn't always there. Sometimes it appeared suddenly, making him wince and grit his teeth, a kind of twisting-dagger pain that shot through him and could not be hurried away by Tylenol or alcohol. It was a devil that took its own time in leaving—a devil he stubbornly refused to deal with except by dulling the whole world with booze.

He made himself a cup of instant coffee and was standing unsteadily in the cockpit when a tug went by too fast creating a wash that made his small twenty-two foot boat bob like a cork and set his stomach heaving. He roared a string of curses at the disappearing tug and checked over the side to see if his fenders were still holding. The owner of the next boat was working on deck and had turned his back as soon as Gerry started shouting, apparently unwilling to get caught up in any socializing with his obstreperous neighbour. But Gerry saw him and shouted, although the man was only fifteen feet away, "Hey, Mac! What day is it?" The shout twisted the daggers in his head and he had to put both hands to his head as he stood unsteadily trying to keep his balance on the bobbing deck. The man shouted "Friday" without turning around. Gerry staggered below, threw himself on the bunk and passed out again.

When consciousness returned, the sun was pouring through the top vent in the cabin. Remembering the shock of the pain that had sent him reeling to bed, he got gingerly to his feet and contemplated the possibility of a sudden return of agony should he move too quickly. The remainder of a bottle of rum was on the counter and half of the cup of coffee he had made hours ago. His mouth was dry and he chose the coffee but could not taste it for the foulness in his mouth. When the coffee hit his stomach, it rejected it violently and he threw up without warning. Covering his mouth with his fingers, with vomit squirting out between the openings, he rushed up to the deck and threw himself flat with his head hanging over the side, retching, hacking, drooling and spitting. When the heaves subsided and he raised his head, he saw that he was being watched without either amusement or concern by several other boaters. "Fuck off! You bunch of beady eyed vultures," he tried to shout as he crawled to his feet. None of the watchers could unravel the tangled words but understood the intent and they turned away, almost in unison, as he struggled painfully to his feet and stood for a minute glaring belligerently at their ignoring backs before he stumbled below. He sat down on the bench in the tiny nook that served as work table and eating area and laid his head on his sprawled arms, pushing off the table the collection of tools and condiments that were spread along the edges. I shouldn't still be drunk, he thought. I haven't had a drink since yesterday. He stayed there for a long time, occasionally trying to stand to one side and look at himself. But he could not tolerate what little the self-examination disclosed and so he dozed fitfully and during periods of lucidity he tried to make some plans. Tomorrow night, he decided, that's Saturday. I'll go home and have a shower and get some clothes. I hope the bitch isn't there. Then I'll just take it easy on Sunday and drive up so I'll be in time for court on Monday and get that goddam thing over with. Then there followed a long, bitter, detailed recall of the indignities he had suffered at the hands of the local police in that town, accompanied by colourful fantasies of violent revenge that were interrupted by flashing moments of insight when he pondered his own irrationality. Finally, he dropped exhausted into a deep, insensate sleep and the pain was gone.

Tom did call her that evening. She had been waiting anxiously for the call and was glad when Craig came home from school asking if they could have supper before six because Rob had Bev's car and they were going out.

"What happened to your new shirt?" she asked. "Come here and let me see it. How did you do that?"

"Oh, I was shooting hoops with a guy and he grabbed it," he lied. "Can you fix it? I kinda like it."

"I think so. Put it in the laundry. I'll get you something to eat but you'll have to eat alone—six is too early for me."

Rob arrived while Craig was eating, and sat down across the table from him. "Hey, you've got another new shirt on," he observed while fingering bits and pieces off Craig's plate.

"Yeah," Craig quickly filled in. "Some guy got too excited when we were shooting hoops and ripped my other one."

"Yeah? I told you. You shouldn't be playing with those big guys. Some of them are tough and mean, you know. You should stay away from them. You might get hurt. Ouch!"

Craig had given him a hard kick under the table, saying, "Knock it off!"

But Rob slid a little lower on the bench seat and put a foot across between Craig's legs out of Marion's sight and sat grinning and moving his foot back and forth in Craig's crotch. "Is Craig going to get dessert?" he called.

"I was going to give him an icing bun and ice cream. That's all I have. Do you want some?"

"Yes, please, UU," with dramatic enthusiasm. "Make mine bigger than Craig's because I have to drive the car and look after him and see he doesn't get into trouble so I need the energy."

"Poor boy!" Marion said bringing their desserts to the table. "What a terrible responsibility."

"You better give me half of yours," Rob said, taking his foot off Craig's seat and leaning across the table with his fork at the ready. "That's too much for you." All he received by way of answer was a jab on the back of his hand from Craig's fork.

Marion had watched and listened to them, warmed by their closeness and happy that the rift between them had been healed.

The phone rang and she was pleased to hear Tom's voice but said immediately, "I just finished getting the boys some dinner because they want to get away early," in order to indicate that anything other than social conversation would not be wise. She need not have worried. The desserts were finished in a hurry and they headed for the door, Craig calling back, "Say Hi to Edie for me. We won't be late." To which Rob added, "And we won't be good!"

"So I'm Edie tonight, am I?" asked Tom laughing.

"Not any more," Marion answered. "They've gone. We can talk now," also laughing quietly at their secrecy.

"Good. I just had an idea. You work tomorrow, don't you?"

"Yes, I do."

"How about I pick you up after work and we go for a long crazy drive and see if we can end up for dinner and maybe other things at our special motel?"

"But we're going next weekend to Seattle, aren't we?"

"Sure," he said. "But it wouldn't hurt to have a little practice session first."

In the end, it was agreed that he would pick her up at work and she would bring an overnight bag this time.

"When we go to Seattle we will be back in time for me to get to work, won't we?" she asked. "I work on Mondays, don't forget."

"We'll be back. I work Monday, too, you know."

"You work? I thought you were just a gigolo!"

"Marion!" he said. "You know I'm not after your money. I'm after your body."

They laughed together and said goodbye looking happily forward to tomorrow.

Rob had wanted to take the car out on the freeway and see how fast it would go, but Craig persuaded him not to and they had spent most of the evening driving around the streets of the suburbs where they lived.

"When are you going to get your licence?" Rob asked Craig when they had parked and gone into the mall.

"I dunno. Sometime, I guess. But I'm sure going to find a better instructor than old Stinkpot. 'Close the window! Close the window! How can you hear me with the window open' he mimicked. And I'm sitting there nearly throwing up from his BO."

They were sitting on a bench in the mall eating giant ice cream cones and watching people go by. Two guys and a girl from school were walking by and stopped to talk.

"Hey, you guys seen any girls around? We need another one," one of the boys asked.

"No, nothing but guys," Craig said.

"And they're looking for the same thing you're looking for," Rob added.

"Good luck to them! Where is everybody tonight?" one of them said.

The girl with them said, "I told you guys before. They're probably at home getting set for tomorrow."

"What's on tomorrow?" Rob asked.

"Big party at Max's. Didn't you hear about it?"

"No! We didn't hear a thing. BYOB?"

"Sure, and any spare smoke you've got, though Max said he made a good buy yesterday so there should be some there—but it won't be for free if I know Max."

"Are any parents going to be there?" Rob asked cautiously.

"No. They're on a cruise. Out in the middle of the ocean. How's that for luck?"

"Great!" Rob said. "C'mon, Craig. Let's move it."

"Yeah, great," Craig copied, but without the same enthusiasm. "Where are we going?"

"To pick up some booze for the party! What d'ya think?"

"Hey, before you go. You guys know that old man that has his junk in a shopping cart around the corner from the liquor store? Give him a buck and he'll get your bottle for you. They say you can get pot from him too, but I've never got him to sell me any."

"Okay! We'll give him a try. See you tomorrow night."

They found the old man and he was readily agreeable to buying them a bottle of Vodka, money up front. He came back with a bottle in a paper bag and passed it to them cautiously. "You shouldn't drink that Vodka crap. It's no good for ya! Rot your guts. I got you Scotch."

They had to take it from him without argument. Craig had a jacket with a pocket big enough to hide the bottle but its presence made him nervous. When they quietly asked the old man if he had any pot, maryjane, smoke, complete with pantomime, he stared at them, his ice-blue eyes narrowed and unblinking, until they got the message and walked away.

"Let's get out of here," Rob said. "We'll dump the bottle in your garage and then I gotta get over to the Library fast. I told Bev I'd be back for sure by nine."

"Yeah, okay," Craig said. "You let me out and I'll hide it. I'll see you tomorrow. I guess I gotta do some yard work tomorrow. Gonna give me a hand?"

"Are you kidding?"

They drove in silence to Craig's home. "Sounds like a great party, doesn't it? We should try to find a couple of girls to take. Whad'ya think?" Rob said.

Craig's response was not enthusiastic. "I guess we should. But maybe we left it too late."

"Yeah, maybe. See ya. Careful with that bottle."

Rob drove off and Craig, after hiding the bottle in the zipper pocket of an old golf bag, went into the house.

"Hi, Mom!" he called when he did not see her in the living room.

"Hello, dear!" she called. "I'm upstairs. I'll be down in a minute."

Craig was sprawled on the couch in the living room when she came down. "Was that you in the garage?" she asked. "I saw the light on and then a car drove away."

"You mean just a few minutes ago? Yeah, that was me and Rob. We were looking for something."

"What?" more for conversation than out of curiosity.

"I thought I had an old bicycle pump. His is broken," he lied. "I'll look for it tomorrow."

"You won't forget you promised to do the lawns tomorrow, will you?" she asked.

"No, I already told Rob we can't do anything because I have to do them."

Now it was time for her lie and she began to flush slightly in preparation for it. "You'll have to manage on your own tomorrow," she said. "I left a meat pie for you to heat up. It's a huge one full of veggies. And there's another one in the freezer if Robbie is here. Don't forget to lock up when you go to bed."

"Are you staying out all night?" he asked with his voice full of surprise.

"Oh, didn't I tell you? There's a bridge marathon going on downtown at the Oldbridge Hotel and you get to bid and play a hand with some visiting experts. So three of us are having a night out on the town."

"Oh, you devils, you!" he teased, taking it for granted that the other two were from her bridge group. But at the same time, his mind shifted into various alternatives: maybe if he and Rob got a couple of girls, they could come over here; maybe Rob would stay over; maybe they could have a party of their own. No, he had to reject that last idea—there'd be a bunch of rowdy free-loaders and they'd wreck the place.

Marion thought she had carried it off fairly well in spite of feeling flushed, although she knew Craig would never notice that anyway. The television had been on during their conversation with neither of them watching it. "That must be the last of the news," she said finally. "There's nothing now but the sports, so I think I'll go to bed." She yawned widely and got up. "Did you hear the weather?" she asked.

He yawned in sympathy while shaking his head.

"I hope it's a nice day for your gardening," she said. "Be sure to lock up. Goodnight, dear." He was still sprawled on the sofa so she blew him a kiss.

CHAPTER 33

Gerry wakened at three o'clock in the morning and switched on the light without fumbling for it or cursing the dark. He was fully dressed and remembered why. For the first time in weeks he could smell the stink of the cabin and himself, and the smell triggered muddled recollections of some of the events before he had passed out.

The ache in his head was only a routine hangover ache—gone was the penetrating grinding pain that at times, to stop from screaming, he had to push his fists so hard into his cheeks that he bruised himself. He was sober. He saw the rum bottle sitting on the ledge beside the sink and he knew there was enough left in it to jump start the day, but a gut-ache of hunger compelled him to pass it by and root around for food. He had never stocked such luxuries as bacon and eggs or anything that had to be cooked. On foul weather days, if he refused to go out to eat, he existed on canned meat and beans with bread if he had it. On this dark early morning, when his stomach griped for food, he found only sardines and two unwrapped pieces of bread that were so dry they crumbled. So he crushed them into a bowl, scraped the sardines over them, spilling some of the strong oil on his pants and the floor. He squirted the mixture with catsup and spooned it into himself without tasting it. Earlier he had been thinking clearly enough to put the kettle on to make coffee and wash up, but when the kettle whistled annoyingly at the boil he angrily turned it off. In his small galley, he could reach the stove and the sink from the small all-purpose nook and he leaned over to drop his bowl and spoon in the sink with the can. The twisting of his neck to perform that simple act set up a series of quick shooting of pains that he could recognize, now that he was as lucid as he had been for days, as the precursor to the daggers of pain in his head. "Jesus Christ!" he said aloud, holding his neck bent and stiff. "Here it comes again." His hunger appeased, his goal now was sleep—sleep that might defer the onset of that unpredictable and frightening pain. He got carefully to his feet, grabbed the rum bottle and tossed it onto the bunk and followed it. He kicked off his shoes and, after a struggle got out of his oil soaked pants. He tried to straighten the sheet and blankets but, in his stocking feet, he slipped on the oily floor, then after using his socks to wipe up the oil he threw the socks into a corner with his pants. Furious and exhausted, but as sober as he had been for many days, he crawled into the bunk and burrowed into the tumble of covers where nightmares tortured him until noon. But, at noon, trying to extricate himself from sleep and the tangle of bedclothes, he found the half bottle of rum which, without getting out of bed, he opened and finished.

Marion had been busy dusting and re-arranging the shelves when Cynthia came by and she was able to ask her if it was alright if she arranged for one of the other volunteers to exchange with her next Saturday.

"Why don't you ask Kathy?" Cynthia suggested, referring to her schedule. "She takes over from you at one o'clock, doesn't she? She told me she wouldn't mind working more hours while her husband is off on a six month course in England. You work it out and let me know."

That was easy, Marion thought. And I didn't know Kathy's husband was away on a course. I wonder why she hasn't said anything. Of course, I haven't said anything to her about my husband being away either—or why.

The morning passed quickly and as one o'clock was nearing she was glancing at her watch waiting anxiously for both Tom and Kathy. They happened to arrive at the same time, coming into the shop as if they were a couple. Marion greeted them both and felt required to introduce them. Kathy agreed readily to cover for Marion on the following Saturday which Tom overheard and remarked slyly, "Well, that's great. That clears the way for us."

Marion blushed at his remark while she was thanking Kathy and turning over the cash and sales record. As she came out from the stockroom wearing her coat and carrying a small bag, Tom again said, this time with a wide roguish grin, "Oh, good. You brought your overnight bag this time."

"Tom!" she scolded as they walked away, her face blushing red, "You shouldn't say things like that!"

"Oh, don't you think they know?" he asked innocently, taking her arm as they walked toward the door.

"Of course they don't know! I mean, I hope they don't know. Oh, Tom," she said, laughing, "I don't think I care if anybody knows."

"Atta girl," he said.

They drove out of the city enjoying the nearby farmlands, the closer hills and the distant mountains on the warm late September afternoon with the trees everywhere in the countryside seeming to be poised waiting for the first frost to make them burst into rich colors.

"Next week," they agreed. "Next week it will be gorgeous!"

They talked easily, touching many topics lightly, agreeing for the most part and able to listen to the other's point of view without endeavouring to make a change. They stopped for coffee at a wayside cafe that boasted of its coffee in dozens of signs along the way, and wandered through a small art gallery in which the artist reluctantly left his easel to welcome them and was oblivious to their presence when they stood to one side and watched him at work. A small gymkhana in an open field beside the road thrilled them for an hour until a small girl took a bad fall and the competition stopped to await the arrival of the ambulance. That event upset them both and put a strain on their conversation for many miles.

When the light was beginning to fade and the clouds in the western sky gave promise of a sunset, Tom asked, "Are we ready to head out for our motel?"

"I think so," Marion answered. "I'm famished. Do you know where it is?"

"I'm pretty sure I do!" Tom said. "We've been sort of circling it all afternoon. We have to look for that huge water tower and turn south there on Route 87 or 89, I'm not sure which but I'll know when we come to it."

Marion was content to sit back and let him find his way. In ten minutes, they could see the water tower in the distance and in another twenty minutes they turned into the driveway of the motel.

"How's that for navigating?" Tom asked.

"Just like a homing pigeon," she said.

He made no move to get out of the car for a moment, but turned to her and said, "Would you like me to register first so you can take your bag to the room and freshen up before dinner?"

"Good idea," she said without a pause, knowing that the answer would commit her.

He went alone to register and returned shortly to drive around to the west side of the motel and park. "I asked for a room on the west side so we could see the sunset," he said.

***

Craig had worked hard in the garden, mowing and doing the edges. He could almost hear his father's voice nagging him as he worked—'Try to keep those edges straight this time. Don't use twine for a line. Put a 2X4 down and cut along it. Make sure your edger is sharp. You can't do a proper job with a dull tool.' He took the half-moon shaped edger into the basement workroom and started the grinder. When he put the edger to the grinder, without glasses on, he did so carelessly and when the edger caught hard against the wheel it threw out a cascade of sparks and a sliver of metal flew up and stuck in the corner of Craig's eyeball. For a brief moment he was blinded, but the tears started to flow and he found he could open the other eye and see, but the injured eye twitched so badly he could not keep it open. Trying to see it in the bathroom mirror was useless, so, as always when his mother was not at home, the emergency took him straight to the Turner's.

Craig walked in without shouting because he heard the noise of the collator and found Rob working. "Where's your mother," he said when Rob stopped the machine. Then, seeing Craig's streaming eyes, he said, "She's not home. What's wrong?"

Craig explained briefly and Rob steered him over to the strong light by the window and grabbing his head with both hands, said, "Now hold still while I take a look!"

"Okay," he said in a minute, letting go of Craig's head. "There's something in there alright. Not as big as a toothpick but a little bit bigger than the 'i' in eyeball. Do you want me to take it out or call 911?"

"What d'ya mean? There is no 'i' in eyeball."

"There isn't? Well, shit! I bet they're going to make me take readin' and ritin' and rithmatic all over again. Well, do you want me to or do you just want me to hug you and make the hurt go away."

"Go ahead!" Craig said.

"Which one? I gave you a choice—doctor or lover?"

"Take the goddamn thing out and stop horsing around."

"Okay, come here, then." He got Craig's head in a good light by the window and pushed his head against the frame. "Hold it just like that so you don't jerk away when I touch your eyeball." He pried open Craig's eyelids and, using his thumb and fingernails, neatly yanked out a small piece of steel.

"There!" he exclaimed. "All done."

Craig stood with his eyes streaming. "Do you think I should go to the hospital?"

"Let me put it this way. I'm not going to take you and I'm not going to call an ambulance. If you do go, don't give them my name because I don't want a bunch of people coming around for my autograph."

"Do you think I should wash it out?" Craig asked, anxiously.

"Good idea! The little thing I took out was probably clean but just before you came I was in the bathroom playing with myself and I didn't wash my hands—you know how it is. You'll probably come down with some social disease and your eyeball will always be red just like it gets red when you jerk off."

"Oh, Rob! For God's sake!"

They were sitting out on the back steps with the first rays of the evening sun beginning to colour up the clouds and a long silence developed between them.

"Rob?"

"What?"

"I gotta ask you something." Craig sat still and quiet for a moment wiping the tears from his eyes. Rob said nothing. "You know, after we got back from the lake, what was wrong? You know, between you and me?

"What do you mean?"

"I mean did I say something or do something. You wouldn't do anything with me and you hardly talked to me. You've been hanging out with Vic and that gang. I didn't know what was wrong. And then, yesterday, there you were— just when I needed you. And it was like it always was." Now there were tears of emotion mixed with the other healing tears and the voice was uncertain.

Rob was silent for a long time and then let out a long shaky breath. "It wasn't you, Craig. It was me. I didn't know what to do. I was getting afraid— you know—we were so close, such good buddies—better than buddies—but I thought maybe we shouldn't be, you know, so close. And I thought maybe I should try to get a girl friend but I really didn't want one when we were, you know..." His voice trailed off. "I thought maybe, you know, that I was getting queer—like being a homo. And then with all the girls that hang around in that crowd of Vic's I couldn't even get a good hard on thinking about screwing them but I can if I let myself think of you."

"Me, too," Craig said.

"What d'ya mean—me, too?"

"Well, I been thinking lately...well, that maybe..., you know! Maybe I'm getting that way too. It's not like it was when we were doing it when we were little kids, but it's different now and I want it to be the same as it was when we were kids, but it can't be, can it?"

"I don't know, Craig." Rob's voice was shaky and his eyes were brimming with tears.

"Maybe we should stop being best friends."

"No!" Rob almost shouted. "You're my buddy and my best friend and you always have been and I'll tell you something else, you always will be and you can't do a goddammed thing about it. And I'll tell you one more thing. There's no girl can ever be closer to me than you—and that don't make me no freakin' homo!"

"Me, too," said Craig.

"What the shit does that mean?"

"You know!"

They both laughed cautiously at the sight of the other, both with eyes that were brimmed with tears and spilling. Then they roared with laughter because they had cleared the air, but this time the most they permitted themselves was to press against each others shoulders as they sat in the growing dusk.

Finally Craig said, "Hey, I gotta go home and get my supper and get ready for the party.'"

"Okay."

"Where's your Mom?" Craig asked. "You gonna eat?"

"Yeah, I guess so."

"Better come over. My Mom put something out for you."

"Arf! Arf!"

"Good dog! See ya! Get dressed—it's a party."

Rob got up slowly and went inside, closing the door softly behind him and with his head leaning against the door jamb and the tears pouring down his cheeks, said softly,, "Craig! Oh, Craig!" And, as always, his tears were private, always private.

***

After Tom had registered they settled quickly into the room and went out on the tiny balcony of their room to watch the sunset sweep across the sky. Tom had brought a bottle of Scotch and he was inside pouring drinks for them. Sitting alone, she suddenly felt very exposed on the balcony of a strange hotel in the middle of the hinterlands. What if somebody should drive by and recognize me. I wonder how many other people in this motel are here for the same reason we are. Everybody, I'll bet. Why else would they stop here. It's perfect—a quiet, secluded little hideaway designed for a man to bring his mistress. Mistress! Good God! Is that what I am?

Tom came out onto the balcony with a drink in each hand. "There you are, madam," he said, handing her one and faking an English accent. "Sorry! My silver tray is out being polished."

"Thank you, Sir Thomas. You may be seated."

He took her hand and, bending a knee, kissed it like a courtier.

She laughed and said, "You know, I've often wondered if, when people talked like that, so elegantly, so little-finger-sticking-out sort of talk, how did they ever get into bed?"

"Oh, probably the king said something like, 'Hey, lady! I'm hot tonight! Wouldst thou care to fornicate avec moi?' They spoke a lot of French, too, you know—to go along with the french kissing, and the french cuffs. And she would probably say 'Pate de foie gras' which means, if I remember my high school French, 'Don't ruffle my petticoats'."

They watched the sunset, saw wild and ghostly beasts in the tumbling clouds and laughed happily together. People walking past on their way to the restaurant had smiled privately, enjoying their happiness. Then, finishing their drinks, they went inside and made exciting love for an hour before they mutually decided that food was necessary too.

When they came into the dining room, the waitress remembered them and smiling, shook hands with them. "Glad to see you again," she said.

"We couldn't drive by without stopping at our favourite spot," Tom said.

"I'll just check on the special and bring you the wine list," the waitress said as she seated them in a quiet spot.

During dinner they talked about the weekend in Seattle and what they might do. Tom would have to spend a full morning with the engineering company but after that he would be free. Marion insisted that just one morning of shopping wouldn't be enough for any woman and Tom was agreeable to accompanying her. He might even do a little shopping himself—a tie or a pair of socks. "What a spendthrift!" she declared. "You already have a pair of socks." It wasn't a big joke but enough to smile about and maintain the light mood that had been a constant throughout their day. They did not drink as much this time as the time before because they knew exactly what they were going to do, so after their leisurely meal, they walked arm in arm around the small garden of the motel and then went back to their room and made love again.

***

It was a great party, as far as the participants were concerned. The neighbour next door did not share that view and had reported the noise to the police who had driven by and stopped to check. Just at that time most of the party had gone down to the rumpus room to watch a porn video so the ghetto blaster noise was minimal. The police logged the neighbour's call as a grump call.

The porn video, which had been talked about quietly as being really far-out and exciting, proved to be so blatantly obscene and sexually explicit that many of the adolescents, whose wildest day-dreams were bedtime stories by comparison, felt physically repulsed. The video had a dampening effect on most of the participants. The music still played and some people danced but the punch, made in the usual way by everybody dumping his or her contribution in a huge bowl with a block of ice, became the central gathering point.

"Jesus," Craig said to Rob when they met at the punch bowl, "that was some video, wasn't it? I nearly threw up."

Rob had walked up with a girl but Craig did not know they were together until the girl said casually, "Hell, I've seen worse ones than that."

"You have?" Craig said disbelievingly.

"This is Donna, Craig," Rob said.

"Hi!"

"Hi!" simultaneously.

"People don't really do that kind of stuff, do they?" Craig's voice was almost falsetto in his disbelief. He drained his glass and refilled it.

"Hey, Craig! Grow up, for shit's sake. Those weren't puppets, you know," Donna said. "Probably they weren't even actors. Some of these people do it just because they get their kicks knowing that people can watch them."

"Kinky!" Craig said in disgust.

"How about them three guys all doin' it to each other at the same time?" somebody said behind them.

"Yeah, how the hell did they do that?"

"Ask old lady Monroe next time you have Socials—she'll tell you!" And there was loud laughter at the thought.

"I gotta get something to eat," Craig said, getting another glass of punch. "This stuff is making me thirsty. See ya." He wandered off in search of food but couldn't find any so returned to the punchbowl but Rob had disappeared. He helped himself to another glass of punch and thought that maybe he might be getting a little drunk.

Rob found him half an hour later, slouched on a chair, his eyes half shut holding tight to his glass of punch.

"Hey, man! You're pissed!" Rob said. "Want me to take you home?"

"I can go be myself," Craig responded disdainfully, getting clumsily to his feet.

"I better go with him," Rob said to Donna.

"You got a girl now," Craig said with a giggle. "You gotta go home with her." He turned and ambled away not quite staggering.

"Well, you heard him," Donna said as they watched him go down the steps and turn in the direction of home, "you gonna come home with me?"

***

Gerry had to pry open his eyes when he wakened in the late afternoon just as other people were standing in awe watching the colourful display of a setting sun whose magnificent colors were splashing across half the western sky. He had thrown up on his pillow in his sleep and his eyes were stuck almost closed with vomit and it was in his hair and was now adding to the foul smell of the fish oil he had spilled on himself and on the floor. Not that those two odours were alone in competing for olfactory attention. His small boat offered no washing facilities other than a sink designed to deal with a minimum of dishes. Right now, the sink was piled to overflowing and every dish and utensil was caked with the detritus of other meals. He needed water so he lifted the dishes in casual bunches out of the sink and put them on the floor. The first bend was nearly his undoing, the inside of his head behind his ear pounded with pain and sent him reeling to the table where he sat, head on fists, waiting for the torment to stop. This time it passed more quickly but he resisted making any sudden or demanding movement. He examined his tongue in a small mirror and found it so hard-caked he could not scrape if off with his teeth and spit it out. He climbed up on deck and coughed and hacked and spit until the neighbour shouted "Get a roto-rooter, for God's sake!" He started to roar an obscene response but the first shouted word kick-started his head.

Gradually some coherent plans emerged. If he washed his face and combed his hair, he could walk along the floating dock to his car. He had no clean clothes left but he searched among the pile of dirty clothes for something that was not vile with food or vomit or dirt. One clean, but wrinkled, white shirt found under the mattress did nothing to offset the picture presented by filthy mismatched socks, golfing slacks and a denim jacket—both heavy with grime— canvas shoes and a toque. But more than the clothes and the scent of foulness, it was the whiskered face whose lines and creases drew attention to bloodshot eyes with lower lids drooping to show the half-moon of red inside the lids.

He climbed out of the boat and walked unsteadily along the floats until he climbed the steep ramp out of the marina to the parking lot. It was not the physical appearance alone that made people move to one side as they met him on the street, it was the look of cold malevolence that kept people at a distance. He was still driving an unfamiliar lease car and he had trouble remembering what make and colour it was. He found one that looked like his and tried the key only to have someone shout rudely "Hey! What are you doing over there?" He looked around to see the face of a belligerent man approaching, and he tried discretion: "Sorry, I thought it was mine."

"Yeah, sure," the man said looking Gerry up and down.

The surly response triggered an automatic angry response in Gerry that he could feel in a pounding heart, in his shaking hand and in the little darts of pain high on his neck that signalled the big one was coming. He turned and walked away being watched suspiciously by the other man and when he found his car and opened the door he turned and gave the other guy the big finger.

The proprietors of the Chinese restaurant he went to were not offended by Gerry's appearance or smell. They required only that the money for the meal was on the counter before the food was touched. According to the gnawing pain in his gut, Gerry thought he was hungry and he ordered a huge breakfast in spite of the fact that it was growing dark outside. He found that he could eat less than half of what was on his plate and, having learned some street courtesies during the past weeks, he slid the unfinished plate over to the man on the next stool.

When he drove up to the house, Marion's car was in the garage but the there were no lights on in the house. She can't have gone to bed yet—it's too early, he thought. He unlocked the door and stepped cautiously inside. He did not know why he was being so cautious, except that he did not want another confrontation or any other kind of upset that would start his head pounding.

He went back to the door and slammed it closed and waited inside for any response it might create, but there was none. Looking around the kitchen, he saw a note on the frig. 'Don't forget to lock the doors and turn off the lights XO Mom.' So, he said to himself she's away for the night. I wonder who she found that would be willing to sleep with her. Then, knowing that there was going to be no showdown, he went to the liquor cabinet and taking a bottle of Vodka, he headed upstairs. Halfway up the stairs, he stopped and unscrewed the cap and tasted the contents. Satisfied that it had not been watered down, he continued up to the master bedroom. There, he stripped and stuffed his foul clothes into the hamper, thinking as he did so, That will put the wind up her ass when she sees that mess. He shampooed his hair and showered, then filled the tub with hot water and lay soaking, feeling some of the aches disappear, trying not to drift off to sleep.

When the water cooled off he got out and dried himself, used Marion's brush and comb leaving them in another location so she would know and be angry about it, and also her powder and deodorant, then went in search of clean clothes. Passing the triple mirror in the bedroom, he stopped to examine himself. He had not been to the gym for a long time, nor had he eaten sensibly and he had certainly overindulged in alcohol and it all showed in the figure of an aging man—particularly his face! Migod, look at me, he said to himself. I'm a goddam mess! He turned the mirrors to look at his back and gave his whole body a close examination from every angle, convincing himself that the tan lines had disappeared, that his shanks were droopy and that the body he had groomed throughout his life was disintegrating. He found his bathrobe in the closet and, having covered up the original of that image he had seen in the mirror, began looking further for clothes. But he sat on the edge of the bed with his back to the mirrors and had a long drink of vodka, straight from the bottle without the slightest choke, and sitting there, thought for a long time of the many nights he had lain beside her, wanting something sexual from her and all she gave was her permission. Permission! For Christ's sake! Finally, he roused himself and found some clothes; some to wear tomorrow and the next day in court, and some boat clothes.

Here I am right in this room, this room in which I begat two children, he said to himself. Begat! Such a nice word! So much more conversational than fucking! But fucking is primary and begatting, or whatever the word is, is secondary. Thank god you don't begat every time, otherwise you'd begat yourself out of your begatting bed. And this time he did choke and splutter when he had another swallow of vodka while laughing at his own joke. He tried to recall, without straining, any event in this room that was worth remembering and he couldn't think of one except perhaps the mirrors he had made. That was a good job he did on those, he told himself and then he heard a door close noisily downstairs and Craig's voice saying "Oops!"

Turning out the bedroom lights he left the door open a crack to watch the stairs. Craig came to the stairs and plodded up them, muttering, "I locked the door and I turned out the lights and I got seven more steps to—sh-h!" He watched Craig turn at the top of the stairs and go to his room touching the wall for support. Minutes passed and Gerry continued to watch and listen. Suddenly, Craig raced out of his room to the bathroom and sounds of retching emerged. He's drunk, Jerry said to himself, I thought he was when he stumbled up the stairs. He heard the toilet flushing and watched as Craig emerged and stumbled down the hall to his room wearing only his shorts. Gerry closed the door to his own room softly and lay on the bed waiting to make sure Craig was asleep so he could get dressed and leave. He thought of how Craig had looked in the dim light of the hall. He seemed taller and slimmer with broader shoulders, and good ridges of muscle across his belly where only a short time ago he had little rolls of baby fat and he obviously had an attractive package in his shorts. Thinking about it, Gerry could feel his gut straining against an erection.

Waiting a few minutes more to make sure Craig was either asleep or passed out, he went quietly down the hall to the door of Craig's room that had been left open. The window blinds had not been closed and there was enough light from the street lamp to see clearly in the room. Craig lay sprawled on his back on the bed, one knee bent and laid sideways and the opposing arm half dangling off the side of the bed. Gerry stood watching for a few moments, his own gut straining, and he heard Craig's quiet moans and saw his body making small coital pushes. He went softly into the room and, moving the chair close to the bed, sat open-legged with his bathrobe undone looking down at a boy again, not really seeing his son. Quietly, gently, he took the boy's dangling arm and he drew it over onto his lap and wrapped the limp fingers around his own pulsing penis. Then carefully reaching over, he pulled down Craig's shorts and exposed his genitals with its curly blond hair and a slim, strong erect penis with the hardness of youth. He took it in his hand and moved it gently and leaned over and blew on it. Craig emitted a small groan and squeezed hard around the thing in his hand. Then the dream, that had been a highly personalized extension of the night's porno video, finished and Craig held his breath and let out a whimpering sound. His knees came together and up to his belly, bumping his father's head. The hand that had been placed around his father's penis jerked away to grab at his own genitals but found his father's hand instead and there was a tangle and bumping of arms that, with the climax in the dream and in reality brought Craig fully awake.

He sat up in bed, groggily staring without immediate recognition at the nude figure beside his bed. Then, yanking his under-wear up and grabbing a handful of sheet, he attempted to cover himself as he squeaked, "What are you doing?"

"Nothing," his father said abruptly, getting to his feet and pulling his bathrobe together. "You were dreaming."

Craig stared at him in horror. "You were..! You were..!" And the words seemed to stick in his throat. "You were giving me a blowjob!"

"Don't be stupid!" his father retorted turning to leave.

"You dirty, filthy, rotten bastard! You were going down on me and I woke up! Jesus Christ! What a father! Get out and leave me alone."

"Craig," Gerry said wearily, wiping his face with his hand and ending up almost scrubbing his lips.

"Now you're wiping my come off your mouth so there won't be any evidence."

"Evidence!" Gerry roared, turning around in the doorway to face Craig. "What's all this shit about evidence? Who did what to whom? Who does what to whom when you and lover boy Rob get together and lick dicks. You pair of fruitcakes! So don't give me any evidence crap! Remember, I'm older and smarter and tougher and a hell of a lot meaner than you. Your mother should have told you that! Where is she anyway? Out whoring around someplace?" He turned and stalked down the hall to his room.

Craig leaped out of bed trembling with fear and rage. He slammed the door and propped the chair back against it. "Pervert!" he shouted. "God damned pervert! Fucking molester!" Then he rummaged in the closet and grabbed an old tenpin, then sat on the edge of his bed listening and shaking with many emotions and periodically shouting threats.

Gerry heard Craig's door slam behind his own closed door. He had the shakes again, partly rage, partly booze and partly the same pulsating trembles he had whenever he thought of Ronnie, the young male prostitute from Celia's. He picked up the bottle from the bed and found he had not tightened the cap and the bottle was empty and the bed wet. Hurling the bottle into the corner of the room he waited for a splintering crash, but the folds of the drapes caught the bottle and it fell unbroken to the floor. He moved to get it and throw it again but caught sight of himself in the mirror, naked under his bathrobe, hair uncombed and hanging over his glowering face, with his lower jaw seeming to be pushed out of human shape. He stopped and stared at the apparition, unable to take his eyes off the awful image. Then slowly he dressed in the clothes he had put out, rolled the second set of clothes untidily together and quietly left the room and went downstairs. He did not even glance at Craig's door, but he stopped for a moment before he went out the door and heard the last of the threat ..."if you even come near me!" and closed the door on it, the last time he would hear his son's voice.

CHAPTER 34

When Gerry left the house he was at least thinking clearly enough to know that, having bathed and shaved and found clean clothes, he should not go back to the boat. As he drove out of the city onto the freeway he had some fleeting feelings of remorse about what had happened with his son, but by the time he reached the edge of another town where he found a liquor store, a cafe and a motel those feelings had disappeared and were replaced by an annoyance that he had been enticed by his son's sexuality. He settled into a drab motel room and went out to eat, picking up a local paper along the way. He had never had any interest in small town newspapers and this one seemed worse than most. Within its skinny pages he could find neither movie notices nor a TV schedule. The headline story concerned itself with water rights, and covered most of the front page. Two inside pages were filled with pictures of brides and grooms each one coiffed and gowned or suited for the wedding picture that would sit on their mantel until the picture of their first child would supplant it. He was in for another long, lonely night, but, he thought, I'm getting dammed used to long, lonely nights and I'm not too sure that I don't prefer them to inane chatter at home, in bars or on the TV.

When his dinner came, served indifferently by a gum-chewing adolescent, it looked gray and colourless—not much different than some of the concoctions he would stir up for himself on the boat rather than go out to eat. He tried to eat some of what was on his plate but his stomach rebelled and the rebellion turned into anger and the anger started the pain in the side of his head. He rested his cheekbones against his fists with this elbows on the table hoping the pain would go away, and closed his eyes.

"Sir?" the waitress said at his elbow. "Is there anything wrong with your dinner?" Her voice was quiet and tentative and she stood nervously watching him.

"No!" he said gruffly. "Take it away. I'm not hungry. Just bring me some coffee."

He swallowed a couple of Tylenols while waiting for the coffee and when it came he drank it down in large gulps, paid his bill and left. Back at the motel, he undressed and crawled into a sagging bed, with the bathroom tumbler half full of scotch and the TV turned on.

Traffic noises and church bells wakened him in the morning and he found himself still on top of the bed with the TV picture flopping and the bottle empty. He had a tolerable hangover but the other pain, the grinding pain on the left side of his head that made him grit his teeth, was gone. The mirror in the bathroom told him that he was grey-faced and baggy eyed, but better, really, than a score of other mirrored confrontations he'd had with himself over the past weeks. He shaved and dressed hurriedly and, not ready yet to face food, set out for his date in court.

The court house was an old and dignified building set back on a side street of the town and surrounded by maples, now, in the final days of September, in their full blaze of colour. The marble steps leading up to the entrance was slippery with fallen leaves and a caretaker with a leaf blower was attempting to clear the way. The shrill whine of the machine seemed to penetrate into the core of Gerry's head and the casual hangover he had been guarding had turned into an agonizing, pounding pain that forced him to sit, head in hands, on a bench around a maple tree on the lawn waiting for the pain to subside. A half hour later, he got gingerly to his feet and after making his way up the steps of the court house, he found the door locked. In a fury he shook the locked door violently and cursed it. The caretaker watching him, turned off the shrieking machine and called over "It's all locked up, mister!"

"Why? For Crissake," Gerry shouted at him in an ugly tone.

The old caretaker, offended by the tone, shouted back, "Because it's Sunday! Asshole!" and turned on the blower while standing looking defiantly at Gerry.

Gerry stood, now trembling with anger, looking at the day and date on his watch, cursing his stupidity and whatever other fates seemed to be joining in opposition against him. He walked back to the parking lot, wondering why he had not noted its emptiness when he arrived. Then, sitting in the warmth of the closed car, the shakes subsided and a decision emerged: Get out of this god-forsaken town before one of its smartass cops recognizes me, then find a motel and get a bottle and hole up until tomorrow.

When tomorrow came, a telephone in a motel room wakened him and a cheerful voice called out, "Seven o'clock, Mr. Williams!" He squinted hard at his watch, saw that it was Monday and hung up without a response. The cover on a match book gave him the name and address of the motel, half empty cartons of Chinese food told him he must have eaten and slowly the pieces of yesterday came into focus. He tried some of the cold Chinese food for breakfast but gagged on it. Then after finishing the last four ounces of rum he left in time to get to court early.

The parking lot was crowded and the steps had been blown clear of fallen leaves. He opened the door and stepped inside to a confusion of sounds that pounded into his head as hard as the whine of yesterday's blowers. At the information desk, inside the main entrance, a female officer, who reminded him so much of one of the girls at Celia's that he began to feel horny and wondered for a moment if she was worth a try, told him to proceed immediately to Courtroom D.

A couple of months ago, Gerry could have handled the noise and apparent confusion of a busy court house without panic. Today, the people rushing by, the hushed conferences and angry arguments going on around him, combined with the uncertainty of what might happen to him aggravated his shakes. At the entrance of Courtroom D he approached a police officer with a clipboard who seemed to be in charge of directing people to other locations. "This is Courtroom D, isn't it, Officer?" he asked.

"Yes, sir. Have you business scheduled in this Court?"

"Yes," Gerry answered. "I was ordered to appear here this morning."

"What name?" The officer had dropped the 'sir' and turned his head away from Gerry's breath.

"Williams, Gerald Williams."

The officer ran his pencil down the list of names on his clipboard, his lips moving as he read. "Yeah, okay, Williams. Here you are. Judge Overton was scheduled for this court today but he was admitted to hospital last night so all his cases have been reassigned. You are to appear in Courtroom F at two o'clock but there's a note here that says you should see the prosecutor first."

"What for?"

"I don't know. That's all it says. See the prosecutor!"

"Where is he?"

"She! Down the stairs and turn right."

Gerry turned away and as he left the officer rolled his eyeballs and blew out a long breath while waving his hand in from of his face. Gerry did not see him but some other bystanders did and laughed. He heard their laughter and turned around. He saw some people smirking at him and his anger flared and then his head started to pound again.

The prosecutor was a short, amazingly skinny young woman, with long black hair wound in a pigtail that hung down to a milk bottle size waist adorned with a huge silver buckle on a thick leather belt holding up oversize jeans. Half her small face, unadorned by make-up, was covered by glasses the size of headlights. She was speaking on the telephone when he first saw her and he was so intrigued by her tiny mouth and pursed lips he did not realize that she had finished on the telephone and had addressed him.

"Yes?" she had said abruptly.

When he had not answered immediately, she continued, "Did you wish to see me?"

"Yes," he finally said, and told her how he had been sent.

"Are you being represented by counsel."

"No."

"Then you intend to plead guilty. Is that correct?" The voice, coming from the diminutive mouth, was surprisingly strong and contrasted sharply with the huge watery blue eyes behind thick lenses.

"No, I am not going to plead guilty."

"You said you do not have a lawyer. Are you going to represent yourself?"

"Yes."

"Mr. Williams, let me give you a word of advice." The watery blue eyes floated behind the lenses like bubbles in a fishbowl. "Judge Gerhardt does not like people holding up court procedures when they try to defend themselves. She gets very irritable. And nine times out of ten, the case is put aside for a couple of months and the accused is warned to prepare his defence properly so as not to waste the court's time. Now, we can drop a couple of these lesser charges and keep the DWI and dangerous driving, and you plead Guilty and we can be out of court in five minutes. However, if you choose to plead Not Guilty, I can tell you right now that you're in for a rough time and she'll throw the book at you. Do you get what I'm saying?" She stood looking at him and waiting.

"So? Guilty and maybe $200 and lose your license for six months or do you want to buck the system?"

He glared at her, his anger mounting and his head pounding. "Fuck you and the system!" he said.

"Noted!" she replied, turning away. "Two o'clock."

At two o'clock, he was in the courtroom. He had spent the time dozing in his car in the warm late September sun and dawdling over a club sandwich and a Bloody Mary. It had been hard to make the drink last but he was determined to keep his wits about him in court. The courtroom was warm and most of what went on was dull and incomprehensible to him. At 3:20 PM he heard his name called and squeezed past some spectators and made his way to the front. As he was doing so, the court clerk was reading his name and the list of charges against him. The judge was listening intently to the varied charges. She was a woman of about fifty, with a large head of grey hair untidily sitting on top of an ample frame. Her eyes were the colour of ice. She read the documents in front of her and then, without looking up, asked in a monotone, "How do you plead?"

He said nothing.

She looked up and tilted her head toward him as if she were wearing glasses. "You! Mr. Williams! How do you plead."

"Oh!" he replied, startled by the direct question. "Me? Not guilty."

"You are pleading Not Guilty to each and every one of these charges, Mr. Williams?" There was no warmth in her eyes or voice.

"Yes."

The judge looked at him for a long moment and then beckoned to the DA to approach. "I expect you have already advised this man?" she asked.

"Yes, Your Honour."

"He prefers to stay with the original charges?"

"Yes, Your Honour."

"Did he tell you that he intended to act as his own counsel?"

"Yes, Your Honour."

"You have heard what the prosecutor and I have been saying, Mr. Williams. Have you anything to add?"

"What about?"

"Did the District Attorney not inform you that this court cannot possibly take time today to hear you argue your defence against all these charges?"

"Yes, she did. But I don't see why I can't. I was told to come today at ten o'clock and I was here, on time. Furthermore I was expecting a man on the bench, not a woman."

"Oh, I see, Mr. Williams. You think a man would have benefited you somehow?"

"Yes."

"Did you not notice, Mr. Williams, during your time in court as an observer, that some people have either the courtesy or the intelligence to remember that the bench is usually addressed with some form of courtesy."

"Yes."

The judge lowered her head and appeared to examine something on her desk for a long silent time. Finally she looked up and with her cold, icy eyes looking directly at him, said, "My calendar tells me that I am free to hear your case on December the 10th at ten o'clock in the morning in this very courtroom. You will be here, Gerald Williams! Preferably with counsel to represent you. Bailiff, escort this man from my court and when he is gone, we will enjoy a five minute recess."

The bailiff took Gerry firmly by the arm and marched him to the door with the judge's eyes following very step of the way. When the door closed, she announced, "Five minutes, exactly—no more!" and swept out of the room.

* * *

Normally, a good night's sleep for Craig was evidenced by the tangle of bedclothes when he wakened. But, shaken by fear and anger from last night's encounter with his father, he had lain flat on his back throughout the night, staring at the ceiling and watching the occasional flashes of car lights flick through the room, certain that each car was bringing his father back to renew his unbelievable attack on him. He had rushed down once to make sure the doors were locked and bolted and then again to undo the bolts in case his mother changed her mind about staying overnight at the bridge convention. He had wanted to stay awake to protect himself or to let her in, but there had been dreams, terrifyingly real, dreams that startled him out of his sleep and locked his turmoil back into consciousness.

When he finally forced himself to get up and dressed it was almost noon. Going downstairs in the quiet house, he walked softly, peering around corners, half expecting his father to be lying in wait, ready to attack him again. All the while his mind raced through the puzzle of what had happened. Had his father done it to him before when he was sound asleep and didn't know about it? What if his father had done it to him many times and he had never wakened and thought it was all a dream? He wolfed down a bowl of cereal for breakfast and left the house, locking it securely, determined not to go back inside until his mother got back and took some of the eeriness away. He spent the day riding his bike around to other parks away from his neighbourhood, not wanting to run into anybody he knew, not even Rob—not yet.

Marion arrived back shortly after Craig had gone. Checking around the house, it seemed to her that he hadn't spent much time at home. There was a sour smell upstairs that she couldn't figure out so she opened his window wide and let it air. Opening the door to the master bedroom, she was struck more forcibly by the smell, and searching around found the source of the odour that was polluting the whole of the second floor—the bundle of fouled clothes Gerry had stuffed in the hamper. The discovery made her shake with anger. Why would he do such a filthy thing? He must be living in squalor, she thought. Whatever had happened to the fastidious man who had even liked his socks ironed and folded flat? She opened his clothes cupboard and noticed that more of his clothes were missing. Searching further, she found the Vodka bottle in the corner of the room and a wet stain on the bedspread. Damn him! she said to herself. How dare he sneak in here and turn my home into a pigsty! She went downstairs and got her rubber gloves from the kitchen and dumped the bundle of stinking clothes into a trash bag and took them out to the garbage can. Her anger was flaring. She stood in the master bedroom and asked herself why, in the name of common sense, was she putting up with Edith's narrow bed and tiny room? Why wasn't she using her own room? And right then, not even having changed out of her good clothes, she started reorganizing the room. With her arms full of his clothes that had been hanging in the closet, she went to the basement and hung them without care in the spare closet. She brought up two large boxes and emptied everything out of his drawers but found the full boxes too heavy to move alone, so she dragged them out into the hallway until she could get Craig to help her. She stripped the bed and took down the drapes ready for dry-cleaning. Then she stood in the room deciding how she could rearrange it. She had always hated the bed in that location in the room. Gerry had insisted on it being directly opposite the mirrors so he could see himself in bed and watch himself when they were making love. Love! She ground out the word. He never knew what love was! Fornication—that's the word for him. Too bad he couldn't fornicate with himself, she thought bitterly. Then she opened the door to the bathroom and saw the wet towels flung around, the shaving stuff left on the sink, the water on the floor where the shower door had not been properly closed, the unflushed toilet and it was too much. She backed out and closed the door and went downstairs and made herself a cup of tea. I'll do the rest tomorrow after I get back from the hospital, she thought. I've had enough for today.

Late in the afternoon, Craig returned home and saw her car in the garage. He found something to fiddle with on his bike needing time to get himself set for meeting her. She would be horrified, he knew, if he blurted out what his father had done. Finally, he went quietly up the back stairs and walked casually into the kitchen. "Hi, mom," he said, struggling for a normal voice. "When did you get home?"

"Craig!" she exclaimed, startled by his sudden appearance. "You scared me when you sneaked in like that."

"Sorry," he said. "I wasn't sneaking in to try to scare you."

"You usually sound like a herd of elephants when you come up the stairs," she said. "Did you have a good weekend?"

"Yeah, I guess so," he replied, trying to be offhand. "How was your bridge thing?"

"Oh, that. Oh, yes. It was very interesting." And she opened the frig door and busied herself rearranging things inside. "Dinner won't be long." She stood up and looked over the frig door at him. "Did you see your father when he came in, either yesterday or today?"

"Was he here? How do you know?"

"Yes," she said. "I don't know when. He left some dirty clothes lying around."

"I guess I was out or maybe I was asleep. I've got some homework to do," he said with a level voice, and turned away.

She watched him go, thinking, "What's he been up to, I wonder?". Then from the top of the stairs she heard him call, "Hey, Mom! What are these boxes doing in the hall?"

She went to the bottom of the stairs and called up to him. "Those are your father's things. I'm moving back into my own room. Do you think you can haul them downstairs and just put them anywhere in the basement, please?" And she added, under her breath, "Preferably out of my sight."

There was a slight delay before he responded, this time with a noticeable change of tone in his voice, "Yeah, sure thing. I'll do it right now."

Returning to the kitchen she heard him thumping the boxes down the stairs one at a time. "I put them in the cupboard in the family room," he announced when he came back up.

"Thank you," she said turning away to avoid any further discussion. "By the way, I need some of your muscles after school tomorrow to help me rearrange the bedroom. Okay?"

"Sure, I'll come right home. Should I get Rob to help?"

"I think we can do it ourselves. But if he's around, good."

On Monday morning they left the house together but in different directions, one reluctantly to school still nursing his hurts and doubts from Saturday night, the other, savouring pleasant memories, on her way to be helpful, she hoped.

"I couldn't find Rob," Craig announced to her when he got home from school. "We can probably do it ourselves."

They worked together, shifting the furniture into different arrangements, until she was content with the change. When they were finished with the moving and scrubbing and vacuuming, Marion looked at it and wondered why she hadn't defied her husband years ago and rearranged the bedroom the way she wanted it.

She watched her son across the supper table, puzzled by some change in him that had taken the sparkle from his face and left a sombre, cautious look. I'm too tired to try to pry anything out of him tonight, she told herself. Maybe there will be a better time tomorrow.

But on Wednesday, Edith phoned her mother and, after swiftly completed preliminaries, said she wanted her to come out as soon as she could. "I have to talk to you, Mom. There's something I've got to tell you. I should have told you years ago but I just couldn't."

"What is it, Edith? Is there something wrong between you and Harvey?"

"Oh Mom! It's not anything like that. Can't you just come out so we can talk? Right away? Like today? I'm afraid if I don't do it today, then I might never do it."

"Can't you come in, Edith? It would be a little more convenient for me. I'm just in the middle of cleaning the house and I'm in a mess."

"Mom! Please! This is something I've got to do and I want to get it over with." Her normally direct manner of speaking had forsaken her and Marion heard her daughter pleading like a child and on the edge of tears.

"Alright, dear. I'll just put things away and I'll be right out." She hung up the phone and gave a worried sigh.

On the way over to her daughter's she tried to come up with some ideas about what might possibly have upset her normally controlled daughter and created a half a dozen wild guesses, none of which she could accept as rational. When she arrived, Edith was alone and in answer to her mother's puzzlement, Edith said, "The girls are over at a neighbour's. We often exchange day care so that we can get away without them sometimes. Harvey said I should send them over if you could come out so we could talk without having to jump up every two minutes."

"Is Harvey at home?"

"Oh, no! He's at work. There's just going to be you and me."

"Well, what's it all about, Edie. You've got me worried."

"It's hard to tell you, Mom," Edith said in a shaky voice, her face looking severe but not angry. "Let me get us some coffee first and then we can go out on the sun porch and sit in the sun." But as usual with Edith, she could not restrain herself and started right in when she got to the kitchen sink to make coffee. "I haven't told you before, Mom, but I'm in a therapy group now." She paused to look at her mother for a reaction. "Harvey suggested it."

"Harvey?"

"Yes, Harvey. He was the first person I ever told and he insisted that I should go and see somebody. I didn't for a long time but finally I took the plunge and I feel so much better for doing it."

"But Edith! What was wrong? You haven't said what was wrong!"

"Let's take our coffee out into the sunroom," Edith said. "Maybe that will help me get started."

Edith walked out to the sunroom and sat down with her coffee mug clutched in both hands so they wouldn't shake. "The therapy group I'm in is for people who have been abused as children," she said, by way of starting.

"Edith! You were never abused as a child—never!" Marion said in a voice of parental denial.

"Oh yes, I was, Mom! Not by you, but by Dad—lots of times!"

"Whatever are you saying? He never laid a hand on you!"

"No, he never hit me or abused me physically. I'm talking about sexual abuse." Her voice was shaky and there were tears brimming in her eyes.

"Edith! What are you saying?"

"Mom, this is awfully hard for me, but I've got to do it. The therapist tells me I should and Harvey thinks I should because I have been blaming you for not protecting me from him when I was a child. But Harvey says that you couldn't have known anything about it or you wouldn't have permitted it to continue and he's tried to convince me I was wrong for blaming you. You see, I told Harvey first and I had never told anybody in my whole life and it was Harvey who insisted I find a therapy group. So I did and you know the way these groups are—they all gang up on each other and they convinced me to talk to you."

"I still don't know what you are talking about, Edith," Marion said, her face stiff with shock. "Are you saying that your father ...that he...that he forced you to...? Oh! Edith!" she wailed.

"Here, Mother," Edith said, passing her a box of Kleenex after ripping out a handful for her own use. "It wasn't what you think. At least I don't think it was. It was quite different than any of the other people talk about in group." She stopped and took a long shaky breath. "It's hard to do, Mom. We have to say it so many times in group that it is getting a little easier there, but to say it to your own mother is hard—I keep feeling that I'm the one to blame and I know I'm not. I'm supposed to confront him, too—that's the word they use, a confrontation with him to get it out of my system, but I won't! I just won't! I won't give him the satisfaction of knowing that I can deal with the awful things he did to me and made me feel how bad I was being."

"Edith! For God's sake, tell me," Marion almost shouted, torn between fear and frustration.

"Okay, Mom, I will. It's just that I'm afraid of hurting you and you're the last person in the world I would ever want to hurt." She took another big shaky breath and blew her nose so hard that Marion jumped. "Remember when you were pregnant with Craig and you were sick a lot and used to go to bed early? Of course you do, what am I saying. Well, that's when it started. He would come to my room when I was getting ready for bed and say he would read me a bedtime story. He made me get into my nightie and sit on his lap in the slider rocker that used to be in my room. Oh, how I hated that thing! Remember how I used to stick holes in it with sharp pencils and scribble all over it with crayons. I never knew why but I know now. I was so glad when it went to the garbage dump. Anyhow," and her voice was thick and shaky, "he'd undo his zipper and take out his penis and I would have to sit on it while he read me a bedtime story. Only most times he never got around to reading anything. He'd pick up a book and he would have a blanket over us in case you might come in and he would slide the rocker back and forth and back and forth and I would feel his penis getting harder and sometimes he would squirt right out all over my legs. Then he would say 'Now look what you've done, you bad girl! You'll have to clean it up!'. Sometimes he would take me to the bathroom and wash me all over and make me wash his penis. He told me that this was our secret and I should never tell anybody ever about it—not you or anybody. And I never did. I always just thought I had been bad. Then when Harvey came along and he was so gentle and finally I had to tell him about it and he said that it wasn't my fault and I shouldn't feel guilty, but I did, and he kept on trying to get me to go to somebody that knew something about child molesting and I finally did. Oh! Mom! Do you think I'm an awful person." She got quickly out of her chair and went down on her knees before her mother and laid her head on her lap and sobbed as her mother had never heard her sob since she was a child.

"Oh, no, Edith! No, no, no. You were a child! Oh, you poor child. I wish I had known. I wish you could have told me." They cried together until there were no more tears to shed for the moment.

After the tears came the anger. "Oh, the rotten bastard! The dirty rotten bastard! How could he? To his own child! To any child! I knew he was fooling around with other women when he was out on the road because men do that sort of thing and I thought that was why he rarely touched me. You didn't know that, of course. But we had sex maybe once a month and I never thought much of it until lately." She stopped suddenly so that she would not blurt out her affair with Tom. "Oh, you poor dear! Carrying around those terrible memories all these years and thinking you were to blame. I could kill him! I could just kill him! Oh! I hope I never have to see his face again. U-ugh!" she shuddered.

Then she thought of the advice Edith had been given to confront her father and she said, "Edith, you're not going to face him with what he did to you, are you? Please don't! He would tear your heart out. He would, Edith! He's a cold, heartless. selfish.... Oh I wish a had the proper words to describe him. How could I have loved him once? How could he do such terrible things right in our own home?" She sat without answers to her numbing questions.

Edith's emotional control had returned gradually. She raised her head from her mother's knee and stood up. "No, Mother, I'm not going to confront him or lay charges or anything like that. Harvey says that doing things like that will only make the healing longer and more painful. He thinks I've had enough pain and it's time to put the whole thing away and I think he's right. The group think I should and so does the counselor, but I'm not going to let them push me around like he pushed me around. I'll just let the son of a bitch carry his guilt feelings to the grave. They belong with him in hell." Her decision made and stated, she blew out a big breath of air and got back to reality.

"Excuse me a minute, Mom. I'll phone and see if the girls are okay and if they had their lunch there. Then I'll make us a sandwich or something. Is there anything you would like?"

Marion shook her head, partly because she couldn't even think of food and partly in amazement at her daughter's ability to make the same sudden switches emotionally as she could conversationally. She was still puzzling over her daughter's emotional control when Edith returned to the sun room. "They've had their lunch," she reported and Patsy will send them home in half an hour, just in time for them to say hello to their Granny before their nap. Would you like to tuck them in today? I always tell them that the next time you come out I'll let you tuck them in if they've been good, so be sure to ask them if they've been good and then watch them. Jenny will look at Iona to see what she's going to say and she will have big round eyes and her mouth all pursed up and then Iona will say 'Oh, yes, Mummy. We've been very good' and she will nod her head and then Jenny's face will soften up and she will nod too. They are just so cute! What would you like for lunch? I know! I've got a little bit of tuna casserole left over and I'll heat that up and some biscuits. That's what we'll have. And soup. I'll get it started. It won't take a minute."

As she was leaving, Marion called after her, "By the way, Edith, when did this granny thing get started."

Edith stopped and turned toward her mother putting on a contrite face. "Oops," she said. "I got caught, didn't I? I guess I really am bad. We call you 'granny' when you're not around—the girls picked it up somewhere." She laughed heartily and Marion marvelled at her daughter's resilience.

They had lunch and talked of other things until the girls came home ready for Granny to tuck them in for a nap. She asked if they had been good and the act they put on was exactly as Edith had described which sent Edith into gales of laughter. "See! Didn't I tell you, Mom? Aren't they rascals. Go on, now, you two! And Granny will tuck you in."

The three of them went noisily up stairs and Edith turned to her kitchen chores with tear filled eyes not knowing exactly why she was weeping.

* * *

When Marion returned home it was late in the afternoon and she felt emotionally and physically drained. Her early rise in order to tackle the house-cleaning she had planned for the day and the long drives to and from Edith's were tiring in themselves. But now, and worse, was the turmoil that Edith had created by her account of what had happened to her as a child without her having the slightest idea of what was going on upstairs. If there is blame to be laid anywhere then I have to take a fair share of it, she told herself. Surely a mother's duty is to guard her children from harm, particularly the ugly kind of harm that Edith had been subjected to. Why couldn't I have seen what was going on? Was that why Edith was so tense and angry when she was a child? She remembered now how Edith had wrecked that slider rocker in her bedroom until it was such a mess that it was sent to the dump. She thought that there could be no tears left in her, but she stretched out on the sofa and the tears came again.

She was awakened from a tortured sleep by the sound of Craig's thumping arrival at the back door. She waited for his usual shouted greeting but he did not call out.

"Is that you, Craig? I'm in here," she called.

He appeared at the door as she was struggling to sit up. "Hi," he said without any of his usual bright cheerfulness.

"Oh, I dropped off," she said. And then, to explain her swollen red eyes in case Craig might notice, she added, "I must be coming down with the flu or something. Maybe there's a lot of pollen around. Something making me dizzy and tired."

"Can I get you something," Craig asked without any tone of concern in his voice.

"No, dear. Thank you. I'll be fine. But do you think you could manage to get yourself some dinner? I don't think I could look at food tonight. Maybe I'll just go to bed."

Craig nodded. "Yeah, okay."

She got up from the sofa and headed for the stairs, knowing that she should pull herself together and tell Craig about Edith but she had had enough hurt and tears and wanted no more for today. And there was something eating at Craig and she didn't want to hear about it tonight. Tomorrow, she told herself, I'll sit down with him and we'll have a good talk. Then, stopping halfway up the stairs, she said, "I drove out to see Edith today. She wanted me to. We had a long talk. I'll tell you about it tomorrow."

Craig's only response was a desultory "Okay" that puzzled her because he always showed an interest in his nieces.

Tomorrow will be soon enough, she told herself. It can all wait until tomorrow. I don't want any more today. She made her way upstairs, undressed, splashed her face and rolled into bed with the sheets and blanket pulled high to shut out the world. Suddenly she sat upright in the bed. Tomorrow! she said to herself. I've got to go to the hospital tomorrow. It's too late to phone anybody—I'll have to go! And bridge! Oh, migod, what'll I do? She started to weep again, then got out of bed and went to the bathroom and stood under a cold shower. She called down to Craig, "Craig, dear? Are you still there?"

The answer was a monosyllable "Yeah?"

"Will you set your alarm and call me when you get up for school? I've got to be at the hospital at nine."

"Okay."

"I'll set mine, too. Good night, dear. Sweet dreams."

From downstairs came a bland response, "You, too."

CHAPTER 35

In the early morning light, he awakened with a start and looked at his alarm clock when it went off, remembering his promise to call his mother.

"Yes, I'm awake," she answered when he knocked and called her. You get yourself some breakfast, Craig. I don't think I'll bother with anything but coffee." She heard him mutter an apparently assenting reply as he turned away from her door, and she tried to convince herself that she should hurry and take time to make sure he had a decent breakfast and got away to school in time. But her sleep had been as ragged as his and she was afraid that she would lose her control and resume the tearfulness of yesterday.

Craig was lying curled on his side staring into space with a book flopped open beside him listening to his mother's movements as she washed and dressed and went down the stairs. She had called him twice and he had responded each time with a noncommittal answer that did not satisfy her so she went upstairs and knocked on his door and opened it when he called "Come in!"

"Why aren't you up?" You are going to be late!" she scolded.

"Ah, I don't think I'll bother going today," he replied in a toneless voice.

"What's the matter? Are you sick?" she asked, coming into the room and placing a hand on his forehead.

"No," he said, trying to draw away from her hand. "There's nothing important that I'll miss. There's an assembly this morning with a bunch of experts coming to talk about drugs, then I have Socials and we'll probably spend the whole period hashing over what the experts said and disagreeing with them. Then I have a study period and then lunch and then Math which we won't have because Mr. Saonsang is sick and the substitute never arrives. Then there's PE and we won't have that either because the basketball team will be warming up before their game this afternoon. Rob is on the team," he finished laconically.

"Oh, Craig!" she said impatiently. "Just get out of bed and go to school. You can't moon around here all day again. What's the matter anyway?"

"Nothin'."

"Well, get up. I've got to go or I'll be late. I'll see you later. Oh, yes, much later—I've got bridge this afternoon. Bye, dear." She leaned over and kissed him on the forehead and noted that there was no indication of a fever. "Now, get up!"

She went downstairs wondering what was wrong with him, quiet and moody, scarcely coming out of his room.. If he had been a girl, she thought, I could guess what was wrong, but who knows about moody boys at that age. But she let the worry pass as she prepared herself for the day. And then there was Edith's horror story, surfacing when she least expected it, pulling her down to anger and tears. All she could hope was that there would be nothing during the day that would start her tears again. She knew that Edith had been wounded deeply, that she could carry the scars of her father's abuse for the rest of her life. Her anger and hurt had been easy to see. But the puzzling thing was that while Edith was telling that ugly story, determined in spite of shame and hurt to expose it all finally, there was an undercurrent of another emotion, something akin to an attitude of self-importance that she did not understand. She shook her head to clear if of the puzzle.

"Don't forget to lock up when you go, Craig," she called up the stairs before she left, to which she received a baffling mumble.

When she arrived at the hospital, she checked herself in the mirror of the car and hoped that her makeup had obscured the ravages of yesterday. Try as she might, her usual light chatter with Ellen at the switchboard did not emerge and she plodded through a greeting conversation without spontaneity. It took her only a few minutes to open the little shop and ready it for the day and then, instead of dusting and rearranging and restocking the shelves, she went into the small back room and sat morosely on a stool. She did not know that she had been crying and making scuffling sounds until Jimmy, the maintenance man, heard her when he walked in to assist a customer who had been waiting impatiently for change.

"Thank you, Jimmy," she said when he found her. "I heard him but I just couldn't face him. I hoped he would go away." She blew her nose hard and wiped her eyes. "I'll be alright in a minute. Could you stay out there until I get myself straightened around? I'll just be a minute."

"Sure," he said. "Take your time."

But Jimmy was used to dealing with upset people and he walked over to Ellen and told her that he had found Marion in back of the shop crying her eyes out, and Ellen phoned Cynthia, who said she would be right over, and, she asked, would the girls on the counter, and Jimmie, if he had the time, keep an eye on things until she got there? One of the girls arrived with a cup of coffee for her and stood in the door to the store room where she could keep an eye on her own station across the hallway if she was signalled while also watching the shop. She was sympathetic and quiet and Marion was grateful that she asked no questions.

Cynthia arrived, elegant as always, took one look at Marion and closed the door and put up the 'Back in five minutes' sign. "Whatever is wrong, Marion?" she asked, her voice filled with concern as she pulled a carton over and sat down beside her.

Her sympathy triggered another set of sobs and shudders from Marion accompanied with an anger with herself. "What is <u>wrong</u> with me?" she said in a reproving voice. "I just can't seem to get hold of myself."

"Something seems terribly wrong, Marion," Cynthia said, gently. "Do you want to talk about it with me."

"No, Cynthia. Thank you. I can't." The jerky answer came as the gasping sobs continued.

"Is there anyone here in the hospital you want to talk to? I think you should, Marion. You are very upset."

Marion sat with her head in her hands and signalled 'No'.

"Should I call your husband to come and get you?"

Marion sat bolt upright. "No! Don't do that!" she almost shrieked. "I never want to see the bastard again!"

Cynthis was a sympathetic and kind person but she was also worldly enough to realize that she did not want to probe deeper into what was obviously a marital fight. "Then I won't call him, Marion." She waited. "Perhaps you had better go home. Can you make it on your own or shall I drive you? We'll just close up for a little, while I take you and I'll finish out your morning."

"Yes, I think I better go home," Marion said. "I'm no good here. I'm sorry, Cynthia. I seem to be more trouble than help."

"Alright, dear. Would you like me to drive you?"

"No, no, please don't! I'll be alright." She looked around vaguely for her purse and coat and Cynthia reached for them and handed them to her. Struggling into her coat and searching for her keys in the pockets and then in her purse, she sighed and said, "Oh, dear! Nothing is coming out right! It's all going wrong."

"What is it, Marion?" Cynthia asked kindly.

Marion looked at her for a moment with her mouth working as if she were trying to say something and then turned away with a long sigh. "I can't say. Really I can't! It's too awful." She turned to leave and then stopped at the door. "Cynthia, I'm sorry, but I don't think I should come in and help any more. There's too much going on that I can't handle. I'm afraid I'll let you down again. Can you find someone else?" Her voice was shaky and she was on the verge of tears again. "I feel terrible," she continued, "just leaving you without any warning. I'm not that kind of a person, really—but I don't think I can do it any more. I want to but I can't and you should have somebody you can depend on, not somebody like me who hides in the back crying, and not, not, being useful to anybody anymore."

Cynthia went to her and took her hands. "Now, now," she said. "You go home and have a rest and we'll talk about it some other time. I'll find someone to come in for you for a couple of weeks and you can call me and tell me that

you are really serious about not coming back in. I know you have enjoyed it."
She opened the door and took Marion's arm and together they walked to the
exit. "Drive carefully now, Marion! And call me, please, if I can do anything."

"Thank you, Cynthia. I will. And I'm sorry."

Cynthia watched her go and turned back into the hospital already searching
in her mind for someone who could fill in.

***

When Marion arrived home, she called Craig but received no answer. She
checked his room and the garden and the garage and decided that he had
changed his mind and gone to school. She made some coffee for herself and
while it was brewing, she took a deep breath and called Kate.

"Oh, isn't that funny," Kate said when she answered. I was just going to call
you, and then I remembered that this was your morning at the hospital. Are
you at home or at work?"

"I'm at home. I did go in but I didn't feel well, so Cynthia came in and I
quit."

"You mean quit for the day or quit, like not going back any more?"

"Yes, I quit for good."

"Why, Marion? You were enjoying it so much!"

"Well, something's come up. I can't tell you about it right now, but I phoned
to say I can't make bridge today and to see if you would tell a couple of the
others."

"Isn't that funny?" Kate said. "I was going to call you to tell you I couldn't
make it either and not to pick me up."

"What's the matter, Kate? Are you sick?"

"No. I'll tell you about it sometime."

They chatted for a while, knowing that they were not the kind of close
friends that would ever get back to a conversation about another's personal
problems. They agreed that Marion would call Cora and Kate would call Dot
and let them tell the others.

The call to Cora was short and to the point. Marion said she was coming
down with something and didn't want to pass it around and Cora said something politely sympathetic and that she was already late for her hair appointment.

Marion sat over her coffee for a while trying to make up her mind whether
she should call Edith now or later and only succeeded in stirring herself up
emotionally again. "When am I going to stop doing this," she asked herself.
Maybe if I get out into the garden and start the fall cleanup I'll get out of this
mood. And with that she changed into her gardening clothes, closed the windows and doors so she would not hear the phone and was soon engrossed and
sweaty in the garden.

Earlier, long after his mother had left the house, Craig had finally roused
himself, got out of bed and made himself some breakfast. Then, after fiddling

with the TV, he reluctantly decided that, perhaps, after all, school was more attractive than being alone in the house with his thoughts. He was just on his way out the door when the phone rang and he turned to answer it.

"Hello?" he said hesitantly as the thought flashed through his mind ˜What if it's him! I'll hang up if it's him!"

Edith's voice came crackling over the phone. "Craig? Is that you? What are you doing home from school? Are you sick? Your voice sounds funny."

"Oh, hi, Edie," Craig said without bothering to answer any of the questions.

"Well, are you?" Edith persisted.

"No. I slept in after Mom left for the hospital and I was just on my way out when you called."

"Oh, of course. I forgot that she goes on Thursday and she didn't mention it when she was over yesterday."

"Was she over to see you yesterday? She didn't say anything about it."

"She didn't? That's funny because we had a long talk and it was important and I thought she would have told you. But I guess she is waiting for the right time."

"What about?" Craig asked, more out of courtesy than interest.

"Oh, she'll tell you when she's ready, I guess. Anyhow, I think I should leave it up to her to tell you. You better get going if you're late already. Why don't you ever come over? The girls will forget they've got a handsome sexy uncle if you don't see them once in a while."

"Edith! For crissake, don't say things like that!" Craig said, raising his voice more than he meant to.

"Like what? Like sexy?"

"Yes," he said. "Like sexy! I gotta go. Goodbye!" And he hung up the phone and left the house.

Edith shrugged off his rudeness and made a face at the telephone as she hung up. Then she remembered that her mother played bridge on Thursdays so she wouldn't be able to get her until later in the day. I hope I didn't upset her yesterday, she said to herself. Come to think of it, she really did look terrible when she left.

When Craig arrived at school he already had a wad of chewed paper packed into his cheek and had practised his excuse for being late. 'I had a dental affointment' sounded legit he thought, but nobody asked. There was a buzz going around the halls about the guys on the basketball team all getting caught peddling pot but nobody really believed it because it had been started by Vic and some of his gang. He looked for Rob and when he could not find him somebody from one of Rob's classes said he was up in the library.

"Library!" Craig exclaimed. "What the hell is he doing in the library?"

"He said he had to look up some stuff on alligator dancing and hairstyles among the headhunters," the student replied sarcastically as he wandered away. "And how the hell would I know? What does anybody do in the library, dumbhead?"

Craig shrugged and gave up looking for Rob. He went to his home room for study period and spent an hour with his unfinished Math homework in front of him but the image of his father naked beside his bed kept erupting into his thoughts. He had forgotten to bring a lunch or any money so when the lunch bell rang he looked for Rob again and when he couldn't find him decided to go home. When he arrived home, he did not notice his mother in the garden or her car in the garage, expecting her to be at the hospital or at bridge. He was in the frig getting a can of coke when he heard steps coming up the back door. His first thought was that it was his father coming back to attack him again and he raised the can to throw it as soon as he appeared.

His mother appeared in the doorway suddenly seeing her son ready to attack her. They both froze in position—she with her face twisted in horror at the prospect of being attacked by her son and he terrified at the thought of the mistake he might have made.

"Craig!" she shrieked.

"Mom! I'm sorry!" he cried. "I thought it was Dad—I mean, I didn't know you were home. I thought—-, Oh, Mom! I'm sorry I scared you." He put down the can and went over to wrap his arms around her and say again that he was sorry.

She was shaking but forgave him quickly. "Well, you certainly gave me a scare," she told him severely. "Who did you think it was at the door?"

"Oh, I dunno. Nobody really. I guess I was just feeling a little jumpy being in the house alone."

"Didn't you see me in the garden or my car," she scolded.

"No, Mom, I didn't. I wasn't expecting you so I didn't see you."

"Well!" she huffed. "You made me jump. Have you had lunch?"

"No, I forgot to take it and I forgot to take some money and I couldn't find Rob so I came home." He paused and looked at her. "Now it's my turn to give you the third degree. How come you're not at the hospital and not ready to go to your bridge? So answer me that before I get tough with you."

His teasing made her answer easier. "Oh, something came up and I quit." She had turned her back on him so he could not see her face.

"You got fired?" he asked in amazement.

"No, I did not get fired. I just quit! And I'm not going to play bridge today either."

"Okay, then I'm not going back to school today either," he mimicked with exaggerated petulance.

"Well then, you can just go change your clothes while I get lunch and you can spend the day doing slave work in the garden."

"Oh, Mo-o-m!" he moaned dramatically. She smiled at his retreating back and felt better than she had felt all morning.

He stopped. "Oh, I forgot to tell you. Edie called just after you left."

Marion stopped her lunch preparations and without turning around said, "Did she say anything?" keeping her voice level.

"No, except she said you were out to see her and that you were supposed to tell me something. What was that all about?"

"We'll get into that later. Hurry up, your lunch is ready."

They took their lunch outside to a picnic table and, sitting in the late September sunshine, they talked about what needed to be done in the garden, but skirted around any talk about Edith.

***

Gerry had left the courtroom in a rage, a rage that he could feel pounding on the left side of his head above and behind his ear. The pain was so fierce that his vision was blurring and he sat in his car waiting for the pain and the blurring and the shakes to go away. He wanted a drink badly but was determined to resist the demand until he could at least get out of this godforsaken town. He slid crossways in the seat and laid his head back, holding his breath and gritting his teeth, determined not to move. When he came to, it was almost two o'clock. He had either been unconscious or asleep and the pain and shakes were gone, but when he roused himself to awareness, the anger began to surge again and with it the pounding in his head. He started the car and headed back to the city, stopping only once for gas, a visit to the men's and a large coffee and bag of nibblers. In a new mall in a sprawling suburb he found a liquor store and 8a deli. Then, supplied with food and booze, he headed for the marina and his boat.

Late Wednesday morning when he laboured back into reality, he blearily pondered his watch, shook it and banged it on the edge of the table and wondered what had happened to Tuesday. The cartons from the deli were in a garbage bag, but here was an empty can of pork and beans and a box of crackers scattered around and the heel of a bottle of dark rum on the floor beside the bunk. He had no recollection of yesterday except for a vague recall of some plans he had made when he was driving back to the city and he now struggled to bring them into focus. He remembered two things: one was to go to the bank and do something there and the other was to see Titty about something else. Looking with craving at the heel of rum he knew wouldn't help and with a desperate effort of will resisted finishing it off. His electric razor was still working. He splashed water on his face, combed his hair and smoothed down the clothes he had slept in for two days. Ready to leave the boat, his eye found the rum bottle and he forgot his earlier resolution and finished it before he stepped out into a world of sunshine so brilliant that his eyes hurt and his head began to throb. At one of his cheap eating spots where he stopped for breakfast, he figured he must look presentable because a bum tried to panhandle him. He ate more food for breakfast than he could remember eating for a week. He sat trying to remember what he wanted to do at the bank and why he wanted to see Titty.

When he got to the bank, a brittle teller with cold eyes refused to give him a copy of last month's statement until she had taken his signature to the manager for authority. Her hostile attitude began to make him angry and the anger

sharpened the throbbing pain in his head. Determined not to let anything interfere with the two plans he had made, he took the copy over to the customer
service area and reviewed it. He saw that the company was making routine
payments to his account and that the monthly transfer to Marion's account
had been made. He considered stopping that transfer but decided against it
solely because he did not want to face the cold-eyed bitch at the counter and
risk letting her make him mad. After withdrawing some money from the automatic machine he headed for Titty's, watching carefully in case he might run
into somebody from the firm. Titty's door was locked but he knocked, then
pounded, then kicked and roared "Open the door, you fat drunken son of a
bitch or I'll kick it down!". Doors down the hall opened and heads popped out.
One man came out and remonstrated from a distance by saying, "Now, what's
the meaning of this?" Gerry took two step toward him, now red with rage and
drooling, and with a voice filled with venom, shouted "Fuck off!" The man did
and the other doors closed. He stood for a minute, his head pounding like an
anvil, knowing that inside the various offices fingers were dialling 911. So he
left and went to a bar and ordered a double "And keep them coming."

His Wednesday began to disappear about the same time that his daughter
was disclosing to his wife the way in which he had molested her for years when
she was a child. His stay in the bar ended when he was asked to leave by the
owner, who, with the barman and an irate customer assisted him forcibly out
the door because of his loud and obscene language. He staggered to a nearby
booze shop then drove blindly to the marina where he stumbled down the
gangway to his boat, climbed aboard and pissed over the side in full view of
other boaters who, until his noisy arrival had been enjoying the quiet and the
sunset. Then. having cleared the area of observers, he locked himself in the
cabin and opened the bottle to finish the day and start tomorrow on its way to
oblivion.

CHAPTER 36

Marion straightened up from the bending position she seemed to have
been in all afternoon. With her hands on her hips, she twisted her body
to get rid of the kinks while looking around at what they had accomplished in
the yard. The sun was low in the sky and the evening cool was setting in. Then
wiping her forearm across her sweaty brow, she gathered together the tools
she had been using and went around to the back yard to put them away in the
garage. She heard Craig hammering inside and, looking in, found him busy
putting up new racks for the tools. "Hi," he said when he saw her. "Just dump
those things there and I'll hang them up in a minute. I'm just about finished."

She looked around and saw that he had cleared out the front and sides of
the garage and the piled broken and useless junk out in the driveway ready to
be carted away—a rusty and broken tricycle, garden tools without handles, handles without tools, a hand mower that had been replaced years ago by a power
mower, some bicycle tires, well chewed hockey sticks and other litter she could

not recognize. He had backed the car out and hosed down the garage and he was filthy and wet and pleased with himself.

"That looks pretty good, eh?" he said to her, grinning.

It was the first time she had seen him looking happy for a week and she realized that while pushing herself physically in the garden, she too had dropped all the distress that had been piling up on her.

"Good?" she exclaimed. "That's marvellous! All that dirty useless junk that nobody would throw away that was always getting in the way."

"I turned over the compost pile too, but I think I'm going to have to build a new one. The side up against the fence has all rotted away."

"Oh, I've got piles of stuff out front from the flower beds. What am I going to do with that?"

"Just leave it. I'll get it when I've built some space for it."

"Not today, Craig. That's enough. It's getting too dark to see what you're doing. I'm going in and have a shower and start dinner. Don't be long." She left him engrossed in his reorganization scheme as if he now had accepted a new role in the home.

When he had hung up the tools and put the car back in the garage he continued to putter, reluctant to quit. His mother had finished her shower and returned to the kitchen and she could see him still working in the dusk.

"Craig!" she called. "It's time to stop. You've done enough for today."

He gave her a casual wave and turned out the light in the garage and stood for a minute in the fading light surveying his days work. Coming into the warm kitchen with the smell of dinner already in the air, he suddenly felt released from the oppression that had been burdening him all week.

"I better phone Rob," he said, leaning against the counter while he drank a huge glass of milk.

"Have a shower and change first," his mother said. "Dinner won't be long."

But as he passed the telephone table in the hall, he dialled Rob and waited for six rings before hanging up. "He's not home anyway!" he shouted to his mother.

At the Turner's house, Rob's parents were sitting in hostile silence—a silence that would not be interrupted by the demands of a telephone. Claudia was crying softly and Glen was pacing with anger showing in every stride and in every line of his face. The police had called to inform them that their son, Robert Turner, had been arrested with two others for possession of marijuana and for an attempt to sell marijuana to a member of the drug squad. He was in jail and bail could be arranged.

"Let him stay there!" Rob's father raged. "He knows the law! He knows how we feel about drugs! How could he be so stupid? I'll be god dammed if I will go down there and bail him out after all the things I've said and done publicly about drugs. I won't embarrass myself like that! And neither will you!" he shouted at his wife. "Don't you dare sneak out and bail him out! I knew it! I knew something like this would happen! He's been too much of a smartass lately. I should have known he was up to something. Let him rot there. Stupid!

Stupid! Stupid!"

"Glen," Claudia pleaded. "He's just a kid. He made a mistake. He didn't rob a bank or kill somebody. Why can't—?"

"No, he didn't," he interrupted. "But that's next, isn't it? It always is with these addicts. They say they're hooked and they can't help it and that's their excuse for robbing and stealing."

"Oh, Glen, please!"

"You better phone Beverley and Richard. See if they know anything about this. I'll bet Richard's school board won't be too happy about a relative of one of their teachers getting caught up in drug trafficking." Their argument continued until they were worn out by anger and stubbornness.

Rob lay sprawled on a bench in the holding cells. He was alone. The other two students arrested with him had long since been bailed out. One of the young officers had brought him a hamburger and coke on the strength of Rob's promise to pay him back. He consistently rejected any suggestion that he phone his parents, saying only, with a shrug, "They know I'm here."

"If they don't come for you before five o'clock you have to be moved to the juvenile section," the officer explained and got only a shrug in response.

Craig tried the phone when he came down after cleaning up but there was no answer. "No answer at Rob's," he reported to his mother. "Maybe their phone is out of order. I'll go over after dinner."

They ate together in the kind of silence that happens when each person is struggling privately to find a way to tell the other something that must be said. Craig seemed to her to be less closed-off and sullen than he been for days and she herself felt more in control. He sat fidgeting with the salt and pepper shakers and draining the last drop from his empty glass wondering how to tell his mother how his father had molested him and exactly what words to use. How can I say those words to my mother? Blow-job? And another word, too—ejaculation. Jesus! I can't say that to her! So he took another deep breath just as she, too, took a deep breath and said. "You said you were talking to Edith today. What was she calling about?"

"I dunno," he answered relieved by the end of the silence. "I think she forgot it was your day at the hospital. Then she said something about you having to tell me something. I don't know what she was talking about and I was just on my way out the door for school."

"Well, I have something to tell you, Craig and it isn't easy. I've been trying to find a way all day but I guess there's no way except just to say it. I guess I've been thinking that you're still too young to know about these things, but you're not. You're almost an adult—almost a man." She stopped and watched his puzzled face, wishing she did not have to go on. "Edith called on Wednesday and asked me to come over and talk to her. She didn't ask as much as she demanded. She said it was important and she was very insistent. I didn't know what on earth was wrong and she wouldn't say anything over the phone. So I had to drop everything and drive over to see what she wanted. She was waiting for me. She had taken the girls over to a friend's place so we could have some privacy and she made us some coffee and we went out on their little sundeck to talk." She stopped and took a deep breath.

"Well, what was wrong? Is she pregnant?" Craig asked with a tone of impatience.

"No, no! Not anything like that. It was about your father. You wouldn't know anything about it and neither did I but it started just after you were born and he would get her ready for bed and when she had her nightie on—. Oh, I don't know how to tell you, it's so ugly."

"What?" Craig demanded. "Tell me what?"

"He would sit in the rocking chair and take his penis out and make her sit on it with a blanket over her lap while he rocked in the chair and got an erection and sometimes he would ejaculate between her legs and then he would tell her she was a bad girl and make her wash him off. Oh, God, Craig I hate to have to tell you this!"

Craig sat looking at her, wide-eyed, his face twisted in horror, his mouth moving but making no sound.

"Edith said it went on for years. She didn't say when it stopped. She could never tell anybody because she thought it was all her fault. She told Harvey and Harvey was sensible enough to make her see that she should get some counseling and now she is going to group therapy sessions."

"The bastard!" Craig exploded before she had finished. "The dirty, rotten bastard! Son of a bitch! Bastard! That's what he is? Rotten, dirty, stinking son of a bitch! Bastard! I could kill him!" He was on his feet stamping around the room. "I will kill him! If I knew where he was right now I would go and kick his brains out! I would! I'll get a gun and if he ever shows up here again I'll shoot him! He's a dirty, rotten—." He knelt beside his mother, his head in her lap. "Oh, Mom! Poor Edie! Poor Edie! How could he?" He raised a tearful face to her. "He hasn't done anything to the girls, has he?"

"No, I'm sure he hasn't. If he had touched either of them, Harvey would have killed him on the spot and you know what a gentle man Harvey is."

Craig got slowly to his feet. "Mom, I gotta go! I'm sorry but I've got to get out of here!"

"Oh, Craig, don't go trying to find him. He can be brutal, you know. Just stay here, with me, please." She got up and caught Craig's arm as he was putting on a jacket at the door.

"I've got to get out of here and think, Mom!" he said, pulling his arm free. "I'm not going to try to find him. Not tonight!"

He pulled himself free of his mother's grasp on his sleeve and rushed out the door, jumping down the three steps and turning swiftly to the side yard and the street. On the street he started walking, not taking the familiar route to Rob's, nor toward the park or the mall. He turned down another residential street and walked without having a goal in mind. He walked with such long, fast strides that anybody watching might think he was jogging except for his clenched fists and mutters that turned occasionally into shouts. Now he was using obscenities and profanities that he had unconsciously refrained from using in front of his mother. The words poured from him, cursing his father with a venom that he never knew was possible for him. He kicked at objects in the gutters, picked up cans and hurled them down the street, threw children's toys that had been left on the sidewalk back into a yard. And he cried. The tears poured out and drenched his face and jacket. They were tears without sobs. He had no breath for sobs, so frenzied was his cursing. The pace of his walking slowed and the cursing became repetitive and stopped. He came to a small footbridge over a meandering stream in a deserted park he had never been in before and he laid his head on his arms on the railing until the heaving emotions had been dispelled. Finally he straightened up and looked around to get his bearings. He thought of turning for home but he was not ready. He knew he would now have to tell his mother what his father had done to him and he had no idea of how to tell her or what to say. He collected a handful of pebbles from the gravel path and stood on the little bridge tossing them into the stream making such a game of trying to place the next pebble in the exact spot of the previous one that unwittingly the hostility and anger faded and he turned for home.

***

When Craig flung himself out of the house, Marion stood watching the closed door with her emotions in disarray until, recognizing that he had really left, she returned to the nook table and sat trying not to think of anything for the moment. The radio that she habitually turned on to take away the quiet of an empty house was tuned to a talk-show station with the volume so low she could barely hear it. The telephone rang and the loudness of the ring startled her. Oh, Edith, she thought getting to her feet. I really don't want to talk to you tonight. I don't want to talk to anybody. She picked up the phone and when she said "Hello" her voice came out in a squawk. Clearing her throat loudly, she said in a clear strong voice, "I mean, hello."

"Well, hello and hello to you, too!" came Tom's voice. "I finally made contact."

"Oh, Tom. It's you."

"Yep, it's me. How are you?"

"Fine," she lied. "What do you mean 'finally'?"

"I called you a couple of times this afternoon but I couldn't get an answer."

"I'm sorry, Tom. I was out in the garden all afternoon. I guess I didn't hear the phone."

"Yes, I thought you might be," Tom said. "I was just calling to see how you were doing and to say that I have some extra preparation to do this weekend before our big trip to Seattle next week and I'll be tied up all weekend."

She didn't fully understand what he was saying, so she said, "Oh, Tom, that's too bad."

There was a long pause before Tom said, "Marion, are you alright? Is there someone there so you can't speak?"

"No, it's alright. I'm alone. It's just that so many things are happening. I don't know. I've really had a dreadful day and I can't talk as much as I would like to. My head is just whirling. And, oh Tom, I'm sorry but I can't go to Seattle with you. I really want to—I mean <u>wanted</u> to—but I can't. I shouldn't anyway but I can't now if you know what I mean. Oh, I don't even know what I mean myself. I'm at my wit's end. I think maybe—-."

"Whoa, Marion!" he interrupted. "Wait a minute, now. Settle down. What's going on?"

"Tom, I can't tell you right now. It's Gerry and, well, I can't say over the phone. I've got to get things straightened around for my children." She had started to cry and her voice was thick.

"Marion, would you like me to come over and we can—-."

"No!" she said explosively. "No, please don't. Craig will be back in a few minutes. I'll be alright."

"Are you sure?"

"Yes, Tom. I'll be fine. I'm sorry about next weekend—truly I am! Would you call me next week? Maybe I'll be able to explain then. Would you, please?"

"Okay, Marion. I'll call you Tuesday, if that's what you want. You won't be at the hospital Tuesday."

I can't explain anything to anybody any more, she said to herself. Aloud she said, "Tuesday will be fine. Goodbye, Tom."

She hung up the phone quickly and left him puzzling.

"So who the hell is Tom?" a surly voice said behind her.

Startled, she jumped and turned from the telephone to see Gerry standing in the kitchen listening to her conversation with a leer on his face.

"I knew there was something going on," he continued. "Had a big weekend planned, did you?"

If she had paled because she had been startled, she was now white with anger at the sight of him. For a moment she stood looking at him, unable to speak, her mouth opening and closing but no sound emerged. Then her bloodstream filled with adrenalin and there was nothing in her mind but vitriol and bitter rage. Her voice finally emerged in a scream as she moved toward him.

"You monster!" she shrieked. "How could you? How could you do a thing like that to your own child? Your own child! Any child! You're rotten! You're a rotten, miserable piece of scum! You're not fit to be called a father! Not fit to be called a human being! Scum! Bastard! Pig! Piece of shit, that's what you are—a piece of shit! Get out of here! What are you doing here?"

He was backing away from her fury but he answered her with a snide smile, "Oh, I see. He ran right to Mummy, did he, with his sad little tale, as soon as you got home from wherever you were whoring around."

"<u>He</u>?" she stopped and asked. "Who's <u>he</u>?"

"Who the hell did you think I was talking about?"

"You tell me!"

"Craig, of course."

"Craig?" she said unbelievingly. "What sad little tale? I was talking about what you did to Edith when she was a child and what you made her do to you in that rocking chair! You— you— pervert!"

"Oh, that," he said with a dismissing shrug. "That was a long time ago. I thought you were talking about Craig."

She looked at him as if she could not believe either the sight or the sound of him. "What about Craig?"

"Nothing!" he said and turned to the door.

"What about Craig, I said?" and her voice was a screech. She picked up the sugar bowl from the table and threw it hard at him, hitting him on the shoulder as he was reaching for the door. The contents of the bowl spilled over him and onto the floor. He turned and looked at her with a hate that she had never seen on any human face before but she also felt a matching emotion in herself. She rushed to the stove and grabbed the biggest butcher knife from the rack with terrible intent but he had opened the door and she could only see his back moving quickly away. So she threw the knife clumsily at his retreating figure and it rattled harmlessly into a corner. Rushing to pick it up she slipped on the spilled sugar and as she struggled on her knees to the corner for the knife she heard the sound of his car starting and the squeal of rubber. She sat on her haunches surrounded by broken crockery and sugar with the butcher knife in her hands and cried. The door was open and the evening breeze was cool but she did not feel it. When Craig opened the door, saw her and shouted "Mom!" she fainted.

When Gerry raced away from the house, he returned straight to the marina. He parked his car and rushed down the floating docks without noticing the curious looks of some of the other boaters who were closing up for the night. Aboard, he sat on the small bench in the galley and poured himself a drink using a stained coffee cup that was handy on the table. His head was pounding again and he lowered it onto his hands with his elbows on his knees, moving only to take an occasional gulp from the cup. He muttered sometimes to himself about 'the bitch' or 'the whore' and sugar bowls and knives but none of it was loud because speaking loud drove spikes into his head, and none of it was coherent. He sat until the bottle was empty. Then slowly he got to his feet, fumbled for the ignition key that he kept on a hook beside the galley shelves and stumbled up on deck. He tried to insert the key into the ignition, forgetting that it had protective cover that had to be held aside and the frustration of failure built up into a roar of fowl language that almost blew his head wide open and created nasty comments from nearby boaters. Finally, inserting the key, he tried to start the motor. He ground it with the choke out and the choke in without success and continued until it was barely turning over and then when it appeared that the battery had given its all, the motor caught and he shoved the throttle open and let it roar. Untying the lines, he shoved the boat away from the dock, climbed unsteadily aboard and sailed out of the marina at a speed that left a wake of violently tossing boats and equally violent language. Passing under the First Narrows Bridge he headed for the strait, oblivious to other boats he met who flashed lights to alert him to turn on his travelling lights.

When he got out into the straits, he throttled back and took down two short trolling rods. With difficulty in the dark and because of trembling fingers he set up the rods with heavy line and, without bothering with leaders, tied on, with clumsy knots, large plugs with double triple hooks on each, illegal tackle that had been in his fishing box for years. When he had finished, he got carefully to his feet on the bobbing deck and shoved the rods into two rod holders, stripped off a long length of line on each rod and tightened holding nut so tight that there would be no possibility of anything pulling line off the reel. Then he steered the boat toward the longest horizon and tied the rudder in place. With everything set, he sat twisting his neck to make the pain in his head go away. In the silence, he heard a rhythmic bumping against the hull and remembered he had not taken in the fenders. He staggered forward to bring them in and as he struggled to haul them in, a big wash from a passing tug threw the little boat side-ways and he toppled over the small railing clutching at air and cursing. The cold water hit him like a hammer filling his mouth and nose until he rose to the surface coughing and spluttering. He saw the boat moving slowly at trolling speed away from him and he struck out after it with, for a minute, a strong stroke he had learned years ago but tired quickly. And just as he gave up trying to catch it, a fishing line from his boat ran across his arm and he grabbed it and tried to cling to it as it kept slipping from his grasp. Suddenly the line ended and the double triple hooked plug ran between his legs and hooked solidly to his genitals. He tried to scream, but his mouth was filled with seawater. The boat moved on, the sturdy trolling rod scarcely bent, the heavy line taut with the diminishing struggle of the catch until flesh ripped and the hooks came free.

CHAPTER 37

Craig was getting anxious to see Rob. It seemed to him that he hadn't seen Rob for a week. He knew that wasn't true because he had seen him around the school usually with Donna hanging on to him, but he hadn't seen him to talk to him. So after dinner he helped his mother with the dishes for which she was more grateful for the company than for the help and headed over to the Turners. The house was quiet but he saw their car in the driveway to the garage so he figured they must be home although there were none of the usual sounds of printers or other office machines coming from the house. He knocked his 'It's me' knock and opened the door and shouted, "Hey, Rob!" As he listened inside the door, he heard no sounds from downstairs or from the second floor until the clump of footsteps coming up the stairs from the basement. Rob's father came to the top with a heavy tread and with his face set in an angry scowl. Craig was quite used to the look and did not take it personally.. Glen Turner was usually angry about something that the political idiots were doing to bugger up the world and Craig was not in the mood for another piece of rhetoric so he said only, "Hi, Mr. T. Rob home?"

The scowl seemed to deepen when Rob's father answered, "No, he sure as hell is not!" and turned to continue up the next flight of stairs.

Craig had learned not to pursue such remarks with questions and as he stepped outside to go he heard Rob's mother call, "Is that you, Craig? I'm down here."

Going down the basement stairs to what was now the Turner's living room and kitchen, he found Rob's mother sitting looking puffy-eyed on the sofa. "Hello, Craig," she said when he came into the room. "Rob's not home. In fact, he's in trouble. Do you know anything about it?"

"In trouble? No! What's wrong?"

"Come and sit down," she said, patting the sofa beside her, and noting the immediate alteration in Craig's face and demeanour at the mention of Rob in trouble, as if Rob's trouble was automatically Craig's trouble too. "You're getting so tall it's hard on my neck looking up at you. Rob and some other boys were caught with pot at school," she continued when Craig sat down beside her.

"It seems the caretaker was an undercover cop and asked Rob for some and Rob was dickering on the price for fun because he only had one butt."

"Joint," Craig said.

"Okay, joint, butt, whatever. The thing is that they got taken in and charged. The other boys' parents went down and got them out but Glen will not do anything to help him and won't let me do anything. I've never seen him so angry. And I know why, in a way. After all, he's spent a lot of time trying to get drugs out of the schools and off the streets and it hurts when his own son is caught trafficking—but I can't think that what he did should be called by the same name as what the big-time criminals do."

"Where is he?" Craig asked, getting to his feet and prepared to do anything for his friend. "I better go do something."

"It's alright, Craig. I phoned Beverley and Richard went down and signed him out. Glen found out and he was furious with me." She stopped and looked at Craig's worried face. "Maybe it's not as bad as it seems but it's the second time for him and I've got to admit that it's got me pretty worried."

"Yeah! That was dumb!" Craig said, leaving her to ponder just what he meant. "I better get out there and see if he's okay."

"It's a long way, Craig. You're not driving yet, are you? Maybe your mother will drive you."

"No, I'll take a bus. She's—, well, she's kinda feeling down these days."

"Oh, I'm sorry. Has she been sick?"

"No, it's just—, well, I dunno how to say it. I guess it's just family stuff. You know, like my dad."

"Maybe I better call her, but not tonight. We could give each other a boost."

"Yeah," Craig said and bent over and kissed her on the forehead twice. "One's from Rob," he said with a grin.

When he got to Bev and Richard's, Bev answered the door and greeted him warmly. "Hi there, Handsome," she said with a big warm smile. "What brings you out here? As if I didn't know. He's in the living room playing uncle."

Craig moved out of the hall into the living room and found Rob flat on his back balancing his delighted niece in the air on the soles of his feet. Catching sight of Craig, he·shouted, "Hey, look who's here! My very favourite person in the whole wide world, except I can't remember his name. Do you know his name?" he asked the child, jiggling his feet so that she screamed excitedly.

"Rob! Knock it off! She'll never get to sleep," Bev called.

"Okay," Rob called, letting the child down. And then to the child, "Are you going to give Uncle Craig a big kiss hello?"

"Unh-unh!" she replied, shaking her head firmly.

"Well, I'll have to do it, then. Do you want Uncle Rob to give Uncle Craig a big kiss hello?"

"Unh-unh."

"I guess he'll just have to wait until I get him alone, won't he?" And the child nodded solemnly. "Then off you go, your mummy says it's bedtime. Give me a big smooch!" After which he sent her on her way with a gentle pat on her bottom.

"Hi, buddy," he said to Craig. "What're you doing in these parts?"

"Oh, I was just passing by."

"Sure!" Rob said with a grin. Then, "Do you want to go for a walk?"

When Craig nodded, Rob called to Bev, "Hey, sis! Me and my buddy are going for a walk, okay?"

"Okay," she called. "It's getting late. Is Craig going to sleep over?"

Craig shook his head in negation, and Rob called, "No, I'll send him home when I'm tired of playing with him."

Outside, Rob said, "I thought we'd better bugger off for a while. Richard likes to meditate for an hour each day and he's been pretty busy today visiting at the police station, so he needs some quiet time."

They walked together for a while until Craig bumped Rob's shoulder and asked, "So?"

Rob shrugged. "So I got conned by a goddam cop."

"How did he con you?"

"He was dressed in overalls with a push mop and came around the corner just as me and two other guys were comparing the joints we got from a guy in the can. And he says, like, Hey, where did you get those. I been looking for some. And I says, No way am I going to tell. And he says, How much do you want for that one? Then I started to kid him and I told him, Maybe, one, two three or four bucks but I'd settle for five. So he reaches into his hip pocket and pulled out his wallet but he just flipped it open and showed me his badge and said, Okay fellas, better come with me to the principal's office."

"But they're not supposed to do that! That's illegal! They're not supposed to trick people like that!" Craig blustered. Rob stopped and looked with dumb amazement at his friend. "Oh, really?" he said. "I guess I should have read him his rights."

Craig shrugged at the put-down. "Yeah, well okay. Then what happened?"

"The principal phoned my parents and told them that I was being taken to the dungeons and they would have to come and get me, and my Dad said, Let him rot, I guess, Then Richard came and they let me go with him. That's all. Nothing to it."

"What's going to happen now?"

"I dunno. Richard says they probably won't waste much time on the arrest of a kid with one joint but I think they'll probably send me up for ten years."

"Ten years !" Craig squeaked, stopping to face Rob. Then seeing Rob grinning, he knew he was being teased and said, "Oh, sure!" and walked on.

"Hey, what have you been doing? I haven't seen you for a while. You mad at me? Donna said she saw you last week but you walked by and didn't speak to her."

"I didn't see her," Craig said in a voice of protest rather than explanation. "I was looking for you but I could never find you alone. You were always with her."

"Yeah, so? It ain't a sin if a guy talks to a girl, y'know!"

"I know! But I had to talk to you alone. It was just some- thing about us—-about me."

"Come on then, baby! Talk to me!" Rob growled in a stage voice, throwing his arm over Craig's shoulder.

"Cut it out, Rob! This is serious!" He twisted away from Rob's arm and they faced each other. "My Dad's a homo!"

Rob looked at Craig, his face darkening with a confusion of emotions. "What d'ya mean"?

"I mean, remember the party last Saturday and I got drunk? Well, I guess I passed out when I got home and I woke up in the middle of the night and my Dad was sitting beside my bed and he had just given me a blow job."

"You're kidding!" in a voice of disbelief and disgust.

"I am not. He was naked and when I woke up I had my hand on his great big ugly dick and I had shot my wad all over the place and he was wiping it off his face."

"You've got to be kidding!"

"I am not and I wasn't dreaming either."

"Holy shit! Holy shit!" Rob kept on saying as he walked around in a small circle like a dog preparing to lie down.

They walked on saying little for a while except for Rob's explosions of "The rotten bastard!" "The filthy son of a bitch!" and such other epithets as he could dredge up.

"Rob?" Craig ventured after a silence. "You know when we were talking about us maybe being too close and not fooling around any more like we used to? Because, well, maybe we were getting that way, you know, like queer?"

"Yeah," Rob answered, his voice more casual than curious.

"Well, I figured out that it was my fault," Craig said.

"What a genius! How do you figure that?"

"I just think it was. Because if he's queer, then it's probably hereditary. So he gave me his queer genes just like he gave me his butterfly."

"For God's sake, Craig. It's not hereditary. Genetics has got nothing to do with it. I've got more to do with it than genetics."

"How do you figure that?"

"Who taught you everything you know about sex?"

"You?" Craig said in mock disdain. "I could get better information from the comics."

They walked on through the quiet night, occasionally muttering but not talking untile Craig said, "Yeah, there's another thing I been wanting to tell you."

"What? You gonna tell me that you got another girl that's prettier than Lee?"

"No, not that! But I wish she would write—she promised, you know."

Rog shrugged. "Promises, promises!" he said cynically. "So what is it?"

"It's about what my dad did to Edie when she was little." They stopped walking again and Craig told Rob everything his mother had told him without interruption except that again Rob paced in small circles of frustration.

"Jesus!" he exploded when Craig was finished. "The guy's a monster. He's not sick—he's just a goddam pervert. How many other kids did he fiddle and diddle with. How come he missed me? I was around a lot! Maybe he knew I'd kick him in the balls if he touched me. Oh, poor Edie! All these years holding it in! And thinking she was to blame. Jesus, he's rotten! What does Edie say? Have you talked to her?"

"No, she talked to Mom and she wanted Mom to tell me. I guess it's easier to tell your mother than your brother. She's going to some kind of therapy"

Rob's anger was very real and Craig watched, seeing in his friend's response the quality of their friendship. They continued with their walking and talking until it was too late to catch a bus back into town. When they got back to Bev's and went inside, she heard them enter and called out to Rob to lock the door.

"Craig missed the bus," he called softly to her. "He's staying over."

"Okay. Get a sleeping bag from the closet. Goodnight!"

In the rumpus room in the basement, while Craig was in the bathroom, Rob had pulled out the daybed and zipped two sleeping bags together.

Seeing the arrangement, Craig protested, "Ro-o-ob!"

"Oh, come on! I can protect myself," Rob said grinning.

"Okay," Craig said reluctantly. "But no funny stuff."

"Promise! No funny stuff."

They crawled into bed and turned out the light. Craig turned his back and Rob curled up against him. Rob threw an arm across Craig and pulled him into a tighter curl. "Know what day this is" he asked.

"What d'ya mean?" sleepily.

"It's the twenty first of September," Rob said. "The end of summer. Jeez! What a great summer, wasn't it?"

"Yeah!"

CHAPTER 38

"Now you listen to me, young man! We do have a telephone and I think you're smart enough to remember the number and if you decide to stay out all night you are supposed to phone that number and tell the person that answers—that's me, you know, your mother, remember me?—that you're not at the police station, or in the hospital or the morgue."

"Or lying drunk in some ditch," he mumbled, just within her hearing zone.

"What did you say?" she snapped.

"Well, that was another possibility you didn't mention."

"Yes and there are a lot more that I don't need to mention. So try to get the point, will you. I do worry! I know you're not a child, but neither have you shown me that you're an independent adult, yet. So I'm entitled to worry when you don't come home. And I like my sleep, too, instead of waking up every fifteen minutes to see if you are home." She was on a pretty good maternal scolding roll and had been enjoying it, covering most of the significant bases—accident, hospital, jail, morgue, runaway—and then she went one step too far and she knew it as soon as she said it. "Or maybe you were out at some brothel picking up some disease like AIDS to bring home." And it flashed through her mind, Or spending the night in a motel pretending you were at a bridge convention.

Craig had listened filially to her, not exactly overflowing with contrition but knowing he should have made a little more effort to inform her but he bridled at the brothel implication. "Mother! For God's sake!"

Seeing his legitimate anger, she tried to back off a little. "Well," she said, "that's what your father did!"

"Don't tell me you think my life is going to be like his!" he retorted. "Just because I inherited his goddam butterfly, do you think I'm going to be a drunk and a woman chaser and child molester and that I'm going to turn into a cold, self-centred son of a bitch like he is! Like father, like son? Is that what you mean? And a freaking homo, too?" He wished he hadn't added that last bit.

She had listened to him without interruption or argument, sensing the depths of his feelings and she waived her parental guiding rights in favour of finding other information. "What do you mean, Craig? Do you mean that...?"

"I mean that he is a homosexual! That's what I mean! I know because he tried his tricks on me the other night, but it didn't work. I woke up in time."

She was pale and shaking, completely unnerved by the strange twists her life was taking. "I don't understand. What happened? Do you mean that when he was here the other night he, he did something to you? What did he do?"

"You don't need to know, Mom. Believe me! You don't even want to know. It's more than enough to know that he made a homo attack on me when I was sleeping and I woke up. But it scares me shitless when the 'like father, like son' thing comes up." He never used such language in front of his mother but she seemed not to notice. Somehow or other they seemed to reach a mutual decision that they were finished talking. This time he went to her and patted her gently on the head before he went up to his room.

Later in the day, he phoned Rob at Bev's but there was no answer. Then he phoned the Turner's on spec and Rob's father answered. "Yes, he's here. But he can't talk to you now. I'll tell him you called. Don't you call again—I don't want you tying up the line." He hung up abruptly without further words. Craig shrugged. By the time he went to bed on Sunday night, Rob had not returned his call.

He searched the halls at every opportunity on Monday looking for Rob but nobody had seen him. Finally, at noon, he called Bev who didn't want to talk to him but did tell him that Rob and his father were still at odds with each other and that Richard had decided that he was not going to get in the middle of a family quarrel so he told Rob that he couldn't stay after last night. So Rob left after breakfast and if he wasn't at school she didn't know where he was. Her voice was a little shaky as she explained it to Craig, saying that Richard hoped they could force some kind of reconciliation if they didn't take sides. She snuffled a bit and Craig heard her say something like 'Fat chance.'

"Bev, listen to me," Craig told her with a tone of urgency in his voice. "If you see Rob or he calls, you tell him to come on over to our house. He can stay with me until...well, he can stay with me. It'll be okay with my Mom. I'll call her and tell her in case he gets there before I get home from school." He said goodbye to her and told her not to worry, that he would look after Rob, which made her smile for the first time in the day. He called home but the line was busy.

Marion was fidgeting as she listened to Edith on the phone. Edith had made her usual checking-in call, and although Marion desperately wanted to avoid it, she had to tell Edith that her father had attacked Craig sexually. Edith wanted to know the details but Marion could not provide them and Edith said she thought that Craig should call her right away or, better still, he should come out and they could have a long talk and maybe he should go to the group session with her. "It's important, Mom," she insisted. "These things get buried away in your unconscious and they rot there and your whole personality can change unless you dig them out and deal with them before they get buried. Believe me! I know!"

"He seemed alright this morning," Marion ventured.

"Well, he wasn't, Mom!" Edith said with her usual authority. "He was just hiding it. Everybody in my group did the same thing." Then from a fastball to a slow curve. "Did you miss not going to the hospital this morning?"

"Well, yes and no," Marion answered, glad that Edith had changed the topic. "But I have been busy moving out of your bedroom and back into my own."

"You have? Good for you! That was always a miserable little room. I hated it." No wonder you hated it, Marion thought, and that slider rocker too. But it was never a miserable little room. It was bright and light and cheerful.

From the back door came Rob's cheerful call, "Hello, UU! Are you home?"

"Edith, Rob's at the door. Just a minute." She turned the mouthpiece away from her face and called, "I'm in here—on the phone." And then returned to

Edith. "I'll have to say goodbye. I want to talk to Rob—he is in some kind of trouble at home." And to herself she said, Will I never learn! That's just like throwing bait out to Edith.

And Edith responded on cue. "What kind of trouble? What did he do?"

"I'll call you, Edith. Give the girls a big hug from their <u>Granny</u>."

"Sorry about that, Mom." Edith laughed and hung up.

Rob was already sprawled on the bench in the nook, looking somewhat more ragged that usual, when she got to the kitchen. "Why aren't you in school, Rob?" she asked without any preliminaries.

"Augh," he replied with a shrug. "I thought I'd wait until the heat was off. Too many questions."

"So tell me what's going on."

"Well, I got caught with a joint by a guy I thought..."

"I know all that. I mean where have you been and how are things with your Dad?"

Rob told her about the long family argument and his father's adamant refusal to let him come home, and Richard's decision that he couldn't stay with them, not because he blamed Rob but to try to force his father-in-law to be more rational. Marion noticed that Rob was a little solemn in recounting the events and the subtle flippancy that marked his usual approach to life's problems was missing.

"I'll make us some lunch," she said, taking for granted that he had not eaten and if he had he would eat another lunch anyway, "and then I'll phone your mother and get her to bundle up some clothes and your school books and you can stay here until things get sorted out." She watched his sombre face light up. "I'll drive over and get them if you don't want to go. I might put in a word for you. Just a word, mind you—not a biographical paean of praise. Now," she concluded, setting the tone for the conditions of his stay, "go get washed."

He got up from the bench smothering a grin and wrapped his arms around her without saying anything and she could feel the child in him trembling.

In the middle of their lunch the door bell rang. Marion pushed the other half of her sandwich over to Rob as she left to answer it, wondering aloud who that could be. Rob, without trying to listen, heard the conversation at the door, and then stopped eating to listen closely.

There were two police officers at the door, a man and a woman.

"Good afternoon," the police woman said. "We're from the city police." She paused and Marion said nothing. "Is this the Williams' residence?"

"Yes, I'm Marion Williams," she said in an uncertain voice. "What's the trouble?"

"Perhaps we could come in and you could sit down," the policewoman said.

Rob moved from the table to a protective stance behind Marion after she motioned for them to come in. They followed her into the living room where they all were seated silently. The policeman cleared his throat and asked, "Is your husband's name Gerald Williams?"

GORDON BRYENTON

288

"Yes. What is this all about?"

"Does he own a boat?"

"Yes."

"Do you know the name and registration number of the boat?"

"No, I don't like boats. I've never been out on it. Oh, yes! I remember. When he bought it, it had some name he didn't like and he changed it right away to, let me see if I can get it right, oh yes. He changed it to the Master Baiter."

The policeman smothered a small smile over his notebook. "Is your husband at home, Mrs. Williams."

"No," she said stiffly. "He does not live here."

The policeman paused, looking at his notebook and then said in a quiet voice, "Mrs. Williams, a boat with that name registered to a Gerald Williams at this address has been reported to have foundered off the shore of Bowen Island."

Marion listened but the information did not appear to be meaningful to her and she gave no indication of having understood. Rob, who had been standing aside, grasped the possibilities more quickly and moved to sit by Marion and take her hand.

The policeman continued in the same quiet voice, "The body of a man has been found in some low tide pools in that area. Identification documents taken from a wallet on the body indicate that the body could be that of your husband, Gerald Williams." Marion heard and understood and she toppled back on the sofa with her head lolling and a sound, neither a moan or a cough but something between emerging from her throat. "Cawc-cawc-cawc-cawc-cawc," she said until she ran out of breath, at which point she took another breath and the sound was interrupted by snuffles as her nose filled with some of the tears that suddenly poured out.

Nothing more was said for a minute. Then the policewoman asked, "Mrs. Williams? Would you like your son to get you a glass of water?"

The noise she was making stopped and she raised her head slightly and said in a strangled voice, "He's not my son. He, he's my, my friend." She meant to say 'my son's friend' but the words didn't come out and she couldn't be bothered correcting them. The policewoman, new to the force, had not yet been exposed to the variety of human relationships she would soon be familiar with, pursed her lips and straightened her back in disapproval. Rob brought Marion some water. The policeman waited.

Finally, he said, "I'm sorry, Mrs. Williams, but I have to tell you that either you or some member of your family must identify the body and sign some documents, proof of identification, autopsy forms, things like that before the body can be removed for disposal." He paused and said gently, "Can you manage that, Mrs. Williams?"

She shook her head, her hands covering her face.

Rob leaned forward to the policeman. "Sir?" he said. "I'll phone the school and ask them to send Craig home, that's her son. I'm his friend. And I'll phone her daughter Edith and tell her. Maybe I can get my mother to come over until the family gets here. They're good friends."

The policeman stood up. "That's a good idea," he said. "Your name?"

"Rob Turner." He watched it being entered in the policeman's notebook and said to himself: Twice in a week. Better be careful, Rob!

"Tell the family that only one identification is required and that there may be some questions. The body is at the morgue in the hospital. Whoever goes to identify it should be told that it is not, well, it has been in the water for some time, and it is not a pleasant sight."

Rob was hanging tight to his own emotions but he managed to nod stiffly and show the two officers out when they had said formal words of condolence to Marion that she really did not hear. When he returned from seeing them out, he went directly to Marion and sat beside her, putting his arms around her and letting his own tears flow. "It's all right, UU," he said. "I'll call my mother and Edith and get Craig. You hang tight, OK?" Marion nodded dumbly.

Rob's father answered the phone and said gruffly, when he heard his son's voice, "What do you want?"

"Listen to me, Dad! Just listen for once, please!" and he continued without giving his father a chance to interrupt. "I'm over at the Williams. The police were here. They found Craig's father's body on the beach. He was drowned. UU's in a bad way. Will you tell Mom to come over right now. UU needs her. I'm going to phone Edith and then I'm going to the school to get Craig. OK?"

There was silence at the other end of the line.

Rob said, after of moment of waiting, "Dad?"

His father answered in a husky voice, "Yes, Rob, I heard. Is there anything I can do?"

"I don't know, Dad. Ask Mom."

There was another silence with small noises until his father said, his voice strained with emotion, "Rob? Rob, when you finish there, will you come home? Please?"

"Yeah, okay," Rob answered openly, without caution or resentment, "after I get Craig and see if he needs me."

Claudia Turner arrived less than five minutes after Rob's call and while he was still on the phone trying again to find a break in Edith's busy signal. She and Rob had a quiet exchange at the door before Claudia went into the living room and sat down beside Marion and took her in her arms. Rob tried Edith once more and then left without a word, taking Craig's bike.

At the school he went directly to the office. The principal's secretary frowned at him in preparation for a dressing down for past misdemeanours and probably present ones as well, but Rob spoke before her frown turned to words. "Miss Claring, I've got to get Craig Williams out of his class and take him home. His father has been drowned. I don't know his schedule or I would get him."

Miss Claring was not prepared for emergency action of any sort other than perhaps spilled ink, but another secretary said, "Just a minute, Rob. I'll get his schedule from the counseling office and it will be easier for me to go get him. You stay here."

Rob took a seat by the door, a safe distance from Miss Claring who kept glancing sadly his way and sighing. Craig arrived with a puzzled look on his face and Rob got up before the door closed and said, "Let's go!" taking Craig by the arm and shoving him out the door. "Thank you," he said to the secretary and nodded to Miss Claring who was still not certain that the principal would have approved.

Outside the office door, Craig demanded, "What the hell is going on?"

The hall was empty and Craig's voice echoed in the stillness. "I'll tell you when we get outside," Rob answered. "I brought your bike," he added, then tagged on the perplexing explanation. "so you can ride home."

They walked out the door of the school and Rob headed for the bike-racks. He pulled Craig's bike out of the stanchion but did not relinquish it. He stood looking at his friend without having any idea of what he should now say, his face a mixture of emotions that Craig could not fathom. Suddenly, Rob blurted out, "The police came to your house this morning. I was there. Your dad drowned and they came to tell her."

Craig looked at him without much comprehension and said "What?" So Rob told him quickly all he knew, surprised by how little reaction Craig showed.

"I better go home and see about my mother," Craig said.

"Do you want me to come with you," Rob asked.

"Of course," as if it had been a stupid question.

"I tried to call Edie but her line was busy," Rob said as they walked.

"Yeah."

"Somebody's got to identify the body—a family member," Rob said.

Craig stopped in his tracks. "Not me!" he said, explosively. "No way! Not me! I'm not going to do that! I won't." And he stomped on down the street, his back little-boy rigid.

"They have to do it, Craig. They have to be sure it's the right person. Supposing it isn't him. They don't know."

"It better be him!" Craig said grimly.

They arrived at the house and went in. Craig's mother had got over the initial shock and was in reasonable control and prepared to comfort Craig, but seeing his dry eyes and stony face she knew that he needed little consolation. Still in a long embrace with little being said between them, Marion said, "Edith called and Claudia talked to her. She is going to get somebody to look after the girls and then she will pick up Harvey and come in."

"Oh, good," he said. "Rob told me he tried to get her but her line was busy." And then he added, "Mom, when I was talking to Bev I told her to tell Rob that he could stay with us until, well, you know. And I didn't tell Rob yet. So, okay?"

"Yes, okay. Rob and I talked this morning about it?"

"What's this all about?" Claudia interrupted with a puzzled look at both of them.

"Hey, people! Just a minute!" Rob called out. "I don't need to stay here, really. My dad asked me to come home. He even said please." and he grinned widely.

"Really, Rob? Really?" his mother said to him. And he nodded not trusting his voice.

She took his hands and pulled him to her, her eyes filling with tears and Rob's own eyes were wet with some inner feelings he could not describe. The other two, watching them, mirrored their uniting moment and with their emotions already close to the surface, smiled and released a few tears. It was then that Edith burst in on the smiling and tearful group. "What's going on?" she demanded.

Edith had hurried on ahead while Harvey parked the car and when he came in he had missed some of the confused attempts to tell Edith what had happened, but he waited and asked and what was known merged into a coherent sequence for everyone present. Edith was wailing loudly but received so little attention that she stopped and went to the kitchen, announcing, "I'll make some tea."

There was a long silence and Marion ended it with a long sigh, saying, "Somebody's got to identify the body, they said. I suppose..." and her voice faded.

"Marion, would you like me to do that for you?" Harvey asked.

"Oh, Harvey! Would you? Oh, thank you. I didn't know how I could possibly do it."

"Yeah, thanks, Harv," Craig said, adding cautiously, "Would you like me to come with you?" And when Harvey shook his head and said, "I can do it, Craig. You stay with your mother," his relief was almost measurable.

"I suppose I might as well do it now," Harvey said. "There's nothing to be gained by waiting." He shrugged and added, "And it might not even be him. We should know for sure."

Marion shuddered at the thought and Craig groaned, "Oh, God!"

Harvey went to the kitchen and spoke to Edith. "You okay?"

She nodded tight-lipped and Harvey said, "I'll be back as soon as I can."

"Maybe this would be a good time for us to go, Marion," Claudia said. "Your family is here and..."

"No, not yet!" Edith called from the kitchen. "I've just made some cucumber sandwiches."

"Well, I suppose I better stay for cucumber sandwiches," Claudia said, smiling, and received a grateful smile in return from Marion. Neither of them noticed Craig, then Rob, slip out the door and disappear.

"Is that right about your dad?" Craig asked.

"Yeah, he really did ask me to come home. I don't know if there are any strings attached but I bet there are. Anyhow, I guess I'll go and see."

"Right now?"

"Might as well."

"I'll go with you."

When they arrived at the Turner's, Rob's father happened to see them coming. "Bringing moral support, Rob?" he said in a soft tone that gave Rob a throb of hope. And without waiting for an answer, he turned to Craig and said, "I am truly sorry for your family, Craig. I think you know that if there is anything I can do, just call."

Craig nodded his thanks, holding onto his emotions tightly and thinking, I better get used to people saying this.

"I wonder if your mother would like some help with the notice for the papers. I've had to do quite a few of those."

"I'll ask her. I'm sure she would."

"Good! Call me." He turned his attention to Rob. "Well," he said, and his voice was neither demanding or pleading, "Are we going to talk?"

***

At the hospital, Harvey was directed to the morgue that had so few visitors there was no need for a receptionist. He pushed the double swinging doors partly open and looked in on the gloomy room. A woman in a white lab coat, working at a microscope, looked up at Harvey's "Excuse me?" "Yes. Come in. Can I help you?" she said.

"I've come to identify Gerald Williams, or I should say the body of Gerald Williams," Harvey almost whispered in the quiet room.

"Oh, yes. Now let's see," she muttered scanning a clipboard she had taken off the wall. "Hm-m. That was a drowning. Not very pleasant to look at. Pretty bloated and the crabs got to him a bit. Now," she continued, "you'll have to fill out this form. Just usual stuff—name, address, relationship to the deceased, stuff like that. We get you to do it before because lots of people can't do it after. Got a pen?" Harvey nodded. "Shout when you've done," she said, walking back to her work bench.

He called to her in a few minutes. "All done?" she asked. "Let's see then," looking at her clipboard. "Over here."

She paused with her hand on the handle of a giant filing cabinet. "Ready?" she asked and when he nodded she pulled open the drawer and let him see the contents.

The body was bloated and the face, ravaged during the past months by abuse, had been further disfigured by the nibbling of crabs. The change had been so dramatic, he could not say for certain that the thing on the table was Gerald Williams. His stomach lurched in his gut. He wanted to cover his mouth but held himself against such an act. "I don't know," he said, shakily.

"Not sure? That's all right. But take another good look just to make sure. Any tattoos, or something like that?"

Harvey was breathing heavily. "Has he got a birthmark shaped like a butterfly right here," he asked, indicating a place on the small of his back.

"Jackpot!" she exclaimed, shoving her hip against the drawer so that it slammed closed. "That'll do it. Thanks very much, Mr. Allen," she said, looking at his information sheet. "Better get yourself a cup of coffee before you head for home. Lots of people get the shakes a long time after they leave. Okay?" and she turned back to her workbench without waiting for an answer.

When Harvey got back to the house, everybody's emotions seemed to be under control. Edith was phoning the Memorial Society which had all the pertinent information on file and now promised to make all the arrangements as detailed in Gerald William's membership form unless there had been changes that had not been documented. She covered the mouthpiece and spoke to her mother, telling her the substance of what had been said. Marion, whose eyes were by now dry, sighed and said, "Give me the phone, Edith. I had better talk to them."

"One minute, Mr. Miller, my mother would like to speak to you," Edith said bringing the phone to her mother.

"Mr. Miller? This is Marion Williams." She said nothing for a moment while Mr. Miller offered his condolences. "Thank you," she continued when he had finished, "I would like to make some changes in the arrangements requested by Mr. Williams when we joined the society. I don't have a copy of the form handy but I think I can remember enough of the details. The family wants the simplest possible plan. There will be no memorial service unless we decide at a later date to have a private service. And cremation immediately." She waited listening. "No, no, Mr. Miller. I do not want the ashes in an urn. The simplest, quickest, most private arrangements that you can manage." She paused again, listening. "Perhaps you're right, some sort of notice in the obituary column would seem necessary. But, Mr. Miller, please keep it as simple and brief as possible. Just a minute, please, my son wants to tell me something." Craig had been touching her on the arm to attract her attention.

"Rob's dad said he would help with the notice in the paper. He says he's done a lot of them," Craig told her.

Marion looked at Claudia, who nodded agreement, and then returned to the phone. "Mr. Miller, a friend of the family will take care of the obituary notice, so you don't have to bother." She listened for another minute and said, "Alright, then, Mr. Miller. If you draw up the papers and bring them around, I'll look over them and sign them. I should be home all day tomorrow, but please call first."

She sat back and handed the phone to Craig to put away. "Well, that's that. It wasn't difficult at all. The next thing will be the will and other stuff like that." She sighed but seemed to be in complete control of her emotions.

"Does that mean that there's not going to be a casket, or pall bearers, or any kind of a service or flowers or anything?" Edith asked.

"That's right, dear," Marion replied.

"But, mother, what will people think?"

Marion shrugged. "Whatever they think really doesn't matter. I refuse to go through a public charade pretending that I am a heart broken widow. But if you two children want a big circus, well just say so and I'll arrange it."

"No, not me!" Craig said.

"I guess not me, either," Edith said. "But I thought it might be good if the twins could see a funeral."

"No, Edie," Harvey said quietly, shaking his head.

Edith blew out a long breath. "Well, I'll certainly have something to talk about in group next time." She looked at her watch and announced, "Harvey, we've got to go and pick up the girls."

Finally, after the last minute agreements to call, the hugs and words of sympathy, the three of them left, Edith, Harvey and Claudia, leaving Craig and his mother alone in a suddenly quiet house, at which point Marion sat down and sighed heavily, her face in her hands, telling Craig that it had been a long day. He agreed solemnly as they set about closing up the house for the night.

CHAPTER 39

The following week placed so many demands on Marion's emotions that she spent many hours in her room with the drapes drawn. The Memorial Society had called to say that the coroner would not release the body until an autopsy had been done. The policewoman who had come to the house called to explain the delay and reported that there was no doubt that the cause of death was by drowning, but, apparently some unexplained deep gashes were found in the genital area which, in themselves, were not the cause of death, but might be indicative of foul play prior to drowning. The captain of the Coast Guard vessel who had found the boat and pulled it out of the shallows told the coroner's office that the boat had been rigged with two heavy fishing rods each with very large triple hooked plugs still tied on. "He must have been fishing for whales," he had added sarcastically. After what seemed to Marion to be too many unnecessary delays, an autopsy was completed and the coroner was satisfied that the cause of death was by accidental drowning and that no inquest was required. A medical social worker called at the house to answer any question Marion might have about the cause of death. Marion had no questions but that did not inhibit the social worker from explaining in detail that the autopsy concluded that, although a valid blood-alcohol analysis could not be made because of the length of time the body had been in the water, the stomach contents revealed a large intake of alcohol within one hour prior to death. The autopsy also exposed, she said, a large tumor, somewhat larger than a golf ball, situated between the left dorsal lobe and the left frontal lobe. "It was not malignant, thank God!" she breathed, while Marion gazed foggily at the ceiling and thought, What the hell difference would it have made if it had been malignant?

"Did you notice any change in your husband's behaviour over the past, say, several months?" the woman persisted.

"No, I did not! I could not!" Marion protested. "I already told you that my husband and I were not living together; that our marriage had failed totally and finally some months ago and that we had very little contact or communication with one another."

"I see," the social worker said. "But would you say that your husband was depressed?"

"I would not know!" Marion stated in a firm voice while two red spots of anger started showing on her cheeks. "Now, listen to me, please, Miss... I've forgotten your name."

"Rannic," came the helpful response

"Miss Rannic..."

"No, Mrs. Williams. It's Rannic Turban."

Marion sighed. "Very well, Miss Turban. I don't know why you are here. You have given me a lot of information that I really didn't want to have, and if you have come to help me, as you say, well, if you will pardon my rudeness, you're not! In fact, I find your visit quite upsetting and I wish you would go."

"But, Mrs. Williams...."

"No, please, no more. No more."

"Very well, Mrs. Williams," the social worker said, picking up her notebook and pens and stuffing them in a carryall with a collection of files. "But if you are feeling depressed, and many people do, sometimes long after the death seems to have been finalized, don't be surprised if it happens to you. I wouldn't be. Mrs. Williams, do give me a call and I'll come any time, any time at all." She put out a hand and shook Marion's till the bones crackled. "Here's my card. I'll see myself out."

She gathered her large frame together and Marion watched her go. She seemed not to walk out the door and down the sidewalk as much as she appeared to manoeuvre out to and around her car like a bobbing tug. Marion thought it would look fitting if she had the words 'The Rannic Turban' stencilled across her stern. Then she started to laugh and closed the door quickly in case the tug heard her, and she went to the sofa and laughed hard and loud until the hysterical laughter turned into tears.

During the week, the Turners learned the possible charges against Rob for possession and trafficking had been dropped by a furious City Prosecutor when he had been told of the entrapment used by an overzealous and inexperienced police officer. "For Christ sake," he had been overheard to roar at the sergeant, "send that stupid bugger out looking for jay walkers. We pick up a half a ton of weed a week and we work our butts off trying to get a conviction on a guy who's got his name written all over the package and what happens? Do you know what happens? Some judge who smokes tells me your boys didn't dot an 'i' or cross a 't' and the guy walks. And you want me to prosecute three kids with three little joints who were conned by your man who was pretending to be a janitor? Who put him in there in plain clothes? And I suppose you expect these kids to get life for their vicious crime against society. Get outta here!"

The story presented to the parents of the two boys and to Richard, who relayed it to Bev who phoned her mother who told her husband who called Rob in for a familiar lecture, was not quite as detailed but sufficient to provide relief for several people and hilarity in the halls of the high school.

Glen Turner had persuaded Marion to expand the obituary notice from the bare bones she had originally insisted on, arguing that unless some informational details were given she would be bothered by many people who were more curious than sympathetic. In the end she relented and the notice stated age, accidental death by drowning, business and lodge affiliations. survivors, cremation and that a private service had been held. Glen had originally written 'Sadly remembered by..' and 'Loving wife and family..' but Marion had blacked out these and other usual phrases so solidly that he had to go back to his original to find out what he had said. The obituary appeared once only at Marion's insistence, midweek in one local paper, during the week after the cremation.

Looking only for the single item in the obituary columns, she found it and issued a sigh of completion. She did not notice a small news item in the same paper that reported that the body of a man by the name of Timothy T. Irvin had been discovered by the cleaning crew in the billiard room of the Sycamore Golf and Country Club. The chief steward explained to the police and to the press that the member frequently overindulged and passed out in the club. He said that Mr. Irvin was a very heavy man and that it took three employees to load him onto a flat cart and wheel him into some unoccupied room to sleep it off. He said that if Mr. Irvin could not be aroused before the bar closed, someone usually covered him with the billiard table cloth and left him for the night. Edith noticed the item and read it to her mother during her daily call to confirm that it was the same Golf Club her father belonged to. The gossiping chief steward has been quickly relieved of his employment at the Sycamore Golf and Country Club.

Two days later she called twice, once her morning check on her mother, and the second time to tell her that the obituary of Mr. Irvin was three inches long while the obit for her family was no more than half an inch which she thought was insulting and unfair. And, she asked, didn't she remember the jokes her father made about a man they called Titty because of his size and his initials? Her mother said she couldn't remember, finally concluded the long call, sighed and went to bed for the rest of the day with the drapes closed.

Tom called and offered his sympathy and any assistance she might need. Her responses to him were dull and flat and he had a hard time maintaining any conversation. He offered to come over but she thanked him and said she would call him when things settled down a bit and hoped he had had a successful trip to Seattle and sorry she missed it.

The women from the bridge club called and each of them talked on and on at length until Marion thought she would scream with the boredom of hearing about other widows and other deaths and lovely funeral services. Several brought casseroles and other helpful food dishes for which Marion was grateful and Craig delighted. All were shocked to learn that there would be no funeral service. Craig had decided that he would not go to school for a week and when the week was up, he was still not ready to leave his mother alone all day. Claudia came over in her cleaning clothes and organized Craig into a hard morning of housecleaning. Rob was over frequently and when he and Craig were not isolated in Craig's room or the family room in the basement, he could be found cuddled up beside Marion, not talking but just sitting together holding hands while they watched television.

There were flowers, of course, most of them tight formal arrangements that Marion hated which Rob took over to the hospital for her in her car accompanied, of course, by Craig. (Craig did some muttering about getting some more lessons but, he insisted, not from the stinkpot he had had before.) Gerry's firm sent a bouquet of mixed flowers that was so huge and ugly that Marion asked Craig to put them out in the garage until she could break up the bouquet into small enough bunches to send to the hospital. Two weeks later, they were thrown into the compost heap.

A letter from a Kevin Claxton offered condolences on behalf of the firm but the main intent was to suggest that within the next two weeks it would be convenient for him to meet with her and her family to agree on what might be done with her husband's shares in the company, and other such personal matters that had been left in abeyance pending Gerry's return from leave of absence due to illness. Marion, alerted by Edith at Harvey's suggestion, had already contacted Murray Andrews, a lawyer who had done legal work for friends and who had prepared their wills for them some years ago. She had asked him to do whatever was necessary about her husband's will. She mailed Kevin Claxton's letter to him asking him to find out what other matters required her attention and, while he was doing that, he might also inform Mr. Claxton that, whatever the schedule of the firm, she was not yet ready to discuss anything with them, and that he, Murray, as her legal representative, would inform him, Kevin, or the Chairman of the Board, of a more appropriate date in due course.

Murray Andrews grinned after talking to her and said to himself, "Tough little lady! She's not about to be pushed around."

He phoned Kevin Claxton and asked what other matters required Mrs. Williams attention during this period of mourning. Kevin nearly choked when he heard this, as Murray thought he might, but the answer came smoothly, "There's the matter of a monthly deposit to Mrs. Williams' personal account that should have been stopped but was not stopped in time."

"Tsk, tsk," said Murray.

"Gerry's own personal account and their joint account have been closed and..."

"Thank you for sharing that information with me," Murray said sarcastically. "I might have forgotten my first year law." He could almost hear Kevin gritting his teeth.

Kevin continued. "It occurred to me that under these circumstances Marion might find it difficult to meet expenses, and I was therefore willing to buy her shares and offer her a better than market price for them, but only to help her out. I know that there is no mortgage on their house but it was registered only in his name, and I also know that Gerry had a number of spousal RRSPs. I thought she would prefer to keep those until her own retirement and sell the shares. At any rate, that would be my advice to her."

There was a long silence that lasted until Kevin said, "I say! Are you there?"

"Of course, dear boy," Murray said, affecting an English accent. "I was momentarily overwhelmed by your thoughtful concern for Marion and her family."

"Oh, I see," Kevin said uncertainly.

"Any other matters of concern to the firm?"

"Well, Gerry did have a leased car. As a matter of record, he had two, but one was stolen before the police could....Well, that's another matter. As for the present car, which is actually leased by the firm, it should be returned to the rental agency."

"Mrs. Williams will have no objections to that."

"But we don't know where it is!"

"Then, dear boy," and again the affected accent. "Let's us return to the simplest of instructions learned in first year law. Call the police."

"Thank you!" came a snarl in response.

"Do keep in touch," Murray said. Then he added casually, "Does everyone in your outfit have access to everybody's personnel files?" He waited a moment before disconnecting, then sat back in his chair and laughed uproariously. "Twit!" he said.

Later in the week he received information that Gerald Williams' last will and testament had been probated and he phoned Marion to tell her that only she, Craig, Edith, Harvey and the two grandchildren were beneficiaries and to ask if she and the family would prefer to have the formal reading of the will at her home or at his office. Marion had spent a lot of time quietly removing Gerry's golf trophies, professional magazines and other personal items so that the house reminded her less frequently of the past years. She did not want the ghost of her dead husband floating into the house and contaminating it so she opted for Murray's office immediately as did Craig and Edith. Murray asked specifically if Harvey would attend to meet Mr. Alvin Dodd who would represent the Columbia Central Trust Company, and who, along with Harvey, had also been named as an executor of the estate. Marion realized that if Gerry had included the granddaughters in his will, he must have made changes since they went together to Murray to set out their wills just after Edith and Harvey were married and before the twins were born. She wondered what other changes he might have made and it was a depressing thought that during the last terrible year he could have made many changes.

"When is a good time?" Murray had asked. "I know Harvey works and Craig's in school so maybe an evening would be good. How about this coming Monday? Would that suit everybody, do you think?"

Marion thought it would.

"Okay, let's say 7:30 PM, my office. If there's a problem with that, call me. Remember, Marion, it is a formality but it is really quite informal. I'll keep it easy."

Craig had been reluctant to return to school. He had no idea of how to respond to questions or comments teachers and friends might make about his father's death. Sorry to hear about your father, Craig. Did the crabs really eat off all his face? Did you have to look at the body? How come you burned him up instead of burying him? Why didn't I see anything in the paper about a funeral?

Rob went back to school and got a lecture from the principal along with two other boys who were caught behaving with defiance. The principal had a set piece to cover a variety of misdemeanours and he usually waited until there was a group of four or more who needed disciplinary warnings. He liked to fix them sternly with an eagle eye, but recently some eye problem resulted in a ptosis of the left eye, so while the right eye eagled, the left eye winked which usually caused uncomfortably restrained hilarity while he droned on about flouting authority, paths of least resistance, respecting the rights of others, repressing the impulses of youth, and other platitudes. On this particular day he raised a fist to the sky and shouted "'Per ardua ad astra!' which means," he said, "Through adversity to the stars! Think now, what your lives might become should you choose such a motto to guide you through life! Choose to be an eagle!" He fixed Rob with the eagle eye but at that moment the ptosis kicked in and Rob burst into uncontrolled guffaws.

"Turner! Go home! Report back to me with a one hundred word apology. The rest of you go to the counseling office." He turned back to his desk as they left quickly, their need for laughter hastening a crowded exit. "Turner!" he called before Rob reached the door. "Where's your friend Greg Williams? He's missing a lot of school."

"Craig," Rob said.

"What?"

"Craig Williams. I guess he's missing a lot of school."

The principal glared with his good eye and breathed heavily through his nose before waving a dismissing hand.

Edith called her mother every day and there was little to say on each occasion. She was openly solicitous and enquired about how her mother was sleeping and eating and about other physiological matters and was never reticent with advice. Marion found her daughter's daily enquiries depressing, but Edith did have many ideas that helped her mother deal with some dull days.

"If it was me, Mother, I'd get a copy of the findings of the autopsy and take it to your doctor and find out if that tumor was causing his crazy behavior. It might have, you know!"

Marion had thought vaguely along the same lines but had never talked about it to anyone. If there had been something wrong inside his head that made him behave so miserably, then she should have hated the thing in his head instead of him and those kinds of thoughts made her feel guilty and more depressed. She made an appointment with Dr. Strawburn who was very solicitous and gave her a prescription for some sleeping pills ('Just in case, he said'), told her that she had lost 18 pounds since she was last in and shouldn't lose any more, and said there was absolutely no way to connect her husband's aberrant behavior to a tumor on his brain. If he had been cold and unloving, it was because he was a cold and unloving man, not because he had a tumor. "You don't need to create a load of guilt for yourself, Mrs. Williams, by thinking that you could have changed him into the kind of person you wanted him to be. From what you've told me over the years, you've nothing to feel guilty about."

She sat listening to him, snuffling into a wet wad of Kleenex, hearing something of what he said but, in the back of her mind, thinking she could have been a better wife and then maybe he wouldn't have committed suicide. Her depression deepened.

Dr. Strawburn, tall and thin and grey, sat and waited. his wrinkled old lab coat drooping to the floor on either side of his chair, his socks sliding down to the tops of his old, uncared for shoes. He pulled at his lower lips as he thumbed through her file. She'll be all right, he told himself. She's not the depressed type. On the way home, she ran a red light and wept while the officer wrote her a ticket. She told Craig that she was going to sell the car because she was too stupid to drive and went upstairs and undressed and went to bed at three o'clock on a bright October afternoon. Hearing her irrational idea about selling the car, he did not argue with her, but decided to do what he knew he should have done weeks ago. He got on his bike and went to a nearby driving instruction school where he arranged for two class sessions in the evenings and a series of driving lessons. He asked to meet the driving instructor and was told that that particular instructor was out on a lesson. Craig waited and when the instructor returned, a neat, placid, middle aged man, he introduced himself, shook hands and, to Craig's irritation and puzzlement, did a lot of sniffing. On the way home, Craig stopped to talk to Rob but Rob and his father were at each other about Rob getting kicked out of school for insolence. He waited until Rob escaped and they sat outside on the back steps while Rob grumbled about his dumb courses and teachers and how hard his father was riding him. When Craig announced his intention of getting a driving licence, Rob reacted with the pride of a parent, clapping him on the back and giving him a hug.

Rob told him of the episode in the principal's office and said, "To hell with the silly old fart. How can anybody write a hundred words of apology. That's grovelling! I don't give a shit what happens."

"Your dad will be furious."

"Well, he'll just have to get over it. I'm not a student! I never was. Did I ever get any thing except a C or a D in anything? You know I didn't. There's no sense wasting my life day after day with the piddly courses I'm taking. So I'm just going to quit and get a job."

Rob's father had come out the door just as Rob made that statement. "What the hell did you say?" He set down some packages he was carrying and faced his son. "You're going to quit school and get a job? Is that what I heard you say? Well, that's about the dumbest move you could make." His anger was very apparent.

"Look, Dad! I hate it. It's just boring and dull and I'm no good at it. I never was. Craig at least knows how to study. I don't even know how to do that!"

"So stick with it! Go to your teachers and get some help! Do anything or you'll end up like me. Look at me, Rob! I'm nearly fifty years old with a grade eight education and all I can do is run a crummy little two-bit print shop out of my house and my wife has to work to make ends meet. And it will never get any better. I've got some good customers, a few, people who are trying to do something to change things, but most of the customers I get are the nuts who want everything for nothing because they are saving the whales or the horned owl or they're against blacks, or the pope, or contraceptives in the schools, on dog-racing or drugs. Whatever they want to print, I'll print it. I'm like a cheap prostitute. That's what you're facing if you don't buckle down and finish your education. Spend the rest of your life selling used cars or fitting shoes of other peoples stinking feet. Jesus, Rob! You've got to have an education to be a plumber or an electrician or anything, even a con-man or a politician. So you better think twice before you decide to quit school. Oh, I know you're seventeen and you can quit legally. But use your brains, Rob, for God's sake! And you, too. Craig! That goes for you too!" He started picking up the packages he had set down when he came out and when he had put them into the car, he came back and stood for a minute facing the two boys, looking now not angry, but defeated and sad.

"Another thing, Rob. I know I have expected you to help out in the shop when I needed some help. But I thought you realized that it was your contribution to the family, or a kind of return for the love and care your mother and I have given you, although she's a hell of a lot better at it than I am. You know that it costs a lot to raise a child, although you're not a child any more, but we feel obligated to house you and clothe you and feed you and look after your medical and dental needs and to see that you have some spending money—for pot, and other essentials," he added sarcastically. "And we will continue to do all of that as long as you are going to school. So, Rob, I think like this. If the time has come, if you want to be independent, then you go the whole way to independence. I think you have to find a job because I can't afford to employ you. And you'll have to find a place to live and look after your own life, that means rent, food, clothes, car payments, doctor bills, and everything else. Maybe sooner than you think, a wife and child! Who knows? Then some of that money we would have used for you can go to letting your mother get away on a holiday and splurge on some of the little extravagances she should have had." He paused, looking down at Rob who was still sitting on the stairs. "I wish you'd think about it—preferably while you are continuing to go to school. We don't need to rush into this. I'm not kicking you out, son. Talk it over with your mother—she's got the brains in the family—and we'll see, okay?" He reached out and tousled Rob's head before he climbed into the old car and drove off.

"I'll tell you one thing," Rob said croakily, getting to his feet and turning to go inside. "He's a lot better at that kind of thing than old eagle-eye. See ya'."

"Yeah."

Rob did talk with his mother who persuaded him to think about it some more and laid out such a comprehensive list of benefits to living at home that he reluctantly made up his mind to give school one more try. He forgot about the apology to eagle-eye until he was on his way to school in the morning and he turned around and went home.

"Now what?" his father shouted as he came in the door. "Did you get kicked out before you even got there? That's a new record for you!"

"No, I didn't," Rob answered in a voice as loud as his father's. "I didn't get that damned apology done and I didn't see any sense in going and getting shouted at by him when I could come home and get shouted at by you when you're so much better at it than he is."

"Well, go get it done, then," his father roared in return and turned away quickly, smiling privately at the fire he had seen in the boy's eye. He sure behaves like he is ready to fly the nest, he said to himself. Maybe he is ready to go.

CHAPTER 40

When Marion learned that Gerry had altered his will without telling her she started to fret about it. To revise it to include the grandchildren was thoughtful but unlike him, particularly unlike the changed man who walked out on her in raging hate months ago. When was it? Oh, yes! It was on her birthday when she decided to hell with him. She remembered that the daffodils were showing buds and the tulips were just coming through, and now it was well past time when she should have put her bulbs in for next spring. In the past two weeks she had not even bothered with the garden and Craig had not done much except rake a few leaves even though he had not been going to school. Edith had called daily, excited about the Thursday evening when there would be the reading of the will, an event she spoke of in capital letters. She decided to bring the girls as soon as she learned that they had been included in the will, and she told her mother that she was going to bring her camera and take some pictures. "Well, it is a significant event and I would like a record of it," she had said when her mother demurred.

When they gathered at 7:30 in the evening in Murray's office, he had thoughtfully provided some coffee and soft drinks while they waited for Alvin Dodd, who had phoned Murray during the day to say he would be twenty minutes late. Marion had steeled herself for 7:30 and the extra twenty minutes of waiting was an eternity. The wills they had made out together years ago were identical: in the event of a death, everything was bequeathed to the other partner; should they die together, the estate would be divided between their two children. There were no bequests to any other persons or organizations. Now there had been at least one change and Marion's worry was that there might be more.

Murray and Harvey chatted together while Craig amused the twins during the brief wait. Edith, who, in her mother's opinion was gaudily overdressed for the occasion, wandered around the office reading the titles on the bookshelves and the diplomas on the walls. Marion sat sometimes watching the others and sometimes staring into space, unaware that her tension showed by the steady locking and unlocking of her purse catch.

When Alvin Dodd arrived, a middle aged grey man with a charming smile and manner, introductions were made and Murray sat down behind his desk while the rest sorted themselves out into various chairs placed randomly around the office.

"This will only take a minute," Murray announced to them, "but I am legally required to read aloud the last will of Gerald Williams formally. Let me do that and also read a codicil to the original will that was attached on June 30th of last year. Then I will explain the legalese in layman's language." He read quickly through the document and the codicil and paused. "What it all boils down to is this: all of the estate of Gerald Williams is bequeathed to his wife, Marion Williams." Marion let out a sigh and Edith's face tightened into disappointment. "There are no bequests of any kind made in the original will. However, the codicil to the will specifies that a sum of $10,000 shall be taken from the estate to be set aside and invested for the future education of the grandchildren, Iona and Jennifer, or for their emergency care at the discretion of their parents. Please note that there is no indication that the sum shall be divided equally or otherwise." He looked around and asked, "Any questions?"

There was a general shaking of heads. "Well, I suppose you know that there are certain duties the executors of the estate, Alvin and Harvey, will have to perform before the whole process is complete. I'd like to meet with you both when we're finished here just to get things started. OK?" The men nodded.

"Well, then," Murray said, getting to his feet. "I guess that's all."

"The house, the cottage, the investments, his bank account, things like that?" Marion asked questioningly.

"Just as I said, Marion," Murray answered. "There has been no change since you and your husband made out the original will with that one exception of the codicil mentioning the two grand-children. The responsibility of the executors is to see that titles to properties and all registered assets are transferred legally into your name. And, of course, to pay the estate taxes."

"What if Harvey and I have more children? Or when Craig has a family?" Edith asked somewhat sharply.

"I'm afraid your father made no provisions for them."

"Humph!" Edith snorted. "I thought he would leave us each a little something to remember him by."

"I don't want anything to remember him by," Craig said sharply. "I'm surprised you do."

Edith sniffed. "No, I guess I don't. It just seemed that it's the usual thing."

Murray had remained standing. Marion took the cue and said, "Maybe the rest of us can go home in my car and Harvey can come over when he's finished." She got to her feet, shook hands with Murray and Alvin and said to Harvey, "Don't be too long. The girls are getting tired. Edith, it's getting dark. You drive."

In the car, Edith said sulkily, "Well, that was hardly worth dressing up for!"

"What did you expect, Edith? Champagne and caviar and a rock band?" Craig asked sarcastically from the back seat with the squirming twins.

"Oh, shut up, Craig! Don't be a smartass!" Edith replied.

"Smartass," Jenny mimicked.

"Mummy! Hear what Jenny said?" Iona exclaimed.

They arrived home and scattered to various parts of the house. Marion went upstairs and sat on the edge of her bed letting out a long sigh, but underneath there was no real feeling, nothing that attached itself to the sigh, no sadness or sorrow or sense of relief. Sitting placidly for a few moments with the subdued family noises drifting up the stairs, not really thinking about anything, she realized suddenly that an annoying 'Click-click' had penetrated her reverie and that it originated on her lap as her hands again opened and closed the catch on her purse in a metronomic beat.

The telephone startled her. As she reached for it and picked it up, Edith called from the downstairs hall, "I'll get it, Mom! It might be for me."

Marion sat with the phone in her hand, thinking, Why on earth would Edith think the call would be for her? In response to Edith's trilled "Hello?" she heard Tom's voice say, "Oh, hello. Could I speak to Marion, please?"

"One moment please," she heard Edith say. "May I say who is calling?"

"It's all right, Edith. I'll take it up here," she interrupted.

"Hello, Marion," Tom said.

Marion made no reply but instead said, "Edith! I've got it!" and waited for the click from the other phone. "Hello, Tom. Sorry about that. Sometimes it's hard to get a little privacy from your children. How have you been?"

"Working. Lonely. Missing you and a certain motel," Tom said with a laugh. "How about you?"

"Oh, I don't know, Tom. There's so much to do and none of it is easy. I find myself feeling sorry for myself too often. I guess I'm a little down tonight because the family just got back from the reading of my husband's will."

"I see," Tom said and waited a moment for her to go on. When she said nothing more, he asked, "Any surprises?"

"No, not really. Well, one, I guess. But it was a good one. He set aside some money to go towards the twins' education."

"I see. Well, that sounds like a decent thing to do."

"I guess so. Not enough for a down payment on a halo though."

Tom laughed, thinking she was sounding more like her old self. "Hey, lady! How do you feel about a rousing night on the town—say, Saturday?"

Just then the doorbell rang and the twins ran to answer it shrieking, "Daddy! Daddy!" then raced up the stairs to her room calling "Granny! Daddy's back!"

"Tom? Tom? Can you hear me over this racket? I want to say 'yes'—at least part of me wants to say 'yes', but Tom, I'm not quite ready. I'd spoil it, I know I would and I don't want to do that. Can we leave it like that for the moment?"

"I guess we have to, Marion," came Tom's disappointed voice.

"I'm sorry, Tom. Will you keep in touch?"

"Sure, Marion. Take care. Goodbye for now."

She hung up and went reluctantly downstairs in time to see Edith greeting Harvey at the door.

"That certainly didn't take long," Edith said with a tone of annoyance.

"No, there wasn't much to do. We just agreed on the time for our next meeting. The way it works is that the Trust Company looks after the details, and Alvin brings it to Murray and he advises me and we either agree or change it.

They both say that it is a very simple will and there will probably be no complications because there's nobody to contest it."

"So you really don't have to do anything?" Edith asked in a tone of disappointment.

Harvey smiled at her and shrugged. "I guess I'm not going to be tied up in an executive office, am I?" He took her arm. "C'mon! Let's get those kids home to bed."

When the door closed behind them, Craig and his mother went into the living room and flopped into easy chairs as if they had been worn out by the evening. The television was still on and Marion reached out for the switcher and turned it off.

After a minute of silence, she said quietly, "Well, that's that!"

"Yeah, I guess so," Craig responded.

"Were you disappointed that he didn't leave you something?"

Craig sat shaking his head. "Mom, he left me a lot, and I didn't want any of it and I can't even get rid of it."

She looked at him sadly. "Yes, he did, didn't he? I'm sorry, Craig. But it will pass in time."

"And will yours pass, too, Mom? And Edie's?" he asked softly.

"Oh, Lord, Craig. I hope so. Oh, I hope so."

The silence of private thoughts descended on them again until Craig said. "There are a couple of things I've been meaning to tell you but couldn't find a chance. One is, I'm taking driving lessons again."

"Good for you, dear. From Mr. What's-his-name?"

"Old stinky? No way! I went to another driving school."

"I'm glad! All the other boys your age seem to be driving."

"And secondly, I'm going to buy a car."

"How are you going to do that? Now don't buy something on time, for goodness sake. You don't need your own car. You can drive mine. And where are you going to get the money?"

"Mother!" he exclaimed in a tone of exasperation. "You don't really think I want to drive around trying to pick up girls in a little old lady's big Buick, do you? No, I just want a little car, a second hand one, there's lots of them around, Fords, Hondas, maybe even a Volks."

She shrugged and made a puzzled face. "And how are you going to pay for it?"

"I saved some money from last summer."

"Enough to buy a car?" she asked in surprise.

He took a big breath in preparation for the next announcement. "No," and he paused. "But I've decided to quit school and get a job."

"Craig!"

"I knew you would say that! Look, Mother. I've missed so much school lately that I can't possibly catch up and I'm going to fail—the counselor told me so. And I'm embarrassed as hell when kids ask me about Dad—I can't stand it any more. Mr. Cranston told me that I could get my summer job back if I continued with the computer program so I could get into that kind of work at the plant when he gets a computer, and I can keep on with my computer course at night school. So I don't really need a car to go cruising and picking up girls—I need one to go back and forth to work and to night school."

"So you've got it all worked out, have you. How come I'm the last to know."

"Mom, you haven't exactly been with it for the last little while. That's why."

"Is Robbie in on this plan of yours?"

"No, not really. He and Donna are pretty thick these days and his dad is making him work a lot. So-o-o, I haven't had a chance to check it out with him. But I will."

She looked at him and suddenly saw not a boy but a man, and she started to cry. "Sorry, dear," she said as he came over to comfort her. "I don't seem to know how to deal with any emotions these days. I look at you and I see somebody I haven't seen before and it makes me proud to see you grow. So why should I cry? I don't know! I just don't know!" She snuffled into a handful of tissues for a minute. "Promise me one thing, Craig, please! Promise me you won't do a single thing about cars, or jobs or quitting school until we can sit down together in the light of day and look at everything together."

"Sure, Mom. We can do that. My mind's made up but that doesn't mean it can't be changed if there's a good reason to change."

She looked at him with a smile of amazement. "Are you sure you're my son?" she said, hugging him hugely.

"You betcha!" he replied. "Where do you think I got my charm and good looks, to say nothing of brains?"

"That kind of flattery gets to me every time. Right here!" she said, poking herself in the stomach. "Mind if I go to bed before I throw up?"

"Good night, Mom," and he waved to her from a sprawl in front of the TV, waiting for her departure before he turned it on.

In the morning she found a note from Craig saying that he was going to see Mr. Cranston to make sure his offer of a job was still open before he quit school. Reading it, she hoped down deep that the offer was not open and that Craig would go back to school. But, she told herself, I can't be too hard on him. After all, I quit a simple little job at the hospital and I've even been hiding away from my bridge club friends. She had busied herself with the most obvious of the household chores that she had been neglecting and was working hard and sweaty at it when the phone rang. Expecting another condolence call, or worse, a call from somebody who wanted to manage her investments for her, she answered cautiously. A man's voice asked abruptly, without preliminaries, "Are you Marion Williams?"

"Yes," she replied, annoyed by his manner.

"Are you the wife of, or rather the widow of, I should say, Gerald Williams?"

She sensed something in the question she did not like. Certainly it was not a condolence call. "Who are you and what do you want?" she demanded.

"One more question to make sure I've got the right party," the voice continued. "Do you know Eleanor Colman?"

"Why do you want to know?" she asked, knowing that she should have hung up.

"You obviously do, by your answer. Now don't hang up," as if he could read her mind. "I've got documents here that could indicate that Eleanor Colman is the only beneficiary of your late husband's estate—the house, everything."

"You're crazy," she shrieked. "Leave me alone!" She slammed down the receiver and fainted.

When she came to, the phone was ringing again. "Hello," she said in a shaky voice.

The man's voice said, "I'm sorry if I upset you, Mrs. Williams. My name is Brian Tobl...."

"I don't want to know you," she shouted, in panic and hung up again. She left the receiver off the cradle until she found her purse and rummaged in it to find Murray's number. She dialled it frantically only to discover it was a wrong number. She tried again and this time got his receptionist. "Listen," she said. "This is Marion Williams and I've got to speak to Murray right away!"

"I'm sorry, but he's with a ...."

"Get him! It's important! I've got to talk to him now. Now! right now! Don't you understand?" Her voice that had started with a shout ended in a bubbling sob.

"Mrs. Williams?"

"Now!" she shrieked.

In less than a minute, Murray's voice said, "Marion? What's wrong?" And when there was no answer except her whimpering, he said, sternly, "Marion! Stop that and speak to me!"

The command in his voice seemed to be what Marion needed. She started by saying, "I'm sorry," and blowing her nose. He waited for a brief moment before saying, "What is it, Marion?"

Then in faltering words, mixed with confused emotions, she told him of the phone calls telling her that there was another will and that Eleanor was getting the house and everything. "I knew it," she cried. "I could just feel it—something had to go wrong. It's not like him to keep to his word. Probably even the money he left to the grandchildren will be gone. God, he must have hated me."

"Marion, who told you all this?"

"He said his name was Brian something but I didn't get his last name."

"Did he say he was a lawyer?"

"No, I don't think so. But he sounded like one. As a matter of fact he sounded like a TV cop."

"When did he call?"

"He called twice and I hung up on him."

"Did you get his number?"

"No, I didn't think of it. What is it, Murray? Is it some kind of sick joke?"

"Yes, maybe. Do you know this Eleanor he mentioned?"

"Yes, of course. She was my husband's secretary—Eleanor Colman."

"Good! Maybe I can find out something from that source. Now listen, Marion. Keep your head and don't get panicky. It's probably a con-job. If he calls again, be sure to get his name and number. Hear me?"

"Yes, I'll try."

"Now I've got to get back to my other client. Does this Eleanor still work at your husband's old firm?"

"I don't know."

"Okay, I'll follow that up and call you. Remember, if this guy calls you back, get as much information as you can."

"I'll try," she replied not very convincingly.

She went to the kitchen and made herself a cup of instant coffee and carried it with shaking hands over to the nook. Then she brought the telephone in from the hall and waited, trembling and depressed. When the phone rang again, she jumped and spilled her coffee.

Carefully she lifted the phone and said, "Yes?"

"Mrs. Williams," a female voice said. "My brother called you a few minutes ago and what he said might have upset you terribly. I'm sorry about that. Mrs. Williams, we have a situation here that may involve you. We would like to go over it with you and explain it, but I think it would be best, for everyone concerned, if your lawyer could meet with us also. Could we do that?"

"But who are you? I don't want to go running around meeting with strangers who might be up to all kinds of hoaxes or might be dangerous."

"Mrs. Williams, my brother's name is Brian Toblin and mine is Sheila Castle. The telephone number here is 555 2933. We'll be here for another hour or more. I'll give you the address if you would like it or if your lawyer or anybody else would like it."

"No, no!" Marion exclaimed. "Let me write it down first. Let's see: Brian— how do you spell the last name?"

"T-o-b-l-i-n," came the response, "and mine is Sheila Castle." She paused, then continued, "And you have the number?"

"Yes. 395 2933." She waited, hoping the other woman would go on but nothing was said. "That's not your home phone, is it?"

"No, it's our cousin's office number. Perhaps you knew him—Timothy Irwin? He belonged to the same golf club as your husband?"

"No, I don't think so," Marion said without really thinking, and then suddenly said, "He's not the one they called Titty, is he?"

"Regretfully, yes."

"Oh, I'm sorry," Marion said. "About his death, I mean. I saw the notice."

"Yes. Well, thank you. Now then, if we are on better grounds, let me say that we are his only relatives and we have the job of clearing up his business and his estate. Not something I am looking forward to, let me assure you. He was a private detective, you know, and his files contain a lot of horrible stuff. That's how we came across your name."

Marion said nothing more as new thoughts tumbled through her mind. Finally she said, "You want money, don't you? You're trying to blackmail me, aren't you?"

"Mrs. Williams! How can I make it clear to you? Just get your lawyer to call either me or my brother at that number. We'll be here for another hour or two and all day tomorrow. Goodbye, Mrs. Williams.

Marion waited a couple of minutes to make sure that when she talked to Murray she would sound coherent. The secretary told her that he was still busy with a client but asked solicitously if Marion wanted her to interrupt him.

"No, not this time. But will you take some information for him just to save time?"

"Certainly, Mrs. Williams, just a moment while I turn off my machine and get a pad." There was a pause during which Marion cleared her throat several times so she would sound composed. "Now then, I'm ready, Mrs. Williams."

"Oh, please call me Marion. You are...?"

"Cathy."

"Cathy, please tell Murray these names: Brian Toblin and Sheila Castle. And this telephone number: 555 2933. They will be there for another hour and also tomorrow. And there's another name, too. I can't think of it at the moment but he was their cousin and he was called Titty."

"Did you say Titty?"

"Yes, silly name, isn't it? Oh, yes! I remember his name was Timothy Irwin and he's dead and they are his cousins, I think they said, and they are cleaning out his office, and he was a private detective and they said they found a lot of horrible stuff—those are their exact words—horrible stuff in his files. I think they are going to blackmail me. They sounded so smooth they scared me." She paused and shuddered, waiting for Cathy to say something. "Oh, yes. They also mentioned the name of Eleanor Colman. She was my husband's secretary..."

"I think you must have told Murray that already, Marion. He has already instructed me to look up her business and home phones and her address."

"Oh!" Marion exclaimed. "Really!" Impressed that Murray took some kind of action even when he was busy with another client. "Well, if there's anything more I remember, I'll call."

"Alright, Marion. I'll get this to Murray as soon as he's free. And then I think he will want to talk to you."

"Should I come down to his office?"

"Why not stay home? If he wants you to come down, I'll make an early appointment for you."

When the conversation was finished, Marion reached to replace the telephone in the cradle and watched in amazement her own hand trembling so hard the telephone clattered as she put it down. She sat at the nook table with the 'what ifs' rattling around in her head until she made herself frantic. What if they aren't blackmailers. What if there really is another will and she loses everything—the house, the cottage, all the money, everything—antiques, silver, paintings—everything, but not the money her father left her. No, they can't have that. That's all she would have left to live on. But what if they sued her and some crazy judge told her that it wasn't hers, it was theirs. Weirder things have happened, she was sure. Finally she stirred herself and moved around the house, straightening things, using her bare hand or the edge of her apron to wipe off the dust she could see in the slanting sunlight. And she was weeping again, weeping so hard that the tears were running out her nostrils and down her upper lip so that she licked at it without awareness—waiting for the phone to ring, waiting until she thought she would go mad. "Phone me, Murray Andrews! Damn you! Phone me!" she screamed at the telephone in the empty house.

Craig had not phoned Mr. Cranston for an appointment, but even so, when he arrived unannounced, his former employer greeted him warmly and came around the desk to shake his hand.

"I was sorry to hear the news of your father's death, Craig. Are things getting back to normal for you?"

"Yeah, I guess so, Mr. Cranston. But my mom's still kind of shook up. You know, with the will and all the legal things that go on when somebody dies. And people phoning, you know, friends and business people and a lot of others who seem to be looking for widows in shock or something."

"Some people feed off other people's misery—carrion eaters!" Mr. Cranston said, shaking his head.

"What's that?" Craig asked.

"Oh, like vultures circling a corpse is one way to describe them."

"Oh."

"Not a very pleasant subject. Sorry, Craig. What brings you here? No school today?"

"Yes, there's school but I haven't been going since.., well, for a while. And I got so far behind I knew I was going to fail so when I talked to you a couple of weeks ago and you said that you might find me a job here, I thought I had better come down and make sure of it before I did anything else."

"You were taking a computer course as an extra, weren't you?"

"Yes, but I talked to the counselor and I can switch from the day program to the night program without any problem."

Mr. Cranston nodded. "I know we have talked before about bringing you in to be a part of a computer set-up for the business if I ever get around to it. But I've got to be honest with you. I really can't afford you right now. But here's the proposition I'm willing to make. You work in the factory at the same rate you were earning during the summer for four and a half days a week. The other half day you will spend researching computers for information about what kind of a system we will need. Then by the time we are ready to invest we will have some kind of working knowledge to go on. I know so little about computers that a salesman could convince me that I really need his fancy ten thousand dollars set-up that will do everything except make coffee. Your half day is really sort of a research day and you'll have to keep notes in a sort of report form. You see, what I want to do is this." He talked to Craig like an equal about his general plans for expansion for more than an hour. Craig was riding high when he left. Not only did he have a job starting next Monday, but he had an interesting project that might lead to something better. But what was best of all was that Mr. Cranston had talked to him as one adult to another and asked him to drop the Mr. and call him Carl.

Leaving the factory he caught a bus across town that would take him within four blocks of the school. By the time he reached the school it was nearly time for the final bell and he hurried to catch a counselor knowing that they sometimes even beat the bell in their hurry to leave.

"Oh, Mr. Arkison! I'm glad I caught you before you left," he said to a counselor who had just opened his office door to leave. "I need you to sign some papers for me."

"What kind of papers?" Mr. Arkinson had stopped but was still sorting out a key that would lock his door.

"I don't know. I'm quitting school and I thought somebody would have to sign something."

"Well, if you want to quit, then quit. You don't need the school's permission. Clear out your locker, take the lock to the office and turn in a copy of your timetable to one of the secretaries there. That's all." He locked his door and turned away. "What's your name?"

"Craig," came the response.

Mr. Arkinson visibly drooped. "Maybe you do need somebody's permission," he said, sarcastically. "Your last name!" he barked.

"Oh, Williams, Craig Williams," Craig responded, red with embarrassment and anger.

"I'll make a note of it," the counselor said, walking away.

Craig watched him go, his disillusion with the system again validated. "What a kind, caring, helpful asshole!" he said to himself. Aloud he called, "Have a nice life, Mr. Arkinson." and saw a hand flopped in the air in reply.

Craig went to his locker and was cleaning it out when the bell rang. He watched for Rob and asked a couple of guys but nobody had seen him, so he left a note on Rob's locker while he returned library books and textbooks. When he got back to the lockers, Rob had not returned, so he opened Rob's locker, shoved a bunch of his junk inside and left the building with an armload of clothes and his mind in a turmoil of emotions. He walked the long route home so he could pass the small coffee shop that was a hangout, hoping to see Rob there. The sky was a depressing leaden colour with no break in the west that sometimes promised a colourful sunset. The trees had been stripped by the October winds and left in untidy piles and rows against the hedges and curbs. On the edge of a pile, matching the worn brown leaves he saw a man's worn brown wallet. It had a name, address, credit cards and more than three hundred dollars in it. He shoved it in his pocket and continued on his way to a neighbourhood cafe called The Sweet Spot, where looking into the steamy windows he could see Rob and Donna in a back booth. They did not notice him until he stopped at their table and said "Hi!" Their response was without animation although Rob shoved over a little as an invitation for him to sit down.

"How much money have you got?" Rob demanded.

"Oh, about three hundred bucks," Craig said, grinning while he shoved his armload of clothes into a corner of the booth. "Hi, Donna," he said to her and she scrinched her face in response.

"You've got more than that! You saved nearly everything all summer," Rob said.

"Oh, you mean in the bank! I thought you meant on me."

"Whad'ya mean? On you?"

Craig pulled out the wallet he had found and took the wad of bills out and counted them onto the table. "There!" he said with a smirk. "Just as I said three hundred and twenty two bucks."

"Where did you get that?" Rob demanded.

"I found it," Craig said, gathering up the money and credit cards.

"Are you going to give it back?" Donna asked.

"Of course I am," Craig said indignantly. "Jeez! What a question!"

"I didn't mean to say you wouldn't or anything like that. It was just that..., well, Rob and I were talking and... You tell him, Rob."

"In a minute!" he said to her. "Why don't you phone the guy, Craig? Maybe he'll be so happy he'll tell you to keep the cash and bring him the rest of the stuff."

"Why in hell would I phone him. Look! There's his address! I can walk over there in five minutes and give him back his wallet. What's with you two?" He reached over and took a big gulp of Rob's milkshake. "Ugh! What is that? Why do you always get such pukey ones?" He slid out of the booth and said, "Stay here. I got something to tell you."

"Yeah? Well, maybe we got something to tell you, too, wise guy."

They grinned at each other. Craig said "What?" and Donna said, "Go already!"

Craig returned with a big smile in half an hour. "Poor old guy," he said. "He didn't even know he'd lost it. He was shaking like a leaf he was so glad his wife was napping and would never know he had lost it. But she woke up and hollered at him, 'Who's that at the door?' And he took two twenties out of his wallet and shouted back at her, 'Just a young man selling siding,' and she said, 'Tell him we don't need any and close the door. It's cold!' So he gives me the twenties and a big wink and shook my hand real crunchy and watched me with his head out the door until I was down his sidewalk and out his gate and I could hear her shouting, 'Did you close that door yet?' and he gave me a grin and a wave and closed it." He looked at them and said, "Maybe I shouldn't have taken it, eh? They looked like they didn't have much money and there was a sign in the window, like 'Housekeeping Room for Rent' or something like that."

Rob shrugged and Donna said, "Yeah, sure you should have. It sounds like he was glad to get it back."

"Yeah!" Craig agreed and they sat in silence. "So what's your big news?" he asked them.

Rob and Donna looked at each other. "Tell him, Donna," he almost whispered to her. She shook her head, and said, "No, you have to. He's your friend."

Rob reached over and carefully untied a scarf from Donna's neck revealing welts that were red turning black and blue. "She's got a few more, on her back and shoulders, given to her by her parents." He tried to get her scarf back in place but she had to take over and used the corner to wipe her eyes. He told Craig that she had spent the night in the bus station and a laundromat and met him at school in the morning.

"But why?" Craig asked, his face taut with concern. "Why would they do that?"

Donna came into the conversation. "Craig, my father's an alcoholic and my mother is a prostitute. I don't know if he drinks because she sleeps around or if it's the other way. I just know that I can't go back and I won't go back. She'd kill me if I went to the police and I mean it: she would kill me with her bare hands and I'm scared. I always have been scared of her when she gets mad. My Dad is too."

"Donna, did your father ever, you know, try to get you to...?" Craig stumbled to a halt, but Donna knew what he was asking.

"No, but some of the guys that came looking for my mother would put the grabs to me and sometimes both my mother and father would accuse me of teasing them and then I'd catch it good."

"Rotten bastards!" Craig said through gritted teeth.

"Oh, I guess there are worse ones," Donna said.

Rob had been listening and now said, "Donna's mother was always telling her to get out and find a place of her own. She said having young girls around just mucked up her trade, so she could either work or get out."

"But what are you gonna do? You can't hang out in bus stops and laundromats!"

"That's why we were kinda looking for you. I thought maybe you could loan Donna enough do get a room and hold her until she gets a job. Oh, by the way, I'm going to be looking for a job too. I decided to quit school."

"You didn't! So did I!"

"So did you what?"

"Quit school, what d'ya think!"

"You're kidding me! C,mon, tell the truth! You did? You really did? And I did and Donna did! Holy Hell, isn't that a hoot and a doozer. The three of us sitting here and we all do the same thing without telling anybody." He roared with laughter and pounded the table and within minutes all the other students who were hanging out in The Sweet Spot joined in and banged on the tables in their glee.

One of the waitresses, Angela, came over to the booth and slid in along side Donna. "Hi," she said. "I've got an idea. I've got to quit here at the end of the week and go back home and look after the family because my mother has to go to hospital for an operation. Why don't you go talk to Bruno right now and see if he'll take you on?"

The four of them talked it over for a few minutes within easy earshot of many other customers, and finally the two girls left the booth and went out back to see Bruno. Those customers who knew something of what was going on, lingered and listened. The other customers were filled in by whispered conversation. To Craig and Rob it seemed that Donna had been gone a long time, when, in reality it took less than ten minutes for her to emerge with her face shining as if a spotlight had been turned on, shaking her fists in the way winning athletes do, and saying loud enough for most to hear or to pass on, "I've got a job!" The tables were banged again as people shouted, "Hey, Donna!" and a couple of Australians roared "Good on ya, Bruno!" A middle aged man walked over to the booth where Donna was still wiping her eyes from the excitement and handed her a five dollar bill, saying with a friendly smile, "There's your first tip, congratulations!" Then he leaned across the counter to Angela and shook her hand and left in it another folded bill that was so large she was at first reluctant to accept it.

Rob and Craig sat happily watching Donna deal with her good fortune in finding a partial solution to her problems so easily.

"I'll bet I could go over to the Salvation Army or the YW and they'd let me stay until I get paid," she said.

"Hey! I've got a better idea! Leave your junk here and come with me," Craig said.

"Where?" the other two said in unison.

"Never mind! I'll tell you as we go. Hurry up," and he rushed on out the door and waited for them to catch up.

"Remember I said that the old guy that lost his wallet had a sign in his window. It said Light Housekeeping Room for Rent or something. Let's go look at it. Donna hasn't got any references. Have you, Donna?" She shook her head. "I'll bet he'd accept me as a reference because I'm a fine upstanding young man who returned his wallet. So what d'ya think? We could use his forty bucks as the down payment on the rent. Neat, eh?"

Donna stopped and hugged him in the middle of the street while Rob looked on approvingly. "Yeah, real neat!" he said.

When they reached the house they were walking more sedately and presenting a reasonable approximation of responsible young adults. The old man answered their ring.

"Hello, sir," Craig said. "Remember me?"

"Oh, yes! Did I lose something else?" he asked with a smile.

"No, sir. But when I was here I saw your sign and I didn't realize until later that it might suit my friend who works just over there at the Sweet Spot. This is Donna, and I'm afraid I've forgotten your name since I only saw it in your wallet."

"Lasseret, Wally Lasseret," the old man said putting out his hand.

"I'm Craig Williams and this is my friend Rob Turner. We both live just over there," giving a wave in the general direction of home.

"Who's there?" came a female voice from inside.

"A young lady to look at the room. I'll take her down to see it."

"Remember, No Smoking and No Wild Parties," said the voice making it sound like it was printed in red and underlined.

He closed the door. "I guess you heard." Donna nodded. He went on: It's a basement suite, with it's own entrance, just one room, with its own shower and toilet, and a small frig and a hot plate. There's dishes and pots and pans, and bedding. Not much, but there's enough to get started."

He lead them around the corner of the house to a short covered flight of stairs, unlocked the door and turned on some lights inside. "There you are," he said. "The boys told me your name, but what is it again?"

"Donna," she said absently, as she gazed happily around the room. "Donna Penser." She held out her hand. "It's so—so homey. It's beautiful."

"It's great!" Rob enthused.

"Yes, it is," Craig agreed. "But we don't know how much it is yet?"

"Well, let's see," Mr. Lasseret said. "If you're working at the Sweet Spot, that means you're getting minimum wages and tips, so I guess you won't be rolling in it yet. So, let's see. The young man that was here last was a student and he thought $50 was too much. How does $45 a week sound?"

Donna's face was sparkling, and Rob was trying to suppress his delight. Craig had no idea what the rent would be, but the other two seemed more than satisfied. "Does that include heat and light and everything?" he asked, because he knew that you were supposed to get these things straight right from the start.

"Sure does," came the answer. "And she can use the washer and dryer if she just tells Mrs. Lasseret beforehand."

"Well," Craig said, and he seemed to be making the decisions, "I guess we have a deal."

"Yay!" the other two said.

"Welcome, little lady. I hope you enjoy it here. And say, I should have told you earlier, I ask for four weeks rent in advance."

Three stricken faces looked back at him. He studied them for a minute and said, "You don't have it, do you?"

"Not quite, sir," Craig said thinking quickly. "How much do you have, Rob? Donna?" They each rummaged in wallets and pockets and were down to counting change. It was not going to be enough and four people knew it. Finally Craig said, "Mr. Lasseret, we haven't got much more than the forty dollars you gave me for returning your wallet. Let's make a deal! Donna's working and I start on Monday, so we can get manage it if you give us a little leeway."

"And I'm going back to work," Rob put in.

"You are?" Craig said in surprise. "Where?"

"At the Superstore, of course!"

"You didn't tell me!" Craig said indignantly.

"I haven't had a chance. There's been too much going on. Besides, I thought I told you I was thinking about it."

"Well, thinking about it doesn't load the dinner table."

"Look, you guys!" Mr. Lassiter interrupted. "Do you mind if I lay down for a nap while you argue?"

"Sorry!" three voices said in unison.

"Look, I'd be a poor business man if I didn't ask how you are going to back up your promises. So, I know Donna is working, okay! And you, Rob, think you're going to get a job at the superstore just like that, are you?" He went on without waiting for an answer. "Where do you work, Craig?"

"Starting Monday, I'll be working for Cranstons Cartons again. I worked there during the summer."

"Cranstons Cartons? Carl Cranston?" Mr. Lasseret asked.

"Yes, over on...."

"I know where he is. He's an elder in our church. So he's hiring you, is he? Well, that's good enough for me. But, god almighty, I wish he'd change that name—Cranston's Cartons, Cranston's Cartons. Nobody can say it without mangling it."

There was a long pause with nothing being said. "So gimme that forty bucks back and we got a deal."

Craig dug into his pocket and handed over the two twenties.

"Easy come, easy go, eh, kid?" The old man said with a smile. "Okay, this month's rent and next month's rent in four weeks time, starting tonight. Right?"

"Right!" repeated a happy trio of young voices.

"One more thing. Donna, this is your home and you have a right to have visitors. But, remember it is rented to only one person."

"I know, Mr. Lasseret. And Rob knows, too," Donna said.

"Rob?" and he paused looking curiously back and forth. "I thought you and Craig were..."

"No," Rob injected. "Donna and I are going together, so I'll probably be here a lot."

The old man turned to Craig and said, "Well, tell me this, even if it is none of my business, if Rob and Donna have got a thing going between them, how come you're doing the dealing and putting out the cash?"

Craig looked at him as if he could not understand the need for such a question. "Rob's my friend," he said with a shrug.

Mr. Lasseret blew out a big breath, clapped Craig on the shoulder and said, "The next time I see Carl, I'll have to tell him he picked another winner again."

CHAPTER 41

When Wally Lasseret left after wishing them good luck, the three of them were so pleased with themselves they could not do much more than grin and say, "Wow!" "Neat, eh?" "Jeez!" and a few other monosyllables accepted in their age group as expressions of pure and utter joy.

Donna's face was glowing like the morning sun. She kept discovering things, the door with the bolt on her side that opened into a small alcove with a washer and dryer; a toaster and a small electric oven, pretty dishes, pictures on the walls, a braided rug, colourful pillows tossed on a three-quarter size bed.

"And look at this!" she kept exclaiming as she found a new treasure.

The daylight was fading fast and the little basement room was growing dark. There was a knock on the inside basement door that startled them. "Yes, who is it?" Donna asked with a sense of ownership.

"It's me," came Mr. Lasseret's voice. "I've a couple more things for you."

Donna unbolted the door and he said, "I just realized that I had taken the trilight out of here to fix, so here it is. You really will need it to brighten the place up. And here's a little clock radio that Mrs. Lasseret thought you might like."

"Thank you," Donna said. "That was very nice of her."

"She told me to ask you to come up and say 'Hello' when you get settled. No need to go around outside, come up the basement stairs and knock."

"I will. I should meet her. When I stop jumping for joy," Donna said as he turned to go and closed the door behind him.

"I gotta go!" Craig announced. "I gotta get home and tell my mom that I quit school and got a job." He stopped on his way to the door. "And, oh! I left a bunch of stuff at the Sweet Spot—I've got to pick that up. Didn't you leave stuff, too?"

"My jacket's there. Get it for me," Rob said.

"I put a bag under the table. I'd better come with you and get it," Donna said.

"I can get it and drop it off here. It's kinda on my way home. I'll be back in a jiff." The door closed behind him.

Donna stood looking at the door for a moment. "He's some guy, isn't he?" she said in a scratchy voice, while she was blowing her nose.

"Oh, you noticed, did you?" Rob said with a grin giving her a small hug and a kiss on the top of her head.

Craig was back within fifteen minutes, his arms loaded with his stuff from the locker, some of Rob's and a big plastic bag of Donna's. He was wearing his own jacket, and had put Rob's on over his own. He dumped everything on the bed or near the bed and suddenly the room looked like home to all of them.

"Angela said if I saw you to tell you that you can go in tomorrow morning after the breakfast rush and she will show you around," he announced. "And I gotta go."

"Craig," Donna said, coming up to him face to face. "You'll never have any idea of what I thought my day was going to be like when the sun came up this morning. But it wasn't anything like I thought it was going to be—thanks to a pretty nice guy." She put her arms around his neck and kissed him gently without passion.

"Yeah, well...," he said, holding her until she released him.

"I'm going to get him a white horse," Rob said, joining them and flinging an arm around each.

"Promises, promises! That's all he gives me," Craig laughed. He sorted through the pile of things on the bed and on the floor and found his own things. "Hey, Rob," he said with a serious face, "What'll your dad say when he finds out you quit school?"

"I don't think I'll tell him until I tell him I've got a job first."

"Yeah! That's a good idea. But c'mon over if, well, you know, if things don't work out exactly, you know."

"Sure, buddy."

"Well, see you guys!"

Donna moved over and said, "The same goes for you. Like, c'mon over if, well, you know, if things don't work out exactly, you know."

The other two were laughing together as Craig left. Upstairs Wally Lasseret said to his wife, "It's nice to hear happy sounds in the house again, isn't it."

"Where have you been all day?" Wally's mother demanded as soon as he came in the door.

"Why?" he asked innocently because he was not much later than usual.

"What have you got there?" she asked, looking at the jumble of clothes in his arms.

"Stuff from my locker." He looked intently at her, puzzled by her mood. "Are you alright?"

"No, I'm not!" she snapped. "Those two have been calling me and threatening me and Murray was supposed to call me back and he hasn't and I'll bet he forgot and went home. Didn't you think to call when you knew you were going to be late."

"Mom! Whoa! I'm not much later than usual. It's just that it's getting dark earlier."

She held her wrist up and peered closely at her watch, shook it and said in a resigned tone, "Yes, I guess you're right."

He went to the basement stairs and threw the armful of clothes down. "Who's been calling you and threatening you?"

"Who's going to pick those up?"

"I will," he said in a raised voice. "Who threatened you?"

"Don't shout at me," she shouted and started to cry.

"Mom, I'm sorry. But what's going on? You're not making any sense."

"Oh, I'm at my wit's end! A man phoned me this morning and asked a lot of questions and said he had another will made by your father and that everything was changed. I phoned Murray but I couldn't tell him anything because I didn't find out his name or anything. Then a woman phoned and said that it was her brother who had called and that they were cousins of Timothy Irwin, remember the man your father used to make jokes about? Called him Titty Irwin? And she said they found a lot of horrible stuff in his files. He's dead and they were closing his office. He was a private detective or something like that. Anyway, it sounded like they were getting ready to blackmail me and I got their names. And Eleanor Colman's mixed up in it too."

"Dad's secretary?"

"I think so. Then I phoned Murray again but he had a client and I gave all the information to his secretary and nothing has happened and I've been waiting and waiting!" Her voice ended in a wail and she put her elbows on the table and her face in her hands and wept.

He went to her and shook her gently. "It'll be okay, Mom. Don't worry. Murray will look after it." After a minute or two when she had regained some control, he said, "Why don't you go up and lie down and I'll bring you up a cup of tea."

"Thank you, dear. That would be nice." She got somewhat clumsily to her feet and plodded upstairs.

Craig put the kettle on and took the phone as far away from the stairwell as the cord would reach. He dialled Murray's number and got an immediate response at the first ring. "Murray? This is Craig Williams."

"Hello, Craig. I just reached for the phone to call your mother. Is she there?"

"Well, she's upstairs lying down. She's pretty strung out. She said she has been waiting for your call. I'll call her."

"No, don't do that, Craig. Let her rest. She's had a rough day. Did she tell you what was going on?"

"Yes, a little, but it was pretty mixed up."

"I expect it was. Now, listen. Don't disturb her. Tell her I've spoken to the people and I'm satisfied that there is no intent to blackmail her. I'm meeting with them tomorrow and I'm taking along a colleague of mine from the pros-ecutor's office. Got that?"

"I think so."

"Good. Tell her I'll call her in the morning and not to worry."

"Okay."

He made her a pot of tea and took it up to her on a small tray with a favour-ite cup and saucer. She was stretched out on her bed with a pillow over her head, her eyes puffy and red. "That was Murray on the phone," Craig said.

"Oh, he finally called, did he," she said, struggling to sit up in bed.

"No, I called him just as he was about to call you. And he said that he had talked with the people and he didn't think they were going to blackmail you. He's going to have a meeting with them tomorrow and he is taking somebody from the prosecutor's office with him. He said everything was okay and not to worry."

"Easy for him to say. But his whole world has not been turned upside down and shaken up."

"Drink your tea and I'll go make some supper," Craig said. Then I'll tell you about my exciting day."

"There's a casserole in the freezer, but I guess it won't thaw in time, so I don't know...." Her voice trailed off.

"I'll find something," he told her.

Downstairs, he poked about in the frig and freezer and at the same time wondered if his mother had talked to Edith. He thought of calling her but decided against it—no sense getting her frantic as well. He worried about his mother. She was getting kind of weird and forgetful lately and all her constant breaking into tears for the slightest reason worried him, but the thoughts passed as he set to work on their dinner. He made scrambled eggs using six eggs and whipping cream, some diced green onions and a sprinkling of parmesan cheese. He thought it looked good on the plate with some toast and sliced tomato and cucumber but when he took it up to her she tasted the scrambled eggs and said, "Craig! You used whipping cream! There's more calories in that than I should have in a week." She ate a piece of toast and a slice of tomato, thanked him and laid down again with a pillow over her head.

When he got downstairs, Rob was sprawled out on the nook bench. "Where is everybody?" he asked.

"You mean the five piece band to announce your arrival?"

"Ha-ha, funny boy. No, Dad and Mom weren't home and she said this morning that she should get over and see your mom, so I thought they might be here."

"Nope. Do you want those scrambled eggs? Mom didn't touch them."

Rob got up and found a knife and fork and brought over two glasses and a carton of milk. They finished the scrambled eggs and Craig said, "There's more toast. I can't find any cookies or pie. Maybe she put them in the freezer—I'll go look." He went downstairs picking up the scatter of clothes he had thrown down earlier and when he returned empty handed, he shrugged defeat.

Rob did the few dishes and put them away while Craig sat and watched.

"What did your Mom say about quitting school?" Rob asked.

"I didn't tell her. When I got home, she was all weeps and tears about somebody who told her there was another will and so she got hold of Murray finally and I phoned him a little while ago because he hadn't called her back and he said it was all a bunch of crap, and not to worry. He's going to do something."

"I thought he had read the will."

"He did."

"Then how could there be another one?"

"I dunno. Wanna watch TV?"

"No, I gotta go home and face the music, if they're there."

"See ya tomorrow."

"Maybe sooner. If they read the riot act, I may have to come over and place my warm and tender body next to yours."

"You'd use any excuse, wouldn't you?"

"Yeah," Rob leered. "And don't you love it!"

Craig watched him go and locked up the house. He moved quickly through the television stations and found nothing, so he went upstairs to get his computer manual and found his mother solidly asleep and snoring loudly. He shook her and called her, hoping to get her up and into bed properly, but she was totally unresponsive to his efforts. He covered her and, before turning out her light, examined the pill bottle on her night table, which read: Take one pill before retiring for sleep. He had never known that his mother needed sleeping pills.

When he settled down on the sofa with good intentions of looking through his computer manual, the phone rang. "Edie, I bet," he said to himself as he got up to answer it.

But it was a man's voice that said after a slight pause, "Is that Craig Williams?"

"Yes?" he answered in the same tentative questioning tone the man was employing.

"Oh, hi," the man said, now assured he had the right number. "I'm a friend of your mother's. Tom Thomas. Could I speak to her please?"

Craig stiffened, remembering his mother's account of a strange man calling and threatening her somehow. "Are you the same man who called her today about the will?"

"No, I haven't spoken to her for a couple of days. Is she there?"

"Yes and no," Craig said. "She's asleep and I don't want to wake her. But I'll tell her you called—-Mr. Thomas, is it?"

"Yes, that's right. I called to make sure she's doing alright and to give her my new number. To see if there is anything I can do. She's okay, isn't she? It's been pretty rough on her, I'll bet."

"Yes, and it's getting rougher. I'll tell her you called."

"What do you mean, Craig?"

"I mean she's had a lot of crank calls and they upset her and I think there is some kind of showdown tomorrow."

There was a long silence and the man said, "Tell her I can be there if she needs me. Give her my new number, will you, Craig. Have you a pencil handy?" When Craig told him to go ahead. he stated the number slowly and heard him repeat it when he had finished. Then he said, "And Craig, don't worry. This is not another crank call. Your mother and I are very good friends. I'd like to help her if I can."

"Alright, I'll tell her. But you better be on the up-and-up."

Tom smiled as he hung up, thinking that Craig didn't sound anything like the description of the Craig Marion had given him.

Early on Friday morning, Murray called the office of Timothy T. Irwin and got an answering machine with the message "You have reached the office of Timothy Irwin. This is Brian Tobler speaking. If you have any current business with Mr. Irwin, please leave your name and number at the sound of the tone and I will get back to you as soon as possible." He left his name and number.

Less than two minutes had elapsed when Murray's phone rang. "Mr. Andrews," a female voice said. "This is Sheila Castle. You called my brother a minute ago just after he stepped out. Can I help?"

"Yes, Ms. Castle. I would like to meet with you and your brother as soon as possible—today, or this morning would be good. Is that possible?"

"Yes, Mr. Andrews. Anytime. My brother just stepped out to get us some coffee. He'll be right back and we have no appointments scheduled.

"Very good. I'm bringing a colleague along who is familiar with these matters. Is that alright with you?" He did not say that the colleague was on staff in the prosecutor's office.

"That's fine. We probably can use his advice."

"Any time?"

"Whenever is convenient for you, Mr. Andrews. We'll wait and have the documents ready."

"I'll be there within an hour. Same address?" And he gave the address he had copied from the telephone book, hanging up when she agreed.

Then he called the prosecutor's office and asked for Roy Cogison. When the call was put through, he said, "Roy? Murray Andrews. How are you fixed for time? Can you spare me an hour at most this morning? You can? Good! I'll pick you up and fill you in on the way. I'll tell you right now, I don't know whether you will be doing me a favour or I'm doing your job for you. Ready anytime? Good! Let's say you meet me in front of your place in exactly ten minutes."

In ten minutes, a roly-poly young man with a bristling crew cut stepped into Murray's car and they exchanged easy greetings.

"Let me fill you in," Murray said. "You knew Titty Irvin, didn't you?" Seeing a nod of agreement, he continued. "Apparently he died without kin except for two cousins, a Brian Tobler and a Sheila Castle. They came to town and as the only heirs to Titty's estate, which isn't much, they are trying to clean up his office and settle his affairs. You know what kind of business Titty was in and what might be in his files. Some of it explosive stuff you can bet. Problem is, from the way they approached one of my clients, they are either totally naive and clumsy or they are the slickest con artists you have seen for a while." He gave Roy a summary of Marion's contact with the two people and his own conversations with them on the telephone.

"Sounds like they could be as innocent as angels or they could just as easily be as nasty as Titty was. Can I use your phone?"

Roy dialled his office and said to someone there, "Look, here are two names: Brian Tobler and Sheila Castle. Run them through the con-artist, blackmail, etc. knowns and wanteds and phone me at

"What's Titty's number?" he said to Murray. Murray dug a small note pad from his pocket and read off the number to him. "Call me there within an hour from now."

They parked the car and walked into the somewhat run-down building and up the stairs to Titty's office. "Just a word of caution, Murray," Roy said quietly. "Remember that you represent Marion Williams and you can ask them anything you want about matters concerning her, but don't go further. I might decide to ask about other clients, but only after I have identified myself as representing the prosecutor's office."

Murray nodded and knocked. The door was opened by a matronly woman of about fifty five, with gray hair that needed another tidying and huge glasses hanging from a rope around her neck.

"Are you...?" she asked, trying to remember a name.

"Murray Andrews," he said. "You must be Ms. Castle."

"Yes, Mrs.," she corrected. "Come in.".

They walked in and a pudgy, almost bald man of about 60 years of age, with wild, bushy, white eyebrows dropped his reading glasses on the desk and stood up. Murray again used the aggressor's advantage, "And you must be Mr. Tobler. We've talked. I've brought along a colleague of mine who is something of an expert in wills and other such legal documents." Everybody shook hands around the shuffling to provide another chair.

"Mr. Andrews, I hope you'll be able to convince Mrs. Williams that I did not mean to distress her, but I guess I did, so I asked Sheila to call back and explain, but Mrs. Williams was too upset." Murray nodded without committing himself. The old man continued,

"You see, I found these papers on file," and he thumped a collection of papers with a middle finger. "Well," he continued, "they weren't really filed, just dumped in a cardboard box, same way Titty kept everything. I never knew what kind of rotten business he was in. I used to think he was sort of an industrial spy or something like that, but not him, oh,no siree, he dug in all the sewers in town. You should see the stuff he dug up. It makes me ashamed to know him."

He was interrupted by his sister who said, "I don't know why he put us in his will. We haven't seen him for years and we don't need anything he has. And we certainly didn't need the chore of cleaning up the leavings of his messy life," and she finalized her disapproval with a loud sniff and a glare.

Roy watched and said to himself, If you're pulling a con, lady, you're pretty good!

"No, we didn't," the old man agreed vehemently with his sister. "Anyway we found this stuff and it looked to me like Tim was trying to create a phoney will for this guy, Gerald Williams. But the puzzler was that all these details or instructions or whatever they were, were written on the back of some company stationery. See?" and he passed a sheet to both men. "So I phoned the company number and asked for Gerald Williams and the girl on the switchboard hemmed and hawed and then told me he was dead. So I said to myself, Holy Shit! I'm not cut out to be a detective and decided we would phone some of these people to see if they wanted some of these personal papers back. So I phoned Mrs. Williams because she happened to be on top of the pile, and she thought I was trying to blackmail her. Then it struck me that everybody I phoned would think the same thing and I'd end up behind bars for the rest of my life. Great example to set for my children and grandchildren! Jesus Christ!"

"Brian!" his sister said. All three men heard the interjection as an admonishment to watch his language and Brian jerked a look over his shoulder as if to check on the presence of children. "Could I see everything you have found that pertains to Mrs. Williams?" Murray asked.

"Sure, right here," the old man said, passing over a sheaf of papers.

Together, the two lawyers read through the instructions to Timothy T. Irvin to create a will as of today's date, leaving all the assets of Gerald Williams to Eleanor Colman. There was a list of assets, properties, investments, etc., and several examples of the signatures of Eleanor Colman and Gerald Williams.

"Did I hear you say that there were files such as this on other people?" Roy asked carefully phrasing the question so that he did not openly ask to see them.

"Yes! Lots of them! Look at this. This is about a previous Alderman. And this! This filth about a minister of the United Church."

After the two lawyers had looked quickly at the documents, Roy Cogison said, "Mr. Tobler, I have to tell you that prior to this moment you were suspected of being involved in a blackmail game. I work in the prosecutor's office and..."

"Oh, God! I knew it! You're going to read me my rights!" the old man interjected, so visibly shaken that he almost missed the seat of his chair when he sat down. The phone rang with startling loudness. Brian Tobler reached for it with a shaky hand and with an equally shaky voice said, "It's for you, Mr. Corgison," and handed the phone over.

"Cogison," he said, and sat listening to a message. He caught Murray's eye, shook his head almost imperceptibly. said "Thank you," and returned the phone to Tobler.

Continuing with the earlier conversation without breaking stride, he said, "No, I'm not, Mr. Tobler! I'm not going to read your rights. I'm of the opinion that you have been made a pawn in some vicious game your cousin was playing. No, no charges will be made against you. Murray, what do you think?"

"No, I can't see that either Mr. Tobler or Mrs. Castle had any intent to commit any unlawful act."

Brian Tobler sat breathing heavily, finally saying to his sister, who was crying, "It's all right, Sheila. Don't cry."

Then to the two men he said, "What am I going to do? You're both lawyers. How do I get myself out of this mess? What should I do?"

Roy paused for a minute before replying, "I offer these suggestions, Mr. Tobler. Remember that they are suggestions, not legal advice. First, get yourself a lawyer. If you can't locate one, let me say that the first listed person in the law firm down the hall is a man I went through Law School with. Together, you might go through this mess and cull out bonds, investments, uncashed cheques, even money, perhaps enough to pay the services of a lawyer to advise you. If you find more than is necessary to pay his fees, I'm sure you have a favourite charity if don't want to touch your cousin's money. Secondly, I would suggest that you invest in a paper shredder. You know what that is?" The old man nodded and suddenly realized the point the other man was making.

"If you choose to accept any benefits from your cousin's estate, it is possible that you could also be held accountable for any debts your cousin may have left."

"Good God! I don't want anything from him nor does my sister!" He looked questioningly at her and she shook her head violently in negation.

The two lawyers got up to go.

The old man stood up and picked up the Gerald Williams file.

"Do you want this?" he asked Murray.

Murray nodded and accepted the file. "I have a paper shredder in my office, too," he said.

When Murray stopped to let Roy out in front of his office, he said, "Thanks for the help, Roy. I wasn't sure what the hell was going on. I only knew that one more thing might tip my client right over the edge. She's pretty fragile right now."

"You're welcome. For a minute, it did look like the whole mess was going to end up on my desk. But they're both clean, I'm positive. Okay, see you around. You owe me one."

"I do!" Murray agreed.

When he got back to his desk, Murray sorted through the papers he received from Brian Tobler, puzzling about his hesitance in putting them through the shredder. But something nagged at him. Something that said that it was possible that T. Irvin had completed the job given him by Gerald Williams and if he had, then now that they were both dead, the phoney will would most likely be in the hands of Eleanor Colman. He put the papers away, thinking that one of these days he might arrange to have a little talk with one Eleanor Colman.

Then he phoned Marion and told her the outcome of the morning meeting with Irvin's cousin. "They are really quite nice people, Marion," he said. "And they were honestly sincere in wanting me to extend their apologies to you for their clumsiness. They were just not used to dealing with the kind of things they were finding in Irvin's files. Their intent was to alert you and others that their cousin had files that could be terribly damaging. It is pure luck that they did not end up being charged with blackmail or extortion, because without knowing them, it certainly appeared that they could be on the other side of the law."

"What about Eleanor Colman? How did she fit in?"

"I'm not sure yet whether she knew what your husband was doing or whether he just used her. Anyway, I think I might arrange a little conference with her, just to test the water."

"I'd like to be there when it happens. I thought I had a pretty good relationship with her. You know, wife and husband's secretary sort of thing. But I just now realized that she never called or sent a card." Marion said.

"It might be a little hard on you, Marion. Are you sure."

"Yes, I think so. It's the only loose end that's kicking around. Maybe if I tidy that up, I can get on with my life."

"OK, Marion. I'll try to arrange it. I'll be in touch."

CHAPTER 42

The next day Craig got up early and, trying to be as quiet as possible, sorted through his school books, put some away for later use and piled the rest to return. He looked through his closet and decided he had enough work clothes so that he would not have to rush out and buy some. At nine o'clock, he opened his mother's door a crack to check on her and found her still sleeping soundly, sprawled crosswise on the bed with her mouth open and snoring vigorously. Going downstairs, he stood in front of the open frig, occasionally dancing vigorously to the loud blast of a rock station, trying to decide what to eat. At the end of a set, he heard a voice screaming, "Turn it down!" and knew that his mother was awake.

"Can I bring you some coffee?" he yelled up to her and received a mumbled affirmation.

While he waited for the water to boil for her instant coffee, he bolted down his own breakfast of a banana and a cold wiener on toast with cheese spread.

When he took her coffee up, he saw that she had straightened her tangled bed and brushed her hair. "Hi," he said cheerily. "Did you have a good sleep?"

"I must have," she said. "I woke up half way through the night with my clothes on and I can only vaguely remember getting undressed and going back to bed. Those are good pills Dr. Strawburn gave me. I'm going to get some more of those."

Craig was lying sideways across the foot of her bed. "I've gotta talk with you about school and job," he said. "I promised I would. But I couldn't wait and you weren't quite ready to talk, you know."

She nodded, sipping her coffee.

"Well, I knew I was never going to catch up on my year—I was going to fail and I knew it. So I went down to see Carl Cranston about a job because he told me to keep in touch, and I'm going to start on Monday.

"You are? You're going to just work in a factory?"

"Well, it's a little more than that, Mom!" And he told her of the plans to employ computers in several areas of operation of the plant and the Carl Cranston had given him a special project.

She looked at him over the rim of her coffee cup. Why can't I bounce back like he does? she thought. He gets slammed and then gets up and starts tackling life again. I just weep and wail and wring my hands.

"I'm switching my day computer course to a night course, so I can keep up with that," Craig said

He can do that and I can't even continue with a little hospital volunteer job or a weekly bridge game, she silently chastized herself.

"Hey!" he said suddenly. "I'm doing all the talking. What d'ya think?"

She smiled at him fondly and said, with a little shrug, "You seem to have sorted it out for yourself nicely. What do you say in baseball? Have you covered all the bases?"

"Yeah, I think so." He stretched and got up from her bed. "What are you going to do today?"

"Oh, I don't know. I haven't given it much thought yet. Maybe I'll just stay here."

"Aw, come on, Mom. Time to get up and do something!" He took a corner of the bedclothes and started to pull them off, but she clutched at them and screamed, "Craig! Don't do that!" but, he noticed, she was laughing.

As he left the room, the telephone rang. "I'll get it," he called on his way down the stairs. "It's probably Rob."

But it wasn't Rob, it was Edith. She was still fussing about the fact that nothing was left to them in their father's will. "Wouldn't it have been nice," she said, "to have a few thousand dollars back-up, in the bank, for emergencies or holidays?"

"Yeah, I guess," he said. "But it didn't happen, did it?"

"No, of course it didn't," Edith said in her sharp voice. "Now listen to me! What do you think Mom's reaction would be if we went to her and suggested, nicely, that she could make it up to us."

Craig said nothing.

"Well?" exploded from the ear piece.

"I'm thinking, I'm thinking," Craig said

"You are not! You little smartass!"

"Just a minute, I'll ask her." He partially covered the mouthpiece with his hand and pretended to shout, 'Hey, Mom! Edith wants you to give her ten thousand dollars!'" Then he covered the mouthpiece carefully and shouted, "Mom! Mom! Edith says she's pregnant!" Then he listened for a couple of minutes to the confusion before putting the receiver down and leaving the house.

In the morning, Rob went directly to the superstore to talk to the Manager. A sign on his door warned him, "Employment enquiries between 10 AM and 11AM ONLY" so he wandered around the aisles wasting time and watching people. Two well-shrivelled grandmothers were craning their necks at the spice racks, their bifocals inadequate for the task. "Oh, Rob!" one of them called spotting him, "You're back! Isn't that nice? Nellie, Remember Rob? He's back working again. Such a nice young man. Robbie, we can't find the toasted sesame seeds. They put them up too high."

"Oh, they're not in this section, Mrs. McDonald," Rob said. "They're over in Oriental Foods. You wait. I'll get one for you," and he dashed off to the far side of the store.

"Need any help, ladies?" the manager asked as he came along the aisle.

"No, not now, thanks. We couldn't find the toasted sesame seeds, but Robbie said they're in the Oriental section and he's gone to get some for us. I'm glad he's back. Such a nice young man." And the other grandmother burbled agreement.

Rob came around the corner with a bottle in his hand and was hailed by another couple. "Hey, Rob! Nice to see you! Are you working here again," the man said.

"Not yet," Rob said, stopping to shake hands, "but I hope to." "Good luck," the woman said, smiling.

"See! I told you!" one of the grandmothers said to the manager as he turned to go, "Everybody loves Rob."

"Thank you, Robbie," the other one said as he handed them the sesame seeds. "We told the manager what a fine young man you are."

"You're a pair of sweethearts, you know," he replied as he took off after the manager.

The manager had been stopped by a shopper who was giving him advice on the proper management of the meat department and he was receiving it with stoic good grace. Seeing Rob standing aside, he interrupted the customer, saying, "I say! Those are excellent ideas. Thank you. I'd like to spend more time but I see I've already kept this young man waiting for his appointment." He turned away to Rob and said "Come up to my office, Rob."

As they walked away together the manager muttered, "I sometimes think I would rather be stocking shelves."

Rob made no response.

They reached the office door. "Okay," the manager said. "I've heard from your support group. Any more out there that are going to corner me with a good word on your behalf?" Rob saw that he was trying to hide a smile.

"Oh, that was just my morning crew, sir. The afternoon crew starts at one." Rob said, smiling broadly.

The manager laughed loudly. "OK, Rob. You want a job, eh?"

"Yes sir."

"What about school? Seems to me today is not a holiday."

"No sir. I'm just not a student. I quit."

"Not a particularly smart thing to do. But then, I'm not a counselor. Are you eighteen?"

"No sir, not quite."

"Then you can't work nights. See Jennie over there and tell her you're start-ing Monday alternating morning and afternoon shifts weekly. She'll tell you your days off. Same take-home as before."

"Thank you, sir! That's great!" Rob's smile was big and open. "OK." He opened the door for Rob. "Thinking of night school?"

"No, I wasn't," Rob answered cautiously.

"Try thinking about it," was all Rob heard as the door closed.

Rob was too tall and lanky to float out of the store like people do in the movies when they are happy, but he did walk through the store and down the street with a big grin that was occasionally mirrored by some people he met on the way out. He still had on a happy face when he knocked on the partly open door of the counselor's office.

"Got a minute, Miss Hutton?" he asked with his head through the door.

"Who are you?" she asked. "It doesn't matter, come in. You're not the one I was expecting unless you're pregnant." And she burst out into a snorting laugh that made her reach for a Kleenex and blow her nose. "Private joke," she said. "What's your problem?"

"I'm resigning," Rob said.

"From the human race or what?" she said with another 'haw-haw' and a good blow.

Rob slapped his thigh and gave her a twisted smile and a wink. She said sharply, "Don't be smart. Sit down!"

She was a dumpy, grey haired woman, close to retirement, with glasses snagged in her hair. She sat down and put her arms on the desk and looked at him without saying anything for a long minute. "Why?" she said.

He knew what she was asking and said, "Because I won't make it."

"Did you give it a good try?"

"No."

"Why?"

"Because I can only give a good try to things I like doing and that interest me." He shrugged, not able to explain his motives.

"Do you want to blame the teachers or the system or your parents?"

"No," he said. "I'm a big boy. I'll take the blame."

"Okay," she said, drawing it out like a sigh. "Here. Take these." She rummaged around among the scatter on her desk. "This one on Quitting School, and this one on A Second Chance. Oh, and this one on Teenage Pregnancy. It's always good to have around even if it isn't pertinent." She sat pushing her lower lip in and out and then said, "See one of the girls at the counter, sign something, clear out your locker, turn in your key, and good luck." "Thank you, Miss Hutton." he said, getting up to go.

"Oh, what's your name?" she called.

"Rob Turner."

She wrote it down. "The system wants me to keep a record of how I do my job," she said. "If preggie doesn't show up for her appointment, I'll add a half hour to your time and go for coffee." She gave him a broad wink. "That's how you work the system."

He gave her a small salute, signed something, got a cardboard box from the custodian, loaded it with the stuff from his locker and headed for home.

"What the hell's that?" his father asked as Rob came in the door, but the tone was more curious that belligerent. His father was pasting up a print master using a six-inch magnifying glass that clipped to his head and his eye looked like a horse's eye when he looked at Rob. His mother was working on the hand operated coilbinder. None of the machines were working and the room was quiet enough to hear the radio in the background.

She stopped working and said, "You did! Didn't you? I talked to Craig's mother this morning and she told me about Craig and I thought, I'd bet anything that Rob is going to do it too."

The horse's eye wandered lazily back and forth between mother and son. "Do what?"

"You quit school, didn't you?" his mother asked.

"Why, Rob? It was only one more year."

"Because I hated it, because I was no good at it and because I was going to fail."

"You wouldn't fail if you really tried," she argued.

"You can't try if you hate it. It doesn't work like that and you know it."

The horse's eye continued to wander back and forth.

"Did you talk it over with the counselor?" his mother asked.

"Yes," he answered and smiled at the recollection.

"What's so funny?" his mother asked sharply.

"Nothing, really. She couldn't have cared less. She gave me a pamphlet on Teenage Pregnancy."

The horse's eye disappeared as his father snatched the magnifying headset off. "She what? Don't tell me that's what...!"

"No, Dad," Rob interrupted. "That's not it. I shouldn't have even told you what she gave me."

"Well, why did she give it to you?"

"I don't know, Dad. She's twitty."

His father harrumphed and sat down. Watching him, Rob relaxed a little, thinking there might not be a shouting match after all. He looked at his mother who had also visibly relaxed when her husband sat down.

"Now what?" his father said, pushing himself back into the chair.

"What do you mean, Dad?"

"I mean, what do we do now. Sit down, Rob." Rob pulled out a hardback chair and straddled it. "I think I blew it the other day when we talked. I said if you quit school you can go and be independent and I didn't mean it quite like that. Your mother made me realize that." Rob heard his mother sniff but she said nothing. "Let's see if we can come to some kind of better understanding."

"Okay, Dad. But you said if I wanted to quit I had to go the whole way and leave home. So I got a job and..."

"You did? When?" his mother asked.

"This morning. At the Superstore. I start Monday."

His father looked at him sharply. "So you got a job and you quit school this morning and it isn't even lunch time yet. Don't tell me you're packing this afternoon!"

"Glen!" his wife said sharply. "Don't blow it again!"

"I'm sorry," he said. "I meant it as a joke."

"I can leave if you want me to," Rob said with a note of stubbornness in his voice.

"Look ! Son! Listen! To! Me!" and each word came out as a statement. "You haven't lived with me for seventeen years without knowing that I find saying things like 'I love you' difficult to say. But I'm saying it. I love you. You're my son. That doesn't mean that I have to love you, just because you're my son. That's a good enough reason, but I do because you're tall and handsome and gentle and funny and kind and you're not afraid of the world and I see in you all of the things I'm not and I don't want you to bugger up your life. Can you understand that? Don't you know that our lives would be barren without you? If you can't believe me, then believe your mother." He got to his feet and moved toward Rob. Rob stood up, saw the tears brimming in his father's eyes and each put out his arms to embrace the other. They stood silently and awkwardly together with the chair back between them until his father patted his back and released him and quickly left the room. Rob turned the chair around, sat down with his arms on his knees and his head in his hands. He said softly, "Well, sh-i-it" and wiped his eyes on his sleeve.

His mother moved to him and touched his head gently, then she too left the room and went to her husband. "Thank you, Glen," she said, although the words were muffled by his embrace.

CHAPTER 43

Rob had left the little apartment early, saying he had to get home and tell his parents about quitting school and getting a job. "What'll they say?" Donna had asked as she hugged him goodbye and thinking that neither of her parents had cared anything about her school or the casual clerking she had done on sale days.

He shrugged and said, "I'm not sure. The last time we talked about it we had a big row. We always have a big row so I guess we'll have another one today. Last time my dad said if I wanted to be independent, then I had to be totally independent, get out and support myself—everything—rent, food, clothes, doctors, dentist and a whole bunch of other stuff."

"Your mom,too?"

"No, she doesn't say anything when Dad and I are arguing. After Dad cools down she gets to him and then later she tells me that things aren't so bad and that he was just blowing off steam and he didn't mean everything he said."

Donna had nodded as if she understood the vagaries of parental relationships, but Rob had seen her glancing around the room while he was talking as if she had been more interested in her new home than in his problem. "See you later," she said as he prepared to leave.

When he left, Donna unpacked the bundle of clothes she had brought with her while trying to scrape up the courage to go back to her home for the rest of her clothes and belongings. She knew that she would be in for another battle with her mother unless she went across the street to a neighbour's and waited until her mother went out. Finally she decided that the best thing was to go, right now, before she chickened out. While she was putting on her coat, with her face set in determination, she looked at the little clock radio and knew her mother would already be into the sauce. Tomorrow, she thought, tomorrow will be a better time. I really should go up and say hello to Mrs. Lasseret.

Mrs. Lasseret was at the kitchen sink doing dishes. She was a tiny, woman with a pronounced widow's hump and a strong voice that went along with her deafness. "Come in, come in," she shouted when Donna knocked on the basement door. "Well now, aren't you the pretty thing? No wonder you had two young men to escort you. Now then, have you had your supper?. You haven't had time to go shopping, have you?"

"No, not yet. I'll get something later. I thought I'd better come up and say hello."

"Then you can have a bite of supper while you say it. There's a bit of chicken left over, some jellied salad and bun. How will that suit you? You sit right there and we'll talk."

"Really, Mrs. Lasseret," Donna protested. "I'm not hungry."

"Nonsense," the woman said and continued getting a plate ready.

"So Wally tells me you're going to work at The Sweet Spot, isn't it? We've never been in but I hear it's nice, and clean, too. We don't eat out much. He's too tied to the TV, you know," she said in what she considered a low voice. "So if you're working in a restaurant, you'll be eating there, won't you? Wally was saying we should get a small frig for the place, but you won't need much of a frig, will you? You can just slip out your door and there's a frig just at the foot of the stairs and you can use that. I only use the freezer part. Do you think that will do?" she said, putting a big plate of chicken, sliced tomatoes and a roll in front of her.

Donna didn't know whether she was referring to the frig or the plate of food. "Oh, yes! I hadn't noticed that there was no frig so that will do me just fine. I guess I'll get my meals at the cafe but I didn't think to ask. Oh, this is delicious," she said around a mouthful of cold chicken.

"Wally," she shouted, "come here and see if she isn't the spitting image of our Katy."

"I thought so, too," said a voice from the living room.

"He heard me," she said. "I make him use earphones so I don't have to listen to that racket all night. Katy is our only grandchild. I don't know what's wrong with the rest of them. Four children and one grandchild, for goodness sake. Milk, coffee—or a beer, maybe?"

"Milk, please," Donna said, knowing it would be useless to refuse. "I'm not old enough to drink."

"But you're old enough to be on your own," the old lady said as she poured a glass of milk and sat down again facing Donna across the table.

"My parents were in difficulties," Donna lied. "And I thought it best for me to go. You know, just leave and be on my own. But I didn't really run away," she added hastily. "I'm going back tomorrow and get the rest of my clothes."

Mrs. Lasseret looked at her as if she believed her and nodded.

"Now about smoking," she said. "I don't care if you smoke and die of lung cancer. It's your life. But No Smoking In Bed. That's the rule because I don't want to die because you smoke. There are no ifs, ands or buts. You smoke in bed and out you go. Okay?"

"I don't smoke, Mrs. Lasseret," Donna said in quiet defence.

"Oh, I thought all kids smoked. They all seem to when they pass by here on their way to school. You don't, eh?"

When Donna shook her head around a full mouth, Mrs. Lasseret went on. "Good!" she said. "Now how about your friends? Which one is yours, by the way? The tall dark one that looks like a gypsy, or the bouncy one?"

Donna started to laugh, "Oh, the tall, dark one," she said. "But they are both my friends and neither of them smoke."

"Well, good," Mrs. Lasseret said. "I got you to laugh. I heard you laughing downstairs and it sounded so pretty. Now can I get you something else?" Donna shook her head. "Are you sure?"

"Well, I'd ask you to stay and watch TV with Wally and me but I'd hate to watch you struggling to be polite saying 'no thank you'."

On her way downstairs, Donna picked up a couple of magazines from a pile in the basement and spent the evening thumbing through them and listening to the little radio, while struggling with her fear of another battle with her mother. Then, too, was the nagging problem of how she was going to manage for a week on $8.37 that was all the money she had in the world. She hoped there would be tips. She set the alarm, crawled into bed and slept somewhat fitfully around frightening dreams she could not remember in the morning.

The basement room was still dark at 7:30 when the alarm went off. Outside the sky was cloudy and dark and it had rained again during the night. The room was warm and the bed was soft and she was tempted to stay there and wait until the world changed. But by nine o'clock her stomach was growling with hunger so she struggled into a pair of tight jeans and a tee shirt with the scarf tied to hide the bruises and headed out to The Sweet Spot.

In the window of the cafe she spotted a sign stating: M to F Open 7AM to 6PM. Sat. 7AM to 1PM. Closed Sunday. That's a long working day, she thought, without adding up the hours. Inside the breakfast smells were overpowering. She could see Mr. Bruno in the kitchen, but Angela was not behind the counter and the waitressing was being done by an elderly woman who was obviously struggling to keep up with a large, noisy crowd, mostly men. She took a stool at the counter and waited for the woman to take her order.

"I was just waiting for Angela," she said, when the woman asked. "But I'd like a cup of coffee, please. Is Angela not working today?"

"She came in but she was so sick she had to go home," the woman said over her shoulder as she poured a cup of coffee. "Friend?" she asked as she put the coffee down.

"Not exactly. I'm going to start work here on Monday and she was going to show me around today," Donna explained.

"She said something like that and that she'd be in later. You've met my husband, then," nodding toward the kitchen and gathering an armload of dishes. "I only do this in an emergency." And she headed for the kitchen.

When she came back out a moment later, Donna leaned over and said, "Excuse me? Would you like some help now?"

The woman looked at her, sagging with gratitude, "Are you sure you are just a friend, not a saint," she said. "Come with me."

In the kitchen, she handed Donna an apron and pointed to a sink loaded with dirty dishes and smiled. "Call me Phyllis," she said. "Yours?"

"Donna."

"Donna, perhaps you could clear the tables out there, first. Start with the ones that have people waiting. Tell them I'll be right there. If you have trouble with the dishwasher, just ask Bruno."

An hour later, as Donna looked up from the dishwasher she saw that the little cafe was almost empty. Phyllis appeared with another armload of dishes. "You were a godsend, Donna. I was at my wit's end. I don't know where they all came from this morning."

"Two games at the park rained out," Bruno called over.

"I'm starving," Phyllis said. "You didn't even get a chance to finish your coffee, did you? Have you had breakfast?"

Donna hesitated. "No, but..."

"Bruno, dear. How about breakfast for the slaves?"

"Coming right up," he called.

"Oh, let's get off our feet while we've got a chance," Phyllis said leading the way to a table at the back.

Just as she was about to sit down, Donna went back to the kitchen door and brought back a bowl. "What do I do with this?" she asked. "It was on the tables when I cleared them."

"Well, put it in your pocket, girl. Where else?"

"But there's nearly seven dollars there! It was meant for you, surely."

"Really, my dear," Phyllis said, putting her nose away up in the air. "You wouldn't expect the wife of the owner to accept gratuities, would you? I get my perks elsewhere, don't I, Bruno," she said, reaching around to pinch his bottom as he laid two plates of waffles and sausages in front of them.

"Perks? Is that what you call it. We used to call it..." and he leaned over and said something in her ear.

"Dirty old man!" she laughed. "Eat, Donna. Don't wait for him. He never eats. He just nibbles away at everything when he's cooking."

They chatted while they ate. Donna had taken the scarf off her neck when she was working over the steaming dishwasher and the bruises were very evident, but Phyllis made no comment about them. As they were clearing up their table, Angela arrived, immediately grateful to see Donna in an apron. "When the boys next door came home and I heard the games were washed out, I knew Bruno was going to be swamped but," she made a wry face, "I just couldn't get out of the bathroom."

"Are you...?" Phyllis asked, looking at Angela with maternal concern."

"Yes, I guess so. Dammit! Just what I need when I'm on my way home to look after my mother." Phyllis reached out sympathetically and took her hand.

Donna left them alone and returned to the kitchen and continued cleaning up. "Good girl," Bruno said, smiling at her as he scraped his grill. "Thank you!"

"Yes, thank you," Phyllis added as she came into the kitchen. "I really was beginning to feel swamped. In a minute I would have gone and put up the 'Closed' sign. I've got a million things to do, so I'm going to leave you with Angela. See you again, Donna." She collected her coat and purse and called to her husband, "I'm off, Bruno. Don't spend the whole day here, now."

The two girls worked together, with Angela showing Donna the routines necessary for efficiency. They talked as they worked and Angela asked outright about the dark bruises on Donna's neck.

"You're kidding," she exclaimed, when Donna told her. "I thought maybe you had been mugged or assaulted and I was going to ask if you had gone to the police. My boy friend is a cop," she added.

Donna shook her head.

"Didn't your dad stop her?" Angela asked

"No, he's always too drunk when she beats me up. I think she waits until he's passed out before she starts on a rampage."

They continued to talk and when Angela discovered that Donna was going home this afternoon to get the rest of her clothes, she said, "Who's going with you?"

"Nobody," Donna said.

"The hell you say!" Angela stated with finality and marched over to the phone and dialled a number. "Good morning, sleepy head," she said. "You really are up, are you?" She talked intimacies for a minute and then said, "You're picking me up, aren't you? How about coming a little early? I got a little job you can help me with. It calls for the tough cop approach." She stood listening and winked over at Donna. "No," she said, laughing. "Don't call out the swat team. Just you! I'll tell you when you get here, Sir Galahad. Bye," she said. "No, just a minute!" She turned to Donna. "Do you have suitcases or anything to pack in?" Donna shook her head, puzzled by the question. "Bring some boxes, honey. Two or three. Okay? Bye, again."

"Now then," she said, "let's have no argument. It's all arranged. That was Steve, Steve Valdez. He's my boy friend and he's a cop, I told you. He's picking us up, not me, us! And we're going over to your home and go in and get your clothes and everything else you want. And I guarantee there will be no fight. Okay?"

"Okay!" Bruno shouted from the back.

"You eavesdropping, Bruno?" Angela called, laughing.

"My shop," he called back. "I listen to everything."

Steve arrived before they had finished cleaning up. Angela was out in the back and Donna was doing her best to swab the floors with a huge string mop. The closed sign was up and he knocked on the door. Donna looked up and saw a swarthy man with a crew cut, wearing a downfilled jacket that reached his knees and made him look so huge that it flashed through Donna's mind that he would have to go through any door sideways. She knew who it was and called Angela to let him in and stood aside and watched the giant embrace the tiny woman. After introductions, Angela said, "We're just about finished. Have a coffee?" He nodded while taking off his jacket and Donna thought he would still have to go through doors sideways.

"What's up with the boxes?" he asked.

"I'll tell you when I'm through," Angela said as she disappeared into the kitchen.

Steve sat on a stool with his back to the counter and a cup of coffee hidden in his huge hand watching Donna finish mopping the floor. She was sweaty and flushed and wished she had thought to put her scarf back on.

"When did you start working here?" he asked.

"About four hours ago," she said. "I wasn't supposed to start until Monday, but Angela couldn't make it this morning and I happened to be here so I pitched in."

"Why couldn't Angela make it?"

Donna saw Angela's head appear at the serving window behind Steve's back.

She signalled with her finger to her lips and Donna realized quickly that if she said much more she might reveal something that was personal and private, so she shrugged and said, "I don't know," and turned her back on him to mop another section of the room.

When they were finished, the two girls emerged from the back with their coats and the three of them sat together at a table while Angela told Steve what they were going to do. Steve shrugged casually and said, "Okay, let's go, then, if Donna wants to."

"Donna wants to," Angela said firmly. "Don't you, Donna?"

She nodded her head but showed a scared face, and said, "I guess so."

They drove to Donna's home and the three of them walked up to the door. Trembling, Donna knocked timidly and they waited. Then Steve knocked a policeman's knock that must have echoed through the house. The door was flung open by an angry woman, dressed only in a loosely tied bathrobe, her hair straggling out of a bandanna and yesterday's smeared make-up on an aging face. "What the hell is going...," she started to fume. Then, seeing Donna, "Oh, it's you. What d'ya want?"

Steve did not give Donna a chance to answer. He asked firmly, "Are you Donna Penser's mother?"

"Who's asking?" the woman said.

"I am," Steve said, walking through the doorway into the house, his bulk making the woman back up. "I'm on the city police," he continued as he flipped open his wallet to show a badge after he was well inside the house. "I'm not on duty at the moment but a phone call from my car will put me on duty like that," he snapped his fingers under her nose, "and then the trouble will start. Now then, while the girls collect Donna's things, perhaps you will tell me all about the bruises on her neck and a few other things that might mark you as an unfit parent."

"Go to hell," the woman said and stormed out of the hall and into the living room.

"Okay, girls, get going," Steve said over his shoulder as he followed her into the living room. "You, lady! Sit down!"

"Who the hell do you think you are?" she said angrily.

"I'm a cop. And I'm going to tell you again to sit down because you've got some questions to answer. Now, SIT!" he roared and walked menacingly closer to her.

She sat suddenly, her face a caricature of anger and hate.

"Where's your husband?" he asked.

She shrugged. "None of your business."

He walked to the stairs and shouted. "Donna? Is your father upstairs?"

"He's not in his room," she answered after a brief pause.

"Where is he likely to be on a Sunday morning?"

"I don't know. He could be anywhere, I guess. And he's probably so hung over he won't even know where he is."

"Okay. How much time do you need?"

"Another five minutes."

He walked back into the living room and sat down in a chair close to Donna's mother and leaned toward her. "I know how your daughter got those bruises on her neck. You were drunk and you've got a bad, bad temper. She's leaving to protect you because you're such a rotten, drunken slut that the next time you could be up on a murder charge. So there's not going to be a next time. Got it?"

"And you tell your husband when he crawls home. And you try to remember that if I ever see Donna with a bruise, or a scratch or if she even tells me you threatened her, I'll be back. And next time, lady, I won't be such a nice guy." There was menace in his face and manner.

He got to his feet so suddenly that she screamed.

"Oh, did I frighten the old lady?" he said sarcastically.

She screwed up her used and jaded face and stuck out her tongue at him. He continued to stand over her, looking at her without emotion, until he heard the two girls come down the stairs. She stuck her tongue out three more times as he turned away from her and met the girls in the hall.

"Finished?" he asked Donna as Angela carried a box out to the car.

She nodded, shakily.

"Want to say goodbye to your mother?"

"Mom?" Donna said.

"Get the hell outa here!" came the response.

Donna was white and shaking as she picked up the last box and headed for the door with Steve following to close the door. "M is for the million things she gave me," Donna said bitterly. "Mostly hurts and bruises."

"You'll be okay," Steve said reassuringly as they drove away. "You've got friends."

Steve and Angela helped her carry in her boxes of belongings and stayed only long enough for them to admire her tiny room. Steve insisted that she take his card and told her firmly to call him if she ever had problems with her mother. "It may not be police work by definition," he said, "but I've got her scared."

"You were right, back there in the car," Donna said as the other two prepared to leave.

"What's that?" Steve asked.

"About me having friends," she replied. "How can I say thanks."

She hugged Angela who admonished her to take care and wished her good luck. When she tried to hug Steve to say thanks she got her arms filled with his thick down jacket but he managed to envelope her easily and the three of them were laughing happily as they left.

Upstairs, Mrs. Lasseret said to her husband, "Did you hear that, Wally?"

"Eh?" he said as he took his earphones off.

"The kids. The kids downstairs. They were laughing their heads off. Like I told you , it sounds good to hear kids laughing again."

"Yeah," he agreed and put his earphones back on.

Craig had busied himself in the yard for most of the day. His mother had come out to the garden but after half an hour in the afternoon she found that she was too tired and went inside to lie down. Rob sauntered into the yard and they sat in the sun leaning against the garage wall and, although they had talked together only last night, they brought themselves up to date.

"How's Donna?" Craig asked.

"I dunno," Rob replied. "I went over to the Sweet Spot but it was closed. So I went over to her place but she wasn't there. So maybe she went home to get some more stuff."

"Sounds like all she might get is a split lip. Jeez! What a bitch her mother is!"

"Yeah, and her father too, sitting around watching the old bag beat up on his daughter."

"What'd your dad say about you quitting school and all that?"

Rob screwed up his face and looked away. "He said a lot of things. But not what I was expecting." He stopped and continued to avoid looking at Craig.

"Well, what did he say?" Craig persisted.

"He said he was sorry he was always nagging at me and that it was hard for him to say 'I love you' and then he said 'I love you' and a whole bunch of other stuff."

"Your dad? Your dad told you he loved you?" Craig's voice was squeaking with surprise.

"Yeah! What's wrong with that?" Rob asked defensively.

"Nothing, I guess."

"Men can say 'I love you' to other men. It doesn't mean anything like you're thinking."

"I'm not thinking anything. Jesus, if my dad had ever said 'I love you' to me, I would run around town shouting 'The sky is falling! The sky is falling'."

They rolled around laughing at the ridiculous idea. Craig's mother heard them and tried to listen, wondering at the cause of such hilarity.

"Where's your bike?" Rob finally asked. "I better go over and see if Donna's okay."

"And if she's not home what're you gonna do?"

"Leave a note."

"I see," Craig baited. "You're going to reach into your pigskin attaché case and retrieve your note pad and your pen and write a little message that you will thumb tack to her door."

"Oh, shut up and get me something to write on!"

"In the kitchen," Craig said. "Get it yourself!"

Rob disappeared into the house and emerged eating an apple. "Want one?" he called.

"Okay," Craig answered and got up to get his bike for Rob.

Rob came out and flung a leg over the bike. He grinned at Craig with pieces of apple showing in his mouth and a mischievous look on his face. "Hey, Craig! I love you," he said and rode away.

"I know!" Craig called after him.

Monday morning arrived crisp and clear. The October night had touched the lawns with frost and the paperboys left their tracks across the lawns of their routes. Donna was up and dressed and on her way long before she was due at work and found Bruno already there with the coffee urn ready to go and the smell of bacon in the air. "Eat something," he urged. "If you don't eat now you won't get a chance until after the mob thins out around ten."

Rob's alarm wakened his mother who roused herself and shook him into wakefulness before going downstairs and making him some breakfast to start him on his way on the first day of a real job. "You should have shaved," she admonished him when he stumbled down the stairs.

"I shaved two days ago," he protested.

"If you're going to work meeting the public, you should be shaving every day," she said. "Tuck your shirttail in. You're not a schoolboy."

Craig jumped out of bed at the first ring of his alarm clock and dressed quickly in the work clothes he had found the night before. Downstairs he made a lunch and ate his breakfast at the same time while listening to the small radio in the kitchen. He listened at the foot of the stairs for any signs that his mother was awake and heard none. But he made a cup of instant coffee and carried it upstairs for her leaving it on her bedside table after collecting her sleeping pills that she had spilled during the night. She was sleeping heavily, not quite snoring but breathing heavily with rattling breaths. He touched her shoulder to say goodbye but she was too deep in sleep to notice. Collecting his lunch pail and shrugging into his winter jacket, he left the house quietly and walked the two blocks to the bus stop, still young enough to walk on the frosted grass of the boulevard so he could look back and see his giant steps.

CHAPTER 44

Marion woke up groggily and it took her a moment to get oriented. The scummy cup of coffee on her bedside table confused her until the world settled into its orbit and she realized that Craig must have brought it to her before he went to work. It was past ten o'clock and her head was fuzzy and her body felt large and awkward. It occurred to her vaguely that perhaps it was the sleeping pills but Dr. Strawburn had assured her that they were the mildest on the market. With a surge of determination she swung herself out of bed and headed for the shower. She had never been one to abuse herself with blasts of cold water after a hot shower but this morning she thought it might stir her into getting her day started so she stood for a minute with cold water punishing her from the needle spray setting. It was agony. Maybe masochistic people love to do it to exorcise their sins, she thought as she shivered trying to dry herself, but it's not for me. With a towel wrapped around her wet hair, in bathrobe and slippers, she carried the cold cup of coffee downstairs with the other hand touching the banister because of a peculiar feeling of uncertainty in her steps. It must be hunger, she thought. I'm famished.

In the kitchen she saw the crumbs and stains of Craig's breakfast and wondered if he had made himself a lunch for his first day at work and then was engulfed in guilt for not having been more thoughtful and maternal when her son was, as of this very morning, not a school boy, but a man on his way to work. She put coffee on in the small drip machine, some bread in the toaster, cut up a banana in a bowl and covered it with yogurt sprinkled with a little cinnamon and a couple of pinches of toasted shredded coconut, got out the butter and the marmalade and while waiting for the coffee and the toast, went to the front door for the paper. The paper boy had been careless again. The paper was not on the steps where she might have reached out for it in her robe and slippers, but out on her sidewalk. Two men were standing across the street talking and she was reluctant to step out for the paper dressed as she was. Back in the kitchen she reached into the frig for the cream and realized the light had not come on. She took the bulb out and wrote it on her shopping list, turning on the little radio above the frig as she passed by. When she went to the living room and looked out the window, the two men were still engrossed in conversation directly across the street. With a sigh of annoyance, she returned to the kitchen and started on her dish of banana and yogurt when she realized the radio had not come on and the little red light was not showing on the coffee machine. She checked the toaster and it was cold. With a muttered groan of frustration she went down to the foot of the stairs in the basement to the fuse box only to see, not a panel of round fuses, but a double line of breaker switches, none of them marked and none of them, to her unpractised eye, different from any other. Her frustration was mounting. How do I know which is which? she muttered aloud. Going up stairs again, she turned the volume control of the radio up high and went back to the basement where she turned off all the breaker switches and then turned them on, one by one, and was rewarded with the sound of the radio playing in the kitchen. Only when she reached to close the door did she see that each breaker switch had been labelled on the inside of the door. She went upstairs shaking her head at her own stupidity and turned down the radio. The toaster was hot, the red light was glowing on the coffee maker, and the clock on the radio was blinking 12:00, and, she suddenly realized, so was every other clock in the house! Stupid! she chastised herself as she proceeded with her breakfast at 11:30 on a bright October Monday morning.

Going upstairs to get dressed after doing a quick tidy up in the kitchen and living room, she frustrated herself with her indecision about what to wear. As if it matters, she told herself sitting defeated on the edge of the bed. I'm not going anywhere and nobody's coming. She finally got into an old pair of slacks and a sweat shirt that were comfortable but didn't really match and when she looked at herself in the mirror all she could see was a dowdy old lady with saggy clothes who needed a haircut badly. At least I'm not bulging at the seams, she told herself, but I'm still too fat. She opened Craig's bedroom door and saw that the cyclonic confusion had not changed for better or for worse. She wondered how long it had been since he changed his sheets. His bathroom mirror was so spattered she could scarcely see herself so she wiped it clean, picked up a grungy towel and some dirty underwear but refused to do more. I really should, she told herself. I should do a whole house cleaning while I've got on some work clothes on. But the urge passed as quickly as the thought.

Downstairs she fussed and fidgeted, not doing anything really constructive, as if she were waiting impatiently for something. She was able to retrieve the paper and she settled with it in a comfortable chair in the noon sun in the living room, but the paper was filled with another shooting, the usual local political bad- mouthing harangues and the morbid accounts of massacres and mutilations in political hotspots of the world. It depressed her. She folded the paper to the crossword but blanked out on even the most obvious clues. None of her gears seemed to mesh—nothing was going right.

The phone rang. Edith! she suspected, getting wearily to her feet. I don't know if I'm ready for you yet. It wasn't.

"Marion! How are you?" Tom's cheerful voice saluted her.

"Tom! How nice to hear your voice. I've missed talking to you lately."

"I've missed talking to you, too. I was sort of waiting for you to return my call, but then, I figured you would still be pretty busy getting things straightened around."

"I didn't know you called, Tom."

"Yes, I called a few days ago. I've forgotten exactly when. I talked to Craig because you were sleeping."

"Well, he didn't tell me about that. He'll catch it when he gets home."

Tom laughed. "Don't be too hard on him. He was being very protective. Marion, the reason I called in the middle of the day was to tell you I'm moving and I've got a new telephone number."

"You are? Where? Not out of town, I hope."

"No, not out of town. But that's the nicest voice of concern I've heard for a long time. No, the place I'm in is too big for me now without Dad. I don't need two bedrooms. So I found a little bachelor apartment—I guess that's what they are called,—anyway, it's in an older apartment building and it's got a small bedroom, and another room with a corner kitchen area. Just right for me. The apartment building is called the Erindale—it's in the West Burnaby area. It's even got a bit of a view of the mountains if you sort of crane your neck."

"That sounds great, Tom. When are you moving?"

"The other people moved out yesterday and the landlord said he would paint it today. So I thought I'd take a couple of days off work—we're not terribly busy, right now—and I'd clear out the old house and move in. But I wanted to give you the new telephone number and the address. Have you got a pencil handy?"

"Just a minute, Tom. I'll get my address book."

"You're going to put it in your address book? That makes it pretty permanent, doesn't it?" he said with a laugh..

"Yes, I guess it does," she responded and laughed with him.

She wrote the address and telephone number under Thomas, M.

She could always tell Edith, if she was nosing around, that the M stood for Marion and make it up from there.

"Do you need some help, Tom?"

"Marion, I'll be brutally frank. I don't want anyone to see where I'm living. Dad was careless and sloppy in his old age. He spilled everything everywhere. And for the last months he was incontinent—day and night. I'm getting a company truck and taking mattresses, carpets, sofa's and a lot more out to the dump and another load to the Sally Ann. So I've cut down the actual moving to a minimum—clothes, dishes, pots and pans, books and a few pieces of furniture Dad wasn't able to ruin. I shouldn't say it like that; most of the stuff was his anyway."

"I see," Marion said. "But if you need any other kind of help, just shout."

"I was sort of hoping you'd offer. Because I will have to shop for living room furniture and a bed and curtains and stuff like that. And I thought maybe you and I could look at the new place and some catalogues and sales and start from there."

"Oh, I'd love to do that, Tom! When?"

"Well, it will take me a couple of days to clear out the old place, so how about Friday?"

"Friday's fine with me."

"You sound a little disappointed. Maybe tomorrow or Wednesday would be better for you?"

"No, no, Tom. Friday's fine," she lied. And didn't say, except it's four days away .

"Okay, then. I'll pick you up and take you over to the apartment and then we'll go shopping and make a day of it."

"That's great, Tom. I'm looking forward to it."

"So am I, Marion. Goodbye for now."

The Erindale, she said as she moved away from the phone. It sounds vaguely familiar. I wonder why.

Just before noon Murray called Eleanor at the work number he had copied from Brian Tobler, hoping to catch her before her lunch break. He introduced himself and said, "This is a personal call, Miss Colman. I'm a lawyer and I am looking after the estate of Gerald Williams and I have some papers that concern you and I hoped we could meet. We could meet in my office, which is a little far from your place of work or we could meet for lunch. Which would be better for you?"

There was a long pause at the other end and he could sense that she was not about to be rushed. "Before we settle on a place and the drinks, Mr. Andrews," she said in flat tones, "tell me why I should have any interest in Gerald Williams' estate and exactly what papers you have that would interest me. Unless, of course, it's a cheque with a lot of zeros in it, which I'm sure it isn't."

"Well, it does involve money in a round-about way, but I can't really explain it on the phone. That's why I thought we should meet."

"Do lawyers ever do anything except in a round-about way?" she asked sarcastically. "Okay. I won't turn down a free lunch. Give me your address and phone number. I'll check you out and when I've picked the place, I'll call you. It will be expensive and Thursday is my only day."

Murray gave her his address and phone number, restraining his laughter. "I'll look forward to meeting you, Miss Colman." he said. "Shall I pick you up?"

"No, thank you. I'll make my own way and keep the taxi receipt for you. The reservation will be in my name for 12:15. One hour and fifteen minutes, max! Good-bye, Mr.Andrews." She hung up.

Murray leaned back in his chair and howled with laughter. "Hoo boy! I bet Gerald Williams had his hands full with her," he said aloud.

He called Marion and restrained his laughter when she answered and spoke in his lawyerly voice. "Hello, Marion, how are you feeling today?" he asked solicitously.

"Oh, hello Murray. I don't know," she responded in answer to his question. "I slept like there was no tomorrow and I'm still dog-tired and on edge. What's up?"

"I've just talked to Ms Colman and we are going to have lunch on Thursday and maybe I'll get this whole thing sorted out then."

"Do I have to be there?" she asked in a panic voice.

"No, no, Marion! No, I don't want you there." And then feeling that she might misinterpret him he added, "It would be much too hard on you. You let me handle it."

"I thought I should be there to confront her but I wasn't looking forward to it."

"No need, Marion. I'll call you as soon as I feel I've got the whole story. You just stay put and rest. You sound pooped."

"Well, alright," she said uncertainly. "Maybe that's the best way. Maybe I'll call up my bridge group. We play on Thursdays but I haven't played for weeks now. I can't remember the last time. That way I won't be sitting around wondering what is happening."

"Good idea, Marion. You do that. It's time you got back into some routine. Now, don't fuss about it. I'll find out what part Eleanor Colman played in this, if she had any part at all."

When they disconnected, Marion was sniffling and her voice was croaky. She's in pretty bad shape, Murray thought. I hope her kids are giving her some support.

Marion went out the back door and walked around the garden, trying to control her mounting anxiety and wondering if she was ready to get back into the bridge group. She spent fifteen minutes pulling off dead flowers and trying not to think, but she had not put on a jacket and the cool October air sent her back inside.

When she passed the telephone, her mind was suddenly made up, and she sat down and dialled Isabel.

"Hello, Isabel," she said, keeping her voice steady. "I thought it was time for me to get back into the world. Where are we playing this week?"

"Oh, Marion, that's marvellous! Are you sure? We've missed you so much!"

Isabel said warmly. "Particularly Kate, because she has to take the bus if one of us can't pick her up, and you know how our uppity Kate just loves the bus, so we're playing at her place this week. Don't you phone her and tell her, let me. And I'll push her into making something special this time instead of those watercress sandwiches she made last time. You weren't there! You were lucky! Can you imagine! Watercress sandwiches and green tea. And that was the day we had invited Tracy Conniski to come and replace you."

"Oh! You've replaced me! Nobody told me that," Marion said, obviously upset.

"No, no, Marion! It wasn't like that. We didn't replace you. It was just that it was getting awkward playing with seven, so one day we decided it would be a good idea to get someone else and then when you were ready to come back we would always have a replacement if one of us was sick or had to go away. And Tracy was more than willing. She's a very good player and she fits right in with us so easily. And Minnie won't be there this week because her husband's in hospital with a prostate thing and she goes every afternoon, so you'll get a chance to meet Tracy."

"Are you sure, Isabel? I wouldn't want to..."

"Of course I'm sure. Now listen, I've got an idea. Don't you phone any of the others and I will and I'll tell them to each bring something special but I won't say why, unless they guess. Oh, they probably will, we've all missed you so much. They'll know why it is special. Oh, it will be so good to see you, Marion. And I won't let them talk about sad stuff. You've had enough of that, I'm sure. If anybody starts, I'll shut them right up and change the subject."

They talked on for a while, mostly about the other women, not gossiping really, but giving Marion a chance to catch up on the lives of seven other women she had been friends with for years. When they said goodbye, Marion was not completely convinced that she was ready to go back to the game, but, I've got to do it sometime, she told herself. She set about to make a favourite dinner for Craig to welcome him home after his first day of work.

In the middle of her preparations, Edith called. "Where were you?" she demanded. "I called earlier and there was no answer. I wanted to come in and pick up that big roasting pan. You won't be using it and we're having a bunch of neighbours and their kids in for a turkey dinner. (Oh, that'll be nice.) I'll get it on Thursday when I come in to pick up Harvey's work boots that are being resoled. Did I tell you he had his eyes tested and he has to wear glasses now? (Really!) The girls think he looks funny and we call him Owly Daddy. Remember Denise that I used to go to high school with? Chubby blond with a squinty eye? I saw her the other day when I was shopping and I haven't seen her for years so we stopped and had a cup of coffee. Well, it wasn't really coffee, it was Espresso and it was so strong it made me dizzy. (Isn't that strange.) Have you ever had it? You should try it some time. Anyway, she's in the middle of a divorce and it is really, really messy. She inherited a lot of money and he is demanding alimony. Did you ever hear of anything so ridiculous? How's Craig?"

Marion really had not been listening closely so when Edith shifted her conversational gears she was not ready with an answer.

"Hello? Are you still there, Mom?" Edith asked when a response was not immediately forthcoming.

"Yes, of course I am. I was just checking the telephone books while you talked," she lied. "I seem to have so many."

"Well, how's Craig, I said. Has he talked to you about anything?"

"What do you mean, Edith? Of course, he's talked to me—about quitting school and his job and..."

"Quitting school? You let him quit school?" Edith's voice was scolding and severe. "Why doesn't anybody tell me these things?"

"Just a minute, Edith. The buzzer went off and I have to take the muffins out."

"Oh, well, if you're busy. I'll call you again. But it sure would be nice if somebody thought to bring me up to date occasionally. It's not as if I live half way around the world. Anyway, I'll pick up that roasting pan when I'm in Thursday and we'll have a talk then."

"I'll be playing bridge Thursday afternoon. But you have a key. You can find it."

"Oh, are you back playing bridge with your regular group again? That's nice, Mom. I was just saying to Harv that I hoped you were finding something to do after you quit the volunteer thing at the hospital, because you do need something to get you out of the house, particularly now that the winter weather is setting in and sometimes, when the rain is pouring down, you feel like you're locked in a jail cell, I know I do."

"Edith! My muffins."

"Oh, yes. Well, bye-bye. I'll get the roasting pan. Why don't you leave it out for me so I don't have to search for it?"

"Alright, dear. I'll leave it on the kitchen counter."

"Okay, and tell Craig to call me. I'd like to hear something about why he quit school and his job. What's he doing anyway?"

"I'll tell him to call you, Edith. I've got to go. Bye-bye."

She sighed guiltily and went to the kitchen and mixed up a batch of muffins.

On Thursday, Marion spent a long time trying to decide what she would wear to the bridge club. She had lost weight and some of the clothes she would have liked to wear hung too loosely on her. The day was dull and threatening and her summer clothes were no longer suitable. She finally settled on slacks and a jacket with a blouse that Edith had given her for her birthday last year. It was loud with too many competing colours but she chose it because she did not want to look like a widow in mourning and because she needed to feel she was giving Edith a little pat on the back.

She arrived at Kate's deliberately late so she would not have to go through a long sequence of individual greetings. Isabel had been wrong in thinking that they would all guess why she had demanded they each bring something special. None of them were expecting her and the warmth of the greeting from old friends brought her to tears. Tracy Conniski was introduced but stood to one side as the others talked to Marion with warm smiles and comforting understanding. Isabel watched Marion carefully, seeing her wiping tears away but smiling. When she decided the tears had flowed enough, she called out, "Now listen to me, all of you! This is a party and there will be no sad talk here. You can talk about anything else—even that shirt-thing Marion is wearing. My God! Where did you get it?"

"Edith gave it to me. I had to wear it sometime," Marion said laughing with the rest of them.

"I thought that only a son would do that to a mother," Isabel said. "Let's play bridge or I'll never get home on time for my husband's supper."

They settled down to play serious bridge, as always with chatter only between hands, changing partners according to a pattern that would permit everyone to play with every other player. When Marion and Kate were playing against Tracy and Cora, Marion tried to talk casually to Tracy between hands but received only short rebuffing answers to her questions. Making conversation, she said, "Oh, it's been such a long time since I played, I feel like a beginner again," which resulted in a disinterested shrug from Tracy who was dealing. Marion fumbled with her cards and spilled some of them on the table while she was sorting and Tracy threw hers on the table face-up and said, "We'll have to deal again."

"We never bother with things like that!" Kate said.

"Well, we have to now. You've all seen my hand," Tracy replied shortly.

"I'm sorry. I seem to be all thumbs today," Marion said as Tracy re-dealt silently.

"No big deal, honey," Cora said. "And that's my joke for today."

Tracy did not smile.

When they had moved to the last hand, Marion found herself partnered with Tracy. She knew she would have to play with her sooner of later but was not looking forward to it. The others seemed to feel Tracy's brittleness also, and there was little gab and gossip.

Tracy dealt. "Two spades."

"Pass."

"Pass," responded Marion.

"Pass."

The table was quiet as Marion spread out her cards. Tracy was looking at her with daggers. "You can't pass an opening two-bid," she said so abruptly that it created a silence at both tables.

"Can't or shouldn't?" Isabel said from the other table.

"Can't!" the response came explosively as Tracy began to play the hand.

"You should have doubled, dear," Cora, who was also a dummy, called over to Marion from the other table, and the others laughed.

Marion sat, frozen with embarrassment and close to tears, while Tracy slapped cards down and made a small slam. "Sorry," she ventured to Tracy who was busy picking up the cards and made no reply.

"Someone come and give me a hand," Kate called from the kitchen. "I don't know what we are going to do with all this food. Just look at this!" she exclaimed, coming in with a plate of sandwiches and a cake. "Now I know why Isabel told everybody to bring something special. You're back, Marion. So it's a celebration and an attempt to fatten you up."

"Was I supposed to bring something?" Tracy asked. "Nobody said anything."

"No, no," Isabel assured her. "You're a guest. We wouldn't ask a guest to bring food. But we enjoyed having you while Marion couldn't make it, didn't we, girls?"

There were nods and expressions of affirmation, none of which exuded much sincerity. "Maybe we will call on you again to fill in," someone said.

Tracy did not linger over a cup of tea and a sandwich. "Kate," she said. "You'll have to excuse me. I promised to pick my husband up and it's getting late."

"Oh, so soon?" Kate purred. "Let me fix you a plate of goodies to take with you."

"No, no! Please don't bother," Tracy said as she retrieved her coat and struggled into it with no help from Kate. She stopped at the living room door. "Good-bye, everybody. Thanks for inviting me."

There was a chorus of good-byes, nice-to-meet-yous and as the door closed behind her, Isabel said it for them all, "She's dead meat, that one!"

"What's she got stuck in her craw?" Dot asked.

"She got the wind up her butt because we were making a fuss over Marion, that's all. She was just plain jealous!" said Dot.

"Oh, I can't wait to phone Minnie and tell her."

"Tell her we just discovered you can't pass a two-bid," someone called.

"What a bitch!"

"I'll bet she wouldn't even pass wind," Kate said with her mouth full and they all laughed as they reached for more.

Marion had been so caught up in the excitement of being back with good friends again, in spite of Tracy's thinly veiled hostility, that she had forgotten the time and it was only when Tracy left that she looked at her watch and panicked when she realized she might have missed Murray's call.

"Oh, Kate! May I use your phone? I have to call my lawyer," she said and the others heard a note of panic in her voice.

"Use the one in my bedroom, Marion. Don't close the door all the way or we won't be able to hear a thing," she teased.

"She really is up tight, isn't she?" someone said in a quiet whisper when Marion had left the room.

"Who wouldn't be after what she's been through?" "I never knew he was such a drunk." "And a skirt chaser, I heard." "Did she ever catch him running around?" All in whispers.

"Come on, now! Let's speak up or she'll think we really are trying to listen," Kate said. And then in a louder voice, "Cora, you promised to Xerox your recipe for those lovely sandwiches we had at your place."

"I decided to make you wait until it is published in Gourmet," Cora answered and they were laughing when Marion came back in the room, flushed and obviously upset.

"Kate, I hate to rush away but I should go," she said.

"Now look here," Kate said with mock severity. "You've got yourself in a tizzy about something, so you just sit right down there and have this cup of tea while I fix you a plate of goodies to take home."

"Kate..." Marion began to protest.

"Sit!" Kate commanded. "Besides, look at all this food. And don't you think Craig would like some in his lunch pail?"

"I heard you tell someone he quit school and he's working," one of them said. "What is he doing?"

"He's working in a factory out in Richmond," Marion replied. "This is his first day and I should be home when he gets there."

"Of course you should, dear," Isabel cut in. "Hurry up with that tea, then. Well, it doesn't matter, you've got it all in your saucer anyway. Give it to me. Kate? What's taking you so long with that plate? Marion's got to go!"

Isabel hustled around getting Marion's coat and her own. "I've got to go, too. Thank God for ovens with timers. He'll be sitting there with his knife and fork at the ready by the time I get home. Do I get a plate too, Kate?" She gave Marion a hug and held on. "Hang in there, babe!" she whispered. "It'll all settle down pretty soon. You'll be fine."

Marion said her goodbyes, shaky and tearful. The afternoon had been stressful, even though she had been with friends. Tracy's hostility had upset her; she had missed Murray's phone call; Craig would arrive home to an empty house after his first day at work—too many things were gnawing at her. She was hurrying home and neglected to slow down through a playground area. A siren sounded behind her and she pulled over and burst into tears.

"May I see your licence please?" a very young officer asked as he came up to the car. "Did you not see the playground sign?"

"No, I didn't. I'm sorry. I was in a hurry. I wanted to get home," she said jerkily as she rummaged in her purse for her wallet.

"Just the licence," he said, rejecting the wallet.

She said nothing further as she fumbled with the card case in her wallet, not realizing the she was sniffling and that she had wiped her drippy nose with the back of her hand.

"How long have you lived at this address?" he asked after he had looked at the licence.

"Twenty five years, more or less."

"You live about four or five blocks away and you didn't know there was a playground here?"

"I forgot, I said. I said I was sorry," and her voice rose to a warning level of hysteria.

He handed her licence back and watched as she shakily reinserted it in her wallet. "You should be able to remember this playground area," he said, looking at her with youthful severity. "Now I want you to drive slowly home and I will follow you. Try to drive with more care and attention in the future. You appear to be very upset about something. Think how much more you would be upset if you had killed a child by your forgetfulness."

"Oh, God!" she moaned as he turned away.

She drove home slowly and could see him follow her and watched him speed away when she turned into her driveway.

Her hand was shaking as she fumbled to unlock the door. She had her purse dangling from her wrist and carried the plastic plate of sandwiches and cakes that Kate had given her. Rushing to get into the house as though demons were following her, she tripped over the sill and dropped the plate and watched it fall upside down on its saran wrap covering. "God damn it!" she almost screamed, feeling stretched beyond her limits. She picked the plate up and put it on the counter and plodded upstairs to kick off her shoes and fling herself on her bed, desperately trying to regain control.

She was still lying there when Craig arrived home half an hour later. "Hi, Mom!" he called up the stairs.

"Oh, hello dear," she responded trying to pull herself together for his sake. "I'll be down in a minute. Did you have a good day?"

"Yeah, it was okay.'

He noticed that she had made no dinner preparations but he had found her keys hanging in the lock and figured that she could not have stayed in bed all day. The morning paper was opened on the dinette table but the mail had not been picked up from the floor by the front door so she must have been up for a little while and gone out, he thought.

"What's this plate of stuff on the counter?" he shouted to her from the kitchen.

"That's for you," she said, coming into the kitchen behind him. "I brought it back from the bridge club."

"Oh, good! You played bridge today, did you? Have a good time?" he asked over a mouthful of three triangles of chicken sandwiches now garnished with some cake frosting. He noticed that her eyes were red and puffy as if she had been crying again.

"Oh, yes. It was good to see the old crowd again, except there was a new woman there who was filling in and she turned out to be a proper bitch! And then, I forgot to call Murray and by the time I remembered his office was closed, and I got stopped by the police for speeding through the playground area."

"Yeah, you look like you've had a rough day. That's too bad."

"How was your day," she asked, more to change the subject for her own emotional control than out of pure interest in him.

"Okay, I guess," he said casually.

"That all? Just okay? The first day on a job you might have for the rest of your life, and you say, okay I guess?"

"Well, you know. It wasn't very exciting. I didn't get picked up by the cops or nothing," and he grinned at her with a mouthful of sandwich.

"Don't eat them all," she admonished. "Save some for your lunch."

"For my lunch! Moth-er! I couldn't eat those things in front of the other men."

She smiled but did not really realize that his statement indicated his new perception of himself as being a part of the adult world. The door bell rang.

"I'll get it," he said.

She heard him open the door and say, "Oh, hi, Murray. Come in," and she felt a rush of panic, thinking only that he would have such terrible news that he had to see her face to face. She heard Craig call her but she stood frozen with the fear of what Murray was going to have to tell her. She heard him take Murray into the living room and still she could not move. She saw Craig come into the kitchen and heard him say to her, "Mom, Murray's here to see you!" With a desperate effort, she said in a dry whisper, "I'll be right there," but she did not move. Finally, Craig took her arm, his face solemn with concern, and moved her toward the living room. "It's only Murray, Mom," he said quietly. "It's all right."

"Hello, Marion," Murray said with a smile when she came into the room. "I called you earlier but there was no answer and I had to come out this way to my father's birthday party so I thought I would just drop by. Craig tells me you were out playing bridge today. Good for you!"

"What did you find out?" she asked in a croaky voice.

"Let's sit over here so we can all look at some papers on the table," he suggested, moving to the sofa and putting his brief case on the coffee table.

"I'll leave you alone," Craig said as his mother moved to the sofa.

"No, Craig, you should stay. I think you should hear this. I wish Edith and Harvey could have been here to hear the explanation too, but I'll have to leave it to you to explain it to them," he said as he opened his briefcase and laid six sheets of paper on the table. "These two pages are handwritten instructions to T.T. Irvin instructing him to create a will for him leaving everything to Eleanor Colman. She confirmed today that it is his handwriting."

"No!" Craig cried in a shocked voice. "He can't do that!"

"It's not clear what he was trying to do, except to be malicious, Craig. Here is a page of samples of his signatures that Irvin was to use, and also a page of forged signatures of Eleanor Colman. I've no idea why they were included. It doesn't make sense. Then here's a list of assets which corresponds with what we already assembled with one or two differences; for instance, it claims here that your account, Marion, was a joint account and we know that not to be true, and he lists your Buick as his property and I think you told me that you had bought it with money from your father's estate, and registered in your name only."

Marion nodded while Craig sat listening in shocked disbelief.

"I don't know what was in his mind, except to make trouble. But there was another strange thing. He instructed Irvin to date the will prior to the date of the legitimate will that we made out and was registered legally. So if Irvin had followed his instructions and the will emerged somehow, it would not have been considered valid but it certainly would have caused a lot of trouble for you and for Eleanor Colman. I can only think the man was sick to the point of being psychotic to plan such a thing."

"Why would he do it?" Marion asked. "How could he do such a thing?"

Murray shrugged. "I don't know—except that he wanted to create trouble even after his death."

"Did she know anything about that will? Was she in on it?"

"No, she didn't! I'm very sure of that. She was furious when I showed her these papers and she didn't mind if the whole restaurant knew it. I can tell you I felt about this big," showing with his forefinger and thumb. "And she had some choice names for him, real locker room stuff that I don't need to repeat."

"I don't understand it. Why did he do it? Did he really hate me that much."

"I think it is possible that he did it to get back at Colman. They had a relationship going back for years and ..."

"What do you mean a relationship?" Marion interrupted.

Murray sighed. "I didn't know whether you knew or not. But it seems they were sexually involved for the last three or four years."

"No!" both Marion and Craig said simultaneously.

"I'm afraid so. I don't think she would make up a lie about a thing like that. Anyway, something happened and she called it off and made trouble for him and maybe he thought up this way to make trouble for her, thinking she might be charged with forging a will or something like that. It was a very sick thing. She said she thought he was an alcoholic, but it seems more than alcoholism to me."

"Did she love him?" Marion asked in an old querulous voice. And then in a stronger voice, "Oh, why am I asking that! I don't care if she did. I know he didn't love me and my feelings for him right now are so far removed from love that he might as well have been from another planet."

"Are you okay, Mom?" Craig asked, moving to sit on the arm of the sofa beside her.

She took his hand and nodded. "But bring me some more Kleenex, will you, please?" And then to Murray, "I really don't know her, except to speak to her on the phone. What kind of a person is she?"

"Strong, very strong and definite. She's nobody's fool. I had the feeling that she was the one who dictated the relationship. I invited her for lunch, you know, and she selected the place and told me it would be expensive." He stopped and had an almost private chuckle. "That's the first time I've paid out $115 for two lunches and I only had a sandwich and a Bloody Mary."

"Murray, what if there is another will? What if Irvin really did make one?" she asked.

"I really don't think he did. Nothing to base it on, of course, except gut feeling. But if he did, it would be useless anyway except to create the problems your husband apparently wanted to create. But the date of the will, if Irwin followed instructions, would make the will null and void. There's always the possibility that he made a will and did not follow instructions and dated it after the will that has been already probated, but that doesn't really matter either because the probate court has already stated that the will I read to you was the last and final will of your husband. If there is another will, where is it? Why hasn't it shown up. Furthermore, if it ever did surface, these documents will show the intent to create a false will. They have been notarized, and I will keep them in safekeeping, if you like, or you may keep them and put them in your safety deposit box."

"No!" she almost screamed. "You keep them. I never want to see them again in my life!"

He put the papers together and picked up his briefcase. "I'm sorry to be the bearer of, well, it's not bad news, let's call it distasteful news. But I really think it's all over, Marion. I think that's the end of it. Now, you've got to get over all the worry and upset and get on with your life. You too, Craig. Don't let these things get you down."

"He quit school and he's working," Marion said.

"Sure you did the right thing, Craig?" Murray asked.

"Yeah, I'm sure. I'm going to night school, though."

"Good, keep it up. I've got to get going, Marion, or there will be no birthday cake left for me."

"Thanks for coming by, Murray. I hope you don't miss your father's party."

"It was something that I knew we couldn't deal with over the phone and I knew you were anxious to hear the outcome of my meeting with Colman. Now, if there's anything, anything, anything I can do, you will call me, won't you?"

"Yes, I will and thank you," as they shook hands.

"Goodbye, Craig," Murray said. "You must tell me about your job and your plans sometime."

"Yeah, sure, Murray and thanks," Craig said. "If we can't explain it to Edith, maybe she could phone you?"

"Anytime."

After he left, Marion sat struggling with her emotions, while Craig paced furiously back and forth, all but stamping the floor in his anger.

"Maybe it was the tumor that made him act so awful," she ventured, trying to find some explanation for his behavior.

"Tumor, hell," Craig exploded. "It wasn't any tumor! He was a miserable, rotten, excuse for a human being. What did Murray say? Malicious, that's what he said. A miserable, dirty, rotten, perverted, malicious bastard! Bastard! Bastard!. What he did to Edith and to me and what he did to you wasn't caused by any tumor. He didn't die from it anyway. He died because he was a drunk and he killed himself. He did it so he could hurt us some more. Oh, Mom!" he said, as his fury subsided and knelt by her and put his arms around her, child-like with his head on her lap, and his voice cracking, "you have no idea how I hate him."

"I think I do," she answered, stroking his head.

"Is it wrong to hate like that," he asked.

"It can't be wrong when he gave us all those reasons to hate and none to love," she answered and believed her own answer.

They sat for a while in silence. "I should call Edith," she said finally. "But maybe I'll do it tomorrow. I don't think I could talk to her tonight. I just want to go to sleep and never wake up." Craig was too young to hear the words of depression that were becoming more frequent.

"Don't you want any supper?" he asked.

"Oh, Craig! I'm sorry! You haven't had your supper and I haven't even started it," she exclaimed, feeling pangs of guilt again.

"Are you going to eat?" he asked.

"I couldn't eat a bite. I just want to go to bed."

"Okay, then I'll go out and get a burger or something. You go on to bed. You look beat," he said, and added, apropos of nothing said, but perhaps expressing his unconscious daily need to touch bases with his friend, "Rob's still at work."

CHAPTER 45

Craig was up with the sun and off to work after struggling to find something for breakfast besides the curled sandwiches and cookies left out on the counter overnight. While he breakfasted on fried eggs and toast and jam, he looked forward to the afternoon when two projects would make the day different: an appointment with a computer firm to talk to them about how to set up a system for the factory and another appointment for what he hoped would be his last driving lesson. He had been very hesitant about talking to the computer people but Carl had said that he knew nothing about computers and Craig knew at least what the damn things looked like so it was his job. Before he left, he looked in on his mother and found her sprawled and snoring. It must be those sleeping pills, he thought. She never used to sleep so soundly and snore like that.

When he saw Carl at work he told him about the appointment he had made with one computer company and that he was going to make some appointments with some others and get brochures from all of them and later maybe get some estimates from the best ones.

"When did you make the appointment?" Carl asked.

"A couple of days ago, after I got home from work."

"You don't need to take work home with you. I don't. Just arrange to take time off from what you're doing and come into the office. You can't leave when there's a run going, of course. But on most of the one-man machines, it doesn't matter if you're away for a while."

When Carl left, Larry, the foreman walked over to Craig. "The boss likes you, eh, Craig?" he said, neither smiling nor serious.

Craig shrugged, puzzled by the question. "I guess so."

"Know why?"

Craig shrugged again, embarrassed and cautious. "Why?"

"The men figure it's because you look like his son—same built, same age, blond hair like you, big grin, good kid. He got drowned last year when he was swimming with a tank, you know, for air, and he was down deep and the air ran out. Very bad, to lose a son. The men think he bounced back a bit when you came back to work. We saw him watching you. He's a good man, Carl is. So..."

"So what are you telling me, Larry?"

"Nothing, I guess. Except some of the men thought he was playing favourites, but we figured out why, and everybody thinks it's okay. It's good for everybody that he's getting over it."

"Nobody said anything about his son when I was here in the summer," Craig said.

"We just didn't talk about it in front of strangers. It didn't seem right. It was too private." He gave Craig a pat on the back and walked back to his machine.

Marion was awakened by the telephone. Tom's cheerful greeting was unexpected until she remembered that she had promised to go with him to see his apartment and help him pick out some drapes and furniture. Her first thought was that she didn't even feel like getting out of bed, let alone traipsing all over town to furniture sales. Then she remembered that she had to phone Edith and she wasn't looking forward to that conversation either.

"Oh, Tom! I'm sorry! I didn't forget, really. I just woke up. Well, your call woke me up, actually. Tom, I can't make it today. I know I promised but you wouldn't believe the day I had yesterday. It just knocked me for a loop."

"That's too bad," he said in a sincere voice. "What was it? A touch of flu?"

"No, no! I'm not really sick. It's just that I had a meeting with my lawyer and learned some things that I...well, things that I probably should have known a long time ago if I hadn't been so blind and stupid. Anyway, Craig heard it all, too and he was pretty upset and I was so caught up in my own misery I couldn't help him at all. And today I've got to talk to Edith about it. I've just got to."

"What's it all about, Marion. Do you want to talk about it?"

"Yes, I do, Tom. You're the one person I know I can talk to about it. But forgive me, not today. I'm sorry to go back on my word."

"That's all right, Marion. I've got lots to do. You can see the place later. Maybe tomorrow?"

"You really are a very understanding man, you know. Tomorrow might be okay, but I suddenly thought that if I could persuade Craig to go out with me to Edith's tomorrow, then Harvey would be there too, and I could get it all over with, with Craig's help. Would you mind very much if we made it Sunday. The big stores will all be open." She was almost pleading.

"Sure, Marion. I've still got lots to do at this place. Sunday's fine. If I pick you up at, say 10:30, will you be up and about?" He said it gently, teasingly, without sarcasm.

"I sure will—I'll be waiting! And Tom, thanks for being so understanding."

"It's easy with you, Marion. See you Sunday."

The call boosted her out of the doldrums she had been in for days. With a burst of energy she went through the house with a vacuum and dust cloth, picked up papers, took out the trash and put on some laundry. Then while the washer was running, she sat down with a cup of coffee and phoned Edith.

"How are you, dear?" she asked when Edith answered.

"Hoo-o, Mom! I'm all out of breath. We went down to the park for a walk. Just the girls and me and they had a great time and when it was time to go home, Iona said she wanted to find the way home and not to tell her. Well, we had a good walk alright. We went around one block twice and Jenny was getting mad at Iona because she thought we were lost. Anyway finally we came to the corner store three blocks from us and both of them recognized it and started running for home and I had to run too, in case they might run across a street without looking, so I'm pooped and I haven't even got the dishes done. I was all caught up in a crossword puzzle when they started begging me to go to the park. What are you doing?"

But her mother heard the question with the emphasis on the last word rather than on 'you' and thought Edith was talking to the girls so she waited and did not answer.

"Mom? Are you there? Edith asked.

"Oh, yes! I thought you were talking to the girls."

"No, I asked you what you were doing. You sound kind of dopey and sleepy. Are you up?"

"Of course I'm up," her mother said snappily. "I've tidied and vacuumed and I've got a wash going and as soon as I've cleaned up and changed, I've got to go shopping."

"Oh, you're a bundle of energy today, aren't you? That's good. How'd you're bridge go?"

"It was nice to get back, really, except they had invited someone in to replace me. I guess their idea was to see if she could be a permanent substitute for anyone who couldn't make it. And Minnie wasn't there so she was subbing for Minnie. But she turned out to be a snarly bitch and she's not going to be invited back. Just as well, she was very rude to me."

"What did she do?"

"Oh, I'll tell you about it sometime. I called to see if you were doing anything tomorrow. And if you have no special plans and Harvey will be home, Craig and I might come over in the morning. I've got something to tell you."

"What?

"It's too hard to tell you over the phone. That's why I want to come out. Is Harvey going to be home?"

"Yes, I expect so. He might have a little running around to do. He usually does. It won't matter—you're staying for lunch, aren't you?"

"That would be nice, thank you," thinking, it would be nicer if you asked me. "I'm just on my way out shopping, can I bring anything."

"I shopped yesterday and I think I've got everything."

"Then we'll see you tomorrow."

"So you're not even going to give me a hint about what it's all about, eh?"

"No, dear, I'm not. I'm off to shop. Bye-bye."

She hurried out of the house and went shopping, leaving her shopping list on the counter. When she arrived at the market and realized that she had forgotten it, she pounded the steering wheel with the heels of both hands, shouting "Damn! Damn! Damn!" much to the amusement of an elderly couple putting their grocery bags in their car.

It took her twice as long to shop, trying to remember everything on the list by walking up and down every aisle. When she got home, Craig was just coming out the door. "What are you doing home?" she asked with Edith's abruptness.

"It's OK Mom. I live here," he said laughing.

"I mean in the middle of the afternoon," she said. "I've been talking to Edith."

"I see," Craig said, grabbing several bags and starting for the house. "I've got an appointment across town and I wanted a clean shirt. I've got to hurry. Are you having a party? You are sure loaded up."

"No, there was nothing to eat. It's a wonder you haven't starved. Thank you," she said as he carried in the last bags.

"We have to go out to Edith's tomorrow. Is that all right with you?"

"Oh, damn! Do we have to?"

"It was my idea. I'm sorry I didn't check with you, but I didn't want to phone you at work. You know, Mummy phoning her little boy the first week he's at work."

"I'm glad you didn't. I'll be late getting home, six-thirty or seven. I've got a driving lesson at five-thirty." She wanted to ask him a couple of other things and wish him good luck, but he was gone. She closed the door and started the wearisome task of putting the groceries away. On Monday she would find a load of wet clothes in the washer and another two piles on the floor, sorted ready to wash.

At six-thirty dinner was ready and she was watching the last of the news while waiting for Craig. The aspirin she had taken for the ache in her shoulders had not helped, but, she thought, maybe a drink would. There was no gin or vodka or tonic, just scotch and rye and brandy and rum and a half a dozen liqueurs. "Why don't you have a scotch, Marion?" she said aloud. "Don't mind if I do," she answered, and took the bottle to the kitchen. She had never been much of a drinker and when she did drink, somebody else had always poured it for her. Pouring some in a glass, she looked at it against the light and decided it didn't look like much so she put in another teaspoonful, dropped in a few ice cubes and filled the glass with water. It tasted insipid, so she poured in enough whisky until she thought it had a nice colour, and went back to the news.

She was well into her second drink when Craig thumped up the back steps. He came into the living room with a big grin. "Well, I passed!" he said in a voice that matched his grin.

"Good for you, dear! Congratulations," his mother said, getting up to add a kiss to her words. "Now I suppose you're going shopping for a car. Come and din your getter, you're late." She went out to the kitchen without noticing the twisted words. Craig noticed them, took a sip of the drink she had left behind and screwed up his face.

"That looks like a whopper of a drink, Mom. What was it?'

"That's just a little scotch. Is it too strong? I couldn't find the measuring thing. You know, that kind of eggcup with some marks on it."

"You mean a jigger? It's right there in the liquor cabinet." And he went back into the living room and brought it out to her.

"Oh, there it is," she said. "I better start using it."

"Yeah," he said. "When did you start drinking?"

"I haven't started, smarty-pants. Sit down, here's your dinner."

They ate in silence for a while, Craig wolfing his food while his mother picked at hers. "I should be hungry," she said finally. "But I'm not, and I just remember I didn't have any lunch. Maybe that's why I feel so dizzy. I think I better go lie down. Do you mind clearing off the table, dear?" She wandered off cautiously toward the stairs. "Don't forget we have to go out to Edith's tomorrow," she called from the top.

"Why are we going to Edith's?" he shouted, but she was already in her room and did not answer.

He tidied up the kitchen, turned off the TV and then went over to the supermarket to find Rob and found him busy packing bags. "Hey," he said while Rob worked. "Guess what? I passed my driving test and I'm getting a license. How about that!"

"Hey, man! That's great!" Rob almost shouted as he stopped packing, slapped Craig on the shoulder and gave him a casual hug. "He just got his driver's license," he explained to the smiling customers waiting in line. "When are we going looking for your car?" he asked over his shoulder as he kept working at top speed.

"When's your day off?"

"Tuesday and Wednesday."

"I got night school Tuesday."

"Rob," the cashier said, "will you check the price on these pickles?"

Rob rushed away with Craig in tow, saying as he went. "I get off at nine and I'm going to meet Donna in the mall. See you there. We'll have a night on the town!" and he dodged through the crowd of shoppers back to the checkout.

"How about Wednesday?" Craig called after him and heard no reply.

When he biked over to Donna's hoping to leave his bike there and walk to the mall with her she was not home, so he headed out alone. He wandered around through the usual hangouts but couldn't find Donna and saw only two people from school who were as uninterested in his job or the results of his driving test as he was in their story that a teacher and a student had called each other stupid and the teacher had slapped the student's face. After walking the corridors of the mall for an hour looking for Donna and Rob, he left and rode back to Donna's where, peeking through the basement window, he saw them sitting on the floor, leaning against the bed, smoking a joint. After watching for a minute, he got on his bike and rode home nursing a resentful hurt. At home he got a Pepsi from the frig and flopped in front of the TV, switching channels without watching until he found a show that the TV Times called the Comedy of the Century. If it was funny, it did nothing to relieve his loneliness and he turned it off, locked the doors and switched off the lights. Upstairs, he knocked gently on his mother's door and opened it. Her bathroom light and her reading light were still on. He listened for a moment to her snores, turned out her lights and went to bed. He had a long complicated sexy dream about himself and Rob and Donna. They had butterflies on their rumps, too.

CHAPTER 46

The traffic was heavy enough in the city that Marion was too occupied with driving to talk. Craig would much rather have been doing anything else than going out to visit Edith and Harvey but his mother got so upset when he told her he had other things planned that he relented.

"I told you yesterday that we were going out to see her," she had said sharply to him. "I can't do it alone!" and she had started to cry. It was only then that he knew the purpose of the visit: to tell Edith and Harvey what Murray had told them. He thought his mother would have done that on the phone with Edith but she told him it was not the kind of thing you could do over the phone.

"What if she lived in Toronto or England?" he said. "What would you do then—go flying off to see her?"

"That would be different, and don't be impertinent," she said. "Of course, I wouldn't, I would write but I can't write to her in Abbotsford."

The traffic thinned out after they crossed the bridge and got on the freeway. The big Buick cruised quietly at 100 K with most other cars passing easily. "Why didn't you want to drive?" she asked.

"I dunno," Craig said with a shrug. "Maybe because I wasn't ready to drive with you in the car. You'd get too nervous, I guess. But mostly because this thing is so big, or because a Buick sounds so big. I've just been driving compacts. I could drive it if I had to, so it's alright if you have a heart attack."

"Don't laugh! I just might. I don't know how Edith is going to react."

When they arrived, Edith was out cleaning the windows on the door and keeping an eye on the twins who were riding their trikes on the sidewalk. Both girls tripped rushing to see who would be first to get to Granny and there were tears instead of greetings as mother and grandmother each picked one up and carried them into the house. "Aren't you going to give your uncle a big kiss?" Edith asked. One of them shook her head and the other gave Craig a look, then a smile and went shyly over to Craig and reached out her arms to be picked up. "That a good girl, Iona. She's always the first," she said to her mother. "And there goes Jenny to give Uncle Craig a big hug and kiss hello. Good girl, Jenny. Now why don't you two take your uncle out and find Daddy? Off you go, now!" And they each took a hand and dragged a willing uncle out of the room. "Oh, Craig! Hi! Sorry—I didn't even get a chance to say hello with all this excitement. How's the job?" Edith called as they were leaving.

"Great!" he shouted back.

"Well, it's not time for lunch yet. Let's have some coffee. Harv was up early so he'll want one. Does Craig drink coffee yet? I got the nicest salad for lunch. I got it out of some magazine—I've forgotten which one—but you take a cucumber and scrape out the seeds and cut it into thin strips like shoelaces and salt it and let it drain in a colander and then you make a kind of salsa out of a boiled garlic bulb, a whole one! Imagine that! and chop it up with a couple of those pear shaped tomatoes and a scallion and a hot green pepper. It really looks pretty! Come and see."

Marion went out to the kitchen with her and looked at the four salad plates she had prepared and was in the middle of complimenting her when Edith said, "Oh, there's Harv! Up the ladder fixing the swing." She rapped on the window and Harvey twisted around on the ladder and smiled at her. "Come and wave to him, Mom!" and her mother did as she was told. Edith made some cup-drinking gestures and Harvey nodded agreement. "I thought he'd be ready for some," she said. "What did you want to talk to us about?"

Marion sighed, not quite ready to get into it yet. "It's about something Murray found out, that I knew nothing about. But let's wait until after lunch and the girls are down. Then we can deal with it."

"Deal with it!" Edith said sharply. "That sounds ominous. I had hoped that Dad had won the sweepstakes and had stashed it away in a secret bank account. I could deal with that!"

"You should be so lucky," her mother said as the twins dragged Craig through the kitchen and up to their room.

Harvey came in and greeted Marion in his warm but almost formal way. "Good drive out?" he asked. "Sometimes that freeway gets packed on Saturday mornings."

"Yes, it was an easy drive once we got over the bridge. But I must tell you. Craig got his licence, well not really, he passed his driver's test and he can get a his proper licence on Monday. I asked him if he wanted to drive but he didn't. He said it was because I was in the car and the car was too big, but I think he didn't want to drive without a licence."

"Good for him," Harvey said.

There was a moment of silence, unusual in Edith's home, then Edith said, "Are you going to buy him a car?"

"No, I certainly am not. He saved up all summer and he is determined to buy his own car. I might help him if he asks but somehow I don't think he will ask."

"Well, you didn't come out to talk to us about Craig buying a car," Edith said. "Are you going to tell us now?"

"After lunch, I said, Edith. When the girls are tucked down for their nap and we can talk without being interrupted," Marion said with a touch of maternal asperity in her voice.

"That's a good idea," Harvey said agreeably. "I've got about fifteen minutes work to finish the swing and then Craig promised them that he would give them each some really big pushes. And that will take us just about to lunchtime. Okay, dear?"

"Alright, I'd better get started then," Edith replied. "But we'll still be eating early."

"That's okay by me, Edie. I was up early. How about you, Marion?" Harv asked.

"Fine with me," she lied, thinking she couldn't remember ever having lunch before twelve. "Need some help, dear?"

"No," Edith said. "I mean no thank you. But I'll tell you what I'd like you to do. Go out into my garden and look around and tell me what I can do to make it nicer. It just looks drab to me and I'd like to perk it up a bit. You know, move things around and maybe buy some more flowering shrubs, a couple of azaleas or rhododendrons, something like that. I'd like to have some colour all year round like you have. Yours is always so pretty. I remember when we moved out here and I could have a garden, I was almost scared to start because I knew I could never match yours. You're so good with plants. You must have a green thumb, like they say."

"It's not as much a green thumb as it is a strong back, Edie. I'd love to look around and see if I get any ideas."

When she went out she saw Harvey on a ladder tying up the swing. "Always some fixing up to do, isn't there?" she said to him smiling as she walked by.

"Always," he agreed. "But it's the best part of my week."

"Edith asked me to give her some ideas about her garden."

"Oh, good!" he said. "She's been fussing about it for a long time and was sort of afraid to ask you."

"I know the situation. You ask for some advice and then you're afraid the other person will be offended if you don't follow it for whatever reason." She smiled and walked on so that he could get back to his task, but had not had a chance to look at the garden before the girls came running up, each taking a hand and chattering. The children were more cheering than a solitary walk in the garden and they made the leaden chore of what she had come for disappear for the moment. So she involved the children in a game of 'What would it look like if we moved this over there and that over here?' With their active imaginations they were able to move everything from the back to the front and have pumpkins growing along the sidewalk. Edith called and they traipsed in, flushed and ready for lunch. "I really didn't get much of a chance to look around, Edith, but I'll give you one suggestion. I've got several things that need to be split. So next time you're in we'll look at them and see if you want them and then in the spring I'll split them and come out and give you a whole day's work putting them in where we think they should go and what ever else you might decide to buy."

"Oh, that's wonderful, Mom! Really?"

"Of course! And..." she said, "there's that big clump of Tiger Lilies out at the cottage that need splitting and the peonies are so choked they need to be done, too."

"I thought about them but I didn't want to do anything without asking."

"Please Edith, go ahead as if it were your own place. It will be some day soon anyway."

"What do you mean?"

"I mean I really haven't much interest in using the place all by myself. I might just turn it over to you two."

"Oh, Mom! That would be wonderful. Then you could come and visit us. I suppose that means taking over the taxes and stuff like that, does it?" Edith's eyes had narrowed.

"I suppose it does. Perhaps we should think about it," her mother said.

Harvey and Craig came into the house. "Harvey, Mom said she was thinking of turning the cottage over to us. Wouldn't that be great?"

"Edith," Marion quickly interjected before Harvey had a chance to reply, "when I said turning it over to you two, I meant you and Craig, of course. Not just you and Harvey."

"Oh! That's different," Edith said, her face tightening into primness. "For a minute I thought we might get the cottage and Craig would get the house."

"Edith! For heaven's sake! I'm not about to die! Although sometimes I think it would be a good solution to all the mess my life is in."

"Mom! Come on, now!" Craig said quickly. "Your life isn't in a mess. Dad's might have been, but not yours." He walked over to her and touched her shoulder as her eyes started to fill.

There was a silence in the room. Harvey saw his two daughters looking on with wide eyes. Iona looked at him and asked, "Is Granny going to die, Daddy?"

"No, dear. We're just having big people talk. Edith, maybe we should have lunch."

"Right," she said. "It's all ready. Come along, everybody. Craig, I need another chair from the dining room. Sit over here, Mom, the girls want to sit beside you."

She busied herself putting the rest of the lunch on the table already set in the sunny kitchen nook. When they were all seated, Harvey said, "Can we hold hands please, while Jenny says grace? Jenny, it's your turn."

Jenny bowed her head low over the table edge and said, "God bless this food. Amen."

Iona called out shrilly, "You didn't say 'God bless our family'," and Jenny burst into tears.

"It's okay, Jenny," Harvey's voice was quiet and soothing. "You've said it right lots of times. Iona, she was just so scared she'd make a mistake that she made a mistake. But she said a good grace. Didn't she?"

"She sure did!" Craig said and clapped his hands and Jenny looked up at him through her tears and laughed while Iona leaned across Granny and patted her sister's hand.

"It's a very pretty salad, Edith. What a lot of work!" Marion said and Edith made a smiling tight face and denied that it was. "It has a tiny bit of hot peppers in it, chopped so fine that you can hardly see it. Is it too hot for anybody?"

"It prickles, Mummy," Iona said.

"Is it too hot for you?"

"It isn't hot, it's cold," the child said, laughing. "It just tastes like I'm eating my funny bone."

Everybody laughed along with her and the meal moved through a jelly dessert to preparations for nap-time.

Harvey took the twins upstairs while Craig helped Edith with the clearing up. There was no talk. Marion sat at the table agonizing about what she had to tell Edith.

"Let's go into the living room," Edith said, and the other two followed her without any discussion. They waited for Harvey to come down and when Edith heard his footsteps on the stairs, she called quietly, "In here, Harv."

Harvey stopped inside the door and looked at the three solemn people. Then, without a word he moved across the room and took a seat beside his wife.

"Well, Mom? You're the chairman," Edith said.

"It's awfully hard to have to tell you this, but I think you have to know it. Craig knows all about it because he was there, thank goodness, when Murray told me." She stopped and took a deep shaky breath. "I got a telephone call one day from a man by the name of Tobler. He was the cousin of a man your father knew and he was, apparently, a man with no morals..."

"Like your father," Craig interrupted bitterly.

"Mine! He was yours, too, you know!" Edith shot back.

"Children! Don't! Don't, for God's sake quarrel. Just hear me out."

Craig turned so that he did not have to look at anyone, and Harvey reached out and took Edith's hand and leaned toward her so that they were touching.

Marion continued. "This man told me over the phone that there was another will and that everything would go to Eleanor Colman."

"What!" Edith shouted. "What do you mean, another will? Who's this Eleanor Colman."

"Wait!" Craig shouted without turning around. "Let her finish."

Marion went on to tell about her frantic fear of another will that would leave her destitute, of the threat of blackmail and Murray's intervention with Tobler and his sister. She told of Murray's meeting with Eleanor Colman. "You remember her name, but I don't think you ever met her. She was your father's secretary, remember?"

"Oh, that Miss Colman. What's she got to do with it?"

"In the new will, he was supposed to leave everything to her, and there was a long list of property and investments and other things."

"He didn't!" Edith exclaimed, her face set and white. "Why?"

"Because she and your father have been lovers for years. And if you are shocked by that, think of how I felt."

Edith was quiet for a moment, then said, "Well, at least this time it wasn't little girls or little boys." She paused. "Sorry about that, Craig."

He shrugged and continued to face away from them.

Marion looked at her son to see how he would respond. She saw him, sitting twisted in the chair, the shoulders broad and the hips narrow, his jaw muscles were clenching and unclenching, no longer hidden by childish fat. Quite consciously, suddenly, she saw him for the first time, not as a child, but as a man and was glad for his nearness. She had been weeping so copiously throughout that Harvey got up and brought her back a box of Kleenex, handing it to her without a word and giving her a gentle pat on the shoulder. Edith had been blessed with large tear ducts. Although she was crying, her cheeks were dry, but she blew her nose as though she had a vicious head cold. Craig continued to look away and the only signal he gave of any upset was the occasional wiping of his face with the crook of his arm.

They worked their way through the fact that the phoney will might never have been made, and if it had, might never emerge, and if it did emerge, could be proved to be false by the documents that Murray was keeping, documents in their father's handwriting that gave instructions for the phoney will to be created.

It was the question of "Why?" that they could not answer: the reason for the hate, the viciousness, the intent to generate as much trouble as possible after his death.

"Maybe it was the tumor," Marion said. "People do strange things when they have growths on their brain."

"No way! No fucking way!" Edith exploded. "I'm not buying any goddam tumor to excuse what he did to me!"

Her mother said, in a shocked voice, "Edith!"

Her husband said, quietly, "Careful, honey. The children."

Her brother turned to her and said, "Good for you!"

They sorted through the detritus that had been left behind, accepting hate as a necessity, refusing understanding.

Harvey added little to the family's search for answers. He did say that their minister had reminded the congregation that hate can be personally destructive, and that forgetting can sometimes replace forgiving. He said, too, that Murray had told him that he, too, found it impossible to understand the other dark side of the man.

From upstairs came the sounds of small children awakening and it became the signal to them that their two hours of emotional soul-searching turmoil had to end. Harvey went upstairs and they could hear him teasing the sleep out of two little girls who had flung themselves at him when he opened their door. Edith went to the bathroom and washed her face. Marion gathered up wads of wet tissues and went to the kitchen to dispose of them. She stood looking out the window into the garden while drinking a large glass of water and trying to force herself to think of some rearrangement for Edith's garden. Craig went outside and took long, deep breaths and then carried Harvey's ladder back to the garage and hung it up.

When it was time to go and Edith's family gathered around to say goodbye. Marion whispered to Craig, "Do you think you could drive home, dear? I am exhausted!"

Craig looked at her and knew she was admitting the truth and he nodded agreement, "Okay," quietly to her.

When the kisses and hugs were completed, he put his mother in the car and went around to the driver's side. No-one commented on the change is the seating arrangement. He started the car, checked the mirror and her seatbelt and backed carefully out of the driveway. Putting the car into gear, he tooted 'Shave and a haircut, six bits' and immediately regretted it. Hearing it, Edith said, "Now why did he do that? That's what HE always did when he was leaving."

As they walked into the house, Edith said, "Oh, I'd like a good long walk on the beach and clear some of the muck out of my head."

"Let's pack a lunch and go tomorrow," Harvey said. "The girls and I can do some cleanup while you have your walk."

"Oh, Harvey," she said, her gratitude shining on her face.

Craig drove home carefully under the speed limit. He was intent on his driving and his mother initiated no conversation so as not to distract him. When he drove into the garage and turned off the motor he grasped the top of the steering wheel, raised his shoulders high and lowered them, expelling a deep breath. He had a small smile of satisfaction on his face. Opening her door to get out, his mother simply said, "Thank you, Craig," knowing that it was enough, that his own satisfaction with himself was all the commendation he needed and that praise would embarrass him.

CHAPTER 47

It was the last Sunday in October. In spite of a struggling sun the morning chill was still in the air and the news reported that in some areas of the city there had been a touch of frost. Marion was not sure that she was ready for another winter, never her favourite time of year. The rain and snow and grey skies, the loss of all the colours in spring and summer and fall dampened her spirits. The thought of Thanksgiving was enough to depress her mood even further. Yesterday had been hard on her. She had slept restlessly in spite of two sleeping pills and the effect of them was to make her feel heavy headed and dull. She remembered her promise to Tom to help him furnish his new apartment and, although the idea had somehow lost its appeal, she struggled out of bed and through her morning routines, to be ready when he called.

She was poking through yesterday's paper when the phone rang and she prepared herself for Tom's always cheerful greeting. It was Edith.

"Hi, Mom. Did you have a safe drive home with your new chauffeur? I didn't think anything of it until you drove away and then I remembered he doesn't have his license yet, does he? Listen, we are just on our way out the door. We decided we would take a picnic and drive out to the cottage for the day. It should be closed up for the winter and I thought I'd better ask you if there's anything special you do. Is there?"

"Nothing very special that I can think of. You were up last so just be sure to take home any open foodstuffs so the ants won't come in. And close the damper on the fireplace in case a bird comes down. Check that the windows are locked and close the drapes. And let's see, oh yes! If you empty the frig, turn it off and leave the door open. That's about all, I guess. Don't turn off the power and leave that little heater, the good one from my bedroom, turned on low in the middle of the kitchen. And, oh yes, another thing—my goodness there are a lot of things to remember to do—turn off the power to the hot water tank. No sense having it on all winter. Oh, you'll know what to do, and Harvey will too.

I'm glad you're going out. I'm so discombobulated these days, I probably would have forgotten it."

"Okay. I just thought we'd better take the responsibility if—well, you know— just in case. The kids are in the car, waiting. I better run. Bye, Mom. Have a nice day."

Her hand was still on the receiver after replacing it in the cradle when the phone rang again and she answered it before it had stopped vibrating.

"Well, good morning," Tom said cheerfully. "You must have been waiting breathlessly by the telephone for my call."

"Oh, yes! I've been a-twitter with expectation all morning," she responded trying to match his mood. "Are you on your way?"

"I sure am. I'm more than on my way. I started out early so I'll be there in ten minutes. Too soon?"

"No, I'm ready now, as soon as I fix my hair, put on my lipstick, find my purse, choose some earrings, get my coat, leave a note for my son, and one or two other things."

"I'll drive slow," he said laughing.

She was ready, waiting at the window, when he drove up and she walked out to the car before he had a chance to get out. "Hi!" he said and leaned over to kiss her when she got in. "It's been a long time."

"Yes, it has!" she agreed firmly. "And it's been a rough time."

"How did your day go with your daughter yesterday?"

"Well, I got through it—we got through it, I should say."

"What was it all about, Marion. Anything you want to tell me about?"

"Yes, I've wanted to tell you all along but I just couldn't do it. I'll give you the Readers Digest version—short and to the point. It will be easier." And she told him the whole story of the telephone call that she thought would be the precursor to blackmail, her lawyer's intervention, the terrible struggle to try to understand her husband's motives. Her voice was flat and controlled and she was able to give him the whole story, without once breaking down.

"Good God!" he exclaimed when she had finished. "What on earth possessed the man?"

"I don't know. I don't suppose I'll ever know. It was a fiendish terrible thing to do. It's frightening to know that he must have hated me that much."

"He was sick, Marion. He must have been. Some kind of mental illness that warped his mind."

"Maybe," she shrugged. "The kids certainly won't buy that."

They were quiet for a few blocks. "Now then," she said. "Let's get on to happier subjects. Where are we going?"

"We're just about there," he said. "We're headed for the Erindale Apartments just off Smith Avenue. South of the Burnaby General."

"I don't know that part of the city too well, but I do know approximately where the Hospital is. The Erindale Apartments," she mused. The name struck her as familiar but she did not know why.

"Not new, but nice, and reasonable," Tom went on. I made a couple of trips yesterday, boxes of dishes and clothes, odds and ends of things. And I made a trip to the garbage dump with the company truck, and the Sally Ann people came around while I was away and picked up the things I had left on the veranda for them. So I'm getting there."

"A move takes a lot of time," she said, but then she laughed. "How would I know? I've never moved. Well, once. From a small place we rented when our house was being built, and it was partially furnished, so we didn't move much." Her mood changed abruptly and she turned and looked out the window of the car, hating herself for bringing up the subject of her husband again.

"Well, here we are," Tom said, stopping in front of a four-storey red brick block that was slowly being faced with Virginia Creeper. "What do you think?"

"It looks very nice, Tom. Sort of comfortable and, well, I guess conservative is the word I'm looking for."

"That's me alright," Tom laughed. "Conservative but voting with the idiots." They sat for a moment, just looking at the building. Marion was searching her mind to try to discover why it looked familiar to her but nothing clicked.

"Shall we go in?" Tom asked.

They walked arm in arm up the short walk. The glassed entrance was inset and beside the door the tenants names were listed beside the buzzer buttons. Inside, Marion could see a small lobby with two chairs, an artificial fireplace and a ficus benjamina. Tom unlocked the door and they walked past a wall of mail boxes to one of two elevators that was waiting and that rose with agonizing slowness to the third floor.

"We haven't got far to walk," Tom said on the way up. "I'm right next door to the elevator."

He unlocked the door and ushered her in. "I had a great urge to carry you over the threshold," he said, following her into the room.

"You wouldn't have been able to go to work tomorrow with a broken back," she replied. "Oh, it's a nice bright room. And the paint is a nice neutral shade that will take any colour of furniture. Nice carpet, too. It looks brand new." She walked over to the window and looked out. "And you have got a view, just as you said."

A small counter with an overhead cupboard separated the kitchen area from the living area. An off-white frig and four burner stove came with the apartment. He had unloaded his dishes and pots and pans and placed them out of sight but obviously, to a woman's eye, not where they belonged. The bedroom was small and empty and the closet held more empty hangers than full ones. The bathroom exhibited a single small towel.

"I might have thought to bring a chair before I invited company," Tom said. "But what do you think?"

"Well, let me think," she said, walking around the room. "First of all, do you have any strong colour preferences or any strong dislikes."

"No, I don't think so," Tom said. "I never really thought about it. I don't like those new fluorescent colours, though."

"I hope we won't go in that direction," she said. "But do you happen to be colour blind?"

"Oh, yes, I am! I forgot. I'm supposed to be slightly blue-green colour blind. That was a long time ago, though."

She smiled at him. "It doesn't get better, you know. A lot of men are blue-green colour blind. What do you say we go for the earth tones? You can mix earth tones and have some contrasts that are soft and comfortable."

"What on earth are earth tones?"

"Browns, beiges, rusts, tans, those kinds of colours. Just like the colours you've got on. Beige slacks, about three different browns in your jacket, light tan shirt and a tie that is doubtful."

"Doubtful?"

"Oh, yes, indeed!"

He made a rueful face. "Let's go shopping," he said. "But let's start with a tie."

They started on their shopping trip in high spirits, stopping first for a tie and then for a coffee. Over coffee they listed the essential furnishings he would need and delicately she asked the price range he could tolerate.

"I don't really care about the price as long as it isn't ridiculous. But I don't want to get into that modern square glass and chrome stuff. Maybe when we look I can give you an idea of what I like and what I don't."

"Let's get started then," she said. "Let's start with the Warehouse. They've got almost everything you'll need and their prices are very good. That way it will save us running around making price comparisons all over town."

"Good God! I don't want to do that," he said. "Let's go!"

"I thought I could talk you into it," she said. "Show me a man that likes to compare prices—except for cars."

"Well, that is totally different," he said in defending himself and males in general. "Men are required to do that! It's in their genes."

"Oh, yes," she nodded. "I see."

When they arrived at the Warehouse, a large banner proclaimed 'Up to 20% Off Everything' and any thoughts of comparison shopping were discarded. They shopped together easily, first deciding on a sofa and arm chair that matched, and then on a recliner and a double bed, ("Are you sure," she asked. He nodded. "I'm hoping for a guest," he replied with a salacious grin.) A chest of drawers was added to the list, followed by a night table, two end tables, a small round dining table and four chairs. He deferred to her decisions easily and gracefully. The young clerk, working partly on commission was in ecstasy as he wrote out the bill and made arrangements for delivery.

They got a huge cart and as he wheeled it through the giant warehouse she filled it with bed linen, blankets, towels, dish towels, pillows, colored cushions for the sofa and chair, a laundry hamper, and a set of dishes and another of glasses that he found and wanted so that he could throw out the mixed collection of old, chipped and ugly ones he had carted over.

When they had exhausted themselves, and the list, they headed for the checkout counters and picked up a magazine stand and a full length mirror for the bedroom on their way. Then they came to an aisle of framed paintings.

"Have you anything for your walls?" she asked.

"Old calendars of naked ladies," he said with a grin.

"Want to look at these and just see if there's one you like? You should have something on the big wall and another on the wall beside the door. Then you can put your collection of nudes in the bedroom and the bathroom or, I'll suggest two other places—on the back wall of the clothes closet or the trashcan."

"You're a hard woman, Marion Williams."

It took them three quarters of an hour to select two limited edition prints of oil paintings. One was a seascape with the tide moving out from the flats, set off by angry clouds and the threat of an imminent storm almost obliterating a sunset. The signature was illegible. The other was by a local artist, Jack Hambleton, with whose work she was casually familiar. It was a Portuguese street scene, hot and sunny, with strong palette knife strokes in colours that would complement the rusts and browns of the furniture. Twice he had eyed a velvet painting of a nude and twice she had simply looked at him square in the eye and shook her head. "You are indeed a hard woman, Marion Williams," he told her as they finally reached the checkout.

They were able to pack everything in the car with the long mirror propped on the back of the front seat between them.

"I'm starving!" Tom announced as he got into the car. "I've been trying to think of a nice place to take you. Any ideas?"

"I can't, Tom. Really. I've got to go home and give Craig a little attention. I feel like I have neglected him all week."

"Oh, Marion! I was counting on saying thanks with a good dinner in a splashy place. Are you sure?"

She nodded.

"What do I have to do to change your mind? I know! Why don't you phone home and see if he's there. Maybe he's got plans."

"I could do that, I guess," she said tentatively.

As soon as she said it, he turned into the next gas station. "Here's a telephone booth right here," he said, stopping in front of it. "And here's a quarter. I'll get some gas."

"You're a hard man, Marion Thomas," she laughed and got out.

Craig answered the phone with his mouth full. "Hi, Mom! Where are you?"

"I've been out shopping with a friend and I didn't notice the time. I'll be home in a half an hour to get dinner."

"Okay," he said around another mouthful. "I've eaten or I am eating right now. Donna and I are going to the early double feature—both good blood and guts stuff. Rob's working. I was just writing you a note."

"Well, there's no sense in me hurrying home to feed the beast, is there? I might as well have dinner out with my friend."

"Okay with me, Mom. See you later."

"I've got permission," she said to Tom getting into the car.

"Good on ya, mite!" he said, leaning over the mirror to give her a kiss on the cheek. "Let's go rip up the town."

They settled on an old established Greek place on Broadway that neither of them had been to for years. When they arrived without a reservation, they were escorted to the bar to wait for a no-show and given the wine list.

"Something from the bar now, sir?" the waiter asked.

"Two double scotches. One on the rocks, one with water on the side," Tom said, looking for approval at Marion, who nodded.

They sat looking around the renovated restaurant, but Marion's mind slipped back to another time in the same place. Years ago she had come here with Gerry. "What is your bar scotch?" he had asked the waiter and when told, he had pursed his lips and frowned. "What else do you have?" he had continued, still frowning as the waiter listed six or eight more scotches. After an eternity of serious consideration, he had selected one of the choices, "A double, no rocks," he said. Without addressing her, he had said, looking at the wine list, "What do you want?" "A bar scotch with lots of water will do me," she said. When the waiter left, he had said to her, "Bar scotch! If you don't know anything about scotch you might at least follow my lead and order what I order to save embarrassment."

"Pretentious bastard!" she muttered.

"What did you say?" Tom said with a shocked look on his face.

"I'm sorry, sorry!" she said, suddenly realizing she had spoken aloud. "Not you, Tom. I had a flashback to another time and another person. Oh, hell! I didn't mean to bring him up but I have to explain." And she did and Tom listened without comment and the waiter arrived with their drinks.

"Cheers," he said and they clicked glasses gently.

"How's your bar scotch?" he said, grinning.

"Good," she said. "Just my type."

"We're a good pair," he told her. "No couth!" and she raised her glass to him.

The maitre d' found them a table before they finished a second drink. The service was fast and efficient, the food appetizing and their conversation easy. They were lingering over coffee when Tom said, "It's early. Want to come back to my place and I'll unload the car and maybe you can get some more ideas about what I'm going to need."

"As long as we're not too late," she agreed. "I seem to have had a lot of sleepless nights lately and I've got to catch up on my sleep." Her answer skirted around the possibility that things might progress to sex and while one part of her was willing another part told her that she really didn't want to roll around on the carpet.

"Okay," he said. "Then I promise to get you home by—is 10:30 a good time?"

"That's about right. That's about the time I turn into a pumpkin or a were-wolf—I forget which."

They drove across town in a drizzling rain with the wipers chattering and agreeable music on the radio. They approached the Erindale Apartments from a different direction and again Marion had a sudden feeling of having seen the place before. When they parked in front of the building the rain was torrential. It pounded on the roof so hard they had to shout to hear each other.

"Let's wait a few minutes," Tom said. "We can't go out in that downpour. I've got a slicker in the trunk but I'd be soaked before I could get it. When it slacks off, I'll dash out and get it and put it on you while you run for the door. Then I'll grab as many parcels as I can and bring them in if you'll hold the door so I don't have to use the key. I should do it in four or five loads. Isn't this a lovely way to spend an evening?"

"It isn't much of a recommendation for tourists, is it?"

"No, but here we are together again—separated only by a mirror. We can't even neck. Or do we pet, at our age?"

"I was never sure what the difference was at any age," she admitted. "Or really what a 'pass' is. If I read it or heard it on TV, a pass could be anything. Did you ever make a pass at me, apart from, you know, taking me to bed?"

"Oh, yes!" he said, laughing. "Many. But maybe you didn't recognize any because I was so clumsy and out of practice."

"You? Clumsy? Not in my books, mister!" There was enough light from a street lamp that she could see him blush.

"Listen! It's letting up. What do you say we make a dash for it? I'll grab the slicker out of the trunk."

He opened his door and rushed around to the back of the car, and in a few seconds appeared at her door. Pushing the hood over her head without regard for her hair, he wrapped the slicker around her and rushed her to the door. Once inside, he put the slicker on himself and tied it in place. "Okay, ready? You stay here in the warm and dry and I'll go out and brave the nasty elements and bring in all the parcels. All you have to do is cheer me on and open the door when you see me coming." And he exited with his slicker flapping.

She waited, watching him sorting among the bags to find the handles to grab until he had enough to make a run for the door. Inside he dumped them near the elevator and went out for another load. Marion stood by the door and looked over the directory of tenants in the building. There was no name opposite Apartment 307. Tom raced in with a carton of dishes. She wondered who his neighbours were on either side. She supposed the apartments on either side would be 306 and 308. Both apartments were listed as Mr. and Mrs. "Have you met any of your neighbours?" she asked as Tom came in with a box of glasses. "Not yet," he said, disappearing out into the rainy night. She continued to browse through the names on the third floor and she read the name E. Colman without recognizing it. Suddenly the directory almost shouted at her, 315: E. COLMAN! ELEANOR COLMAN! She stood frozen and let the door handle slip out of her hand. The door closed and locked just as Tom approached with the mirror.

"Whoops," he said, and set the mirror down carefully and reached for his keys without noticing her distress. It was only when he picked up the mirror again and was going in the door that he saw that she was white faced and trembling. He put the mirror inside and went out and, holding the door open, put his arm around her and said, "Marion! What's wrong? You're as white as a sheet You're cold. You've been standing in that damp draft in the doorway too long. Come in, come in."

She resisted his efforts to ease her inside. "Look!" she said, pointed to the name on the directory. ELEANOR COLMAN!"

He read 'E. Colman' and said it aloud and suddenly the light dawned. "Oh! You think... You think that might be the Eleanor you were telling me about?"

She allowed herself to be taken through the door into the warmth of the lobby. "I know it! I know it! I know it!" she kept saying. "That's her. She's a she-devil! A bitch! A rotten whore!"

An elevator door opened and a man and woman stepped out in the middle of Marion's tirade. The woman threw nervous sidelong glances at Marion. The man said only, "Rotten night for moving."

Tom nodded and waited until they were out the door. "Sit down, Marion. I've got one more load to bring in. Then we'll load it all on the elevator and take it up and get ourselves a drink and you can tell me about it. Okay?"

She nodded numbly.

He hurried to the car and grabbed the remaining parcels, locked the car and came back to the door. Marion was sitting in the lobby chair and made no motion to open the locked door for him nor did she even appear to notice him. Once inside he called down an elevator and blocked the door while he rushed to get the pile of bags and boxes into it. Marion sat, slumped in the chair, both hands nursing her stricken face, while she stared through the steamy windows out into the rainy night.

"Marion!" he called softly when the elevator was loaded. "Come on, let's go."

She appeared not to hear him and made no move. He went to her and shook her shoulder and she jerked alert. "Let's go," he said again and assisted her to her feet and into the elevator. As the elevator ground slowly up, she suddenly said loudly, "My purse! I haven't got my purse. Did you bring it in from the car?"

"I didn't see it," he said.

"Stop the elevator!" she shouted at him and reached around him and started pushing buttons randomly. He restrained her gently. "Wait," he said. "I'll unload and go right down and see if your purse is in the car. The car's locked. It's alright."

He unloaded the elevator into the hall, opened the door to his apartment and took her inside. He left her standing in the empty room staring vaguely at the wall. The elevator descended with agonizing slowness and he had nothing to block the door while he raced to the car. Her purse was laying in plain sight on the seat and he grabbed it and ran hoping no one was watching and suspecting him of stealing it. The elevator was gone and he looked for the exit sign and ran up the stairs.

When Tom left her standing in the room, Marion stayed without moving for a few minutes, and then left and walked down the hall looking at the numbers until she found 315. She knocked at the door and waited. There was no answer so she knocked again, louder. Finally, a woman's voice called, "Who's there?"

"Why don't you open the door and see?" Marion shouted boldly.

She heard the security chain rattle against the door and the door opened only as far as the chain permitted. Through the crack she could see only a part of the woman's face. "That's you, isn't it? Eleanor Colman. I thought it would be you, hiding like you are ashamed of yourself and you should be!" she shouted.

The door closed far enough for the chain to be taken off then opened fully for the two women to see each other. Marion was in street clothes, a little bedraggled from the rain with her hair mussed from the plastic hood Tom had thrown roughly over her. She was angry and shaking. Eleanor was in an old dressing gown and slippers. No other clothing was evident. Her hair was wet and held back in place with a kerchief. She stared at the woman in her doorway for a moment before recognizing her.

"You!" she said in an angry voice as two red spots appeared on her cheeks. "What the hell do you want? Got your lawyer with you?" She stepped far enough out to block the door and looked down the hall. "I hope to hell that's not your junk down there," she continued. "You're not moving in here!" It was an assertion, not a question.

"Don't worry," Marion replied with acrimony evident in her voice and manner. "I wouldn't be caught dead living anywhere near you. You prostitute, whore!"

Tom stepped out of the stairwell just in time to hear the last few words Marion was shouting at a stranger. "Marion," he called, hurrying down the hallway. "What's going on?"

"I'm just talking to my husband's whore," she said angrily, her voice rising in pitch. "This is the one I told you about—the one that's going to write a will and swear on a stack of bibles that it was his and he left everything to her. And she's been sleeping with him for years!"

"So what!" Eleanor retorted. "He said he could have a better time sleeping with an ironing board than sleeping with you."

"And so he turned to a slut like you!"

"Marion, that's enough. Let's go!" Tom pulled her somewhat roughly away from the door but she resisted and continued shouting.

Doors opened down the hall and heads peeked out briefly and went back in. "I'm sorry, lady. She's been through a rough time." And then to Marion, harshly, straight to her face, holding both her arms, "Now you shut up and come with me!" And as he forced her down the hall she started to wail.

"You can't speak to me like that, you bastard!" she shouted at him.

"I'm sorry! That's the only way I could get you to stop. For Christ sake! What were you thinking of? I've got to live here, you know. Fine introduction to my neighbours!"

"Who cares? What kind of neighbours are they anyway. This is probably a brothel. That's the only place that bitch would live!" Her voice was loud and the door was open and he knew that the TVs had been turned off in favour of live entertainment.

"God almighty," he said to himself through clenched teeth. And then to her, "Can you just be quiet? I'll get the stuff out of the hall and then I'll take you home."

"Call me a cab," she told him. "I can go home by myself. I don't need you!"

"I can't, I don't have a telephone yet."

"Well, why don't you go down the hall and knock on the bitch's door and tell her your sad story and maybe she'll call a cab for you and give you a good screw while you wait."

"For God's sake, Marion! Settle down!"

"Why should I?" she cried, and sank down onto the floor like a lump, her hands over her face, sobbing uncontrollably.

He watched her briefly, uncertain about what to do, afraid that any word from him would topple her into hysterics. So he went to the open door and threw, pulled, shoved with his feet and carried in all the packages dumped in the hall. Then he went to her and said, "Come! I'll take you home."

She made no response so he tried to pick her up by thrusting his hands into her armpits, but she went limp. He went to the kitchen and brought a glass of water and handed it to her. She slapped at it and knocked it out of his hand. His patience came to a sudden, abrupt end.

"Look, you stupid woman. Get your purse and get out of here. I'm fed up completely with your nonsense."

Something got through to her. "My purse," she said. "Where's my purse?

He handed it to her without comment. She took it and stood looking at the floor, her eyes red, her cheeks flushed, her hair messed and the front of her dress wet. "Take me home," she said tonelessly, neither pleading nor demanding.

He took her arm but she jerked it away. She followed him out the door and waited at the elevator until he pushed the call button. When the elevator came she stepped to the rear and waited for him to press a button. It creaked slowly to the main floor and when the door opened she huddled back, waiting until he got out and then she followed him out the door and to the car still parked at the curb. She put out her hand to open the back door but it was locked, so she stood in the rain waiting for him to unlock the back door and then she climbed in. He closed her door, went around to the driver's side and got in and drove away without a word.

"There'll be a taxi at the hospital," she said in a flat voice from the back seat. "Take me there."

"I'll take you home," he said mildly.

"Get me a taxi," she screamed.

"Alright! Alright! I'll get you a god damned taxi."

At the hospital, there was one taxi in the waiting zone. He parked beside it and got out and went around and opened her door. The taxi driver had got out and opened his back door for her to hurry in through the rain. He noticed with some concern the state she was in as she climbed into the back seat.

Tom opened his wallet and gave the driver ten dollars. "She'll give you the address," he said.

"Hey, mister!" the cabbie called as Tom walked away. "If you've been beating up on her, I've got your license number."

Tom stopped and returned, taking out his wallet again. He opened it and shoved it in front of the cabby's face. "Take a good look. That's my driver's license," he snarled, and walked away.

When the taxi pulled up in front of her house, the cabbie stepped out quickly and went around to open her door. She was fumbling in her purse to get a tip for him and he watched her with brown, anxious eyes peering out of an East Indian face. "You OK, lady?" he asked.

She nodded her head, looked at the meter and handed him a tip.

"You know that man?" he asked, his face furrowed with concern.

She nodded again.

"He was a very angry man!" he said, in a warning tone.

She nodded again, then said "Thank you," and turned to her door.

The house was dark and the cabbie waited until she had unlocked the door and gone inside. When a light went on, he shook his head and muttered, "No good, lady. No good," and drove away.

CHAPTER 48

Craig and Donna left in the middle of the second feature so they could meet Rob when he got off work at nine. The first movie had been, as advertised, full of violence and gore and heavy with deep-fried Freud. The second promised to be worse including, critics said, "torrid S and M". A sign at the ticket window read: Ages 18 and over. I.D. Required—Driver's License, Bank Card, etc.

"I haven't got my license yet," Craig had said in a panic. "I don't get it until tomorrow. I'll just tell her."

"Don't say a thing, kid," a guy beside him in the second line advised. "Just walk up, put your money down and say 'Two please' and try not to look like your pissing your pants." There was laughter from those within earshot, and Donna was laughing, too, but she was hanging onto his arm tight and she gave him a little shake while looking straight into his eyes. The woman at the ticket window gave him two tickets without question and they hurried to the entrance in case she changed her mind, and had stopped only long enough to hear the guy who had advised them explain to the other cashier, "But it IS my driver's license. It's just that my hair was very bleached from the sun and I'm wearing contacts now." They laughed about him on the way to pick up Rob. "Remember that video we saw at the party at Max's?" Craig asked while they

walked, their shoulders hunched against a wet wind, and went on without waiting for an answer. "That was ten times worse than this and nobody needed a
driver's license," laughing loudly at his own joke.

"Yeah! Bleagh! That was B-A-D crude! I nearly threw up. But that was just
sex stuff. This was nothing but S and M. That kind of kinky crap makes me
shiver," Donna said.

"Me too," Craig agreed. They walked on saying nothing more until Craig
said, "Okay! So I'm stupid! What the hell is this S and M thing?"

"You don't know?" Donna asked, looking at him to see if he was playing
games.

"No, I don't! Am I supposed to?"

"I don't know if you're supposed to. I thought everybody we know knew
what it means." She started to giggle at his naiveté. "S stands for sadism and M
stands for masochism," she explained. "Now you know."

"I knew that!" he said huffily. "I just didn't think that, well, that they, like
people who did that sort of thing, that they had to hide it behind initials."

"Oh, sure," she said nodding her head in smirking agreement.

"I did so!" and he started to laugh. "Just wait until I tell Rob how dumb I
was!"

Rob was waiting for them outside and saw them laughing together as they
approached. "Hi, gang!" he said as he went to meet them. "So, it was a funny
movie, was it?" he asked, throwing an arm around each as they walked away.
"You told me you were going to a grisly horror story."

"It was supposed to be," Craig said.

"Craig got his categories all mixed up," Donna explained laughing.

"I did not, Donna. Let me tell him. You'll make me look stupid if you tell
him."

"Well?" she said teasingly.

So Craig launched into his explanation of his confusion that only succeeded
in confusing them all and they were laughing when they went into Donna's little basement apartment.

"Wally, turn the sound down," the landlady said when she heard them. "Just
listen to them laughing! They're such happy kids!"

Donna split her only bottle of Coke three ways and they sat trying to make
times to see one another. When Donna was off in the afternoon, Rob was working, and when he was off, she was working, but they managed to see each other
those nights.. They had also seen each other when Rob finished work, but not
for very long because she had to get up early. Craig was the only one of the three
who worked weekdays only. Donna had Sundays off and Rob had Wednesday
and Thursdays one week, Wednesday the next week and Thursdays the following week. Sprawled on Donna's bed, Craig watched while they sat on the only
two chairs at the tiny kitchen table trying to mark a little calendar with their
times for being together. He did not feel left out because he knew he could see
Rob any time. So he stretched and yawned and finally said "I think I'll head
home."

Donna said, "Thanks for the show, partner."

Rob said, "Next time I'll pick the show for you."

Craig said, "Yeah, Disney!"

They all laughed, and upstairs Mrs. Lasseret said, smiling, "There they go again, Wally. Just listen to them!"

Craig said a casual goodnight and walked to the bus stop only to see a bus pull away before he could get there. He was wearing only a light shower proof jacket and the wind that signalled winter was cold. "Damn!" he muttered as he started for home, walking and jogging, through a drizzling rain. "I've got to get me a car—soon! Maybe I can start looking around after work tomorrow. Maybe I should see what Rob thinks. Maybe I should move my ass and do it myself. That'll shock him!"

He arrived home and entered through the back door as usual. The house was cold and filled with winter gloom. Only the front hall light was on with the rest of the house in darkness. He shouted upstairs but there was no response. The front door was unlocked and he gave a shrug at his mother's forgetfulness and decided to wait up for her. Turning up the thermostat, he spent an hour searching for his warm winter jacket and the steel toed boots he had worn last summer. He found his jacket in the downstairs closet in a plastic bag with moth crystals and the boots where he had left them, covered with the dust and mud from Lake Lovely Water. The jacket was tight across the shoulders but it would do. He dug out a canvas fishing hat that would keep the rain off if he had to walk or wait in the rain, and he found a wool work shirt that Rob had borrowed from Richard and forgotten so he marked it as his own until he got another one. He carried everything upstairs stopping at the frig on his way to his room. There was nothing in the frig that looked immediately edible—no fruit except withered grapes, no pie and only some dried-up pieces of chicken as leftovers. He noted that they were out of milk, so he couldn't have cereal in the morning and he started wondering if his mother was ever going to get around to shopping again. She seemed to have been melancholy and out of it for days. He returned to the basement and got a loaf of bread from the freezer to make his lunch and some frozen waffles for his breakfast. He thought he had better phone Edith one of these days and tell her about the way things were going at home. Then he thought that Edith would probably just say that it was only his imagination and that he was just being childish because his mummy wasn't looking after him.

While he waited for his mother to come home, a little concerned because she usually left a note if she was going to be late, he fiddled with the TV looking for something funny. Finding nothing, he settled for a basketball game taped earlier between college teams he did not know and got quickly bored. About to turn the TV off, he noticed that the doors for the liquor cabinet were both open, and checked it in case someone had come in when the front door was unlocked. Everything seemed okay except that there was no Vodka but he remembered seeing her shopping list with Vodka on it. So he closed the doors to the cabinet, turned off some lights and the TV and headed upstairs, planning to read in bed until she came in. On the hall table he saw her purse and stopped. She must be home, he told himself. She wouldn't go out without her purse. I'm sure it wasn't there when I came in. It couldn't have been. I would have seen it. What the hell is going on?

He raced up the stairs and stopped at her bedroom door. It was latched but not locked and he was reluctant to turn the knob and peer in, so he knocked. Then he knocked again and called. Then he called her in a loud and anxious voice and opened the door. The lights were on and he could see her lying in her nightgown, uncovered, curled on her side and breathing in laboured, gargling gasps. The vodka bottle was on the floor beside her, empty. Her pills were spilled on the night table. He stood frozen with terrifying thoughts for a moment, then rushed to her bedside and shouted, "Mom! Wake up!"

She did not respond and he continued to call her name and shake her. Then he took the glass of water that was on her bedside table and splashed it on her face, thinking too late, "My God! What if that's Vodka!" He tasted it and it was only water. He tried to pull her around so that she was on her back intending to cover her up but immediately rolled her back on her side when her breathing began to be interrupted by choking sounds. He yanked the edges of the bedcover from under her and pulled them over her, continuing to call her name and shake her. Sitting on the edge of the bed, he suddenly became furious with her and slapped her hard across the face and shouted, with tears streaming down his face, "Wake up! Wake up! Damn you!" and the words seemed to echo around the room as if the ghost of his father had shouted them.

He picked up the phone and called Edith. Her voice, heavy with sleep, yet decisive, settled him slightly.

"Yes? Who is this?" she said.

"Edie, it's me." His voice was shaky.

"Craig, it's nearly midnight. Where are you?"

"I'm at home. It's Mom! I got home about two hours ago and I thought she wasn't home and I waited up for her but she was home and I didn't know it and then I went up and found her passed out on her bed and..."

"Craig! Don't babble! What do you mean passed out?"

"Passed out!" he shouted. "Just like I said! She's lying there gurgling and snorting and I have shouted at her and poured water on her and can't make her wake up. I think she's been drinking and I think maybe she took too many pills because she spilled them all over."

"What kind of pills?"

"I don't know!" he complained.

"Look at the bottle, idiot, and read the label."

"Just a minute." He picked up the pill bottle and reached over under a stronger light to read it. He could hear Edith talking to Harvey and he waited until she was listening. "It's called Halcion, I think. It says 'Take one at bedtime as required for sleep.'"

"Jesus! I wonder if she took too many. What else does it say on the bottle, Craig?"

"Well, it's got the date—October 21. That's just a little more than a week ago and the prescription was for 50, it says right here on the bottle."

"About how many are left?"

"There's none in the bottle but I can see maybe 10 or 12 spilled on the table and the floor."

"That's it, Craig! She's taken too many. She tried to commit..." but she couldn't say the word. "Craig! Listen to me!

Hang up and call 911 right now. Then call me right back!"

"Edie, do you think that..."

"Do it!" she shouted at him and hung up.

The answer at 911 was immediate. The woman calmly determined the nature of the emergency, the address, his name, age and relationship to the person in trouble, kind of pill he thought she had taken, whether alcohol was involved and continued until he shouted in exasperation, "Please just send the ambulance! don't waste time talking to me."

"The ambulance was on it's way a long time ago," she replied calmly. "All your information is being relayed to them so that they will know exactly what to do when they arrive. Now please make sure your front light and other house lights are on and leave the front door unlocked. You might want to put a pot or a dishpan beside the bed in case she vomits. If she does, make sure she is on her side. Don't let her roll over onto her back. Don't try to give her anything to drink. How about you? Are you Ok?"

"Yes, I'm fine. Thank you. It seems to be taking a long time."

"It always seems much longer than it is. You're quite close to the dispatch centre. They should be there very soon. Better hang up now and put the lights on and unlock the door."

"Thank you," he said, but she was no longer on the line.

He rushed to unlock the door and put lights on and then back upstairs to phone Edith. She answered on the first ring.

"I called," he said, "and they're on their way." At that moment, a voice shouted from "Hello" from downstairs. "They're here, I'll call you back."

"Upstairs!" he yelled. And in a minute two men came into the room with medical bags and a stretcher. One went immediately to his mother and listened to her heart and took her pulse. "What's her name?" he asked, while he fastened a blood pressure cuff on her arm.

"Marion Williams."

"Are these the pills?" the other one asked.

Craig nodded and the man picked a few pills up, put them in the bottle and stowed the bottle in his bag.

"Marion! Marion! Wake up!" the other man was shouting and Craig winced as he slapped her hard on one cheek and then the other, twice. "She's out. Blood pressure's okay but let's get her out of here."

"Has she vomited," one asked.

Craig relied shakily, "I don't think so."

"Check the bathroom," one said to the other while unfolding the stretcher.

"Nothing there. She's still holding them."

"Sure she wasn't drinking, son? There's an empty bottle here."

"I don't know. She doesn't drink much—hardly anything."

"Okay, son. We got her in time. She'll be alright. Don't worry." He continued talking as they rolled her onto the stretcher and strapped her down. "You can ride with us to the hospital and give us some more information. That will save time at Admissions."

Craig hesitated for a minute. "I've got to call my sister," he said.

"Go ahead while we get her downstairs and into the ambulance."

They were working their way around the turn of the hall by the stairs when he rang and Edith answered. "What hospital?" he shouted to them. "St. Paul's Emergency entrance," one of them called back.

"You nearly busted my eardrum," Edith complained.

"They're taking her to St. Paul's Emergency."

"I heard. I'll be there as soon as I can."

"I'm going with them in the ambulance."

"Okay, see you. Did they say anything about her? About how she was?"

"Yeah. One of them said they got her in time and she'll be alright. That's all he said."

"Okay, you better go and stay with her. I'm nearly dressed and ready to go."

He put the phone down and turned to go when the phone rang again. It was Edith. "Take her purse and her dressing gown and her slippers," she said before Craig could say hello and then she hung up.

The trip to the hospital was fast and quiet. Craig had hoped that they would put on the siren but there was so little traffic it was never required except for a small 'whoop' as they slowed down through red lights.

At the hospital there were forms to fill in and questions to be answered. Some answers were found in the cards in his mother's purse. When Admissions had sufficient information he was told to wait in the waiting area and he would be called when he could see his mother. An hour passed slowly in spite of the emergency traffic into the hospital. Edith arrived, her face tight and looking angry instead of showing the worry she felt inside.

"What's happening?" she said to Craig as she sat down in the chair beside him.

He shrugged and said, "They just told me to wait."

"How is she?"

"They didn't say."

"Jesus! Craig!" she said through gritted teeth as she got swiftly to her feet and headed for the Admissions desk where she was immediately involved in a exchange with the Admissions clerk and a young doctor who happened to be near the desk. The doctor turned away and disappeared down the hall but returned almost immediately to speak with her. Craig heard her say, "Thank you, Doctor. You've been very helpful," and she turned away and added, "Not like some other people."

"I would think you could have got off your butt and found out what was going on," she said as she sat down.

"Well, they just told me to wait," he said defensively.

She sort of sagged in her seat and sighed. "Well, it looks like she tried to commit suicide," she said with tears showing.

"Oh, no!" Craig said and reached out to take her unresisting hand. "Oh, Jesus, Edith! I can't believe it. Why?"

"I don't know, Craig," she replied, but she started to shake her head. "Yes, I do! It's what that bastard did to her. He tried to wreck her life even after he was dead. The son-of-bitch!" Her voice was low and venomous.

There was quiet agreement between them for a minute, then Edith sat up and said, "Well, one good thing is that all her vital signs are good, the doctor said. And she'll be okay once the poison gets out of her system. She apparently had a lot of alcohol and a lot of sleeping pills. They pumped her stomach," she stated matter-of-factly. "She had had a big dinner which slowed down the effects of the pills or she would have been a goner. He didn't say it like that, but it's the same thing." She stopped and stared at the floor. Craig said nothing.

After what seemed an eternity, a nurse approached them. "Are you Mrs. Williams' family?" she asked.

"Yes, I'm her daughter," Edith said getting to her feet so that Craig felt obliged to rise, too.

"Edith Allen," the nurse said, looking at her chart. "I guess it was your brother that admitted her." Craig nodded. "It was fortunate that you looked in on her and knew enough to call 911. If you hadn't, she would never have made it. But she'll be alright. We are going to keep her overnight and Dr. Strawburn has been alerted and he will see her tomorrow. Probably he will keep her in for a couple of days for psychiatric evaluation. We strongly recommend psychiatric evaluation in cases of attempted suicide. I see you've brought some of your mother's things. That will cheer her up when she comes awake. About another half hour or so and you can see her. I'll call you." She turned away as if she could see Edith formulating questions she did not want to answer.

In the intervening time, Craig came to grips with the fact that his life as an adolescent was about to undergo a sudden change. The casual dependency on his mother for the comforts of his life that he had taken for granted would disappear and be replaced by her dependency on him. The realization that she would need care and attention, that she might not get better even though they said she would be alright, that she would be alone all day while he was at work loomed like a black cloud in his future. A dozen 'what ifs' raced through his mind and baffled him. He thought of the freedom he had had to come and go at will, giving no thought to the fact that his dinner would be ready, his clothes washed, and that his mother would be there, happy and welcoming. And what if she wasn't? He couldn't live there alone. He'd have to sell the house and everything in it—How in hell could I ever do that? Maybe...

At that point Edith jabbed him. "Wake up!" she said, "Let's go!"

"I wasn't asleep," he said. "I was just thinking." But, as he staggered to his feet, he was dimly aware that someone had come by and said "You may go in and see your mother now. She's still pretty groggy. We'll be moving her to the third floor as soon as a bed is available."

"You look beat, Craig!" Edith said as they followed a nurse down the hall. "Perk up for her sake, can't you? Are you sure you can make it to work today?" He looked at his watch, saw that it was nearly four o'clock and groaned with fatigue.

Their mother was lying with her eyes closed on a high bed behind a partition of drapes with a single sheet covering her. She looked old and gray and fragile. Seeing her without make-up, with her hair messed and somehow looking gaunt, they were both struck speechless by the change. She opened her eyes and looked at them, and her eyes were gray instead of the pearly blue they remembered. Then she closed her eyes and two gigantic tears formed and hung on the lower lids for a moment before sliding down her cheeks and neck to join in the wet stain on her pillow. "I'm sorry, children," she said in a voice between a whisper and a croak.

Edith went to one side of the bed and laid her cheek against her mother's and stayed there throughout several difficult, jerky breaths without a word. Craig stood silently on the other side holding his mother's pale and unresisting hand. It was Edith who broke the heavy silence.

She raised her head from her mother's cheek, dabbed her eyes and said, "Well, just look at you! That's what comes of letting a woman out of the house without her purse. Now then," and she rummaged in her mother's purse and pulled out a lipstick, "just hold still and we'll get some colour on you." She touched her mother's quivering lips with colour and spread it with a finger. "No sense in letting this go to waste," she continued and she smoothed a little colour on her mother's cheek bones. "Now let's see what we can do with that hair." She combed and patted the hair back into something that looked cared for and chattered as she did so, "My, my, Mother! You're overdue for a dye job. Your black roots are showing." She giggled and touched her cheek against her mother's again.

"I don't dye my hair, Edith and you know it," her mother said with some crossness in her voice and then continued, "I'm sorry," and closed her eyes and got tearful again and breathed deep with tiny little moans emerging with each exhalation.

Craig caught his sister's eye across the bed and made a gentle shrug with his shoulders and eyebrows as if to say, "You tried."

After the little moans had disappeared and the breathing was less stressed, she opened her eyes and said, in a reasonably normal voice, "Shouldn't you be at work, Craig?"

"It's four o'clock in the morning, Mom."

"Oh! I saw your watch and thought it was four o'clock in the afternoon. What day is it?"

"Monday morning."

"Monday morning? How long have I been here?"

"Just a few hours," Craig answered.

"I feel like it has been a week," she said with a deep sigh. "I think I would like to go to sleep."

"Okay, Mom," Edith said, tucking the sheet around her mother's shoulders. "I'll see you later today. Do you need anything? Craig can bring it."

The eyes were closed but the mouth opened slightly and a single high squeak emerge accompanied with one feeble shake of the head. Craig leaned over and kissed the unresponsive cheek gently.

Outside, Edith said, "I'll drive you home."

"It's out of your way," he protested.

"It looks like I'll be doing a lot of driving in the next while," she said. "When are you going to get a license?"

"Today."

"Oh! Why the sudden change?"

"I dunno. It'll soon be too cold and wet to ride a bike to work, so I thought I'd get a car." He stopped. "And there was one other thing. I could just sorta see this coming with Mom."

"What do you mean?"

"Well, she's been sorta weird since, well, you know, since all that stuff. She quit at the hospital and she's been only once to her bridge. She's not doing nothing, not even shopping sometimes. And I can catch her sleeping any-time."

"Maybe she's just tired."

"Yeah," he said noncommittally.

"Here you are," she said, stopping in front of their home. "Better catch forty winks before you go to work. Do you want me to phone you at seven? I'll be up."

"Sure. Great. Thanks."

"Hey," she said as he got out of the car. "Why don't you drive her car?"

"What! That black barge! You're kidding."

"Well," she said, sitting up straight and sticking her thumbs under her arm-pits, "that's what Dad said she should drive."

He laughed for the first time that morning and closed her door.

CHAPTER 49

Edith called him at seven as she had promised and had to let the phone ring twelve times before she roused him. His voice was growly and thick with sleep as he thanked her and turned off his radio alarm whose blare had been unsuccessful in waking him.

"Wait a minute, Craig!" she said in her staccato manner as if she hadn't been up all night worrying about a sick mother. "Here's what Harvey and I are going to do. He's going to take an extra hour at lunch time and drive me in and I'll pick up Mom's car and he'll go back to work. But...now listen! Are you listen-ing?"

"Yes, I'm listening," he said, impatiently.

"Well, we're only going to do that if, that's IF, you're sure you don't want to drive Mom's car while she can't use it. So, are you sure?"

"Yeah," he said, laconically, wanting to go to the bathroom and wishing she would stop.

"Okay, but only if you're sure. That way, I can get in to see her without Harvey having to make arrangements for a ride to work."

"Yeah, that's good. I gotta go."

"Where's her key ring? Did you see it in her purse?"

"I can't remember."

"Well, think, Craig. Wake up! You were looking in her purse for her Care card and Social Insurance Number. Were there any keys in her purse?"

"I don't know. I wasn't looking for keys. You were searching for her lipstick—did you see any keys? Just a minute!" and he left the phone abruptly and went to the bathroom and relieved himself with a sigh, then went downstairs and checked that the extra keys to her car were hanging on key board in the kitchen. He picked up the downstairs phone. "Hello?" he said.

"Where did you go?" Edith demanded.

"I went to take a leak, if you have to know. And to see if the extra keys were on the rack."

"It took you long enough, you must have a bladder as big as a football! So?"

"Are you finished talking about my unirary problems?"

"Don't be a smart-ass. And that's urinary. You shouldn't have quit school. So! Were the keys there?"

"Yeah, I'll mark them and leave them on the kitchen counter. I gotta get to work. Say, Edie, she looked pretty gruesome, didn't she?"

"Yes, she did. She was really wrung out. She just looked beat, you know. Kind of scary, wasn't it?"

"Sure was. Think she'll be alright, Edie?"

"Yeah, sure. She's really quite tough, you know. She'll make it. You'll see," in a voice that was a little husky. Then in her usual tones she added, "You better get moving or you'll be late, kid."

Craig managed to get to work on time without breakfast, hoping to catch the coffee and donut truck at morning break. Larry, the foreman, pinning up a notice on the company bulletin board beside the time clock, looked at him and said, "What'ja do, kid? Party all weekend?" He was smiling.

"No," Craig answered, surprised. "Why?"

"Why? Because you look like somethin' the cat drug in."

"Oh no, I didn't go to a party. I had to take my mother to the hospital and I didn't get home until four in the morning."

"That's too bad, kid. Was she sick or did she hurt herself?"

Craig didn't know what to say, but Larry's interest seemed genuine, so he said, knowing that he was going to have to say it to a lot of other people, and wishing he could have said it to Rob first, "I think she might have taken too many pills."

"Oh, Geez! That's tough, Craig. It was probably just a mistake. Old people get their pills mixed up all the time. She'll be okay, I betcha. Yessir, she'll be okay. Them doctors know what they're doing these days. You'll see."

At the coffee break, Craig was hanging around the door with two or three others waiting for the coffee truck when Larry sauntered over and said quietly, "You goin' over to see your Ma at lunch time?"

"No, I won't have enough time to do that," Craig said.

"Tell what you can do, kid. You can take the wife's car."

"What do you mean," Craig asked, puzzled.

"Take that one," he waved a sandwich over his shoulder. "Try it out. Tell me what you think."

With a little more discussion, Craig learned that Larry was selling his wife's car. He had not stopped to read the notice Larry was tacking up earlier. They walked over to the notice board together with Larry working a key to the car off his key ring. The hand printed ad read: "For Sell Civic Honda with a hatchback and four good tires. 7 yrs old. Good cond all round. 5 speeds, radio white. No rust. See Larry $2850 or make a deal." In smaller print it said: "My wife's car she can't drive" .

"You take it. Come here, I'll show you which one." He took Craig over to the door and pointed to a clean white Honda on the parking lot. "Too small for me," he laughed, patting his large belly. "Only once did I get in it—this morning. My wife, she goes to the store and back, that's all. Oh, maybe cross New West to see the grandchildren. Her eyes bad now. She can't see good enough to drive. So drive it and tell me if it's good price."

"But Larry..." Craig began to protest.

"We better get back to work before Carl catches us. It's a good thing for you to see your mother. Here is key."

Craig was working in the back in the warehouse when Carl came by. "Larry tells me that you took your mother to the hospital in the middle of the night and you should see her over your lunch break," he said.

"Yes, I was going to try to do that but I didn't want to ask for special, you know," he shrugged.

"Look, Craig," the boss said kindly, "we all feel a little safer around here if people can give their full attention to their jobs. So, take some time and see you mother. Call it sick leave, or whatever. And if you need more time, you probably don't know it, but you are entitled to borrow against your vacation time."

"Thanks Mr. Cranston—Carl," he corrected himself.

The correction was met with a smile and some further paternal words. "You look a little ragged around the edges. Better take off now and come back in the morning."

"Thank you, I'm anxious to see her and find out how she's doing. Oh, by the way, I met a friend of yours who asked me to say hello to you—Mr. Lesseret?"

"Oh, yes! Lasseret. Wally Lasseret. Nice guy. We go back a long way. Better be on your way." He put up his hand as if he were about to touch Craig on the shoulder but refrained.

Craig clocked out and stopped on the edge of the area where the huge machines were rolling out sheets of corrugated cardboard and waited to catch Larry's eye. Larry looked over, saw him and gave him a big grin and a wave. Craig felt a little catch in his throat.

Sitting in the little white Honda with the rain banging on the roof, he looked over the tidy car—neat and clean and polished and just right! It's beautiful, he told himself, and I've got enough money to buy it. He couldn't find anything wrong with it. But, he thought, I should let Rob check it out, but if I do, some guy in the shop is going to buy it before I can. He tried the radio and it worked but he turned it off so it wouldn't distract him on his way to the hospital.

It took a while at the hospital. She had been moved to a ward in another wing and he had wandered around lost for a long time before he found her. She was sleeping with her mouth open, behind a screen of drapes. He pulled a chair up to her bed and took her hand. There was no response to a gentle shake or to his voice calling her softly. Another voice was calling feebly over and over, "Nurse? Nurse?" A nurse parted the drapes. "Are you family?" she asked.

He nodded. "Son," he said.

"Dr. Strawburn was just here and he ordered some more sedation for her, so I don't think she'll be awake for a while yet," the nurse said.

"Did he say what was wrong with her or how she was doing?" he asked in a small plaintive voice.

"I think he may still be on this floor. Let's see if we can catch him. He can tell you first hand what he plans." She disappeared out of the shroud of drapes and Craig followed. "There he is," moving towards the nursing station. He did not recognize the old man behind the counter. The nurse said, "Dr. Strawburn, this is Mrs. Williams' son," and left them looking at each other.

"I'm Craig," he ventured.

"Um, yes," the old man said, looking over his nose-glasses at him and holding his pursed lips in his closed fist. "You're quite grown up."

"How's my mother, Dr. Strawburn?" Craig asked. "She's sound asleep and I didn't want to wake her."

"Yes," came a muffled reply while Craig was examined through several head nods.

Finally the doctor seemed to have reached some sort of decision about something. "Yes," he said again. "Your mother has been under considerable stress in the past months. What with the death of your father and other, um, problems she has had to cope with. The plain truth is that it has become too much for her and she has suffered what we call a nervous breakdown. Now then, I have made arrangements for a colleague of mine to see her and if he agrees, then, well, I think she should go into a rest home for a month at the very least. There is one in White Rock that I favour. I've had excellent reports from other patients I've sent there. So, I'll be in touch with them and see if they have room. It's getting very difficult these days with governments trying to cut back on hospitals, fees, drugs and everything else in health care. And one government is as bad as the one before in spite of their silver-tongued promises. They, of course, blame the medical profession, not realizing we are so inundated with their bureaucratic paperwork, that we have scarcely time to see our patients. At any rate, um, what's your name? Oh, yes, Craig, isn't it? Well, I'll check in on your mother tomorrow. She'll have a good night, I'm sure." And he wandered off looking as if he had either many things or nothing on his mind.

Craig went back to the ward and checked on his mother again. She had rolled over and the snoring had ceased but she was unresponsive to any approach. He tucked the covers more securely around her neck, kissed her forehead and left. Out on the parking lot, he saw three white Hondas in the area where he had parked and did not know which one he had come in and had to examine each one in the pouring rain until he found the right one. He went to the licence office and because it was Monday morning on a very wet day there were only three people in the line-up for a license and it took him less than thirty minutes to exchange his driving school certificate for a temporary license with a permanent one to be mailed. He drove over to the Sweet Spot as carefully as he had driven before he got a license. He thought he recognized Vic from the school walking out of the cafe as he parked across the street.

"Hi, Craig!" Donna called with a big, welcoming smile when he walked in. She put down some plates of food in front of three customers, poured them some more coffee and came over to him. "Hey, you're not at work," she said without asking why.

"No, I went but I had a couple of things to do. I'll tell you after but I'm starving. What did you take that guy over there? That looked good! Can I have the same?"

"Sure," she said, filled his coffee cup without asking and bustled away looking very competent. He would rather have had milk but managed to drink only enough of the coffee that she did not fill his cup again.

The next time she stopped near him, he said with a secretive smile, "Look across the street. See that white Honda in front of the red truck? I'm gonna buy it."

"You're kidding! Are you really? It looks cute. Did you get your license?"

"Yeah, an hour ago."

Bruno banged his bell three times meaning that there were three orders to be picked up. "One of them will be yours," she said and rushed away, returning in a minute with a plate of pancakes, fried eggs and bacon.

"Gonna take me for a ride on my break, Craig?" Donna asked.

"I can't," he tried with his mouth full and then when he had swallowed some and shoved the rest in his cheek pouch, he finished. "I had to take my mother to the hospital last night and I have to meet my sister and see what they are going to do with her."

"What happened to your mother?"

"She took too many sleeping pills."

"Oh, Craig!" Donna said, her voice full of sympathy, knowing from other experiences exactly what he was facing.

They did not talk further as Craig finished his meal and Donna cleaned tables. Bruno came to the serving window and looked out and gave Craig a smile and a wave. Craig waved back and stood up. "I gotta go," he said to Donna, putting some money on the counter. "Is that enough?"

"Just a minute," she said, going to the till. "Here's your change."

"Keep it."

"Hey, come back here! I said 'Here's your change.' Good friends don't tip good friends," she said putting his money on the counter. "Good friends kiss good friends goodbye—discreetly, of course." She puckered and leaned toward him. He puckered and touched lips with her. "That's better," she said.

"I'll tell Rob," he teased.

"He'll be pleased," she retorted.

Bruno was still smiling at the service window.

Craig drove to his bank, withdrew some money and cashed in a bond that he had bought with money from the sale of his drum set and an electric guitar. He drove home to see if he could connect with Edith but the keys were still on the counter, so he left a note with the time on it: 'Home at lunchtime. Missed you. Going to hospital' and rushed away. He stopped at the Superstore and looked for Rob but somebody said he was on a break so he decided not to wait. At the hospital, his mother was still sleeping, although the nurse said she wakened up to eat a little lunch and that her daughter had been in and fed her. The psychiatrist had not been in to see her yet. He could see no good reason to wait around for her to wake up so he left and made a phone call home to see if Edie had arrived there but there was no answer. Driving back to the factory he began to feel the effects of a busy day after a long tense night and he drove with excessive care in the pouring rain in a car that was not his—yet. But his mind was made up that he would make a deal with Larry for the car right away.

When he walked into the plant, a guy leaving the washroom stopped him and said, "You're Craig, aren't you? Lucky fucker!"

"Yeah. Why?"

"Because Larry said you had just bought his car and I offered him more than he wanted but he wouldn't budge. You sure got a deal on that baby. He's in the lunchroom if you're looking for him."

Craig gave him a safe grin and a shrug and walked off to find Larry.

"So what you think, hey, Craig?" Larry called to him as soon as he walked in.

Craig walked over and sat down at the same table.

"I know what you think. You think it's too much money. Okay, then for you, we make it $2500 even. How's that?" Larry said.

"No, no Larry! I wasn't going to bargain with you. I just wanted to buy it at your price. It's a fair price. But I met a guy out in the hall and he says you told him I had already bought it and he even offered you more. I was just going to ask you to give me a couple of days to get the money together. I haven't got enough right this minute. Why didn't you sell it to him?"

"I don't like him," Larry said bluntly. "He swears too much."

Craig laughed. "I swear, too, Larry. I even say 'shit' in front of the b-a-b-y."

Larry whacked him on the back laughing. "That's okay, That's just funny. Other stuff, cursing, I don't like." he said, shaking his head solemnly. "Okay, we got deal? $2500." He put out his hand.

Craig reached into his pocket and took out the $300 he had taken out of his account and handed it to Larry. Larry slapped the hand away gently and said, "First we shake hands!" and they did. Then Larry said, "Now we got deal," and picked up the money and stood up. "We sign papers after work, okay?"

"Okay."

Craig clocked back in rather than wait around until quitting time. He was working in the shipping office when Carl came by.

"Back again?" Carl asked.

"Yes, I promised to meet Larry after work and do some things."

Carl smiled. "Everybody in the plant knows by now that you bought Larry's car. Congratulations."

"I guess I just lucked out. I didn't even have to go around looking and kicking tires."

"That's luck alright," Carl said as he walked away. "Good car, good price, good man."

At five o'clock, Craig and Larry met in the lunch room and filled out the transfer papers. Then Larry phoned his wife and told her he would be a little late because Craig was going to drive him to get insurance and new plates and then Craig would drive him home.

At the insurance agency, Craig was struggling to get the least possible insurance, but when it was added up, it was still more than $100 short of what he had taken out of the bank to cover it. Larry looked at his embarrassment and pulled out the $300 Craig had paid him and passed it quietly to him. "I can't, Larry!" Craig protested, but Larry hit him hard on the back and Craig smothered a laugh and said, "Okay, okay."

"So now you got a car, eh, kid? So drive me home. We take my plates off and put yours on in my garage out of the rain."

When they arrived at Larry's place after Craig's careful drive through the heavy afternoon traffic in the rain, Larry said, "Now you come and meet my wife, okay?"

"Okay," Craig agreed.

They went into a warm kitchen smelling of dinner cooking, with a small table set by the window for two and pictures of Jesus on the cross hung on two walls and another larger one visible in the dining room. "This young man, he bought your car," Larry said to a grey-haired woman wearing a print dress with another print apron over it. "He bought your car and now you are a rich woman," and he laughed boisterously. "Except I gave him the money back," and he watched her face screw up in puzzlement, and then explained it to her, partly in English and partly in another language. "This is my wife," he said to Craig.

"Hello, I'm Craig Williams," he said to her, putting out his hand carefully after glancing at her swollen arthritic hands.. "I'm sorry, I don't know your last name, Mrs...? Everybody goes by first names at work."

"Koski," Larry said. "Larry Koski. Polish name."

"Pleased to meet you, Mrs. Koski."

"We change the license plates and then Craig goes to see his mother in hospital," Larry said.

"Your mother in hospital?" Mrs. Koski asked with sympathetic eyes peering through thick lenses.

"Yes, I had to take her in last night. She was, well, she got quite sick. I saw her today but she was asleep." He thought that was all a stranger needed to know.

"Oh, that's too bad. And nobody at home for to make the supper for you and father?"

"No father!" Larry interjected roughly.

Mrs. Koski took a deep breath through her nostrils and straightened her back. "You do your work," she said. "I put place for you at our table. You stay for supper." she said to Craig, not as much an invitation as it was a command.

"But Mrs. Koski..." he protested.

"He is late already," she said, nodding to her husband while pulling up a folding leaf on the table and rearranging the settings.

"Come on, Craig," Larry said.

They went out to the garage where Craig had parked the car at Larry's direction. Larry had finished the front plate before Craig had started the back. He simply took the screw driver from Craig and did it himself. "There!" he said. "Supper's ready."

In the house, Larry washed at the kitchen sink. "Too dirty to go to bathroom after work," he explained, inviting Craig to the sink.

Craig washed and was seated with them at the little table, laden with food. "Say grace," Larry said to Craig bowing his head.

Jesus Christ! What do I do now? He asked himself in a panic. And then he decided if Jenny could do it then he could too. "Dear God," he said aloud, "Please bless this food and this family and make my mother better. Amen."

"Amen!" said the other two in unison and Mrs Koski reached out with her twisted arthritic hand and touched Craig's arm gently.

"This guy talks to the big shot," Larry said to his wife with a grin. "He don't mess around with the middle guy."

"Larry!" she scolded after she realized what he was talking about and added something in Polish. "Eat, Craig. Help yourself."

He helped himself to what he thought must be polish sausage, heavy with garlic, and boiled potatoes, sweetened parsnips and sauerkraut and thick bread with seeds in it that Craig did not recognize. And then there was a hot apple something with thick cream that was named but Craig could not get his tongue around the word. There was little talk at the table and what little there was centred around the car. No mention was made of money. Craig was so openly pleased and happy about the car that it made them happy. When Craig had finished a huge helping of the dessert, Mrs. Koski left the table and went into the dining room, returning with a vase of flowers. "These I pick yesterday from my garden, before the rain," she said, taking the flowers out of the vase and wrapping them first in wax paper and then in newspaper. "Everlastings. You take them to your mother. That's a good boy."

Craig stumbled to his feet. "Oh, Mrs. Koski," was all he could think to say for a minute. "She has a big garden, too. She will really like these. Thank you!" He took the flowers from her and as automatically as if he had known her all his life, he leaned over and kissed her on the forehead. "And thank you for the dinner. It was wonderful. And thank you for your little car, I'll take good care of it." He turned to Larry and shook his hand, wanting to say something more but no words came.

"Better hurry, there, kid," Larry said.

"Yes, I will. See you tomorrow."

He went out the door and they watched him back out of the garage. Then Larry turned out the garage light and flicked the switch for the overhead door. He watched the rain streaming down hard in the light of a streetlamp as the door folded into place. "The other kid," he said to her, "he would pay more money, but he swears too much."

"Psshht!" she replied with a shrug. "Money!"

He arrived at the hospital just as his mother was being settled in for the night. Her face had been washed and her hair brushed but she lay like an unresponsive lump in the bed without much life in her voice or manner.

"Craig," she said when she saw him, her voice as drab as her surroundings. "Somebody said you were here before. Did Edith come?"

"Remember?" the nurses aid interjected. "Your daughter was here and helped you with your supper."

"Yes," she said tonelessly.

"Here, Mom," he said showing her the flowers. "These are for you from Mrs. Koski, a lady whose car I bought today." Slow down, he told himself. You're going too fast for her. "Her husband works at the same place as me, and he had her car for sale and I bought it."

"Did you have enough money?"

"Not quite, I'll get a loan from the bank tomorrow. I'm $500 short."

"Where's my purse? Get me my purse."

"What do you want your purse for, Mom?"

"Never mind! Find ittt!"

He found it for her in her bedside locker and she rummaged in it until she found her check book. Opening it, she signed her name and handed it to him. "Fill it in yourself," she said.

"Fill in what?" he said. "I didn't ask you for money."

"Oh, don't be so difficult!" she said and started to cry. "Just fill it in! Put a thousand dollars! I don't care! Just do it, Craig, so I can have some peace of mind."

"Alright, I'll write $1000 in if it will make you happy."

"I don't care if I'm happy." Her voice was weary. "I want you to be happy." She stirred around again in the purse, emerging with her bankcard. "Here," she said, shoving it at him. "Pay the bills. Get some food in the house before you starve to death. I was going to shop today but... Oh, dear God, my life's a mess!" She drew the sheet over her face and he could hear the gasping sobs coming from underneath. He tried to pull the sheet away from her face but she struggled to hold on to it. He sat on the edge of her bed looking down at her. She could obviously feel him near because she said when the sobs had subsided. "Go home, please, dear. I'll get some sleep. I promise."

Suddenly, she pulled the sheet down and looked at him with swollen eyes. "Who's Mrs. Koski?" she asked suddenly.

"The lady I bought the car from."

"Old or young?"

"Old, I guess."

"Did she give you dinner?"

"Yes, why?"

"You smell of garlic. Koski? That's Polish, I bet. They live on garlic." She pulled the sheet up again.

He reached out and touched her, "Good night, Mom. Have a good sleep."

He left feeling a little relieved that she was showing signs of concern for someone other that herself. He wondered if he should tell the nurse on duty, but it seemed too inconsequential to be bothered.

CHAPTER 50

The next week was a frantic period for Craig. He paid off Larry with big smiles on both sides and congratulations from some of the other workers. Some of them had learned through workplace small talk that Craig's mother had been taken to the hospital for what had been a botched suicide and some ventured to ask cautiously about her. Craig could do nothing more than shrug and say that the doctors said she needed a lot of rest. Privately he hoped she would be coming home so that their lives could settle into a more normal routine. In case she was discharged sooner than expected, he bustled around the house, making it tidy, doing a sink full of dishes and a couple of loads of laundry. One night when he had stopped in to see Rob at work, he loaded up on some groceries—mostly breakfast cereal, bread, milk, cheese, packaged meat and a huge assortment of nibblers. Wandering down the pickle aisle in search of a brand of pickles his mother always bought, he found some smoked oysters and put three cans in his basket for his mother because he remembered she liked them. Rob's mother had phoned to see if his mother wanted visitors and he promised he would ask her. She had already sent flowers and a note, and when Craig remembered to ask his mother about visitors she told him to tell Claudia that she would be out soon and would rather she come over to the house and have a proper visit.

When he dropped by the Turners to pass on the message Rob's mother told him quietly that their house and business was up for sale and they were planning to move to Prince George where Glen had been offered a job on a community newspaper. "Does that mean that Rob is going too?" Craig asked in a voice so filled with sudden panic that it reverted to an adolescent squeak.

"That has to be his decision," Claudia replied, smiling. "He can certainly come with us if he wants to, but I rather suspect that, given a choice, he would opt for staying here—with friends."

Craig breathed a huge sigh of relief. Prince George was a million miles away. He couldn't remember any time in his life that they had been separated, even on vacations because they always took Rob with them, or he went with the Turners, except for one time when Rob had to go east to his grandmother's before she died.

"He probably will stay with us. We've got lots of room," Craig announced in a tone of certainty.

But when Craig and Rob got together later in the week, the problem had already been settled: Rob was going to move in with Donna. They had talked with Mrs. Lasseret and she was agreeable to the arrangement, but Wally said that it went against the grain of their religious beliefs, so the rent would have to go up to make up for the extra heat, electricity and wear and tear. Craig went away with his nose out of joint, partly because Donna seemed to be usurping his place in Rob's life and partly because Rob, for the first time, had not told him first off what was happening.

When he went to the hospital and told his mother about the Turner's plans to move to Prince George she broke into tears.

"Oh, I'll miss her so much you wouldn't believe it," she wailed.

"But Mom!" he exclaimed, puzzled by her upset. "You hardly ever see her and she never phones or anything."

"What's that got to do with it?" she snapped. "We've been good friends for years even if the two men didn't have much in common. I knew that Claudia would always be there if I needed her and that's a good feeling—to know you have a friend like that whatever happens." She stopped talking suddenly and looked at Craig with a stricken face. "Does that mean that Rob is going too?"

"No, he doesn't have to go. He's going to move in with Donna. They've got it all worked out," Craig assured her.

"Oh, that's good. The thought of you two not being together—well, I can't imagine it." She stopped and thought again. "You mean, they're going to live together. Does his mother know?"

Craig shrugged. "I don't know. She didn't say anything about it when I talked with her."

"I'll have to phone her. I have to phone her to say thanks for the flowers anyway. Rob could stay with us. You'd like that. He could use Edith's room. I like Robbie," she added as if it were a new thought. And then after a long sniffling silence, "Imagine that. Living together! Do I know Donna?"

He shook his head. "No, you've never met her. She's nice—you'd like her."

She got a Kleenex and wiped her eyes and blew her nose and, with a big sigh disposed of the Turners and their problems.

"I was going to ask Edith to do this, but it's a long way in for her and I need these things right away because I'm supposed to be up walking the halls for exercise. So here's a list of things I need. Would you mind? I've written down where you can find each of them so you don't have to turn everything upside down to find them. And, oh yes, there's a little blue overnight bag on the top shelf in my closet that will hold everything."

He was beginning to feel pleased that she was so coherent and not crying so much when she suddenly wailed, "Dr. Strawburn and that fat ugly psychiatrist who came to talk to me...oh, I hated her!" She stopped to control her weeping. "They say I have to go to a private rest home until they're sure I won't, you know—they're afraid I might try to do it again. And I didn't try to do it last time! They won't believe me that it was a mistake!" She snuffled for a minute or two, then looking up at him suddenly, she asked, "Did you buy a car?"

"Yes," he said with a big grin, "I thought you'd never ask! I guess you weren't listening when I told you that I bought it from a man at work. Remember—his name was Larry Koski and his wife sent you those flowers right there. Forget-me-nots, I think you said."

"Oh, yes, I do remember, because you had dinner with them and smelled of garlic. Not forget-me-nots. They're called Everlasting but there's another proper name I can't remember. I thought you had brought them from my garden. It's funny Edith and Harvey didn't think to send some. She's only been in once, you know."

Craig made no response. He was about to say that it was good to hear her talking normally again but bit his tongue, thinking that the word normal would set her off on either a crying jag or a lecture. But all she said finally was, "You'd better go. You haven't had your dinner yet. Has Claudia had you over for dinner?"

"No, but I've been kind of busy," he said excusing her.

"Well!" she huffed. "Some friend! The least she could do was make sure you were fed properly."

"Oh, I'm eating okay," he said. "Not like your home cooking, but not bad."

"Well, don't worry, dear. I'll be out of here soon and start looking after you again. Oh, dear God! I'm a terrible mother. And imagine! Not even remembering to ask you about your car." The tears started again and she said, "Go, Craig, Go! And try to bring those things tomorrow, will you? I hate these hospital rags they make you wear and I'm certainly not going traipsing up and down the hall until I can look decent."

Craig kissed her goodbye and made his escape.

At home, Craig settled down in front of the TV with a bag of chips to watch a hockey game and between periods searched out the things on the list his mother had given him. She had described the cosmetics she wanted very precisely knowing that he was naive about such matters so he was able to collect them, along with some other toilet articles, easily. Further on down the list, she had specified '6 pairs white cotton underwear—2nd drawer on the left (not the colored ones) and he knew exactly what she meant and where they were to be found.

In her room, standing in front of her chest of drawers, he opened both the second drawer and then the one beside it, knowing what he would find in each. His mind raced back to the days of hidden chocolates and the compulsion to feel and fold the lingerie he found there. He remembered too, the gut tensions of early adolescence now recognized as strong sexual arousals. He plunged his hand into the other drawer and lifted up a tangle of soft frills and hot colours and waited a minute, searching his body to find the stirrings within him that he could remember vividly, but nothing was happening. Nothing! he exclaimed to himself. One part of him was elated by the lack of response but another part was confounded by the change. He tried, almost with a sense of desperation, to create an excitement in his groin, but still nothing happened. Finally, without folding and replacing the articles neatly, he dropped them back in the drawer and closed it, thinking as he did so, that the pleasure had gone and the guilt of his childhood was hidden away in that drawer forever—a secret he had never revealed, not even to Rob.

Going downstairs, he stretched out on the couch in the living room and stared at the ceiling in the flickering blue light of the muted TV pondering something that he could not put into words, but knowing, whatever it was, that it marked a change in his life—a change that at one moment excited him but at the same time he resented. He was at the point of drowsiness when, for no reason, he sat up and looked at the window and framed in it, and making him jump, scared, he saw Rob making ugly faces at him. He flopped back on the sofa again, not bothering to go to the door to let Rob in. After a long series of bangs and shouts, Rob appeared in the living room door and made a flying leap at him. He punched him on the arm with a fist made of hard knuckles until Craig struggled and writhed out from under him. "How'd you know I was there?" Rob asked.

Craig shrugged. "I just knew," he replied.

"Why didn't you let me in? Fine host you are! Here I come over to party with you, leaving my lovely lady alone, and find you've locked me out."

"You know where the key is—obviously! And if I knowed you was comin' I'd've barred the door and got out the shotgun."

"What are you sitting in the dark for? You holding a séance or something weird?"

"Yeah, something weird, alright. I was thinking about you."

"You're yanking my chain! Nice sexy thoughts, I hope."

Craig was silent a long time and Rob let the silence grow. Finally Craig said in a husky voice, "When you knew your Mom and Dad were going to Prince George pretty soon and you weren't going to go with them, why did you choose to move in with Donna instead of coming to live here? And you didn't even tell me about it for a long time, did you?" he asked accusingly. "You didn't even try to discuss it with me, to see what I thought about it. My best friend!" he added with a touch of bitterness in a shaky voice.

Rob said nothing but both were aware of a tension between them, like a barrier that was restraining their frankness with each other.

"Well?" Craig said, loudly but not in anger, and reverting to an old childhood joke, "tell me if you don't know!"

Silence in the blue light of the TV.

"Rob?"

"Oh, Jesus Christ, Craig! Don't you know? Can't you figure it out? I'm scared, Craig. That's why. I'm scared shitless. I wanted to live with you—that was the first thing that I thought of when they told me about Prince George. And then I knew I couldn't. Somehow or other I knew that if I lived with you I would never let you go—and I have to, Craig, don't you see? If I did I would never find a woman, and I had to find one or I end up as a frigging fruitcake. But I found one and it'll work out, you'll see. I thought of you and wanted to tell you but I thought if I did I would give up and go with you forever and that was okay except I knew it wasn't okay—I shouldn't do it. I thought maybe I should go to Prince George with them but that would mean we would hardly ever see each other, so I figured if I moved in with Donna, she could sorta take your place but I didn't want anybody to take your place. She's okay, you know." He was silent as if uncertain how to go on.

Craig was silent too, until Rob said, "Well, say something."

"What do you want me to say? Don't you want us to be friends any more? Holy Jesus, Rob! We've been friends all our lives and I just figured we'd be friends for, well, you know, like the rest of our lives. Even after we got married I figured we'd just keep on being best friends like always."

"What the hell do I have to say to make you understand," Rob said, his voice squeaky with frustration. Craig could see him across the room in the dim light, sitting with his elbows on his knees holding his head in his hands. Finally he sat up. "Look at me," he said. "I'm shaking like a leaf. Do you know why? You're going to make me say it, aren't you. Okay, I'll say it." He took a deep breath and let it out jerkily before saying slowly and deliberately, "I love you too much and it scares me!"

In the dim light Craig could see Rob's eyes brimming with tears. He reached up to turn on the lamp beside the sofa.

"Don't put the light on!" Rob said quickly, and Craig took his hand away from the lamp. "Let's just talk like this, in this light like it was a campfire. You know, like we were up at Lake Lovely Water again."

"That was great, wasn't it?" Craig said, getting up from his sprawled position on the sofa and moving to a chair nearer to Rob.

"What did you do that for?"

"What?"

"Move over closer."

"I didn't move closer—I just moved, that's all."

The old, wicked Rob emerged for a minute in the dim light. "Oh, yeah?" he said with a stagey lascivious grin. "It's not the old enticement ploy, eh?"

"Oh, for Christ's sake, Rob!"

"You see. I have to keep on trying," and the grin stayed.

Craig shook his head in smiling scepticism, and a comfortable silence arose.

"Hey, Craig. Remember that sex game we did together? Well, it never went further than fun and games, did it? But you know what? I sometimes wanted it to, didn't you? I really wanted to."

Craig nodded in dumb agreement, not trusting his voice.

"Yeah, I thought so and that's what scares me. You see, when I have sex with Donna, it's just sex, there's no fun and games. And almost always when we're, like, doing it, I find myself thinking of you and pretending it's you."

"That's not right. You shouldn't!"

"So tell me how to stop, jerk!"

"I don't know! But if you love her you shouldn't be thinking of somebody else."

Rob sat up straight in the chair and then stood up and towered over Craig. Craig looked up and saw his red-rimmed eyes.

"For God's sake, Craig! Haven't you been listening? I don't love Donna. I like her, I like her a lot. She's a really nice person, and she's probably good for me. BUT—and this is a god-damned big but—I can only love one person, I told you that. And I have to stay with Donna or I'm lost."

Rob moved over beside Craig's chair and took Craig's head and held it tight against his body. Craig felt the trembling in Rob's body and heard the huskiness in his voice as Rob said, "I've got to go, buddy." He could not respond to Rob's final squeeze and he watched the tall, lanky figure move out of the room and heard the back door close.

He stayed in the chair for a while and then moved again to the sofa and stretched out. He found a spot on the ceiling that needed examining and let the tears roll out of the corners of his eyes.

CHAPTER 51

Craig heard the ringing and reached out and fumbled in the dim light of the cold November morning to turn off the persistent sound. It wasn't the radio alarm or the school buzzer or the stove timer. Frustration rather than sound pushed him over the edge of sleep into wakefulness. It was the phone and he rushed to his mother's room to answer it, sleepy and resentful about being wakened. He heard Edith start to talk as soon as he picked up the phone and croaked something that approximated 'hello' but he didn't start to listen until he finished an enormous yawn and sigh.

"Whad'ja say?" he finally said.

"Weren't you listening, for God's sake? Wake up! Are you up? I bet I let your phone ring twenty times."

"Jesus, Edith! It's Sunday morning and it's only quarter past eight! Or are you living in a different time zone."

"Well, I've been up for hours. What are you doing today?"

"I'm going to go back to bed as soon as you hang up—maybe before."

Edith plunged on. "I'm coming in to see Mom today. Harv is coming down with something, so he won't be going in to visit Mom because he's so germy.

I'll bring the girls with me and leave them with you while I go to the hospital and you make us some kind of lunch and maybe put the girls down for a nap. What's the weather like in there?"

"Just a minute," Craig said, putting the phone down but continuing to talk in a loud foreign correspondent's monotone.

"I am now making my way across the room and pulling back the drapes in order to give you an up-to-date weather report. There is no sun. The sky is completely overcast. And, baby, it's cold outside. I don't know what the temperature is but I estimate it to be about five degrees below b-r-r-. It's raining with that kind of blowy, straight into your face wind with blobs of snow in it." He picked up the phone again. "It's a nice day—for November," he said.

"Don't you ever stop horsing around?" she snapped.

He made a horse's neigh sound and said, "I'm going back to bed. See you when you get here. And I'm not making you lunch, but I'll take you to McDonald's. Oh, and there's some things for you to take to Mom that she asked for. Don't let me forget to give them to you."

"What kind of things?"

"Oh, shit, Edith! You can look at them when you get here. I'm going back to bed." He hung up and when he got back to his own room his bed was still warm.

Edith arrived with the twins who were anticipating a romp with Uncle Craig. It took five minutes of racing around before he tired them enough to get back to Edith. She was sorting through the things he had collected and methodically ticking them off the list. "What about these other things?" she asked.

"I figured you would know what she meant, so I left them for you to find."

"How is she?" Edith asked.

He shrugged. "I dunno. She's still pretty weepy, so you have to be careful about what you say."

Edith sniffed and went on looking for things on the list, but she was also checking out the kitchen cupboards and the frig.

"What are you poking around there for?" he asked, a little miffed at her nosiness even though she was his sister.

She didn't answer and went on with her inspection tour.

"So where's your car," she asked.

"In the garage. We can go to McDonald's in it."

"How did you buy it—on time?"

"No, I paid cash for it, of course."

"How'd you do that? You've only been working a month, if that," she said, looking at him with her hands on her hips.

"I saved from last summer," he said cautiously, not wanting to have to tell her that his mother had made up his shortage.

"And you had enough to buy a car?" she asked suspiciously.

"Jesus, Edie! Why the third degree? I saved it! Alright? I don't smoke. I don't drink. I don't go to whorehouses. I don't gamble. Why couldn't I buy a car? What's the big deal?"

"Nothing," she said, shortly. "I just wondered if Mom had bought it for you. She didn't do anything like that for me when I quit school."

"Well, she didn't," he lied. "Let's go get some lunch. How about that, Jenny?" guessing at which twin was leaning against his knees, listening. "Ready to go to McDonald's?"

"Yay!" came the ready answer and an equally spontaneous agreement from the living room.

"We have to go in my car," Edith announced on their way out. "The car seats are already in it."

"Well, can't we change them?" Craig asked.

"Oh, Craig! Let's just go in mine. You can show it off some other time. Where is it?"

"In the garage, I already told you."

"Okay, show it to me then, or is it some old wreck that you're ashamed of. Come on Jenny, and Iona, where are you? Uncle Craig's going to show us his nice new car."

He opened the garage door and said dramatically. "Ta-dah!"

Edith walked around the car, trying not to show she was impressed. "How much did you pay for it?" she asked bluntly as always.

"None of your business," he said, grinning.

"Oh, get off it! What's the big secret?"

"Okay, then. I got it for $5000."

She pursed her lips and nodded her head. Craig thought she might even kick a couple of tires. "Good for you, you sure got yourself a deal, it seems to me. We've been looking for a small car for me for a long time but we haven't found one yet." She looked over and saw Craig smirking. "What are you grinning like an ape about?" she snapped.

"Oh, nothing," he answered.

"Yeah, I'll bet! You're up to something."

"No, I'm not. Cross my heart," still grinning.

"Oh, come on. Let's go if you're going to buy lunch. McDonald's yet, big deal," she said with a sneer.

"You said we had to go in your car," Craig said when they walked to the street where she had parked. "This is Mom's car."

"Well, this one already had the car seats in it," she said, lamely. I couldn't see the sense of trading." She was busy securing the children into their seats.

"How'd you get that big dint in the front fender," he asked.

"Where?" she asked, leaving the children and rushing to look.

"Oh, no! It's just some dust," he announced and continued a walk-around the car with his hands behind his back and a malicious grin on his face.

McDonald's was a big event for the children. It was packed with families and noisy and exciting. The staff had painted red dots on their noses and cheeks and a girl in a clown suit painted, with Edith's smiling permission, a red dot on the nose of each of the twins that proved to be so hilarious for them that they paid little attention to their burgers served in a train box. It took a long time to finish lunch but Edith remained tolerant and patient with the children and Craig was relieved that she seemed to be enjoying herself.

"I hate this big black hearse," Craig said on the way home. "It's so ostentatious. I wish she'd get rid of it."

"I don't mind it. At least people notice you. She can leave it to me in her will." She stopped speaking suddenly. "I'm sorry. I didn't mean it like that. If my feet were bigger maybe I wouldn't put them in my mouth so often."

Craig smiled in acknowledgement, and let the subject drop. He had hassled her enough for one day.

Edith dropped them at the house without going in. "Now you girls be good and have fun with Uncle Craig. Mummy will be back in a little while, then we'll have to go home and show Daddy your cute red noses. And who knows, maybe Daddy's cold will have made his nose all red like yours. Then Mommy will be the only one with a white nose and so she'll have to paint her nose too."

"And Uncle Craig!" one of them said.

"Sure," she said. "Why don't you give him a big red nose while I go see Granny in the hospital?"

"I want to come," one said.

"Not this time, dear. Hospitals don't allow little girls in unless they're very sick. You're not sick, are you?"

Both put on long serious faces and shook their heads in unison.

"Off you go, then. Mummy will be back very soon."

"Not if Mummy doesn't shake her you know what and get out of here before visiting hours are over," Craig said pointedly.

She was back within an hour and a half and found the three of them on the floor in front of the TV. Her face was set and she looked like she was ready to spit nails. "Didn't you put them down?" she asked.

"They didn't want to go," said a clown with the big red nose who was lying flat on his back with a twin nestled on each arm. "Say hello to your mummy before she says hello to you," he urged the children and escaped from them.

"So why are you back so soon?" he said getting to his feet.

"I don't know why I bothered," she said angrily. "She'd been crying and wouldn't say why. I went to kiss her and she told me to get away because my face was cold. Then she was mad because you put in the wrong gown. And I showed her that she hadn't put it on the list and she said that anybody with any brains would know that somebody in hospital would need, not just want, their own good dressing gown not an old bathrobe."

She was busy collecting the children's clothes and dressing them.

"Where are you going," he asked, spitting on a Kleenex and trying to rub the red lipstick off his nose.

"Home, of course! Where I've got a sick husband to take care of. Home! Where somebody might appreciate me."

"Oh, Edith, come on! She's just having a bad day."

"I don't care. She's depressing!"

"Edith! For Christ's sake!" he shouted. "She's depressed! That's why she's in there! She's sick!"

"Well she isn't so sick that she can't nag me about not sending flowers. And who the hell is the Mrs. Koski who sent her those god-awful weeds that she's so proud of?"

"That's the lady I bought the car from."

"Does Mom know her?"

"No."

Edith looked him hard in the eye and snorted. "Maybe somebody will take the time some day and fill me in as to what the hell is going on in this family. Say goodbye to your Uncle Craig. We've got to go. Hurry up, please, Jenny. Iona, don't drag your scarf—put it on. Oh," she said as she herded them out the door to the car. "Thanks for lunch."

Craig belted one child in while she looked after the other. He got his hugs from one and went around to the other side to get his hugs from the other but Edith had already slammed the door and was moving around the car to the drivers side. When he opened the door, Edith exploded, "Now what, for Christ's sake!"

"You swore, Mummy," one of them said. "Daddy said not to say that." The other twin nodded in pursed lip agreement.

"You tell Daddy what Mummy said," Craig told them.

"Thanks a lot, brother," Edith said starting the car. "Do you think you might call me sometime if you're not too busy."

"My free time is between 11 and 12PM," he said. "Will that be convenient for you?"

She drove away without responding, not quite laying rubber.

It was only a little past four o'clock when Craig went back into the silent house. He turned on the TV to fill up the silence while he wandered around picking up the toys that were kept to amuse the twins when they came to town, all the while wishing that Rob had a phone so he could touch bases with him. Just talking to him would clear up some nagging questions that had kept popping up all day long. Putting on his ski jacket against the sleety snow that was the preliminary to a bigger winter storm he drove over to the Turners to show them his new car. He knocked and shouted his usual greeting and heard Rob's mother call "Just a minute, Craig!" She came up the stairs with a big smile of greeting for him but also displaying in her face some other pleasure unrelated to him.

"I'd ask you to come down," she said quickly, "but we've got a buyer downstairs and we think he is just about to close the deal. Isn't that exciting?" She moved over to Craig and, tiny as she was, almost crushed him in an embrace. "Just think! A new city, a real job—not all day everyday, a new house, new people…oh, I hope he pulls it off." She released him, taut with anticipation.

Glen called from downstairs. "Claudia, where are you? Can you come and sign a couple of things?"

"Oh, he did it!" she breathed, holding her arms taut into her body with her hands made into fists pushed into her face. "Oh, Craig! He did it!"

"Who's there?" Glen called.

"Craig just dropped in," she called on her way down.

"Bring him down and let him meet his new neighbour."

She stopped and looked back and gave Craig a big 'Come on' signal.

"Well, honey," Glen said going to her and putting his arms around her. "Just a couple of more things to do and then we're out of business. You sign, I sign, he signs and he witnesses," indicating two men seated in the room. "Think we can handle that?"

"We've handled tougher assignments," she said,

"Oh, by the way, gentlemen, meet our friend and neighbour, Craig Williams. He and my son are so close, we sometimes get mixed up as to who belongs to who." He put his arm affectionately around Craig's shoulders. "I should warn you that he has regarded anything in our frig or tool box or home as common property, so don't call the police if you find him in your frig. And reciprocally, we think our son, Rob, lives at his place, although we used to run across him here, too."

"Pleased to meet you, sir," Craig said moving to shake hands with one of the men.

"Roger Todd," the man said, covering up Glen's forgetfulness. "And this is Mr. Richards of Richards Realty."

The Turners were having a quiet personal conversation and Glen turned to Craig and said. "I hear you just bought yourself your first car. Congratulations! Now, I wonder if you would do us a favour. Robbie doesn't have a phone and I don't know his work schedule. So would you leap into your chariot on this miserable November evening and find Rob and tell him that we want to see him, like now?"

"Sure," Craig said, preparing to go.

"And Craig," Claudia said, smiling. "This isn't a secret. You can tell him."

"Oh, you know I would have told him anyway, even if it was a swear-to-god and spit secret," he said as he left.

He drove past Donna's and could see no lights on in the little basement suite, so continued to the store. One of the guys packing bags told him that Rob was working but didn't know where he was. He wandered the aisles and found Rob stocking shelves but also yakking with an elderly couple about the hockey game.

"Hi, buddy," Rob called out with a big warm smile as Craig approached. "Whatcha doing?"

The old couple moved away before Craig answered, saying, "Nice talking to you, Robbie."

"Come on in again," he said with a big smile for them. "And remember. Don't put any money on that American team—go Canadian all the way. Unless Gretsky's playing, of course."

"Oh, we don't bet money!" the old lady said. "We just bet on things like who has to do the dishes."

"I bet he's got the softest hands in town." Rob said, and then turned to

Craig, "What's new?"

"Big news!" Craig said, and then tried to sing the 6/49 ad, "Big, big, big! Big, big, big, big!"

"I know!" Rob said, lowering his voice conspiratorially. "You got laid this afternoon."

"Not even close! Besides if that had happened, you'd have been there." They grinned at each other, erasing any misunderstandings that might have arisen last night. "No, you couldn't guess. Your mom and dad found a buyer. They are signing things right now. And they want you home PDQ—like now, your dad says."

"Wow, that's great," Rob enthused. "Who bought it?"

"A guy by the name of Roger Todd, that's all I know."

Rob continued stacking the shelves and frowning over something on his mind. "I get off at seven," he said. "Have you got your car here? Of course you have! Stupid question! Pick me up, eh? And I'll have to stop and tell Donna. We were going to a show."

"Sure. See you at seven."

Craig worked his way through the crowd in the store wondering why so many people would choose to go out shopping on such a miserable night. The house felt so empty when he opened the door that it felt like it could echo. He turned up the heat, put on a tape and got out the notes he had made after his visit to two computer companies on Friday afternoon. Comparing the notes on the eight companies he had talked to, he couldn't see much difference in what they recommended. The only real difference was the price—two companies were more than twice as high as the lowest estimate. He didn't feel comfortable about making a recommendation so maybe he could suggest that Carl could phone some of his business friends and get their ideas. Keeping his eye on the clock, he looked through the exercise he was supposed to study for his Monday night computer course and found that it was one that had been covered in his day course and the study intent slipped into a daydream and suddenly it was time to pick up Rob.

Rob was standing outside shivering when Craig honked at the entrance and he rushed to the car and turned up the heater full blast. "Take me home first," he ordered. "I have to tell Donna we're not going out." He sat quietly letting Craig pay attention to the slippery roads and limited visibility.

"Has this car been fixed?" he asked.

"What d'ya mean?"

"Like I said, has it been fixed? There's a law, you know, that all Hondas have to be fixed so that they can't reproduce and clutter up the roads."

"Oh, sure!"

"S'truth. You better get it done right away. The way they do it is to cut about three inches off the tailpipe. Doesn't spoil the performance at all. Matter of fact, some drivers say the car is improved on the straight-away and others say it handles curves better."

"Yeah, sure. You never stop BS-ing, do you? Here we are," Craig said pulling up in front of the little apartment. Rob jumped out and went inside, returning in a couple of minutes to say, "She's not home. I left a note. Home, James!"

When they arrived at the Turner's Craig did not turn off the motor and Rob made no move to get out. "You gonna come in with me?" he asked. "I'm kinda scared. I've lived in there for eighteen years and I can't think of home as being any other place. Just like last night when I told you I couldn't think of anyone else that could ever take your place. It's scary, Craig! Like something is ripping my whole life apart."

"Seventeen and a half years on December 15," Craig said as an inconsequential correction.

"Yeah," Rob said flatly. "You coming in?"

Craig shook his head. "Unh-unh," he said. "You got to do this one alone. Besides, what are they going to say except that they sold the place and they're moving to George? And," he continued, "they're gonna give you your freedom. Isn't that what you been looking for?"

"Yeah, I guess. But I'm not so sure I want it." He gave a big sigh. "Oh, well. Better go and see what it's all about. Did they say Bev and Richard were coming?"

"They didn't say."

"Can I come over to your place after?"

"What the hell kind of question is that? You, Rob Turner, suddenly asking me, Craig Williams, if you can come over to my place after seventeen and a half years!"

"Yeah, that was kind of stupid, wasn't it," came the response accompanied with a big, wide, familiar grin. "See you later."

The house was warm and the tape was still playing on the repeater mode when Craig returned. He changed the tape to country with the volume up loud while he searched the frig and the freezer for something for supper. He took out one of the steaks his mother had bought, supposedly big enough for two, thinking hungrily that it would be great with a plateful of fries. Given his druthers, he would have preferred to tackle the steak over a campfire and eat it, blackened and ashen or bloody rare but memorably delicious—the Lake Lovely Water way. But this was November, so he zapped the frozen steak in the microwave and fried it until the kitchen was smoky then covered it with fries heated in the toaster oven. Sitting down at the kitchen table to eat, he discovered that a paring knife was preferable to a table knife, that catsup was needed—in fact, a lot of catsup was needed—that the milk he had left out on the counter in the morning was now sour, and that he missed his mother.

Rob came in a couple of hours later. "Did anybody call the fire department?" he asked as he wandered into the living room where Craig was watching TV.

Craig didn't bother to answer. "So what happened?" he asked.

"I could use a smoke right now," Rob said. "Got any?"

Craig knew that he meant pot, not tobacco. "No, and if I did, you couldn't smoke in here. My mother would kill me."

"You think she could smell it after the bonfire you had in here! When's she coming home?"

"I don't know. They are talking about sending her to a rest home for a month."

"Oh, shit! I better go see her. I got a day off tomorrow. I can go and lie to her about how well her little boy is making out on his own. That'll cheer her up."

"More likely one look at you will cause a relapse."

"Is that good or bad?"

"Come on, Rob! Stop horsing around! What happened?"

"Turn off the goddam TV then, and I will," Rob said as he settled himself sideways in a stuffed chair. When Craig pushed the mute, he said, "Off! I said," and Craig complied.

"Did Bev come over?" Craig asked.

"No, it was too stormy. But they had a long talk with her on the phone." He waited a minute and then went on. "They really did sell it, Craig. I didn't think my dad ever would. I didn't think he would work for anybody else. But he says it's getting too hard, there's too much competition and a small operator can't make it any more. So he's quitting and they're going. And, you know what? They are practically packing. The guy that bought it is single and so he's going to buy everything, I mean furniture and all that kind of stuff, so all they have to pack is their personal stuff and haul it up in a trailer."

"Geez, that was fast, wasn't it?"

"Yeah," Rob agreed and stopped talking for a minute trying to get his thoughts in order. "My dad and mom were really pushing me to go with them but they quit after a while when I said I really didn't want to go and I wouldn't. They said what am I going to do with all my stuff and I said I'd put it in storage. My mom said why don't you put it in Craig's garage or his basement where it's handy. And I couldn't tell her why, like the real reason being what we talked about last night."

Craig nodded, unhappily accepting his reasoning.

Rob went on. "Dad said the guy said he was going to need some help and he asked Dad if he thought I would be interested because Dad had told him that I knew all the machines and helped out when he was pushed. Dad said it would have to be full time because I was already working and he told the guy what I'd have to get to make it worthwhile, and the guy didn't even blink and it was more than twice as much as I'm making now."

"Hey, Rob! That's great!" Craig enthused, sitting up straight, his face alight with happiness.

"No, it isn't,"Rob said. "It isn't great at all." Craig's face fell. "Why not?"

"Well, think, for Chrissake, Craig! There I'd be and here you'd be—a half a block away as always. And I'd be over here all the time and things wouldn't have changed a bit except I wouldn't be living there any more. And Donna would be mad—she always gets mad at me if I talk about you." He paused. "I didn't tell you she asked me the other day if we were queer."

"What did you say?"

"I told her you were but I wasn't."

"Oh, for shit's sake! Why did you say that?" But when he looked at Rob, he could see him trying not to a grin.

"Come on," Rob said. "I gotta go. Drive me home—I mean to the place where I live."

The snow storm had subsided leaving the lawns and sidewalks white and sparkling. They drove off the main streets and zigzagged through residential areas finding untravelled streets on which to leave their own virginal tracks in the snow. When they arrived at Rob's, Craig did not turn off the engine.

"Coming in?" Rob asked.

"Uhn-uhn," Craig replied, shaking his head. "You've got too much to tell Donna. She won't want me hanging around, butting in."

"You're probably right," Rob said with a sigh but not moving. "I guess I'll be around home quite a bit helping them get sorted out and packed. I gotta pack my own stuff too and get it over to your place."

"Yeah, okay."

"I don't think Donna will come and help. She doesn't really like parents, you know. I guess because of the way her parents treated her. I tried to get her to go with me to meet Mom and Dad but she never wants to go."

They were quiet for a minute.

"It sure would have been easier if I could have moved in with you," Rob said.

"Yeah, that would have been great. You still can," Craig added casually, but hopefully.

"No, I can't," Rob said, opening the car door. "Goodnight, buddy." His voice was gruff. Then added, with his usual escaping flippancy, "Get this heap washed, it's filthy. I hate riding in dirty cars."

Craig drove home by the shortest route. The roads were well marked and sloppy. The lawns were not as sparkling as they had been half an hour ago. The house seemed cold and depressingly quiet, and he suddenly felt very lonely. Sleep did not come easily and he wakened twice during the night, thinking he had heard Rob open the back door and call him.

CHAPTER 52

On Friday, Dr. Strawburn visited Marion on his morning rounds asking routine questions and spending a lot of time pulling his lower lip and nodding. Finally he said, "The rest home in White Rock I spoke to you about can admit you tomorrow. You will enjoy it there. It is very quiet and the staff is well trained. I expect either Edith or Craig can drive you or would you like me to make other arrangements?"

"You mean an ambulance?"

"Yes, but it is not covered by your health plan."

"Well, good heavens," she said briskly. "I certainly don't need an ambulance. One of my children can drive me or I can drive myself."

"No, I don't think that would be wise. You think about it. I'll sign your discharge and you can pick it up at the desk." He stood looking at her for a minute, still pulling at his lips and nodding. "Yes," he said, as if he had made a decision. "Right! I'll see you on..." He pulled a well-thumbed diary from his pocket and, after very deliberate consultation, continued, "...Wednesday. Yes, that will give you time to settle in. Wednesday is my usual day out there. In the afternoon." He pulled back a curtain and disappeared and she could hear him shuffle out of the room.

She stayed sitting up in bed puzzling about what she should do next and suddenly noticed that she was not upset. With that, she got out of bed and went down the hall to the public telephone, pleased, as she looked at the thin shanks of an old man in a short hospital gown who was wheezing and coughing into the phone, that she had her own dressing gown. The old man finished but stood, with the receiver in his hand, trying to explain something to her and only stopped when the shrill sound for 'receiver off the hook' startled him and he handed it to her and turned away.

She wiped the mouthpiece and dialled Edith's number, she wondered anxiously if all the people in the rest home would be like him. I don't think I could stand that she decided, just as Edith shrilled her abrupt greeting into the phone.

"Good morning, Edie," she said.

"Oh hi, Mom!" came the quick response as she launched into the details of her day. "Isn't this the most gruesome day? Or is it not raining cats and dogs in there? The girls haven't been out of the house for two days and they are getting snarly with each other and I've simply got to get out and do some shopping, but I hate to leave Harvey with them. His cold turned into the flu, I think. They say it's a new bug and if you get it you just have to stay in bed and suffer until it's gone."

"Edith," Marion interrupted. "Dr. Strawburn is discharging me today and I'm going to have to get out to White Rock to the rest home there."

"That's great, Mom," Edith said, somewhat more cautiously than enthusiastically. "I didn't think you'd be going so soon."

"Well, I'd rather go right away than be cooped up here. I'm not sick, you know."

"I know, but..."

"Well here's what I want you to do," Marion interrupted before Edith could get into gear. "See if one of your friends can take the children—Harvey will be alright, probably better with some peace and quiet—and you come in and get me from the hospital and take me out to White Rock, but I'll have to go home first and get some clothes to take with me."

"Mom, I can't do that. It will take all day! Can't Craig do it?"

"Craig is working, you know!" she said sharply.

"Yes, I know. But I don't think I could find somebody on such short notice, really, Mom. And I hate to leave Harv—he's really sick, coughing up junk and he's got a fever. I wouldn't like to ask anybody to come in and catch his bug. Mom? Why don't you take a taxi?"

"Edith, I've got two children, one of whom I hoped would put herself out a little to bring her mother home from the hospital. I also have my own car, only you have it, otherwise I'd struggle along on my own."

"I know, Mom! I'm sorry! But I can't seem to think of a way..." Edith wailed.

"Alright, then listen to me. I would take a taxi except I don't have any day clothes. Now you've surely got a friend out there who has a car and might do you a favour. You bring my car in and get your friend to come to drive you home. You can come straight to the hospital and I'll drive home. I don't mind driving home in my own car in my dressing gown, but I am not going to get into a taxi."

"Maybe if I phoned Craig at work..." Edith ventured.

"No! Edith," Marion said, surprised at herself that she was dealing with this situation without breaking into tears. "I think the responsibility is yours. Do you know that Craig has been in to see me almost every day? Do you know that you have only come in to see me once, and I gave you my car so that you could come in and see me occasionally? So I am expecting you today, Edith."

"Let me phone you back, Mom."

"You can't phone me back. I don't have a phone."

"Well, couldn't I phone the nurses' station and they could go and get you."

"Edith! This is a hospital, not a hotel."

"I know, Mom, but surely... Alright," she finished in defeat. "I'll be there as soon as I can." She hung up abruptly and Marion sighed, and said, "Children!" in a tone of exasperation to two women standing near waiting for the phone.

She walked back to her room with a good, firm stride, pleased with herself that she had dealt with a problem without thinking the world was coming to an end. A nurse came into the room with a tray of charts and instruments. "Good morning, Mrs. Williams," she said. "You feeling pretty chipper today?"

"What do you mean, nurse?"

"Oh, I heard you on the telephone—I wasn't listening on purpose, I couldn't help hearing."

"Oh, that!" she laughed. "My daughter sometimes thinks she can manipulate me."

"You certainly sounded spunky," the nurse said, smiling. "Pop up on the bed and relax now. I'll take your blood pressure and temperature in a minute." She stopped before going on to the next bed and made a short note on a chart.

I was spunky, Marion declared to herself. Last week I would have been in tears. Maybe I don't need to go out to that rest home. Maybe it's time I stopped feeling sorry for myself. So what if Tom dumped me just because I told that Eleanor Colman what I thought of her. She deserved it.

"Now then," the nurse said, returning to the bedside. "We'll just get these things done for the last time. It will be the last time, Mrs. Williams. Dr. Strawburn discharged you either today or tomorrow, but the hospital requires a definite date so that someone else can be admitted." She shoved a thermometer in Marion's mouth, and picked up her wrist. "So," she continued after thirty seconds while wrapping her upper arm in the blood pressure cuff, "when I overheard you making arrangements with your daughter to pick you up to-day, we started the discharge procedure." She put the earphones in her ear and listened intently. "Good!" she said. "Everything's as right as rain. Oh, I should remember not to say that. I'm from Saskatchewan and rain is accepted as a blessing there, not as a curse." She put her instruments on the cart and started for the door. "Now you just call me when you're ready to leave and we'll get you signed out."

She was back in the room within five minutes. "There's a young man out here who insists on seeing you. He says he is not a relative but you found him under the Christmas tree so he belongs to you. What shall I do with him?" She could hardly talk for the big smile on her face.

"Robbie!" she exclaimed. "Oh, let him come in, please!"

She heard the nurse say something outside the door and then Rob came in, grinning widely as if he had pulled a good one on somebody.

"U.U," he cried. "Here I am, all ready with hugs and kisses and cuddles to make you better, and they tell me you are leaving. What shall I do with all this affection? You're not in need, are you nurse?" He leered at her and took a step toward her.

"One step more, mister, and I'll have you arrested for not wearing your clown suit," she laughed as she left.

"Robbie!" Marion exclaimed, her face alight as she put her arms out to him. "I'm so glad to see you!"

They walked together arm in arm down the hall to a small sitting area, and sitting side by side, he told her about Donna, his job and the sale of the family home and business. She told him only that things had been pressing in on her until she had to get some help and that she thought she was all better now. She noted, at some point as they talked, that Rob had said nothing about Craig and hoped that it didn't mean anything, but dared not ask, and as they continued talking, that little anxiety slipped away.

Finally, Rob looked at his watch. "Worktime, U.U.," he said. "I gotta go to the sweatshop. So, fare thee well, my lovely one."

"Must you go, my prince?"

"Ah, yes! I must away. I have a woman who demands to be kept in minks and pearls," he said, giving her some Groucho Marx eyebrows. Then, as she stood up, he wrapped her in his arms, kissed her forehead, then on both cheeks, and said, "See, I do the French stuff too," as he walked away with a wave.

She watched him go with tears in her eyes, not minding them, because for the first time in weeks, they were lovely tears of happiness.

As she walked back to her room, a nurse said as she passed by the station, "He's quite a guy, that Christmas boy of yours."

"Yes, isn't he?" Marion said in smiling agreement.

"Oh, by the way, your daughter called to ask us to tell you that she was go-ing to feed the twins and her husband and put the twins down for their nap and that she and a friend would leave—in separate cars, I think she said—about quarter to one which would get them here before two. She might have said more, but that's the gist of it."

"Thank you, nurse. I asked her not to bother you with messages, but…" she shrugged. Even second-hand, Edith had managed to douse the spark that Rob had left.

"No problem, Mrs. Williams," the nurse said.

Marion busied herself getting her few things together and packing her little bag, while leaving out enough clothes to be warm on the way home. Why should I care if I have to go home in my dressing gown, she told herself. They always take you to the front entrance in a wheel chair and all I have to do is step into the car. I should phone Craig and leave a message—no, I better wait and phone him from home just in case Edith…

Lunch came as usual earlier than her need for food demanded but she ate it all, then worried for the first time in a long time about her weight. After lunch, she went down the hall and weighed herself and came back to her room happy with the result. She would have liked a full length mirror to check visually against an acceptable weight loss, but that could wait until she got home. Sitting in her chair beside her bed, waiting for Edith, she tried not to fidget. She checked her nails and decided that if she filed them any more, she would be down to the quick. The Reader's Digest on her night table was old and fat-leafed with licked finger turning but she picked it up in order to do something—anything—that would quell a rising panic. I can't let myself get upset. I won't! She told her self. When Edith gets here, I am going home and I am going to phone Dr. Strawburn and tell him to tell the White Rock place that I'm not going, and I'm going to get a message to Craig to say that I've come home. And I'm going to cook supper for Craig—Edith won't stay, I know that. Maybe if I call Claudia she can pop over and we can catch up. I'll bet the house is a mess. The whole house will probably look like Craig's room. I'll have to do a lot of house cleaning, so I'll phone the cleaning woman who came in the spring when my elbow was hurting so much I could hardly lift my arm. Now, where in the name of goodness, is Edith. It's after two already. If she doesn't come, then I don't know what I'll do. And the feeling of disquiet and panic that she had been living with in the past weeks began to emerge again just as Edith walked in the door.

"Oh, Edith!" she exclaimed, getting up from her chair and going to Edith with her arms out, "Good! You're right on time." She gave her daughter a hug but somehow it was like embracing a picket fence. How is it that Robbie knows how to hug and Edith doesn't, she thought.

"Well, let me tell you it was a rush, what with getting the girls their lunch and putting them down early so that Harvey wouldn't have to get up to them. He's very sick, you know. I shouldn't really have left him. But I see the nurse gave you my message. She was very snippy on the phone. You'd think I was asking a great big favour, to walk twenty steps to your room with a simple message. Twenty steps—I counted them. Are you ready?"

"Yes, all ready," Marion said, trying to keep her voice light and pleasant.

"I think I just have to sign something at the desk and that's all. Where's your friend who's going to drive you back?"

"She's down in the cafeteria getting some lunch. We had to rush away and she was starving. When she's finished she'll drive right to your place and then we can head for home. If we hurry, we can beat the traffic. Is this where you sign out?" Her voice was distinctly loud, but the nurse at the desk finished what she was doing before turning to Marion. Edith was on simmer, and Marion hoped she wouldn't make a fuss.

"All ready, Mrs. Williams? Well, then," she looked at her watch and marked the time on her chart, "just one minute while I get a chair."

She walked down the hall to another nursing station and started back with a wheel chair but stopped and had a brief conversation with another nurse that started Edith fuming.

"Now what!" Edith said in exasperation, and Marion could feel her control slipping but said nothing.

The nurse returned in a moment with a smile, saying as she approached, "I know what you are going to say. Every patient says it when they are discharged: 'Why do I have to use a chair?'. It's the rules, Mrs. Williams. And ours not to reason why, but maybe someday we should. Now you've got your pills and everything from your closet?" she asked as she tucked a blanket around her, and Marion nodded. She kept on chattering as they went down the hall and into the elevator. "Is your car close by," she asked Edith, finally recognizing Edith's existence.

"It's in the front lot," Edith said abruptly.

"Have you the correct change for the gate?" the nurse asked.

Edith opened her purse and rummaged in one of the compartments.

"Four quarters," the nurse said, and waited, the embodiment of patience. "The gift shop will make change."

She chatted with Marion as Edith went off to the gift shop and rushed by on her way to the car. "I hope you like the rest home," she said to Marion. "I don't know it, but one of the other nurses said that it is a lovely home."

Marion said nothing. She didn't want a lecture on doing what the doctor ordered.

The nurse didn't notice her silence. "I've only been out here a month—but I love it. I can't wait for the skiing to open," she continued. "Is that your daughter's car at the door? I can see someone waving but the windows are all fogged up."

Edith came rushing in the door. "Stupid people!" she fumed. "Imagine getting into the gate line-up without having the right change. Ready?" she asked the nurse.

"This is as far as I go," the nurse said, taking the blanket off and withdrawing the wheel chair as Marion stood up. "Now, take care, Mrs. Williams. Lots of rest and relaxation. Bye-bye."

"Snotty bitch," Edith said. "She might have wheeled you out to the car so you wouldn't have to wander out in your nightie."

"I imagine there are rules, Edith," Marion said, determinedly patient but anxious to get home.

On the way, Marion said, "There's been a change of plans. I don't have to go to the rest home, after all." She thought that Edith would be so pleased not to have to drive her out to White Rock that she would not question the change in plans or suspect a lie from her mother.

"You don't? Oh, that's marvellous. I was beginning to wonder how we could ever have time for you to change and pack a suitcase and get out there—well, there just wasn't going to be time. So I was going to suggest that I could leave after I took you home and you could get ready to go and then Craig could drive you out when you were ready."

"Well, none of that is necessary. I'm not going."

Edith glanced at her sideways. "Is that the doctor's idea?"

"No, it's my own. I don't want to go and I don't need to."

Edith was silent. "I guess if you're sure then... It's certainly makes my day less complicated," she said with relief in her voice. Marion knew that the matter would be dropped and that Edith would not try to persuade her to follow the doctor's orders.

Marion had her keys out ready to open the front door as Edith pulled up to the house. "She should be here, by now," Edith muttered as she looked up and down the street for her friend's car. "I hope she hasn't got herself lost. She's not very reliable, you know."

"I'm sure she'll be along in a minute," Marion said as she went inside. "Oh, it is so nice to be home. You wouldn't believe it, Edith."

"Oh, I can believe it," Edith said as she watched out the window. "I'd sure like to be home right now."

Marion sank into a chair, trying to conceal her irritation. Watch it, she told herself. You knew it would be touch and go with Edith. You could have phoned Claudia. You should have phoned Claudia.

Her discussion with herself ended with a shout from Edith. "Here she is," she announced as she rushed to the front door and made signals. "Now Mom, you take care and don't overdo it," she said and put her arms out to give an awkward hug and kiss on the cheek to her mother who had started to get up. "Stay there, don't get up!" Edith said. "I've got to run. We've got to beat the rush hour traffic or it will take forever."

"Aren't you going to ask your friend to come in?" Marion said.

"No time, Mom. I've got to get home."

"Well, tell her thanks for me. It was very kind of her to drive all the way in from Abbotsford for a stranger. And thank you, Edith. It was so much nicer coming home with a daughter who cares instead of in a taxi."

"You're welcome, Mom," Edith said but she looked rather quizzically at her mother who maintained an impassive face.

As the door closed, Marion sank back in the chair and gave a big sigh. My, you look well, Mother! Thank you for the car, Mother! Sorry I couldn't get in to see you more often, Mother. Is there anything I can do for you before I go, Mother. She wanted to give another big sigh, but stopped herself, saying, C'mon woman! You made your decisions—now do something! And stop sighing!

She got up to look out at the soggy November day and saw Edith talking animatedly to her friend before they drove away and then noticed her own car at the curb. Damn! she said. Edith forgot to leave the keys and I forget where the extra keys are. Craig will know.

She went upstairs and washed and put on a pant suit and redid her makeup. Then, feeling much better, she phoned Dr. Strawburn.

"Doctor's not available at the moment," the receptionist said.

"Please ask him to call me," she gave her name and number slowly, "and tell him that I have decided not to go to the rest home in White Rock."

"Very well, Mrs. Williams. I'm sure Doctor wants to talk to you about it before you make up your mind."

"Perhaps you didn't understand my message," Marion said. "I have decided not to go. I have made up my mind. But I would like him to call, because I want to thank him for his kindness and his attention over the past while."

"Very well, Mrs. Williams. I will relay that message to Doctor."

Why does she always talk like she's balancing a crown on her head? Marion mused as she hung up.

Next she phoned the cleaning woman who said she would have a whole day free, not tomorrow but the next day. Then she checked the frig and the freezer and decided she could rustle up a dinner. Finally, with her heart thumping, she phoned Craig's workplace and asked if she could leave a message for him. The message was simply: Your mother came home from the hospital this afternoon.

"Oh, that's wonderful, Mrs. Williams. He'll be so glad to hear that. Are you sure you don't want to hang on and I'll go out to the plant and find him and you can tell him yourself?

"That's very kind of you, but no, thank you. There's much more to tell him, but it can wait as long as he knows I'm home."

"Well, I don't think good news should wait. I think I'll go find him right now and tell him. Is that all right?"

"I don't think I could stop you, dear." Marion said, laughing. Marion busied herself with a general tidying up without getting serious about dustballs and finger prints. She found things in the cupboard that a man would not recognize as food and, bustling around the kitchen and enjoying it, she produced a meal that she could put in the oven and have ready in time for Craig's arrival home. Then she phoned Claudia who answered on the first ring.

"Marion!," Claudia cried happily. "I had the phone in my hand to call you. Rob said you were coming home today and I've been phoning every half hour or so hoping to catch you in. How are you, dear?"

"Fine, but a little pooped. Edith just dropped me off," Marion said, knowing that Claudia would read between the lines.

"I'm know. I'm sorry I didn't get over to see you but things are hectic. May I come over now and help you pack for the rest home?"

"Thanks, Claudia, but I'm not going."

"You're not?"

"No. After Robbie came to visit me, I decided I wouldn't go. It was like he gave me a booster shot of life and we talked and laughed and I just decided I didn't need to go to a place where there are a bunch of old, depressed people. So I'm not going."

"The kid has a lot of charm if I do say so myself. And he really does love you a lot. I'm glad I'm not a jealous person."

"So am I," Marion said. "Claudia, I'm tidying up a bit and getting dinner for Craig so we can have an evening together. How about I come over for morning coffee before I go shopping and we can catch up on everything and everybody?"

"Great, Marion. I'll put on a big pot. Oh, it's nice to have you back!"

She was just about to go into the living room and turn on the five o'clock news when Craig thumped up the steps and burst into the house. "Mom! You're home!," he exclaimed wrapping his arms around her, still in his wet work coat. "I couldn't believe it when I got the message at work."

"Craig! You're soaking me," she said, laughing and pushing him gently away. "Take off that wet coat—no, don't! Put my car in the garage for me first, please. Edith took the keys with her by mistake and I don't know where the other set is—do you?"

"Yeah, but how did you get home?"

"I'll tell you all about it after. Put the car away and get out of those wet clothes."

He walked over to the key rack on the wall and took down a pair of keys with a tag marked 'Buick' and dangled them with a grin in front of her face.

"So I forgot," she said, unembarrassed. "Lock me up for getting old."

He disappeared and came back into the warm house that smelled of dinner cooking and hung his wet jacket in the stair well. "Now I'm dry," he said. "Can I give you a proper welcome home or do I have to wash my hands first."

"Never mind washing," she said, going to him and snuggling against him. "I've seen dirty hands before."

They held each other for a long, quiet minute and then by some signal parted and started talking. She told him about the doctor's arrangements for her to go to a rest home in White Rock, about Rob's visit, and her struggle to get Edith to come into town and drive her home and leave the car for her. Dinner was ready and she took it up while he washed and changed his work shirt for a clean sweat shirt. They talked throughout dinner and the joint clearing up. They talked about his job, his car, the Koskis, the special job Carl had set out for him, and they talked about the Turner's and how their lives would change when they were gone. And they talked about Rob and Donna and she could see the hurt in her son's eyes as they talked of Rob and she wondered if there had been a falling out between them but could not ask.

Finally, all talked out, she pleaded legitimate fatigue from her long day and went upstairs to bed. She sank into the luxury of her own bed and dropped easily into a deep and restful sleep. Craig stayed up with the television on, paying little attention to it, until he yawned several times, locked the doors and went to bed. He wrestled with sleep for a while, thinking how great it would be if Rob got a telephone so they could touch bases more easily.

In their little apartment, Rob and Donna were talking. Even though both the Lesserets were slightly deaf and Wally had his TV on they kept their voices low.

"I don't like it, Donna. I don't trust him."

The person they were talking about was Vic. Both of them had gone to school with him before he quit after he was kicked out and Donna had been one of Vic's 'gang' and had double dated him a few times before going out with him steady, an agreement that only lasted a month. But now Vic had come back into her life.

He had come in for lunch three times, each time when the lunch rush was nearly over. "Hey, Donna," he said on the third time, "you can't be making much here. How'd you like to make some extra cash?"

"What have you got in mind, Vic?" cautiously, knowing he was a bit twisty.

"I'll pick you up when you get your break—say 2:30. How's that? It's sorta private so we can't talk here," he said quietly.

"Okay," she had answered lightly. "What the hell!"

Now she was telling Rob what had happened. Vic had picked her up and they parked in an outdoor parking lot without getting out of the car. He told her that every time he was in the cafe for lunch he would leave a key along with the tip. She was to say nothing about it to anybody and if anybody found it she should just say I'll give it to him next time.

"The key fits a locker at the bus station, and I'm supposed to go there and pick up a package and take it to...you know that donut place on Robson with the huge great donut sign hanging up in front?"

"Yeah, I know it," Rob said cautiously, wondering what was coming next.

"Well, I'm supposed to take it to Apartment Number 1 above the donut shop right away. He said there are only two apartments, so I can't make a mistake."

"So what's in the package?"

"That's what I asked and he said 'Don't ask'."

"How big is it going to be?"

"He told me it would fit into my purse, but maybe I should get one that's a little bigger."

"Jesus, Donna!" Rob exploded. "You know what you're into, don't you? You'd be peddling drugs."

"I know it. But it's a chance to make a little easy money. and we could use it."

"I don't get it! What do you do with the package? Where's the easy money? Are you supposed to peddle it and split with him?"

"No, there's supposed to be a sticker on the package with a price on it.

Whoever comes to the door will recognize the package and I'm not to hand it over until they pay whatever the sticker says, 50, 60, 70 dollars, maybe more and that will be mine."

"Yours?"

"Yes, but I also have to get an envelope before I hand over the package and I have to go quickly back to the bus station and put it in another locker and then Vic will be waiting for me across the street from the cafe and I'll give him the key. Now, that's an easy way to make a few bucks for Christmas, isn't it?"

Rob was pacing with a frown darkening his face. "I don't like it," he growled. "I don't trust that stuck-up, smirking smart-ass SOB at all, at all!"

"Oh, come on, Rob. It's just for kicks—just to get a little fun money."

"You know it's not going to be pot, don't you? It's going to bethe hard stuff—coke, probably or something like that. Jesus, if you're caught with that, they'll throw the book at you!"

"How could they catch me? I pick it up and it takes fifteen minutes at the most to get over to Robson and back. Come on! Rob," she pleaded. "Let's live a little!. Let's have a little fun!"

"Okay," he said reluctantly. "A couple of times. But you'll have to be careful. And what's in the envelope, by the way?"

"I don't know. I just put it in another locker then I give Vic the key. Maybe there's nothing in it. I figured it was just their way of making sure I delivered the package and not run off with it. Some sort of code, I guess."

"Jeez, Donna! You gotta be careful! I don't like it!"

"You're beginning to sound like grandpa Craig," she said with a pouty face.

"What do you mean by that?"

"Nothing," she replied and went to bed mad.

CHAPTER 53

Claudia and Marion were tucked into fat chairs on either side of a winter fire that was burning down to red coals and hot enough for them to keep their legs tucked up out of the blast. It was the kind of late November day that needed that kind of fire, nothing but drizzle and low, heavy clouds. They had talked through two cups of coffee. Children, grandchildren and sons-in-law had all been covered as a social exercise before they got down to the nitty-gritty of Marion's breakdown and the reasons for it. With such an old friend as Claudia, Marion found it easy to talk about her sudden need to acknowledge to herself that Gerry was, and always had been, a selfish, conceited, demanding person who was incapable of loving. She talked about her affair with Tom and the exciting realization that she was suddenly responsive in a sexual relationship. It was the malicious and insidious business of the phoney will that upset what precarious mental balance she had had. There was no way that she could understand how he could have hated her so much for so long. "Oh, there was something else, too, if I am going to be honest with you. I flared up at Eleanor Colman and Tom got rude and angry with me. Tom had just moved into the same building where she lived and either she was on the make for him or vice versa. I don't care which it was, it was just too much for me to stomach and I'm sorry because he was a gentle, friendly guy with a good sense of humor—something I needed after Gerry."

She stopped for a moment and felt her eyes getting moist so she changed her position in the chair and plumped a couple of cushions while telling herself, "Get on with it, Marion." And she did. Claudia watched sympathetically and made no comment.

"And that thing about the tumor being the cause of everything that went on in his life is just something I won't ever accept. Nobody will ever make me believe that everything he did, all the cold, callous, deliberate, hurtful things, all his womanizing, all the things he did to Edith as a child, and to Craig, and the drinking, and everything else was caused by a tumor. The fact is, Claudia—and it hurt me terribly to realize I had been so stupid not to see it right from the very beginning—he was a tall, trim, well-groomed, tidy, handsome piece of shit! I think I had a breakdown, not because of how he treated me, but because I made myself deliberately blind to his defects and made myself believe that I was the one who was weak and wrong."

She stopped talking for a minute while Claudia busied herself with the fire. "I just realized, Claudia, that this is the first time I have talked about it without blubbering and wailing. That must mean something."

"Probably means that you're over your breakdown and ready to take charge of your life again," Claudia said. "How's that for an Ann Landers answer?"

"You could start charging," Marion said, smiling.

They were quiet for a minute, watching the fire and sipping their coffee. Finally, Marion said, "Claudia, there is something I have to ask you to set my mind at ease. Please tell me if I'm out of line for asking. Did Gerry ever molest Beverley?"

"I had the feeling that you would want to ask that. The plain straight truth is No! You see, Glen never really liked Gerry but didn't know why and then when he noticed Gerry eyeing Bev in a lecherous way and finally, after I told him Gerry had made a couple of passes at me, we decided to cool it. We knew we could never split up the boys, and Bev and Edith were never that chummy, so we found excuses to avoid the foursome events and the family cookouts and things like that. I was afraid it might hurt our friendship but I had to chance it."

"I was hurt for a while when I became aware that our families were drifting apart," Marion said, "but then I realized that the boys remained as close as they ever had ever been and I never felt that you had changed. But I never knew that Gerry was the real reason for the rift." She shook her head. "I should have. I was so blind."

They were quiet for a minute, both staring reflectively into the fire and, with the intuitive understanding that is part of an intimate friendship, put aside that topic and went on to other things.

"Oh, I am going to miss you, Claudia. It will never seem the same without you around the corner. When are you leaving?"

"We were going as soon as we could get packed because the publisher of the paper wanted Glen right away. But we hit a couple of snags. Roger Todd is being financed from his father's estate and apparently he's having a little difficulty with the trust company because he already got some money from the estate and messed up somehow. So he's got to find half the mortgage money elsewhere and they'll put up the other half, but only if he gets a commitment from us that we will stay and help him get started. They said two months and we said 'no deal' and settled on January the first. If he has any sense he would offer Rob a job."

"Craig said that Rob is definitely not going. Is that the way things stand?"

"Seems so," Claudia said sadly. "I guess it's more like the nest being thrown out rather than the chick leaving the nest."

"Well, I suppose it has to happen, doesn't it? But they seem so young."

Claudia nodded and said nothing.

"Does Roger Todd know anything about the business?" Marion finally asked.

"Not much. He's pretty naive. I think he's a spoiled little rich boy who is running away from a failed marriage and thinks the idea of living in Vancouver and skiing all winter is going to be just great! I'll tell you how naive he is—he accepted our asking price without making a counter offer and we had upped it considerably from the market value."

"Really!" she said disbelievingly. "Where's Glen today?"

"He flew up to Prince George to talk with the publisher and he might stay over a day to check out the real estate situation. But I made him promise me not to get excited about anything until I saw it! This time I want a real house with a front door that leads into the living room not onto a bunch of printing machines. And a garden! Oh, how I have envied you your garden!"

"Speaking of gardens, I do wish this rain would stop. There is so much I want to get done in my garden. Craig did some but only the obvious things. But right now I've got to go shopping instead. My cupboards are bare. Do you want to go shopping?"

"I do but I can't. I promised Glen I'd set Roger Todd up on a couple of machines and keep an eye on him. He was supposed to be here at 8:30, and what is it now? Ten past eleven. He's going to be a roaring success in business." They laughed together.

"How old is he?" Marion asked, getting up to go.

"Thirty or so."

"And you're going to call Roger Todd, like a nice mummy, and tell him he's late for work. Aren't you?"

"I certainly am not!" And they touched cheeks in goodbye.

***

Craig was busy at the shipping desk when Carl stopped to talk. "Glad to hear your mother is home from the hospital. No more bachelor meals for you, eh? I'll bet you're tired of your own cooking."

"I didn't do too bad," Craig said smiling, "if you like fried greasy stuff. My Home Ec teacher would have given me an F."

"How's your computer project coming along?"

"I think I've done as much as I can. I sorted it out on the weekend and I thought I should see you today and show you what I've done."

"Okay," Carl said. "How about two o'clock? How long will it take?"

"I don't know, Carl—maybe an hour, maybe less."

"OK. I'll tell Larry where you'll be." He turned to go, then stopped and said, "What's this stuff about sorting it out on the weekend? I thought I said that only the boss works on weekends and I'm the boss."

Craig reddened. "I know," he said. "But I had seen all the computer people on my list and I had to put it together and I felt kind of funny going into the office to do it, so I just worked Friday afternoon and decided to do it at home. But I did leave early when I got a message that my mother was out of the hospital. I told Larry about it."

Carl suppressed a smile. "Okay, see you at two."

At two o'clock Craig went to his locker and picked up the notes he kept in a used 8x11 manila envelope addressed to his mother and went to the office. He was waiting for the girl nearest the counter to finish on the telephone when Carl looked up over his glasses through the open door of his office, and shouted, "Come in, Craig."

"Let's look at it over here," he said, getting up from his desk and pulling up a door sized piece of plywood hinged to the wall. He hooked his desk chair with his foot and rolled it over and pointed to another chair for Craig. He noted with approval the unpretentious re-use of the envelope as Craig extracted a sheaf of lined, loose-leaf papers with handwritten notes and handed them to him.

"First, tell me what your plan was," Carl said, shoving the papers to one side. "Then we'll go over your notes together. First of all, how did you select these particular companies?"

"There were so many I just decided to go through the Yellow Pages and not bother with the big companies, so I stuck with the local independents."

"Good move," Carl said, nodding approvingly.

"There were some that were very specialized so I didn't bother with them, and," Craig said with a smile, "I didn't bother with a couple of them who were offhand with me, maybe because my voice still sounds—well, sorta young."

"They'll never know they might have missed a big sale, will they?" Carl said, chuckling.

"Anyway, these are the ones I ended up with. I thought a local company would be good in case of problems."

Carl nodded as he shuffled quickly through the papers. Each one gave the name, address and telephone number and the name of the representative Craig had talked with, the computers each company sold, the computer recommended and other information, ending with a range of costs for hardware, software, setting up programs appropriate for the business, and other items.

"I couldn't answer a lot of their questions, but I figured they could ask you later. Oh, one thing I should tell you because I thought it was funny. One of them said there didn't seem to be anything erotic about the company so there shouldn't be any big problems with programs. That sorta puzzled me because I was sure he said erotic, so I searched around when I got home and I guess he meant to say 'esoteric'. I'm glad I didn't get into a discussion about it with him." He was grinning widely.

Carl heard it with a smile, and then leaned back in his swivel chair and laughed so heartily his belly jiggled. Two of the women in the office stopped working and listened with pleasure to the sound of Carl laughing again, something they hadn't heard since the death of his son.

CHAPTER 54

Last Thursday, while Marion's bridge group was meeting, she had phoned in the middle of the game and they had passed the phone around so she had a quick chat with all seven of them. She was delighted that they had not invited Tracy Connish back to fill in. For the last few weeks when Marion had been unable to play, the dummy of the foursome moved to the other table for the bidding and they had had some hilarious and some confusing games. They were all warmly delighted to hear from her and happily anxious for her return. Marion extracted a promise from them that next week's game would be at her place.

Now it was Wednesday of the first week in December and she had been home almost two weeks. Today the radio played Christmas music endlessly as she got ready for her Thursday group, just as it had in the stores yesterday when she had to shop again because earlier she had not thought to buy the kinds of things she wanted to put out for her group. She had phoned Edith and settled that they would come for Xmas, so there would be just the six of them. Enough, she thought, just us six, but I would have had Robbie and Donna if Claudia and Glen had moved to Prince George as they had originally planned.

On Monday, Glen had gone to Prince George again and had phoned home with exciting news about the perfect house he had found. He could not conceal his concern that the house would be gone unless they moved quickly. They decided that Claudia would have to leave Roger on his own and she would fly up the next day and meet him. They had arrived home this morning, bouncing like teenagers, called Beverley and then Marion but wouldn't tell Marion anything unless she came right over. She put on her coat and dashed and was met, breathless at the door by an equally breathless Claudia who said, beaming with delight, "We bought a house!" and proceeded, with excited interruptions from Glen to tell her all about it.

"Three bedrooms, and the master bedroom is huge and its bathroom and dressing room are just about as big! And there's another bathroom upstairs and a lav downstairs and another one in the basement off a rumpus room. And it's only three years old and it has new carpets all over. Brand new! Imagine! And you wouldn't believe the cupboards in the kitchen! And all the appliances go with it! Only three years old! I'll bet mine are thirty years old. And there's one of those barbecue things with a fan built into the kitchen counter so that Glen can barbecue all winter long without going outside."

"Who? Me?" Glen said, smiling and picking up the refrain to let Claudia catch her breath. "And there's a hot tub on the sundeck, but it's not operating now. But it will be great in the summer."

Claudia jumped in again. "Marion, it's on a south slope and I can have a garden and there's a nice market about three blocks away. And the bus stop is right there by the market and Glen can take the bus to work if he wants to. Oh, I have to pinch myself to believe it. I wish Rob would get a phone soon." She paused and blew a big breath. "I'll put on some coffee," she said and left for the kitchen.

"I think I'm going to have a party," Marion announced suddenly. "It will be a combined New Years Eve party and a going away party for you, and you have to do the invitations—whoever you want, because it's your party—but not more than twenty."

"Oh, Marion," Claudia said, her face glowing, "that would be wonderful! But should you, it's a lot of work for you."

"Not a bit, I'll lasso somebody in to help, you can bet on that."

"It's a great idea, Marion. But, Claudia," Glen demurred, "it might make us late. We promised to be there on the first."

"It will work out, dear," Claudia assured him. "The first is on Saturday so we will have two days. You drove it in one day, didn't you?"

"Yes, but the roads were bare."

"Come on, you old stick-in-the-mud. Tell Marion its okay."

Glen grinned. "It's more than okay—it's a wonderful idea. Thank you, Marion."

"Great!" Marion said, getting to her feet. "Oh, this is going to be a really good party. But I feel all mixed up—celebrating you going out of my life."

"It's not the end, Marion," Claudia said, moving over to put her arms around her. "I know we won't be able to throw on a sweater and dash over. But there are telephones, letters, buses, airplanes, trains... Have you forgotten that you traded in your covered wagon?"

"I know, I know!" Marion said as she turned to hug Glen. "But I tell you, you're taking a big chunk out of my life. And I don't think I want to fill the space you leave with anyone else. So," she finished, "I've got to go. Excuse me if I don't stay for coffee but I've got Xmas shopping to do and a big party to plan. You give me the list, Claudia, and I'll do the phoning—but soon! Lots of people may have made New Years Eve plans already." She stopped at the door, "I forgot to ask. What about Christmas?"

"We're going to Bev and Richard's."

"Good, I thought you would be. Rob, too?"

"I suppose so but I haven't seen him yet. But, oh yes! I'm sure he will. It might be our last family Christmas for a while."

***

Rob and Donna were having a coffee together at the counter before her noon hour rush started. It was Rob's morning off and he wasn't due in for work until two. He had promised Donna that he would do the laundry today and she had already sorted it out into darks and lights because she didn't trust him. He had put on a load of lights and decided to go over to see Donna and call home from the diner. She got up to wait on a customer and he went to the phone in the corner. When she returned to her coffee, she twisted on the counter stool so she could watch him on the phone. He stood, lank and dark, leaning against the wall while he talked, looking as though he had extra joints in his body, his face displaying changing emotions as he talked and listened. He scratched his crotch unconsciously, looked straight at her without seeing her and waved his arms in extravagant gestures as he talked to the floor and the ceiling and the cars passing by. Finally, he came back to the counter and announced, smiling happily, "That was my Mom. They went up to Prince George and they bought a house and she was telling me all about it. She's pretty excited—so is Dad, she says. And...Guess what? We're invited to Bev's for Christmas! Isn't that great?" Donna's face did not register either enthusiasm or indifference, and he went on. "Craig's mom is having a New Years Eve going away party for them and we're invited. It won't shake the pictures off the wall but I got to go. Okay?" he asked with a big happy grin.

Donna listened without a change of expression and got up and cleared away their cups as some customers came in. "I guess so," she said with a shrug.

"Well, would you rather do something else?" he asked, taken aback by her indifference.

"No," she said. "I just think Christmas is a bore."

Before they could say anything further, more customers came in and Donna was immediately busy. He left, catching her eye with a little wave, and walked home to finish the laundry, feeling blue.

***

Carl and Craig had had two meetings together to talk about the computer companies Craig had made notes on. Carl was certain in his own mind that a computer would be a useful investment for his company because every other business man he had talked to kept telling him that they didn't know how they ever managed before. His trouble was that he knew nothing about computers except that they could be made to perform a function in split seconds that would take an ordinary mortal hours. But he did know that running a company required a lot of tedious and meticulous work involving inventory, sales, personnel records, payroll and other things that a machine should be able to do. Craig had a reasonable understanding of the complex tasks a computer could be made to perform but he had only a vague appreciation of what was involved in managing a business operation.

"Craig, I have to admit I don't think we are ready yet to talk to a salesman. I think he could sell us a Ferrari when we really could get by with a Ford pickup."

They were sitting together at the fold down table in Carl's office. "You've made a good start, Craig, and it has got me thinking. I thought it was relatively simple like buying a VCR that you have to learn to operate. But it's much more complicated than that, isn't it?"

Craig nodded and looked anxiously at Carl wishing he could think of something to solve the problem. "Maybe," he said tentatively, "I could ask one of my teachers if...."

"That's it!" Carl said, sitting up and slapping the desk. "You've got it! We need to hire a business consultant."

Craig nodded in agreement but wondered what he had said that triggered Carl.

"Great!" Carl continued, getting to his feet. "I'll get hold of one. Sounds pretty impressive for our little outfit, doesn't it? Hiring a consultant!" He chuckled at the idea. "Thanks Craig, I'll give you a shout when we can get together again."

As Craig got up and turned to the door, Carl asked, "You and your girl coming to the Christmas office party? Lots of party food and free beer but no hard stuff."

Craig struggled with a reply and finally said, "I don't drink, Mr. Cranston—Carl."

"Well, you won't be alone in that—neither do I and a few others, like Larry. Think about it. I'd like to see everybody turn out."

"Sure thing," Craig responded as he left. Carl watched him leave with a soft look on his face. "Marny will like him," he said to himself.

***

Vic had not come in for lunch and Donna was a little relieved because Rob was getting uptight about the deal. She had made three pickups for him and made herself $170 with no hassles. "It was easy," she told Rob. She was ironing and he sat leaning over a chair back watching her. "I just went to the bus station, opened the locker and took out a package with no name or nothing on it except this little sticker that said $60, only the third time it only said $50. So I goes to Robson Street and I knock on the door of Number 1, and this scrawny old man opens the door and he doesn't say anything, just reaches for the parcel and I snatched it away and say, real hard like, "That'll be sixty bucks, Mister!" He puts his finger on his lips and looks down the stairs, then comes back with the money and an envelope. That was the first time—the next two times, I just hold it up so he can read the figures and he pops back in and comes out with the money and the envelope. We never say anything at all. I take the money and the envelope and I give him the package and go back to the bus station and put the envelope in a locker and go back to the cafe and give the key to Vic. Hundred and seventy bucks right there!" She patted her pocket. "Simple as that!"

Rob listened uneasily, his face closed with concern. "I still don't like it," he said. "I don't trust Vic. I think he's into big time drugs."

"We don't know that. We don't know what's in the package."

"Jesus! We're not stupid, Donna! Whoever they are, they don't dare deal directly with each other. So they get a sucker girl to run errands for them and they pay her sixty bucks for half an hours work. Hah! You know goddam well what's in those parcels, and it ain't somebody's lunch."

"I know," she said. "But I'm not going to do it many more times. Maybe just long enough to buy a little TV for us for Xmas."

He smiled and relaxed a little and they were silent with only the little radio playing rock in the background. "Hey, by the way," Rob said. "Craig was in yesterday and we're going to the hockey game on Saturday. I traded time with a guy."

"Okay," she said.

"I didn't think you'd want to go—you hate hockey."

"Okay."

Rob sprawled on the bed slapping his hands and knees in time to the music. "I wish I could get a job with regular hours like Craig. Then maybe we could get to see each other once in a while."

"Why don't you try to get on where Craig works? Then you could be together all the time." There was a note of sarcasm in her voice that he did not hear.

"No!" Rob said, very quickly, and added enigmatically. "That wouldn't be any good."

She hung up the clothes she had ironed and put the iron away, then came and sat on the bed beside him. "It would be good if we could find a little TV," he said. "We could tap into Wally's cable line."

The room was warm and cosy. Donna had put up some posters and bought some colourful pillows for the bed. She moved closer to him and ran her fingers tickling up his back and into his hair.

"Don't!" he said sharply, jerking his head away.

She hit him with a pillow and moved off the bed to a chair and sat with a pout on her face not looking at him.

"Sorry," he said mechanically. "I just don't feel like it."

"You never do," she replied.

***

The day of the bridge club was sleety and cold. The women arrived at Marion's early, as if by some signal, ready for a good gossip and talk before playing, but as always the gossip was about other people one level removed from their lives—the store manager who was caught with his hand in the till, a next door neighbour's teenage daughter with two boyfriends each disclaiming responsibility for her pregnancy and the talk, at this season of the year was about the displays and sales and bargains.

Dot said she had heard that Marion had been running around with a man and asked bluntly how things were going in that area of her life. The chatting among the others subsided with Dot's question and with Marion's answer, "There was a man for a while, a very nice man, but it's over." Isabel put a stop to any further discussion by saying, "That's a very private matter and if Marion wanted it known she would have told us without anybody prying!" Cora said, "I second the motion." Kate said, "You don't find out if you don't ask." Minnie said, "Did anybody see that movie about the Russian couple and the American couple and nobody spoke the other's language but that didn't stop them from sleeping all over the place. I haven't laughed so hard for years. I think it was a spy story." Somebody else riffled the cards and said, "Changing the subject, ladies: are we going to play or not?" As if it had been a starter's gun, everyone got up and took their places and played serious bridge with the bidding and the playing being the only topic of conversation.

Marion had felt a flutter of apprehension with Dot's blunt question but it passed when none of the others picked at the bone. The first hand was dealt and passed and when she looked at her hand again before throwing it in she realized that she could have opened and then she settled down and put her attention on the game. Only occasionally did the idea of Tom sneak in and out of her mind without concern.

With the game finished and the food devoured to the accompaniment of many sounds of pleasure and words of appreciation, and eight small gifts given to the names drawn the week before, they talked about their individual plans for Christmas and New Years and agreed that they could not meet until the first Thursday after the New year and gave Dot a small applause when she asserted loudly, "It's my turn, please!" Then, dressed in their winter coats and scarves, with toques and mitts and boots shielding them from a winter evening, the seven friends bid Marion and each other goodbye and Merry Xmas, scarcely able, in their bundling, to touch cheeks. When the door closed behind them, Marion sank into an easy chair, happily exhausted from the pleasures, with one exception, of the afternoon and sat quietly for a while watching the fire before she started the cleaning up.

She had just finished when Craig thumped up the back stairs.

"Hi, Mom!" he said. Then seeing the bridge tables and folding chairs piled beside the basement stairs, he continued, "Leave those there. I'll carry them down. Did all the ladies come?"

"Yes, they were all here and we had a little Christmas gift exchange."

"What did you get?"

"I don't know. We promised not to open them until Christmas, but," she laughed, "it feels like a quilted tea cozy."

"You lucky lady!" he said.

"Yes, I am, saucy!" she agreed. "How was your day?"

"Okay. I had another meeting with Carl and oh, yes! There's going to be a company Christmas party. I think I might go."

"Good, will you take somebody?"

"I dunno. I wonder if Lee is coming home for Christmas," he said pensively.

"Why don't you phone and find out?" she asked.

He grunted something and then said, "I dropped into the store and saw Rob. He gets off at six and he's going over and help them pack."

"Donna, too?"

"No, she doesn't want to go."

"That's too bad," she said. "I'm going to change out of this party dress and make a phone call while you take those chairs down, then I'll make supper."

She sat on the edge of her bed and steeled herself for a moment, then dialled Tom's number. "Hello," she said, when he answered, trying to keep her voice level. "This is Marion."

There was a momentary silence and he said, and she heard indifference in his voice, "Well, hello. How are things?"

This is idiocy, she told herself. "Just fine," she said. "Getting ready for Christmas, of course."

"Yes, I guess everybody is."

She plunged on. "I'm having a sort of New Years Eve and going away party for friends, and I wondered if you were free?"

"On New Years Eve?"

"Yes."

"I'm afraid I've already made other plans. Sorry."

"That's too bad. I was looking forward to..."

"Yes, well, maybe another time. Have a good Christmas and a Happy New Year."

"Thank you. The same to you." She hung up quickly not trusting her voice to say goodbye. Rude bastard, she said to herself. Not even a 'Nice to hear from you', 'How have you been?' Where is that cheerful, funny, warm other guy? She sat nursing her embarrassment for a few minutes then, splashing cold water on her face, went down to prepare their supper.

Craig was watching TV. She poured herself a glass of wine from the large bottle she had served to the bridge group and joined him while things cooked. We make a fine pair, she thought. He doesn't have a girl to take to a party and I don't have a man.

"Oh," he said during a muted ad, "Did I tell you me and Rob are going to the hockey game on Saturday night?"

"That's nice," she answered. "Sure you wouldn't like to go to night school, instead?"

"What? Oh, you mean the 'me and him' thing. Gotcha, Mom!" he exclaimed with a big grin as he turned on the sound.

"Oh sure," she told him with mock sarcasm as she left to serve their dinner.

There was casual catching-up-on-the-day conversation during dinner but Craig's mind was on his intention to try to contact Lee and her mind flitted back several times to the cold response she had got from Tom. She finished the dishes and went upstairs to get her book with the intentions of reading in front of the fire until something interesting came on TV. Starting down, she heard Craig dialling on the phone and she returned to her room, closing the door, so as not to overhear and embarrass him.

Craig had decided suddenly that he had to try to contact Lee soon or it would be too late. He looked up the number in the phone book and found the right Lee from two columns of Lees by recognizing the address. A soft woman's voice answered his ring, "The Lees Residence." He remembered that Lee's mother never answered the phone and the voice was too mature for Lee, so it must be a maid, he thought.

"Could I speak to Mr. Lee, please," he asked.

"One moment please," the voice said.

It was followed almost immediately by a male voice, "Hello?"

"Hello, Mr. Lee. This is Craig Williams. Do you remember me from last summer?"

There was a short pause. "Of course, I do. How are you? School going well?"

"I quit going to school and I'm working now. But I was wondering," he plunged on, "if Lee was coming home for Xmas."

"Those were original plans but now the family is gathering at relatives in the East."

"Oh, I was hoping to see her when she came home for Xmas," the disappointment very evident in his voice.

"I'm sure you both would have enjoyed that meeting. Are you having a family Christmas?"

"Yes, we are. My sister and her family are coming in."

"Good. It's important to have family around at this season of the year."

"Yes," Craig said. "Will you remember to tell Lee Merry Christmas from me, please?"

"Well. I certainly will remember your call," Mr. Lee said, not committing himself. "And will you pass on our best wishes to your family?"

"Yes, I will," Craig said feeling awkward.

"Well, goodbye, then. Have a good New Year."

"You, too, Mr. Lee," Craig replied automatically and hung up.

At the Lee residence, Lee said to her Father, "Who was that, Daddy?"

"Craig Williams," he said as he put the phone down.

"Daddy!" she cried. "Why didn't you let me speak to him?"

"Remember we decided it's better this way, dear."

"You decided, not me!" she said bitterly.

He looked at her severely, but said nothing.

"I'm sorry, Daddy," she said, turning away. "But I can't see the harm in saying hello to an old friend."

"You must trust your father," he said.

At the Williams, Craig went down to the basement workbench and worked on an old wood and brass reel he had found in the rafters that he thought would be good for salmon trolling. His mother had heard him finish his call and she came downstairs with her book and settled in for a good read. The house was quiet for an hour with only the sounds of Craig's tinkering in the basement and the brushing of a branch of a tree against the side of the house.

Marion jumped when a familiar knock sounded at the back door.

"Yoo-hoo!" Rob's voice trilled in a silly falsetto. "Anybody home? I've come to steal your heart—anybody's heart will do."

"In here!" she called. And Rob came smiling into the living room.

"U.U. You lovely creature. You look more ravishing than ever!" and he sat down on her knee and threw his arms around her and snuggled his face into her neck.

"Get off me, you big goof!" she said, laughing and pushing him so that he slid carefully off and sat on the floor at her feet.

"Please, U.U Don't reject me!" he cried with a exaggerated quiver in his voice. "I've been rejected all day."

"Oh, sure! Who's rejected you today."

"Let me tell you. I'm glad you asked!" he exclaimed dramatically. "I asked if I could apply for a manager's job now that I'm so good at collecting carts and packing bags. And U.U., they laughed! Oh, it was so cruel! It hurt me right here," and he slapped his chest and stomach in several places. "Well, somewhere there."

"Poor boy," she said without sympathy. "Craig's downstairs."

"Rejected again," he said, getting up and walking away with drooping shoulders.

"I heard you come in," Craig said from the workbench when a stair tread creaked as Rob tried to sneak down quietly.

"What're you doing?"

"Fixing this. I found it in the rafters. It's all corroded."

"Put some Rustoff on it."

"What's that?"

"I dunno. I haven't invented it yet."

Craig didn't bother to answer. "I tried to phone Lee," he said. "But her father told me that the family is going East for Christmas."

Rob did not answer for a minute. Then, "So what're you going to do now."

"Who will you take to the big bash?"

"Ah, I don't think I'll bother going."

"I thought you said the boss expected everybody to go."

"Yeah, he does. But shit, man! I can't go alone."

"When is it?"

"Next Saturday, the nineteenth."

After a short silenced, Rob exclaimed, "Hey, I've got it! I work late on that shift. Take Donna!"

"Donna!"

"Sure, why not? We haven't got a Christmas party at the store so we won't be going out. And she loves to dance. So why not."

"Geez, I dunno. I can't even dance," Craig protested.

"Hell, man! It's easy. All you gotta do is put your arms around each other and sort of shuffle in time to the music. You'll get the hang of it—but if you try anything fancy you'll fall flat on your ass with her on top of you. C'mon, I'll show you," and he rushed off to the family room. "Hurry up!" he called back to Craig who was moving reluctantly.

Rob turned on the record player and sorted around in a pile of records. "Here's a good one," he said. "Not too fast and not too slow." He shuffled slowly in time to the music. "Come here," he said. "Put your arms out like this—around me. Okay, you're the woman and I'm the man."

"I know that, for Crissake1! I'm not stupid. We had to take dancing in Grade 9."

"Yeah but you gotta get back to feeling the beat. Like this," Rob said, holding Craig tight and forcing him to sway back and forth and move his feet in time until their feet tangled and they tripped and nearly sprawled.

"You're getting it," Rob said. "One more time." And Craig, without thinking put his arms out in the female position and they moved, a little more successfully, in time to the music.

"Oh, yeah, one more thing. If you get a hard-on, stick your bum out because it's the gentlemanly thing to do and besides, if I find out you've been pushing your hard-on against my woman, I'll bust your head."

"Well, stick your bum out, then," Craig said.

"Oh, you noticed, did you?" Rob said, and they exploded in laughter and stopped dancing. "Let's go talk to Donna before you get cold feet."

"You guys were having a rollicking good time down there," Marion said as they came upstairs.

"Yeah! We were dancing," Rob said with a grin that said, 'Ask me more', but she refused to bite.

"That's nice," she said, turning back to her book. "Better than fighting."

"We're going over to Rob's and I'm going to ask Donna to go to the company party with me," Craig said.

Marion turned away from her book and looked at them again. My God, she thought, they really do share everything. "Good luck," she said. "Lock up when you get home. I'll be in bed."

"OK, goodnight, then," Craig said and blew her a kiss.

"That's no way to say goodnight to your mother! Here, let me show you." He walked over to Marion and said "Good night, my precious U.U." And gave her a gentle kiss on the cheek accompanied by loud smackings and pretended slobberings. But Craig had gone out of the room, and Rob shrugged in pretended dismay. "I can't ever learn him nothin'," he said as he left.

Donna was delighted with the idea. "Anything but another show!" she answered with less than ladylike courtesy. "Can you dance?" she demanded of Craig.

"Certainly," he said. "What a dumb question. We've been practising."

"Who?" she asked. "You and Rob?" They both nodded.

"That figures," she added. "Come and dance with me and show me what you can do," she said to Craig while she searched the dial for some music.

Craig stood up ready to dance, his right arm out and his left arm crooked to encircle her. "Not that way, idiot," Donna said. "I'm the lady this time."

"Oh, yeah," Craig said, changing positions.

They danced to the music, doing not much more than keeping time by moving their feet three or four inches while Rob watched. Donna cuddled closer and tucked her head into Craig's neck and their dancing improved.

"Hey there, buddy," Rob yelled over the music. "Stick your bum out!"

"Oh, yeah," Craig said and Donna giggled.

CHAPTER 55

On Friday afternoon, during her break, Donna found another key among a handful of change Vic had left as a tip. It was a $60 pickup that went as smoothly as a trip to the corner store for milk. After she put the envelope in a locker, she walked down to Hastings Street and looked at some TVs in a second hand shop. She found one that was the right size and price but the shopkeeper refused to plug it in to ensure that it would work.

"Whad'ya want for eighty bucks, lady? Ya want I should plug in every set I got? I ain't got the time!" he growled.

"I don't want to check every goddam set, you moron!" she snarled, not at all impressed by his growl. "I want to check that one. Get it down or get me a ladder and I'll get it down. Do you want to sell it or not?"

"Get it down!" shouted a voice from the back of the store.

"Geez!" the man said under his breath and got up reluctantly and with a long pole jiggled the TV off the top shelf and caught it before it crashed to the floor. He plugged it in and she pulled up the rabbit ears and found several stations. "It's filthy dirty," she said. "How long has it been up there?"

The man shrugged.

"It's hot!" she announced. "Somebody took the serial number off the back" She reached into her pocket and slapped her $60 on the set. "Sixty bucks! My only offer!" she said.

"Sold!" said the voice from the back.

"I told her eighty," the man complained.

"If you wanted eighty, you shoulda got off your ass and sold it. Get the lady a box."

She walked out feeling very pleased with herself, and caught a bus back to work. Vic was waiting in his car down the block. "What took you so long?" he demanded truculently.

She handed him the key and looked at her watch, and responded with heavy sarcasm. "What's your problem? Are we on some sort of schedule?"

"Look!" he said. "The deal was for you to go straight there and straight back and no farting around window shopping. What's in the box?"

"It's certainly not your Xmas present," she snapped and walked away, listening to him lay an angry strip of rubber.

Rob was in the cafe when she walked in. In good weather, he rode his bike to work and rode it back for lunch with her on a break. On rainy days, he took a bus and it was too expensive to bus back to the cafe, even if Bruno did load his plate with the daily special at bargain prices.

"Look what I got," she exclaimed happily after he had got up and given her a peck. She put the box on a table and opened the lid. "Sixty bucks and it didn't cost me anything."

He puzzled at the statement and then understood. "Did you—did you pick up a key today?"

She nodded, smiling.

He pulled the set part way out of the box, his face set with disapproval. "Good make," he said. "And just the right size for us. Did you test it?"

"Sure!"

He closed the box and returned to his lunch. "I'll carry it home for you," he said. "I've still got time on my break."

"Don't be mad at me!" she said to him quietly. "That's probably the last one, because Vic was pissed off when I was late." "Okay by me," he said without changing his mood.

***

Marion had spent the morning shopping too. She had found talking dolls for the girls, a pant suit for Edith with a silk scarf that matched exactly, a sweater for Harvey and a dark brown leather jacket for Craig. She had vacillated over the last purchase for a long time, torn between the brown one and a black one with studs. The black one had looked dashing on a slim, black-haired, saucy looking model but it was more Rob than Craig. She had nearly bought it for Rob but restrained herself, and settled on a colourful pair of biker shorts. She and Claudia had always exchanged small family gifts but she wanted something special for Claudia this year and did not find it until she was tired and ready to call it a day. In a small leather shop in the mall, she discovered a leather bound writing case with high quality, simply ornamented paper and envelopes that she knew Claudia would appreciate. Name and address would be printed on the envelope and 'Claudia' with two small violets on each page. She chose the type with time-consuming care, paid for it and said she would return with the address tomorrow. In a shop next door in the mall, she found a suction mount car compass for Glen that read, East, West, South and Home. Happy with that small gift, she gathered her purchases and headed for home, planning to return tomorrow with Claudia's new address and pick up a few stocking presents for her family and some napkins and other things for her New Years Eve party.

The next nice day, she told herself, I must go out to the cottage and check it out and see Audrey Thomason. I'd better phone her first and make sure she doesn't have company.

Carl and Craig were sitting with a member of the Business Administration Department of Langara College who had just been given a tour of the plant and was now enjoying a cup of coffee as he asked Carl a series of question about the operation of the company. He was an older man, probably close to retiring with an easy smile and a big laugh, who had a way of explaining complexities so that they appeared to be simple. "Your son said something about recycling, but I didn't hear it because of the noise of the machinery. What was it you said, Craig?"

Both men were looking at Craig, but Carl controlled a small smile and a wink. "I'm not... Craig began until he saw the wink. "We were just passing the baling trapdoor and I was going to say that all the trimmings go down the trapdoor into the baling room in the basement and are baled and sold by the employees."

"Sold by the employees," their visitor repeated, puzzled.

"We set up a little scheme that seems to work," Carl interjected. "Everybody who works here is listed alphabetically against one week, one person for one week. And each person names his or her favourite charity. "Every Friday afternoon, one of the men is relieved of regular work by the foreman, the women are excused because its a heavy job, and he goes down to the baling room and bales and weighs all the trimmings and rejects for the week and records it up in the office. Then, to keep it simple, when we reach the end of the list we call the recycling people and divide the proceeds according to bale weight. I don't send their contributions for them—it's up to them. Then, to personalize it a little, the person who has the highest weight gets a Friday afternoon off with pay. It's a kind of simple lottery but people have a little fun."

Their visitor leaned back and let out a rumbling laugh. "Now that's quite a scheme," he said. "And this must be quite a family you have working here. Congratulations! It seems to me to be a very healthy operation. And there's an old saying, 'If it ain't broke, don't fix it'. I'd like to talk to your bookkeeper, your shipper, your receiver and your foreman and perhaps one or two others and then I'll write you up a little report that should guide any computer outfit you decide to get involved with." He got to his feet, somewhat stiffly. "Okay if I come back on Monday? It's between sessions and I'm free."

"Fine," Carl said. "Thank you for taking the time. You must be a busy man. We appreciate it. I'll set it up with my people for Monday."

Craig had got to his feet, retrieved the visitor's coat and held it out to help him on with it.

"Thank you, Craig. You between sessions, too,?"

"No, I quit school this term." Craig answered. "I'm going to night school to learn computers."

"He's working his way up to be my full-time assistant," Carl said, giving Craig a pat on the shoulder.

When their visitor left the office, Carl turned to Craig and said, "What was his name?"

"I don't know. I heard it but I forgot. I was waiting for you to use his name."

"I forgot it, too. We better get our act together," Carl said, moving behind his desk. "By the way, did I embarrass you with that 'son' thing?"

"No, I got a kick out of it. But I nearly let the cat out of the bag."

"So did I with that 'assistant' remark," Carl said."

Craig waited a moment and asked, "What was that all about?"

"All in due course, Craig. All in due course." And he smiled as he sat down and reached for a pile of files in his in-basket.

Craig went over to Rob's on Saturday afternoon and found Rob measuring the room for TV wiring. Wally had told him it was okay to tap into his cable but not to do it when one of his favourite shows was on. "Silly old bugger," Rob complained, "everything on TV is his favourite show. I'll do it tomorrow morning when all the kid shows and the come-to-Jesus freaks are on." He continued measuring and then, after some earthy language, measured a third time when the first two did not match.

"Hey!" he said. "Guess what? I'm driving up to George next Saturday."

"How come?"

"Dad was going to rent a U-Haul to take up some stuff from the basement and the garage. And Roger decides now that he doesn't want most of the furniture even though he bought it. So Dad's going to take some of the stuff to the Sally Ann and some to the dump and then he's going to load the good stuff into the U-Haul and haul it to Prince George. Good!" he said suddenly after the third measurement. "Two of them match! How about you dashing out and getting me a splitter and 18 feet of that flat TV cable? Got any money?"

"Of course I've got money. Have you?" Craig asked pointedly.

Rob grinned and gave him twenty dollars. Don't forget the change," he said. "It's not a tip."

Craig shoved the money in his pocket. "Just a minute. I thought you said you were driving to Prince George."

"Yeah, I am. I'm driving Dad's car with a load of dishes and glasses that Mom won't trust to a truck and then Dad and I will drive back together. We'll have to stay overnight. I had to take a day off and you should have heard the Assistant prick when I told him. 'Holy Gee, Rob!' he mimicked in a squeaky falsetto, 'that will be our busiest Sunday.'" They both laughed.

Suddenly Craig sat up with a worried look. "Is Donna going?"

"Naw," he said, not looking at Craig. "I asked her but she said she had a date with you. Big deal!"

"Well, she does!" Craig exclaimed almost petulantly, relieved that his Saturday date had not been broken.

"Yes, I know," now mimicking Craig's petulance.

"Where is she?"

"Out buying Christmas presents. Are you going to get that stuff for me before it's too late?"

"Okay! Okay! Nag, Nag."

When Craig was in the hardware getting the splitter and cable he saw a small table that was about the size Donna and Rob would need for their TV. They usually gave each other a gift at Xmas but nothing so utilitarian as a table. He hesitated about buying it then decided he could give it to Donna and get Rob a fly purse he had seen in another store. So he bought the table, stuffed the cable and splitter in its drawer and drove to the mall to get the fly purse and three flies, a Tom Thumb, a Doctor and a Nymph. On his way out of the mall, he passed a stationers and quickly bought a Christmas card, borrowed a pen and wrote "To Rob and Donna XXOO Craig" in it and, taping it to the table top, rushed back to Rob's.

He tried singing Here Comes Santa Claus when he knocked on the door but not even he could recognize it. He was greeted by Rob's shout, "Where the hell have you been. We're going to be late!"

"We've got lots of time. These are for you guys." he said. "They're your Christmas presents but they're early. The table's for you, Donna, and, Rob, yours is in the drawer. Not the splitter and the cable. Oh, yeah, I owe you change from a ten."

"Oh, Craig! It's just what we need. I've been wondering where we were going to put the TV. Thank you! You're so sweet!" Donna exclaimed, wrapping her arms around him and giving him a very solid kiss.

"You didn't need to buy me this," Rob said, examining his fly purse. "All you needed to do was to bring me back the change from my twenty."

"Oh, was it a twenty?"

"You're so sweet," Rob said and wrapped his arms around Craig who managed to struggled free.

"We're going to be late," Rob warned Craig, then said to Donna, "Santa Claus took too long with his shopping so I can't hook up the TV tonight even if Wally would let me."

"That's okay," Donna said. "You guys drop me at the Mall and I'll see you later."

When they let her out at the entrance to the Mall, Donna kissed Rob but Craig noticed that she kissed Rob with much less passion than when she kissed him to thank him for the present.

Donna went straight to a leather store in the Mall that was advertising 25% to 40% off all leather jackets and stopped in front of a rack of black jackets with studs. She beckoned to a salesman and said, "This one, please. But would you try it on for me? You're just about his size, I think."

"Sure thing," the clerk replied. "I get to do this a lot."

He unlocked the rack, took out the jacket and put it on. It looked so much better on him than on the rack, particularly when he stepped around and walked with a little wiggle, that Donna said, "I don't know whether to take you or the jacket." Finally, she told him with a dramatic sigh, "I guess it will have to be the jacket."

"You know you have just ruined my Christmas," the clerk said. "Cash or Visa? We gift wrap if it's cash."

"Then cash, by all means."

She took the nicely wrapped box from him and they wished each other a smiling Merry Christmas. When she got home, she knocked on the basement door to the upstairs and opened it when Mrs. Lesseret called "Come in!" After some easy greetings, Donna asked her if she would hide Rob's present for her until Xmas eve.

"Of course, dear. I'll hide it where I always hide Wally's. Nobody will ever find it."

"I always find mine," Wally called. "One time I even took it back and got the right size."

"You did not! You rascal!" she protested.

He laughed. "Have you got your little TV hooked up yet?"

"No, Rob was waiting until it wouldn't interfere with you."

"Well, tell him now is a good time."

"Oh, I can't! He's out at the hockey game."

"Well, come on. Let's you and me do it."

He got his tool box and they went downstairs. "That's the wrong kind of splitter, but I've got the right one. I'll just trade you. It'll come in handy."

Within twenty minutes, Wally had bored a small hole in the common wall, attached the splitter and hooked the cable to the TV.

"Turn it on," Wally said.

She turned the set on and the screen blazed with colour.

"Good! We did it!" Wally said and squatted down in front of the set and adjusted it until he was satisfied with the picture. "And lots of stations," he said twisting through the dial. "Nice little set. What did it set you back?"

"Sixty dollars."

"Hot, eh? I see the identification plate is gone."

She shrugged. "Maybe."

They watched the picture for a minute. "Thank you, Wally. Rob will be surprised when he gets home." He left and she closed the door behind him and settled in to spend the rest of the evening in front of the television.

The hockey game was a dull affair. Half the seats were empty and the crowd seemed to be constantly on the move back to the concession stands even when the home team was playing with a one man advantage. There were a couple of fights that amounted to nothing more than five or six players yanking at each other's sweaters. In the last period, the visiting goalie slashed a player who had been tripped and slid into his net. The crowd booed loud and long and the referee gave the home team a free shot on goal that went in and eliminated a tie and set the score at 6 to 5 with four minutes to play. The crowd headed for the exits and when the horn sounded most of the spectators had their backs to the ice.

"Dumb game!" Rob grumbled on the way home. He had been grumbling and criticizing all the way home in traffic that mixed hockey fans, Christmas shoppers and revellers.

"Well, we won anyway," Craig said.

"That was a shoot-out! That's not hockey!" Rob argued. "They should yank the goalie and send in the second string goalie—he's always dressed—and then take out one of the defence men to sit out the penalty."

They argued about the game and some of the bad refereeing and managing until they arrived at Rob's. "Come on in," Rob said, not so much an invitation as an expectation.

"Yeah, okay. Might as well," Craig answered indifferently, reflecting the down mood Rob had been in all evening.

When they stepped in, Donna greeted them happily. "Hi, guys!" she called. "Come and look!"

"Hey, great!" Craig said as he saw the TV operating without rabbit ears. "Good picture!"

"Who hooked it up?" Rob asked peevishly.

"Wally."

"You didn't need to ask him. I was going to do it tomorrow."

"Well, he just offered. What could I do? Besides he had all the tools and he had the right thing, that divider thing, you know. You guys didn't get the right one. So we traded."

They watched together quietly until the end of a program and Craig got up and yawned and announced, "I'm off. See you guys tomorrow."

"I'm working tomorrow," Rob said giving Craig a long meaningful look.

Craig drove home wondering what Rob was so down about. Maybe he's feeling bad about his family moving up to Prince George but he discarded that idea. Could be he's getting the flu, he thought. There's a lot of it around and he's got people coughing all over him in the store.

There was a note on the frig when he got home informing him that Edith and Harvey and the girls were coming in for lunch tomorrow after their visit to Santa Claus. His mother had gone to bed but she was not asleep when he went upstairs.

"Did you see my note?" she called when she heard him coming up the stairs. "I hope you're going to be home."

"Yeah, I'll be home. What did you do tonight?"

"Nothing much. Wrote some late Christmas cards. Did Donna go to the hockey game with you?"

"No, she hates hockey. Good thing she didn't go. It was a dumb game. We played sloppy, like it was a practice session for fun," he told her through a big yawn. "Are we going to have a tree this year?" he asked, after a contagious yawning session.

"Not a big one," she said. "I bought a live one, about three feet, and I'll take it out to the cottage and plant it later."

"Remember the time Dad came home drunk and tripped over the cord and pulled the tree down? And then he dragged it out the front door with all the ornaments falling off all over the place and threw it on the front lawn?"

"It is indelibly printed in my memory!" she said slowly and flatly, pronouncing each syllable. "Goodnight, Craig."

He got up from the edge of her bed and blew her a kiss. "Sorry," he said. "I think I'll watch Johnny Carson. Goodnight," and gave another huge yawn as he closed her door.

***

"Donna?" Rob said when they were in bed. "Was that the last pickup you're going to do." He was on his side facing away from her.

She moved closer and curled against his back. She felt him tense a little as her arm went around his waist. "Yeah, I guess so. He was mad at me when I was late. I'm glad I quit. I was beginning to feel kind of scared. That old guy gives me the creeps."

"I'm glad, too. Did you ever tell Craig what you were doing?"

"No, I didn't. The less people that know, the better."

"Yeah, that's right. But I didn't want Craig to know."

"Didn't want your best buddy to know your girlfriend was pushing drugs, eh?" she said teasingly.

"Something like that," he said and caught her hand that was beginning to wander. "Good night, Donna."

In the morning, yawning and scratching and stomping around in his shorts while eating toast, Rob saw a letter on top of the bookcase he had made from bricks and boards. It was addressed to Mr. & Mrs. S. T. Watherton on Sheridan Lake in Lone Butte, B.C. "Hey, who's this?" he asked picking it up and waving it at her.

"Rob! Don't get it all greasy! It's a Christmas card to my uncle and aunt. She's my father's sister."

"I didn't know you had any relatives."

"I guess we never got around to talking about relatives."

"Do you ever see them?"

"No, I haven't seen them for years. My mother used to put me on the bus and send me up to them for summer holidays but one time when I was twelve Aunt Ella lit into my mother for not sending up some decent clothes and some spending money for me. She said the price of a bottle of booze would do me more good than the booze would for my father. They had a big fight and I never got to go back. I really liked them and we always sent Christmas cards to each other. I got to thinking she would have sent one this year and if she did my mother would probably rip it up. They're the only relatives I have. I don't count my mother and father. Not any more!"

She looked and sounded so forlorn that Rob said, with passionate sympathy, "Oh, Donna! That's terrible!" and crawled into bed with her and cuddled her gently. She turned to him, tucking her head into his shoulder, being careful to keep her hands above his waist.

CHAPTER 56

Edith and Harvey arrived with a pair of excited girls ready, at Edith's urging, to tell Granny and Uncle Craig all about their visit to Santa and all the toys they were going to get for Christmas.

"Show Granny your pictures of you with Santa Claus," Edith told them.

"Isn't that a good picture, Mom? I think I'll get it enlarged. You know, they were just wriggling like worms until it was their turn to sit on Santa's knee and then, of course, wouldn't you know, they wouldn't let go, I had to drag them up and put them on his knees. Well, would they look up at the camera? No way! They just sat there with a finger in their mouth and wouldn't smile for anyone until finally I said, 'Oh look! Here comes Uncle Craig!' and the both looked up with excited looks on their faces and the camera clicked and that was it. Then, Santa dumped them off his lap and shouted 'Next'. Really! He was almost rude! Some Santa!"

"Craig," Marion called over the squeals. "Not so much rough housing with them, please!"

"Oh, they love it, Mom. They rough house with their Daddy all the time. Don't they, Harv?"

"All the time," Harvey agreed dutifully. "Not a minute of peace."

"I wasn't concerned about them getting hurt, Edith. I was trying to save my hearing."

"Oh, that! You tell me if they get too loud. By the way, I thought, now that we're in town, we should drop over to the Turner's and say Merry Christmas and goodbye. Is that all right with you? We could leave the girls with Craig— OK, Craig?"

"Good idea, Edith. Off you go, then."

"Thanks, Mom. How soon do you want us back for lunch?"

"How about half an hour? You two trot off and I'll get started."

"C'mon, Harv! We have to hurry or we won't get any visiting in at all." Harvey moved obediently to the door.

"Oh, don't rush your visit. I can delay lunch a little."

"Oh, no. Half an hour is fine."

"Did I tell you I was giving a New Years and going away party for them?"

"Yes, you did. When you phoned. Let's go, Harv."

They were back in fifteen minutes. "We didn't stay long. They were in the middle of their lunch. They're not very sociable people anymore, are they? They hardly said a word when I was telling them about our visit to Santa. Maybe they just don't like saying goodbye. Lots of people find it difficult. What do you want me to do? Have you got milk for the girls?"

"Maybe if you round them up and wash their hands. I'll have it ready by then."

"Jennifer! Iona! Where are you? I'm coming to find you," she shouted before she got out of the kitchen.

The girls were under the table in the dining room playing hide and seek with Craig who had turned on the TV and wasn't seeking hard at the moment. They peeked out and giggled and Marion beckoned them over with a shushing finger to her lips and patted the chairs where they were to sit and did the same to Harvey. Then she went to the living room and whispered to Craig to come quietly. They all sat at the table, the little girls trying desperately not to giggle as they heard their mother call upstairs and then go down into the basement.

"Craig? Craig? You didn't let them go out, did you? Oh," she exclaimed coming into the kitchen and seeing them all seated and laughing at her. "Somebody's playing a joke on your Mummy." She sat down and flicked her napkin and spread it carefully on her lap. "Well, you had me worried," she said sharply. "They could have run out onto the street."

"Oh, come now, Edie! We were just having a little fun."

"Well, I didn't think it was funny," she said, her face pinched up small and tight, the way Marion remembered it when she was a teenager.

There was a brief moment of quiet and Harvey said to the children, "Now, whose turn is it to say grace?"

"Mine! Mine!" they shouted simultaneously.

"Now, wait," their father said. "Iona, you said grace last night, so it's Jenny's turn. Okay, Grandma?"

Marion nodded and watched Iona's little face turn into an almost-tears pout, different only in years from the one her mother showed a few moments ago. Oh my, Harvey, she thought. You've got your work cut out for you.

Lunch proceeded quietly with Craig and his mother talking to Harvey about his work and the church. Edith moved slowly back into the social conversation and the girls signalled their need for a nap by bickering and toying with their food. Finally Edith's patience ended and she took them upstairs for their lay-down.

"You didn't put any of my things back in my room after you moved back to your own room," she said accusingly to her mother.

"Of course not, Edith. Why would I?" Marion asked, puzzled.

"Well, I always think of it as my room. It didn't cross my mind that you would just throw all my things out."

"I didn't throw any thing out, Edith. Almost everything is in boxes down in the basement cupboard. Well, I did throw out the posters of Elvis and the Beatles and somebody else. I didn't want the room to be a shrine to your childhood. I wanted it as a guest room. It has to be painted, of course."

"Maybe Harv and I will go down after I help you with the dishes and sort them out."

"Don't sort them, Edith—just take them. And there are lots of games up on the shelf, please take them, too. The girls are just about ready for them. Oh, I'll tell you what! Separate them into two bunches and I'll take one up to the cottage—I'm driving out to see Audrey Tomason one of these days."

"Maybe you won't mind doing that on your own, Edie. Craig and I were planning to watch the golf game," Harvey said.

Marion saw Edith's face tighten and she quickly said, "Come on, Edith. We'll leave the dishes and do it together and get it done before the girls get up or they'll think Christmas has come early."

Edith brightened and said, "Oh great, Mom! That will be fun."

They headed for the basement and Harvey and Craig went into the living room. "I hope there's a golf game on. I just said that hoping that your mother and Edie would find some private time together. Edie's a bit up-tight these days. We think she might be pregnant and I wanted her to tell Marion."

"Oh, that's great, Harv," Craig said. "Maybe it will be a boy this time."

"Doesn't matter to me," Harv said. "Oh, look! We lucked out. There is a golf game on."

"Do you play?" Craig asked perplexed by his sudden interest.

"No, but I'm thinking about it. We've got seven crews now so all my work is planning and supervision and trouble shooting. I miss the exercise and I thought golf might do it. I certainly don't want to get into a contact sport, and pumping iron and that kind of thing seems so boring. But I need to do something."

They spent a friendly time together not really watching the game. Harvey knew next to nothing about the game and Craig remembered the basics and some of the niceties from PE and from some rounds he had played, so they talked about clubs, fairways, hazards, the rough, pars, bogeys, birdies, eagles and with their amateur expertise what each pro should have done whenever he got into trouble. Their shouts of excitement when somebody made a hole in one woke up the children and brought the women up from the basement. After that there was a bustle to get the car packed with the cartons of Edith's collection from the basement and getting the girls into their coats.

"I'll call you to see what I can bring," Marion said.

"I don't want you to bring a thing. I want to do it all myself this time."

"All right dear, but don't overdo it," her mother said, smiling as she hugged her goodbye. "I'm so happy for you!"

"Maybe we can have a game of golf together sometime, Craig," Harvey said as they shook hands. "I guess some of these sport shops rent clubs?"

"Somebody must," Craig replied. "I know we all played at school and we didn't have our own clubs."

"I'd like to try it some time if you'd like to," Harvey ventured.

"Sure," Craig answered, suddenly realizing that, now that he was out of school, his social life had dwindled seriously.

Marion closed the door after waving goodbye to them as they drove away and turned to the kitchen to tidy up. Craig followed her, saying, "I'll give you a hand for a while. I told Rob I'd pick him up and we'd go Christmas shopping."

"Don't bother—there isn't much to do," his mother said, but Craig went right on clearing the table.

"Did you have a good talk with Edith?" he asked innocently.

His mother stopped and look at him quizzically and then said, "Oh, Harvey told you! Didn't he?"

Craig grinned and said, "Yes. I think he was trying to explain why Edie was so up-tight. It will be nice for them if it's a boy."

"Well, what's so special about a boy?" she demanded smiling.

"Oh, nothing. I was just thinking of poor Harv with four shrieking females around."

She looked at him and said "Why don't you go shopping?"

"Thanks, Ma," and draped the tea towel over her shoulder.

"And don't call me 'Ma'!" she said to his back.

When Marion first thought of going out to the lake and visiting Audrey Thomason, it was when she was hurting and needed Audrey's sympathy and understanding. She had always been puzzled by that need to talk to Audrey. After all she had only seen her once for a pleasant neighbourly visit, but the older woman's ostensible dismissal of the problems that tied her to a wheel chair without crushing her spirit or diminishing her interest in the world around her was a philosophy she might, in time, learn from her. When she called to ask a convenient time to call, Audrey's answer made Marion feel that her visit would be the best Christmas present Audrey could possibly receive. They agreed on Wednesday and Marion found herself looking forward to her visit more than she had expected. On her way, she stopped and bought a potted plant that was covered with flowers, and a card that matched the plant. The young girl at the checkout did not know what kind of plant it was and could not find any other employee who did. When she arrived at the lake, she checked her own cottage and was pleased to find that Edith had left it tidied and immaculate with every-thing put away or lined up. Good for you, Edie, she thought. I don't know where you learned your compulsive housekeeping. I don't think it was from me.

Audrey called a cheerful "Come in, Marion," when she knocked on the door. "I saw you drive in and I thought you'd check your cottage first, so I put the kettle on and the tea's all ready. How are you, my dear?" She put out her twisted hands and Marion took them carefully in hers and they touched cheeks. "Now if you don't mind bringing in that tray, we'll have some tea right here between the fireplace and the sunny window—the best of the winter world."

Marion went into the kitchen that was filled with the aroma of baking bread while Audrey kept on talking in her strong voice. "Ron—my grandson, remember him? He's here for a couple of days. He comes out every month like clockwork to see what he can do. Wonderful boy! I sent Frank and him out to do anything they want until lunchtime so we could have a little peace and privacy. You pour, will you, dear?"

They talked easily and quietly for more than an hour. Audrey never asked a penetrating question, only casual explorations that lead Marion into the depths of her feelings in an examination of the sequence of events of the summer. She talked without tears, without anger, without self-pity and Audrey offered only compassion and empathy.

They had come to an end, although there was much more detail that could have been explored. Audrey seemed to know that any further talk might lead to reopening of only recently healed wounds. "It's marvellous to see you in such control of your life after what you have been through," she said as she glanced out the window at her husband and grandson coming in the gate. "You not only have survived, you have got on with your life and grown from your experience. Many people don't, you know. They sink into themselves and wallow in self-pity. But you're a survivor, Marion. You'll be alright."

Marion was absorbing her words and comparing them with all the 'You poor dear's she had heard from friends. "If I have survived, Audrey, it was only because I looked next door and found a model."

The stomping and shouted greetings from the back door put an end to their talk. Ron greeted Marion politely and said with adolescent uncertainty that he was sorry to hear about the death of Mr. Williams. Marion thanked him and the subject was dropped when Audrey said, "Look at the lovely plant Marion brought me, but neither of us knows what it is! Ron, be a dear and bring me those two books on flowers from the bookcase and let's see if we can identify it."

The three of them poured over the books while Frank busied himself in the kitchen making lunch. They could find nothing in either book that identified the plant by the time Frank called them for lunch so Ron said that he would plant it in the spring on the south side so Marion could see it from her place and they would call it a Williamensis. Frank had made a huge omelette and a stack of toast. "Audrey's bread," he explained.

"It's delicious, Audrey," and stopped, puzzled. "But how...?"

"It's a bread machine," Audrey said laughing. "It's marvellous and it makes me feel like I'm really doing something useful."

"Gran's going to let me make it next time," Ron said. "It's easy. You just dump stuff in and plug it in and Presto! you have bread."

The conversation was light and easy. After lunch, the two women were chased back to the fireplace while Frank and Ron continued with an afternoon game of fiercely competitive 'Spite and Malice.' At three o'clock, Marion made her first casual overtures about leaving over Audrey's protests. They had talked together only twice but Marion, for her part, felt a bond with Audrey that was stronger than she had felt with any other woman for many years. She knew without exploring it that Audrey returned those feelings. After warm good wishes that went far beyond season's greetings, she drove back to the city into the brilliant last light of a winter day, holding tight to the bonds of a wonderful friendship, feeling relaxed and happily content with her life and herself.

***

On Friday, Carl Cranston received a letter from "The Man From Langara", as the office women referred to him. He had spent some time with the firm's accountant, who had been alerted to his visit by Carl, and with some of the men on the line. He apologized in the letter for his typing due to short staffing during the Christmas season and his wish to get his report to them because of his retirement in two weeks time. His report was signed with an undecipherable squiggle. They still could not remember his name, nor could any of the men on the line. The accountant was on holidays in Hawaii. The three women in the office changed his name from "The Man From Langara" to "Mr. Squiggles". The report contained no invoice but it did explain that the members of the Department felt that such studies benefited them by the acquisition of real life studies instead of textbook examples. In the report he was very complimentary of the way the small company was presently being operated and he warned against excessive dependence on computers instead of people. He pinpointed several areas where computerization could be beneficial in assisting, rather than replacing present staff. He remarked that Larry Koski was a remarkably efficient foreman whose concerns were equally spread between the company and the workers, and that Craig demonstrated good management potential for his age and would quite probably fill Carl's shoes competently in the family business when it came time for Carl's retirement. He said he had been impressed by the way in which the company operated internally on the basis of trust and mutual loyalty, attributes not easily found in today's unionized and computerized world.

Because there had been some worried concerns expressed in the lunch room about what computers would do to their jobs, Carl put up two copies of the report in the lunch room, underlining the part about "several areas where, in the writer's opinion, carefully selected computer programs could be utilized to assist, not replace, present staff." He also underlined 'Carl's retirement' and wrote "Who, me?" in the margin.

Craig was to receive a lot of good natured teasing in the next few days, particularly from the older employees and the three women in the office. Carl would be presented with a cane from Larry at the Christmas party, who, trying not to show his pleasure about the comments made about him, complained, to everyone's amusement, that "Nobody ever spells my name right."

Rob worked only half a shift on Saturday and at noon, he rushed over to the cafe to gulp down some lunch and say a second goodbye to Donna—the first being early in the morning when Donna was usually grouchy. "Drive carefully," she urged. "It's winter up there!"

"Okay," he replied. "And I'll be on the lookout for polar bears and those other things with red coats and funny hats."

"Those too," she agreed and kissed him lovingly in the corner of the kitchen with Bruno not looking but smiling.

By the time he reached his parent's home after stopping to shove some overnight things in a plastic grocery bag and pick up a ski jacket and after-ski boots, his father was waiting with the U-Haul truck packed and ready. "Your mother made us each a lunch and a thermos," his father said, so we won't have to stop on the way except for gas. Are you all ready to go?"

"Ready as I'll ever be," Rob said. "Except I don't know where I'm goin'. So lead on, McDuff!"

"That was my plan, Hamlet. Me first, then you. But, come to think of it, it couldn't have been Hamlet. It was one of those kings, I bet."

"Yeah, they were always saying things like 'Whether thou goest, I wilt go,' and stuff like that."

"Well, I know that one's not Shakespeare. That's from the Bible," his father said.

"For heaven's sake," Claudia interjected. "Will you two romantics mount your steeds and get out of here before I freeze my you-know-what!"

"Okay," his father said. "You kiss her on the left cheek, I've already used the right one."

"Oh, I'm so glad you told me," Rob said as he dutifully kissed his mother seven or eight times. "Bl-e-a-gh! Imagine! Used cheeks."

The engine of the truck roared as it pulled away, all its travelling lights glowing in the early afternoon. Rob drove off close behind him in the little family car, smiling at the little fun they had had with each other, wondering what had happened that the fun seemed to have stopped a long time ago, and marvelling that his father had loaded and unloaded a truck load at the dump and another at the Sally Ann, had loaded the truck a third time and then the family car and was still going strong into a nine or ten hour drive.

***

"Aren't you going to wear a tie?" Craig's mother asked him when he came down all shaved and slicked, wearing a new sports jacket that he and Rob had picked out. She was startled to note how much he had changed physically over the summer, leaner but only a little taller with broader shoulder and, maybe it was the shadow of a beard, with a firmer jawline.

He shook his head to her question and said, "Nope!"

"You really do look very nice," she said. "Very handsome! But you should really wear a tie to a party."

"Nope!" he said and nothing more.

She gave up trying, suddenly seeing him again as a baby in a high chair, resolutely, without changing expression, pushing out of his mouth every spoonful of mashed banana she put in.

"Oh, well," she said, laughing. "That's not too bad. Just two things to rebel against—ties and mashed bananas."

He smiled but really did not know what she was talking about.

The corsage he had bought for Donna was huge, but Marion held her tongue. He was pleased with himself that he had thought of it but puzzled when the girl in the flower shop asked the colour of the dress she would be wearing. On her recommendation they settled on a silver bow and ribbon that, she had said, would go with anything.

When Donna took it out of the box and held it against her shoulder, it looked as though she was trying to hide behind a display in a florist shop. "It's beautiful," she said, "but I don't know where to wear it," holding it against her shoulder, then at her waist and then carrying it, in two hands, like a bride. "Would you mind if I take it apart and make it smaller? It seems a shame but it's just too big for me."

They were both laughing because it looked comical on her small body in a tight short dress. He watched as she took the corsage apart and put about one third of it into a smaller, daintier arrangement that she could pin on her shoulder.

"Perfect!" he exclaimed when he saw it. "You should go into the business."

"Yes," she said proudly, standing on tiptoe to see herself in the bathroom mirror. "It does look better, doesn't it?"

They arrived ten minutes after the set time and found the rented banquet room almost full. Carl was near the door greeting everyone as they came in and Mrs. Cranston sat nearby.

"Glad you could come, Craig," Carl said. "I wanted you to meet Mrs. Cranston." He looked at Donna and smiled appreciatively.

"This is my friend, Donna," Craig said. "This is my boss, Carl Cranston, Donna."

They exchanged smiles and polite greetings and Carl took Craig by the arm and said, "Now first you two come and meet my wife and then I'll send you off to the punch bowl."

They walked over a few feet to where Mrs. Cranston was sitting talking with some other women. She was in mid-sentence when they approached and she stopped suddenly and looked at Craig hard, then regained her composure as Carl said, "Marney, this is Craig Williams and his friend Donna. Sorry, Donna, I didn't get your last name."

"Penser," Donna said but Mrs. Cranston was not listening.

"So you're Craig," she said, now smiling warmly. "Carl talks about—Carl told me you were working at the plant," she said lamely.

"Pleased to meet you, Mrs. Cranston," Craig said, a little perplexed by her greeting.

She released his hand after a long moment, then, offering her hand to Donna, "And Donna. How are you, Donna? I'm sorry, I know you told Carl your last name but I didn't quite catch it."

"Penser," Donna said again.

"Donna Penser," Mrs. Cranston said. "Such a pretty name and such a pretty girl. And your corsage is lovely and dainty. If Craig picked it out for you, then he must have exquisite taste."

Neither of them said anything correcting about the corsage as Mrs. Cranston continued, "Now, Craig, you must come and find me when things settle down and tell me all about yourself."

"All right, I'll do that," Craig said. "Bye for now."

"She's nice, isn't she?" Donna said as they moved toward the punch bowl.

"Somebody said she hasn't been to a company party for four years, not since her son was killed," Craig said filling two cups from a punch bowl clearly marked "Non-Alcoholic Punch".

"How?" Donna asked.

Craig shrugged and almost spilled his drink when a voice beside him said, "Scuba diving—nobody knows what happened. I'm Terry."

"I'm Craig."

"I know that and guess what, I'm trying to horn in on your conversation so I can be introduced."

"Oh, sorry. Terry, this is Donna."

"Hi, Donna," Terry said. "I saw you come in."

"Well, what can I say?" Donna said with a big smile. "I didn't see you see me."

"What would you have said if you had seen me seeing you?"

"I'd have said, Who's spiking your drinks?"

"Would you like a shot for yours? Vodka." He reached inside his jacket and waited for a response.

"No, thanks. I'm driving," Craig said.

"Maybe when they start dancing," Donna replied.

"Save a dance for me," Terry said as he filled two cups and wandered away.

Craig and Donna moved around talking and looking for some of the younger people to join. He saw Mrs. Koski sitting alone at a table and he took Donna over to introduce her. "Mrs. Koski sold me her car," Craig said after the introductions.

"No good for me," Mrs. Koski said, raising two canes and looking down at her grossly swollen ankles. "You take good care of my little Honda?"

"Oh, yes. And I must tell you how much my mother appreciated the flowers you gave her." Mrs. Koski's smile softened. "She still has them in her bedroom. Everlasting, she calls them."

"Yes, yes!" Mrs Koski said, nodding her head vigorously. "Everlasting. Just no water and they dry and remember summer all winter. We had a nice talk on the phone, your mama and me. You say hello for me."

They wandered back in the general direction of the punch bowl and he was hailed by one of the girls from the office. "Have you got a table yet?" she asked.

Craig shook his head. "Is that the way you do it? Sort of make up a party?"

"Sure," she said. "Come and join us. We've got another couple and I'm holding down the fort." Craig made the introductions casually. "Tina, Donna."

"Hi," Tina said. "That's my boyfriend, Evan, over there in that horrible loud jacket. He's supposed to be getting me a beer."

"I'll go hurry him up," Craig said. "Want one, Donna?"

"Sure, why not?" Donna said. "It's beginning to sound like a party."

He and Evan returned, Evan with two beers and Craig with one and a cup of punch. Carl was just turning away from the table. "Just checking that everyone's making up a party," Carl said. "Sounds like everyone is having a good time!" Craig responded as he handed Donna her beer. He had to raise his voice over the party noise.

The caterers were finished setting out the food and people were settling in around tables of eight. Someone Craig did not recognize walked to the middle of the room and banged a spoon against a glass until the party noise subside. "Ladies and gentlemen" he called. "I think dinner is ready."

There was a general shoving back of chairs and conversation again until the spoon and glass restored the quiet.

"I forgot to announce that we want to proceed in an orderly fashion this year. So we decided to draw table numbers. The first number drawn was Table

Number One—that's the Cranston party." There was a general roar of approving laughter. "Of course, all the tickets in the hat were labelled Table One. We did that so that Marney wouldn't get trampled and to let her know how glad we are that she is back." There was loud clapping and cheers as the Cranston party moved to the table. "The rest of you are on your own."

There was a moment of shy hesitance until Larry stood and helped his wife to her feet and they walked, she with only one cane, to the serving table. The conversation level returned and lines formed on either side of the long buffet table. Wine bottles appeared on many tables and a party mood developed.

"I meant to remember to bring a bottle of wine," Evan said, as dinner progressed. "but I forgot."

"I could slip out and get one," Craig offered.

"No, no!" the people at the table protested.

"There's still some company beer," someone said. "Let's grab a few before it's all gone."

When the caterers had cleared the serving tables and the waitresses were moving around with pots of tea and coffee, Carl moved out to the centre of the room and waited for silence.

"I am not going to make a speech," he said and smiled when there were several teasing hurrahs, "but I am going to say a few words later. First, though Marney has told me that she would like to say something before I put you to sleep." There was polite laughter and some clapping as Carl walked back to the table and escorted his wife to the centre of the room that was suddenly quiet.

"I wanted to tell you," Marney began in a small shaky voice. She stopped and cleared her throat and continued in a stronger voice. "I promised myself that I would speak in a voice you could all hear. Let me start again." She cleared her throat again and said, "Now then! Can you all hear me?"

There was a chorus of assent and she continued.

"I wish I could tell you all individually but I don't think I could and this will have to do. Over the last many months, it has really been more that three years, your sympathy, your concerns, your love has reached and sustained me more than I can put into words. Your cards, flowers, messages through Carl—there wasn't a day that I was not made aware how much you cared. I could not always respond. Somehow you even learned of my birthday and brightened that day with your messages. Many of you ladies took me shopping when I did not think I could do it alone. Many of you men came in groups of two or three on a Saturday and did the lawns and weeding and pruning. How can I tell you how much I appreciated everything you have given me. It means so much to me. And it means so much to Carl, too. I know now what a depression is—it is a thick, dark, terrible thing that blots out sunshine, love, smiles, laughter and beauty. But somehow the persistence of your love and concern filtered through that melancholy fog. I'm so happy to be back at a company party again with all of you, and so grateful to have this chance to say thank you and I love you all."

She stepped back and, wiping her eyes, took Carl's arm to be escorted back to her table to the accompaniment of applause that continued until she was seated. Most people, men and women alike, even the partners of employees, like Donna, busied themselves surreptitiously drying their eyes while getting reseated and waiting for Carl to return to the centre of the room.

As soon as Carl returned and quiet was restored, Larry got to his feet and taking one of his wife's canes, walked to the centre saying, "Just a minute there, Carl. Before you get started, I would like to say something. That man from Langara wrote something in his paper that we didn't know nothing about. He let the cat out of the bag and said you were retiring. Now then, you can imagine our surprise when you would tell a total stranger something like that before you told us. But we forgive you and we want you to take this to help you in your old age." He thrust the cane out to Carl and turned to go back to his seat, but stopped to say. "It's an old one. It's being recycled. And by the way, tell him that my name is spelled K-o-s-k-i, in case the TV and newspapers are interested." He sat down with a big grin on his face and the room exploded in laughter.

Carl smiled easily at the room full of friendly faces. "Thank you, Larry, for this eventually useful gift. It is so like you to think ahead and be prepared. I'll keep it and treasure it because it carries within it, the warmth of Mrs. Koski's hand (that's spelled with an 'i' by the way.) But, and let me say it loud and clear, the report of my retirement is grossly exaggerated. Oh, I'm going to start taking more time off, and Marney and I are planning a couple of trips, but that's all. So the boss with the big whip is going to be around for a long time yet. Okay?"

The response was a storm of clapping and laughter.

"Now then, and I know that every year you are kind enough to listen to my annual speech in order to get to the good part. The accounting firm, whose boss, having received his compensation for the year, is sunning in Hawaii, has informed me that, due to your efforts and cooperation and teamwork, our small company, after taxes and other bureaucratic demands, has shown a satisfactory profit that can be shared with you in these three ways: first, a Christmas bonus that will show up on your next pay check accompanied by my thanks to all of you, to the amount of $200." He paused during a rumble of chatter and clapping, looking around at the gathering of happy faces. "Secondly, there will be a salary increase, beginning January 1, of exactly 8.72% for everyone. I don't know why it couldn't have been rounded off to 8.75 but that's the way the accountant's mind works." The small joke in the last sentence was almost lost in the sounds of clapping and voices of happy approval. "Thirdly, I have been investigating a dental plan for us but it seems we are not big enough to support one on our own, nor, not being unionized, can we join an existing plan. At the moment the best that can be done is this: a sum of money, the exact amount will be determined later, will be set aside for orthodontal and surgical corrections for children of employees up to age 16 on a 50/50 sharing basis. There are many gray areas that have to be clarified but we have a start on helping to eliminate a very significant drain on the family income of some families. There's nothing quite so beautiful as the smile of your child. For some of you old guys—sorry, your choppers are not covered."

He paused and stayed standing in the middle of the hall waiting for the talking to subside.

"Now, one or two other things and then I'm finishing speechifying. Raise your glasses and clap your hands for the five people who organized this event. Stand up and be recognized, people. They get better at it every year."

A wildly enthusiastic round of applause greeted them as they stood. Donna recognized Larry, Terry and Tina.

"Next, I have to tell you that there will be dancing and the music will be supplied by the boys from the print shop who tell me they have everything from waltzes to reggae, what ever that is. A big hand of appreciation, please." A drum roll roared out over the speaker system and continued until people shouted "Okay!" "Enough!" and ended with a maniacal laugh and "Just testing, folks. Just testing! You ain't heard nothin' yet!"

Carl waited until the laughter died down, and said "One final announcement and then we can clear away some table and chairs and get to the dancing. I have felt a couple of pushes and shoves in the direction of retirement. Well, as I have told you, I am not about to retire but I am about to start taking some time off from the business. So that I can do that without feeling guilty I am going to shift some of my work load over to someone else. That someone else is going to become Assistant to the Manager—Manager, that's me, remember? Not Assistant Manager, but Assistant to. He doesn't get a raise. He can't hire. He can't fire. He can't sign checks. And when I don't need his assistance, he'll be out there doing what everybody else does. Oh, yes! He will be getting a small car allowance. His name is Craig Williams. Stand up, Craig."

A woman's voice called out, "Oh, good!" and started clapping.

It was Mrs. Cranston.

Craig stood, embarrassed and blushing, as people called out, "Good for you, Craig," and those nearby reached out to pat his shoulder.

Carl shouted, "That's all, folks. Have a Happy and safe Christmas. And thank you." He turned and walked over to Craig who was still standing. "I hope I didn't embarrass you, Craig," he said as they shook hands.

"It took me by surprise, Mr. Cranston—Carl. I had no idea. But gosh, thanks. Thanks a lot!"

"Well, we've been working well together. So it's a kind of Christmas present and presents are supposed to be a surprise." Then he added, enigmatically, "And it's a kind of Christmas present for Mrs. Cranston and me, too." He stopped and seemed to want to say something and ended up saying, "I mean, me be able to take some time off, and we'd be able to take a couple of trips or something."

"That's great, Carl. Really, thanks a lot!"

"Maybe you'd take a minute and have a chat with Mrs. Cranston, would you?"

"Sure thing, Carl. Right away."

"Don't hurry, now. There's a lot of people who want to congratulate you. And you have to dance with Donna." Donna had been standing beside Craig listening. "Save me a dance, Donna?"

"Sure thing," she replied.

The music started but they waited shyly until more people moved into the small dancing area. "Was that really a surprise, Craig?" Donna asked.

"Honest! I didn't know a thing about it. He never said anything to me."

"But it's great, Craig! Congratulations," she hugged his arm and pressed against him.

"Would you like to try dancing with me now? There's enough people out there," Craig said.

"Sure! Let's go! Remember, I'm the woman and you're the man," she laughed as they made their way to the dance area.

They danced sedately together, not moving too far from their original spot, stopping occasionally as other dancers stopped to congratulate Craig. The next record was hurtfully loud with a beat that Craig could not recognize although Donna was moving her body subtly to some rhythm. Evan came over and shouted, "That sounds like our kind of music, Donna!" he said.

She looked inquiringly at Craig who said, "I'll go speak to Mrs. Cranston. Be back in a while." He watched them in envy as they moved onto the floor and then in amazement as they whirled away in what seemed to him to be a flurry of arms and legs and gyrations that he would never dare try to emulate.

Mrs. Cranston saw him approaching and beckoned to him and patted a chair beside her as if she had been saving it for him. He smiled at her and sat down. "I hope you're not going to ask me to dance," she said. "I'd rather just sit."

"Okay," he said. "That's fine with me. I'm not much of a dancer. Every time the music starts, I think I can feel the rhythm but when I get up, my feet are all thumbs."

She looked at him quizzically until he said, "That's not the right one!" and she knew what he meant and said, "You mean the two left feet thing." And he said "Yeah, that one," and laughed at his own confusion and she laughed comfortably with him.

They talked together without any interruptions and she congratulated him on his new job and thanked him for taking some of the load off her husband's shoulders so that now they would have a little more time together. She asked him how his night school course was going, said softly that she had heard about the death of his father and then let that subject drop quickly. She said that Donna seemed to be a very nice girl and Craig explained that she was not his girl friend, that she was his best friend's girl friend and that the girl friend he had was at a private school for girls in the East and that her father probably did not approve of him because they were Chinese. He looked so tormented that she reached out to shake his arm gently in consolation and assured him that things would work out. "They did for me," she said. "But it took time. Time heals all wounds, they say."

"Yes, I know they say it, but if I tried to say it, it would come out like, Time wounds all heels," he said, laughing.

She straightened in her chair with laughter written on her face, "Craig!"

she chided.

"Oh, Mrs. Cranston. I didn't mean... I'm sorry. I was trying to make a joke." His face was crimson.

"I know, dear. And it is a funny joke." She reached out and touched his arm again. "Oh, I am so happy we could find a few minutes to talk. I have really enjoyed it, Craig. But I shouldn't keep you from your dancing."

Craig got to his feet and as he shoved the chair back, it fell over. As he picked it up, he saw her watching him with a strange look on her face. "Sorry," he said. "Oh, and I think I should ask you if you would like to dance?" It was a plaintive question.

"I would love to, Craig, but I can't. I have already said 'No, thank you' to too many requests—but thank you. And Craig, if you see Carl, please tell him that I'm ready to go home."

"I will, Mrs. Cranston. I've had a nice time," and he bent over as he shook her hand and nearly kissed the motherly forehead automatically but stopped himself in time.

He saw Carl on his way back to the dance area and gave him the message. "Did you have a good chat?" he asked.

"Oh, yes," Craig answered, with a grin. "I guess we talked about everything except politics and you."

"That was politic of you," Carl said as they shook hands and bid each other goodnight.

"Did you have a good time?" Craig asked Donna as they plodded through a dance together before going home.

"I had a great time," she answered. "And that Mr. Cranston! Can he ever dance! The old dances, you know. I felt like I was a movie star and he was Fred Astaire."

"Sorry," he said, as he tramped on her foot again.

"That's okay," she replied and snuggled closer. They were able to move together in time with the music not daring to say anything in case Craig lost the beat, but finally Donna said, "Hey, buddy. Better stick your bum out!"

Craig turned crimson and had they not been holding tight to each other they would have doubled over with laughter.

CHAPTER 57

Carl and Marney Cranston left the plant party feeling tired and happy. Many of the older employees were also heading for the cloakrooms, leaving the dance floor and the music to the younger and more active people with good eardrums. When the boss left the volume increased another few decibels and the beat of the music changed and a hoarse voiced soloist repetitively screamed a single phrase.

"Good party, wasn't it?" Carl said on the way home. "Did you enjoy it?"

"Yes, it was. And I did enjoy it—until the music got so loud I just wanted to run outside. I don't know how they stand it! Are they all going to be deaf by the time they reach forty?"

"Or before!" laughed Carl.

They were quiet for a couple of blocks. "That was a good speech, dear. I knew you could do it," Carl said.

"Thank you, but you couldn't see how I was shaking inside. I just about quit after the first flub."

"But you didn't! And what you said was honest and frank and they knew it and loved you for it."

"I hope so." She sighed happily. "It feels like those dark drab days are over."

"I hope so, dear."

"Your speech was good, too, Carl."

"Same old speech," he laughed. "I just change the numbers around each year."

"No, it wasn't the same old speech—it never is! You always thank them because you mean it and they like to hear it from you."

"I do mean it. They're good people and I'm grateful to them. The only way I can show it is by looking after them. The pay is better than union and the perks are different but as good, I think."

They were quiet again for a long time until Marney said in a very soft voice. "He really does look like our Chris, doesn't he?"

"Yes, he does. It startled me when I first saw him. That's why I warned you again."

"I'm glad you did. As it was, I took one look at him and nearly fainted. Same hair, even parted on the same side, and the same eyes. He's a couple of years younger than Chris was." She stopped for a moment and went on. "Chris was maybe an inch taller and a few pounds lighter. But the smile! Like something flicks a switch inside and everything lights up. Just like Chris. And he's a little shy, and polite and sort of awkward."

"His father apparently was a drunk and a lecher," Carl said.

"Don't tell me things like that," she said sharply, but after a minute of silence, she continued, "You know, after we had a little talk, he got up to leave and knocked his chair over. Remember how Chris could never seem to get out of his chair at the table without pushing it over? And I laughed and probably embarrassed him." Carl smiled at a memory. "And, you know, when he leaned over to shake my hand, I thought he was going to give me a kiss, and he almost did but he stopped suddenly and blushed." She stopped and Carl reached out and took her hand while they waited for a light to change. "Thank goodness, he didn't. If he had, I probably would have burst into tears and embarrassed everybody."

He patted her knee as they drove.

"Did you hire him because he looked like Chris?" she asked.

"Not really, but it might have had a bearing on it. He just seemed like a nice kid who didn't have any skills and needed a summer job. So he worked for the summer and did a good job and I told him to come and see me again if he needed work and he did. And I hired him again. I like having him around. We work well together and it's sort of like having another glimpse of Chris every day."

"Why did you promote him?"

"Because he has some skills that are useful." He paused and smiled at her in the dim light. "And because I like him and he reminds me of Chris."

"Do you suppose any of the others suspect?"

"Maybe. But if they do, so what? It's still my company."

"And you won't tell Chris—I mean, Craig."

"Oh no! I couldn't do that."

They reached home and got out of the car and went arm and arm inside. "Nice party! And nice ending!" she said.

Much later, Craig and Donna drove to her place, Donna curled close with one arm clutching his and one hand on his thigh. It took all his concentration to keep his mind on his driving. He took her to the door, one part of him knowing he should kiss her quickly, leave her there and go home. The other part of him was in a raging arousal that wanted to deny all the things he should do. So he kissed her at the door and suddenly it was a deep, passionate, lingering kiss. He tried not to, but his arms tightened around her and he found her lips again and his mouth couldn't say, "Donna, we shouldn't!"

"Come on in," she whispered. It's cold out here."

She unlocked the door and lead him unresisting inside. It was warm and dim. What if Rob comes home and catches us? raced through his mind along with a dozen other restraining thoughts. But Donna took off her coat, turned on the TV to the Late Late Show and came to him again and kissed him with more passion than he thought possible. Then she unbuttoned his ski jacket, slipped it off his shoulders and let it slide off to the floor behind him. While his hands were engaged in shaking his coat off, she undid his zipper and reached in and fondled him until he groaned.

"Come to bed," she urged. "Quickly!"

He stumbled over to the bed and fumbled out of his pants and shoes while she stripped of her dress and lay back waiting for him. He crawled on top of her and as quickly as he entered her, it was over.

"Craig!" she protested. "What's the matter with you? That was no fun at all."

"I'm sorry," he said meekly. "I couldn't..."

"Get me some tissues. In the bathroom," she demanded.

He got up clutching himself and waddled to the bathroom with his shorts below his knees but in the dim light, the butterfly birthmark on his rump was not visible. He returned in a minute with his shorts in place and with a roll of toilet paper. He stood, his face red and his jaw clenched in some sort of emotion, watching her wipe herself. "You don't need to stand there gawking," she said. Then, pausing and looking at him with a different expression on her face, she stated, "I bet I know. That was your first time, wasn't it?"

He nodded, dumbly.

She laughed. "Come over here," she said, extending her arms to him. "Just like Rob. Pretending he was such a man of the world. He never even got in, the first time we tried."

"Who? Rob? My Rob?" he asked incredulously.

"Yes, your Rob," she said. "All talk, no action. But he's getting better although he's never very interested."

"Who, Rob?"

"Will you stop saying that and come to bed."

"Donna, we shouldn't!"

"What do you mean, we shouldn't? Don't you want to?"

"Yes, but... Supposing Rob finds out?"

"How's he going to find out? I'm certainly not going to tell him and I bet you're not."

"No, but..."

"Yes but no but! Get your butt over here and we're going to try again and this time you're going to get it right, or we'll keep on trying until you do. Got it?"

"Okay, but..." and he quickly stopped and said, "Sorry! Okay."

He crawled into the bed beside her with a sigh that was a mixture of anticipation, confusion and a lot of guilt.

"Shouldn't I be wearing a condom?" he asked. "I didn't bring one. I didn't think, you know, that we'd, well, that we'd ever do it."

"Rob has some, somewhere, but I don't know where they are. I hate the things, so I take care," she said and snuggled against his non-resisting and ready body.

Sometime in the dark of the early morning, he awakened and carefully extricated himself from a tangle of arms and legs without waking her up. He dressed quietly in the blue light of the TV screen and let himself out of the apartment without disturbing her. The Lasserets were restless sleepers and Wally, hearing the crunch of tires in the snow in the driveway as Craig drove away, wondered if Rob had got back early.

Craig let himself in quietly, turned off the lights and crept up the stairs stepping only on the outside of the stairs treads to avoid any squeaks in the silent house. In his room he undressed again and sat on the edge of his bed, naked, looking down at himself. What a prick! he thought. What a sneaky, dirty rotten son of a bitch! To screw my best friend's girl. There was nothing left of the high, happy exhilaration that he had carried away from the party. There was no pleasurable review of his first true sexual relationship. There was only shame and disgust. And the thought of having to look Rob in the eye and lie and keep on lying tore at his insides like nothing he had felt before. He walked naked across the hall to the bathroom, looked again at himself with revulsion in the mirror, then stepped into the shower and stood under the punishing full blast of an ice cold, needle spray until the agony gave him at least temporary absolution. Back in his room, he put on a pair of pyjamas instead of crawling into bed naked. Lying on his back, with his arms stretched hard outside the covers, he stared at the ceiling for a long time, then turned out the light and let the darkness of the night match his guilt.

In a wayside motel, fifty miles south of Prince George, before the light of dawn, Glen Turner, stood partly dressed, shaving and at the same time watching for his son to stir. Rob lay sprawled in his shorts on the twin bed with the covers flung back, snoring gently. The father looked at his son lying lithe and long and dark with his long black hair splayed across the pillow and felt a gentle protectiveness toward him. Putting on his coat, he left the room and went to the office for the advertised Continental Break-fast and came back with four doughnuts and two heavily sweetened coffees. He shook Rob's mattress with a foot until Rob showed signs of coming awake.

"Come on, Rob! Wake up! We gotta get going!" he called.

Rob sat up and looked wildly around. "What time is it?"

"If I told you, you wouldn't believe me," his father said. "Here's your breakfast."

Rob looked with unfocussed eyes at his watch and flopped back and the bed. "Geez, did I ever sleep!" he said and scratched his genitals with both hands. He sighed and got up. "Is that mine?" he asked, and when his father nodded, he shoved a doughnut halfway into his mouth and went into the bathroom, and, not bothering to close the door, made a long, splashing urination and emerged, still working on the doughnut, Glen sat watching his son wake up and get dressed while eating and drinking and wondered casually at what age men would start to think that eating and toileting simultaneously were aesthetically incompatible.

"I thought that if we got an early start, we could get unloaded and you could see the place and we could take the truck back and be on our way to get home before dark. There's a big snowstorm scheduled for the coast," he added. "Is that going to be too much for you? We can split the driving going home."

"No, that's okay," Rob probably said around a mouthful of his second doughnut and a big yawn, presenting to his father a mouthful of masticated food in an unshaven face with uncombed hair matching casually sloppy clothes.

"My son, the savage," the father said to himself, flatly, without malice. But aloud, getting to his feet, "Let's get on our way, then. Shall we?"

They left in the morning darkness and arrived at the new home in the new city just as the sun washed over the city and showed it spread out and sparkling with fresh snow, looking like an adolescent, half-way between, and uncertain whether it wanted to be, a little city or a big town. They unloaded and Glen showed his son proudly around the house. "This would have been your room, I guess," Glen said as they walked through the house. "Still could be, if you want to change your mind and come," he added.

"It's a great room, Dad, but I don't think so. Thanks."

They took the truck back and Glen got into the car with Rob behind the wheel. "If you drive for a couple of hours, I'll get a little shut-eye. Then we'll switch. Okay?"

"Sure, Dad, but hey! I gotta put the radio on to keep awake. Is that okay?"

"Won't bother me," his father said, sliding down in the seat and pulling his cap over his face. "Let her blast!"

Ten miles down the road he wished he hadn't used the word 'blast' but it was too late to take it back.

CHAPTER 58

Rob and his father exchanged the driving every two hours as agreed, each managing to sleep in reasonable comfort in the laid back front seat. Rob slept in silence, his father was able to sleep by shutting out Rob's constant station search in his efforts to escape from the women's talk shows on CBC. They had stopped after four hours at a small place in 100 Mile House that advertised 'Breakfast 24 Hrs' and gorged themselves on bacon and eggs with pancakes and sausages and more coffees to go. The weather news promised heavy snow for the lower mainland. At Cache Creek, they ran into some mixed flakes and light pellets of snow hitting the windshield but the roads were clear and the Sunday traffic was light. By the time they got to Lytton the snow was coming down harder and the radio stations were warning that a heavy storm was imminent. Just past the school and the mill yard the highway barrier was down and an RCMP car with its lights flashing was parked beside the road. A very young Mountie, huddling down in his heavy coat, stopped the car and approached the driver's side. The snow was blowing straight into his face and he had to turn slightly away as he talked to them.

"Sorry, sir," he said. "We have a report of a heavy snow warning for this area, so all traffic on the highway is being restricted to vehicles with good winter tread and or chains."

"Do we have chains, Dad?" Rob asked.

"No, we don't, dammit," his father replied.

"Look, officer," Rob said. "We've got practically new Mud and Snows on and four-wheel drive. Surely that's good enough, isn't it?"

"Oh, I didn't notice your hubs," the officer said, bending over with his face into the driving snow and taking a casual look. "Yeah, you should be okay, but take care, eh?" and he walked away and opened the barrier.

Rob drove under the barrier giving the officer a toot and a wave, and smiling to himself.

His father looked over and watched him smile. "And what would you have done if he had seen we didn't have four-wheel drive.?"

"Oh, I guess I would have acted surprised and said 'Gee, I must have got the cars mixed up. I thought we were driving the other one.'"

Glen smiled and shook his head as he slid down in the seat again and tried to catch some more sleep. After half an hour he gave up any idea of sleep. The wipers were working hard to keep the windshield clear and Rob had slowed to a cautious speed and kept retuning the radio to CBC as the reception faded in and out through the canyon with the hope of catching a recent weather report. The opposing traffic was light and the few cars they met were covered with snow. They were following in the tracks of some vehicle out of sight ahead and, in the mirror, Rob could occasionally catch a glimpse of the lights on cars following behind.

"Do you want me to take over for a while?" his father asked.

Rob looked at his watch quickly and replied, "No, it's okay, Dad. I've only got half an hour to go."

For someone with very limited driving experience, Rob was handling the car with remarkable skill, Glen thought. He watched his son sitting alertly at the wheel but showing no signs of tension as they moved through the curves of the canyon. He put his head back, closed his eyes and tried to relax. He was just nodding off when he felt a blast of cold air and came alert and saw Rob's window open.

"What's wrong?" he asked.

"I was getting dopey and you were asleep and I thought maybe we were getting a bit of carbon monoxide so I cleared it out. We're going to have to stop for gas pretty soon and it will be your turn to drive," Rob said.

"It doesn't seem to be getting any better, does it, Rob? Think we should stop and wait it out?"

"I could wait it out in a restaurant," Rob said. "I'm starving and I've got to pee so bad it hurts."

"Okay, let's stop at the next place we come to. I didn't notice until you said it but I'm in the same fix."

In Yale, after the last tunnel, they gassed up and found a small cafe and flopped into a booth.

"Whew!" Rob said, picking up a menu, his shoulders sagging. "That was hard work!"

"Why didn't you let me take over if you were getting tired?"

"It was my turn. You needed a rest," Rob said simply.

"Yeah, but..."

"I know, Dad," Rob interrupted with a wide grin. "Yabut, Yabut! That's what Craig always says when he hasn't got a good argument."

His father chuckled. "What are you going to have?" he asked as a waitress approached.

"I'll make it easy," Rob replied. "I'll have what you have."

Thinking of the heavy breakfast of sausages and pancakes and bacon and eggs, Glen wanted a salad or something light. But looking at the fatigue in his son's face, and knowing how he would react to a cottage cheese salad, he said to the waitress, "Two coffees now, and two double cheeseburgers with onions and mushrooms, and fries."

"That'll be okay, I guess, Dad," Rob said, with a yawn covering a wide smile. "But I was sorta looking forward to a fruit salad with cottage cheese."

"Well, why didn't you...?" his father said, raising his arm to recall the waitress but stopped when he saw his son's grin and something like the devil lurking behind it.

"I've never got over my craving for junk food," he said.

"Sure, Dad."

They sat in comfortable silence, waiting and looking around, and demolished the food when it came.

Glen paid the bill and stopped to talk with somebody while Rob wandered back to the car and settled into the passenger seat. His father came out in a few minutes and climbed in. "Well, we're in luck," he said. "That guy said that a lot of snow was dumped on Vancouver last night but the highway is good right up to Chilliwack. I guess we drove through the worst of it and he's heading into it."

"Poor bugger," Rob commiserated, and closed his eyes.

It was dark when Glen stopped in front of Rob's and nudged him awake.

"Hey, I musta dropped off," he said around a wide unstifled yawn. He reached over the seat to get his heavy jacket and his bag. "That was a good trip. Fun," he added.

"Yes, that was a good trip. You did the hardest driving. I can't remember when we've had that much time by ourselves. I enjoyed it. I wish it could have been longer." He reached out to shake hands but Rob twisted it around to a thumbs-grab and grinned.

"See ya, Dad. Love to Mom." He walked away, with a wave over his shoulder, looking like a badly nailed together scarecrow.

"Oh, you're home!" Claudia said with relief when Glen came in the door. "I was getting really worried. They said the canyon was closed. Was it a hard trip?"

"Not too bad. The canyon was closed, but Rob drove through it anyway." Then he told her how Rob had conned the RCMP cop and what a remarkably competent driver he was.

"Did you have a good time together?" she asked.

"Yes, we did. We didn't talk much but he is such an easy person to be with. I never realized that before. I'm sorry I didn't." He stopped, thinking. "Do you think he could change his mind about coming to Prince George?"

She shook her head slowly, several times. "Not a chance," she said. "Unless Craig and his mother moved, too. And probably Donna as well," she added. "Although I'm not too sure about Donna."

Donna was curled up on the bed in her housecoat, reading a book with the TV on when Rob walked in. He walked over and kissed her without passion. "Miss me?" he said.

"What do you think," she said. "I had nobody to cuddle up against."

"Well, I'll fix that right away," he said. "I'm pooped." He crawled onto the bed beside her with his clothes on.

"Rob!" she scolded. "Don't get on the bed with your dirty clothes on! Besides you stink. Go take a bath!"

"I might as well," he said in a tone of resignation. "I have early shift tomorrow." He undressed, dropped his clothes on the floor and went into the tiny bathroom.

"Did you have a good trip," she called.

"Yeah," he answered. "I drove most of the way. It was snowing."

"It snowed here too."

He came out drying himself. "Did you have a good time at the party with Craig?"

"Yeah, it was great. Well, except for trying to dance with Craig. But his boss is a fantastic dancer. There were a lot of nice people there. And a big turkey dinner. And you know what? There was free beer and I don't think anybody got drunk. I mean really drunk like we'd get when somebody's parents were away and there'd be a party."

He was picking up his clothes and emptying his pockets while she talked. Then he put on a pair of clean shorts and crawled across her into bed.

"Did you get drunk?" he asked.

"No," she said. "I had a beer and some guy gave me a shot of vodka in my punch."

"Did Craig?"

"Are you kidding? He had a beer," she said disdainfully.

She got off the bed, took off her housecoat and turned off the TV and the lights. Crawling in beside him, she curled up against him and reached down and slid her hand under his shorts.

"Don't, Donna," he said, twisting away from her. "I'm pooped, I said."

She stiffened, then turned her body away. After a few minutes, she turned her reading light on and picked up her book.

CHAPTER 59

Craig's normally sound sleep had been disturbed throughout the night by a tangle of anxiety provoking dreams that trashed the bed and left him sweating. It was daylight before the dreams disappeared and let him sink into deep unconscious slumber. When he wakened after noon, the house was quiet and the normal sounds of the world outside were being dampened by a thick layer of soft snow. He foggily remembered there had been no sign of snow when he drove home last night but now there was a foot of new snow and a cold winter sun was shining out of a cloudless sky. Reluctantly, he got out of bed and, seeing his new sports jacket flung half on a chair and half on the floor, he remembered coming home last night about four in the morning after the party and Donna. Donna! He sat down on the edge of the bed again and thought about going to bed with her. His first time—and what a mess he had made of it! What a clumsy idiot! He recalled the party, the promotion (if that was what it was), and Donna. Damn! How did I let myself get into that? What a shitty thing to do! Suppose Rob finds out! If it had been any other girl, I'd have been up hours ago and telling him about it. But I'll never be able to tell him about this. And there will never be another first time for me. He threw himself back on the bed and yanked the covers over his head. In the darkness he wondered if Rob had been as clumsy on his first time, and then, sitting up, he remembered what Donna had said: that Rob's first time was with her and he had mucked it up too, and that he really didn't like doing it anyway. Rob had been lying to him all along! Telling him he had slept with lots of girls—and naming them! Lying to him! He couldn't believe Rob would lie to him. Maybe it wouldn't be too hard to lie to him about Donna. He swore to himself to keep his mouth shut about it and deny it if Donna ever said anything.

"Craig! Are you getting up?" he heard his mother call. "It's lunch time. Get out of bed, for goodness sake!"

"I'm up." he called. "I'll be right down."

"Put on something warm," she called. "There was a big snow storm and you've got a lot of shovelling to do." She heard him mumble something and went out to fix them both something to eat.

"Well, you certainly had a good sleep-in," she said when he appeared. "I wish I could do that, but I still wake up early and read for a while and if I do go back to sleep, I feel so dopey when I wake up. Did you have a good time last night?"

He gave an unenthusiastic, "Yeah, it was a good party," through a yawn, and she glanced at him and could detect none of the sparkle he normally showed if he had had a fun time.

He suddenly realized that he had given a drab answer that she would detect so he set about to correct the impression. "Oh, yeah!" he said, struggling for more animation, "We all got a $200 bonus and a raise and he's working on a dental plan for children of employees. Thank you," he said as she put a plate of bacon and eggs and biscuits in front of him.

"That's lunch," she said, after bringing her own sandwich and coffee to the table. She waited for him to go on.

"Oh, yeah. He also gave me a promotion," he said around a mouthful, his face flushing.

"He what?" she said. "A promotion?"

He swallowed and said, "I guess it's a promotion—everybody called it that when they congratulated me." He began to come alive a bit and talk more like a regular Craig. "He said I would be his Assistant—no, that's not right. I'm going to be Assistant to the Manager—not Assistant Manager. But I don't get a raise." He grinned at her proudly.

"Oh, Craig, that's marvellous!" she said. "And you've only been there a couple of months"

"But I worked there in the summer too, don't forget."

"Yes, I know. Did any of the others resent it, do you think?" He shrugged. "Nobody said anything about resenting it. Everybody seemed glad for me."

"I think that's just great!" she enthused. "I can't wait to tell everybody."

"Oh, Mom!" he said, embarrassed. "Don't go doing that."

"I certainly will," she replied. "I'm just sorry I've written all my Christmas cards."

He shook his head and escaped before she could enquire about the rest of the party and how long it went on and what they did after. He found his snowboots, mitts, heavy coat and the snow shovel and went out to clear the sidewalks and the double driveway.

The scrape of the metal snow shovel on the cement walks sounded like words. Cheater, it muttered on the short strokes. Double-crosser, it growled on the long pushes. He cleared front, back and sides, then did the walks for the old man next door.

When he went in, his mother was sitting at a card table near the fireplace with the trilight beside her, working on some papers, her glasses drooping low on her nose.

"Are you going over to see Rob," she asked.

"No, he won't be back from Prince George yet."

"Oh! Well, if you're going to watch TV, would you watch downstairs? I'm right in the middle of a mess I want to clear up."

"Okay," he said, and headed for the stairs.

"But bring in an armful of wood first, would you, please? I'll keep the fire going and we can have our dinner on our laps."

Good, he thought as he left, she is finished asking me about last night. If she doesn't ask, Rob won't because he'll get it all from Donna and she won't tell and I'm home free.

He turned on the TV in the rec room and looked at a basketball game without seeing it, his mind on last night and his embarrassment with his clumsiness. He wondered how he should act when he saw Donna again. Would she say anything? God, she was insatiable! He never imagined it would be like that! Four times she made him do it. He didn't think that was possible. He wondered if Rob could do it four times. He was beginning to get an erection thinking about Rob doing it, when his mother called.

"I thought you were going to bring in a load of wood!" she shouted up to him over the noise of the TV. He sighed.

Rob came home with an armful of groceries. "I didn't get everything on the list," he said. "I'll get the rest tomorrow." "That's okay, we've got enough for supper so we don't have to go out into that miserable night," Donna said, putting the groceries away.

"Oh, I thought it was kind of fun," Rob said. "The snow is all crunchy and squeaky when you walk. Don't you want to go out and have a snowball fight?" he teased.

"No way!" she stated firmly. "I just about froze my butt off walking home from work. That's enough for me! If you want to go out and play in the snow, go find Craig."

He was getting out of the black slacks and white shirt that he wore at work and putting on jeans and a sweatshirt. "Did you guys have a good time at Craig's party?" he asked. "I probably asked you last night but I was too tired to listen. Oh, yeah! I remember. You told me. You said his boss was a great dancer and you were drinking vodka with him."

"I didn't say it quite like that!" she protested. "I said some guy gave me a shot of vodka, not Craig's boss."

"How did you get on with Craig—dancing?" he asked. She looked at him casually trying to find a shade of suspicion in his voice or face, but there was none.

"Well, we worked our way through three of four dances without moving very far. People kept stopping to congratulate Craig and it takes him a long time to work his way back to the beat. Not what you would call a great dancer."

"Did you have to tell him to stick his bum out?" Rob grinned.

"He was too busy counting his feet to get sexy," She said. "I think he'd rather dance with you, anyway."

"Hey, what did you mean—about people congratulating Craig," dismissing her remark.

"Oh, didn't I tell you. His boss announced that he was promoting Craig to Assistant something or other—Assistant to the Manager, that's what it was."

"He didn't!" Rob exclaimed, his face lighting up. "The lucky little bugger! I wonder how he managed that! Shit, that's great! I better go phone him right now or he'll be mad at me. I'll just run over to the pay phone at the drug store." He got into his snowboots again and pulled on a ski jacket and toque. "I won't be long," he assured her as he headed out the door.

"Give him my love," she called.

He was back in ten seconds. "I'll give him your love if you give me some change. I haven't got any."

"You never have any of anything when you need it," she said giving him a handful of change from her tips bowl.

"Yeah, but I got you, babe," he said as he seemed to disappear in the darkness, leaving his grin behind like the Cheshire cat.

The phone rang at the Williams and Marion answered it, and she heard Robbie say, "Hello, U.U., my lovely one."

"Hello, Robbie," she said. "I was just talking to your mother. Are you home, or have you got a phone now?"

"No, I'm at the corner drug store. I just had to phone and hear your voice again even if I had to brave the storm."

"I'll call Craig," she said.

"How do you know I want to talk to Craig," he said with dramatic petulance.

"I'm psychic," she said, putting the phone down.

He heard her call Craig, saying, "Guess who's on the phone?"

"Hullo," Craig said. He wanted to say it in a normal way but it came out with a note of caution.

"Hello to you, too," came Rob's bouncing voice. "You know what my lady just told me?" Craig stopped breathing. "She said you didn't have to stick your bum out when you danced with her."

"She did?" Craig croaked.

"I think that's unforgivably rude of you—not to give the lady of your best friend some casual indicator that she's a lovely sexpot."

"Yeah, but—-."

"But-but-but, like an outboard!" Rob interrupted. "You know if I had taken your lady dancing, if you had one, I would have certainly given some indication, probably physical, that if you thought she was lovely, then I did too. Matter of fact I probably would have taken her to bed for you."

"But you do that to all the girls." Craig was trying to pretend envy.

"I know, I know. They can't keep their hands off me, and who am I to disappoint them? Ah, me!" he sighed. "Anyhow, I'm not standing out here in the cold and sleet and dark of night to talk about my love life. Donna says you were the hit of the party and everybody clapped for an hour just because the boss gave you a promotion. What's that all about?"

"It really wasn't an hour. Maybe thirty minutes, forty five at the most."

"Good thing I taught you how to bow. So tell me!"

So Craig told him and Rob did not interrupt. He finished, saying, "Oh, yeah, I also get a car allowance for running around town. Sorta gofer food." He laughed.

"Hey, man," Rob said, "that's great! Really, really great! I'm proud of you!"

"Yeah, well, thanks. It was sure a surprise."

"I'll bet!" Rob agreed. Then he said in a low, growly voice, "You're sure he's not after your boddee?"

"Pretty sure," Craig laughed.

"Good! Remember, I get first dibs. Hey, I gotta go before I freeze the family jewels. See ya soon, eh? When are you going to give me my Christmas present?"

"I did already."

"That little thing! I thought now that you're an executive with your own desk and a travelling allowance, you'd want to share some of those riches with your best buddy."

"Nice try!"

"Cheapskate, goodbye!"

Craig sat smiling at the phone. His mother passed by and gave him a searching look. "That's all it takes, does it? Just a call from Rob and the dolefuls disappear."

He grinned at his mother and went up to his room where he laid flat on his back and stared happily at the ceiling.

On Monday, late in the morning, Glen walked into the Superstore and walked up and down a few aisles with a shopping list in his hand but his eye out for Rob. He finally found him stocking the herb shelves and stood for a moment looking at him in amazement. Rob wore the standard dress for the store: black slacks, white shirt and a red bow tie. But Rob had had his slacks fitted to his lean body, the shirt was sparkling white, his unruly hair was slicked into place and his shoes were polished. He wished he had brought a camera.

He walked close to Rob who was intent on his job, and said, quietly, "Young man, I wonder if you could help me?"

"Dad!" Rob said before all his father's words were out. "What are you doing here?"

"Your mother gave me a shopping list and I've never seen where you worked so I figured I'd drop by and surprise you."

"Good. I haven't got a break for an hour yet, but I'll walk around with you and help you shop. Let's see your list." He took it from his father and said, "Okay, let's start on the next aisle."

They walked together around the store, dodging through the crowd, stopping occasionally as people stopped Rob to ask for directions. There was little opportunity for talk. Rob asked his father if they needed any help in packing to go north. Glen said how much he appreciated Rob's help on the weekend, and said again what a competent driver he was. Rob said he was glad they could get away together but if they ever did it again he hoped it would be in sunshine. His father agreed that it was a cold trip that he wouldn't want to do too often. Rob put his father into line and said, "I better get back to my job, Dad. I'm glad you dropped by," and he smiled and squeezed his father's arm. "Oh, better tell Mom that I did the shopping," he said as he turned away, "or she'll think you're so good at it, she'll make you do it all the time."

"Good idea," his father said with a wink. "Oh, by the way, maybe you'd better phone your mother and make a time for us to pick you and Donna up to go over to Bev's for Christmas dinner."

"Okay, Dad. I'll do it on my break. Bye"

"Are you Rob's father," a fragile old lady behind him asked.

"Yes," Glen answered, nodding and trying not to look too proud.

"Such a nice boy," she said. "He's always so pleasant and helpful. And if we can't find anything, he doesn't just tell us where it is, he runs off and gets it for us."

Another equally fragile old lady behind the first one was nodding in agreement. "We always shop here," she said.

He smiled at them as he moved ahead to pay the cashier.

"Merry Christmas," the first old lady said while the other nodded agreement.

"Thank you," he answered. "Merry Christmas to you, too."

Leaving the store, feeling warm and content, he stuffed a couple of bills in the Salvation Army bucket.

"God bless you," the Santa Claus said.

He walked to his car and headed for home, thinking, I would be truly blessed if Rob changed his mind and came with us.

Craig went to work feeling a little uncertain about his role but decided on his way that he would go in as usual and wait until Carl called him when he wanted him. The men were standing around in small groups talking mostly about the company party. "Look out, guys," Larry shouted with a big grin as Craig walked in. "Here comes the boss!"

"Aw, cut it out Larry," Craig said, red-faced.

But from several men other comments erased his embarrassment. "Nice going, Craig!" "Atta boy, Craig!" "Hey, if you can't give us a raise, how about a day off?" Larry gave him a solid whack on the back and moved off to his machine which the other men read as the signal that work had started. Larry had not given him a job to do, so Craig looked quickly around and saw a load piled up in the stitching area and walked over and started stitching. Larry watched him out of the corner of his eye and made a small nod of approval.

Carl came out after the morning break and walked around stopping to talk with those men whose attention was not demanded by a machine. There were a lot of smiles and handshakes as those who had not thanked him on Saturday did so now. He stopped at Craig's machine and said, "Did you close up the place on Saturday?"

"Not quite. There were still a few people going strong when Donna and I left."

"I think it was a good party. Best one we've had in years," he said. "Did you have a good time? I guess you and Donna were the youngest ones there."

"Yeah, I had a great time. I'm not much of a dancer so I talked with a lot of people. And Mrs. Cranston and I had a good talk together because she didn't want to dance either."

"She told me you had sat down and chatted with her. Actually she's a very good dancer, but sometimes she just likes to sit and talk."

He turned to go but stopped and said. "Maybe we should move ahead with our computer plans. We should try to get it in place for the new year. What do you think?"

"That's not much time," Craig responded uncertainly. "We could get the computers installed, I guess. That wouldn't take long, I don't think, once we decide what one. But I guess we have to remember time for training of the people."

"Yeah, maybe I'm rushing it," Carl said. "Come on in after lunch and let's talk about it."

"Okay," Craig said and turned back to his machine wondering if he had said too much.

***

Marion and Claudia had a nice long gossip on the phone. Claudia had been sorting out her perishables and boxing some of them to take and others to take out to Bev.

"I don't see any sense in loading up all the canned goods and dragging them up to Prince George, so there's a whole box I'll take down to the food bank because I know Bev doesn't need them. You know what most of it is? Glen passes a store and sees a big sale and he thinks it's a bargain so he buys a half dozen and brings them home proudly. The last time it was pickled herring. We tried one jar and had to throw the rest out. He's out shopping again right now. He wanted to go over to see where Rob works. Lord only knows what he'll come back with this time." She paused. "I think he wants to try one more time to get Rob to come with us."

"They must have had a good trip together," Marion said.

"Marion, you wouldn't believe it. Glen came home raving about Rob as if he had never met him before. He was absolutely glowing with happiness. I didn't know what kind of magic happened but it sure was nice to see after those years of father-son adolescent warfare."

"Yes, I remember the warfare but I can't recall any magic," Marion said quietly.

"Oh, Marion! How stupid of me to bring up the subject. I'm sorry."

"It's all right, Claudia. Nine days out of ten I never even think of him any more. As a matter of fact, this will be the first Christmas when I won't be walking around on thin ice wondering how he is going to spoil it this year. I might even celebrate. I know what I'm going to do—I just thought of it. I'm going to get some champagne for your party to celebrate a lot of things. Not your leaving, I don't mean that. But you and Glen making such a big change in your lives. It seems like such a big venture, like a thing young kids would do."

"We're not exactly ancients, you know!"

"Well, you are three weeks older than me," Marion said teasingly as their tête-à-tête came to an end. "Think I should splurge on champagne?"

"Why not? I'll split it with you."

"No, you won't. It's my party. Bye for now, I'll call you tomorrow or Wednesday to wish you Merry Christmas."

"Bye, dear. I'll get moving too."

Marion settled down with another cup of coffee to make some calls to her bridge group, leaving a call to Edith to the last.

* * *

Rob spent some time after he finished work looking for a Xmas present for Donna and finally settled on a thick white terry-cloth bathrobe and a pair of house slippers. He tried to sneak it into the house but couldn't.

"Close your eyes and no peeking!" he called from the door. "I'm Santa and I have to come early because you haven't got a chimney."

He stuffed the parcel under the bed and said, "Okay, you can turn around now and open your eyes."

"Where is it?" she asked.

"I hid it, goofy! You can't have it until Xmas morning." He went over to her and put his arms around her and kissed her, but her lips were tight and unresponsive. He drew back, puzzled and a little hurt. Now what did I do, he thought, still holding her. Oh, maybe because I turned her off last night. So he nuzzled into her neck and pulled her body into his, and said, "Sorry about last night, Donna, but I really was so tired I couldn't have done anything."

She pushed his body away from hers. "Don't get all hot and sexy. It's my no-no time of month," she lied.

CHAPTER 60

As the result of their conference on Monday afternoon, Carl and Craig met with the sales manager of the firm whose computer they had selected. On his recommendation, and that of the salesman who had visited the plant, they agreed on a particular model that would be housed in the main office with two satellite stations, one in shipping and receiving and the other in the work area so that corrugation, cutting, printing, stapling and other work jobs could be entered easily. Carl was impressed that they could have a complete record of the progress of any job from the time the order was received to the receipt of payment, including time, material, and other data that would make possible a cost analysis for each order. They also contracted with the company to demonstrate and to teach the employees in each section in one hour sessions following the noon hour break in such a way that no section of the plant would be shut down at any one time. Carl thought it was important that all employees should know the basic operation of the system, including himself and Craig and the three women who ran the office. Because of the slow period between Christmas and New Years they arranged morning sessions for Carl and Craig between the holidays, then five morning sessions for the three women after the New Year with Carl and Craig trying to hold the fort. Other noon sessions for the men would be worked out later. Craig would attend all sessions so that he could be called upon for trouble shooting and training. He and Dorothy, the senior office clerk, would also attend a computer training course two nights a week for ten weeks at company expense with time and a half the course time added to their vacation time. By the end of the session a contract had been completed and the total price set and agreed upon. The sales manager had wanted to include travelling time to and from the plant for the training salesmen, but Carl balked at the suggestion so resolutely that the item was excluded from the contract.

"Well, how did we do?" Carl asked as they drove back to the plant.

Craig had listened all morning and made notes, responding supportively to Carl's questions to him and occasionally drawing his attention to some detail he thought was being overlooked. "I was surprised at the total price," he said. "I had a good idea of the basic computer system costs, but I thought the installation and training would be an awful lot more."

"So did I," Carl agreed. "But, then, I had no way of making a comparison. But I think we made a good deal. I didn't like his attempt to sneak in travelling time costs for the instructors. I think those costs should be his company's responsibility."

"Yeah, I thought it was a funny thing to do, but..."

"I would have walked out if he had insisted," Carl said. "There are other computer companies, after all."

They were silent until they reached the parking lot. Carl made no move to get out for a minute but sat thinking with his hands on the wheel. Finally he said, "My schedule is pretty packed for the rest of the day. How about you making some detailed notes of what went on this morning and I'll use them to make up a memo to the rest of the people so there will be no surprises. And you can field any questions that might come up. There's an extra desk in the main office you can use."

"Sure, I'll get right at it," Craig said as they got out of the car and went into the plant.

Carl stopped to have a word with Larry while Craig went to the lunch room and picked up his lunch from his locker. The lunch break had been over for some time so he ate alone thinking about the morning and feeling very pleased with himself that he had been invited and was expected to participate. He wolfed down his lunch and headed for the office.

"Dorothy," he said to the senior clerk, "I have to make up a report for Carl so I'll need some paper and a pencil, please."

"Your desk is over there, Craig. You should find everything you need in it," Dorothy replied while the other two women looked on, hiding smiles.

Craig looked over to where she had pointed and saw a small oak desk with a matching arm chair against the far wall. There was a blotter on the desk, a calendar on the wall and a hand printed note taped below the calendar, 'This is the desk of Craig Williams. Assistant to the Manager.'

"For me?" he asked bewildered.

"That's for you alright," Dorothy said. "Carl ordered it yesterday and it was delivered this morning."

Craig went over to the desk and touched it without sitting down. "Where's Carl now?" he asked. "I should thank him."

"He's on the phone," Dorothy said.

"Better try it out," one of the others said. "See if it fits."

Craig went over and pulled out the chair and sat down while the women smiled and watched. "Better check out the swivel and tilt," Dorothy called.

He did, grinning widely.

"Looks like an a executive, doesn't he?"

"As soon as he gets a phone."

"Oh yes, Craig," Dorothy said. "Your phone will be here after Christmas." The three women smiled at him and turned back to their desks.

Craig sat down and wondered how to start. He looked in the drawers of the desk and found some paper and with much hesitation wrote at the top of the page 'Report on the Computer Contract.'

He was on the second handwritten page when Carl came out of the office. "So, you found your desk, eh?" he said to Craig with a smile.

"Yes, I did. I wasn't expecting that. I thought... I don't know what I thought. Thank you very much."

"A man's got to have a place to work," Carl said. "How's the report coming?"

"I've got some more to put in, maybe another page."

"Fine. Put it in my in-basket. I'll deal with it in the morning. Dorothy, I'm heading over to the bank and then I have a committee meeting at the church. Do you want me to take the mail?"

"No, I'm not finished. I'll take it."

"Okay, see you tomorrow." He walked to the door and looked back to watch Craig pull his chair up to the desk again and a trace of a smile appeared on his face.

* * *

Vic came in to the Sweet Spot for lunch and as usual he and Donna had only a casual conversation such as any school friends might have, and as usual there was a key among the change on the table that was left as a tip. On her break, she caught a bus down to the bus station and went immediately to the locker number on the key. Looking around cautiously, although she did not know what she was looking for, she reached in and withdrew a small parcel which she slipped into her purse. Taking a taxi to the Robson Street address, she climbed the stairs and knocked on the door. There was no answer. She knocked once more and waited in the quiet of the dimly lit hallway trying to quell a rising panic. The only sound she heard apart from the street sounds coming up the stairs was a radio playing in the other apartment. Once more she knocked, this time very hard, and again there was no answer but the radio in the other apartment was turned off. She panicked and ran and, trembling, took a taxi back to the Sweet Spot where she searched up and down the street for Vic's car but could not find it. She wanted to give him the package and put an end to this scary game but by the time she was due back at work he had not shown.

"You not feel good?" Bruno asked as she hung up her coat.

"I'm okay," she replied. "Maybe a little cold, that's all."

"Better go home and take aspirin and get better."

"Maybe later, Bruno. I'll do the clean-up and maybe then if I still feel shaky, I'll go," she replied as she set about her routine after lunch chore while keeping a close watch on the street. She wished Rob would come in and tell her what to do with the parcel. It was still in her purse on the shelf in the kitchen above the hooks where they hung their coats and every time she passed it, it seemed as though it was getting bigger. After an hour of unorganized shaky work, Bruno said abruptly, "Go home!"

"Thanks, Bruno," she said. "I better go. Maybe it's just the flu."

When she got home, she locked the door and hid the package in the cupboard, then sat in the quiet room waiting for the sound of Rob's key in the door.

Rob's parents had stopped for a tea break. Glen had spent most of the day, helping Roger get caught up. He was a slow worker at best, but today he had jammed a staple in his hand and was trying ineffectively to work with one hand, so Glen took over.

"I don't know how he is going to manage after we go," Glen said. "He knows bugger-all about the business and he doesn't learn very quickly, that's for sure."

"Maybe he will hire somebody competent," Claudia said. "Rob would have been ideal. He knows the idiosyncrasies of every machine up there."

"Yeah, I never realized how efficient Robbie was until I watched Roger. Good thing he's got a rich daddy that will bail him out again. And it's a good thing we decided not to hold the mortgage. Let the bank and daddy do the dirty work."

Claudia was only half listening to her husband. She had stopped listening when he had said "Robbie." He hadn't referred to his son by that endearment for years and he was still bringing up little things about their trip to Prince

George—all of them positive, which pleased her immensely. But, and she couldn't help it, she found herself figuratively crossing her fingers, hoping it would last and that Rob would not do anything to upset the balance.

Craig finished his report and walked over to Dorothy's desk to use her stapler.

"Would you like me to type it for you?" she asked.

"Oh, should it be typed?" he asked. "It's only for Carl." He stopped and stumbled, "I don't mean only, in that way. I meant it's not for mailing out, it's just internal." But he handed the papers over to her feeling like a school boy handing in an assignment.

"You're right," she said. "That's good writing. It doesn't need typing." It was Craig's usual writing—large letters without any slant, looking somewhat feminine.

He put it in Carl's in-basket and went out into the plant to look for Larry.

"If you don't have anything to do, check in shipping. I think there are three orders there that have to go out," Larry told him.

Craig liked shipping, probably more than any other job in the plant, but he figured he might like his desk job more once he had more to do. He worked in shipping until the buzzer went and it was time to punch out.

Rob came home and found the door locked and wondered where Donna could be as he searched for his key. When he opened the door, he found Donna sitting on the edge of the bed in the dark, looking upset.

"Hey," he said, flinging off his coat and turning on the light, "What are you sitting in the dark for."

She looked at him with wide eyes and said, "Rob, I've got to tell you what happened today. Now don't get mad at me."

"Okay, what?" He went to the bed and sat beside her. "Tell me!" when she hesitated. "I'm not going to get mad."

So she told him about Vic and the key and how she meant to tell him it was the last time and she wasn't going to do it any more only before she could tell him he had walked out, so she went down to the bus station and picked up the package and she felt something was wrong but didn't know what and she took a taxi to Robson Street and knocked on the door and there was no answer and she tried again and it was so quiet it was scary but she tried once more and got scared and went back to the cafe and looked for Vic but he never came so she worked for a while and Bruno sent her home because she looked sick and she hid the package and was waiting for him to come home.

She was breathless and tearful when she finished.

"You mean it's here? You hid it here?"

She nodded dumbly.

"Oh shit!" he said. "Shit "Shit! Shit! Shit!" He flung himself back on the bed. "I knew it! I knew we'd get caught!"

All Donna heard, with relief, was Rob saying 'we'.

"What are we going to do?" she asked shakily.

"I dunno. Where is it?"

She got up and brought the package to him. "Shall we flush it down the toilet?" she asked.

"We can't. They know we've got it because Vic gave you the key and the locker is empty. They'll be looking for us so we better give it back to them fast."

He was turning the package over in his hands, examining it. "Is it the same as the others?" he asked.

"It might be smaller and a little heavier," she said. "Because I could put it in my purse and I couldn't put the others in s in." She stopped. "And, the money's the same," she added, pointing to the $60.00 written in ink on the package. "And there's never been any initials on the package before, I don't think."

"It's a trap!" Rob said. "Why in hell did we ever get into this?" He stood up and paced as far as the little room would permit. "Do you know Vic's number or where he lives?"

She shook her head. "He was living at home when I knew him last year, but his father kicked him out."

"We gotta get it back to him or them somehow," Rob said.

Donna was sniffling and wiping her eyes. "I'm sorry, Rob," she said. "I really wasn't going to do any more. I was going to tell him but he skipped out while my back was turned and I couldn't and I thought, well, just this once more. I'm sorry!"

He sat down beside her and absently patted her while he sorted through various possibilities. "They're going to be looking for us," he said. "You specially."

She started to cry again.

"I'm sorry, Donna, but it's true. Vic would know you anywhere and he doesn't really know me, except there was one time I stopped him and his gang from beating up on Craig. I wish we had a phone, then I could get Craig to come over and we could figure something out."

"You didn't tell Craig anything about this, I mean what I was doing, did you."

"Hell, no! I didn't tell anybody about it. I figured it was too dangerous."

They sat in silence for a while, then Rob got to his feet and put his coat on. "Here's what we're gonna do," he announced. "You stay here and keep quiet, no TV and no lights, and lock the door. I'm going to catch a cab and take this parcel down to the bus station and put it in a locker. Then if they come looking for us we'll just tell them that you couldn't deliver it because there was nobody at home so we put it in another locker and we'll give them the key. Then we'll say they still owe us sixty bucks because we tried to deliver it and couldn't. That'll make it look good, not like we were trying to steal it."

"What if they're looking for you and catch you," Donna said, breaking into another flood of tears.

"I guess I'll have to lie like hell or tell the truth or call the cops," Rob said with a grin and kissed her goodbye. "Keep the door locked and no lights. Find me a bag of some kind, will you? A plastic shopping bag will do. That'll look nice and innocent."

"Wish me luck," he said with a grin as he stood getting ready, with his hand on the door handle.

"Oh, Rob! I'm sorry," she said again.

He blew her a kiss like an old-time black and white movie hero, corny as hell, and closed the door behind him.

Fifteen minutes later he paid the taxi and asked him to wait. He walked into the bus station, hoping he was looking nonchalant and not as scared as he felt. His mouth was dry and his knees felt rubbery. He headed for a bank of lockers, trying not to look around at the people waiting with their luggage piled at their feet. He found an empty locker, took the package out of the bag trying not to look furtive, and shoved it into the locker. He closed the door quickly and, with shaking hands tried to turn the key to extract it, forgetting to put money in.

"One moment, sir!" a man's voice said behind him.

"What?" he squawked. It was not quite a question.

"City police," one of two men said, showing a badge. "There's been a bomb alert and we are asking public cooperation permitting us to examine locker contents."

"It's just a parcel," Craig protested.

"Then you shouldn't mind opening the locker."

"Look, officer," Rob started without knowing how he was going to finish, but it didn't matter.

"Open the goddam locker!" the other officer growled in a threatening monotone.

With a defeated sigh, Rob opened the locker. "See!" he said in a last feeble defence, "It's just a package, like I said."

The officer extracted the package from the shopping bag and examined it. "This $60 written on it. That the value of this package?"

"Yes. No. I mean, I don't know. I'm just delivering for a friend," Rob mumbled.

"These initials?" the officer asked.

"I don't know."

The officer took a notebook from his pocket and scribbled something in it. "These are my initials," he said. "Would you compare the two."

It took Rob only a single glance to realize the two sets of initials were identical. "Oh, shit!" he said.

"We will also find my fingerprints all over the plastic bag inside that contained $75,000 worth of cocaine this morning. We left an ounce in it—enough to charge you with possession."

"Oh, shit!" was all Rob could manage, now white with fright and shaking. "$75,000! O-oh! O-oh! Jesus!" he groaned.

"Come with us quietly," one officer said, and they walked him out the door.

"Spread!" the other officer growled and Rob placed his hands on the roof of the squad car and spread his legs. He felt the officer's hands roaming expertly over his body. "In the car!" came another growl.

"What's your name," the first officer said when they were in the car. The growler was driving.

"Rob Turner."

"Got any identification?"

Rob produced his wallet and handed it to the officer. "There's my driver's license."

The officer looked at it and asked, "Is this your present address?"

Rob remembered that he had never changed the address on the license from his parent's address to the Lasserets. "Yes," he said, hoping that the lie would keep Donna out of it.

"Where does your girl friend live?"

"What girl friend? I don't have a girl friend."

"You don't, eh? Look kid, we watched her pick up this package from the bus stop this afternoon and take it to the old man on Robson Street but we had already taken him in and she couldn't deliver it and we lost her. Who is she?"

"I don't know who you're talking about."

"So she had the parcel and then you have the parcel and you don't know her. Is that what you're telling me?"

"Yeah," Rob said, feeling that he was getting trapped. "All I know is this friend of mine phoned and said he would put a small parcel on my front door step and asked me to take it to the bus station and put it in a locker and he would get the key from me later. So that's what I did." He didn't dare look at them while he was creating the story, afraid that they would see the lie in his face.

They had reached the police station but stayed in the car. Both men had twisted around in the front seat to look at him.

"So who is this friend of yours? What's his name?"

"Just a guy I knew from around school. He isn't really a friend—just somebody I knew, you know, like you know a lot of people just from seeing them around," Rob stuttered.

"So you're telling me that this guy you hardly know dumps $75,000 worth of coke on your doorstep and asked you to go put it in a locker at the bus station. Is that right?"

"You said you had taken the coke out and only left a little in," Rob said.

The growly cop who had driven the car turned around further in the front seat with his arm dangling over the back and a look of cold fury on his face. "Don't get smart, kid!" he said with such slow menace that Rob pushed back into the seat as far as he could, and decided to stick to answering questions.

"So what's the name of this friend you hardly know?"

Rob hesitated a long time and then decided he better tell part of the truth. "Sid," he muttered.

"Sid what?"

"I don't know his last name. He's just called Sid."

"And this girl you don't know, is she connected with this friend of yours, this Sid guy?"

Rob just about blurted out "No!" but caught himself and said, "I don't know. I don't know what girl you're talking about."

"I see," said the talking cop. "Well, it looks like you and the girl just provided a little delivery service for old Sid, eh? Out of the kindness of your hearts. Is that it?"

"I don't know about her, but that's all I did."

"Well, we'll see what Sid's got to say. We call him Vic, by the way. He's one of our guests tonight along with the old man from Robson Street."

Rob groaned.

"Now if we could just 'cherche la femme' you guys could get together and get your stories straight."

"For Crissake, Harry," said the growler. "Let's get this guy inside and book him. I'd like to get home for my supper once this week while it's still hot."

"Okay, Robert Turner, out you get," the other cop said as he got out and opened the back door for Rob. "We're going inside and book you for possession for a start, maybe more, maybe a lot more. And I'd like to recommend to you the special we have on for Bed and Breakfast for those who decide to be cooperative. Your friend, Vic or Sid, however, chose the rat hole with bread and water rather than accept our hospitality."

"Cut the shit, Harry," said the growler. "Let's just book him and go home."

CHAPTER 61

Rob had been taken to an interrogation room where the two arresting officers went over his story again and then once more.

"So this friend of yours, Vic, who is not a friend but just some guy you knew from school—and that was only four months ago, right?" the one who was called Harry by the Growler said.

Rob nodded.

"Look, Robert! It would be exceedingly helpful to me, a member of the city police, and to our cranky secretary whose task it is to take this crap from tape and put it on paper, if you could see your way clear to say yes, no, maybe, I think so, yes sir, no sir or up your kilt sir, instead of just nodding. Got it?"

"Yes, sir!" Rob replied, and added in a louder voice, "Sorry, Ma'am!"

Harry continued, but turned to one side to hide the beginnings of a smile, "So Vic leaves a package on your doorstep with instructions to take the package to the bus station and put it in a locker. Right?"

"Yes sir."

"He phoned you at home. Right?"

"Yes sir."

"What time would that be?"

"I don't know what time he put it on my doorstep because I wasn't home, but I found it about six o'clock, maybe six fifteen, or six seventeen."

"Watch it, smartass!" the Growler said from behind him.

"Yes sir!" This time like a marine.

Then there followed another long series of questions: How many times have you done this before? (None.) Has your girl friend delivered? (I don't have a girl friend.) How much were you going to get paid. (Nothing.) Nothing? (Yeah, he was calling in a marker.) What kind of a marker? (He put me in his car and let me sleep it off when somebody spiked my drink one time.) Ever been charged with a drug offence? (Yes. For having a joint in school, but the judge dismissed it.) Yeah, we know.

"Harry, let's get out of here. Hand him over to the desk and let them finish the booking, for God's sake. I'm hungry," The Growler urged.

Harry put his papers together and stood up.

"Excuse me, sir. I have to go to the bathroom bad. Where can I go?"

"I'll send someone in to take you," Harry said as both officers went out the door.

Rob sat alone in the room waiting, uncomfortably. He crossed his legs, groaned, gritted his teeth, clutched his crotch with both hands and rocked in his chair while a wet patch on his pants grew steadily in size. After twenty minutes he stuck his head out of the door and shouted "Hello?"

A cop emerged from another door and turned in the opposite direction.

"Sir!" Rob shouted at his back. "I gotta take a piss!"

The cop looked at the crouching figure clutching himself and said, "What are you doing in there?"

"I don't know! They just left me in there and went home. Please! I have to go to the bathroom. Where is it?"

"Come with me."

Rob followed him around a corner and into a men's room.

Rob rushed to a urinal and while he stood, sighing, as he relieved himself, the cop said. "What were you doing in there?"

"Nothing! They just left me there."

"Have you been charged with anything?"

"I dunno. Shit! Look at my pants!" He walked over to the towel dispenser, unzipped his fly and tried to dry the worst of the wetness while the cop looked on.

"Hurry up, I got other things to do and I have to take you back," the cop said.

Rob zipped and rinsed his hands and together they walked down the hall. "Thank you, officer. I was afraid I was going to rupture myself."

"Okay. What room were you in?"

"I don't know."

"This one will do," the cop said, opening a door. "I'll tell the desk."

"Thanks again, officer. Say, is it possible to have Chinese delivered in here?" Rob said with a grin.

The officer smiled and said as he turned away, "Don't press your luck, kid."

It wasn't the same room but it was the same setup. Rob sat down and waited. An hour passed. The room was soundproofed so that he could only hear faint rumbles of voices and thumping steps. Finally the door was flung open and two men were shoved into the room followed by two policemen.

"What are you doing here?" one demanded.

"I dunno," Rob said with exasperation. "I was told to stay."

"Who told you?"

"I don't know, for Chrissakeake! You guys don't wear nametags!"

"Stay here," one of them said and disappeared.

"Where the hell did you think I was going?" Rob shouted. Then he made a sweeping gesture and said to the two men, "Sit down, fellas. There's lots of chairs, none reserved."

Nobody moved.

Another officer, looking harried, rushed into the room, followed by the one who had rushed away a minute ago. "Are you Turner? Where have you been?" he demanded, not waiting for an answer to the first question or the second. "Come with me!"

"When you're told to stay, you stay!" he commanded as they walked down the hall to the main office.

"I had to take a leak and some guy took me down the hall to the men's and then put me back in a different room."

"Well, how am I supposed to book you if I can't find you?"

Rob began to feel like he was in a skit for Saturday Night Live but restrained the urge to say so.

The evening wore on. He was questioned routinely for full name, parents names, address, postal code, age, birthdate, place of work and other inconsequentialities, all of which was banged out on a typewriter by the officer. He was photographed, fingerprinted and searched, but he was not fed and he was famished. His pockets were emptied and he was told the charge was possession of cocaine with a street value of less than $1000.

"I don't know why they bother," he heard the officer mutter as he finished typing and ripped the sheet out of the machine. "One of you guys take him down to the tank for me," he called out generally as he made some copies of the charge sheet.

One of the policemen got up, picked up a copy and beckoned to Rob to follow him. Rob had a sudden feeling of having been through all this before and crossed his fingers hoping it would have the same easy ending, but somehow he felt things would be different this time. When they went through some barred doors at the back of the building, he was suddenly overwhelmed by apprehension. The large cell contained eight or nine men, two sleeping or passed out on the floor, several pacing and all of them looking menacing. He walked closer to the officer leading him, keeping a wary eye on the cell full of men who were watching him.

"Williams," his guide said, handing the charge sheet to a policeman sitting reading at a bare desk. "Better put him in the Queen's quarters. Those guys in there will tear him apart."

The guard glanced at the sheet, said "Okay," and jerked his head to Rob to follow. He unlocked the door to an empty cell and, without a word, locked it after Rob walked in, white faced and distressed.

He sat on the edge of a lower bunk. What did he mean, 'Put him in the queens quarters'? Does he think I'm a homo? Can these guys pick one out of a crowd? Jesus! Does it show?

At that moment, the label and the quickness with which it was attached to him was more agonizing than the drug charge. For a long time he sat and worried and puzzled. What did I say? What did I do that made me look or sound faggotty? Finally, more oppressing concerns took over. There was Craig and Donna and his parents and his job—and, oh, shit! What a mess!

He got up and went to the barred door of the cell. "Guard! Guard! Can I speak to you, please?"

The guard appeared at the door. "Yeah?"

"Don't I get a phone call? Like, you know, when anybody gets arrested, aren't they given one phone call?"

"Didn't you get one when they booked you?"

"No!"

"Just a minute. I'll check the charge sheet." He wandered off slowly and came back. "No, nothing on your sheet," he said. "The phone's over there."

"Officer, why did the other officer tell you to put me in the queen's quarters?"

The guard shrugged, "Maybe he wants to come down and visit you later on."

Rob shuddered. He walked over to the phone and picked up the ragged, dirty phone book to give himself time to figure out who to call. Not his mother or father, for certain. Maybe Craig, but what could he do? U.U., maybe. But no, that would scare her. Richard, that's who! Like last time. Or U.U.'s lawyer—Murray something. No, Craig, that's who. He can go and tell Donna—she must be going crazy, and he can phone Richard or Murray what's-his-name. "How do I call out," he called to the guard. "I don't have any money."

"It's on the Queen," the guard answered. "Just pick up the phone and the operator will take your name and dial your number."

"There's that goddamn queen thing again," he muttered as he picked up the phone.

When Marion answered the ring while she was reading in bed, she heard Rob's unusually strained voice. "U.U.," he said. "I know it's late and I'm sorry to bother you, but I need to speak to Craig right away. It's urgent."

"Robbie, are you in trouble?" Marion asked.

"Yes. But please don't tell my Mom and Dad."

"Alright, Robbie," she agreed. "Just a minute. I'll get Craig. He's asleep."

In less than two minutes, Craig was on the phone, "Rob? What's up?" he asked anxiously as he heard his mother's phone click off. "Mom said it was urgent."

"I'm in jail," Rob said. "Are you awake?"

"I am now!"

"Well, listen. I want you to do something."

"What did you do?"

"Craig! I'll tell you later. Not over the phone."

"Okay. So what do I do? I hope you're not expecting me to bust you out."

"Yes, that's exactly what I want. I want you to go down to that construction site on Fourth and steal a bulldozer and come up here and wreck this joint. Nut head!"

"That's easy! Gimme a hard one."

Rob spoke quietly without reason, nobody was listening and nobody cared. "Phone Richard and tell him I would appreciate it if he would do the same thing for me as he did last time I got caught."

"It's the middle of the night," Craig protested.

"I know. I hope he won't be mad, but you gotta catch him before he buggers off in the morning."

"Okay, but he'll be mad," Craig said.

"And ask your Mom if she thinks Murray—I don't know his last name, her lawyer—would help me."

"He'd have to know what you did, or what they're charging you with."

"Yeah, I guess so. Tell you what. Go see Donna first—she doesn't know where I am and she must be climbing the wall. Tell her I said to tell you everything," Rob said. "Then when you talk to Murray in the morning you'll know what to say."

"Jesus, Rob! What did you do?"

"I said I'd tell you later. It wasn't something real, real bad, it was just real, real stupid."

"Well, they can't hang you for stupid, Rob," Craig said, attempting a laugh.

"I know. But I don't want them to try. Get moving, will you, buddy?"

"Yeah. I'll get the bulldozer first."

"What's this about a bulldozer," his mother said when he went upstairs. "I wasn't listening but I heard."

"Just a joke, Mom. Rob's in jail. I gotta phone Richard for him and go see Donna. And he wants me to ask you if you thought that Murray Andrews would help him."

"In jail! What's he done?"

"I don't know yet. Donna knows something so I gotta go see her. I can't phone Murray until the morning anyhow."

He rushed off to his room to get dressed and called to her as he ran down the stairs, "See you in a while, Mom. Go back to sleep."

"You wake me when you get back if I do get any sleep," she called. "You hear?" The back door slammed shut and immediately opened again.

"I forgot to phone Richard first," he shouted.

He did not know Richard's number and had to look through two columns of Lewises before he found it. Bev answered and was reluctant to waken Richard until Craig said "Tell him Rob's in jail again and needs his help."

"In jail! What's he done this time? Was anybody hurt?" Bev's voice had gone up several decibels.

Craig was in the middle of trying to explain when he heard Richard's voice, saying, "Who's in jail?"

"That's Craig on the phone. He says Rob's in jail again and needs your help," Bev explained.

"Craig?" Richard's voice came over the phone. "What's going on?"

"I don't know exactly. He just called me to say he was in jail again and asked me to call you and tell you he would appreciate it if you could do the same thing as you did before."

Richard gave a middle of the night groaning sigh. "Why did he call you?" he asked and immediately wanted to withdraw the question. Of course, he would call his best friend first, who else?

Craig said, "I don't know. All he would tell me for now is that it wasn't bad, it was just stupid. And he wants me to check to see if my mother's lawyer would represent him and I gotta go over and tell Donna. She doesn't know anything and she doesn't have a phone."

Richard gave another huge yawn and said, "Well, I'm not going to get up in the middle of a cold winter night to go down and bail him out. It's stupid to do that. Then you would have two stupid people trying to deal with sleepy, dopey cops. It's easier to wait until morning."

"Yeah, thanks Richard! And something else, he said not to tell his parents. He has to tell them himself."

"Too goddam true! I wouldn't get into that blowup if you paid me. Okay! I'll go down first thing and see what's what. It's a good thing school is out. What are you going to do now?"

"I gotta go see Donna and tell her. I'm not looking forward to it," Craig said. "And by the time that's over, I'll have to explain it to my mother. Then I guess I'll go to work."

"Maybe we should just leave Rob to work out his own problems," Richard said.

"You wouldn't! Would you?" came the horrified response.

"No, no," soothed Richard. "I was just teasing. Goodnight."

Craig listened for any indication that his mother was asleep or listening and, hearing nothing, slipped quietly out the door and drove to Donna's.

At Donna's, he parked on the street and, taking his flashlight, went silently up the walk to the unlit basement entrance, feeling like a sneak thief. There was no light to be seen in the basement and he could not be sure if Donna was out or asleep. Rob had said she would be climbing the walls, so surely she was home and not asleep. He tapped several times on the window in the door calling softly, "Donna, it's me, Craig."

He saw the curtain covering the window move slightly and he shone his flashlight on his face. When he heard the lock click, he opened the door and was met by a tearful Donna who flung her arms around him crying, "Craig, oh, Craig! Thank God! Where's Rob? I've been going crazy and I'm so scared!"

Without releasing her, he reached around and shoved the door closed, but she jumped out of his embrace and locked and bolted it.

"Oh, am I glad to see you! Somebody! Anybody!" she said. "No, that's not true. I just want to see Rob. Where is he? He's been gone since six o'clock. God, I wish we had a phone. I'm going to get one right away so if he's away, he can phone me. What are you doing here in the middle of the night? What's wrong?"

"Whoa! Donna," he soothed, "not so fast." He put his arm around her and drew her over to the bed. "Sit down and I'll tell you all I know," and he sat beside her and took her hand. "He's in jail."

"I knew it! I knew it!" she cried and started to weep, snatching her hand out of his and covering her face. "I knew he would get caught and it's all my fault. I should have listened to him and not been greedy." She turned to him and threw both arms around him and sobbed. He felt an erection so suddenly and hard it was almost painful and he moved so that she would not touch it unintentionally, but she clung more tightly to him.

Stop! Stop Stop! You pathetic excuse for a friend, he told himself. Stop before you screw your best friend's girl again while he's in jail. But he did not move away, and one part of him hoped she would discover what was happening and either move away or move closer. Finally, she released him saying, "Reach me a Kleenex by the TV, will you. I think I already soaked your shoulder."

He got up and walked carefully so his bulge wouldn't show and brought her back the box. She took it with one hand and snapped her finger against his bulge with the other. "Don't get any ideas," she said. "Not tonight!"

"I didn't...! I wasn't...! It just happened," he said miserably. "I'm sorry."

"Well, tell me what happened to Rob," she said.

"I don't know. He said you'd tell me."

"Oh Oh!" she said and then was quiet for a moment. "I guess I better." So she told him about the keys and the lockers and the easy money. She said that Rob didn't want her to but she thought it was sort of fun and scary. But Rob got anxious and moody so she decided to quit and then there was another chance and something went wrong and she was stuck with a package of their dope and didn't know what to do. Rob was certain they would come after her and he said the best thing to do was to put it back in a locker and, "if they did try to get tough, we could just give them the key to show we weren't trying to steal their stuff, whatever it was—cocaine, probably, this time."

She started to wail again. "And I haven't see him since and I didn't know if he was lying in a ditch somewhere or what. Oh, I'm so glad he's safe in jail. It's all my fault."

They sat together for a while worrying together about what could happen to Rob, what Rob's father was going to say and all the disasters their imaginations dredged up from gossip, newspapers and TV. Finally, long past midnight, Craig said, "Hey, we both gotta go to work in the morning. I better go. I'll check with you tomorrow. You okay?"

She nodded and gave him a tight hug as he left.

On Wednesday, Donna went to work a little early to make up for leaving early yesterday, looking a little wan from her late night.

"You okay?" Bruno asked as she hung up her coat, looking at her closely as if to demand an honest answer.

"Yeah! Thanks Bruno, I'm okay. Maybe I just caught a chill from the cold wind blowing in every time the door opens," she said.

"Keep your sweater on," he said paternally.

But within an hour, after she had dropped a few things and started to mop before she swept, Bruno came out from the back and saw her trembling and tearful. "Donna, you go home to bed," he said. "You probably got germs to give everybody to spoil their Xmas. No good! Come, I fix your breakfast and then you go home."

"But, Bruno!" she started to protest.

"I already call Phyllis. She's comin', right now."

Donna sat down on the nearest chair. "I'm sorry, Bruno."

"Okay, kid," he said and left her alone to make her breakfast.

Phyllis bustled in full of energy and sympathy. "Maybe just the flu," she said to Donna as she took off her coat. "You sure you're not...?" she said, patting her tummy.

"Oh! Good lord! I hope not. I'm not ready for that."

Bruno appeared with her breakfast. "Eat!" he ordered and she did, suddenly hungry.

"Not so busy this morning, I think," he said to Phyllis as she took down the closed sign. "Too many Christmas parties, too many hangovers."

He looked at Donna. "You okay for tomorrow? Or I do it myself for morning only. Then close after lunch. That's Thursday, the day before Christmas, and for Christmas Day and the Boxes Day and then Sunday—no working for nobody. Big holiday!"

Phyllis stopped wiping the counter. "No work for nobody, eh, Bruno!" she said.

"All except for Mama, sure," he corrected himself with a wry grin and a wink, "She's at work all the time."

Donna finished her breakfast and cleared her table. "I think I'd better stay and help," she said, still looking tense and worried.

"Go home and rest," Phyllis said. "I've got nothing to do at home. We're going out for Christmas. Really, dear! You do look peaked."

Donna hesitated and then put on her coat. "Thank you both," she said. "I'll be in tomorrow morning."

As the door closed, Phyllis watched Donna walk away for a moment and, turning to her husband, she gestured in the direction of Donna and patted her tummy with a smile. Bruno raised his eyebrows and made and 'O' with his mouth before his face broke into a smile. "How you know these things?" he asked.

"Women know!" she said in a tone of confidence. "We watch the eyes and the appetite."

Marion phoned Claudia, not wanting to ask but wanting to know. As soon as Claudia heard her voice, she said, "Oh, Marion. I have to come over right now!" and hung up the phone.

She appeared at Marion's door within two minutes, her coat draped over her shoulders. She flung herself down at the nook table and buried her face in her hands. "Oh Marion, all hell's breaking loose!" she stammered through a shaky breath.

Marion stood with an arm over Claudia's shoulder, patting her gently but saying nothing for a minute. Claudia finally gave a loud sniff and wiped her eyes with both hands while Marion reached out and picked up a box of Kleenex. Claudia blew and wiped and finally met Marion's eye with a weak smile. "Do you know what's going on?" she asked.

"Only vaguely," Marion replied. "Craig didn't say much."

"I don't know much either, and neither does Glen but that doesn't stop him from raving like a madman. Rob's in jail. He is being charged with possession of narcotics. That's all I know. Bev called me to tell me as much as she could find out after Richard phoned her. Richard's down at the courthouse or where ever they took him, trying to arrange bail, I guess. Richard talked to your Murray Anderson—?"

"Andrews," Marion supplied.

"Yes. That was Rob's idea or Craig's—one or the other. And he said he would see what he could do later, as long as Richard could manage the bail thing for now. Do you know if Craig talked to Donna?"

"He said he was going to."

"Good! Bev said that Richard said that Rob was worried about her," Claudia said, and stopped, trying to get herself under control while Marion poured coffee for them both and sat down with her.

"I can't believe Glen," she said, holding her mug in front of her mouth but not taking a sip. "He's in an absolutely uncontrolled rage—stamping around, banging his fists, calling Rob the awfulest names. He stopped for a while and told me again about their trip to Prince George and he was crying and then cursing Rob for letting him down. He said 'he has always let me down and I can't trust him and I won't trust him and I won't love him any more.'" She sat, staring at the mug in front of her face, with tears streaming. Somehow, Marion found the wisdom not to interrupt with soothing words.

"He rushed suddenly out of the house," she went on, "and I didn't know where he had gone and I was thinking all kinds of things, and then he was back. He said, 'I've gassed the car. Let's pack and get the hell out of here!' He wanted to go right that minute, forget Christmas, forget your party, just go! And I got mad and I said I wouldn't and he said he would go without me. And then we had a big fight." She stopped and took a sip of coffee and went on in a controlled voice. "We don't fight, you know. We never have. Oh, we have arguments and silences and angry moments, but we've never had one of these before, where we both said things we wished we hadn't said. At least, I wished I hadn't said some things—awful hurtful things that I didn't know were in me. Now I can't unsay them, and I don't know where we are or what to do or where we're going and through all that terrible shouting match, we lost track of Rob."

When Craig got home in the early morning hours, he tried to be quiet but his mother heard his homecoming sounds and called him. "Did you see Rob?" she asked.

"No, I didn't go down there. It was too late and I didn't think they would let me see him. After I called Richard and he said he would go down in the morning and bail Rob out if he could, I went over to Donna's."

He told his mother as much as he knew and she sighed for Rob and the family and told him to leave her and go to bed. He set his radio alarm loud and slept through it with tortured dreams until his mother came in and roused him. When he got to work he went directly to the shipping room where the noise of the machinery was muted, but he worked slowly and carefully, knowing that his attention would wander to anxieties about Rob.

At ten o'clock, Carl walked through the plant and found him in shipping and stopped to talk. "That was a good report, Craig—very useful. I've made up a memo to be posted and I think it will explain what the plans are and relieve any concerns the men might have that their jobs could be taken over by some machine."

"I guess some of them might have been thinking that way. The movies and TV are always showing a world operated by machines—goofy stuff made for kids," Craig said, but it was a flat, restrained response that Carl noticed immediately.

"Not feeling up to scratch today, Craig."

"Oh, yes! I'm fine. Just a late night," he answered.

"Yes, I guess it's the season for late nights as friends get together," Carl said, interested but not probing. He waited for a moment expecting Craig's usual social response that would lead them into a friendly discussion that Carl had come to anticipate and enjoy.

But there was a moment of silence until Craig said, "No, it wasn't a party or anything like that, Carl." He stopped, gripped the edges of the chest high shipping desk, and said, his eyes dark with concern, "It's my friend—Rob. He got arrested last night and I don't know what it's all about. He wouldn't tell me when he called, but it sounds serious, something about possession of drugs, I guess, from what his girl friend told me. I had to go see her last night and she was scared and worried. I guess I am, too. He's my best friend."

"Is he out on bail?"

"I don't know. I guess he goes to court this morning."

"Shouldn't you be there?" Carl asked.

"You mean, I should just go?" Craig asked, puzzled.

"I thought that was what best friends did."

Craig hesitated for a moment, then said, "Thanks, Carl," and put out his hand. "Thanks very much," gripping Carl's hand harder than he realized before rushing away.

For a fleeting moment as he watched him go, Carl had the impression that the boy had been about to embrace him.

The small courtroom in the police station held few observers but there was an air of constant movement as doors swung open as court officials and others came in, found someone and disappeared into the hallways for whispered conversations. Craig had made frantic enquiries of indifferent policemen and had finally been pointed to the courtroom where Robert Williams was due to appear.

He watched with wide eyes as people were lead in, names called, questions shot and decisions made faster than he could follow.

The judge was a woman. He saw Richard come in and take a seat beside another man at the back of the courtroom. He moved quickly to join them and went with them into the hallway. "This is Reg Hawthorn from Murray's office," Richard said. "Craig Williams." They shook hands.

"I have just talked to the prosecutor," the lawyer said, "trying to get this charge heard in juvenile court. But he is adamant that it should be heard here, in adult court, and he is making that recommendation to the judge, on the basis that it is an adult crime, not a juvenile crime and that Robert is six months short of eighteen and, at that age, should be aware of the nature of the crime with which he is being charged."

Richard shook his head in dismay and Craig knew that something serious was going on.

"Any chance that the judge will disagree with the prosecutor's recommendation?" Richard asked.

"They rarely do," the lawyer said. "But I'll try again, in court, on the grounds that his rights as a juvenile have been abused by being made to appear publicly in an adult court. I haven't much hope that it will change anything but I have to go through the motions"

"There are three more to call before Robert Turner," Reg Hawthorn said and started for the courtroom door. "Let's go in. They said the charge will be 'Possession under one thousand', but they could add 'For the Purposes of Trafficking'. They sometimes do, even if they don't have any good evidence. But it's not on the charges yet, so it looks like they're not going to if everything Rob told me is the truth."

"Rob wouldn't lie!" Craig blurted, and both men smiled.

They took seats inside.

A long haired man was protesting loudly and was being escorted out roughly by two officers and the protest continued outside the courtroom door.

"Quiet in the court!" someone shouted. Then "Robert Turner!"

Rob was lead in by a police officer and placed standing at a table in front of the judge. He had looked quickly around the court room and apparently recognized only Reg Hawthorn who was moving to the front to be beside Rob, having motioned to the other two to stay. "Reg Hawthorn for Robert Turner, your Honour," he said. "May I approach the bench?"

She nodded without looking up.

The lawyer walked to the front of the courtroom and faced the judge directly. He spoke in low tones to her with his back to the courtroom. Nobody in the court could hear what he said. Her reply to him, although quiet, was heard throughout the room.

"Mr. Hawthorn, I have heard your argument and I have read the prosecutor's recommendations. I must agree that this is an adult crime that Turner is being charged with. Turner, although legally a minor, is of an age, and independent of his family, that he may be considered an adult. Your request to move to juvenile court is rejected."

Reg Hawthorn gave a small shrug and returned to his place beside Rob.

Craig was looking at Rob carefully and saw that he was standing straight and appeared to be nervous and pale under his swarthy skin. His eyes were wide and ringed with dark shadows. There was none of his usual nonchalance showing in his manner.

A man stood and read quickly through a statement that the judge followed from her copy but few observers understood.

"Possession under one thousand?" the judge said, looking over her glasses at the man who had read the statement.

"Yes, your Honour."

"No added niceties—like For the Purpose of, et cetera?"

"No, your Honour."

She looked at him again. "Must be Christmas," she said almost under her breath..

"Once a year, your Honour," the man said, smiling.

She nodded while looking at her calendar. "Nothing to do with an uncertainty about the actual amount of evidence, of course," she said and continued without waiting for a response, "Morning session, Mr. Hawthorn, January 7, courtroom to be determined?"

He looked at his appointment book. "I'm clear, your Honour."

He pocketed his book and asked, "Bail, your Honour?"

"Five thousand dollars," she said without looking up from her writing, and almost in the same breath, "Next!"

An officer moved from the side of the courtroom to escort Rob out. Rob turned to Reg Hawthorn to thank him and his eye caught a figure moving to the exit.

"Dad! Dad!" he shouted but the figure moved more hurriedly through the crowd and out the door. Eyes turned in his direction as Rob stood watching the door where his father had disappeared until he was lead away, his shoulders sagging and his eyes moist. Craig was standing out of Rob's line of sight, mirroring his every emotion.

Craig followed Richard and the lawyer as they made their way out of the courtroom and down the hall to arrange bail.

"Tell Rob to make sure to see me before the seventh. And tell him it is important that he brings Donna," he said. "It will take a few minutes before he is released. You can pick him up at the side door of the main entrance. I've got appointments waiting so I have to run. Have a good Xmas and New Year." He extended his hand to each of them and turned to leave.

"Thank you," Craig said. "Do you think he'll get off, Mr. Hawthorn?"

"Hard to say, Craig. But we'll try. It's highly probable that he will get more than a symbolic slap on the wrist. It's his second narcotics charge, remember."

"Yeah, I know," Craig responded with a stricken look.

Reg gave him a pat on the shoulder. "Take care," he said and left with another small salute to Richard.

Rob appeared shortly, looking tired and troubled. He shook Richard's hand and said, "Thanks again, Richard. Sorry to bugger up your Christmas plans. I hope this kind of thing doesn't get to be a habit," he added with a grin.

"And I hope your hope is as fervent as mine," Richard said returning the smile.

"Hi, buddy," Rob said and the two boys permitted each other a quick hug and pat on the back. Craig couldn't say anything.

"I saw my Dad," Rob said. "Was he with you?"

Richard shook his head. "I guess he came on his own."

Rob's face was closed with anxiety. "How am I ever going to explain this to him," he muttered to himself.

The other two understood his distress but said nothing. Finally Richard said, "I've got to be on my way home. Have you got your car, Craig? Will you take Rob?"

Craig nodded and said, "Sure."

Richard shook hands with Craig and said casually as he turned away, "Take care, Rob. I guess we'll see you and Donna for Christmas dinner."

"I hope so," Rob called out quietly. "And Richard! Thanks a whole hell of a lot, man!"

Richard gave him a thumbs up sign without turning around.

"I guess I'm in deep shit again with my dad," Rob said as they walked to the car. "Just when things were beginning to look good."

"Maybe it won't be so bad," Craig offered lamely.

"Are you kidding? You know what he thinks about dope."

They were silent while they walked the ramps to the car. Emerging out of the dim parking arcade into the bright winter sun onto a street festooned with Christmas decorations, their silence continued, their mood matching neither the day nor the season.

"So where do you want to go?" Craig asked as he headed the car out of the downtown area.

"I don't know," Rob answered dejectedly. "I've gotta see Donna first, I guess. And I better find out if I still got a job—I was supposed to go in at eight. And I gotta get things straight with my dad. Oh, Christ! My life's a mess!" He pounded the dashboard in anger. "How come yours is so neat and tidy. You get a job and right away you get a promotion and the boss lets you off to see your best buddy in front of the judge, and you got a car and I got nothin' but grief!"

"You got a girl," Craig suggested.

"Oh, sure! I got a girl," Rob answered wistfully. "But I was better off when I just had you."

They were quiet for a few blocks while Craig tried to figure out what Rob meant. He remembered the pact they had made when they were ten years old by mixing their blood from a cut on their hands, a pact that would seal their friendship forever in a bond that not even marriage would break. Often he had wondered what would happen if Rob found a girl and got married and now he had found a girl. But he was saying he would be better off without her and there would be just the two of them again.

Rob interrupted his reverie by saying, "Are you coming in?"

They were stopped in front of the Lasserets. Craig thought for a brief minute and said, "No, you'd better do it alone. But, listen, if you got all that running around to do, take the car and give me your bike."

"No," Rob said. "I'd better not. Besides, the chain's broke." He opened the door and got out. "See ya. Wish me luck."

"With Donna?"

"With Donna, and my dad, and my job and the whole shiteroo."

He slammed the door and walked disconsolately away.

Inside he had only expected to shave and change clothes before going to the cafe to see Donna and was surprised to find her at home and by the lack of emotion he felt when they embraced. She told him that she was so worried and clumsy and useless that Bruno sent her home and he was going to close up until the day after Boxing Day. She was worried and sorry and soft and gentle and they made love rather more quickly than Donna would have enjoyed.

Rob was torn between the need to see his parents and the urge to get quickly back to work to save his job. He decided on the latter and bathed and ate on the run as he changed clothes. He rushed out leaving her alone and upset. Arriving at work, the assistant manager saw him come in and motioned to him to come over.

"Better see Mr. Penrose before you think of starting," he was told. "He's sore as hell at you."

"What did I do?" Rob said, the picture of hurt and innocence.

But it didn't work with the Manager. "Where the hell have you been?" the Manager roared as soon as Rob walked in. "This isn't a social club where you can wander in whenever you like. You work here! At least you appear to work here occasionally at your convenience. I'd fire you right now except there are about twenty old ladies out there that appear to be your fan club and they'd tear the place apart if I fired you before Christmas. So work to Christmas Eve and then bugger off. As of Boxing day, you don't work here. Got it?"

"Stick it up your ass, Mr. Penrose! Got it?" Rob said without venom as he turned to the door. "And Merry Christmas!"

As he walked out the door, quite composed and without rage, one of his little old lady fans saw him and called, "Oh, there you are, Robbie. I can't find the croutons and I need them for my Caesar salad."

"They're on top of the bread shelves, sweetie. But I'll have to go with you to boost you up because you can't reach them."

"Robbie!" she pretended to scold. "You can't do that!"

"Sure I can! How else can I get you in my arms?"

"Oh, Robbie. You're such a rascal," she giggled.

He reached the croutons for her. "There you are and your virtue is intact. Merry Christmas, Mrs. Trent," he said as he turned to walk out the door, leaving her waiting at the checkout with a happy face trying to rearrange a big grin into a smile.

Rob stood outside the Superstore watching the crowds of people come and go from the Mall shops most of which were now displaying big Boxing Day sale banners. Christmas carols were playing on loud speakers, the Sally Ann bell could be heard from their favourite guilt position in front of the liquor store. The festive mood did not match Rob's mood. He walked the Mall for a while, not seeing the people or the shop windows, trying to find a way out of the family problem that was due to explode. Finally with a sigh and a 'what the hell' shrug he headed for his parents' house.

He knocked, wondering why as if this house had not been his home all his life, and opened the door. None of the machines were operating. His mother was downstairs looking grey and worn, putting things in boxes. She looked up and saw him and started to cry.

"I had to phone Richard to find out what happened," she said through her tears. "Couldn't you at least have phoned?"

"Why would he bother?" his father's voice came from behind as he emerged from another room and headed for the stairs. "He's too busy with his pushers and addicts."

"Dad, it wasn't like that," Rob shouted to his father's retreating back.

"Glen! Come back! We've got to talk about this."

"What's there to say? We said it all and he spit it back in our faces."

"Glen!" she screamed. "Come down here! This is your son!"

He came halfway back down the stairs and sat down. "Claudia, listen to me. He knows how we feel about narcotics, how we have worked with every organization we could find to fight those wretched crooks who peddle the stuff. And what does he do?" he shouted. "He goes out and joins the crooks and gangsters and peddles the stuff. What's the sense of it? It's all so futile when your own son joins the enemy. Tell him to go away—I can't bear to look at him."

"I will not tell him to go away. If you want him to go, then you tell him. But you listen to me, Glen Turner, if you turn your back on him, I'll turn my back on you. And I mean it! He made a mistake, for God's sake. Don't tell me you've never made a mistake! If you try to deny it I'll jog your memory to a few. Have you no understanding that people make mistakes? No forgiveness?" Glen was sitting with his face in his hands while she went on with her tirade. Rob stood near her, white-faced and tearful.

"When was it," she continued. "Just three days ago, wasn't it? You sat beside me on the sofa right there, with a happy smile, telling me what a wonderful trip you had together, how competent your son, your son, was! What a great sense of humor he had! How you wished you had been a better father! What happened to you? He makes a mistake and you will throw him to the wolves! Are you going to hang, draw and quarter him, too? Who are you to pass judgement like that. You said you wished you knew how to love him! Well for God's sake,

<u>TRY!</u>" she screamed, almost hysterical.

Glen raised his head from his hands and went down to her and tried to put his arms around her but she jerked away. "Don't!" she said sharply.

"Dad?" Rob said. "Dad? Listen to me please! Give me a chance! I didn't do anything wrong! Really! Honest to God, I didn't. Will you listen? I didn't want to tell you this but I guess I have to before you tear each other's hearts out. Donna carried and delivered some packages for a guy we knew from school, only three times. We thought it was fishy, but she wanted some extra Christmas money and she was going to quit. But things got fouled up and she couldn't deliver one package and she brought it home and we got scared because we didn't know exactly what was in it but we were pretty sure it was either marijuana or probably cocaine. We thought they'd be after us, so I took it back to the bus station for her and I was putting it in a locker when the police arrested me. That's the truth, Dad!"

"Why didn't you tell the police that?" his mother said.

"I couldn't, Mom. I had to cover for her! I had to! Everybody in her life has always let her down. Her mother's a whore and her father's a drunk and she was molested as a child. She doesn't have anybody except an aunt and uncle in the Cariboo. And me. I've got to do it for her, don't you see?" he pleaded.

There was neither agreement nor disagreement with his plea. His mother nodded in understanding sometimes but his father maintained a cold silence. The tempers and the tears subsided and Rob knew the worst was over when his father raged, "Why couldn't you at least have told us?"

"Told you what? That the girl I was living with was peddling marijuana or cocaine or something. You know what you would have said, Dad! I knew! And Mom knew! What would you have done, except rant and rage and threaten to disown me again. I couldn't tell anybody, Dad. I didn't even tell Craig, for chrissake! Don't you understand?"

Rob was angry now and the anger had replaced fear—fear that they could not understand or would not understand that he did nothing deliberately to hurt or disappoint them. He told them that they had always been so tied to each other that they had had little room for him in their lives, and they denied it. He told them that they had given him love and care in return for work. He said he thought he had loved them but right now he wasn't sure. He told them that the only person he knew he loved for sure was Craig because he was the only person in the world that he knew would never turn his back on him or lie to him or deceive him. He told them that they had deceived him, that they pretended to love him as much as they loved each other. Some of what he said, wasn't true and he knew it, but he wanted to hurt them without knowing why.

And then all the mixed up, pent up, confused feelings and hurts and disappointments had been spilled and he was sorry and he cried and said so, but they didn't know quite what he was sorry about or for. His mother came to him and put her arms around him, her head reaching only to his chin. She said nothing in words but he heard everything she was saying. His father moved out of the room to the stairs, and in passing, grabbed his son's shoulder and gave it a gentle shake.

"I've got to go, Mom," Rob said, and gently took her arms from around him and lead her to the sofa and sat with her hand in his for a minute. "Donna's alone," he said and, kissing her softly on her forehead, he left.

Before he opened the door, he called out in the silent house, "I'm going, Dad."

A gravelly response came from the back of the house. It sounded to Rob like, "Okay."

Downstairs his mother sat slumped on the sofa, staring unseeing at a spot on the rug, her arms crossed and her chin cupped in one hand. "He said the only person he really loved and trusted was Craig," she mused. "Not even Donna, or me or...."

***

"Hi!" Donna greeted him as he came in the door. She went to him before he could take his coat off and kissed him. "Br-r-r. It must be cold out. How did it go?"

"I don't know. I have to think about it. I had to tell them about you. I'm sorry! I swore to myself that I wouldn't but they sort of cornered me or something. I dunno. Anyway, I told them."

She shrugged and said bitterly, "That's okay. Maybe we should take out an ad."

They were quiet for a minute but there was no anger in the silence.

"We got nothing in the place to eat," she said. "Will you go to the corner and get something?"

"If you give me some money," he replied. "I'm broke."

She gave him a list and some money and he put on his coat again and walked disconsolately to the corner store, feeling an old sense of resentment again from the times his mother called him in from play and gave him a note and some money and sent him to another store where he would steal a candy and the man would take it out of the change, and when he got back his reward would be a pat and a 'good boy.'

"I wonder what my reward will be this time," he mused. "Maybe she'll let me screw her again. Big deal."

When he got back, she made a quick dinner for them which they ate in front of the TV with little talk. Once she said, during a commercial, "Do you think you'll get off?"

He shook his head. "No," he told her. "There's no way. I'm gonna do time," saying it out of the corner of his mouth like an old time movie gangster.

After the show on the TV was over, he said, "Donna, I've got a couple of things to clear up with Craig. Okay?"

"What things," she asked.

"Things!" he said abruptly, in a none-of-your-business tone.

She cleared the table and started on the dishes while he put on his coat. He went over to kiss her goodbye and she offered her cheek which he dutifully pecked.

"I won't be long," he told her. "What are you going to do?"

"Oh, maybe I'll check out the mall," she said. "I'll have to do some shopping if Bruno's going to close over Christmas."

He nodded and left, walking fast in the cold night air with small soft flakes of snow fluttering down. When he arrived at Craig's he felt better for the hard fast walk and some of the despondency had dissipated.

He knocked his usual signal and opened the door. "Hi! Anybody home?" he called. There was no answer. The basement door was open and the light on. He walked over and called "Hello?"

"Who's there?" came Marion's voice, followed by, "Is that you, Robbie? You can't come down. I'm wrapping presents and one of them is for you."

"What is it? Let me see!" and he tramped on the top stairs.

"Stay away!" she called. "Craig's upstairs having a shower."

"Meanie!" he called to her and turned away to climb the stairs to Craig's room. He took off his coat, tossed it on a chair on top of a pile of Craig's clothes and flopped on the bed. Craig's radio was on tuned to a talk show and he turned it off. In the quiet, his mind flipped through the times he and Craig had been in this room together with the door closed talking about sex, school, parents, sisters, teachers, games, the future—and what was the future now? he asked himself.

Craig walked into the room with a towel wrapped around his waist. "Hi," he said with a smiling greeting, "I didn't hear you come in."

"I sneaked in like a thief in the night and warmed your bed up for us."

"The hell you did!" Craig answered as he dropped the towel and pulled on a pair of jockey shorts.

"That's a pretty good sized package you've got there," Rob said, making a biting lunge in the direction of Craig's crotch.

"How come you haven't shown it to me?"

"I didn't want to make you jealous."

"Make _me_ jealous? Ho! Ho! Ho!"

Craig finished dressing.

"I got fired." Rob said.

"Fired? Why?

"Old Penrose got snarly and I told him to stick it up his ass. I didn't wait around to see if he did."

"Now what are you going to do?"

"I'm going to be the guest of the Queen for a while, it looks like," Rob said, trying to be flippant.

"Maybe not," Craig argued.

Rob made no further comment and they were quiet for a while. Craig shoved Rob's feet over and sat on the foot of the bed facing his friend.

"How did it go with your mom and dad?" Craig asked.

"Tough!" Rob answered with suddenly moist eyes. "But we got through it.

Mom sorta read the riot act to Dad and he came around. You shoulda heard her! She was laying down the law to him and he couldn't get a word in. Boy! Was she on a roll!" He paused reflecting on the scene. "I had to tell them about Donna," he continued. "I didn't want to but I had to tell them to make them understand why I had to take the rap for her."

"Because you love her?" Craig ventured.

"No, not really. Because she's my friend and she's had a rotten life and somebody should care. Nobody has ever cared for her before. Everybody has deserted her. Friends don't desert each other—they're supposed to hang in there out of loyalty, and love."

Craig thought that Rob might be trying to tell him something.

"I'm not going to desert you," he said.

"I know that! Asshole!" Rob indignantly replied and raised a leg and kicked Craig hard on the shoulder. Craig grabbed the leg and twisted it and they progressed to a rough and tumble wrestle that landed them on the floor with Rob eventually straddling Craig's waist and holding his hands on the floor above his head. They stayed in that position for a minute, puffing, grinning and staring into each other's eyes. Then Craig stopped grinning and Rob read in his eyes, "Let's not, Rob." He released his hold and they got up from the floor and sat side by side on the bed.

Rob stood up after a moment of quiet. "Look after Donna for me, eh, buddy?"

Craig looked at him blankly and then squeaked, "You mean move in with her if you go to jail?"

"No, I sure as hell don't mean that!" Rob exploded. "I mean look after her, see that she's okay."

"Oh, sure," Craig said. "I would have done that. She's my friend, too."

"Friend, okay," Rob smiled. "Just don't let it turn into best friend or more." He reached out and gave Craig a long fierce hug. "Merry Christmas, buddy," he said.

They went downstairs together. Marion was in the living room watching the television.

"What were you two doing up there," she asked. "I thought you were coming through the ceiling."

"He got smart and I put him on the floor and made him eat his words," Rob said. "Are you all ready for Christmas, U.U.? Have you got my present? Are you going to give it to me now? Is it something I can use in jail?"

"Oh, don't! Robbie," she said, the tears starting to fill her eyes. "Don't joke about it! I can't stand it."

"I'm sorry, Auntie Marion," he said, reverting to the formality of childhood. He sat beside her and wrapped an arm over her shoulders and looked into her eyes. "Forgive me?" he pleaded.

"Don't I always?" she answered.

"Always!" he agreed.

He kissed her on the forehead, got to his feet and said, "Merry Christmas,

U.U." Then he put on his jacket, flung an arm over Craig's shoulder and walked him to the door.

"Hang on. I'll put on my shoes and drive you," Craig said.

Rob opened the door. "I gotta walk," he said, gave a little wave and a grin and closed the door behind him.

CHAPTER 62

The wind was blowing harder and the soft flakes had changed to sleet as Rob tucked his shoulders down into his jacket and, feeling buoyed up by his time with Craig, headed for home. He arrived home with snow on his head and shoulders and thumped the doorframe to knock the snow off his boots before he opened the door. Donna was sitting up in bed looking startled.

"What was that?" she demanded.

"What was what?" he answered. Then suddenly realizing he had wakened her, "Oh, sorry! I was just kicking the snow off my boots. Were you asleep?"

"What else is there to do? You bugger off to be with Craig and leave me alone with nothing on the TV except Christmas carols, Santa Clauses and gooey, gooey goo."

"Why aren't you watching Johnny Carson?"

"Because he's not on! There's some other jerk wearing a Santa Claus hat and going 'Heh, heh, heh' at his own jokes."

"Oh," he commiserated, "you've had a bad night. Didn't you go shopping?" He leaned over the bed to kiss her.

"No," she answered sulkily. "It was too damn wet and cold. Get away! You're wet and cold, too."

"Heh, heh, heh," he mimicked. "I know. I've got the answer. I am, after all, renowned throughout the civilized world as the best, the greatest, the creme de la creme of hot chocolate chefs! That's what I'll do for you! I'll do my famous hot chocolate! How about it?"

She grinned at his nonsense and the sulks disappeared. "Okay," she said, "but don't scald the milk. I hate it when it's scalded."

"Yes, your majesty," he said, his nose haughtily in the air. "But it is a matter of pride for me, that in the records of hot chocolate chefs, there is not a single entry of scalded milk against my name," he called from the bathroom.

"Wash your hands," she ordered.

"Picky-picky!" he replied.

He busied himself with the hot chocolate while she lay back and watched him, his face looking undisturbed as if his troubles had been wiped away.

"Rob?" she asked.

"Yeah?" he answered routinely.

"Tell me something. What is it between you and Craig? Every time you get down in the dumps you head over to Craig's and come back all okay and cheerful again. And he's the same way. It's as though he has to get a shot of Rob every so often to make his world go around, and you have to get a shot of Craig."

"I dunno, Donna," he replied cautiously because she was approaching a subject he had no intention of discussing with her. "It's always been that way. Right from the time we were born, I guess. We just always seem to be on each other's wavelength. Here's your hot chocolate, majesty! Note that there isn't even the merest hint of scalding. Tell me if that is not utterly superb!"

"It's almost as good as mine," she said, tasting and smiling.

"Rats!" he said with a tragic face. "You prick my ego like a balloon!"

They lay side by side sipping their drinks. "Speaking of balloons," he said. "How about me dressing up in a fancy balloon and we, you know, wink! wink! do it?"

"Feeling sexy tonight, are you?"

"Yeah!" he growled. "Hot chocolate will do it every time," he said as he headed for the bathroom, dismissing her earlier excuse.

"Or Craig," she said quietly to herself.

Much later, she lay awake beside him, feeling casually unsatisfied, wondering what it was that Rob was trying to prove.

Earlier that evening, the mood between Rob's parents was still dark and tense. Glen had carelessly reinstated the earlier mood by announcing that he thought they should phone Bev and cancel Christmas dinner.

"Phone if you want," she exploded. "But speak for yourself, not for me! I am going to spend Christmas Day with my daughter, her husband, my granddaughter and my son and his friend. If you want to stay at home and sulk, you can stay alone!"

"I am not sulking!" he protested. "I just thought everybody would be more comfortable if...," he finished lamely.

"Why in God's name would anyone feel uncomfortable?"

"I don't know, Claudia! It's just that when I look at Rob I have this terrible feeling of disappointment," he said helplessly.

She put her head back and sighed. "Oh, Glen! Don't you know that you have been walking down the widest two-way street you will ever walk down in your life? A street of your own choosing! You, on your side, bemoaning your fate of having a son who has never, ever lived up to your expectations, so distant from your son on the other side of that wide, wide street, that he has never heard what you have expected of him. And there he is, nearly out of sight on the other side of the street, going the other way, wishing he had had a father."

"But I am his father!"

"Yes," she agreed quietly, almost pensively.

He looked at her for a long time, his face white and drawn. "You mean..." he took a deep, shuddering breath. "You mean I've been a father in name only."

She nodded and took his hand in hers. "I'm sorry," she said.

He stood up and moved away from her. Stopping in front of the cold fireplace, he stared into it with his hands gripping the mantle as if the strength had gone from his legs.

"You have nothing to apologize for." He paused, deep in contemplation. "I'm the one who must struggle with regrets—and repair, if there can be any," he told her softly. And then after another silence, "I wonder if there are any turnarounds on that one-way street of mine."

"I'm sure there are, dear, if you look for them."

The morning of the day before Christmas gave no promise of a bright, sparkling day, but it had at least stopped snowing. Last night's snow was piled deep along the sides of the main streets where the snowploughs had scraped it, but the side streets were covered solidly and spotted here and there with deserted cars whose drivers, late last night, had defied winter and challenged the deep drifts on summer treads. The warble of ambulances and the wail of police sirens could be heard easily above the muted noise of those few cars and trucks who had ventured out. Every neighbourhood was filled with a cacophony of snow shovels shrieking against sidewalks and driveways in preparation for tomorrow. Inside, the worry signs were up, as people, who were either planning to be somewhere else for Christmas or were expecting company, scanned the skies with inexpert eyes and listened in frustration to the weather channel that reported ad nauseam on the weather on every hamlet in Ontario and ended each broadcast with the maddening announcement: 'In British Columbia it is snowing.'

Rob woke early and looked out on the winter scene. He dressed quickly without waking Donna and, adding a scarf and toque of Donna's to his jacket and snow boots, went quietly outside. In Wally's garage, he found his snow shovel and began to clear the driveway and sidewalk. Wally heard the scraping and opened the front door, still in his pyjamas and dressing gown.

"Rob! You don't need to do that!" he called.

"Yes, I do, Wally! Merry Christmas!" Rob answered and kept shovelling so that any further protests Wally made were drowned in the scraping of metal against concrete.

When he was finished, he put the shovel away and went in, puffing and red-cheeked, to find Donna up and dressed and waiting to make breakfast for him.

"Maybe if it snows some more we won't have to go to your sister's for dinner," Donna ventured.

"We have to go, Donna. Richard has gone to bat for me twice and they're expecting us."

"But your dad will be there! And your mom! I wish you hadn't told them what I did," Donna said, looking contrite.

"I'm sorry I had to—there was no other way," he said. Then, after a silence, he continued, "I'll tell you what! Let's just go over there and we'll work it out. Okay?"

She shrugged. "Might as well," she said and added pensively, "It would be a lot easier if we had a phone."

"Oh, I forgot to tell you. I got you a phone for Xmas, but it won't be hooked up until January, the seventh, I think."

"You did!" she squealed. "Oh, Rob, that's wonderful. Oh, what a nice present!" She ran to him and flung her arms around him and kissed him solidly.

They dressed and set out happily together, having a little snowball fight while they waited for a bus and shouting Merry Christmas to strangers.

"What else do we have to do today?" she asked.

"We've got to see U.U. and Craig—I've got presents for them and I'll have to wrap them at my mom's. And I've got to pick up my pay at the store. Did you get something for the Lasserets?"

She nodded. "A plant—I didn't know what else."

"Good," he said. Getting to his feet, he smiled at her and said, "This is our stop. Let's go and meet our fate. Or should I say my fater and mater."

She made a vinegar face at his joke and they got off and trudged the two blocks to his old home. "Imagine," he said. "I've spent my whole life there and I'll probably never see it again after the first of January."

"I've lived in a lot of places and I can't think of one I would ever want to see again," she said bluntly. "Except where I'm living right now."

He smiled at her and put his arm around her shoulders as they walked to the door together.

"Ready?" he asked.

She nodded.

He knocked a shave-and-a-haircut knock and opened the door. His father was working on a collator with the parts spread around him. "Oh, Rob," he said, looking up and putting down his tool. "We were wondering how we were going to get in touch with you to make a time to pick you up tomorrow."

Rob felt his gut tighten and a flood of emotion sweeping over him at the signal of some kind of armistice. He was able to say, his voice tight and unnatural, "We'll work something out, Dad. Merry Christmas. You remember Donna?"

"Yes, of course. We only met once, didn't we, Donna? Merry Christmas!" He moved away from the machine wiping his hands on a work towel and offered her his hand just as Claudia came hurriedly up the stairs with an anxious look on her face.

Seeing her husband and Donna smiling and shaking hands, her face relaxed and she moved over to them. She kissed her son and said "Merry Christmas, Rob," and when she released him from her embrace, his father said, "Yes, Merry Christmas to you too, son." Rob controlled another surge of emotion and turned to watch his mother and Donna hold hands and touch cheeks.

"Come on down and I'll put on some coffee," Claudia said. "You may have to sit on boxes. We're still packing."

"I'll be down in a minute," her husband said.

She stopped in the middle of the stairs. "You don't have to spend the day before Christmas fixing another man's machine," she said severely.

"No, of course not," he responded and followed them down.

"Where is Roger?" Rob asked casually.

"Gone skiing, of course," his father answered sarcastically. "Just dropped everything last week and said he would be back after Christmas. No business head! No business head at all! I told him he should have hired you to help him out."

"I didn't want to then, Dad."

The conversation ended on that note and Rob called out to his mother, "Have you got some wrapping paper, Mom? I've got to wrap Craig's and U.U.'s."

"There's a box in there that's not taped yet. And you should find paper and ribbon but you'll have to cut up one of the old Christmas cards to make a To-From."

He found the box and Donna helped him. While they were busy, Glen wandered out to the kitchen. Claudia stopped and kissed him and said, "Thank you, dear."

He held her gently for a moment and said, "I think I might have found a turn-around in time."

"Good for you!" she said. "What do the kids say? Put the pedal to the metal and never mind the fuzz, something like that."

***

Craig had meant to send some Christmas cards but put it off until it was too late, because he was fussing around about how to address the envelopes: Carl and Mrs. Cranston? He certainly couldn't address it to Carl and Marney Cranston. The same for Larry and Mrs. Koski. Mr. and Mrs. Koski? The problem was solved by delay. Now he would have to phone them. First he phoned the Cranstons and the phone was answered by Mrs. Cranston who seemed to be more than socially pleased by his call and they chatted about Christmas plans and weather until she said, "Here's Carl back from shovelling snow. That was thoughtful of you to call, Craig. Thank you. I'll put Carl on."

There was a slight pause during which Craig could only hear muted conversation. Then Carl picked up the phone and said heartily, "Craig! How nice of you to call. Merry Christmas!"

"I was going to send a card, Carl, but I never got around to it, so I thought I'd better phone and wish you Merry Christmas and thank you for, well, for a lot of things."

They talked for another couple of minutes about Christmas plans and weather and wished each other Season's Greetings again. Carl put the phone down and turned away to look out the window at the still cloudy sky..

After a minute he said, "For a while it almost seemed like the sun was back."

She wasn't listening carefully. "What did you say?" she asked in a startled voice and then reheard in her mind what he had said.

"Oh!" she said, falling back in her chair, "For a moment, I thought you meant s-o-n."

***

Marion was on the phone talking to Edith when Rob and Donna arrived. She heard Rob's familiar call and looked around the corner to motion them in.

Rob went over to her and placed his cold hands on her neck.

"Rob!" she shrieked. "Don't do that!"

"Oh, is Rob there?" Edith said. "I better speak to him and wish him Merry Christmas."

Marion tried to finish her conversation with Edith, but Edith continued as usual, now commenting on the repair problems that always seem to come in bunches at Christmas time. "Well," she concluded finally, "You better let me speak to Rob. Oh, I hope it's nice tomorrow—the girls can hardly wait. Bye for now, Mom."

"Edith wants to talk to you, Rob," Marion said, handing him the phone.

Edith was already talking when Rob took the phone and he listened for a moment and then said, "Whoa! Grk! Rimph! Clunpy! Hey, Edith—those are words trying to get in edgeways. Merry Christmas."

"Oh, you sound in high spirits for the festive season," Edith said. "Are you going to Bev's for the day? Wish her...Oh, never mind, I should call her and get the kids together before they reach high school."

"Good idea," Rob said. "I haven't seen you since you ran off and got married and had two babies—or was it the other way round?"

"Oh, knock it off, nuthead. What did you get Donna?"

There was a long silence—long for Edith, who broke it with a demanding, "Well?"

"Okay, but promise you won't tell her. It's a surprise. I got her a—-wait for it—-a CAR!"

"Oh, Rob! Grow up and stop playing silly games." When there was no response, she said, "Rob? Rob? Did you really get her a car?"

"Well, it's not here yet! It's coming—special order with leopard skin upholstery and stuff like that. I can afford it, you know, I'm in the drug business now. Silk shirts, Mercedes, Cuban cigars—the works, but no broads!"

"Oh, Rob! Don't be such an asshole."

"Asshole! Asshole! Asshole!" came a chorus of little voices behind her.

"Just listen to them, the little monkeys. I gotta go."

"Okay. Have a good Christmas. Give Harvey a kiss from me."

"What!?"

"He'll understand. Bye, bye, Edie," he said laughing as he hung up.

"That was your Uncle Rob," Edith said to the twins when she turned away from the phone. "He's such fun! But I don't think I'll give Daddy the message," and she went out to the kitchen, laughing hilariously at the thought.

Last night Craig had told his mother that the plant was closing early today but that he had some last minute shopping to do before coming home. So Marion sat with Rob and Donna over coffee and chatted, delighted to discover that Rob was pleased to be going out to Bev's with his father and mother, but she let the subject drop without any questions as to how the rift had been mended. Time enough after Christmas when she and Claudia could talk.

Donna seemed anxious to be on their way, but Rob obviously wanted to wait for Craig. Donna told Marion that she had not thought about a gift for Bev and asked what she should take.

"I've got the perfect thing for you," Marion said. "Let me get it."

She came back with a round tin box about a foot in diameter with a picture of a castle on the lid. "These are English biscuits," she said. "Cookies to you and me. They're very good and very fattening. One of the ladies in my bridge club gives each of us a box every Christmas. Her husband is the Canadian distributor so she gets them for nothing or practically nothing. I'm still working on last years box and I have to eat them every time we play bridge at her house. I'm getting to hate them. So, please! Take them and give them to Bev as a Christmas family gift. They're perfect for that sort of thing. You know, they're sort of elegant, and they look expensive without being ostentatious."

"Really?" Donna asked, unbelieving that people could do such a thing graciously. Rob was smiling at her.

"Yes, really. Please take them and you won't have to go shopping, and believe me, Bev will like them and be impressed."

"Thank you, Mrs. Williams," Donna said, flushed with pleasure.

"You are more than welcome, dear. Oh, I remember. I used the box to wrap a couple of work shirts for Craig. Come on, Donna. We might as well be doing something useful. Rob, you go watch a soap or a game or something while you wait for Craig."

She went to the living room and came back with a gift-wrapped box. "The wrapping paper is downstairs. We'll just unwrap this one carefully and find something else for Craig's shirts."

Donna did nothing more than watch as Marion carefully undid the parcel, slipped the cookie tin inside the box and wrapped it again.

"You write the card," Marion said, "while I find something for Craig's shirts."

Donna sat chewing a pen. "I don't know what to write," she said, blushing.

"Oh, I see," Marion said. "Use first names because you're close to the same age. Say 'To Bev and Richard' because it's her house and her family will be there and 'From Rob and Donna' because it's his family. But it doesn't really matter, nobody pays much attention any more to such niceties."

"Thank you," Donna said, writing. And Marion realized again that this was a sensitive, intelligent girl who had little experience with family relationships.

There were loud voices and thumps upstairs and then Craig shouted down. "Hi, Mom and Donna. Rob's got my present so we're going up to my room."

"Okay," Marion called up. Then to Donna she explained. "They have always exchanged their presents privately the day before Christmas. It seems to be the most important thing about Christmas for them. Even when they were little, Santa was almost incidental." She smiled. "They're very close. You'll get used to it."

"That's why Rob's been waiting," Donna said, nodding her head in sudden understanding.

They went upstairs together. "Have you had lunch?" Marion asked.

Donna shook her head. "I didn't think we'd be away so long," she said.

"Oh, good," said Marion. "Let's make some sandwiches and coffee. Those two will always eat."

The two of them worked congenially together, making lunch and setting the table, and talking as a mother and daughter might. When lunch was ready, Marion called upstairs and Craig and Rob came down grinning and happy.

"Well, come on! Show us what you got," Marion demanded.

"I got Jack Nicklaus's book on golf," Craig said.

"He's an executive. He needs to know how to play golf," Rob explained. "Besides it was on cheap at the Book Warehouse on Broadway."

"And a book of naked ladies," Craig added, laughing.

"I had to explain to him that it was art, not pornography," Rob interjected. "He's very naive, you know. And I got something very useful and practical—a tool box filled with tools." He showed them off, one by one, finding unique and casually vulgar explanations for the uses of each tool. "Very nice," he finished, and added with a grin, "But I was expecting new skis and boots now that he's rich, but practical will do."

"Practical because his dad will take all his tools to Prince George and he will just come and borrow mine and never bring them back," Craig explained.

"Where's the book of naked ladies?" Donna asked, no longer interested in admiring tools.

"They're upstairs. Not for family viewing," Craig said.

Marion interrupted the game. "Okay," she said, "lunch is ready. And Donna, I'll find the naked ladies sometime when I do an annual rootout of Craig's room and I'll phone you."

"Great!" Donna replied as they smiled at each other privately.

* * *

Bev and Richard had taken their daughter for a long sleigh ride after her nap, coming back hot and happily tired from slogging through some deep snow out in the University Endowment Lands. Bev was making some last minute checks on her Christmas dinner while Richard watched the news with one eye and playing with his daughter.

"Oh, great! Just what we need! Did you hear that?" he shouted to Bev.

"Did I hear what?" she asked, coming to the living room door.

"They are forecasting four to six inches of snow during the night and if there is no agreement reached with the bus drivers by five o'clock, they are walking out. The word is out that most stores and offices are closing now so employees won't be stranded on Christmas eve but the chains will stay open until midnight whatever happens. The spokesman for the Superstore said they had a responsibility to serve the public and he said it with a serious face as if he hadn't received orders from on high to stay until the last buck was grabbed. I bet Rob won't volunteer for that late shift."

"Oh, I forgot to tell you," Bev said. "Rob quit. When he went in on Wednesday, after he left you, his boss was snarly and Rob told him what he could do with his job and walked out."

"Now what's he going to do?"

"I guess he's planning on being a guest of the government for a while," Bev said, unhappily.

"Not a happy thought, but it's at least realistic,"

"Is it?"

"I think so."

The snow crunched underfoot as Rob and Donna walked home from the Williams. Craig had given Donna a gentle kiss and the two boys permitted them selves a couple of shoulder bumps by way of wishing each other a Merry Christmas. They stopped at the Superstore to pick up Rob's pay from the Assistant Manager who handed it to him without a word and rushed off to attend to more important duties such as making sure the cigarette case was locked and that customers were adhering to the '10 items or less' notice on the express checkout. They needed milk and bread and eggs but decided the little corner store was going to be quicker and less frantic.

Arriving home, they wrapped small presents for Bruno and Phyllis and set out to deliver them. They were welcomed warmly, particularly by Bruno who was already in a party mood. "He started as soon as we got in the door," Phyllis said, with a smile. "He doesn't get too many chances to tie one on, so I guess it's his night tonight. You feel better?" she asked Donna, glancing at her tummy.

"Yes, I do, thank you," Donna said. "Must have been a touch of flu."

"Come have glass wine with us," Bruno insisted.

"And?" Phyllis said.

"And what?" Bruno asked. Then his face lit up, "Oh, yes! I remember! Merry Christmas, Donna. Is good working with you." He handed her an envelope.

Donna took it from him. "Shall I open it now?" she asked.

"Open! Open!" Bruno said taking another great gulp of wine.

It was a card with a fifty dollar bill tucked inside. "Bruno! That's too much. Thank you, but... Well, thank you both." She moved to shake his hand but he grabbed her and gave her a monstrous hug that lifted her off her feet and gave her a wet, grandfatherly kiss on the cheek. Then he gave her a pinch on the bottom that was casually less than grandfatherly.

They drank a glass of wine, ate greedily of Phyllis's Christmas baking and headed happily for home. There they knocked on the Lasseret's basement door and took them up the plant that Donna had bought. They talked for a while, drank another glass of wine, ate more sausage rolls and shortcake, bid the Lasserets a Merry Christmas and went downstairs where they turned on the TV and turned off the lights and crawled into bed and made love.

Later, Rob said, "Hey, a couple of days ago you gave me the cold shoulder and said you were having your period. How come it was over so fast?"

"I just said that because I was mad at you. It's not due until the first of the month."

Still later, Donna, feeling relaxed and satisfied, curled closer to Rob and said, "You know, I think we should always keep some wine around, just in case."

"Happy New Year," he answered enigmatically.

CHAPTER 63

The National Weather Service was again projecting snow for the Lower Mainland but nobody really believed the forecast when they looked out onto a landscape glistening with a morning sun determined to shine through a lightly overcast sky. Smoke curled from the chimneys of fireplaces in those homes where young children had stirred the household into wakefulness and living rooms were awash with torn wrapping paper and paper boxes filled with once used colourful bows and ribbons that would find another year of use.

The Turner's home was quiet and dark. Glen and Claudia had exchanged small gifts to each other on the evening before and, after a celebratory hot rum had gathered together the gifts and other contributions for Bev's Christmas dinner, had gone to bed early in a house that was beginning to echo with emptiness. Of course, they told themselves, it was the absence of Rob that heightened the feeling of emptiness. But there was something more. They told themselves that they should be responding to the spirit of the season and they should feel some greater sense of excitement about their impending move, but something was inhibiting their usual positive response to each other and to life. They lay in each other's arms comfortably and agreed in the dark that it could be that they were just getting old.

Craig and his mother had had dinner by the fireplace and the TV, then phoned Edith's and talked to the excited twins who listed all the wonderful things that Santa was getting ready to bring them. The presents he had wrapped for his mother and her presents to him were already placed carefully around the small tree to be opened in the morning and those they would take with them to Edith's were boxed and piled in the hallway ready to go. They watched television until they discovered that they were both nodding off so they bid each other sweet dreams and went to bed. In other years, each thought independently as they struggled with sleep, they would have waited for 'him' to come home. They would have waited dinner but he would have eaten. He usually brought some quickly bought present for each of them and tossed them, undecorated, under the tree in the original store bag. It was their first Christmas without him and neither of them felt guilty about not missing him. Just before she drifted off to sleep Marion thought she should feel guilty about her completely negative feeling toward her dead husband (she even hated the word) but it was a passing thought that did not inhibit sleep. Craig lay sprawled on his bed, staring into the darkness. 'He was a dirty, rotten bastard' was his last thought before, as young people can, he clicked off consciousness and turned on sleep. But January 7 tumbled around in tormenting dreams. It was well after nine o'clock in the morning before they stirred and went down to coffee and their few presents to each other happily exchanged.

***

Even though they had been busy visiting all day, Rob had persuaded Donna to go for a walk with the promise that there would be moonlight. The walk turned into a snowball fight, which ended in a rough and tumble wrestle in the snow refereed by a snowman who declined to declare a winner. On their return, wet and hungry, they stripped and put their wet clothes in the drier and feasted on a macaroni and cheese dish that Donna created without reading the directions, accompanied, of course, by Rob's famous hot chocolate without the marshmallow. Each was pronounced so delicious that they rewarded themselves by opening their presents to each other and then cuddling in bed to watch the Tonight Show and sleep through a movie. There had been no agreement made between them but it passed through the thoughts of each of them that neither had brought up the problem of Rob's court appearance on January 7.

Bev spent the evening rearranging presents in front of the tree while Richard struggled with the assembly of a wooden wagon that in the end bore little resemblance to the picture on the box. Last year's wooden doll carriage had been easier. To celebrate his success, he poured them another glass of wine and, putting his camera on a tripod, they posed, raising their glasses to each other in front of the Christmas tree as the camera clicked with the lens cover on.

After the twins had talked with Granny and Craig, Edith checked again with her mother to make sure of their arrival time and to remind her of the things she promised to bring. Harvey put the girls to bed while Edith phoned to wish Merry Xmas to two people in her therapy group who were known to live alone without family or close friends. It was her intention to cheer them up by detailing the wonderful Christmas she was planning for her children and her family. The two phone calls took much less time than she had anticipated so there was lots of time to spend with Harvey just looking at the tree and the presents and talking about tomorrow. She allowed the children one present each before Santa Claus came. Next year maybe she would just let them open their presents to each other—like Rob and Craig do. I should have phoned Bev about Rob, Edith thought. Oh, well! I don't know what to say. It's too depressing, all that drug and jail stuff. She rarely permitted the clouds of yesterday or even the threat of impending clouds to intrude upon the sunshine of today.

By ten o'clock on Christmas morning, whatever little sun had filtered through the earlier light overcast had disappeared and the sky was leaden. Phone calls were being made to talk about the weather and the safety of the roads. Edith phoned promptly at ten to say the roads out her way were all clear and without pausing went on to tell her mother all about the excitement of Santa's visit. Marion reassured her that they would be on their way momentarily, that Craig was loading the car now and that they would be there, as promised, in time to open more presents before lunch.

On the car radio, the weather station reported on ski conditions in the east and stated that although no snow had as yet fallen on the west coast, a heavy snow advisory was being put out.

"Have they ever got it right once in the past three or four weeks?" Marion grumbled to Craig as they crossed onto the freeway into light traffic on ploughed and salted roads.

The two of them arrived at the Allen household that was strung with flashing Christmas lights and lighted at night with flood lights. There were cut-out snowflakes on every window and on each side of the biggest snowflake on the front window was the excited, shining face of a welcoming twin. With that greeting it seemed that Christmas had officially started.

Gifts were opened and exclaimed over. Each twin took a turn at being Santa with their mother in the sergeant major role to keep things orderly and fair. Iona ripped her parcels open, examined the present, rushed over to say thank-you to the giver and returned for a closer examination of the gift. Jenny opened her presents more carefully, folding even the torn wrapping paper before examining the gift happily. Then, with wide smiling eyes and a pursed smile she said her thank-yous by climbing up onto a lap and nestling her head into the neck of the person who had given her the gift. Iona obviously followed her mother's pattern of dealing with gifts: rip, look, thank and put aside. Jenny did what her father did: appreciate the pretty paper, fold it, carefully admire the details of the present before thanking each person with graceful sincerity.

Edith's gifts were routinely accompanied with, "Now if you don't like it or it doesn't fit, you can exchange it. I saved all the sales slips."

They tidied up and put their gifts in piles beside their chairs while Edith and her mother set the table for lunch. Iona and Jenny said grace successfully together, with Edith looking proudly on, her lips moving with her daughters'. Then, after lunch, before naps and before Harvey and Craig settled in for a full afternoon of football reruns, Edith and her mother took the girls for a long walk, two adults holding the hand of a child and Edith singing. Dogs barked when Edith sang and owners emerged to hush the dogs and return her cheery wave. It started to snow—light, large beautiful flakes that you could catch on your tongue or admire against the dark colour of a coat sleeve—underscoring the heavy snow advisory issued in the morning.

The time for dinner was advanced as far as turkey cooking time would permit and a watchful eye was kept on the falling snow by Craig, with Edith pacing everything, determined that her Christmas Day would not be spoiled by rushing anything.

It was a delicious dinner, everyone agreed, not spoiled by hurrying or children's fatigue. Edith glowed with pride, and although her mother thought it bordered on preening, she admired her daughter's competence. Edith never does anything by halves, she thought. She always throws her whole self into everything she does. Craig was the only one who wanted things to speed up and he made frequent trips to the window and outside, returning with increasingly worried looks that he thought nobody noticed.

It was Edith who, hiding the fact that she was tired herself from a long, busy day and in need of some peace and quiet, suggested that the storm was getting worse and hadn't they better pack up and be on their way. Craig tried to appear casual about the suggestion, but in twenty minutes, thank-yous and goodbyes exchanged, they were on their way. The storm had not been as widespread as predicted and halfway home the snow stopped and Craig's concerns disappeared.

"Nice day, wasn't it?" he asked as he relaxed.

"Yes, it was," his mother agreed. "Edith does a good job of entertaining. She's always so—so—organized. I guess that's the word I'm looking for."

Craig smiled and said nothing for a few miles, then said, "Do you think anyone missed Dad not being there?"

"Nobody I would know," she replied bluntly, looking out her window as if totally intrigued by the passing landscape.

Craig made no response and they drove in silence through the countryside and into the suburbs.

"I wish Rob would get a phone," he said.

***

Rob's parents arrived to pick up Rob and Donna much later than promised. Donna was sure they had forgotten but Rob's concern was that his father had changed his mind again.

"Sorry we are so late," his father apologized when he knocked on their door, "but just as we were leaving Roger Todd came in on crutches. He broke his leg skiing and bummed a ride home. He had to leave his car up there. God, the man's a walking disaster. Ready?"

"All ready," Rob said. "Come in and see the place while we get our coats on. Maybe Mom would like to see where we live. I'll go get her."

A dark look of impatience flashed over his father's face but it vanished quickly as he said, "Of course she would. We would have phoned," he said to Donna as Rob went out, "but, of course you haven't got a phone."

"Oh, Rob's giving me one for Christmas," Donna said. "It was a surprise. But it won't be here until January the seventh."

"Why the seventh? Isn't that the day that...?"

She nodded. "It was the first available date, I guess."

"Oh, my! This is cute!" Claudia said as Rob ushered her in.

"Good morning Donna, and Merry Christmas. This is very, very cosy. Just a perfect starter for a young couple, isn't it, Glen?"

"Better than the one we started with," Glen agreed. "We had one room with a hotplate and had to share the bathroom," he told Rob with a smile.

The little room looked very crowded with four people standing. "It's easy to look after," Donna said, "now that I've got Rob trained to pick up his clothes."

"You mean you've got him trained to do that! How did you do it? I tried for seventeen years and couldn't," Claudia said.

"It was easy," Donna said. "Anything that's dropped and not hung up or put away, I just fling under the bed. That way I get it dusted under there every day."

Everyone laughed. Rob said, "Oh, she's a hard woman!"

His father said, "Hadn't we better get going?"

Donna got her coat from the curtained off closet and Glen held it for her as she put it on.

"Where's my jacket, Donna?" Rob asked while rummaging around in the tiny closet.

"Look under the bed," she answered with a mischievous grin.

"You wouldn't!" he exclaimed, looking crestfallen as he dived under the bed. "My new jacket!"

He emerged with a sheepish grin and a box to a roomful of laughter. "I didn't think you would," he said to Donna. He took his new black leather jacket out of the box and modelled it. "My Christmas present from Donna," he said.

"It's beautiful," his mother said, feeling the soft leather. "What a lovely gift, Donna. It looks very expensive."

Donna smiled and said "Thank you," but she remembered again the real cost and wondered if Rob would think of it every time he wore it.

Upstairs Mrs. Lasseret had heard the sounds of conversation and laughter and she watched the four of them leave. "Did you hear them, Wally?" she asked. "They must be Rob's mom and dad. They seem like such a happy family."

"Was young Craig with them?" Wally asked.

"No, he wasn't," she said as he put his earphones back on.

At Bev and Richard's, most of the first clutter had been cleared away by the time they arrived with apologies and explanations for their tardiness. The granddaughter was fussed over and her presents admired. Other gifts were exchanged. Donna's box of English biscuits was claimed to be much too extravagant. "Really, Donna! You shouldn't have!" Rob romped with his niece until she was screaming with excitement with Bev occasionally calling, "Rob! Rob! For God's sake, keep it down. We can't hear ourselves think!"

The TV was turned to the football review and the three men with the little girl sprawled on her uncle's lap watched the armchair analysts as the three women set the Christmas dinner table and talked in the steamy fragrant kitchen.

In neither the Turner or the Lewis family had there been any recognition of Christmas as a religious observance. When Bev called them to dinner, Rob was asked to pour the wine while Richard carved. Claudia, Donna and Bev served vegetables as the plates were passed around the table, with Glen's plate the first to be completed.

"Help yourself to the gravy, dad, and please start. Don't let it get cold," Bev said.

Glen raised his glass and said, "Here's to our family!"

Everyone stopped their serving chores and raised their glasses and clinked without any pattern to their salutes.

"I can drink to that," Rob announced touching his wine glass to the glass of milk of his niece who cuddled close beside him while he leered lasciviously across the table at Donna.

"Cheers!" Donna said to him now beginning to relax in the easy atmosphere of Bev and Richard's home.

Rob had been mulling over the problems Roger Todd had taken on in running a business he knew little about and now with a broken leg he would find it doubly hard to manage. When dinner was over, he asked Richard if he could use the phone in the study and behind the closed door, he phoned Roger. A groggy, distressed voice answered after four rings.

"Roger? This is Rob. Did I catch you at a bad time?"

"No, not at all. I was just dozing in front of the TV and trying to find a comfortable position for this damn leg. Did your dad tell you what I did?"

"Yeah. That's too bad!"

"Stupid—that's what it was," Roger said.

"Yeah. Look, Roger. Dad said that you were swamped with orders and I wondered if you needed some help. I know the shop because I've helped my dad for years on all the machines. The thing is I have to go to court on January the seventh? Did my folks tell you about it?"

"They didn't exactly tell me, Rob. But I couldn't help overhearing them."

"Okay, then you know what's going on. Nobody knows what's going to happen but I might get fined and if I do I'll need some money. I got fired at the Superstore, by the way."

"I heard."

"Well, I just figured you need some expert help and I need a job, well, at least until the seventh of next month, and I thought maybe we could make a deal."

There was a long silence and Rob could feel a sense of disappointment rising. "Roger?" he said.

"Just a minute, I'm looking at the calendar. Can you start tomorrow?"

"Tomorrow's a holiday, Roger," Rob said for no good reason.

"I know that," Roger replied. "Look, I'm in a bind. I need somebody and I need him fast. I'll pay you the going rate—whatever it is, we'll have to find out—double time for holidays like boxing day and New Years and time and a half for overtime and weekends. How does that strike you?"

"Great, Roger! That's great! Thank you. What about after the seventh? My big date with the law, you know? If things work out better for me than people think?"

"Let's wait and see. Okay?"

"Sure!"

"So? Will I see you tomorrow."

"You bet, Roger. You sure will and thanks. And Roger, sorry about your leg and your bum Christmas."

"Bum Christmases are standard for me. See you tomorrow."

Rob sat for a minute controlling his excitement and wondering what his father's reaction would be. He left the study and joined the others just as an ad came on the television. Standing in front of the set, he called out, "Attention, please everybody! Hit the mute will you, Richard. I have an announcement to make."

Everyone stopped talking and turned to him expectantly.

"I've got a job," he said with a wide grin.

"What do you mean?" his mother asked.

"I mean I've got a job starting tomorrow and lasting at least until January the seventh. I just talked to Roger Todd because I knew he would need somebody and we made a deal."

"Is he paying you?" his mother asked.

"You bet! Standard wages when we find out what they are. Dad, you'll probably know. And double time for holidays and time and a half for overtime and weekends. How's that?"

"Can we hire you to bargain for the teachers?" Richard asked with a laugh.

Rob looked at his father to see his reaction and his father looked grim and caught his eye. "Why didn't you take that job when I told you I would work something out with Roger for you?" His tone was severe. "Then you might not have got caught in that other..."

"Glen!" Claudia's voice interrupted sharply. "There are some questions that can't be answered and some that shouldn't be asked!"

He looked at her and then at Rob. "Sorry, son," he said. "Congratulations!"

"What's this about the seventh?" Bev asked and then, when a silence fell on the others, realized the answer and blushed. "Sorry, Robbie! I forgot."

The television was turned back on. Other conversations were picked up and Rob found a place beside Donna. She took his hand and held it tight and somehow communicated to him how proud she was. "If you're not careful," she warned, "we'll never see each other. It sounds like he might make you work twenty four hours a day."

"Not quite that bad, Donna, but," he said quietly, "if I do get a sentence, we've got to get some money ahead to help you with the rent and stuff Might as well grab it if it's there."

"That's what I tried to do and look where it got us," she answered with a wry grin.

They were able to laugh hilariously at their private joke and the others turned to look at them, approving of their happiness. A few minutes later, Rob said, "I better phone and see if Craig is home yet. I should tell him." She watched him as he left her to go to Richard's study again and could not repress a small sigh.

The phone rang three times at the Williams before Craig answered it. "That will be Edith," his mother said after the first ring, "checking to see if we got home safely. You answer it and tell her it was a lovely dinner."

"Hello. We got home safely and it was a lovely dinner," Craig said as he picked up the phone.

"Hello yourself, knucklehead! I'm glad you're home safe and well fed but I didn't ask."

"Oh, hi! Where are you? I thought it was Edith."

"At Richard's. I got a job."

"Yeah? What doin'?"

"Same old thing. Working at home but the boss is Roger this time instead of my dad."

"How come?"

"He broke his leg skiing and dad said he was swamped and stupid and in-competent and spoiled, so I asked him and put him down and twisted his arm until he came up with a good offer. Simple as that!"

"Is it temporary?" Craig asked cautiously.

"Whad d'ya mean?"

"Well, you know, like after January the seventh, what'll happen to it?"

"Jesus! Thanks for the vote of confidence, pal! I'm glad you're not on the jury. You'd vote for life."

"That's not what I mean."

"I know," Rob said, suddenly serious. "I couldn't just sit around and do nothin' until the seventh. I'd go nuts. And I figured I could just dump it all on Donna so she can manage the rent and stuff."

"I woulda helped her."

"I know." Silence for a moment. "Have a good Christmas?"

"Yeah, I guess," Craig said in the middle of a huge yawn.

"Did ya like my present?"

"Oh, sure! It was great—just what I needed—what was it?"

"Ungrateful prick! I gotta go."

"Okay. See ya."

Rob went back to the his place beside Donna. She saw him coming and said to herself, "All it takes is a daily shot of Craig and everything's okay."

"That was Rob," Craig announced to his mother when he went back to the living room. "He's got another job. He's going to work for Roger Todd—you know, the guy who bought Rob's dad's business and house?"

"Well, isn't that nice!" she said. "You'll be nice and close again."

"Yeah!" he said, with a contemplative smile.

CHAPTER 64

Rob got up early and stuffed down some breakfast without waking Donna. In spite of the treacherous streets he decided to take his bike rather than wait for a bus on a holiday schedule. When he arrived at what used to be his home, the house was locked and quiet and he had to use the extra key that al-ways hung on a nail under the top step. Inside, he listened and could hear noth-ing but the fluttering sounds of his mother's snoring. It was eight o'clock—time to start work, and without a boss to tell him what needed to be done, he did what he had learned from his father years ago—clean the machines before us-ing them.

"Good morning, dear!" his mother said suddenly and brightly from behind him, approaching him with a smile and touching cheeks with him. "You're bright and early. Have you had breakfast?"

"Thanks, Mom," he said. "I gobbled something before I left."

"I'm going to put on the coffee," she said going downstairs. "Come down and grab a mug when you smell it. Oh, your father won't be up for a while. He was so fidgety I gave him a great big sleeping pill about three in the morning. It always knocks him out for hours and I get some sleep." She stopped at the bottom of the stairs and said, "We might drive up to George today to get out of your way and get organized up there. That is, if Roger doesn't need him and I wouldn't think he would with you around."

"Okay with me," Roger called, emerging from what used to be Rob's bedroom, "if I can beg a cup of that coffee from you."

"Sure thing," she said. "And with that leg and no car, I'll bet you wouldn't say no to breakfast."

"Mind reader!" he replied.

"Mom, you're coming back for your party, aren't you," Rob called anxiously.

"Of course!" her voice emerged from the basement kitchen.

"What did she say?" his father said, coming out of the bedroom, looking groggy.

"She said 'Of course', and she also said she gave you a sleeping pill that would knock you out for hours."

"Yeah, she has great faith in those things," he said on his way downstairs. "Call me if you need me."

Roger and Rob talked about what each should do to get a backlog of work done and Rob got started. Roger got on the phone trying to find a friend who could rescue his car. Answers at eight in the morning tended to be somewhat abrupt, but he persisted and finally found someone who was driving up and would take someone else to drive Roger's car back if Roger could find somebody within an hour.

"Take a friend with you, Jerry! Find a woman," Roger pleaded and listened to the excuses at the other end. "Son of a bitch!" he said as he hung up, "he's not a ladies man!"

He thumped around on his crutches for a while, then said, "Have you got any friends that are good drivers, good drivers, I said, that could go and bring my car back. It's a Porsche, you know, and it's going to be ripped off if I don't get it back right away, I know it!"

"Craig might," Rob said.

"Craig! Why didn't I think of that ! Perfect! He's careful. Call him!" Roger said excitedly.

"It's easier to go over," Rob replied.

"Go then, Rob. Please! And hurry. This guy is not giving me much time."

Rob walked quickly to the Williams, tried the door and found it locked. He knew neither Craig or his mother would be up at this time so he found the key hanging on the nail on the ledge of the porch and let himself in. Going quietly to Craig's room he found him sleeping on his back with one hand clutching his crotch and he paused for a moment thinking of several things he might do with this opportunity. Instead, he shook him roughly, "Wake up!" he whispered hoarsely in his ear and then stuck his wet tongue in it.

"What the..?" Craig said, coming awake, dropping his genitals and rubbing his ear. "Oh, hi!" he said companionably when he saw Rob, and then, "What the hell are y'doing?"

"Wake up! Get up! I've got a job for you. You gotta go pick up a Porsche," Rob said conspiratorially.

"Bugger off," Craig replied and rolled away onto his side.

Rob got on the bed and curled around him, a leg and an arm restraining Craig. "It's a fact," he whispered in Craig wet ear. "We got the keys and everything! It's a cinch!"

They wrestled for a while until Rob said, "Okay, are you awake?" and let go. "Listen," he continued. "It's no joke. Roger broke his leg skiing at Whistler and he had to leave his Porsche there. He's going nuts thinking somebody will rip it off. So a friend of his is driving up right now and I said you would go with him and drive Roger's Porsche back. So get up, get dressed, get your skis and have fun."

"Are you coming?" Craig asked getting out of bed and scrabbling around naked looking for ski clothes.

"I'm a working man, remember? No time for skiing for me."

It took Craig twenty minutes to get dressed, eat a banana, shove a handful of cookies in his pocket, write a 'Gone skiing' note and collect his skis and poles. When they reached Rob's place, Roger would have been hopping if he hadn't been on crutches.

"Oh, good!" he exclaimed, "you'll do it! I really, really appreciate it, Craig. I just hope nobody's stripped it before you get there." He gave Craig the keys and many instructions on how to start it and drive it. "It's got a tiger for an engine and the steering is very, and I mean very, sensitive. Have you ever driven a Porsche before?" Craig shook his head. "Well," Roger continued, "just take it slow and easy."

"Craig always drives slow and easy," Rob said, laughing.

"Where is it," Craig asked.

"At Whistler, I said," Roger answered, thinking the kid wasn't even awake and would probably forget all his instructions.

"Yeah, I heard. Now where is it parked? What colour is it? What's the license number? Is it a keyed door lock or a punched code? And you'd better give me a note of authority to pick it up. I don't want to be in court with Robbie."

Roger looked at this unshaven, tousled hair kid in amazement. "He's awake all right, maybe the only one of us who is," he said to himself. But aloud, he said, "Yeah, sure. I was just going to."

Rob had turned away and was on the other side of the room, controlling his laughter.

While Roger was writing directions, a knock sounded.

"Can you get it, Rob? It's probably Jerry."

Rob opened the door and a tall swarthy man with an earring demanded, "Is Roger here?"

"In a minute, Jerry," Roger called without looking up from a desk out of sight of the door.

"Move your ass. I'm late," came the answer as he stalked back to his car, got in and raced the engine.

"You'll have to introduce yourself," Roger said to Craig.. "Here's the license number and door code, and here's fifty bucks for parking or gas or lift tickets or grub or whatever. Take it easy, eh?"

"You don't have to..." Craig started to protest.

"Take it! He's waiting!" Roger said and gave him a shove.

Craig looked at the car and wondered what it was. Two doors, the hood, and the trunk lid were all of different colours, twin pipes jutted from the rear, and three aerials jiggled with the roar of the engine as the driver vroom-vroomed it while Craig tried to hurry to get his skis in the rack.

"Boots in the back. Let's go," the driver shouted.

Craig got in and as he closed the door they shot out into the street with a roar. Craig struggled into his seatbelt and pulled it as tight as it would go.

"I'm Craig," he ventured.

"I'm glad," came the reply, the only sound the driver would utter apart from curses for the rest of the trip.

Roger and Rob were just settling into work when the phone rang. Rob answered it and then said, "Roger, it's Jerry."

"What the hell now?" Roger muttered. Then, "Hi Jerry, what's up?" He listened, then said, "What do you mean, you can't make it?"

He listened some more. "Then who the hell was here? No, I didn't see him—he didn't come in. Just a minute."

"Rob," he called, "what did the guy who came to the door look like? Did you see the car?"

"Yeah, the car was a junkie, couldn't tell what it was but the engine purred like a kitten until he razzed it, then it growled. The guy was big with long hair and an earring. He sorta matched the car except he wasn't purring."

"What was his name?"

"I thought you called him Jerry."

Roger went back to the phone and talked some more and hung up. "Shit! Now what!" he grumbled. "That wasn't Jerry. That was some guy his brother picked up and spent the night with them. He was heading for Whistler and Jerry said his hangover was worse so he gave him your address and asked him to take your guy."

"Who was he?"

"I dunno and they don't either. Jerry said he thought he builds racing cars." He paused and added by way of explanation. "Jerry and his brother are, shall we say, a little left of centre. Know what I mean?"

"Yeah, I guess," Rob answered, a little shaken by the information. After a minute, he ventured, "You got many friends like that?"

Roger looked at him curiously. "A few," he said. "But I can play both sides of the net. Why? You interested?"

Rob shook his head and turned on his noisy machine again and discovered that his hands were shaking.

Craig was not adjusting to the odd-ball machine he was a passenger in. The man's crazy! I'll never get there alive, he thought. He was strapped in tight and holding his breath and closing his eyes as the driver passed on double lines, cruised sometimes at 140 kph, pulled a cut-out switch on the mufflers so that they roared up behind and beside other cars and passed them when they pulled over, shaking. Muttering and cursing while tailgating other slower drivers, he gave them the finger and a blast on his air horn as he roared by. They arrived at the hotel where Roger had directed Craig. All 'Jerry' needed to be told was the name. He did not turn off the engine while Craig struggled with the seatbelt and the rooftop carrier. When Craig had taken his equipment out and stuck this head in to say thanks, 'Jerry' smiled a smile as big as the world and his eyes twinkled merrily as he reached over and tousled Craig's hair.

"Hey! We made it!" he said. "Best time ever. I'll see ya on the hill, eh, kiddo? Let's take the copter up. I know a great route down the backside. Comes out about a mile from here. Okay?" Gone was the frowning, glowering, sour man.

"Yeah, sure. See you on the hill then," Craig lied, almost stuttering and hoping desperately he would never see that madman ever again in this life or the next.

He went inside and parked his skis and boots and headed for a quick eating joint. While he ate and looked at the slopes spread over the huge mountain, the gondolas ascending full and descending empty, the thousands of skiers in as many colours dotting the brilliant snow, he thought, he'll never find me up there.

Then he was jolted by a great whack on the back and a huge arm around his shoulders. "Hey, there! Little buddy! I thought I lost you. Let's get going. They tell me the powder in the backside is so deep if you fall they won't find you till spring."

Craig looked up. 'Jerry' looked twice as big as he did slouching in the car. He was wearing a one-piece padded ski suit that fitted like driving gloves and seemed to accentuate every muscle and bulge. Even his smile was bigger. "I can't go, I mean I can't ski powder—not like that, I mean," Craig said, in stuttering lies. I just ski, like the bunny hill and maybe a little bigger. Like not too many moguls. Grouse Mountain is my favourite."

"Aw, come on! We'll have a great time. You gotta ski deep powder! It's the greatest! It's like, well it's like losing your virginity every time you do it."

"Oh, I've already done that," Craig said, trying to be funny but it came out wrong, and before the words were out he regretted his stupidity and looked for a rock to crawl under while people around giggled and laughed.

The guy sat down sideways on the stool beside Craig, one knee pressed against Craig's rump and one arm draped on his shoulders. "Tell you what I'll do, little buddy. I'll give you a piggy back ride down. How's that?" His face was so close Craig could smell his minty breath and his smile looked sinister.

"No, no! I can't!" Craig protested. "I think I better get back home with Roger's car. But it sure sounds like it would be fun."

"Well, why'd you bring your skis?"

"Oh," Craig replied shakily, "just habit, I guess."

"Well, shit!" the guy said, standing up so that he towered over Craig. "Jerry said we'd have a great day together." The glower came back to his face as he turned to go.

"I thought you were Jerry," Craig called after him.

"Hell, no!" the guy said over his shoulder.

Craig paid his breakfast bill and hurried out the other door.

***

During periods of quiet in the morning, while Rob and Roger were setting the printers up for another run, they could talk.

"So did you ever find out who this guy was?" Craig asked.

"No. They don't know anything about him—just another quickie. He stayed the night and he wanted to get to Whistler bad. Jerry was hung-over so he figured this guy could take Craig." And he added, "I hope the bugger's not figuring to get my car."

"I hope he's not figuring to get Craig," Rob said.

"Yeah," Roger said. "He could hit Craig over the head and dump him in a ditch and take off with my car."

On that note, they turned on their machines and got back to work, one worrying about a car, the other about a friend.

Late in the morning, Claudia phoned Marion to tell her that they were packing for George and leaving after lunch. "We'll be back in lots of time for your party," she said. "But tell me right now if there's anything I should be doing."

"Not a thing, dear!" Marion replied, knowing from experience what a terrible cook Claudia was. "Just don't phone me on the 31st and tell me you're snowbound."

When Claudia got off the phone after exchanging stories about their Christmas days, Glen was so anxious to get going that he had started to make lunch. He let her take over and talked to her while she worked. "I had a session with Roger," he said, "and he can't think of anything right now that he needs help with. But he says Rob seems to know the basic operation so there should be no problem there and that he's not up to scratch in the accounting end of things, so he's going to spend a day with the accountant at the end of the month to make things tidy. Then he might have some questions. Where's that list of things to do that we made out last week?"

"On my dressing table in the bedroom," she told him and he wandered off in search of it, stopping on the way to make an adjustment on the machine Rob was working on and suddenly saying, with a smile, "Oops! Sorry. Can't help it—it's a habit."

At noon, Claudia called Rob for lunch and insisted on Roger coming, too.

"With luck, I should have my car back today and I'll be able to get out to eat," Roger said.

"And how in hell will you manage a stick shift with a cast on your foot up to your knee," Glen asked pointedly.

"I don't know! But at least I'll have my car. Maybe my first assistant will have to take on added duties, like chauffeur."

"Who, me?" Rob asked. "You bet!"

By twelve-thirty, Rob's parents were on their way with warm goodbyes to their son from both.

At three o'clock, the door opened on the noisy room to reveal a smiling Craig.

"You're back!" shouted Roger, shutting down his printer.

"Hey, buddy!" Rob shouted with a grin when he saw Craig and he, too, shut down his noisy collator. "How'd it go? Didn't you ski?"

"No, I thought I'd better get the car back before the heavy traffic started."

"Well, you made it by three or four hours," Rob said wryly. "So what's the real story?"

Craig did not answer but reached into his pocket and brought out a handful of bills. "That's your change," he said to Roger. "The parking was thirty dollars and taxes and you didn't need gas."

"Keep it," Roger said. "Hell, I'm sorry! You couldn't have bought a lift ticket with what was left. Stupid of me! That's why you didn't go skiing."

"No, no!" Craig protested. "It wasn't that."

"Well, what was it?" Rob asked.

"I dunno," Craig said reluctantly. "I just wanted to get away from that madman. You told me his name was Jerry and he wasn't Jerry."

"Who was he? Did you find out his name?" Roger asked.

"No, I didn't ask. I was too busy shitting myself. He drove like crazy all the way—140, 150, passing on double lines, roaring up behind other cars and pulling some switch that cut out the mufflers when he was riding somebody's bumper and scaring them off the road nearly. The man's a maniac. He didn't say a word all the way up and then he found me in a burger joint and it was like we were old buddies from away back. And he was practically mauling me, you know—hugging me, saying we should take the copter and do the deep powder and I said I couldn't ski powder and he said he would give me a piggyback all the way down. He's crazy! I think he's probably queer, too."

"Where's the car now," Roger said peering out the window.

"I put it in the garage. It was empty," Craig said.

"Was it okay? Nobody stole the ski-racks? They can do that while your back is turned, you know. Just rip them off and put them on their own car and drive away for the cost of a parking ticket. Five minutes, max!"

"Everything looked okay," Craig said.

"I better go out and check it over," Roger said, pulling on a jacket and working his way inexpertly through the maze of machines and out the door.

When the door closed, Rob grinned at Craig and said, "So you think the guy was queer, eh?"

"Either that or nuts or both. He was practically mauling me in the coffee shop. He was sitting sideways so his leg was around me and his face was so close I could feel his breath, And he leered, like this," and he made a toothy, narrow-eyed smile and leaned towards Rob.

"That's a leer alright," Rob said laughing. "Did he tell you he had a cabin halfway down the back side where he takes little boys?"

"No, does he?" Craig's face registered horror at the thought of what might have happened. Then, seeing Rob's 'gotcha' grin, he hit him hard on the arm and said, "Don't be an asshole!"

"Hey, I'll tell you something else, and no shit," Rob said, rubbing his arm. "Roger told me that Jerry and his brother picked this guy up for the night. How d'ya like that? He says that they are a little left of centre and that he likes to play both sides of the net himself, and then he invited me to play. How do you like that? That hurt!" he added. He made a big knuckle and thumped Craig equally hard on his arm.

Craig was listening without any comprehension of what Rob was saying, his face showing only bewilderment. "What do you mean? Play what?"

Rob shrugged and made a couple of coital thrusts.

After of minute of total perplexity, Craig's face registered a light of comprehension. "You mean Roger's a homo?" he squeaked. "And that guy and the other one—Jerry? They all are? Jesus! You're surrounded." He stood shaking his head at the thought, then suddenly said, "What do you mean—he invited you to play?"

The door opened and Roger stumbled awkwardly in on his crutches. Rob grinned at Craig. "Don't worry," he said. "I've got my own playmate."

"Great!" Roger announced happily. "Not even a scratch on it. Thanks, Craig! I'm glad to be rid of that worry. Now maybe I can get some work done."

The conversation stopped as Roger looked back and forth at the other two apparently realizing he had interrupted something private. He hobbled over to the printer and turned it on.

"I guess I better get out of the way," Craig said.

"Yeah, see ya," Rob replied with a big wink behind Roger's back. Roger saw him leaving and gave him a wave.

When Craig got home, his mother was on the phone talking to Edith. He could tell by her fidgets that she had been on the phone a long time, so he said loudly, "Is that Edie? Let me say thank you for her present before I go."

"Just a minute, Edith. Craig wants to talk to you and I've got to get the things out of the drier before they get wrinkled. I'll call you again. And thank you again for a wonderful day and a delicious dinner. Bye, dear." She handed the phone to Craig with a wink.

"Hi, Edie! Thank you for my present and for dinner. Goodbye." Craig said and waited for the explosion.

"Craig Williams! Don't be so rude!" she shrilled at him.

"Who me? I wasn't being rude, I was doing my courtesies."

Suddenly she realized that she was being needled and she softened and needled in return. "Oh, you're doing curtsies these days, are you? That's sweet!

Would you like to borrow my crinoline?"

"You know I don't like crinoline unless it's well done. You always cook yours rare," he answered.

"Oh, Craig! You're goofy!" she said, and laughed happily.

"Did you have a happy Christmas?" he asked.

"It was perfect," she said. "And thank you for the thing you gave me. What is it?"

"I don't know. I just saw it and it was cheap and I knew you needed one but I don't know what it is either."

She laughed again and said, "If I ever find out what it was I won't tell you."

"You always were a mean sister," he laughed.

"The girls won't open your game until you come out and play it with them," Edith said with one of her sudden switches in conversation.

"Oh, I should have driven out this morning in my Porsche."

"Sure, sure," she replied and he went no further with the Porsche story.

"Well, hey, Edie. I called to say thanks and I did. So..."

"Craig?" she asked and paused, then said, "I love you."

He was so stunned by her sudden emotional admission that he could make no reply.

"I'm learning to say that from my group therapy sessions," she continued. "It feels kind of nice to say it."

"It feels kind of nice to hear it, Edie."

"Goodbye, Craig," she said in a shaky voice and hung up.

His mother asked casually as he passed her going up to his room, "What did Edith have to say?"

"She told me she loved me," he said, not stopping.

She looked at his retreating back and shook her head.

He closed the door to his room, piled up the pillows and stretched out with a computer book in his face with his mind on a dozen other things, mostly Rob and people like Roger, and Jerry and the other Jerry, who ever they were, and the puzzle about them playing 'both sides of the net'. He was sound asleep when his mother called him for dinner.

The Christmas holidays passed in a desultory way for most people, visiting, walking, putting away decorations and filling the time after Christmas with incidentals until wives could breathe a sigh of relief as husbands went back to work on Tuesday for three days until New Years. Fathers had OD'd on football for the long weekend and had claimed dibs on the TV at any time. On Tuesday, there would be a breathing spell until the end of the year, during which mothers could catch up on the soaps and kids on their cartoons. Everybody waited for January the fourth when the obligatory New Years Eve party would be over, as would be the Rose Bowl parade and the Rose Bowl, Cotton Bowl, Orange Bowl and perhaps even the Cranberry Bowl games, and the hangovers and the guilts. Then fathers would return contentedly to the routine of work, children with disguised reluctance would trudge off to school and mothers, while clothes driers were spinning and dish washers were turning and vacuum cleaners had been hauled out of cupboards to stand in readiness, would pick up the telephone and the lines would hum with the happy chatter of the real world. Everybody would return to their comfortable routines. Everybody, that is, except the Turners and the Williams and certain close others who were anxiously waiting for January the seventh.

Craig had gone back to work on Monday, the extra Boxing Day, not knowing whether the plant was open or closed for the day. Carl was already in his office and Larry was in the shop repairing one of the machines but Craig saw that none of the other employees had arrived.

"Happy New Year," Carl said, shaking hands with him. "I decided I better come in and go over a few things before the computer people come tomorrow."

They chatted about Christmas while searching the secretaries' office to find the coffee makings and together discovered the magic of the coffee machine and sat back talking until it brewed.

"Call Larry and tell him the coffee is ready, will you, Craig? I'll get the mugs."

Larry came in, bundled up in a heavy sweater under his overalls and a cap with earflaps. "Lucky people—bosses," he said with a smile. "Always work in the nice and warm."

He was wiping his greasy hand on a shop cloth. "Look my hands!" he said, holding them up. "Yesterday, all white and soft because I do dishes all holiday. My wife, she spilled the turkey grease on her hand and I have to take her to emergency for a big bandage, so I have to do all dishes and I get hands like a boss, all nice and clean. But," he waved his hands in the air, "this more like me, eh?"

The phone rang and Carl answered it and talked to someone for a few minutes while Larry continued with the story of his wife's burned hands.

"Are you going to be around all day, Craig?" Carl interrupted, and Craig nodded and said, "Sure!"

"How about you, Larry?"

"Yes, okay. I work."

"Fine," Carl said into the telephone. "Bring them anytime. We'll be here." He turned back to the other two. "That was the computer people. They would like to come today instead of tomorrow. The place they had booked for today is closed."

"Good!" Craig said. "We'll get started sooner. It should be easier for them when the plant is not operating.

They were in the main office and they immediately started planning the location of the machine, drawing out on paper where the computer could be placed to give easy access to it for the three secretaries and Craig. It was Larry, who had been sitting back listening, who solved the problem.

"No good!" he said, bluntly and the other two stopped to listen.

"All carpenters have hammer," he said. "Can't stand around waiting for same hammer to do work. Same as women in office. They all got their own typewriter. Same like carpenter or plumber or mechanic. All got their own tools. So I don't think, if you ask me, one machine is not good. One machine for each is better, then nobody spoils somebody else work." He stood up and smiled. "I go and do something I know about."

"Don't go, Larry," Carl said. "I think you solved our problem."

"Good," Larry said. "But I gotta fix my machine for it's ready for tomorrow. Besides, too hot in here." He went out, almost strutting, obviously feeling pleased with himself.

"He's right, you know," Carl said. "That means we start all over again with our plans."

By noon of the 31st, the computers had been installed and Carl and Craig had been through three half day instructional sessions with the three office women sitting in whenever their regular duties would permit. The men in the plant glared balefully at the computer installed in the work area, certain that the intruder was an enemy or a spy or a Simon Legree that would destroy something they had valued.

"Is a tool," Larry kept on saying to them. "Just a typewriter and telephone and adding machine and like a brain all mixed together. Is a twenty-first century tool! We don't use stone hammers no more. We use modern tools. Much better. Why you scared?"

"Yeah, but...."

In his own way, speaking bluntly and loyally in the language of the workplace, Larry continued to deal with the 'Yeah, buts' more effectively than either Carl or Craig so that by the time the training sessions were scheduled an attitude of distrust and been replaced by curiosity and interest.

Craig had found himself so intrigued by the complexities of management and by the different skills of leadership displayed by Carl and Larry that for three days he gave little thought to the complications in his private life. In mid afternoon, when the computer man quit early, Carl leaned back and said, "Well, Craig, we've started. Let's leave it until the New Year. I'm going to ring the quitting buzzer and wish the men Happy New Year. I guess you've got plans for a party, so why don't you get going too."

He stood up and shook hands with Craig. "Have a Happy New Year, son," he said. "It's going to be a great year."

Craig returned the greeting and only then realized he had made no plans for New Years Eve other than his mother's big party that he wasn't looking forward to with much enthusiasm. But it might not be so bad, he thought, with Rob and Donna there and a midnight movie. He wondered what Rob was doing.

CHAPTER 65

On Boxing Day, a Saturday that year, Marion set out later than usual looking for next year's supply of Christmas decorations and wrappings. The big sales would come on Monday when the stores and malls would swarm with women snatching, grabbing, pushing and shoving in a frantic search for bargains. Marion had spent the largest part of the morning phoning friends and family and it was when she called Bev's to speak to Claudia that she found out that Glen and Claudia were getting ready to leave for Prince George at noon.

"But we haven't done any shopping," she wailed. "We always have at least two days doing the stores and the big malls. How can you leave me on my own, all by myself?"

"I know! I'm sorry, dear. But I've got to get Glen away from here before he drives everybody mad. There are a thousand things to do up there that will keep him busy and I'll have a good chance to look around at the sales. Are you sure there isn't something, anything, I can do for the party?"

"Just be here! Don't you dare be late! Phone me as soon as you get back, do you hear? I don't want a phone call on New Years Eve telling me you are stuck in a snow bank and me with a house full of people. Oh, I am going to miss you so much!"

They bid each other a warm and tearful goodbye and Marion made herself a lonely cup of tea before setting out for the first of the year end shopping sprees. There would be, as usual, two weeks of frantic activity by the merchants in their attempts to entice and trap the shopper, but on Boxing Day, nobody—neither clerk nor customer—was really fit and ready for the battle. Boxing Day was a warm-up. Sunday, December 27, was an alternate Boxing Day with no papers and few home delivery ads, but Marion did another warm-up run in preparation for Monday when the _real_ sales started. Craig had gone to Whistler on Saturday to pick up Roger's car, had lounged in front of the TV all day Sunday and had gone happily back to work on Monday that was, some unions insisted, the legal Boxing Day.

Marion had had two good days of shopping. The dining room chairs were loaded with the bargains she had found and had dumped there when she got home, foot weary and hot. There were birthday presents, Christmas presents for next year, clothes for herself and Craig, surprise gifts for the twins and Edith and a number of other items not yet allocated as gifts to anybody in particular. So on Tuesday evening when she dropped exhausted into a chair in front of the fire to take stock, all she had to do before the party on Friday was to put away the piles of purchases she had dumped in the dining room, clean the house, get her hair done, do the ordinary shopping and then the special shopping for the party, polish the silver, make sure Craig shovelled the walks, get some flowers for the table, pick up her dress from the cleaners, look up a non-alcoholic punch recipe, pick up some liquor and mixers and make the dinner for fourteen people including the two boys and Donna. She sighed with relief that she did not have to childproof the house. Edith and Bev had got together and arranged to share a babysitter for the children at Bev's.

She had draped her apron around her neck when she got home but decided she would like to put her feet up before getting started on dinner and was just getting up from her easy chair when she was faced with two young men with careful smiles hooked across their faces.

"Hi, Mom," one said and kissed her cheek. "Busy day?"

"Hello, U.U.," the other one said, "You look all tuckered out. Would you like me to get you something—a drink perhaps, or a massage, maybe?"

She stood looking at them while she retied her apron, leaning toward them slightly as she tied the strings behind her back. They were children with smirks on their faces, up to something.

"Mom?" one of them said, "we were just thinking that we might not come to your party on Friday. We thought we might go to a double feature and watch the celebrations down town. We thought that the three of us would just be in the way with all the old people wanting to talk, and things..." he finished lamely, watching her face.

"You thought <u>what</u>?" The voice sounded like ice cubes cracking out of a tray and sparks seemed to leap from her eyes with such force that they stepped back from her. They were about to be the sole witnesses of a torrent of maternal fury that, in their young sheltered lives, they never knew existed. "You thought <u>what</u>?" she repeated. "You thought that you would not bother to come to your own party? Well, just a minute, you two! Just stop, look and listen and beware! You sure as hell are coming to your party! You will be here at five o'clock sharp! And I mean sharp! Ready for your guests and ready to do all of the things that I tell you have to be done if you're having a party. And you will be clean and neat and tidy! Both of you! Rob! Get a haircut. Craig! I see your good shoes kicking around in the basement with old mud caked on them. Don't start asking me for the shoe polish when the guests are ringing the bell."

She was working on a full head of steam now, and they stood gaping at her, mouths open and eyes wide, ready to retreat if she moved in their direction. Her fists were punched into her hipbones and she was leaning forward aggressively.

"And," she continued, "I don't want to see you standing around giggling in a little private threesome. I want you out there mingling, talking to the loners, listening to the big shots, pouring drinks—big ones for the shy ones and little ones for the drunks. And none for yourselves! Hear that? Not one! You may have one glass of white wine with your dinner. If you think you are being cheated out of a party, you can get that Vodka bottle out of the bar, the one you filled with water, and put an ice cube in it and call it a Vodka Martini. And take those silly smirks off your faces or I'll take them off for you—or have you both forgotten what a good right hand I have?" She didn't even have to take a big breath as she continued. "And you will take the plates of hors d'oeuvres around and pick up empty glasses and plates and mingle and make yourselves useful until dinner is over and the dishes are cleaned up. Then, and only then, and after you have made a polite exit, you can go to your midnight movie. Now then! Have I made myself clear? Any questions? Now is your chance!" She stood, glaring at them, still furious and waited.

"We just thought...," Craig began uncertainly.

"Bull!" she interrupted. "You didn't think at all! Now get out of here."

"I guess I better go do my shoes," Craig said, edging toward the basement stairs.

"I better help him, U.U.," Rob said, following him, still the irrepressible Rob, shaking his head and tsk-tsking. "He can't do anything right. I have to teach him everything." Then, in a loud whisper, "See, I told you it wouldn't work. You should have let me do it. I could have softened her up."

"Oh, shut up!" Craig said, and gave Rob a hard punch on the arm. "Where's the shoe polish, Mom?" he continued innocently.

"O-o-h! Ouch! That hurt!" Rob wailed. "U.U., he hurt me. Craig hurt me!"

"Get out of my sight!" she shouted, charging toward them.

They stumbled over each other getting down the stairs as the door slammed behind them. At the bottom they stopped and looked at each other and in a minute started to double up in silent laughter.

"Boy! She's good!" Craig said, wiping his eyes.

"She's the best, man! She could give lessons," Rob said, and gave Craig a sudden hard knuckle punch on the shoulder and they laughed quietly again while Craig massaged his arm.

Upstairs, Marion walked into the kitchen and sat down on the nook bench. Her heart was pounding but she said to herself, laughing, "That wasn't bad. I should have tried that sooner on somebody else."

She heard Craig's car drive off, taking Rob home.

On the way, they agreed that they should tell Donna of the failed plan in case she heard it from Craig's mother later. Donna was feeling peevish about being left so much on her own while Rob put in extra hours, and she was casually concerned about not feeling well in the mornings as if she had caught the flu bug that was going around.

"Well, I like that!" she exploded when Rob told her. "Didn't either of you think I might have been looking forward to some kind of a party. Did you think I like sitting around here looking at TV every night, alone?" Then she started to cry and Rob put his arms around her and said he was sorry.

Craig just stood looking at them. He could think of nothing to do or say that would be helpful, so finally he said, "Well, I guess I better go." Neither of them said anything, but Rob gave him a long face over her shoulder as he left.

Rob's parents arrived back in the morning of the 31st, fresh and happy to see him. "We got an early start to make sure we wouldn't be late and then we had lots of time so we stayed over-night at a lovely motel in Chilliwack," his mother told him while his father talked with Roger. "I must phone Marion," she said. "She probably is starting to panic right now," and went down stairs to phone. "Nice haircut!" she added with a smile over her shoulder.

"Hey, Mom!" Rob called after her. "You don't need to give us your famous lecture about party manners, you know, the one about 'sit up straight, don't pick at yourself, say please and thank you' and all that other good stuff? U.U. already did it. Boy, she's good, too. She packs a real wallop!"

His mother had turned around on the stairs and was looking back up at him. "You could take lessons from her," he said with the grin she could never resist.

"Really?" she said, smiling at him. "Listen, Buster! I've got punches I haven't used on you yet. If I let myself go, I'd have you on the ropes begging for mercy. I just might throw a few at you before the party just to make sure Marion hasn't overlooked anything. So keep your guard up!" she finished as she turned around and continued down the stairs.

"What was that all about?" his father asked, coming up behind him.

"Oh, Mom was just about to give me her 'behave yourself at the party' speech," he answered.

"Good idea," he said indifferently. "Roger says you've been doing a great job and he doesn't know how he'll get along without you. That is," he added awkwardly, "if he should have to get along without you. You know what I mean." He patted Rob on the shoulder. "I didn't mean to bring it up, sorry. Nice haircut, Rob. You should keep it that way."

"Thanks, Dad," Rob said, refraining from a flippant response that was on the tip of his tongue as he turned back to work.

His parents spent the next two hours packing the remaining odds and ends of personal belongings and vacuuming and dusting to leave their old home shipshape for Roger. The pictures, the knick-knacks and the good dishes and glasses had long since gone to Prince George. All that was left was the furniture and lamps, some basic kitchen equipment and sheets, pillows, blanket and towels for the two bedrooms. (Bev's bedroom had been turned into an office when she married and Glen had stripped it of everything personal as the first act of turning over the business and property.) Roger had been using Rob's old room so it did not need to be checked. The only things left in the master bedroom had been packed in a large suitcase waiting at the door. They went downstairs one last time, and suddenly Claudia was in tears.

"Oh, Glen! It looks so drab!," she said through her sniffles. "How could we have let it get so rundown?"

"It isn't rundown, dear. It's just been lived in," he said, trying to ease her sadness.

"We'll do better with our new house," she promised herself.

"Let's go, dear, before you change your mind or decide to take the moulding off the door frame where we marked the children's growth."

"Oh, I'd love to take that," she said seriously.

"No way!" he replied. "Let's go." He took her arm and guided her upstairs.

When they came up, it seemed apparent to both Rob and Roger that they were ready to go. The machines were shut down and it was suddenly quiet in the whole house except for a radio playing somewhere.

"Well, I think that's everything, Roger. The place is yours," Glen said.

"I'm sorry it looks so drab and empty," Claudia said. "But it will look better when you get your own pictures up."

"Don't apologize for it, please, Claudia," Roger said. "That was our agreement. I just can't see myself shopping for tables and chairs and pots and pans and stuff like that. I'm more than happy with the arrangement."

"Now then," Claudia said briskly, to camouflage her feelings about leaving. "There are two boxes downstairs marked 'Bev' and 'Donna'. They are filled with odds and ends of extra things—probably useful, I don't know —cookie sheets, corkscrews, paring knives, rubber gloves, casseroles, all sorts of things that have been collected over the years. There are even some bread pans and angel cake tins and muffin pans, most of them never used but they were all filled once with my good intentions. Roger, I've left you the same sort of collection in a drawer beside the sink."

"Thank you, Claudia," Roger said. "I'd love to see my mother's face when I tell her I've got a cookie sheet and a casserole. I hope I got the angel cake tin. That will knock her for a loop. I'll bet she doesn't even know what a cookie sheet is!"

"Better luck with the angel food pan than I had, Roger. I never did figure out how to get the darn thing together." Claudia's sad mood had lifted as they chatted easily about the arrangements. She thought how alike Rob and Roger were in the way they both seemed to take things in their stride, always finding the happy current in the tide of life. Suddenly, she choked up at the thought of not having Rob around. Glen came and put a protective arm around her.

"We've lived here almost all our married life," he explained to Roger. "It's hard to leave the memories."

The quiet moment was terminated by Rob. He said, with a sober face and teary eyes, "I'll get Bev's box and put it in your car for you, Dad."

Glen nodded his thanks to Rob, released Claudia and turned to Roger. "I think we agreed to meet in my lawyer's at two o'clock today to sign things and hand over legally. Is that still okay with you? Are you driving yet?"

"No, not yet. But I've still got my private chauffeur for a while yet."

There was a moment of clumsy silence and Roger looked quickly around to see if Rob had come back. "Sorry," he said, contritely. "I shouldn't have said that—it slipped out."

"Well, it may be something we will have to live with," Glen said bleakly.

Claudia moved quickly to Roger with her hand out to say goodbye, but immediately withdrew her hand and extended her arms, They embraced and touched cheeks. "There will probably be many reasons to be in touch," she said. "In the meantime, let me wish you a Happy New Year and much success in your business."

Glen extended his hand. "See you later," he said.

They moved to the door and Claudia could not resist one last look even if it was a glance at what was now the workroom. Outside, they squinted into the winter sun. "Mr. and Mrs. Williams!" a voice shouted. "You have just won a trip to the lovely city of Prince George. No expenses paid. Smile for the camera, please."

They looked toward the voice and saw Rob with his camera set on a tripod and a black sheet of plastic over his head, and they smiled.

When they drove away, Rob went back inside. Roger was waiting for him. "How'd you like to play chauffeur for a while this after-noon? I've got to be at the lawyer's at two and I have to get some booze for tonight—I've got a party and house warming planned for tonight, maybe eight or ten people."

"Sure," Rob said enthusiastically. "But I gotta be over at Craig's by five or U.U. will have my head and anything else that's dangling loose."

"Okay, we can manage. The lawyer will probably take an hour, maybe more. He's such a slow old fart," Roger said. "So how about you take the car and go home and shower and shave and put on your bib and tucker, then if you have time pick up some crackers and some special cheeses and chips and that hot Mexican salsa. That should hold them."

"I can do that, I think."

"Well, let's finish up here fast and get going."

"I'd offer to get the booze for you but my phoney ID is too old," Rob said. "And, you know, I don't want to take the chance."

"Thanks, anyway, Rob, but I wouldn't ask you."

They worked in silence for a while. Then Rob asked, "Is that all you're feeding them—chips and dip?"

"No, I was going to order in Chinese. Why?"

"Because all the talk of food has made me hungry."

"So am I," Roger said. "Jeez! Look at the time! How about you slipping down to that place on the corner and get us a couple of ready made sandwiches and a coffee for me and whatever you like. Take the Porsche. We'll have to get it out later anyway."

"I'm off," Rob said. "All I need is some cash and the keys."

The plan they had worked out for the afternoon worked well. Rob squeezed the box of kitchen gadgets into the Porsche, dropped Roger off at the lawyers in time and rushed home to shower and change. Donna had not come home from work yet so he left her a note reminding her of their five o'clock deadline. When he arrived at the lawyers office, he was surprised to see his father and Roger waiting outside, but no more surprised than his father to see Rob driving a sleek, low slung, red car.

"Whose car is that?" Glen asked as Rob got out. His face was tight with suspicion and concern.

"It's mine," Roger said.

"Yours?" Glen said. "You drive a station wagon."

"Oh, that was one I borrowed to move my stuff. You can't get much in a Porsche."

"Is that a Porsche?" Glen's face belonged on a country boy at a strip joint. Roger watched him smiling.

"Rob, take your dad for a ride," he said. "I've got to find a john, ten minutes?"

"Okay. Come on, Dad. Hop in!"

Glen buckled himself in and Rob drove off with his father looking like a kid on a ferris wheel. He drove around a few blocks of the neighbourhood, then crossed over to Cambie street and turned south. Once over the bridge, he moved to the left lane, and with one eye on the mirror, floored the little car, pushing his father against the back of his seat as the little car reached 140 K in seconds.

Then he geared down, swung off the first off-ramp and took a clover-leaf back onto Cambie street and back to the lawyer's office where Roger waited.

"What a beautiful little car!" Glen exclaimed, his face flushed with pleasure, a sight Rob had rarely seen. "It's—it's—-just absolutely beautiful! Thank you, Roger. That was great. And can that kid ever handle it."

"Would you like to take it for a spin," Roger said, knowing he was perfectly safe in making the offer.

"No, oh no! No!" Glen said quickly. "Not me! I'll stick to things I can recognize as cars. But thanks. Rob, I better go. See you later. And Roger, it was a pleasure doing business with you. Both Claudia and I wish you every success."

They shook hands formally again, their business completed and he and Rob watched Glen climb into his six-year-old Ford Station wagon and drive sedately away.

"Nice man, your dad," Roger said as he wriggled himself and his cast and crutches into the small car,

"Yeah," Rob agreed. "I just wish he had let me know sooner."

"You, too, eh?" Roger said with a sigh and Rob knew exactly what he meant.

"Well, where to now, boss?" Rob asked.

"Let's forget the liquor store," Roger said. "It will be a madhouse. Let's go to a wine store and I'll pick up a case and that will have to do."

"Oh, maybe your guests will be bringing a bottle to a New Years Eve party."

"Ha! Not likely," Roger said. "Most of them are leeches."

They parked at a wine store and Rob went in with Roger to help him. They emerged with Rob carrying a case of mixed wines.

"That will keep a couple of them busy showing off," Roger said, laughing. "They just l-o-v-e to go on and on about the colour and the nose and the dryness and the aftertaste. And one of them, he's the biggest fruitcake of them all, he insists that a wine should be fru-it-ay. 'It's good but it's not fru-it-ay' he'll say." Rob laughed uncertainly, but only because Roger was laughing.

"Nice guy, though," Roger continued. "Pays his way. Drinks too much and gets absolutely blotto. Give him a glass of horse piss and he'll say 'It's good but it's not fru-it-ay'."

Rob found himself liking Roger more and more.

They arrived home and Rob carried the groceries and the wine down stairs. Then coming upstairs again, he passed Roger the keys.

"Keep them," Roger said. "Take Donna to the party in style."

"Really?" Rob said with a happy grin. "She'll love it!"

"Two conditions, though. "No blasting around town and showing off and have it back in the garage soon after five. And bring Donna over sometime during the evening. I'd like to thank her for all the wonderful dinners and I'd like the guys to blab around that there was a woman at my party."

"I can start the rumour if you'd like," Rob said with a grin.

"Never mind. I can handle it. Better move, it's after four."

"Thanks, Roger. See you in an hour."

Roger stood for a moment with a quizzical look on his face watching him go.

When Rob walked in the door, Donna was still working through the surprise box from his mother.

"Where did this come from," she asked and when Rob told her she said, "It's like having another Christmas. I'll have to remember to thank her."

"You'll have to hurry and get dressed," Rob said. "Your carriage awaits without."

"You mean Craig's here?" she asked.

"No, look!" he said drawing back the curtains.

"Omigod!" she said when she saw the car. "That's Roger's! Did you steal it?"

"No, Donna! I don't steal cars. He gave it to me so I could take you to the party in style. But it's got to be back in the garage right after five or I'll turn into a pumpkin. So hurry up!"

"Are you sure you didn't steal it?"

"No, I didn't steal it," he said impatiently.

Donna believed him and smiled happily. She put on her dress and shoes, brushed her hair quickly and was ready to go in less than two minutes. "I'll put on my make-up when I get there," she said.

They drove around until it was time to go to the party. They smiled at each other and turned a lot of corners and braked a lot and stepped hard on the gas, marvelling at the way the little car hugged the road and leaped in response. Although it was winter and the air was cold, Donna could not resist opening her window and letting her hair blow. They arrived windblown and rosy cheeked.

"Well, don't you look beautiful and healthy," Marion said. "You look like you've been riding in a little red Porsche."

"Oh, you told them already," Donna said to Rob in a disappointed voice.

"No, no," Marion said. "Craig thought he would pick you up so he phoned to see if you were still working and Roger told him. Nice haircut, Rob."

"Thank you, U.U. Specially for you. You see what you've done for me. One word from you and I jump. Donna had hers done just for you, too. Didn't you, Donna?"

Donna looked at her hair in the small mirror in the kitchen and saw it looking like a cyclone had stirred it. "Oh, jeez!" she exclaimed. "It'll take me half an hour to get the tangles out."

"No, it won't," Marion said. "I've got work for you to do. The powder room is down the hall."

"I better take the car back, and get to work, too," Rob said.

"Yep!" Marion said, and Rob left.

He parked the car in the garage and patted it as he left. "I'm gonna get me one of those some day," he told himself.

He let himself into the house and listened for Roger and heard the shower running. "Hey, Roger?"

"Yeah, is that you, Rob?"

"I'll leave your keys on the table in the hall, okay? And thanks a lot. Donna really got a kick out of it."

"You're welcome. See you later?"

"Sure," Rob said. Then, "Roger, are you having a shower?"

"Yeah, why?"

"How do you do that? I mean, with your cast on?"

"You'll never know!" Roger replied. "I'd invite you in to watch, except I know you'd be envious of what I've got."

"Oh, sure!" Rob said, disbelievingly. "See ya!"

Marion had given three young people a taste of what army life might be like. She had barked and they had jumped and at seven, when the guests were invited, they all stood back and admired their handiwork. "I can't think of a single thing that we've missed," she said. "Nice going, kids. You've been gems. Now we're ready for anything. I wish Glen and Claudia would hurry and get here, I've never met some of these people." The doorbell rang and she said, "That will be them now."

But the people at the door proved to be a couple that the devil had sent to test whether they were indeed ready for anything.

"Hello. I'm Tom Webster," a large man said in a big voice as he walked in ahead of his wife. He took off his coat and handed it to Rob who barely caught it before he let go and walked into the living room. Marion appeared and rescued the woman and took her to the bedroom.

"Are we drinking punch tonight or are we having proper drinks?" Tom Webster said to Rob who was still hanging up his coat.

"We've got a nice non-alcoholic punch or some wine, if you'd like." Rob said.

"Nothing stronger? Scotch?"

"Oh, yes. We have scotch," Rob said, acting surprised that anyone would order such a thing. "Would you like scotch?" in an unbelieving tone.

"Yes, I would. And a little water, please."

Rob went to the kitchen grinning. "I made the bastard say please," he said to Craig who had heard the exchange. Then he selected a big colored glass, put in a careful ounce of scotch, one ice cube and filled the glass with water. "Here we are, sir," he said as the doorbell rang and Craig appeared to answer it. "Oh, that will be my parents. Excuse me." And he hurried away to greet his parents at the door before the man could taste his drink.

Donna walked with Claudia down the hall and met there with Marion and the drab and wan Mrs. Webster.

"How are you, Thelma?" Claudia asked solicitously. "I'm sorry I didn't get in to visit you in the hospital. I seem to have been going to or coming from Prince George for the last month. Was there any sign of cancer?"

"Just the one little spot they found but then they decided to take out a lot more than they said they were going to. I don't know. I don't feel like I've got anything left in there. Tom doesn't think so," she said bitterly.

"Oh, well, Tom!" Claudia said meaningfully and Thelma nodded.

The three ladies went to the living room where Claudia successfully backed off from a slobbery greeting from Tom Webster. Craig came in to ask about drinks while Rob went to the door again. The room began to fill up with guests and the two boys were kept busy serving drinks with an agreement between them not to see Webster's waving glass. Rob was finally caught by Webster and said, "Certainly, Mr. Webster. Right away! Sorry to have missed you," and took the glass to the kitchen and set it to one side.

All the guests had arrived, the boys were busy with the drinks and helping Donna with the canape trays. Webster's big voice could be heard above the party chatter holding forth on the inadequacies of the medical profession using his wife's recent hysterectomy as a platform. Marion moved away from the party and started the final dinner preparations. Thelma Webster came timidly into kitchen. "Is there anything I can do to help, please, Marion?" she asked. "I'm tired of being the topic of conversation."

"Oh, certainly, Thelma, thank you," Marion answered and set her a small task of washing a handful of parsley.

The party noise had increased slightly, but over the hubbub came Webster's voice, "Glen, I never did get them straight. Which one of those two boys is yours...the one that got caught peddling cocaine?"

The conversation came to a stuttering halt, not to hear the answer but out of embarrassment. Then out of the corner of the room came Rob's voice, clear and as strong as Webster's.

"That will be me, Mr. Webster. I'm Glen Turner's son and I will appear in court in one week's time to answer a charge of possession. Now then, I'm sure that's all you want to know about the personal affairs of the Turner family. Give me your glass and I will get you another drink."

The two men Webster had been talking to drifted away as Rob took his glass and left. Webster was left standing by himself for a minute and then Donna approached him and said quietly, "Mr. Webster, your wife is in the kitchen and she asked me to tell you she needs you."

When Webster entered the kitchen he found his wife sitting, pale faced on the kitchen stool.

"Take me home!" she said as soon as she saw him.

"What's wrong, Thel? This is a party!" he complained.

"Just take me home!" She looked like a baby kitten facing a tomcat.

He shrugged and made a wry face. "Sorry, Mrs., uh..."

"Williams, Marion Williams," his wife supplied crisply.

"Yes, of course," he said. "Well, we better go."

"Donna, help Mrs. Webster find her coat. Craig, tell Glen and Claudia the Websters are leaving. Quietly!" she commanded. "Then help Mr. Webster find his coat."

The Turners and the Websters assembled in the hall and said words and shook hands. Tom Webster stuck his head in the living room and announced, "Sorry we have to spoil the party, folks, but the missus has to go. You all have a

Happy New Year, now." He gave the room a small wave and they left.

Glen went to the kitchen. "Sorry, Marion. I only knew him in business. He always seemed like such a reasonable guy. I never knew he was such a bore."

"It happens, Glen. Don't worry about it."

Meanwhile Claudia had turned back into the living room. She clapped her hands, grinned and said, "Party time, people!"

There was laughter and the talk increased immediately in volume. "See, Glen," Marion said to him in the kitchen. "No problem." He touched her gently on the shoulder, the most Glen had ever done publicly to show his affection for her.

The party mood continued and the numbers were right for small groups. Marion had deliberately not set out enough chairs to accommodate everyone so some had to sit on the floor or the arms of sofa chairs. Little was said about the Websters.

The dinner of Caesar salad, lasagna with hot buttered buns with a roasted garlic bud stuffed in each was impressively delicious and had people laughingly wondering if they would stop smelling of garlic by Sunday. There was lots of red wine and when Rob spilled his on the carpet, the dinner entertainment centred on the half dozen or more suggestions for removing red wine from a carpet, leaving a puzzled Rob in the middle of the room waiting for a final decision. Finally Marion went to the kitchen, returned with a half bottle of white wine and a roll of paper towels. She poured most of the wine all over the red stain and said to Rob, "Now wipe it up."

By the time he had used half the roll, the stain had disappeared. He stood up, said "Voila!" and bowed to his applause.

"Remember," Marion said, "I limited you guys to one glass of wine for dinner and it was supposed to be white. So if you choose to use your wine allowance for entertainment, Robbie, then I guess you don't have wine with dinner."

"Oh, U.U.! You're mean!" Rob said. "Isn't she a mean, mean Marion?" he appealed to the others.

"Oh! Mean Marion! Mean! Mean!" came a chorus from the group.

"Oh, all right, then. Robbie, you may finish the white wine."

Cheers from the group.

"All of it?" Rob asked.

"Yes," she said.

"You're a sweetie!" he said and got up and kissed her on the forehead. "Even the two bottles in the frig?"

"Just try it," she said amid the laughter.

"Wine steward," Rob called, waving his glass to Craig. "White wine, please!" and Craig laughingly went to the kitchen with Rob following.

"Why the nickname 'you-you'?" someone asked. Then, while the young people cleared away the plates, Claudia explained the way the nickname emerged which lead to confessions of other nicknames in other families. The topic lasted until Marion came back in with an announcement.

"Now, ladies and gentlemen, we have a dessert. It is my famous homemade rhubarb pie with raspberries and blueberries, all fresh from my freezer. It's famous because it's the first time I've ever made it. As a matter of record, it's the first time anybody has ever made it, so everybody better say it's good because there are no seconds. It's cut and ready on the table. All pieces are the same size so there will be no fighting. Each piece has a large dollop of whipped cream on it. No groans, please. This is New Years Eve and no diets are permitted. So get up and help your-selves please, and by the way, I have a house rule, when you get up to get your dessert, you can't go back to the same seat."

There was a general movement and the voices of women complimenting Marion for being so brave. "Marion! Not really? The first time you've ever made it and no recipe! I can't believe it." Claudia said. "It really is scrumptious! But you were always a super cook. Me, I have to look up a recipe for buttered toast."

"Oh, come now, Claudia. Your potato salad is famous."

Somebody groaned in the kitchen.

"Was that you, Rob?" Claudia called out, as people laughed.

There was no answer and she continued, "Marion is just being kind. The only variation in my potato salad is whether the potatoes are overcooked or undercooked."

The banter continued and Marion excused herself to see about the coffee and tea. Donna had found the big coffee pot but had not started it, waiting for Marion's decision. The two boys had stacked the dishwasher and set the next load already rinsed beside the sink.

"Shall we turn it on or will it be too noisy?" Craig asked.

Marion looked at the three of them and felt a sudden emotional charge of pleasure. "No, don't turn it on," she said. "Don't do a thing more—any of you. You have been absolutely priceless. I knew I could count on you but I never realized how much I needed you—all of you! Thank you! Donna, you were charming. You seemed to anticipate everything. A perfect hostess! And you two, always like a shoe and a shoelace." She put out her arms and embraced them all in one big hug.

"Now," she said releasing them after a moment. "You've got a midnight show to go to, haven't you? And what else? Sure you don't want to stay and play games with the old folks?" she added with a sneaky smile.

"I'd love to," Rob said immediately as the other two startled and looked at him in total disbelief.

"Gotcha!" he said to them as he and Marion laughed together at the other two.

"Well, get going!" Marion said. "Donna, use my room to get ready. When all of you are ready, come in and you can say a general goodbye without going the rounds to everybody."

In two minutes, they appeared at the living room door and the conversation stopped. When there was a moment of quiet Craig said, "We've come to say goodnight and goodbye and nice to have met you and thank you for coming to our home to honour Rob's Mom and Dad and, oh yes, Happy New Year."

Somebody clapped and others joined in. Somebody said "Well done!" and others called Happy New Year. Claudia and Glen moved to them and Marion burst into tears and rushed to the kitchen. Claudia hugged Donna and then Craig and then Rob, holding him tightly. Glen followed her, hugging Donna easily, and less easily Craig and his own son. "I don't quite know what to say," he said huskily, "but I'm proud of you."

The three of them made their exit down the hall to the kitchen where Marion had gained control of her tear glands and was ready with maternal do's and don'ts for young people setting out into the dark and wicked world for fun on New Year's Eve. Just before they got into Craig's car, Rob looked carefully back and walked nonchalantly into the shadows of back steps and retrieved a pop bottle.

"What's that?" demanded Craig.

"Just a little party lubricant," Rob replied, climbing into the back seat with Donna.

"What is it?" Donna asked. She took off the cap and sniffed.

"Let's get out of here," Rob said, and Craig started the car and backed out of the garage.

"Well, hurry up and tell us!" Donna demanded.

"It's the punch," Rob said, laughing. "But with some Vodka added. It's good, too"

"Yeah," Donna said, tasting. "Better than the original."

"Were you guys drinking punch?" Craig asked in a serious voice and then answered his own question. "I tried it and it was awful even with scotch in it."

They stopped in front of the Turner's old house. Craig turned around and reached out a hand. "Let me have a taste," he said.

He tipped the bottle and had a large swig and swallowed it without tasting it. "Holy shit! What did you put in it?" he managed to croak between coughs.

"Just some Vodka," Rob answered. "Why?"

"Why? Because it burned all the way down, that's why. I better not have any more of that if I'm driving."

They walked up to the door and rang the bell and did not wait for a response. Rob walked in and shouted down the stairs, "Hi, Roger. It's us!"

"Come on down, guys," Roger called.

They walked through the shop and down the stairs into the family room and into a party. Roger was sitting in a corner with his caste up on the knee of a man who sat in front of him busily engaged in painting flowers on the cast. Five other men were scattered around the room, one stretched out on a sofa with his head on the lap of another man who was playing with his hair. Two more were in the kitchen busy with something that smelled spicy and garlicky. At least three wore earrings and two were very obviously made up. There were no women in the room.

Roger called out, "Hey, everybody! Meet my working buddy and his friends. The tall, dark gypsy-type is Rob and that's his girl friend, Donna and his friend Craig. Get the guests something to drink, Petey. And Donna, come and talk to me please, and let me thank you for all the lovely meals you send me."

"We're too young to drink," Rob said quickly, "but maybe Donna and I will split a beer, thank you. Craig can't drink. He's the, you know, the something driver."

"Oh, yeah, the duplicated driver," someone supplied laughing.

"No, decorticated," from across the room.

"Not de-neutered anyway," said a deep bass voice.

"The designated driver!" Craig said stiffly, finishing the game.

"Where's the other lady," the man with his head on another man's lap asked.

"There's no other lady. We're just friends," Rob said.

"You mean you two guys share one woman?" someone asked.

"Of course. We share everything," Rob said throwing a challenging smile at the questioner.

"That's sweet!" the man said. "We share, too."

"Knock it off, Petey!" the bass voice said.

"I just thought Rob might like to stay and that would even things out," came the reply.

"No, thank you," Rob said. "We're quite happy with our own arrangements."

"Did you guys ever get back up to Lake Lovely Water?" the bass voice asked.

"How did you know we were there?" Rob asked, surprised.

"Remember me? You rowed me across," the man said, smiling a big smile with large white teeth.

"Oh, yeah, I remember," Craig said. "And then you called to us as we walked by your cabin."

"Yeah, just checking to see you made it okay," he said. "And then we watched you fishing across the lake by the little waterfall. You'll have to teach me how to do that sometime."

"You were watching us?" Craig squeaked.

"Yeah. I always carry good binoculars. I could even see the kind of flies you were using." His laugh rumbled around the room.

Craig just stood not knowing what to say, but Rob was grinning as if it were a huge joke.

"Oh, yeah. I walked over to your camp to check the fire because the wind was coming up, but it was okay. Nice sleeping arrangements, too. I peeked." His smile was as wide as his voice was deep.

Craig looked back and forth between the man and Rob. "It was cold!" he said.

"That's the way to keep warm," the voice rumbled and he and Rob laughed together hilariously.

Donna had moved over to Roger's chair and he greeted her warmly and thanked her for the variety of meals she had sent over. "I loved the happy face in the mashed potatoes and gravy," he said and she smiled. She admired the flowers on his cast and complimented the painter who appeared to be so engrossed in his art that he barely looked up.

"He's shy," Roger said. "Aren't you, old thing?" He rumpled the man's hair who blushed but did not look up. "See?" Roger teased.

Craig and Rob were talking with their friend from Lake Lovely Water who told them about other hikes they should try. "Another beer?" he asked.

"No, thanks," Rob said quickly. "We gotta go and get in the line-up for the midnight show."

"Good idea," Craig agreed. "I'll tell Donna."

"Here comes a party-poop," Roger said as he saw Craig approach. "Come to drag you away when we were just getting to know each other. I hear you're heading for a midnight show. I wish I could go with you."

"And leave all your friends?" Donna asked and Roger shrugged.

"Hey, man! I got all I can handle with two," she continued and laughed as she got up and joined Craig. "Nice to meet the man I make lunches for. Thanks for the drink."

"Yeah, Happy New Year," Craig added as they turned away.

When they got to the stairs Rob joined them.

"Happy New Year, Roger," he called. "See you tomorrow!"

There was a general exchange of best wishes as they climbed the stairs.

"Where's the bottle. I need a drink," Rob said as they got in the car.

"Me, too, "agreed Craig, enthusiastically. "Jeez! What a weird bunch. They give me the creeps." He took a big swallow of their drink. "Even that big guy, but he was kinda okay." He took another swallow. "That's enough for me. I'm driving." He passed the bottle over his shoulder to the other two and started the car.

He let the car warm up for a minute with the heater blowing before he drove away. "Be careful with that bottle," he warned. "There are cop cars all over the place tonight." They drove in silence; the other two sharing the bottle.

"Rob?" Craig asked over his shoulder at a stoplight. "Do you think Roger's a homo?"

"I dunno."

"Well, has he tried anything on you, like, well, you know?"

"No, not yet," Rob replied. "But, hell! We got a week to go yet. Anything could happen."

Craig was craning to look in the mirror to see if Rob was smiling and nearly rammed the car in front. "Shit!" he said. "Hurry up and finish that bottle before the cops see it." But he was thinking 'What did he mean by that?'

They drove around trying to find a parking spot until it was getting so late that Rob and Donna got out and held his place in the line-up. Craig was finally able to squeeze into a lot and rush back just as Rob was nearing the ticket window. They found good seats and waited to get popcorn until the trailers started. Donna was sitting between them and she and Craig talked about the people at both parties but Rob was unusually quiet. After a while he leaned over Donna and said to Craig quietly, "Did you hear what my Dad said to me when we were leaving?"

"No, what did he say?"

"He told me he was proud of me."

"Yeah?"

"Yeah!" A long silence with Rob still leaning over and looking with troubled eyes at his friend. "Why in hell couldn't he have told me that years ago instead of..." He twisted back into his seat and slumped down with his knees against the seat back in front of him, staring down with his arms crossed on his chest. Donna leaned toward him and took his arm but he jerked away from her touch. They sat in a strained silence for a few minutes until the house lights dimmed. Rob sat up, leaned towards them with a smile and said "Sorry!" and smiled his way back to them. He put his arm around Donna's shoulders and she snuggled against him. His arm was long enough to reach further and gently squeeze Craig's neck for a moment. Craig got the message and smiled to himself.

For a half hour they watched videos of the New Years celebrations across Canada and at midnight they were shown live videos of the celebrations outside. Then the features started, both of which had been touted as horror/murder mysteries but both failed to keep the audience riveted to their seats and moved most viewers into amorous exchanges except during the screaming gory bits. Both Rob and Donna dropped off to sleep cuddled against each other. When Donna became uncomfortable she twisted away from Rob and leaned against Craig. She rubbed, then held, his genitals, kissed him on the neck and continued to sleep.

They were wakened by the blast of sound from the finale and they stumbled in a slow crushing line from the theatre into the cold winter air. It took half an hour to find the car and worm their way out of the lot and another half hour to drive home to Rob and Donna's. Craig stopped on the left side of the street to let them out and Donna got out, opened Craig's door and kissed him goodnight. Rob got out and leaned into the car and kissed him too, full on the mouth. "Happy New Year," they said to him almost in unison and Craig drove away.

CHAPTER 66

On the morning of the New Year, there were few cars on the road as Rob pedalled his bike to work. He had dressed quietly and left the apartment without waking Donna, after breakfasting on bits and pieces of fruit and sandwich meat with large swills of milk from the carton between huge yawns. He noticed two cars in the driveway so assumed Roger had some overnight guests. The door was unlocked and the house quiet and warm. He went down the hall to close the bedroom doors before starting any noisy machines and saw Roger and another man curled together in his parent's bed and two others tangled in his old three quarter size bed. Downstairs a toilet flushed, so it seemed that Roger had at least four sleepover guests. Going back to the order table to find some work that would be reasonably quiet, he found an order for 200 posters in three colours that required manual handling. Setting up the machine, he found his mind going back again and again to the figures in the bedrooms, to Roger's all male party last night and to Roger's apparent lack of concern that the world would know about his sexual preferences. Jeez! he thought as he worked, maybe I'm getting like that. No, I'm not, he argued with himself. It's only Craig and me, that's all. There's nobody else. That's different. Besides, these guys were old. They were all whiskery and hairy and thirty something like Roger. I'd bet anything, he told himself, that no two of them were lifetime buddies like me and Craig.

He worked quietly laying one sheet at a time precisely in place then rolling one colour on 200 times plus a 5% reject insurance, and then doing it again with another colour, and then the third. It was the kind of monotony that promoted daydreaming and he slipped from the puzzle of Roger and his friends to Thursday, January the seventh, and where he would be spending that night and how many more nights and if there were going to be many guys around like Roger and maybe he should go down to some gym and brush up on some boxing or karate. Come to think of it, he'd better take Craig too. Craig never was any good at protecting himself in a fight. He always flailed his arms around like he was warding off wasps and backing up.

Rob was smiling at the recollection of Craig in a fight when Roger stumped into the room on his crutches looking tousled and hung over. "What the hell are you looking so happy about on this miserable morning? And what are you doing here anyway," Roger said in a hoarse croak.

"Double time for holidays. Remember?" Rob answered.

Roger paid no attention to his answer. He turned around and went down the hall to the bathroom from where gurgles, groans and splashes emerged from the open door. He stuck his head out with a toothbrush in his mouth and called, "Do you know if there's anybody downstairs? Oh shit, that hurt!" he finished, holding his head.

"I heard the toilet flush down there, that's all I know. I didn't go down."

Roger looked at him with uncomprehending eyes. "Whose cars are those out there?"

Rob shrugged, "Dunno," he answered, turning back to work.

"You're not going to turn that damn printer on, are you?" Roger's voice was almost panicky.

"No, I'm doing that three colour job for the symphony."

"Can you do that? Your dad said he would show me,"

"Sure! Nothing to it." Rob said.

But it was all too much for Roger. He looked blankly at Rob and moved his lips as if to say something, then turned and worked his crutches down the stairs.

Shortly after the noise from that basement told Rob that there must be at least two more men down there. All apparently trying to rake their throats without rattling their heads. There were grumblings, groans, hackings and coughing. Then the two who had been sleeping in Rob's old room emerged bleary-eyed and stalked past Rob without a word and went downstairs. There were words emerging from the basement: "Hurry up, for Crissake! What are you doing in there?" "There's another one upstairs." "I can't make it upstairs." "You'll just have to hold it." "Yeah? How'd you like to hold it for me." "Now you ask me! Last night you slapped me!" "Rog! Look! Ted's pissing in the sink1" "Ted, for Crissake! Don't be such a slob!"

Rob thought if he turned on the printer or the collator the noise would drown out the catty bitching, but he continued with his original job. Then a man stamped out of the bedroom shoving his shirttail in and without a word or glance, left the house coatless, got into a car and drove away. In a minute, Rob heard Roger come thumping up the stairs as he shouted down over his shoulder, "And scrub out the sink before you leave, you scruffy son of a bitch!"

"Hey! Happy New Year, everybody," Rob said under his breath holding back his laughter.

Roger came out of the bedroom with a leather jacket and a scarf on. "How'd you like to do some driving for me, instead of working, Rob?" he asked. "I got to get out of here."

"Sure," heading for the hall to get his own leather jacket. "Where're we going?"

"No place! Let's just get some air."

"What about them?" Rob asked, jerking his head towards the basement.

"Who cares? Let's go!"

"I'll have to drive over to my place first and get my wallet. I came on my bike this morning and forgot it."

"Okay," Roger grunted, settling down in the little car as far as his cast would permit.

Rob stopped at his apartment. "I'll just be a minute," he said as he got out and left the motor running to keep the car warm. He opened the door and Donna was not in bed. Then he heard her retching in the bathroom.

"Are you alright?" he asked opening the bathroom door a crack.

"Lee-me-lone," came the croaking answer.

He stood in the middle of the little room wondering what to do. Finally Donna emerged from the bathroom, looking white and shaky. "Hi," she said as she headed back to bed. "I didn't hear you go."

"What's wrong with you? You got the flu?"

"No, it must have been that punch last night. I drank most of Craig's. What are you doing?"

"I have to take Roger for a drive. I'm chauffeur today—double time on holidays," he answered with a wide grin. "Nice way to make a living, eh? Driving a Porsche!"

"Have fun!" she said. "I'm going back to sleep."

"Want me to bring you back a burger," he asked as he was leaving. He didn't hear the exact answer but it was a definite negative.

"Well, where to?" he asked getting back into the car.

"Anywhere," Roger said. Then after a minute, he added, "The Polar Bear Swim is at noon, I think. Let's drive down to Spanish Banks and see if there's a crowd yet."

"I think it's at English Bay, Rog."

"Okay, let's go there then and find a parking spot and get some breakfast. How's Donna?"

"She's got the flu, I think. Throwing up and cranky."

By the time they arrived at English Bay a parking space was not to be found. Rob let Roger out of the car in front of the restaurant that had the smallest line-up and drove off to find a parking place. When he got back, twenty minutes later, Roger had progressed to the inside of the restaurant and he had to excuse himself and explain a half a dozen times while edging his way past sometimes belligerent people to join him.

"What a bunch of cranks!" Rob said. "What are they doin' here anyway?"

"Having fun," Roger said. "Sadist watching masochists."

"Have you ever gone in the Polar Bear Swim?" Rob asked the waitress who stopped to clear the table and take their order.

"Do I look like an idiot?" she snapped. "What do you want?"

"Bacon and eggs, but break the yolks and cook them hard, and brown toast and coffee. Coffee first and soon, please," Roger said.

"You?" the waitress said, looking at Rob.

"You paying?" Rob asked Roger.

"Of course."

"Gimme a stack of sourdoughs with maple syrup and sausages and coffee first and soon, too and he'll give you a big fat tip. Oh, maybe a glass of orange juice, too"

The waitress walked away without a word.

"And Happy New Year," Rob called after her.

"Maybe she was up as late as I was," Roger said, "and is just as hung over."

They were silent for a while. Their coffee came. "How was your show?" Roger asked, more out of boredom than interest.

"I guess we slept through most of both of them."

"Real chillers, eh?"

"Yeah," Rob said through a giant yawn. "You guys have a good time?"

"It was okay," Roger said with a shrug. "But I'm getting pissed off with a couple of the guys who are nothing but leeches, like the gang my wife used to hang around with."

"I didn't know you were married!" Rob said, surprised.

"I'm not—anymore. I was, but it didn't last long. Stupid!" he said, shaking his head.

"Why stupid?" Rob asked cautiously.

"Because she was a tramp and I, or maybe it was one of my friends—who knows—got her pregnant and she got very legal and I married her. That was the stupid bit. She knew my family had a bit of money and she got nasty and filed for a divorce and got a big settlement. Then she got an abortion or maybe she wasn't even pregnant—she could pull off a stunt like that. Anyhow, she disappeared with the guy she was living with when I first met her. And that was my experiment in matrimony—my first and my last, I hope. Good! Here comes our breakfast."

Rob was also relieved to see the waitress approach, not only because he was hungry but because he did not know what next he could say to Roger about his marriage. He was beginning to wonder if the break-up had anything to do with Roger's interest in men but didn't want to pursue it.

The large breakfast plates were hastily put in front of them and the waitress rushed off before Roger could say anything to her.

"Look at those eggs!" he said with a look of revulsion. "I hate eggs looking at me like that!" His eggs were sunny side up and wiggly. He shuddered and looked around in futility for the waitress. "I'll trade you," he said to Rob. "Two eggs for half of your pancakes."

"Sure," Rob answered agreeably and they made the trade and ate in silence.

The restaurant began to empty. Their waitress approached and asked, "Would you mind if I gave you your check now? My husband's in the swim and I'd like to watch him. They start in about ten minutes."

"Oh, we better hurry too," Roger said reaching for his wallet.

"Did you enjoy your breakfast?" she asked as she waited.

"Excellent!" Roger replied, handing her a bill. "Just excellent! Keep the change."

"Liar !" Rob grinned.

"Oh, well," Roger said. "What I ended up with was a hell of a lot better than the Chinese junk last night. Let's go and watch the masochists."

They found a place on the edge of a huge crowd and watched two hundred people stand shivering and jumping around to keep warm while they waited for the start. Some joker blew a whistle and about twenty people rushed into the water while the crowd yelled, "No! No! Not yet!" Then a bundled-up man (someone said it was the mayor) climbed, very officially, up on a lifeguard stand, made a short speech that no one listened to, held up a green flag and after a dramatic pause, during which a hundred or more swimmers dashed into the water, waved it downwards to start the swim.

Family members rushed to the shore with towels for their swimmers who emerged blue with cold and with chattering teeth.

"It was great (Mom-dear-Dad)!" You should have come in." was the usual shuddering greeting to the towel wrapper, with a not unusual answer, "Yeah, maybe next year."

Most of the swimmers were content to dash in, get wet and get out. Some swam a few strokes, some frolicked in the shallows splashing each other and screaming and some hardy souls swam out a couple of hundred yards and back, stepping out of the brittle water as if emerging from a California pool into a hot sun. Rob shivered just watching them. On the way back to the car, slowly because of Roger's crutches in the sand, they stopped to watch a TV crew set up to interview an eighty year old woman who, stood blue with cold and shivering so hard it seemed her bones would rattle, practising her line with the producer: "I've had an early morning swim in English Bay every morning for the past fifty three years in every kind of weather and I've never been to a doctor in my life."

"Well, that's a better claim to fame than I will ever earn when I'm her age," Roger said gloomily as they continued to the car.

Rob couldn't think of any kind of reply.

They drove in silence back to the house with Roger yawning widely every five minutes and Rob struggling not to return a contagious yawn of his own. Before they drove into the garage Roger said, "I hope those guys have buggered off by now." When they opened the door, he shouted, "Anybody here?" and listened and smiled when there was no response. "Good!" he said. "They've gone."

But he stumped down the hall and checked the bedrooms and the bathroom to make sure, then shouted to Rob, "Will you look downstairs and make sure nobody has passed out down there?" and waited at the top of the stairs for Rob's response.

"Nobody down here," Rob said, climbing the stairs. "And they left it all neat and clean with everything put away."

"Oh, that will be Petey," Roger said. "He's such a tidy little thing. Good! The housekeeper's not due until Tuesday." He yawned widely again. "Lock the door, will you, Rob? I'm going back to bed." He looked at Rob, smiling slightly and testing, "Want to join me?"

"Not today, Rog," Rob replied lightly. "Maybe some other time. I think I'll finish that colour job and quit early." And then, to keep things light and easy, "Aren't you going to watch the bowl games?"

"Who, me?" Roger said, turning away to the bedroom, "God, no! I can't stand the stupid game." He closed the bedroom door behind him.

It took Rob another hour to finish the job. His mind was wandering and he was tired and he was struggling not to make mistakes. While he was cleaning up, he tried to remember whether his parents were going back to George today or staying over until his trial. He phoned Bev.

"Hi," he said when she answered. "Happy New Year! Did you have a good time with the old folks?"

"Sure," she said. "We played games and Richard got drunk and I had to drive home."

"Richard did?"

"Yeah, he was kind of celebrating because I think we're preggie again. So I wasn't drinking and he was drinking for two."

"Good! Congratulations! Maybe it will be a boy this time and I'll get to be an uncle instead of an auntie."

"I thought you and Craig liked being aunties," she replied.

He could feel her getting her claws out but before she dug them in, he said, "Are Mom and Dad still there or did they drive up to Prince George?"

"No, they're staying down until your trial. Remember? I wish they would go. He's around the house with nothing to do but pace and worry. Wasn't he supposed to help Roger?"

"Yeah, but he doesn't help—he just gives orders and fusses and Roger gets annoyed with him. Roger has had a hard time with his own father and doesn't need another one, I guess. Are they there?"

"No, they're over helping Marion clean up after the party."

"I wondered when I heard you talking like that," Rob said. "I guess I'll go over and see them, then head home. See ya'" he said. "I hope it's a boy."

"So does Richard, but I tell him it might turn out to be like you."

"What a sweet sister! Goodbye."

Rob finished his clean-up, listened at Roger's door and heard a fluttery snore, turned off the lights and locked the door.

At the Williams, he knocked his knock and opened the door. "Hi, U.U!" he said when she turned around from the sink. "Happy New Year again!"

"Thank you, Rob," she said, coming to him and giving him a hug and a kiss. "You kids got it off to a happy start for me. You were wonderful! I was so proud of you."

"Was I more wonderful than Craig?" he asked with a grin.

"Who spilled his wine on the living room rug?" she said. "Was that Mr. Wonderful?"

"Oh, U.U! I'm sorry!" he said with open contrition.

"It's alright, dear. Somehow, with all the advice, you did a beautiful job of getting the stain out. All that shows is a clean spot on the carpet, so your Mom and Dad helped me rearrange the furniture, and I like it better now."

"Are they still here?"

"No, you just missed them. They left for Bev's ten minutes ago. They're talking about going back north until they come down for..., well, to be here for you."

"I missed them again. I called them at Bev's and she said they were here. Guess I'll have to try again. Where's Craig?"

She pointed to the basement and continued polishing glasses.

Craig was asleep on the sofa, flat on his back with a football game on. Rob approached him quietly, slobbered on a finger and put it in Craig's ear. Craig came suddenly awake, felt his wet ear and saw Rob kneeling beside him, flapping his tongue.

"Don't do that! I hate it!" he said.

Rob disregarded his protests. "Who's playing?" he said.

"I don't know. I was switching channels. I don't know which game this is," Craig said grumpily.

Rob got up and sat down on the middle of the sofa, forcing Craig to turn over on his side to make room. "Oh, is my Craggy all grumpy today after his big night out on the town?" he asked, and reached over and rumpled Craig's hair who jerked his head away and said "Cut it out!"

"Hey, I gotta tell you. This is great! Roger asked me to go to bed with him."

Craig struggled up to a sitting position, pushing Rob out of the way. "You're kidding!" he said, with a big grin.

"No, I'm not! Cross my heart and spit." He raked a gob from the back of his throat and, face to face with Craig, sucked it back in with an explosive sound.

Craig didn't even blink. Then Rob told him about the sleeping arrangements he found when he went to work in the morning, and Roger's invitation after they had come back from the Polar Bear Swim.

"Jeez!" Craig exclaimed after listening raptly, "he really is queer, isn't he?"

"Yeah, but he's awfully nice and cute, too!" Rob replied with a dreadful attempt at coyness.

"Nut!" Craig said and punched Rob hard on the arm and they both burst into loud laughter that was heard upstairs above the sound of the TV.

When they stopped laughing, Rob yawned hugely while trying to say "I'm pooped!" And then, "Are you going to ask me to go to bed with you or do I have to go home?"

"Go home!"

"Ungrateful wretch!" Rob said and pounded a return punch on Craig's arm before stumbling up the stairs.

"Bye, U.U! My only love," he said as he passed her in the kitchen and went out the door.

"Goodbye, my fairy prince," he heard as the door closed.

He stopped suddenly, cocked his head and made a face and smiled. "Close, U.U., but no cigar—yet." Then he pedalled home.

CHAPTER 67

On Saturday, Donna was up before Rob and made herself a cup of tea and the first sip was enough to send her rushing into the bathroom where the noise of her retching wakened Rob.

"Are you alright," he called. There was no answer and he called again, "Donna? You okay?"

She emerged from the bathroom, white and shaky. She blew her nose, wiped her eyes and said, "I can't seem to shake this miserable flu. Aren't you going to work?"

"Yeah!" he said. "In a minute," and he tucked down under the covers. "Roger doesn't get up until nine most days and he never knows what time I get there." His voice was muffled by the blankets.

She yawned as she looked at the lump in the bed and the bed seemed warm and inviting. Outside, it was cold and grey and she desperately wanted to go back to sleep. Peering at her little watch, she read 'Sat Jan 2' and stood looking at it with a frown. "Damn!" she said, looked at her tea and rushed to the bathroom again. Rob was still under the covers when she came out. Walking the four steps to the bed, she yanked the covers off him and threw them off the end of the bed out of his reach.

"Donna!" he protested.

"Now get up and go to work," she said. "If I have to, then you have to, too."

"To, too. Two two. Tutu," he said, laughing. He leaped out of bed and danced around her naked. "What do you think I'd look like in a tutu?"

"Wear one to work and see what Roger thinks," she replied. "And speaking of Roger, just think what he'd say if your lawyer calls him as a character witness. He'd have to say 'He's always late for work and he sometimes wears a tutu'." She had put on her coat and wrapped a scarf around her head and shoulders. Stepping into her snow boots, she opened the door wide. "Come and kiss me goodbye," she dared.

He moved quickly to the door and pushed her one step outside before wrapping her in his arms and kissing her soundly.

"Get back inside, nut!" she said.

"Get off to work, slave!" he replied, waving to her as she walked down the driveway.

"You can make the bed and do the dishes. I hate coming home to a messy house," she called.

"Oh, you are being just too, too hateful," he called after her giving her a limp wristed wave as he stood naked in the open doorway until she reached the street. She looked back and laughed as she walked away and suddenly thought of what she'd get Bruno to make her for breakfast and the thought didn't make her stomach tighten.

Rob closed the door and quickly threw the covers of the bed together, not neatly but adequately. The tea Donna had made was still hot and he loaded his cup with sugar and drank it while picking up dishes and waiting for the toaster to ding. When the toast was done, he put in two more pieces, spread the first two with peanut butter and jam and took them into the bathroom to eat while he washed and shaved. Then, shoving himself into yesterday's clothes, he peanut-buttered the other two pieces of toast and slapped them together to munch on as he pedalled off to work.

Craig woke up when he heard his mother talking on the telephone in her room. He could only hear bits and pieces and couldn't make out who she was talking to but thought it must be one of her bridge group because Thursday kept entering the conversation. Just as he decided to get up, he heard her say, "I'll call you back right away," and her head appeared at the crack of his half-open bedroom door.

"Oh, good! You're awake," she said, coming into his room and sitting on the edge of his bed, determined not to let the tornado-struck room bother her. "That was Claudia on the phone. She said that Glen is so uptight that they are going up to Prince George and he can start on his new job as they planned on Monday."

"But they are going to come back for Rob's trial, aren't they?" Craig asked, pushing himself up in bed with a distressed look on his face.

"Oh, yes, of course," she answered.

"Well, they promised," Craig said and relaxed.

"Claudia invited me to drive up with them and see their new house and help her get some ideas. Just for two nights and I will take the bus back on Monday. Will that be alright with you?"

"Sure, Mom! You need a little holiday. "Don't worry about me. When are you leaving?"

"They are going to call in a few minutes and then we can leave as soon as I put come clothes in a bag. Now then, there's lots of things in the frig to eat up—you won't starve but you'll have to get milk and that's all, I think. Will you be alright?" she asked.

He smiled at her. "Sure I will," he said. "I've been on my own before, remember?"

She frowned, trying to recall. "Of course," she said. "When I was in hospital. What am I fussing about?"

She bent over and kissed him lightly on the forehead. "Get up," she said. "So you can wave me goodbye."

He got up and made some breakfast for himself while his mother packed, fussing about whether she should wear her light coat in the car and carry her winter coat for the Prince George weather or just wear a good cardigan in the car, and she mustn't forget her warm gloves and snow boots—but snow boots are always too warm to wear in the car, and she mustn't forget her pills.

Craig paid little attention to her fussing. She always talked out loud when she was planning and lost her planning rhythm completely if anyone even asked, "Pardon? What did you say?" He was daydreaming in his own world: maybe he should wash his car, but if he did that he would have to wash his mother's too. He looked outside and decided car washing was out.

His mother came downstairs and put her bag and winter coat and snow boots by the front door, ready for a quick exit. "There!" she said. "I think I've got everything."

"Got your toothbrush and lipstick and your nighty?" he teased.

"Oh, migod!" she exclaimed. as she turned and rushed upstairs. "I forgot a nightgown."

She looked quickly through a drawer and picked out a nightgown that was decent and fairly new. Suddenly she remembered that it was the one she planned to pack when she and Tom were going off for a weekend in Seattle. She sat on the edge of the bed, folding and patting the gown over and over again, wondering what went wrong. Oh, she knew what went wrong. She lost control when she saw Eleanor instead of playing it cool and Tom just dumped her—like that! There were tears in her eyes as she went slowly back downstairs and she swiped at them with the nightgown and then looked at the dark spots in dismay and shoved it in her overnight bag before Craig noticed.

A horn sounded out front. "That's them," Craig said, looking out the window. "Have a nice time."

"Thank you, dear. Phone Edith and tell her where I've gone and don't forget to lock up when you go out." But to herself she said, "You wouldn't have said 'Have a nice time' if I had gone off to Seattle with Tom and Edith would have had kittens." He picked up her overnight case and took it out to the car and she followed with her coat and boots. Greetings were exchanged and the two women got themselves organized in the back seat. Glen razzed the motor.

"Alright! Glen," Claudia scolded. "Don't get antsy."

"Have a nice time," Craig said holding the door until they were settled and ready.

"You and Rob behave yourselves," his mother said.

"No," he responded. "We're planning a huge party with drinks and exotic food and Grecian girls—the works!" He grinned and closed the door.

"Grecian girls?" Claudia said, puzzled.

"He probably meant Geisha girls," Glen said as he drove away. "Every adolescent's idea of the ultimate in decadence."

As he watched them drive away, Craig thought how awful it would be for Rob if they got caught in a landslide or a snow storm and couldn't get back for his trial. Then he remembered that he must ask Carl if he could take the morning off next Thursday. He went back into the house and checked the TV schedule for anything worth watching. He phoned Lee's house hoping she might have come home for the holidays, but got an answering machine. Going upstairs, he saw that his mother had propped his door open with a chair, a not very subtle suggestion that it was time to muck out. She had placed clean sheets and pillow cases on the chair. Reluctantly, he tore the bed apart and remade it, collected other pieces of clothing after examining them to see if they were dirty and took them down to the laundry room with his sheets. He went into the workroom to tidy it up but as he stood in front of the work table his father's voice came screaming at him, 'For Christ's sake! How many times do you have to be told to put the goddam tools away when you're finished with them. Look at this place! It's a bloody mess. Get it cleaned up and everything put back in its proper place and call me when you think it's done and I'll inspect it and, by God, if it's not done right, there are a hell of lot of other things that need doing around here that will keep you busy for a month. Now get busy!' He muttered "Bastard" under his breath as if his father might be close enough to hear him, turned out the light and got in his car and drove down to the pool hall. There he met the old pool hall gang from school, watched and played a few games, then ate a big pizza at Bruno's, the pizza man, who asked about his Momma and BS'd with him until it was time to go home and watch a football game. "Boring!" he told himself as he turned on the set and, while waiting for the pretty boys to get finished with their brilliant armchair ideas of how the game should be played, he phoned Rob. There was no answer. Probably they both went out for lunch, he concluded, or maybe Roger got him into bed. "That's a shitty thing to say," he told himself and flopped down in the lounge in front of the TV and tried to stop thinking about Rob and January the seventh.

Donna and Phyllis were doing the usual Saturday morning clean-up and talking about their Christmases and New Years. Donna stopped and sat down for a minute, wiping her brow.

"Dizzy?" Phyllis asked. Then, "Did you eat breakfast?"

Donna shook her head. "I wasn't ready when I came in."

"Bruno," Phyllis called into the kitchen. "Donna needs her breakfast."

"Coming up," came the reply.

"You should always eat regular," Phyllis said, quietly because there was a customer at the counter, "when you're eating for two."

"But, Phyllis! I'm not..." Donna started as Phyllis turned away and returned in a moment with a cup of coffee for Donna.

"Just don't do anything foolish," she said. "Now sit there until Bruno gets your breakfast," and she turned back to her cleaning.

In the kitchen, Phyllis caught her husband's eye, patted her tummy and jerked her thumb back toward Donna. She smiled a pleased tight smile and nodded her head deliberately three times.

Waiting, Donna thought frantically. "How could she know? I just thought that maybe... I can't be! I still think it's some weird kind of flu! But I'm overdue by three weeks—maybe more. Damn it! I wish I could remember."

Just as Bruno called, a thought struck her that sat her back in her seat. "If I am, I can't tell Rob now! Not before the trial. It'd tear him up! Jeez! What a mess!" She worked at that awful puzzle for a minute then got slowly to her feet and collected the breakfast Bruno had made for her without returning her usual smiling thanks to him for the extra attention he always gave her meals.

"Phyl!," Bruno called out. "Maybe you finish and we close up, eh? Not many people. Not worth it. Besides, everybody tired."

"Okay by me, Bruno. I'm finished right now."

"Okay, okay. But wait for Donna, eh? She gotta eat good, you know."

Donna smiled at them and forced herself to eat all her breakfast, more to please them than from hunger. As they were ready to leave, two regular customers rattled the locked door. "No, Bruno!" Phyllis warned. But Bruno took off his coat and opened the door. "People gotta eat," he told her with a shrug.

On Monday, the holiday world came to an abrupt end and clutches of people in stores and offices could be seen gathered in small knots exchanging stories about the long weekend. At Cranstons Cartons, the time clock was not working, so the idle talk continued until Carl pushed everyone back to their jobs. The computer trainer appeared and checked with Carl and about the times and place he would have for his training sessions with the men. The office talk among the three women and Craig centred around the training sessions that had been planned for them. There was an air of expectancy around the plant waiting for reports from the first six men who had been chosen for the first training session. Craig sat in with them and watched their dogged concentration as the trainer, in easy steps and layman's language, dispelled some of the magic and mystery of the machine.

Craig and Carl got together at coffee break and talked casually about their New Years and at length about the training sessions and the increasing interest shown by the men. When they finished, and Carl was putting on his coat to go out on a business call, "Your friend appears in court this week, doesn't he?"

"Yes, on Thursday morning," Craig said. "And I was going to ask you if it was okay for me to take the morning off to be there."

"Certainly, Craig. You should be there. Just tell Dorothy and Larry you won't be in case they are looking for you." He turned to go then added, "I hope your friend gets a fair hearing. "Tell him I wish him Good Luck."

"Thanks Carl, I will."

Carl was half way out the door when he stopped again and said, "Come to think of it, you might as well take the whole day. No matter what happens you will have to celebrate of commiserate, won't you?"

Craig left for the shipping area feeling lucky about having such a great boss. He worked sorting and organizing two large shipments of paper that had been received on the 31st. But moving rolls of paper with a lift was not a demanding job and he found himself worrying unhappily about Rob. He missed the time he and Rob used to have together and he was jealous of Roger and the time he spent working with Rob. He had terrible thoughts of Rob turning more and more to Roger and he remembered the time last year when Rob started hanging around with a gang and had nothing to do with him and how hurt and angry he was.

The noon buzzer sounded and he realized he had forgotten his lunch so he drove to a nearby cafe and ate alone feeling gloomy and out of sorts. He thought maybe he had caught a little of Donna's flu that she was complaining about. Returning to work, he went directly to Receiving and Shipping and continued what he had been doing. Nobody came looking for him until Larry wandered in a few minutes before quitting time.

"There you are, kid! I couldn't find you. How come you didn't come for the computer guy's lessons this afternoon.?"

Craig stopped and slapped his forehead. "Jesus, Larry! I forgot. I'm sorry. I forgot my lunch and went out to eat and forgot all about him coming in today."

Larry looked at him like a disappointed parent. "Carl depends on you," he said. "Not good to let Carl down."

"I'll have to see him right away, and explain," Craig said.

"Sure," Larry said as he left.

Craig locked and bolted the cargo doors, checked the shipping room carefully and turned out the lights.

"Hold on there! Just a minute," came a voice from the dark. Craig turned on the lights again. "Sorry. Who's there?"

"Me," Carl said, emerging from an aisle. "I just slipped in to check on some stock while you and Larry were talking."

Craig blushed. "I'm sorry about the noon session," he said. "It just slipped my mind. It won't happen again."

"If it does, I'll sic Larry on you. His bite is sharper than mine," Carl said smiling. "As a matter of fact, it turned out well. I passed by and saw you weren't there and I figured one of us should be so I just slipped in and sat down." He smiled again, conspiratorially. "The men were very impressed that their boss was sitting in on their training session and they paid attention and worked hard like little kids in school."

He turned to go. "Goodnight, Craig."

"Goodnight, Carl. Sorry about my mix-up."

Carl gave a dismissing wave over his shoulder. "Things happen," he said.

When Craig was driving home, he said to himself, "Just Tuesday, Wednesday and then Thursday."

Craig was sitting on the floor of the living room eating his dinner off a stool with the TV blaring when Rob sneaked up behind him. "Jeez!" he said. "You scared me!"

"Poor baby!" Rob said, taking Craig's fork and starting in on his dinner.

"Hey! Leave some or get your own!"

"What! You'd deny your best friend sustenance when he is starving and begging."

"Get your own," Craig replied, grabbing his fork back and protecting his plate.

"I can't," Rob said, suddenly serious. "I gotta go home. But my bikes got a flat so I have to take yours and you can fix mine tonight."

"Okay," Craig replied around a mouthful, seeing nothing unusual about the arrangement.

Rob sat slumped in a chair, looking pale and tired and somehow thinner.

"I can drive you," Craig said.

"No. Then I wouldn't have a bike in the morning," Rob answered, yawning.

They were quiet while Craig finished eating. Then Craig asked, "Why are you doing this, anyway?"

"What?"

"Working your ass off, day and night."

"I said I would look after Donna. I told you before."

"Yeah, I know but..."

There was a silence between them, then Rob, leaning forward with his elbows on his knees, looked earnestly at his friend and said, "I know I asked you before but I gotta hear it again. If things don't go right on Thursday, you will look after Donna, won't you?"

"I said I would, Rob. Why do you have to ask me twice?"

"I don't know. She's important to me. I don't know why, except she's my insurance against turning into a queer, I guess. Roger's testing me and sometimes I think it's fun and I'm afraid I might slip over the line and I think as long as I've got Donna, I'm safe. I know she's been around a bit before me, but I know she's square with me—she's that kind of a person. And I have to know that someone I love and trust will look out for her if I..., you know, ...can't." He stopped to wipe his eyes with the back of his hand and continued with a croaky voice. "And you're the only person in the whole goddam wide world that I really love and trust!" He got to his feet. "Where's the bike."

"I'll drive you," Craig said standing up.

"Of course you would," Rob said, wrapping his arms around his friend and holding him in a crushing embrace for a long time during which they could each feel the other's heart race and listen to their shaky breathing. Rob released Craig, turned suddenly, saying nothing, and went out the back door. Craig saw the garage light go on and watched Rob ride away without a word or a wave.

When Rob arrived home, Donna heard him putting his bike away and was ready to greet him when he came in the door. Her eyes were shining and she had a careful little smile on her face. "Guess what I got today," she said after he had taken off his cold coat and she could hug him.

"A puppy dog? A banana split? A sweatshirt with 'I love Rob' on it? Am I close?" he asked looked down into her happy face.

"No, you'd never guess," she said. "A letter from my Aunt!" she announced looking smug.

"You make it sound better than winning the 6/49," he said laughing.

"Well, it is, almost. I've never had a real letter before, except for post cards. But look!" She pulled the letter out of the envelope and waved it. "Three pages! From my aunt in the Cariboo! She told me all about her Christmas and weather. She said she phoned my mother to ask about me and my mother said she didn't know where I was and didn't care and called me a little bitch. They're sisters, you know, and my aunt said they had a big row over the telephone and she said that's the last time she would ever bother with her again. Anyway, she said I could come up and visit them anytime, she'd love to have me but I'd have to remember they have a lot of animals if I'm scared of animals or allergic. She gave me her phone number and told me to write her soon and send her my phone number and we could keep in touch. She asked how you were doing—I didn't tell her anything about, you know, this court thing. I just said in my letter that I was living with a wonderful man who was tall and handsome and sweet to me and she said it sounded like I better look after you good and hang on to you. So I think I'll take her advice." She hugged him happily and said "I'd better get you some supper," and got up and tucked the letter away in her top drawer.

"Can I see it, Donna?" Rob asked suddenly. "I've never had a letter either, come to think of it—not a personal one, I mean."

"Sure," she said, retrieving the letter and handing it to him. "You can read it."

"'My dear and only niece:' she starts out. That's nice." Rob said and he read on, "And she says at the end, 'With all my love and best wishes for the coming year, Your loving Aunt Ella' and then she adds. 'Your uncle Steve sends his love, too.', but it's in a different ink—she must have added it later."

Rob sat looking at the letter, not reading it, and after a long silence said, "You know, Donna, we could do that when I have to go away. I could write to you and you could write to me. It would be nice, wouldn't it? To get a letter and read it over and over again."

"Yes, it would. I'd like that. But I don't like what you're thinking—that you are sure to get sentenced."

"Well," he said, shrugging. "No sense pretending."

He handed the letter back to her. "I'll have to tell Craig about writing letters," he said.

"Craig! Craig! Always Craig," she said to herself. Then aloud, "Come and get your supper."

CHAPTER 68

Just before eight o'clock, Marion phoned Craig from the bus station to ask him to pick her up. She had had a long miserable cold trip from Prince George and she was anxious to get home and have a hot bath and get some dinner. The bus had broken down in the middle of nowhere and they had sat in the cold for two hours before the replacement arrived, and road conditions had further delayed them. After Rob left, Craig also had sat around morosely, worrying on two levels, one the constant nagging concern about Rob and Thursday, of course, and the other about his mother who had told him she would be back before he got home from work. At seven he had made himself some supper, and it was only after he had finished eating that he thought of phoning the bus station to enquire about the bus from Prince George.

"We are expecting it at any minute," he was told. "There has been a slight delay due to some engine trouble and the snow storm."

"Slight delay!" she snorted when he told her about it on the way home. "We were supposed to arrive here at 4:30."

At home she went immediately upstairs and Craig could hear her running a bath. By the time she came back downstairs half an hour later, her snarly mood had vanished.

"It looks like you made yourself some dinner," she said. "Did you get enough? I'm going to make myself some scrambled eggs and bacon. Would you like some? Why don't you turn that television off and sit down and tell me what you did all weekend?"

There wasn't much to tell her because he hadn't done anything, he said. Besides, she was too busy talking about the Turner's new home.

"Of course, they've got a lot to do to it yet," she said. "And Claudia has a lot of good ideas, which surprised me because she has never shown any kind of real interest in her home here. She's very worried about Glen. He scarcely said a word all the way up. Claudia says she doesn't know how he will react if Rob has to go to jail. Of course, he has always been a worrier, but this time he is really down in the dumps. Are you sure you wouldn't like a bacon and tomato sandwich? It smells so good."

So Craig joined her in a late night snack and they talked about many things until the yawns started and they went off to bed.

On Tuesday, just tomorrow and then Thursday, Craig told himself as he was getting dressed for work, his semi-expertise was demanded many times during the day as the men tried to remember what they had to do to satisfy the computer. Dorothy was frustrated with the machine that sat in her workplace and waited impatiently for another session with the trainer and for the course she and Craig had registered in to begin. Near the end of the day, Craig realized that he had thought about Rob only a couple of times.

Rob was worried because he hadn't heard from Reg Hawthorn and asked Roger if maybe he should get another lawyer. Roger told him bluntly to phone

Reg and ask when they were going to meet and talk. Reg apologized because he had been too sick with some kind of flu bug to come into work but told Rob to come in any time tomorrow and they would get things sorted out. Rob relaxed a little but watching machines turn out sheets of paper only promotes day-dreaming and anxiety. He wondered if Roger had done anything about finding someone to replace him and decided he better have a talk with Roger about it; he didn't want to find himself without a job in case (not much chance, he told himself) he didn't get sentenced to jail. Finally, he turned off the noisy printer and walked over to the small corner Roger called his office and found Roger sitting sideways with his cast propped up on a chair, frowning over some papers.

"Hey! What's up, Rob?" he asked when he saw him.

"Oh, I was just wondering if you had done anything about finding somebody to work for you after Thursday?"

"No, dammit! I haven't—and I should have, if I had any business sense at all. I just had it firmly fixed in my mind that you'd be back as usual on Friday. I hate facing the reality that you might not be. But you might not be," he finished, looking grim and worried.

"That's right. I might not be," Rob confirmed.

Roger was silent for a minute, looking at Rob. "Jeez, I hate the thought of you not being around—of you being locked up some-place. We were becoming really good buddies, I thought."

Rob felt a little jerk inside someplace when Roger said the word 'buddies'. It was a word that had a special meaning for him and he was not too sure he liked Roger using it about them, but at the same time there was a confusing flush of pleasure at the thought.

"Yeah, I thought so too, Roger," Rob said cautiously.

"Well, hell! What am I going to do," Roger said, staring at Rob while he pulled his lower lip like an old man and pondered. "First of all, I owe you some money. We can get that settled up tomorrow."

"No, not tomorrow, Rog," Rob said somewhat apologetically. "This has to be my last day. I gotta see Reg tomorrow, and Donna and I have to, well, we have to have some time together, you know, in case..."

"Yeah, of course. Stupid of me! Selfish! I was just thinking of having you around for another day. Okay, let's work out your time."

They sat together, shoulders touching, while they added up the complexities of time, time and a half and double time without any disagreement. Roger totalled the hours and multiplied by a dollar figure that startled Rob.

"Where did you get that figure," he demanded.

"From your dad," Roger replied, grinning.

"That's away too high," Rob protested.

"Well, that's what it is, like it or not," Roger said, writing out a check.

Rob looked at it and saw that Roger had rounded up to the next hundred. "Rog! You shouldn't have done that! Jeez! Rog!"

"Oh, why the hell not?" Roger said flippantly. "It's only money. I didn't earn it, so why not share it with friends. I get it from my family as long as I stay far enough away that I don't embarrass them."

"Thanks, Rog!" Rob said, shaking he head in disbelief. "Thanks a whole bunch!" He stood up and held out his hand.

"Sometimes friends hug instead of shaking hands," Roger said, struggling to his feet.

They hugged each other and Rob noticed that Roger held him tightly for a long time, until he said, "Well, are you going to take the Porsche and bring back lunch from Donna or do we order Chinese?"

Rob grinned and said, "I'll take the Porsche. It might be a long time before I have another chance."

He arrived at the Sweet Spot still grinning. "I got something to show you," he said when she was able to come over and greet him.

The check was in his hand ready to show her.

"Happy Birthday!" he said, holding it up in front of her.

"My birthday isn't until May," she said. Then, "Rob! What is this?" when she saw the figures.

"That's what I earned working for Roger, including overtime. It's for you."

"No! Oh, no! No-no-no!"

"Yes!" he said. "Oh, yes! Yes-yes-yes!"

"Rob!" she protested.

"Listen, Donna. I promised I would look after you and if I have to go to jail, then this will at least pay the rent for a couple of months."

"A couple! I would think so!" She was still reluctant to take the check he was holding out to her.

"Tell you what we'll do," he said. "When do you get your break?"

"Oh, anytime. The lunch rush is practically over. Why?"

"We'll go down to a bank right now and open an account for you. Okay? Ask Bruno."

"I guess I could clean up when we get back," she said, and disappeared into the kitchen. She came back out a couple of minutes later with her coat on, followed by Bruno.

"Good boy!" Bruno said, approvingly and went back to his grill.

They walked to the nearest bank and in fifteen minutes she had an account in her name. "And here are a few temporary checks, Miss Penser," the motherly clerk said, "to use until yours are printed with your name and address and telephone number. They will be mailed to you in about a week."

Donna stood for a moment wondering if there was more. "Oh, I feel so important!" she said to the clerk.

"It's a nice feeling, isn't it?" the clerk replied. "Have a nice day."

They walked out together with Donna squeezing his arm tightly and smiling happily.

"Well, back to work, slave," he said to her as they entered the cafe. "I didn't come only to endow thee with all my worldly goods, but to pick up two box lunches for the workers of the world, namely, Roger Todd and Robert Turner."

"Mr. Turner, please have a seat or a stool, if you prefer, and I'll see to your request with pleasure." Then she curtsied to him, and for good measure gave him a hearty kiss.

"Wow!" Roger said when he opened his box lunch. "What would I have to do to get a lunch like this when you're not here?"

"You have already done it," Rob answered.

"Did you give it to her?"

"The whole thing!"

Roger made a face that Rob could not interpret as approval or disapproval so he forgot it and tucked into his lunch.

"I had an idea, Rog," he said later, shoving as usual, a huge bite into his cheek before he spoke. "You could phone some of your competitors that might be finding business slow and if they are planning to lay anybody off, maybe they would steer them your way. That way you might save a lot of time in ads and that sort of thing,"

Roger, normally a tidy eater, took a huge bite and after two chews, shoved it into his cheek, and flashing a big lettuce and bread dough smile, said, "You should be running this goddam business!"

"Sure," Rob said. "Piece of cake!" and laughed at Roger's struggle with a full mouth. "You're a city boy. You don't know how to cram. Watch me!" and he stuffed more food in and started to chew.

Roger watched in pretended amazement, then said around his mouthful, "Did you go to the bank with your fly undone?"

Rob looked down in surprise and Roger said, "Gotcha!" and they both laughed until they had to spit out the food in their mouths. "Just the way," Rob thought, "Craig and I used to." Then he realized he hadn't really thought of Craig all day and he felt guilty about sharing their kind of fun with Roger.

They worked for a while cleaning up and it was time for Rob to go. "Listen, Rob," Roger said. "Ordinarily, I'm a very selfish bastard, but I'm not being the least bit selfish when I say I hope to hell I see you tomorrow." He put out his arms and hugged Rob hard again.

"Thanks, Rog!" Rob said and found he could say no more for a moment. "Well, I guess I better drop in and check on Craig. So long, pal."

Roger closed the door on the silent house and felt a sense of loneliness and, he was surprised to discover, some jealousy.

Rob and Donna talked far into the night. Donna cuddled closer but Rob kept on talking until Donna fell asleep in frustration. When Rob finally slept he thrashed around in desperate efforts to deal with his dreams. He and Craig were lying naked on the beach side by side and the man with the white teeth and the bass voice and some other people, including Roger and the judge, were sitting watching them. Then Roger climbed up high above them on a hill and started rolling rocks down on them. A rock hit Craig and blood gushed from a big wound on his lip. Rob raced up the hill and tackled Roger but Roger held him so tight he couldn't get away. Then the man with the bass voice called to Roger to bring him down and when Roger brought him down, the judge looked at him and said, 'He's too small. Throw him back.' The man with the bass voice threw him into the water and he was swept away. Craig was standing on the bank washing the blood off his wound and the water was red with his blood. Craig was calling but Rob couldn't hear him as the swirling water swept him further away. Roger appeared in a red boat and hauled him aboard but they had no oars and just before they went over a gigantic waterfall, with Roger hanging onto him, the last thing he saw was Craig with blood and tears dripping down his face watching him go over the falls. He tried to call out "Craig! Help me!" but his voice was a hoarse whisper and another voice kept saying "Rob! Wake up!" He came awake, sweating with terror, hanging over the edge of the bed, clawing at the floor with Donna trying to pull him back onto the bed.

"You must have been having a hell of a nightmare," she said as he got back into bed. His teeth were chattering and he was shivering as if he were freezing cold. She cuddled her warm body around his and finally the shivering stopped and he slept. Waking later, she reached up and checked his forehead and found his pillow soaking wet. "He must have had some kind of fever," she thought and drifted back to sleep.

When he finally wakened, Donna had dressed and gone, leaving a note on the counter saying "Good luck with Reg Hawthorn XO D." Her morning cup of tea with about two sips out of it was cold beside the note.

He showered and shaved, put on fresh black slacks and his new leather jacket and headed out for his lawyer's office. Reg was in, but busy, the receptionist said, "But I'll tell him you are here." He sat thumbing through a pile of old magazines, not reading, but worrying and watching people come and go. Reg, passing by in a hurry with a sheaf of papers clutched in his hand, stopped momentarily and said, "Hi, Rob. I won't be much longer. It looks like they're not going to throw in any additional charges, otherwise they would have informed me by now. That's good!" And he was off again.

In another hour, they were face to face in Reg's office.

"Sorry to keep you waiting, Rob, but paying customers come first."

Rob looked at him in total puzzlement. "I never even thought about..., he said. "I should have. Jeez, what do I do?"

"Oh, didn't you know? I thought you did. You're pro bono." Reg said casually as he shuffled through some papers. "Oh, here you are," picking out a file. He looked up and saw a young face urgently in need of answers.

He chuckled quietly. "Look, Rob. Every lawyer in the firm has to take a certain number of pro bono cases—that means free, no charge, a freebie, okay? If it's pro bono, you take what you get; you don't get to pick and choose, and you got me. Now then, shall we get on with it or do you want to get a real lawyer in a three piece suit?" He smiled as though he knew the answer.

"Yessir! Let's get on with it. Sorry I am so dumb about these things, Reg, but I've never been arrested before."

"That makes it easier. Now then, I'm going to give you some instructions. No debate or questions—we haven't got time. You are dressed okay, but if you've got a sports jacket, wear it. Leather jackets don't appeal in court rooms. Get rid of the runners. Wear anything that will take a polish. If you've got a sweater with some colour, soft colours not loud, wear it. You're a fairly swarthy guy and black and white on you makes you look like a buccaneer. Sit up straight, stand up straight, don't fidget or pick your nose. When you are asked a question, just answer it and nothing more. The prosecutor will ask you questions, and I will, and probably the judge will—her name is Judge Moore, same one as before. She's tough, probably tougher on lawyers than on the accused but that's good because it means she hasn't made up her mind before she hears the case. Now then, we've got about twenty minutes. I'm going to ask some questions and you answer them. I'm going to be tough. Ready?"

Rob nodded.

"I can't hear a nod," Reg barked. "Sit up straight. Pretend your chair doesn't have a back. Put your hands on your lap and keep them there."

Rob was getting himself straight up when Reg said loudly, "How old are you?"

"Seventeen, nearly eighteen."

"You are seventeen! Nothing more. Just answer the question. How old are you?"

"Seventeen."

"Seventeen what?"

"Seventeen years old?" Rob responded uncertainly.

"Seventeen, SIR!" Reg paused. "How old are you?"

"Seventeen, sir."

"Are you living with your parents?"

"No, sir."

"Are you employed?"

"No, sir."

Reg looked at him curiously and asked in a different tone of voice. "What do you mean? You are working for the guy that bought your father's business, aren't you?"

"I quit yesterday."

"Why?"

Rob shrugged. "I thought I'd probably be going to jail."

"But if you don't, you'll be going back there on Friday?"

"Oh, yes," Rob said.

Reg put his head in his hands. "Boy, have we got some work to do!"

He buzzed his secretary and said, "Make my apologies to my next appointment. I'll be held up for another half hour."

Then he went at the drill again and at the end of thirty minutes he leaned back and smiled, "Good going, Rob. You'll be okay." He got up and shook hands. "See you Friday, say 9:30?"

"Where, sir?"

Reg laughed and said, "Yeah, sorry. That's kind of important to know." He went back to his desk and wrote the place and date and time on a piece of paper and gave it to him. "See you there."

When Rob got to the Sweet Spot, Donna was so busy they had no time to talk except for Rob to tell her he had a quick rough session with Reg. Bruno sent out a cheeseburger for Rob and told Donna not to put it on her tab. He was protesting Bruno's indulgence when Phyllis walked in.

"I just remembered that tomorrow is your big day," she said to Rob. "Donna, you take off that apron and get out of here. I'll finish up. You need some time together. Did you eat breakfast?"

Donna said "Yes" and Phyllis looked at Bruno for confirmation. He nodded and Phyllis smiled and said "Good girl!"

"Tomorrow," she said. "Try to let us know as soon as you can what happens." She was standing behind Rob with both hands firmly on his shoulders as she spoke and he could not turn around to face her. "But good luck, kids!" she said as she turned and walked into the kitchen.

"I'll bring her in for a late breakfast," Rob called.

"On the house," Bruno called.

When they arrived home, the telephone company truck was parked in the driveway. Mrs. Lasseret rapped on the window when she saw them coming. "They arrived about an hour ago and said they were ahead of schedule and could put your telephone in today if it was convenient. So I told them to go ahead and I would phone you at work and find out where you wanted to have it and what kind, but you can talk to them now."

Donna was so excited that the gloominess of the day disappeared while they watched the installation and the test. Rob was making a list of who they would call, when suddenly Donna said with a sad face, "I haven't got anybody to call, except my aunt."

"Sure you have!" Rob declared knowing how alone in the world she sometimes felt. "Look at this list! There's Craig and his mom, and my mom and dad—but that's going to be long distance, and Roger and Bev and Richard and even Edith if your ear is in good shape, and I bet I could think of a dozen more."

She smiled slowly. "Yeah, I guess so."

"Hey," he called with his head in the frig when he finished listing the possible list of contacts, "Don't we have any fruit?"

"No, sorry. I wasn't going to shop until after..."

"Okay, I'll pop out and get some while these guys finish up." He slipped on his jacket and was gone.

He went directly to a wine store, walked briskly in to the wine cooler, looked quickly at prices and picked out a cheap bottle of champagne, He put it on the counter, reached for his wallet and said with a shiver, "Cold out, isn't it,"

"Yeah, and we've got three more months of it," the clerk said. "I'd like to go south with the birds." She wrapped the bottle and handed it to him with his change. "Have a nice day," she added routinely.

"Thank you," he replied as he left. And once outside he added, "And thank you for not asking for my ID."

He stopped at a corner store and bought some oranges, apples and grapes.

Then he closed himself in a phone booth outside the store, dialled a number and hung a tissue over the mouthpiece. He raised his voice a tone and articulated carefully, "Is this the Penser residence?" he asked when the call was answered after at least eight rings. "This is the B.C. Telephone Company calling to enquire if you are satisfied with the installation service today." He waited, smiling, as Donna replied. "Thank you, Ms Penser." he continued. "To welcome you as a new customer to B.C. Tel, we are sending you a complimentary bottle of champagne. Have a nice day."

He walked home, left the champagne on the doorstep and stepped inside. "Oranges, apples and grapes for my lady," he announced.

"I got a telephone call," she said, her face alight.

"You gotta be kidding!"

"No, I'm not. It was from the telephone company asking me if I was satisfied with the service," she said. "I let it ring and ring because I thought it was them testing. Then she said they were sending over a bottle of champagne."

"Well I'll be go to hell," he said. "She said that, did she?" He rapped on table. "That must be her now!"

He opened the door and picked up the champagne. "What service!" he exclaimed with a grin.

"Oh, you sneaky.... I don't know what to call you," she said slapping his shoulder when she caught on. Then she wrapped her arms around him and said huskily, "Oh, Rob. You are so much fun to be with. What am I going to do?"

They held each other for a minute until Rob said, "Well, first we'll put the champagne in the frig and then we'll start phoning people."

"You phone," she replied, putting the bottle in the frig.

"Okay, then," Rob said. "He'll still be at work. I'll have to look up the number."

"Who?" she asked.

"Craig," came the 'of-course' reply as he searched the Yellow pages.

Why did I have to ask, Donna said to herself. Who else would he think of first?

"Hi, buddy," Rob said when Craig was called to the phone.

"Hi! What's up?"

"Nothing. I just wanted to make sure you are going to be in court tomorrow morning."

"Well, of course I am. I told you that already."

"Okay. People change their minds or break a leg, you know. there's no harm in checking. How about dropping over on your way home tonight. Donna got her phone today."

"She did? That's great. See you in a while."

"Who's next?" Rob said to Donna.

"You decide," she answered. "I'll just listen while I get some supper ready. What would you like?"

"Aha!" he said. "My last supper before the gallows, eh?"

"Don't say things like that. It gives me the shivers. Okay, you can have anything you like as long as it's sausages, instant potatoes, and that peas-beans-carrots-and-corn mix."

"Dessert?"

"Wait until we go to bed."

He gave her a lecherous grin and continued phoning. He phoned Craig's mother and tried to josh her out of her worries and tears.

"I don't think I should go to court tomorrow," she said. "I'll just start bawling whatever they do to you."

Then he called Bev and found out that his parents hadn't arrived yet and she was getting fretful. He gave her Donna's telephone number and asked her to phone when they arrived. She told him their phone in Prince George had not been connected yet and there was no way to get in touch. He phoned Roger and had a long talk. Roger said he would take a taxi to the court house tomorrow. A little reluctantly Rob phoned Edith to give her Donna's number, knowing that it would probably never be used. They had a short conversation, Edith ending it with, "Well, good luck tomorrow. I guess I'll find out from Craig what happened."

Rob sat back with a melancholy look on his dark countenance. "You know, I must know a hundred people and I don't want to talk to any of them," he told Donna.

Donna couldn't think of anything to say, so she said, "Well I guess it will sort itself out tomorrow," and then she wished she hadn't said it.

There was a soft tapping on their basement door and Mrs Lasseret came in with a pan of fresh buns. "I hope you haven't had your supper yet," she said. "And Wally and I wanted to wish you good luck tomorrow. I'm sure everything will be fine."

They thanked her and chatted casually with her carefully avoiding any talk of the details of tomorrow. Mrs. Lasseret, uncertain how to end her visit, finally made her escape when Craig's typical knock was heard. "Oh, more well wishers, I'm sure," she said as she scuttled to the adjoining door. "We'll be praying for you."

"Hi, come on in," Rob said, opening the door for Craig. "We're celebrating. Let me pour you some champagne."

"You should keep it to celebrate after, not before," said the more practical Craig. Then he added, "What the hell! If there's reason to celebrate after, I'll buy! Let's eat, drink and be merry for.... Oh, shit! I don't mean that." But they could all laugh.

Donna permitted one small drink. "The rest is for our dinner and you're not invited, Craig. Sorry," she said.

"That's okay," he answered, understanding. "I should be on my way home for my own dinner," as he turned to the door.

"I gotta see Craig for a few minutes," Rob said as he reached for his jacket. "I won't be long."

They went out the door together and got into Craig's car.

"Just drive around a little," Rob said, "and don't talk."

Craig drove without speaking, understanding what Rob needed from him. In the silence, they both became very much aware again of the depth and strength of the bond between them. It was, without a word being spoken, a reaffirmation of that covenant that went beyond friendship.

Rob took a deep breath and held it for a long time, finally expelling it almost with a sigh and said, "Okay, take me home."

When Craig stopped in front of Rob's place, Rob leaned side-ways in the passenger seat far enough to bump Craig's shoulder.

"See ya, buddy," he said before opening the door.

"Okay."

CHAPTER 69

By 10:30 in the morning of January the 7th, in a small, quiet courtroom off the marble and glass main corridors of the Law Courts in the City of Vancouver, Judge Ellen Harley Moore had completed hearing the case of the Crown vs Robert Turner, and had called a fifteen minute recess. The assembled court officials and interested observers all stood as she walked quickly out, gown billowing and glasses dangling from an earpiece cord.

"It went well, Rob. We had to gamble on the 'Not Guilty' plea by virtue of naiveté and I think she might go for it, although it's touch and go, so hold your breath. We're fortunate that the other prosecution witness failed to show. It will be difficult for her not to be prejudiced against the prosecution."

They followed the other spectators into the corridor and those whose interest was only in Rob's trial gathered around him and poured out their support. Craig did the introductions. Rob's mother and father were not present.

Rob had wakened early and dressed carefully. Donna had risen even earlier and, by the time they caught the bus, she was over the morning cramps and stomach upsets that she blamed on the flu. Reg had met them in the corridor near the courtroom in which Rob's case was scheduled and he and Rob found a private room and left Donna on her own until she eventually met up with Craig and his mother and Bev. Bev told them that her parents had not arrived and that she had had no word from them. Richard, she informed them, had a faculty meeting this morning but would be in as soon as he could get away. She had checked with the police in case there had been an accident but there had been no accident reported. However, the police told her that the heavy snow storm around the Williams Lake area was still causing long delays and that a second storm was forecast. Roger arrived, puffing up the stairs on his crutches, unaware of the handicap facilities. Craig took care of the introductions. Shortly after, Rob and Reg emerged from their conference and Rob introduced Reg to the group. "We could go on tour as the three R's" Rob joked, "Rog and Reg and Rob." Reg had smiled, happy to see that Rob was not up tight, and then had urged everyone to proceed to the courtroom.

At ten o'clock exactly, the clerk called the courtroom to order and Judge

Ellen Harley Moore entered, waved a hand for the observers to be seated, settled her papers, nodded to the prosecutor, to Reg Hawthorn and to the Clerk who intoned "The Crown versus Robert Turner."

Nothing more was said. She looked over her glasses at the clerk who gave a small shrug and glanced at the prosecutor who was whispering to a colleague. She looked directly at the prosecutor and said, "Am I to assume that you have prepared some sort of charge in this case?"

"Yes, Your Honour," he answered and paused fractionally so that she glanced in his direction again. "Robert Turner is charged with possession of a narcotic, namely cocaine, in an amount not exceeding eight ounces." His voice finished on an uptone as if he had something more to add, such as 'for the purposes of trafficking'. Reg Hawthorn sat poised on the edge of his seat ready to enter a robust objection if anything was added. The prosecutor sat down. Reg whispered "Okay!" to Rob.

Judge Moore moved some papers around on her desk and said, without looking up, "Robert Turner, how do you plead?" The question was almost a monotone.

Rob stood up, looking handsome and pale, remembering to stand straight and to look directly at the judge. Trying to keep his voice steady while addressing the top of her head, he said, "Not guilty, Your Honour."

She gave no visible indication that she had heard the plea, but glanced over her glasses briefly at the prosecutor. "Are you ready to proceed, Mr. Crowley?"

"Yes, Your Honour."

"Call your first witness."

"Your Honour," Reg interrupted. "Could I ask permission to address the court prior to hearing evidence?"

"Proceed, Mr. Hawthorn. But please, no protracted orations."

"Thank you, Your Honour. I promise to be brief. I wish to put into the record certain facts relating to: one, the age of the accused, and, two, the fact that there is no actual evidence. Your honour, my client is seventeen years of age. I made an unsuccessful application to have this case removed to juvenile court. I must point out, Your Honour, that my client's rights, namely, the right to anonymity guaranteed to juveniles, has been violated by being named publicly as a suspect in a drug related crime. I could say more, much more on that point, but at your request, your Honour I will be brief. However, I am distressed, and I hope you are also, Your Honour, that the actual tangible evidence upon which this charge rests has disappeared and something else has been substituted, namely a substance, sodium bicarbonate, I believe, into which a minimum amount of cocaine was introduced for the purposes of entrapment."

"Mr. Hawthorn!" the judge interjected.

Reg sat down.

"I think you know you have overstepped the bounds of leniency ordinarily permitted the defence prior to hearing evidence." The tone was that used in making a statement rather than a disciplinary tone. She looked at the prosecutor. "Proceed, Mr. Crowley."

Mr. Crowley, after an extended conference with two other men, during which Judge Moore's impatience with the delay was made obvious by her glare and the way she sat turning a pencil end over end on her desk.

"Call Officer Walton, Your Honour."

"Thank you, Mr. Crowley. I thought, for a long wasteful time, that the wheels of justice might have ground to a halt." Her voice was heavy with sarcasm. Reg looked at Rob with a very small approving smile.

Officer Walton was sworn in and the prosecutor began a long routine of questions. Officer Walton was the cranky, hungry one of the two policemen who had arrested Rob. He answered the prosecutor's question in a bored voice, wishing things would hurry up so he could get home and get a hot dinner for a change. He said he was in his fourth year in the narcotics branch of the local police. He usually worked in plain clothes. He and his partner kept a routine eye on the bus station where it was known that a lot of drug deals were made. On two occasions he had witnessed a certain known drug dealer place a small package in a locker and it was later picked up by a girl who took it over to Robson Street. They had followed her but lost her both times. On the last occasion they had received authority for the station manager to open the locker and give them the package. They had opened the package, discovered it was full of cocaine, substituted baking soda for the cocaine leaving about a tablespoon of cocaine in, then resealed the package, initialled it for identification and with the manager's assistance put it back in the locker. He and his partner had taken turns watching the locker but nobody approached it except for the accused who opened the locker and was seen to put the marked parcel in. They had not observed anybody take the parcel out and neither he nor his partner could figure out how the accused got it. They could tell by the initials that it was the same parcel they had put in earlier so they arrested him on a charge of possession.

"Am I to understand," the judge interrupted, "that you placed a marked package in a locker at the bus station, kept it under twenty four hour surveillance, and then saw the accused walk in with the same package and attempt to place it in the same locker?"

"It would appear so, Your Honour."

"Any explanation forthcoming?"

"No, Your Honour."

She sighed heavily, made extensive notes, then nodded to the prosecutor to continue. Mr. Crowley then lead Officer Walton back through another series of the same questions to which he responded with increasing diffidence.

"Mr. Crowley," Judge Moore interrupted. "I assume you intend to call the other arresting officer for corroboration."

"Yes, Your Honour. That would be Officer Kirenski."

"When?"

"My staff are trying to locate him now."

"Have they looked in the bus station?" she asked caustically, and without waiting for an answer, continued. "Have you anyone else to call?"

"No, Your Honour. But I would like permission of the court to call Officer Kirenski when he arrives."

She nodded. "Mr. Hawthorn, do you wish to cross?"

"Yes, Your Honour." He stood up to face Officer Walton. "Quite a comedy of errors, Officer Walton. Is it not?"

The policeman shrugged without changing facial expression.

"Where is this so-called package of drugs now, Officer?"

"In safe-keeping in the station lock-up."

"You're certain of that, Officer? That it is locked up safely at the station?. It seems to have the capability of moving around of its own volition."

"No, I am not sure. And I don't care where it is at this moment. I care only that I have a receipt from the sergeant when I turned it over to him."

"I see. It seems that while it was in your safekeeping or that of your partner, it was removed from under your watchful eye. How do you account for that, Officer?"

"I don't know," in a very bored voice.

"What shift arrangements were made between you and Officer Kirensky to keep at least one eagle eye on this locker?"

"Six hours on and six off."

"Now tell me, Officer Walton, on the day before you arrested Robert Turner for possession of narcotics, which of you, you or Officer Kirenski was on surveillance duty at the bus station for the sole purpose of watching a particular locker, say around the hour of two o'clock."

The policeman's expression of boredom did not change, but his fingers moved against his knee, presumably counting off something. "That would be Kirenski's shift," he announced with a slight change of expression, perhaps indicating relief.

"I see. But the following day, at approximately the same time, you were both there watching the locker?"

"No, we weren't watching the locker. We were changing shifts when he," jerking his head, "opened the locker and we caught him in the act."

"What act, Officer Walton? The act of trying to rectify a mistake in juvenile judgment? No further questions, Your Honour." He returned to his place at the defence table trying not to look too pleased.

Without looking up from her notes, the judge asked, "Mr. Crowley?"

His face flushed with anger, he responded to her more curtly than he meant to, "Nothing more, Your Honour."

"Then, Mr. Hawthorn. We appear to be ready for the defence. How many witnesses will you call?"

"Just one, Your Honour, Robert Turner."

"Good!" she said. "We may be through by lunch time."

Apparently coming suddenly out of a drowsy state, the clerk struggled to his feet and shouted in a voice so loud that some spectators jumped, "Robert Turner!"

Rob got up from the table he and Reg shared and moved to the witness box.

At the same time Reg said "Your Honour?"

"Yes, Mr. Hawthorn."

The clerk, who, bible in hand, had moved to the witness box, returned to his table.

"Your Honour, since we have established that Robert Turner, the accused, is a juvenile, being seventeen years of age, and, had the arresting officers not been so inept, Robert Turner would now be in Juvenile Court. Instead, the anonymity that is guaranteed a juvenile offender has been completely disregarded, his name and the charges against him have been made available to the press. All his rights as a juvenile have been nullified. That being the case, Your Honour, I ask that I be given the privileges of examination that would be permitted me in protecting my client in juvenile court, that is, primarily, the privilege of leading my client to relate his story clearly and coherently without harassment from the prosecution."

He had been watching the judge carefully. She sat without looking up, moving her pencil from end to end and from end to end, and he got the message. "Thank you, Your Honour," he concluded and sat down.

There was silence in the courtroom. She looked up at the defence attorney and noticed the accused standing in the witness box. "Sit down," she said peremptorily.

"Mr. Hawthorn," she finally said. "The court is not ignorant of Robert Turner's age nor of other factors that bear upon the court's decision to support the argument of the prosecution that this case be heard in adult court, in spite of, I might add, some negligence on the part of the investigating officers, including, Mr. Crowley," she said in an aside, looking over at him, as he reddened but refused to meet her eye, "the failure of one of your witnesses, Officer Kirenski, to appear as subpoenaed. The court is aware that Robert Turner is not yet eighteen years of age but will be in five months time, that he is not living with his parents and has removed himself from their immediate supervision, that his parents are in the process of moving to another part of the province, that he is living with a woman of his own age who also has left the immediate supervision of her family with cause, that he left a job in a supermarket and is presently working for the new owner of his father's previous business, that the curriculum of the school he attended includes several compulsory courses concerning the use and abuse of tobacco, alcohol and drugs. These are facts, Mr. Hawthorn, that lead this court to support the application to retain this case in adult court. The transmission of drugs, for whatever reason, is not a juvenile crime. It is an adult crime and Mr. Turner is an adult in the opinion of this court. I will hear no further applications for special privileges nor variations in questioning procedures. Shall we proceed, Mr. Hawthorn? Your witness."

During the next half hour, Reg Hawthorn determined for the court that Rob was an average student, aware of drugs of most kinds and the impact of drugs on society, that he had tried marijuana once from somebody else's joint but it had made him cough and nearly throw up. Then, under very adroit questioning, Rob related how he had been approached by someone he knew of, rather than knew, from school who said he was rushing to the airport and was supposed to pick up a package in a locker at the bus station but didn't have the time. So he gave Rob a key, asked him to pick it up, and told him that another guy, a big tall guy, would find him at work and say 'Vic says you have a parcel for me' and pay him fifty bucks just as soon as the parcel was handed over.

"What did you do then?"

"I went down to the station, opened the locker and got the package."

"What time was that?"

"I was on my lunch break, so it must have been around two."

"How big was this parcel?"

"About like this," Rob answered, demonstrating with his hands. Too big to go in my pocket so I put it in with some groceries I was taking home."

"Can you describe it?"

"Yes. As I said it was about this big," again showing the size with his hands. "It was wrapped in brown paper, not in a box with corners, just wrapped and taped, quite a bit of tape. It had $50 written on it, very small, in ink and there were two small squiggles that looked like initials. There was no name or nothing like that."

"Then what did you do then?"

"I took it home."

"Were you curious about the contents?"

"Yes, I was. It all sounded fishy and kind of secret or underground—something like that. I didn't like it. But I kept on thinking fifty bucks would buy my girl a nice Christmas present."

"So what did you do?"

"I took it to work the next day and put it in safekeeping where the ladies keep their purses."

"Did you receive fifty dollars from this person for whatever was in that package?" Reg asked carefully.

"No, sir."

"Why not?"

"He never showed up."

"So then what did you do with the parcel?"

"I was getting scared. The more I thought about it the more I thought I might be getting mixed up with some kind of gang thing that could get me in trouble. So I decided to get rid of it."

"How?"

"I decided to take it back to the bus station on my break and put it in a locker and if the guy came looking for me, I'd just give him the key and tell him to get it himself."

"Did you do that? Take it back to the bus station and put it in a locker."

"I tried to. I even found that the same locker was empty so I started to put it in when two policemen stopped me and arrested me."

"So you took a package out of a locker in the bus station around two o'clock one day and returned it to the same locker, unopened, the next day. Now you have heard this morning that during that twenty four hour period, two police officers on six hour shifts had nothing more to do than watch that that locker. Is that correct?"

"Yes sir."

"You had the key and went there and opened the locker and took out a package presumably under the watchful eye of one of the two officers who were alertly guarding that locker." He paused, then continued. "Then you returned the following day to replace the package and these alert police officers saw you and arrested you."

"Yes sir."

"And you found the same locker box open?"

"Yes sir."

"Does it not now strike you as ludicrous that neither of these officers noticed they were watching an empty box for twenty four hours?"

"Yes, I guess so, sir"

"And I suppose it is possible that other people may have used that locker during that period of time and again it is ludicrous to think they were not observed opening a presumably locked locker for which you had the only key."

"Yes. I guess so, sir."

Reg realized that he was stretching the boundaries of legitimate examination, so he switched to a safer topic. "Do you realize, Rob, that it is only a stroke of bad luck that you are in this court today? Had you returned to the bus station to return that package and selected any other locker than the one you previously used, neither of the two alert guardians of the law would have noticed you or cared if they had noticed you."

"An interesting observation, Mr. Hawthorn," the judge observed. "But let us stick to legitimate examination."

"Yes, Your Honour." He paused briefly, gave Rob a small smile of encouragement and continued. "After you were charged and bail arranged, you went back to work the next day. Is that right?"

"Yes."

"You were fired. Is that right?"

"Yes."

"When you thought about going back to work, were you alarmed that this person who was supposed to contact you would find out you had been fired and would somehow find you and make trouble and demand his package?"

"Yeah," he answered, nodding vigorously. "I mean, yes sir. I still get kind of spooked sometimes, thinking him or some of his gang are out to get me for stealing their dope."

"But the police have it, right?"

"Yessir. I just hope they know that."

"That's all. No more questions." Reg Hawthorn said in a tone that almost said 'Well done, Rob', and returned to his seat.

The judge watched Reg sit down, then looked casually around the courtroom while bouncing her sheets of notes into square. "Robert," she asked, "what will you do if this man, or the person who arranged this event in the first place, or any of his cohorts finds you and demands the return of his parcel."

Rob looked at her with wide eyes. "I'll just have to tell them the truth."

"The truth, Robert? What is the truth?"

Rob looked at her in amazement. "Why, it's like I said, Ma'am. What I told Officer Walton and Officer Kirenski and what I told Mr. Reg Hawthorn, and what I said in court. That's the truth, ma'am, I'll just have to make them believe me."

She looked at him as if he might be able to persuade anybody of his innocence. "That's all, Robert. You may stand down."

She paused a moment and said, "I know you gentlemen have the right to make a final summation but because of the time I am denying you that right in the same way that Mr. Hawthorn claims the rights of his client have been abrogated by the vagaries of the system. I know what you would have said, and I know I am legally bound to hear it if you insist. Mr. Hawthorn, any objections?"

"None, Your Honour."

"Mr. Crowley?"

"None, Your Honour. But I would like to point out that the accused was not sworn."

She was half-standing when he spoke. She sat down and turned to the clerk of the court. "Is that true?" she demanded.

"Yes, Your Honour," he said meekly. "You were talking to counsel and I am not supposed to interrupt."

She muttered something under her breath with bared teeth which was clearly audible in the small courtroom and which was equally clearly meant to be synonymous with a blessed defecation. She glared at the clerk. "Give me the Bible!" she demanded. She turned to the defence table. "Robert Turner! Come here!"

He really did not need the nudge from Reg to move him quickly to the bench.

"Take the Bible in your right hand! Do you swear, in front of this court and these witnesses present, that what you have answered to all questions put to you in this court, is the truth, the whole truth and nothing but the truth, so help you, by God?"

"I do," Rob answered, his face creased with confusion.

"Fifteen minute recess," she said, storming out.

"Chambers!" she said on her way out, her finger pointing to the clerk who followed as though leashed.

The group that gathered in the hall were tense and anxious. Rob looked questionly at Bev, who shrugged and said, "I guess they must have got snowed in. He touched hands with Donna who was already tearful and walked over to Craig who was standing a little apart. "What do you think, buddy?"

"They're a bunch of keystone cops. It's a total fuckup!" Craig said with real anger. "We got to talk to Reg about an appeal."

"Come on, man! Let's get the verdict before we start talking appeal," Rob said trying to mollify his friend's upset.

"Yeah, but we should—just in case."

"Yabbut, yabbut, yabbut," Rob teased with his arm around Craig's shoulder. "You're the biggest yabbutter I know."

"Well...." Craig responded feebly but with a grin.

Everyone in the group seemed to be watching him and Rob was struggling to keep up a face of self assurance. He went back close to Donna and when she said, "Got your shot of Craig, eh?" he suddenly choked and couldn't answer.

"We better go back in," Reg announced and the group moved to the entry. Reg held Rob back. "She's going to read the riot act to you, I'm sure. The rougher she gets, the less likely she is to find you guilty. So stand up straight and take it. No smiles, no looking around, no tears—nothing! Got it?"

"Yes sir! And Reg—thanks!"

They walked in together and sat down at the defence table. Reg leaned over and whispered, "When she calls your name, we both stand up." Rob nodded.

There was a complete, cathedral-like silence in the courtroom, with not even a shuffling of feet or clearing of throat. Judge Ellen Hardy Moore entered. She said, "Robert Turner" almost before she sat down.

Rob stood up with Reg beside him. They waited for her to speak—an eternity, so long that Rob felt his knees beginning to tremble.

"Robert Turner," she finally said, "you have pleaded Not Guilty to a charge of being in possession of a narcotic. There is no doubt that you were indeed apprehended with a package which contained a minimal amount of a narcotic. The process by which a larger amount of the narcotic was reduced to a smaller amount is not within the purview of this court at the moment. That act of tampering with evidence will be investigated elsewhere and may indeed reach this court at a later date. The Chaplinesque behavior of the arresting officers in what appears to be a twenty four hour surveillance of an empty locker also belongs in another disciplinary venue. One irrefutable fact remains. You were found to be in possession of a narcotic. Fortunately for you, the amount was so minimal that a charge of 'for the purpose of trafficking' would have been ludicrous. But considering the inept way in which this case was handled, it is amazing that somebody didn't try to insert the second charge."

She paused for a very long minute and Rob could almost feel the blow coming.

"Robert Turner," she said. "You are not a stupid young man. You live in a city in which, daily, we are inundated with reports in newspapers, television and on radio of the way in which narcotics of many kinds are destroying lives and diminishing our society in the eyes of the world. You are the product of a school system that attempts to instruct you of the damages and dangers surrounding drugs of all kinds. I am talking about what appears to be a simple act of sharing a joint with a friend and proceeding by degrees to the more risky drugs and then to those from which there is no drawing back until your body, punctured and diseased, your mind incapable of rationality, your family and friends, even such friends as that young man back there whom you have known all your life—oh, yes, I know a lot about you, Robert Turner—will refuse to crawl into the gutter in a futile attempt to save you."

She paused again and Rob could see the years in jail clicking over like a mileometer.

"You knew that the sum of fifty dollars for the pick-up and delivery of a small package of undisclosed contents was a camouflage to cover some nefarious act. You gambled and you lost. I find you guilty as charged. Underlying your guilt I detect the naive testing of authority. It is this naivety that compels me not to sentence you to a term of imprisonment in an adult institution. I sentence you to six months in the New Starts Correctional Centre for Young Offenders in Burnaby. Should you strive to be an exemplary prisoner, your release could occur in time for your eighteenth birthday in May. This court is adjourned."

CHAPTER 70

The judge's final remarks had exploded on Rob's small group of family and friends so suddenly that they stood whispering to each other trying to get things straight until they watched Rob being led out, white faced and looking suddenly small and scared. Then they knew he was going to jail. No scolding, no probation, just jail! He managed a quick, surprised, wide-eyed look in their direction before the door closed behind him.

Their questions to each other received no answers. Where did they take him? When does he have to go to that place? What about his clothes and things? Can we see him? Maybe we should appeal? How do you do that? Where is his lawyer? Is he coming back? There were tears and comforting hugs as they made their way out of the courtroom into the corridor where they stood in a confused group trying to put it all together. Richard stomped off in search of Reg, found him signing documents and together they asked some questions and got some answers to take back to the group.

Meanwhile, Claudia and Glen were searching the halls of the Law Courts looking for them. They had not escaped the blizzards and had not arrived in the suburbs until ten o'clock in the morning and did not know where the trial was being held. They had tried to phone Marion, then Bev and there were no answers. Then they tried to get Richard at his school and he couldn't be located, then they tried Roger Todd and when he didn't answer, Claudia was almost hysterical. In desperation, they phoned Edith, and "Thank God," Claudia said, when by accident they all met in the hall while Reg and Richard were getting information, "Edith knew!"

Bev took her parents to one side and informed them of what had happened. Marion watched her friend Claudia in desperate sympathy, wanting to go to her but restraining herself from interfering. Claudia sat on a bench with her head in her hands sobbing uncontrollably. Bev stood beside her, patting her shoulder for comfort while continuing to talk to her father, who was listening to her, stiff and stony-faced. "We could have made it," she heard Glen storm.

"But would she fly? No! She would not! Not even to be present at her son's trial."

"You know I'm terrified," Claudia protested.

"Dad! Please!" Bev begged.

Reg and Richard returned to find Bev struggling to inform her parents about what had happened in the courtroom. Reg gave Richard a few minutes to help Bev's mother compose herself and then herded the small group into a quiet corner where they could talk.

"I am sorry, Mr. and Mrs. Turner," Reg said, "that the weather prohibited you from being here. I'm sure that Rob would have benefited from your physical presence. I know you will have a lot of questions but let me say a few things first, then if I haven't covered everything, I'll try to answer questions. First of all, we were lucky in getting Judge Moore. She is tough but fair. You saw how she persisted in supporting the prosecution's position of treating Rob as an adult, but when it came to the final judgment she reversed her position and sentenced him as a juvenile. And I must tell you that it was as light a sentence as she could have given. We were very fortunate that the police acted so, well, I guess the word is, stupidly. Had Rob been in possession of a package of unadulterated cocaine of the size he demonstrated, it would have had a street value of, say, and I'm making a guess, around $25,000 or much more, depending on the quality. We were very lucky. Lucky also that the second officer did not appear, so it was not two against one, as it might have been, so it worked in our favour, particularly in that it angered the judge and frustrated the prosecutor. I was very proud of Rob. He looked good. He answered well and he left a very positive impression. Specifically, in his answer to the judge in her final question. He said, with an open face, without a trace of guile, 'Well, I'll just have to tell them the truth'. A beautiful answer that spoke simply of his natural innocence.

"Now, appeal," he said. "Everyone tends to think immediately of appeal. Let me advise you strongly against it. Firstly, appeals take a tremendous amount of time. It would take two months for the application for an appeal to work its way through the system, and Rob would still be in custody. Then the process of initiating the appeal itself—that is, finding time on the court calendar, could take another two, three, four or more months. Secondly, appeals are very expensive. Certainly, you could count on spending some thousands of dollars. Thirdly, in my opinion, you would lose an appeal. That is my opinion, and it comes to you free, as part of my pro bono work. I cannot continue with an appeal on a pro bono basis. My firm does not involve itself in pro bono appeals. Also, my firm prohibits me from taking your appeal case, should you care to proceed, on a fee basis. You would have to find another firm to represent Rob.

"Another penalty Rob must pay beyond the six months in a correctional facility is that he will be recorded officially as a convicted criminal. That will mean, for example, that he cannot run for public office, serve on a jury, et cetera, and there are certain other limitations that will be placed on his life. Such limitations are removed in the event of a successful appeal.

"I have given you my opinion about an appeal. I will see Rob once more and tell him what I have told you. I would recommend to you that your first enquiry concerning an appeal is not to another lawyer but through your public library. In other words, before you start spending money on second opinions, learn enough to ask intelligent questions.

"Now, I know that uppermost in your minds are questions about Rob's immediate welfare. He will be warmly housed in barracks such as you would find in a military camp. He will be well fed, well clothed—perhaps not fashionably, but certainly not in prison stripes or rags. He will have an opportunity to continue with his education, to start learning a trade, to engage in sports activity, and to work. There will be little idle time. He can have visitors, I know, but I do not know the times or other rules. I will leave you to discover that yourselves by phoning the institution. Now, then, how else can I help you?"

He spent another fifteen minutes with them, fielding questions, most of which he had already addressed. Finally, looking at his watch, he said, "I'm sorry, I must go. I have an appointment at one, and I want to see Rob before he is taken out to New Starts. You will not be able to see him until he has been processed and gone through the orientation program. I will tell him that his parents arrived." He went around the group shaking hands, making comforting comments and left.

Roger had earlier made overtures to leave so that relatives and close friends could deal with their problems in private but Craig had persuaded him to stay and promised to drive him home when he took his mother. The Turner family had three cars, the parent's, Bev's and Richard's. None of them offered a ride to Donna who was sitting quietly to one side and who had said very little during the whole morning except to make minimal responses to questions and social comments. Marion thought, as the Turners organized themselves for leaving, that one of them might have made a little more effort to include Donna.

"Come, dear," she said to Donna. "I guess we'd better go. Craig has to go back to work and I suppose Roger does too. But you're not going back, are you? Poor dear! This has been a hard morning for you, hasn't it?"

"I'll get the car and meet you all in front," Craig said. "It's too far away for Roger." He walked quickly away, his face set in anger.

In Craig's little car, when they had crowded in with the crutches sticking through between the seats, they were silent for a few blocks until Craig slammed his hands on the wheel and said, furiously, "Dammit! You'd think they would have made sure they would be at Rob's trial, wouldn't you?"

"They really did try," his mother said, placating.

"They should have tried harder, then," Craig said in an unforgiving mutter.

Marion sat wondering how Craig was going to cope without having Rob immediately available to share his life with. Donna was thinking much the same, only she was thinking of Rob's need to get his 'daily shot of Craig' as she always thought of it, sometimes with feelings of jealousy. Roger was simply envious, thinking, 'Wouldn't it be marvellous to have a bond like that?'

"Give me a call, Donna, now that you have a phone," Marion said as Donna got out.

"I'm going to check on the place and tell you about it," Craig said to Donna as she said her thanks and goodbyes and walked looking forlorn to her door.

"I hope you find somebody to replace Rob soon," Marion said to Roger as he struggled out of the car.

"I think I'll need a couple," Roger replied. "I'm pleased to have met you at last, Mrs. Williams. It might have been under better circumstances."

"Call me Marion, please," she answered. "But you know what they say—bad beginnings, good endings."

He smiled as he closed the door. "Thanks for including me, Craig. And for the ride. Drop over sometime."

"Sure," Craig said. But as he drove around the corner to home, he thought he probably never would because he knew Roger was a queer, or a fag, or a homo or whatever they were being called these days. Gay, that was the new word. But it didn't sound right to him.

CHAPTER 71

When Donna opened her door it was only 1:30 but the dark January day made her little apartment look cheerless and gloomy. She turned on all the lights and flung herself on the bed without taking off her coat and sobbed. She had shed tears quietly during the worst parts of Rob's testimony, fearful that something would slip and everyone would discover that she was the one who picked up the packages. When the verdict came, she wanted to shout "No! It wasn't him! It was me! I did it! Let him go!" but she restrained herself only by lowering her head in her hands and biting down hard on her thumb knuckle. When she was a child and had to escape from her mother's drunken rages, she would hide in the bushes or the attic or under the house and bite hard on her thumb so as not to cry out in fear or in hurt. When she had cried herself out she forced herself to get up, wash her face and bathe her red eyes in cold water. As she was considering going to work just to keep busy, Mrs. Lasseret knocked.

"I heard you come in, dear," she said when Donna opened the door, and I listened but I couldn't hear Rob. Then I heard the water running so I knew you hadn't gone out again and I just couldn't wait. I had to find out how everything went this morning."

Donna's tears started again and she told Mrs. Lasseret a slightly altered version of what had occurred but the outcome was the same: six months in New Starts. The charge was possession of narcotics but Donna cleared Rob's name with Mrs. Lasseter by drawing on the scheme of entrapment by the police.

"Oh, you poor dear! How awful for you! And for Rob. He's such a fine boy. Why ever would the police do something like that? I think it's just terrible. They're probably covering up them-selves, I'll bet. There's a lot of crooks in them uniforms, Wally always says. Now if there's anything I can do, just let me know and you have a lie-down and a good rest."

"Thank you, Mrs. Lasseret," Donna said as the old lady gave her a hug, "but I've been cooped up in that courtroom all day, it seems. I think I'll have a walk and see if they need me at work."

"Alright, dear. I'll tell Wally that it was a police trap just like he thought. You take care now, dear," she said as she left.

On her way to the Sweet Spot, Donna refined the story of police entrapment, so that both Bruno and Phyllis were sympathetic and angry with the system. "They are bad, some of them, crooked! Just like the old country. When you go see him," Bruno said, "I send him a big hamburger. I know the kind he like." He went back to scraping his grill, his face set in outrage.

There was outrage at the Lewis's house too. When they arrived Glen immediately phoned New Starts and when he discovered that they would not be able to see Rob until Sunday afternoon, he announced to Claudia that they could not wait that long and that they would have to leave immediately.

"What do you mean 'We have to leave immediately'?" she stormed. "I am not leaving here today, tomorrow, or Saturday or maybe not even Sunday—not until I have seen my son! I don't care what you are going to do but I am not going."

"Claudia," he protested, "I have to get back! I just have to!"

"Then go," she snapped, and walked into another room.

"Dad?" Bev ventured, not really wanting to get into their argument, just hoping their quarrel would stop. "Couldn't you phone?"

"What the hell do I say to an new employer? Sorry, old boy, but I'm going to be another week late. You see, my son has just been taken to prison on a narcotics charge and his mother wants to make sure he gets clean sheets," he said bitterly. He was pacing. Bev was silent.

"I've got to go," he said finally and went into the other room where he found Claudia, sitting, elbows on her knees, staring out of the window.

"I'm going, Claudia. Will you come?"

"I'll come when I've seen my son," she said, not looking away from the window.

"I've got responsibilities," he started to say.

"Yes, you have," she interrupted. "And right now you are shirking a major responsibility. You know damn well that any employer you would work for would not mind at all, not even that much." She squeezed a thumb and forefinger until they were a hair-breadth apart. "The real reason is that you can't bear to see your son in prison, isn't it?"

His face was closed, his lips tight. His eyes were wet as he nodded.

"Kiss me goodbye, then," she said sadly, but she did not stand and offered him only her cheek. "I don't know how I can explain to Rob, but I'll try."

He kissed her cheek and she could feel him trembling.

"I'll be home next week," she said as he turned to leave.

"You didn't need to come in today," Carl said when Craig showed up for work in the afternoon.

"I know Carl, and thank you, but I had to get away and do something that would take my mind off this morning," he replied. Both Carl and Larry asked Craig independently how the court case of his friend had gone that morning.

Both men were firm in their opposition to the use of drugs, but both under-stood that the police sometime played dirty pool in their efforts to catch of-fenders and both could sympathize with Craig's distress.

Roger stumped around on his crutches and started on a job that required all his attention but as a consequence of his morning, he made so many mistakes that the job had to be discarded. Even with the radio playing, the shop was almost spookily quiet. He remembered Rob's advice and spent the afternoon phoning around to his competitors to find out if they were letting men go. He learned of a very competent man who had retired six months ago and is now regretting it and wants to return to his old job but his place has been filled. He knew he should ask to have the man call him but he was desperate and asked for the man's name and telephone number.

"Allen Singh. Actually Allen Bandra Singh. Very good man, knows his job. I think you'd find him very competent."

Roger thanked his informant and decided to get on with it and call the man now. Allen Singh was obviously pleased that his previous employer had recom-mended him. He spoke in a carefully articulated voice with the lilt of an East Asian and said he would be delighted to come for an interview and was free at the moment and could come right away. Roger was able to restrain him and made an appointment for the next afternoon.

He phoned the clinic where he had gone with his broken leg and asked the receptionist to locate his records and ask any available staff doctor if it was time to change to a walking cast. The receptionist phoned back within the hour and told him to come in tomorrow morning at ten. Then he shouted, "Hey! I can get my cast off tomorrow," before he realized he was alone. Alone or not, getting rid of the cast was going to be great. He would be able to drive, he hoped. He could drive out and see Rob one of these days.

Marion phoned her daughter to let her know how Rob's trial turned out and to catch up on other things. Edith's interest in Rob's trial stretched as far as her mother's three minute recounting of the events of the morning.

"Well, I don't know what else he'd expect," she said, bluntly. "When you start messing around with drugs, you're going to end up in jail sooner or later. Maybe he'll learn a lesson. He always was one to experiment with things, wasn't he? It's a wonder that Craig didn't get caught too. He always just follows Rob around like they were tied together. Oh, by the way, Rob's dad phoned me this morning and asked me if I knew where Rob's trial was and I just happened to remember you told me last week, I think it was, that it was in the Law Courts and I thought about going because it would be interesting to see a case about someone you knew, but I didn't go. But you know that, I wasn't there. Anyway, he was practically rude on the phone. He just said 'Thank you' and banged down the receiver. He didn't ask about the girls or Harvey or even how I was. What's wrong with the man!"

"They were caught in a blizzard driving down," her mother tried to explain, "and didn't know where the trial was going to be held. So they phoned all over and couldn't get anybody and then he phoned you. They missed the whole trial."

They didn't arrive until it was all over."

"Well, good heavens! Doesn't he know enough to check the weather before he starts out? We never even drive into Vancouver without checking the weather these days!" This was pure Edith, at her best.

Marion gave a quiet sigh and asked about the girls and received a very up-to-date report on the little rascals. When it was over, she begged off saying she should phone Claudia and find out when visiting hours were and when they were going.

"Tell her to tell Rob I'm sorry he got caught," Edith said. "No, I don't mean that. I mean, tell, you know, whatever people are supposed to say when things like that happen."

"I'll tell her to tell Rob that you still love him," Marion said.

"Oh, Mom! Don't be silly!" Edith said with her little shriek of a laugh. "Oh, I better go! Here come my little snowmen now all covered with snow. Talk to you later. Bye bye." And the line was dead before Marion could respond.

The Friday evening weatherman, normally effervescent and giggly to the point of nausea, warned, between smothered yawns, of another front moving in and promised mixed snow and freezing rain. The news consisted of the most recent uprising in some obscure country Craig had never heard of and the continuing local search for an abducted child. The U.S. President was threatening to send troops into some other country so that he could have his war for the history books like all the other presidents.

Craig snapped the TV off and headed for the basement, saying to his mother as he went by the kitchen where she was busy writing letters in the nook, "I'm going skiing tomorrow."

"Good!" she said. "Who with?"

"Nobody. There's always somebody up there."

"Are you going to see Rob on Sunday?"

"Yeah, I guess. But I hope there isn't a crowd. You know, his mom and dad, and Bev and Richard. And you?"

"No. I'll wait," she said. "Donna?" she asked.

"I don't know. Oh! I could phone her. She's got a phone." He went immediately to the phone, took her number out of his wallet and wrote it in the book before he dialled.

"Hi," he said when she answered. "It's me! How're you doing?"

"Okay, I guess. I went in to work but so many people asked me about Rob that it put me down in the dumps all day."

"Yeah, me too. I'm going skiing tomorrow to get away."

"Good idea. I wish I could ski."

"You could learn. I could teach you and you could surprise Rob."

"No thanks," she said bluntly.

"Do you want to go out Sunday to visit him? I could drive you. I don't know what the bus schedule is."

"No, thanks."

"Why not?" he asked, puzzled.

There was a long pause before she answered. "I don't want to be there when his father is there. I don't think he likes me. His mother is okay, but I don't know about him. He didn't say one word to me yesterday and he looked at me like I wasn't there. He's weird."

"Maybe he was just upset. He's always like that. You know, not bothering to say hello and things like that."

"Yeah, well maybe," she conceded.

There was another long silence. "You know what, Craig? I don't think we should go out together to see Rob. I'd rather go alone. And I bet you would, too. I was thinking, see, that if we went out together, we'd see him but we wouldn't have any time alone with him, either of us. See what I mean?"

"Well...." he said uncertainly.

"If I go out alone, I can think about what I want to talk about with Rob and then we can have our visit, just two of us, not three, and I don't mean anything mean or that I don't like you because I do and you know that. But it's like Rob's all I got and I don't want to share him when there is so little time."

"Yeah, I guess I see what you mean. Well, we'll work some-thing out." He paused for a minute. "I'm going to go out Sunday, so should I tell him what we were talking about?"

"Oh, Craig!" she laughed, the first laughter in days. "When did you ever not tell Rob everything.?"

"Yeah, I guess you're right," he admitted, "Well, see you around. Call me if you need anything."

"You'd be the first," she said and hung up.

He sat by the phone a minute. There's one thing I'll never tell him, he said to himself. Not ever!

"I couldn't help overhearing some of what you said," his mother said to him on his way through the kitchen. "Is Donna going out with you to see Rob on Sunday."

"No, she doesn't want to be there when Rob's dad is there. She thinks he doesn't like her or something."

"Oh, he's gone back to Prince George. Didn't I tell you?" his mother said.

"They did?" Craig said dumbfounded.

"Just Glen, not Claudia," she corrected.

"Did he see Rob before he left?"

"No," flatly.

Craig turned and went down the stairs without a word. At the bottom, he kicked the laundry basket across the room.

CHAPTER 72

Driving out to see Rob on Sunday afternoon, Craig drove past New Starts without recognizing it as an institution. A group of low buildings was separated from the road by a stretch of well-tilled garden patches and the build-ings, most of them labelled because of their uniformity, were scattered without apparent formality among fruit trees and ornamental shrubs. The grounds were fenced but the fence was low and concealed by carefully tended espaliered trees and vines so that the institution did not intrude upon the community into which it had been inserted and which later grew compatibly around it.

Craig drove through the entrance gate that was nothing more than an unguarded barrier and found the visitors parking lot where he sat for a long time watching people come and go, wondering what to do. The administration building was closed and there did not appear to be anybody, such as uniformed guards, that he could ask. Most people appeared to head for the gymnasium so eventually Craig, with some trepidation, followed suit. Inside the gym door there was a crowd of young men, all in institutional denims, lounging around, talking and laughing while keeping a close eye on every person who entered, each one waiting, Craig concluded, for his own visitors to appear. When no one came forward to meet Craig, an older man in a sports jacket and carrying a clipboard, approached him and asked, "Who are you visiting?"

"Robert Turner," Craig said. "But I'm not sure where to find him."

"Okay, let's see," the man said, consulting his clipboard. "Oh. here he is. He was added to the list so he's just come in. Probably doesn't know the drill yet. Harris," he called to one of the boys nearby, "you're in C7, run over and see if Robert Turner is in the dorm and tell him he's got a visitor."

When Harris had trotted off, the man continued, "It's always frustrating for a boy on the first visiting day. They are expected to telephone or get a message to the people who will be visiting them each Sunday and arrange a time and place—usually here in the gym in bad weather—but in the summer, almost anyplace, except the dorms, of course. No visitors in the dorms."

"And only on Sundays? No other times?" Craig asked.

"Afraid so. Rules, you know. Not a summer camp." He stopped talking and watched two boys who were arguing loudly and angrily face to face. He waited a moment and walked over and spoke quietly to them and they moved a distance away from each other. He turned his back on them and returned to Craig.

After a moment of quiet, he asked, "Is that your friend coming now?"

Craig looked where the man had pointed and saw Rob working his way in through a crowd of people, standing tall and searching faces for him. Craig gave him a wave, his own face shining, and watched Rob's face come alive with a big smile when he saw him, not realizing the man beside him was watching and assessing the greeting professionally.

"Hi, guy!" they greeted each other and, with too many people watching, shook hands, grasping each other's free elbow while looking at each other closely with soft eyes.

"I figured you'd be along today," Rob said. "My mom and Bev came out earlier and I just happened to be here in the gym when they arrived. Lucky! My dad went back to Prince George right after the trial." He made a wry face and shrugged. Craig made no comment but he could feel a surge of resentment rising within him.

"Turner," the man with the clipboard said, "I know you haven't had time to read all the rules yet, but it's a good idea to make a specific time and place to meet next time with each visitor. See all these guys standing around here waiting? Most of them probably said only, 'See you Sunday', no time, no place and so there's a lot of no-shows. That's hard on the boys." He turned to go.

"Good idea, sir. I'll remember that," Rob said.

"And thanks for your help, sir," Craig added. "I was lost."

They walked away from the crowded entry hall to some empty seats on the sideline, walking with only shoulders touching, and sitting together with shoulders and knees touching and a large chunk of understood silence between them.

"So how come you didn't bring Donna?" Rob asked finally.

"I asked her about it and we talked and I guess she decided she would rather come alone so she could have you all to herself. I know how she feels, I think. I offered to drive her but she said if she came on the bus she could get ready to talk to you or something like that." Craig hoped he had made it clear to Rob.

"Yeah, maybe that's better," Rob said. "Look at that guy over there! He's got six people visiting him and they are all talking to each other and nobody's talking to him." They watched and started laughing in sympathy at the poor lonely inmate, but Rob's laughter was unnaturally restrained. "He'll be glad to get back to the dorm, I bet," Rob added.

"So what happened?" Craig asked. "What did they do when you got here?"

"Well, first they took me down to the dungeons and they chained me to a wall and took turns beating the living shit out of me," Rob said with a straight face. Then seeing Craig's look of horror, he said quickly, "No, no, Craig! I was teasing, for Crissake! No, I was late getting here and supper was over, so they took me to the kitchen and one of the guys fixed me a supper like you wouldn't believe. Then I got taken up to a room in a dorm where there were three other guys. They're okay, I guess. They started right in with that old junior-senior thing like high school only as soon as they found out I would be getting out before any of them they sorta stifled that crap."

"What did you do Friday and Saturday?"

"I got my clothes, these things," Rob said. "And gym strip, and a poncho, you know—everything, work gloves, cap, underwear, toothbrush, the works."

Rob told him he had to decide where he wanted to work, the wood working shop, machine shop, laundry, chickens, the orchard or other things. He could have time for a hobby. He said that everybody had to work in the vegetable gardens and flower beds and lawns when the weather was good. He also said a lot of guys opted to finish their education but he rejected the idea. "Well, you know what a brain I am," he explained.

"I was thinking I might take up engraving," he told Craig. "It always seemed kind of interesting."

"Yeah," Craig agreed.

"I think I might go out for basketball, too," Rob said. "They got six teams here and I bet I could make the second team. Some of these guys are really good—practically pros."

A loud buzzer sounded.

Craig jumped and looked around warily.

"It's the five o'clock quitting buzzer. Suppertime is in one hour," Rob explained.

They had talked for almost two hours. "I better go," Craig said, and Rob made no move to stop him except to say, "I'll walk with you to your car."

They walked slowly out of the building to the car lot, agreeing for next Sunday, on the time and the same place they were sitting today, depending on what time Donna might want to come.

"Tell her I'll phone her," Rob said. "But there's only two payphones in each dorm and there's always a line-up."

They stopped at Craig's car and stood for a moment after Craig unlocked the door. There were only a few cars left in the parking lot. Suddenly Rob reached out and hugged Craig hard. Craig could feel him trembling.

"See ya next Sunday," Rob said, releasing Craig and walking away.

"He's never quite as tough as he pretends to be," Craig thought as he drove home. They hadn't talked about why his father hadn't come and Craig was glad they hadn't.

During the week Craig was kept busy at work. One night a week he attended his computer course and found himself much further ahead than the rest of the class. There was little to study or to practice without a home computer and the winter evenings hung heavy and dull.

"Why don't you finish your high school at night school?" his mother asked one evening when he was muttering about the dumb television.

He didn't answer but he did stop muttering and the next day at noon he went back to the school and sought out Mr. Arkinson who seemed openly delighted to see him.

"What a good idea!" Mr. Arkinson enthused. "Unfortunately, you are too late for night school but we could get started on a correspondence course. It really isn't by correspondence, Craig. You take your lessons and assignments home, and if you get into difficulty, you can either call the teacher giving the course or come in and talk about it. Now let's look at your record and see what you're missing."

Craig watched as he punched a few buttons on his computer and called up Craig's complete high school record.

"Well, let's see," Mr. Arkinson said. "You've got one credit carried over from last year when you took that extra Socials course, but you've got to get your English and a couple of others. How about Economics?"

"You mean cooking and sewing—that kind of stuff?" Craig asked with a face that already said, "No way!"

"No, I mean real Economics. Dollars and cents. Supply and demand. Income and outgo. Profit and loss. Management and labour. All that good kind of nuts and bolts stuff."

Craig was sitting up straight and listening. "Gee, Mr. Arkinson, maybe I should. I got a promotion in my job, you know. I was made Assistant to the

Manager. That's the kind of stuff my boss often talks to me about. Is it a hard course?"

"Well, I wouldn't call it hard and I wouldn't call it easy. It depends how you tackle it and how bad you want it. But it sounds like something you should have if you are moving up in the company. What do you think?"

"I don't know, Mr. Arkinson. I'm not much of a student. You know that—it's all right there, on the computer."

"What's not there, Craig, is that you are approaching this institution as a mature student. I think you will discover some interesting changes in your attitudes toward learning. I don't want to make your decisions for you. Think about it and come back and see me."

Craig sat looking at him for a long minute, not really seeing him. "No, Mr. Arkinson. There's no sense waiting. I think I should take your advice. Economics, now and then I'll do English in the fall. That will give me all summer to do the reading."

"Good for you, Craig! Good decision. Let's get started."

By the time Craig left, a little late for work, he had an outline of the course, a list of readings, a text book and a set of questions designed to show his present knowledge of the subject.

He told Carl why he was late and got a huge smile and a pat on the back. "Good going, Craig," he said. "We need a fresher economic outlook in this company."

On Sunday when he went out to see Rob they had barely got settled into talking about Craig's plans and looking at Rob's sheets of practice printing of various styles when they looked up and saw Donna walking toward them across the gym floor. Rob leaped up to meet her and they greeted each other warmly and unselfconsciously on the gym floor. Craig watched them from his seat feeling slightly miffed that his visiting time was being usurped.

"Hi, Craig," Donna said as she came over and gave him a hug and a gentle peck on the cheek. "I haven't seen you all week. Did you register in that course you were talking about?" They chatted for a moment until Rob gave a big affected yawn and said, "Oh, I guess I might as well go up to my room while you two chat."

The place and the fact that there were three of them inhibited their normal conversation. They admired Rob's pages of printing practice. Donna told them of meeting two friends from school in the mall and finding them so giggly and gossipy that she made excuses and escaped. Craig told them about how funny he felt going back to school, where it seemed he didn't belong any more, to talk to Mr. Arkinson who seemed like a real live human being. Donna said she read the bus schedule wrong and that was why she was early. Craig said he'd better leave so they could have some time to themselves. Rob protested, but Craig insisted and said goodbye and walked away alone to his car. On the way, he yawned.

On the following Sunday, January 24th, Craig surprised Rob by bringing his mother who greeted his U.U. with more than his usual display of affection.

They talked together on the hard seats of the gymnasium that was, for Marion, depressingly spotted with dozens of small groups seeking an island of privacy to visit with a denim clad son or brother or friend. It was a short visit and Rob walked with them back to the car and embraced them both with moist eyes as they said their goodbyes.

Donna walked into the gym an hour after they had driven off. Rob had been hanging around the entrance with some others who had been drifting away one by one as they gave up on an expected visitor. He had been watching for her but did not see her walking toward the building until she opened the door, and he rushed to greet her. Their greeting was complicated by other people wanting in or out, something that did not bother Rob but embarrassed Donna. "Can we get out of here?" she asked, interrupting his embrace.

"Sure," he said, taking her arm to lead her into the gym.

"No, not in there. Can't we go someplace else?"

He looked at her, puzzled by her tension and nervousness. "Want to walk?" he asked.

"Sure," she said abruptly and turned to the door.

Outside, he said, "Hang on while I get my jacket. I'll just be a minute." He ran off and disappeared in a dormitory building and came out, wriggling into a jacket, to catch up with her as she walked slowly down a path through the winter garden. He took her hand and they walked silently for a minute. He could not think of what to say to ease something that was obviously upsetting her. Then she took her hand away from his and turned to face him, her face tight and her eyes ready to flood with tears.

"I'm pregnant," she said in a flat voice.

He looked at her, stunned. Her tears started to fall.

Then he said, his face opening up, "You are?" unbelievingly, joyfully, happily.

Those two words, said like that, started the flood. "Oh, Rob! I was afraid you'd be mad." She moved to him and nestled against him.

"Me? Mad?" he said, and he raised his face to the sky and roared a great "Yahoo!" Then returned his face to snuggle against her hair. "Oh, Donna! I think it's wonderful. Geez! Isn't that great! Are you sure?"

"Pretty sure," she said, pulling away from him a little so she could look at his face. "I'm more than three weeks overdue. I decided I had to tell you today and if you were happy about it, I would see a doctor this week to make sure. And if you weren't, I'd see somebody else before it's too late."

It took him a minute to understand what she said. "Oh, no, Donna! You wouldn't!" he said.

"Oh, yes, I would!" she declared firmly. "I want to have a baby but I don't want to have it all by myself. No sir!"

They walked and talked and even if it was a cold wintry day, they didn't notice.

"It has to be a girl," he said. "I love little girls."

"I'm glad," she answered. "I'd hate to hear you say you love little boys."

He gave her a happy little bum bump as they walked. "Oh, you think you know me so well, smarty-pants," he said and they were laughing as the buzzer sounded.

He walked her to the gates, as far as the rules permitted him to go, and the open gate was tempting. It took a long time to say goodbye.

"Don't tell Craig," he called as she walked away. "I want to tell him myself."

She waved a hand in understanding. "I guess it isn't little boys," she told herself. "Maybe it's only one big boy."

CHAPTER 73

Donna came out of the Doctor's office trying to suppress a smile and not fooling anyone.

"Are you going to make another appointment, Miss Penser," the receptionist asked as Donna levitated by her desk.

Donna stopped and turned toward her and gave her a wide-eyed expectant smile, said "Oh, yes," and turned again and floated out the door.

When she opened the door to the Sweet Spot, Phyllis looked up from behind the counter, and said, "I knew it! You are, aren't you?" and came out with arms outstretched. "Happy?" she asked. Donna nodded a tearful admission into the older woman's shoulder. Bruno came out from the kitchen and seemed to know immediately what was going on and smiled like a grandfather when Donna reached out and pulled him into their embrace. Finally, she said, "Oh dear!" and let them go and blew her nose and laughed.

"Good girl!" Bruno said and headed back to his kitchen.

"When?" said old mother Phyllis.

"September the twenty first," said Donna.

"The last day of summer," said a customer. "Congratulations."

"Thank you," Donna said, looking up, not realizing she had had an audience of four regular customers.

"Yeah, good luck!" "Congratulations!" "If it's a boy, don't name him after me, my wife's already suspicious."

"What? Call him Ptolemy? You're safe!" Donna replied, laughing and escaped to the kitchen.

"What's wrong with Ptolemy? Name of fifteen Egyptian kings," a voice laden with pretended hurt called after her.

Bruno's guffaw was heard and he stuck his head through the serving hole and said, "Fourteen, Pitall! Go learn your history! Egyptians!" he snorted, grinning.

"Fourteen! Fifteen! Who cares?" came the retort. "We had kings before the Italians discovered flint."

"We didn't discover flint. We discovered America," boomed Bruno in reply.

"Bah! Italians!" the voice called. "Phyllis, put it on my tab, will you? And where's the baby jar."

"Leave it on the counter, Pitall. You're the first!"

"Of course," Ptolemy, Pitall to friends, said, putting five dollars on the counter with a grand gesture before swaggering out to the applause of the others.

"When are you going to tell Rob?" Phyllis asked.

"I told him I thought I was on Sunday and he was bouncing around like he'd hit the jackpot. I don't know how much happier he can get when I tell him it's true." Donna was smiling in anticipation.

After work, Donna went home and knocked on the door to the upstairs. Mrs. Lasseret was busy cutting up vegetables for a stew and the smell of meat and garlic cooking filled the kitchen.

"You look all rosy-cheeked and happy, Donna. It must be this lovely January day. Wasn't it beautiful? I went for a walk—all by myself. Couldn't uproot Wally to go with me, though. There's always something on the TV that he can't possibly miss. I hope February is as nice, before the March and April winds and rain. I don't think I went out once last year in March except to shop and lots of times I just sent Wally." Mrs. Lasseret chattered on with Donna sitting dreamily on the kitchen stool thinking about many other things. Finally Mrs. Lasseret wiped her hands and said, "Well, now Donna, would you like a cup of tea?"

"I just came up to tell you that I'm pregnant and we're going to have a baby and I wondered if you minded." Donna blurted out.

"Minded? Of course not, dear. That's marvellous! Wally," she shouted, "Come out here and hear the good news." She stopped suddenly and said, "It is good news, isn't it? You and Rob?"

Donna nodded and Mrs. Lasseret smiled in relief. "I thought for a minute I might have jumped the gun."

Wally came into the kitchen wearing his slippers and an old sweater, the TV guide still in his hand. "Hello, Donna. I hope the good news is that I don't have to go shopping again."

"Guess who's having a baby," his wife said.

"Well, it's not you, I hope and it's not me, for sure, so that leaves you, Donna. The right age and the right glow—it's got to be you!" She nodded, smiling. "And Rob," he said, not asking and she nodded some more.

They congratulated her and patted her hand warmly, perhaps not as effusively as Phyllis, but with obvious affection.

"I thought I should tell you right away," Donna explained. "You told me you built it as a bachelor suite, and now there are two of us and with a baby... I thought you might not want us any more. So...."

"Oh, for goodness sakes!" Mrs. Lesseret fussed. "Did you think we would evict you just because you had a baby? Donna!" she ended with a scold. "But it is awfully small for two people and a baby. Babies take up a lot of room. You'd be surprised." She turned to Wally. "Wally, remember when we built it, we couldn't make it any bigger because our kids had so much junk stored in the basement?"

"Yeah," he agreed.

"Well, they've taken most of it now and what they haven't taken they obviously don't want so we'll call them or the Salvation Army.

Let's go look," she said, like a small general.

The other two trooped down into the basement after her.

"Now look," she said, "we can get rid of almost all this junk, knock out these shelves, build a wall about here and put a door in somewhere here into their room. Wally?"

Wally was looking around, doing some eyeball measuring and checking on wiring. "If it's going to be a bedroom it's got to have a window," he said.

"Well, you can put one in, can't you. Right about here. It'll face onto the driveway."

"Not in this weather," he protested.

"Wally, for heaven's sake! The baby's not due until when Donna?"

"September 21st,"

Wally smiled at her. "Oh, a couple of nails each day and I'll have it done by then," he said and turned to go back to his TV. He stopped on the stairs and said, "Of course, we'll have to talk about a rent increase sometime."

"We'll talk about that when the room is finished and when Rob gets out and gets a job and sees how much they can afford. They're going to have a lot of expenses before September the 21st." Wally had heard those firm tones of finality before and he shrugged and smiled at Donna and continued on up the stairs.

Donna and Mrs. Lesseret talked a little more about painting or wallpapering and a carpet and hoping Wally would remember some soundproofing in the ceiling so they wouldn't wake the baby. Then she excused herself saying she better finish getting dinner ready before the old bear growled. Donna smiled at the thought of Wally Lesseret growling about anything.

***

Marion's life had settled into a pattern that she was content with except that she had too little to keep her busy in the winter months. Her bridge group continued and provided her with the only real social exchange in the week. She was regretful that the short experience in volunteer work at the hospital had proved so embarrassing that she could not bring herself to try again. Instead, she went to Meals on Wheels and agreed to deliver on five days a week, excluding Thursdays and Sundays. A few of the people she delivered to were bright and chatty but she could spare only a few minutes to talk otherwise she would be late for the cranky ones. But she enjoyed it and the exercise of climbing in and out of the car and climbing stairs made her feel like she was keeping fit.

She and Craig dragged Edith's old bed and the rest of her childhood collections downstairs and rearranged the family room, which was never used these days, into a guest room. Craig ensconced himself in Edith's room with a second hand desk and a computer console which waited the arrival of a second hand computer he would buy from the company he was dealing with at work. He was spending more and more time upstairs with his Correspondence Course. He and his mother began to agree on certain television programs they liked to watch together and these plus the evening meal became the sum of their family social life. Always at the back of her mind was the wish that he would find a girl friend. If she mentioned it, always cautiously, he usually said something like, "Yeah, I've got to remember to phone one of these days and see if Lee is coming home for Easter Holidays." Craig's Sunday afternoons were sacrosanct. Nothing could disrupt his regularly scheduled visit to Rob. He told her that he wished his computer would hurry up and come and he would get a printer and start writing a weekly letter to Rob. "It's good practise for work too, you know," he assured her.

Edith's calls came routinely with updates on the twins, Harv's jobs and her own continuing saga with "the group." Marion wondered if Edith would ever be free of "the group". The topic always depressed her but more so when Edith continued at length about what had been discussed last week. She often wondered how long people could go on picking at the scabs of their childhood and exacerbating their wounds. Then she would sigh and try to turn to happier thoughts.

On Sunday, Craig phoned Donna. "Hi," he said. "What are you doing? I haven't talked to you all week."

"Oh, hi, Craig!" she replied, her voice full of bubble as if she were really happy to hear from him. "No, we haven't talked, have we? I picked up the phone to call you twice and each time I remembered you were either at your computer course of your Ec class. How are they going?"

"Okay, I guess. I'm doing pretty good at the computer course but the Ec course is a bitch! I have to read some things a half a dozen times before I understand what it's all about. It might as well be written in Chinese."

Donna laughed merrily at his grumpy frustration and he laughed along with her.

"Hey Craig, have you ever heard from Lee?"

"Nope! I called her house a couple of times but each time her father very politely tells me that any correspondence or telephone calls would not be in her best interests or something like that. In other words, bug off!"

"Oh, isn't that awful!" she commiserated. "She was so cute and you made a great couple. Why is her father like that?"

"I dunno. I guess it's a Chinese thing. Her mother goes back a hundred generations or something like that. Or maybe he thinks I will turn out like my father. Anyway, I called to see what time you were going out to see Rob today."

"Probably the same time. It gets me there about 3:30 and you're already gone. Why don't you stay a little longer and say hello to me today too?" Her voice was pleading but she was suppressing her giggles about the thought of what Rob was going to tell him. "I tell you what," she continued. "Let's go together—just this once, and surprise him."

"I don't know, Donna..."

"Please, Craig. I know that's not what we promised—but just this once, please."

"Okay, just this once, though. I don't want to kick any spokes in the wheels of your love life."

"Oh, Craig! You couldn't! Pick me up then?"

"Okay. Three o'clock?"

"Suits me. I'll be waiting. Kick any spokes in the wheels of my love life! Where'd you ever read that?"

"In my Ec text," he replied blandly.

"You did not!" she giggled. "You're getting as bad as Rob!"

She hung up the phone and sat down and wrote a long letter to her aunt in the Cariboo, planning to add to it after she got back from seeing Rob.

Craig picked her up at three and they walked to the gym together. "Do me one favour, Craig, please?" Donna asked. "Let me go in first for five minutes and Rob and I will come out and get you. Okay?"

"Okay, I guess," he said with a shrug.

"It's a surprise," she said. "We won't be long."

Rob saw her coming from his place where they usually sat. She was nodding and smiling and he let out a whoop of joy as he leaped over a row of benches to greet her. Their greeting was so long and passionate that some observers gave them some gentle applause.

"I got Craig to bring me out today. I wanted to see his face too, when you told him," Donna explained.

"You mean he's here?"

"Yes. He's waiting outside."

"Okay, let's go get him," Rob said taking her arm and rushing her to the exit.

It would have been an impossible call for anyone watching, to say which of the three was smiling the broadest when they found Craig waiting outside.

"C'mon, you guys," Rob said after the greetings were over. "It's nice out. Let's go for a walk around the gardens or go spit on pigs."

"What do you mean 'spit on pigs'?" Donna asked.

"Oh, we just go up to the pig pens and lean over the fence and all the little pigs come along to see if they are going to get a treat, I guess. Anyway, they stand there and look at you with their little piggy eyes and you can practise your spitting. You try to get them right between the eyes."

They walked three abreast around some garden paths with arms linked, until Craig couldn't stand some private joke between them any longer.

"So what's the big joke?" he said when they stopped beside a wishing well and the other two were still smiling.

"Okay, tell him, Rob," Donna said.

"Tell me what?" demanded Craig impatiently when Rob couldn't stop grinning.

"We're pregnant," he finally blurted out.

Craig looked at him blankly. "Who is?" he asked stupidly.

Both Donna and Rob burst out laughing and while Rob caught his breath, Donna said, "I am, dummy. Rob and I are going to have a baby."

It was the face they were waiting for. Craig stood looking from one to the other while puzzlement, doubt, perplexity and other emotions flickered across his face and then in a brilliant flash of understanding, he said, his face aglow, "Oh, you're going to have a baby."

There was more hugging and kissing and laughter.

Rob said, standing as tall as he could, "I'M going to be a father."

"And I'll get to be an uncle or something," Craig said. Then he asked suddenly, "Are you going to get married?"

"Of course," Rob said.

"Don't I get asked?" Donna put in pleadingly.

"I was going to do it properly: you know, me, all dressed up with clean fingernails, down on one knee with a bouquet and a ring and music playing, and you looking sweet and demure and as beautiful as you have ever looked, like right now. But I can't wait for the flowers and all that stuff. I got my best friend here as my witness." He took her hand and got down on one knee and said as sincerely as he had ever said anything in his life, "Donna, I love you. Will you marry me?"

"Oh, yes Rob! I will," she managed to say.

He got to his feet and took her in his arms and said only with great sincerity, "Thank you, Donna."

They held each other in a close embrace until Rob heard a snuffling behind him. "What are you crying about?" he asked Craig. "I can't help it," Craig answered.

"Well, come here then," and both he and Donna put out an arm and included him.

"I'll be your best man," Craig said.

"Maybe I'll ask somebody else."

"You do and you'll end up with two best men, only one will be a better best!"

"Let's go ask somebody about something. There must be some kind of rule, like in school," Rob said. And they wandered off, arm in arm, with Craig offering a mumbled portent, "I'll bet they got a dozen if not a hundred."

Arms entwined, they ambled back toward the gym and on the way saw someone coming out of the administration office Rob ran to catch him while the other two hurried.

"Sir!" Rob called and the man stopped until Rob caught up. "I wonder if you could give us some information. This is my fiancée and my best friend. I'm Robert Turner. I'm an inmate, but they are not. I guess you can tell that, can't you?"

The man nodded.

"We would like to get married but we don't know how. You know—the regulations and all that stuff. What do we have to do?"

"No problem," the man said after looking at them carefully. "When you set the date, you can reserve the little chapel for the ceremony, make arrangement with the nondenominational chaplain—he's here every Sunday morning. You can only get married on Sunday because that's the only time visitors are allowed. Maximum of six and that includes the minister. So, not counting the groom, you got the bride and her lady, the best man, the minister and a couple of parents usually. Don't forget the license. How old are you, by the way?"

"We're both nearly eighteen," Rob said.

"Well in that case you will need the consent of your parents or guardians. That's just the law, It's got nothing to do with this institution." He looked at three long faces. "Sorry, kids! Maybe it's a good thing—gives you time to think it over—make sure. That sort of thing." He looked at them sympathetically. "Anything else?"

"Oh, no sir. Thank you very much for your time." Rob said and the other two added their thanks as the man left.

"Good luck," he said. "But a word of advice if I may—you're young, don't rush it."

There was a minute of dead silence when the man left. "Well, shit!" was all Rob could manage.

"I told you that there would be a hundred rules. There always is," Craig said.

"I'm going to ask some questions tomorrow. Like phone city hall and a church or a marriage counselor. He could be wrong, you know!" Donna said through some sniffles.

They sat silently together on a low stone fence until Donna said, "Let's go inside, Rob. It's getting cold."

He got to his feet without answering and waited for her before starting away.

Craig did not move. He called out, "You gonna take the bus, Donna, or come home with me?"

"I'll take the bus," she called. "Bye!"

Rob turned and walked back to Craig, wrapped his long arms around him and while holding him firmly, pressed his chin against the top of Craig's head and wiggled it.

"Ouch! That hurts!" Craig said as Rob finally released him and turned back to Donna.

"See ya, buddy!" he called over his shoulder.

On his way home, Craig recalled again, with all the details and with shame mixed with gratification, his night with Donna. It bothered him to think of it and he tried to push it out of his mind whenever it popped in, because he hated the thought of having cheated on his best friend. Nothing, he told himself, not even torture, would make him admit to anyone what he had done. He also recalled the overwhelming feeling of relief he had felt, when in the next few days or so Donna did not take him aside and tell him she was pregnant. Everything he had heard in Social Studies about sex and procreation seemed to have slipped through the cracks.

As for Donna, whenever she thought of that night with Craig, she smiled privately. What made her smile was the recollection of Craig's delightful virginal naivety. So sure she was of the birth control techniques she routinely used that she never gave even casual thought to the possibility of a pregnancy.

CHAPTER 74

February barged in and stayed, not welcomed with open arms by anyone. With the exception of two days in the middle of the month when the sun shone in a cloudless sky and the wind was gentle the rest of the month was a parade of drizzling rain, frost, icy roads and brooding skies. Sudden and brutally cold overnight frosts trapped the ducks in the ice of the ponds in Stanley Park. The squirrels and raccoons raided anything edible that was left unattended while the brave winter pansies continued to defy the elements and display the only colour in the gardens. Pedestrians were treated to long choruses of screaming summer tires as grim-jawed and unprepared commuters, pressing ever harder on the accelerator, fish-tailed their way to traffic-clogging stops. And then February suddenly ended. The skies turned blue and gloves and toques and scarves were shed. The mounds of muddy snow, ploughed onto the sides of streets, melted and flooded the gutters just in time for the weekend and for a howling low front from the Arctic to embrace another moisture laden low from the Pacific directly over Vancouver and shut down the city under a two foot blanket of glistening snow. Giant trees crashed over power lines and telephone lines and freckled the city with huge areas of darkness and silence. City transit was immobilized. People struggled to their nearest open store on skis and snow shoes pulling ancient toboggans resurrected from the garage. For a time it was a city of neighbours. Then the snow began to melt again and the streets flooded as the drains plugged. Exasperated citizens in the dark and silent pockets of the city tormented themselves with the uncertain knowledge that the power and phone companies had rushed in overtime to repair the facilities where city officials lived and had now returned to their normal practice of three men watching one man working. It seemed to the cold and bureaucratically disenchanted that everybody else was scheduled for service first.

On Saturday, Craig put chains on and tried out some local streets. He decided he could make it to New Starts on Sunday if it didn't snow again. On Sunday morning he drove out without too much difficulty and found only two other cars, both four-wheel drives, in the parking lot. Nobody was expecting visitors on such a miserable day, and although Rob was overwhelmed by Craig's visit, he seemed lethargic and morose. He was so preoccupied with his own thoughts that many times he didn't hear what Craig was saying as Craig chattered on trying to jumpstart Rob out of his doldrums. There had been only a half dozen visitors the previous weekend, the telephone lines were still down and a sullen mood seemed to prevail within the institution. Rob and Craig left their usual meeting spot and went to a warmer corner to talk but it was more public and they were interrupted frequently as other inmates approached with requests to Craig to give someone a call as soon as he got home. He collected more than a dozen scribbled messages to transmit. Finally, after a few long silences, Craig announced that he had better get going and Rob got to his feet without protesting his friend's decision and walked to the door with him. At the door, he clapped Craig on the shoulder, said "See ya," and walked away in the direction of his dorm without another word.

When Craig got home, he started immediately phoning the list of people he had been given at New Starts. Some of the phones were not in service, but when he did get through, after introducing himself and passing the message, he was faced with a lot of questions he couldn't answer: How did he look? Did he say anything about when he might get out? Is he still living in that same dorm with those guys who could hardly speak English? Finally he was finished and leaned back with a sigh of relief feeling the same sense of gloom he sensed in other people.

He phoned Donna as he promised. Her phone rang a lot of times before she answered it breathlessly. "Oh, hi!" she said happy to hear from him, the first bright sound he had heard all day. "I was upstairs playing cards with Mrs. Lasseret. Our power's off but they have a gas fireplace so we've been sitting around with blankets around us, playing cards and talking. Big storm, eh? Wally's just about going nuts without his TV." She giggled. "I wonder how Rob's doing."

"Oh, he's okay. I drove out to see him this morning."

"You did? Wally's got a battery radio and he heard that all the highways were closed and nobody was going nowhere."

"Well, I didn't have any trouble," Craig said. "But I had chains on and it's a little car and it sorta goes over the drifts instead of ploughing through them. Anyway, there were only two other cars that made it and I collected a bunch of numbers to phone because the phone lines are down out there, too."

"Well, aren't you a nice guy!" she said.

"Yeah," he agreed blandly.

"So how was Rob? Happy to see you?" she asked.

He lied to her, not telling her that Rob was flat and moody and quickly started asking her questions about getting a marriage license to get off the subject of Rob.

"God, it's hard to get through to some of these government offices," she said. "The phone rings and rings, twenty times I'll bet, and then the girl on the switchboard puts you through to the wrong office and they hang up and disconnect you and you have to start all over again. I'll bet I spent my whole break trying to get through to some dumb bugger who was eating his lunch or something and talked with his mouth full so I had to make him say everything twice. And you know what I said to one guy, oh, I shouldn't have said it," she prattled on. "Any way I was asking him about getting parental permission to get married and if there was any way around it. And he said that, maybe, if there was an emergency, you wouldn't need it. And I asked him what kind of an emergency, and he said, 'Well, like your mother was dying'. And I said, 'Hell, that wouldn't be an emergency—that would be my wedding present' and he didn't say anything and I started laughing and I had to hang up."

They laughed together, talked some more until Donna said, "I'm going to go back up to the fireplace. It's cold down here."

"Okay, Donna. See you soon."

"You always say that, but soon is a long time for you."

"Okay," he laughed. "I'll be sooner."

"Good! I love you. Goodbye!" She hung up.

He sat in the chair by the telephone trying to think what he wanted to do next. His mother was napping and reading alternately on the sofa in the living room with the gas fireplace blazing comfortably. He didn't feel like going upstairs to study. He didn't want to have an afternoon nap. He didn't want to continue with his project of cleaning up junk in the basement and garage. He wasn't even hungry. Putting on his jacket and snow boots again, he went outside, closing the door carefully so as not to wake his mother, and started walking.

Without thinking, he found himself ringing the Turner's doorbell and stopped just before he had automatically opened the door and shouted. Then he remembered Roger and his bad leg so he did open the door and shout, "Hello, anybody home. It's me, Craig."

Roger's voice came back. "Hey, Craig! Come on in. I'm downstairs."

Craig slipped out of his snow boots and went down the stairs to find Roger sprawled out on an easy chair reading with his leg up on a stool. "Hi," he said, "I was in the neighbourhood and wondered if you had got snowed in."

"Great to see you, Craig! Take off your coat and sit down. Want a beer?"

Craig shook his head. "No, thanks. How're you doing? I mean with the shop and your leg and everything."

"Okay I think, so far. Maybe just lucky. I found somebody to help out in the shop and turns out he knows ten times as much as I do, and you remember, it really is a one man operation most of the time, so I turn him loose and he loves it. He retired too soon and misses work—can you imagine?. I sit around on my butt and try to look business-like if anybody comes in. Allen Singh's his name, Allen Bandra Singh. Nice man."

"You got a new cast—a smaller one, I see," Craig said.

"Yeah, it makes it easier to get around. I can drive the car but I can't use the brake pedal so I have to use the handbrake. The sudden stops scares the shit out of tailgaters," he said with a big laugh. "But I can get out to eat. My home cooking is getting worse and it was bad to begin with." He found himself carrying the conversation. "I was going to go out this morning but I stepped outside and slipped and caught the handrail just in time or I would have been ass over teakettle like that," snapping his fingers. "So I smartened up and came back inside."

"Yeah, it was rough out this morning. I went out to see Rob, but I put chains on and went very cautiously."

"Well, how's Rob doing?" Roger asked, thinking finally he's going to talk about Rob.

And Craig did, with detail and shining eyed enthusiasm.

"Pregnant! Really?" Roger said when Craig reached that part of his review.

"Yeah, really!" Craig said. "And are they ever happy. Both of them. Rob was jumping-up-and-down happy!" He sat grinning at the recollection.

"Jesus, they're young, aren't they?"

"Yeah, I guess." Craig shrugged. "But old enough to make a baby."

Roger shook his head, frowning about something.

"Robbie's older'n me," Craig said soberly. "Seven days older," and then he laughed at himself for saying such a silly thing seriously.

Roger changed the subject suddenly. "And how are you doing, without your closest and best buddy."

"Oh, I'm doing okay. I'm taking an upgrading course in computers—the company's putting me through that, and I'm doing a course in Economics by correspondence for high school credit. I'll need another one, maybe two—one will be English—next fall. That'll be all I need if I get credit for this Computer course."

"How do you like Ec?" Roger asked.

"It's a bastard! I tell you!" Craig said, sitting up and hitting his knee. "I have to make myself like it or I'll never get through it. This guy can't say anything simple—he has to say it in the most round-about, complicated way. I mean the guy who wrote the book—I'm doing it by correspondence. He uses words I bet he makes up sometimes to make it seem so difficult that only he can under-stand. Pompous! That's the word I was trying to think of when I was mad at him last night. Pompous! Fits him exactly."

Roger had started chuckling long before Craig had reached his dramatic climax, and now he roared with laughter.

"Well, he is!" Craig insisted defensively, while laughing with Roger.

Roger's thoughts had gone far beyond the puzzle of Economics authors. "No wonder you two have such fun together," he said.

"Who?" Craig asked and then answered himself. "Oh, you mean me and Rob."

"Yeah," Roger said quietly and reflectively. "Me and Rob,"

"Well," Craig said, getting up to his feet after a minute of silence. "I guess I better get going. Maybe I can get through another chapter before the power goes off. A lot of the whole lower mainland is out, you know. We're lucky."

"I guess we are," Roger agreed. "Thanks for dropping in. I was getting stir-crazy. Do it again."

"Sure," Craig said and started up the stairs. He stopped half-way. "Anything I can do? Shopping or anything?"

"No, but I'll remember the offer. Oh, you can give my, regards, I guess is the word, to Rob when you see him."

"Sure," Craig replied. And Roger heard him thump into his snow boots and go out the door.

As Craig turned the corner, he saw a police car stop in front of his house and two policemen get out. He hurried and reached the house before they could get up the steps and ring the bell. "Can I help you?" he called.

"Who are you?" one asked.

"Craig Williams—I live here."

"Good!" the other one said. "We were looking for you."

"Why?" Craig's voice reverted to a childish treble. "What did I do." A dozen possibilities raced through his mind, none of them rational.

"You went out to New Haven this morning, didn't you? May I ask who you were visiting?"

"My friend, Rob Turner. Is he in trouble?"

"No, no," one of them said after looking at his notebook. "Three boys walked away this morning. Turner wasn't one of them. Did you happen to see three boys on the road or give them a lift?"

"No," Craig answered relieved that they were not looking for Rob. "I didn't see anybody that I remember. Nobody was hitching, I don't think, or I would have picked them up. There was a lot of snow, you know."

"Yeah, we know," the other one said. "Mind if we look at your car?"

"No, it's in the garage." He turned and walked quickly to the garage with the two officers following.

They all went in and Craig turned on the light. "There!" he said. "It's not locked."

One of the officers went to the car, opened the back door, took of his glove and felt the floor mats. He closed the door and came back to the door. "Thanks for your cooperation, Craig," he said. "And just a word of caution: it's a good idea to keep your car locked even in your own garage."

They turned to go and Craig called, "How did you know I was out there this morning?"

"A guard gave us your license number," one replied. "Thanks again."

He watched them drive away.

"They were police! What did they want?" his mother said in a voice of panic as soon as he opened the door.

He told her quickly why they had come. "Oh, thank goodness that's all!" she said with sigh of relief. "I saw their car and the two of them get out and it was suddenly just like they came and told me about your father. I think my heart must have stopped when I thought it was about you and then I saw you and I didn't know what to think." She sat down and fanned her face. "Oh, my!" she said a couple of times. Then, "Where did you go? You were here one minute and gone the next."

"I had to go for a walk. And you know, it was the funniest thing. I kinda just walked automatically over to Rob's without thinking and rang the bell and nearly walked in. Then I had to open the door and call just so Roger wouldn't have to come to the door. Anyway, he called to come in and we sat around and yakked about a lot of things. Nice guy!" he added in spite of his earlier reservations.

"How does he ever manage in this weather?" she worried.

"He says he's driving but he can't use the foot brake so he uses the parking brake and scares tailgaters with sudden stops," Craig reported, laughing at the thought. "And he says his home cooking is getting worse instead of better."

"Oh, Craig, phone him up and invite him over for dinner. Would you like to do that? We've got lots for three. Do you think he'd like to come?"

"There's one way to find out," Craig said and went to the telephone. "I don't think he has changed the number yet," he called over is shoulder.

"Hey, Roger! My mom says if you're lonely and hungry and tired of your own cooking then come on over for dinner. How about it?"

He paused and listened. "Sure I'm sure," he said. "And you can just come as you are—just like family. We don't dress for dinner," he added laughing. He listened again, then said, "Tell you what, Rog. It's pretty slippery out. So stay there and I'll be right over and give you a shoulder to hang onto so you don't slip and break your neck. Okay? See you in five minutes, then."

He went back to the kitchen and said, "He said he'd love to." He wriggled into his coat again and stomped into his snow boots. "I'm going over and watch that he doesn't slip and hurt himself. It's very icy out."

She smiled at the good Samaritan as he went out again.

Craig rang the bell and opened Roger's door and shouted, "It's me, Rog. Ready when you are!"

He picked up the snow shovel and scraped the snow off the steps and the sidewalk. A narrow strip in the middle of the sidewalk in front of the house had been cleared. "Who shovelled your sidewalk? You?" he asked when Roger came out wearing one snow boot and a wool stocking over his cast.

"No way!" Roger replied. "A couple of young kids took me on that job. I paid them before they started and they took off after doing that much."

"That's an old game Rob and I used to pull. It's best not to do it around where you live," Craig said in an almost advisory tone.

"I'll try to remember," Roger replied laughing.

Roger started slowly down the steps. Craig threw down the shovel and rushed over. "Careful!" he warned.

"Now, I'll tell you what we'll do," he said when Roger was safely down. "We can't walk down that narrow path so we'll go on the road. You put your arm around my shoulder and hang on tight, then you'll have me and a good leg and cane and that should get us there. It's slippery so watch out."

With Craig careful shepherding, they managed the five houses to the corner and the next six houses to Craig's front door without a major mishap. Marion had watched for their arrival and opened the door. She put out a hand to help Roger and Craig said quickly, "I've got him, mother. He's fine."

Once inside, Roger withdrew a bottle of wine from his deep jacket pocket. "It's white wine, Marion, and it was cold. I don't think it got warm on the way over."

"Thank you, Roger," Marion said with a welcoming smile. "That was thoughtful of you. I'll put it in the frig anyway."

With jackets and three snow boots off, Craig relinquished his caretaking responsibilities. Marion did some things in preparation for dinner while Roger and Craig talked, mostly about their common denominator, Rob. It was Marion's suggestion that they delay dinner until after the six o'clock news. They listened to a long series of accidents and storm related problems, saw serious faced officials promising immediate rectification, and sat in sudden concerned silence as the announcer said that the police were searching for three juveniles who had walked out of the New Starts Correctional Institute today. Their names could not be released because of their age. None were considered to be dangerous.

Craig was immediately on his feet, his face set with concern. "He wouldn't, would he, Mom?" he asked her, only to confirm a certainty in his own mind. "He wouldn't be so stupid."

"No, I'm certain he wouldn't. He knows it would just make things more difficult for him," his mother said.

Craig flicked off the TV and paced. "But when I was out there today, he seemed like he wasn't really glad to see me, you know. Like he had something on his mind. Mostly he just sat and grunted while I talked and I kept thinking something was wrong, like maybe he was sick or he had got into trouble and didn't want to tell me."

"There isn't anything Rob wouldn't tell you, Craig. You know that. He might have been just feeling down in the dumps because of the place and the weather—that sort of thing," his mother replied. "How about turning the TV back on to get the weather and maybe Roger would like to catch up on the sports in the civilized part of this country."

"Oh, sure Mom. Sorry!" he said. He turned on the set and sat down again, his face still set with concern.

"Well, that doesn't look so bad," Marion said when the weather report was over. "You two watch the sports and I'll finish getting dinner. We'll eat in the kitchen if that's okay with you, Roger."

"Fine with me, Marion. Thanks for not fussing," Roger replied.

"Sure! Put your elbows on the table and slurp your soup," Craig put in, emerging for a moment from his preoccupation with Rob's possible troubles. Then he added, "Rob's a terrible slurper—he dribbles," and laughed at the thought.

While Marion was in the kitchen, Roger said quietly to Craig, "You're pretty sure Rob wouldn't be one of the three, are you?"

"Yeah, I'm sure, I think. Anyway he would have told me. And if he had, I would have just sat on him until he smartened up. So it can't be him." That seemed to put QED to Craig's problem and they went out to the kitchen.

They had a pleasant quiet dinner that Roger appreciated and complimented graciously. They talked of Roger's growing up in Toronto, of his private school education, his travels and other casual things without once returning to the topic of Rob. Marion had asked Roger to pour the wine and when he had uncorked it, squeezed the cork, sniffed it and tasted it, Craig said, somewhat bluntly, "My dad told me you're supposed to read the cork to see if it matches the label. That way you can tell if it was bottled 'en maison'."

Roger smiled and handed Craig the cork. "Quite a connoisseur, your father," he said.

Craig made a 'hmph' sound with such disdain and Marion's face turned suddenly as cold as the outside, so Roger quickly decided to abandon that topic of conversation.

After dinner, like a regular family, they laughed through the antics of people on Home Videos while trying to forgive the Saget's interminable cuteness, challenged each other to responses in 'Jeopardy' and agreed that Alex Trebek was the best host in television.

Then Roger thanked them for a pleasant evening, complimented Marion again, and accepted Craig's determined need to give him a shoulder home.

At his door, Roger asked, "Want to come in and talk for a while? Have a game of crib?"

But Craig, still casually wary because of what he had seen at the New Year's Eve party, said, "No, I don't think so, Rog—but thanks. Maybe another time. I should go stick my nose in that goddam Ec text. See ya again. Goodnight."

Roger stayed standing in the doorway. "I meant to ask you, Craig, if you would ask Rob the next time you go if it would be okay if I dropped out to see him. And if he says okay, ask him what time would be good."

"Sure! I'll ask him."

"Maybe we could go out together."

"You'll be out of your cast and driving any day now," Craig responded as he left, which Roger interpreted as Craig having no intentions of sharing his time with Rob with anybody.

Inside, Roger stopped at the top of the stairs and called to the light he had left on in the basement, "Hello, down there! Welcome home!" just in case Rob had been one of the three and remembered where the house key was still hidden.

CHAPTER 75

The next Sunday, Craig arrived early, a half hour before their usual agreed time of meeting. He went into the gym and sat in the bleachers where they always met and watched the entrance carefully. He saw Rob saunter in early but he stopped to horse around with a couple of guys who were also waiting for their visitors until he glanced into the gym and saw Craig. A great grin spread over his face as he left the group and walked rather than sauntered over to Craig, who was mirroring his smile but with a background of concern on his face.

"Hey Buddy! Good to see you," Rob said as they gave each other the briefest of hugs, the most they permitted in this public place. "What have you been up to?"

Craig didn't answer the question that was asked. He had other things on his mind. "Up to? I'll tell you what I was up to. Sitting on pins and needles waiting for this day to see if you were one of those three guys who ran away last week and knowing you wouldn't go home or to my place because those are the first places they would look for you."

"What the hell are you talking about?" Rob said with a phoney distressed look on his face. "Me? Run away from this place?"

"Well, it could have been you. Just like you to do a thing like that. But there was no way of knowing because they wouldn't give out names. Shit, you had me worried. Last Sunday, when I was here you acted like you were in another world. You hardly heard a thing I said to you. That's why I thought it might have been you and you didn't want me to know."

"Oh, that!" Rob said dismissively, "I was just pissed off with the weather knowing that Donna wouldn't be able to come. But then she wrote me a letter and it got here Wednesday."

"Well, that's okay then," Craig said as if he were passing some sort of paternal approval.

"But I'll tell you something," Rob said, and continued, partly to tease but mostly because he had always told Craig everything, "I was planning to walk that day but I didn't want you to know. And it was hard not telling you. And then I did walk out when it started to get dark but I didn't get far because I could just hear you yakking and yakking at me for being so stupid... so I turned around and got back in time and nobody saw me."

Craig leaped to his feet facing Rob, his face red with anger, his mouth trying to say something. Finally in almost a shriek, he shouted "YOU STUPID ASSHOLE!" and smacked Rob across the head with an open handed blow and stood glaring down at him. Some other groups of visitors nearby stopped talking and looked but saw Rob laughing hilariously and holding an arm up to protect his head in case another smack was forthcoming.

Craig sat down and slouched low in his seat. "Idiot!" he said, breathing deeply and snorting.

"I know," Rob agreed.

"Goddam idiot!"

"You betcha."

Then they were laughing.

After a silence, Craig said, "Roger was over for dinner last Sunday. Mom invited him."

"Good. How's his leg?"

"He got a new cast. He's driving and he wants me to ask you if you would like him to come out and see you."

Rob was beaming with pleasure. "Sure I would. That would be great. He's a great guy. Did he say when?"

"No, he just said to tell him a time and he'd come."

"Okay, just tell him if he can tear himself away from old lady thumb and her four daughters, then late in the morning next Sunday would be great. Yeah," he mused. "It'll be great to see him. I guess we've got a lot to talk about." Then, seeing Craig's deliberately uninterested face, he changed the subject. "Stay here," he said. "I've got something to show you." He walked quickly out of the gym.

Craig sat looking around at other groups, glad that he was alone with Rob instead of being one of a bunch of visitors. His mother said she would like to come sometime and maybe bring a picnic when the weather got better. He was still thinking about her idea when Rob got back carrying a file folder and a paper bag.

"Look at these," he said proudly, opening the folder and displaying many sheets of beautifully scripted writing in a wide variety of styles. "Neat, eh?" he asked.

"Yeah!" agreed Craig enthusiastically. "I didn't know you could do that."

"I'm just learning," Rob said, pleased and a little embarrassed. "And look at these," he continued pulling some wrapped black and white blocks out of the bag.

"What are they?" Craig asked.

"They're slabs of wax and I paint them black and I practise carving in them. See! White carving on a black background. Isn't that neat? Then when I'm finished practising I just scrape it off and paint it black and start again. And I'm making a thing like a sideways guillotine. It's the size of a block of wax and you put some paper on the bottom that's just as thick as the carving was deep so you can scrape it off even."

Craig was looking at him without any clear idea of what he was talking about. "Come on, Craig!" Rob teased. "If you can understand a computer, you certainly should be able to understand this." He went over it again until the great "I see" light went on as the blond head and the black head bent together over scribbled drawings.

"Or you could make a thing like a wood plane that wouldn't even have to be adjustable. And you'd just pull it across to take off an even surface, or twice or three times if the letters were cut deep," Craig said enthusiastically.

"Yeah, that's way better than my other idea. I thought if you just scraped the paint off with a paint scraper like I do now, you could put it in the oven and let it melt into a nice smooth surface. But I guess it would have to be made out of metal if you do that." They sat puzzling some more until Rob said, "You know what? My instructor said I should patent it."

"I'd bet you'd make a fortune," Rob's best supporter declared.

"Now what scheme are you guys cooking up," a voice said.

They looked up to find Donna standing in front of them. She had walked in, seen them in the stands and walked quietly to them and stood watching them, feeling almost jealous of the all but visible bond that bound them together.

"Donna!" they said simultaneously, leaping to their feet.

Rob took a long time greeting her, this time without concern for onlookers. Craig eventually got to say hello and got his hug and gentle kiss. Then goodbyes were said and they watched Craig walk across the gym floor to the exit with a bouncy step and a private smile.

"He looks like he got a good shot of Rob today," Donna said.

"Yeah, we had fun."

Craig drove home in the late afternoon sun, for the first time seeing the crocuses in the border of flower beds, and clumps of daffs full out on the south facing walls of some homes. Even the forsythia was turning colour. He smiled as he remembered the family story of him asking his mother about the handful of cuttings she had brought into the house to force.

"That's forsythia," she had told him.

"Who's Sythia?" he asked.

When he turned into the garage, his mother was just coming in with an armful of tools, red-cheeked and muddy from her first day in her garden.

"Hi!" he greeted her. "How's your garden and how's the forsythia?"

"Oh, it's coming along—any day now," she answered.

"That's nice. She'll be pleased."

"Who?" she asked.

"Sythia!"

She remembered and smiled and they laughed gently together as he put an arm around her while they walked the few steps to the house.

CHAPTER 76

April doesn't arrive in Vancouver as much as it suddenly explodes in a tumult of colours all over the city. In parks, in private gardens, along the boulevards, bulbs burst forth, shrubs push out their buds for a later display and flowering trees wave their colours over the sidewalks of the city.

The grounds of New Starts were, as the nearby community agreed again this year, even more beautiful this year than they had ever been. On weekdays the grounds were dotted with the figures of young men, mostly shirtless, pruning, edging, mowing and transplanting yet more flowers from the greenhouses. On Sundays few visitors stayed in the gym. Most found sunny places on the lawn where blankets were laid and folding chairs placed, while others sought benches that ringed the shade trees. Rob and Donna preferred to walk. They walked on the paths through the gardens, they visited the chickens, they poked their noses into the greenhouses, they explored the perimeters of the institution and, sticking their heads over the casual fences, argued about whether the air of freedom on the other side smelled fresher. They stopped occasionally and rested on a raised border. They were too young to need a rest after a gentle stroll but there was a need for closeness not possible while strolling and a frequent need for Rob to place his hand on a slightly swollen belly and wonder what it would be and what they would call it.

Donna had missed very few visiting days. On Friday, her aunt and uncle had arrived from the Cariboo for the weekend and she did not leave them in order to visit Rob nor did she want to take them with her. She called Craig on Saturday so that he could tell Rob she wouldn't be going out to see him on Sunday. Then Craig told her that Rob's mother had just arrived from Prince George and that, it was planned that tomorrow he would take her and his mother out to see Rob. After he and his mother had a visit with Rob, they would leave Rob's mother with him while they drove around to a nursery to buy some plants and come back for her in an hour.

"Roger is going out in the morning to see Rob, so I'll go over and tell him what the schedule is and he can tell Rob before we get there," Craig said.

"OK, general!" Donna said. "You're in charge. I hope somebody is keeping the minutes." She told Craig to give Rob a big kiss for her and he told her to mail it. "Chicken!" she said and hung up. He deliberately didn't tell her that Rob's father hadn't come because he had a conference or something.

I better go over and tell Roger right now so he can tell Rob first thing when he gets there, Craig told himself and headed out to see Roger.

He rang the bell, stuck his head in and called.

"Come in, Craig. We're down here," Roger yelled.

Downstairs, Roger was sitting down with his leg on a stool.

"Hi, Roger. How does it feel to have that thing off?" Craig asked.

"It should feel great but after a week it still hurts like hell when I walk and I'm supposed to walk a lot. How's your world these days?"

"It's okay, busy," Craig said and looked casually at Roger's visitor who was sitting on the sofa with his shoes off and his feet tucked under him.

"Tommy," Roger said. "This is a friend of mine, Craig Williams. He lives down the street. Craig, Tommy."

Craig walked over and put out his hand which was grasped limply. "Nice to meet you," he said.

"Likewise, I'm sure," was the response in a soft voice.

"Are you going out to see Rob tomorrow?" Craig asked turning to Roger.

"Yes, I was planning to," Roger replied. "Why?"

"I just wanted you to give a message to Rob because you'll see him first. Donna won't be going out tomorrow because her aunt came down to see her, and Rob's mother arrived and I'm going to take her and my mom out to see him, but we're going to be there at least a half an hour earlier than I usually arrive so he can have a good visit with his mother." Craig looked closely at Roger to see if he had got the message straight.

"I guess I can remember all that," he said. "That will be a nice surprise for Rob—not the Donna message, though." He paused. "Sit down and have a beer."

"Not today, thanks. I've got a few things to do. Nice to meet you, Tom."

"Yeah."

"See you around, Craig," Roger said.

When Craig reached the top of the stairs and turned for the door, he heard the conversation below.

"I suppose that's your new boy." Soft and cattily.

"Oh, Tommy! For God's sake!" with impatience obvious.

"We-l-l!" petulantly.

He closed the door, saying to himself, "Oh, for God's sake."

Earlier, in the middle of March, Roger had arrived for a visit. Rob was expecting him and was waiting at the door for the little red Porsche to drive into the parking lot. He was out to meet him before Roger struggled out of the car. They were both delighted to see each other and the embrace was long and tight.

"You look great!" Roger said. "You must have put on a few pounds."

"Yes, I have," Rob agreed. "I started to work out in the gym as soon as I got here to protect myself against—-, you know. Hell, I wasn't going to let myself get caught in some of the things I heard goes on in these places. And I didn't, but there's not much of that stuff here anyway, not that I can see. Oh, one of the guys got caught giving a blow job to one of the guards in the hay loft last week." He laughed. "The catch word now is 'Hey! Meet me in the hayloft'."

"So you're still pure, eh?" Roger said with a leeriest grin.

"Well, I wouldn't say I'm exactly virginal. I am going to be a father, you know." Rob grinned back.

"I know," Roger said flatly, looking away.

Rob cocked an eye at the tone and said nothing.

They limped into the warmth of the gym. "I'm getting this damn cast off this week," Roger said as they settled into some seats and he struggled to get his leg comfortable.

"That's great," Rob said. "You'll be able to ski, and dance and probably play the violin."

Roger gave a grunting chuckle at the old joke. "All the doc said was, when it comes off, start walking and don't stop. It was a double fracture and walking is good for it, I guess. I was thinking of picking up my golf clubs again but none of the guys I know play golf—afraid they'll break a fingernail or something." He was quiet for a minute. "Do you play?" he asked.

"No, not me," Rob replied. "A few times with Craig. He played a lot more. Tried out for the school team. I stuck to basketball. Hey, why don't you ask him? He can hit a hell of a ball. He's compact, you know, and he just plants his feet and swings. He looks like an old farmer pitching rocks at crows, but when he connects he sends it 250 yards straight as an arrow."

"Maybe I'll check with him," Roger said not very enthusiastically. "You sure you don't want to?"

"Well, my movements are rather restricted at the moment, you know," Rob said with a grin.

"I know. I mean after you get out."

"I don't know, I just don't know what I'll be doing."

"I thought you were coming back and work with me."

"We talked about it but I didn't think it was settled." Rob replied.

"Well, I sure as hell did. That's why I only hired Allen until you got back," Roger exclaimed.

"Great! Roger," Rob said sticking out his hand. "I'm sure happy about that. I was thinking it might be tough to get a job that would support a wife and child." He stopped. "Oh, yes. I should ask. Same deal as before for overtime and holidays?"

"You bet. But there might not be as much overtime as soon as I can get around better."

"Well, better not rush it, Rog," Rob said with mock concern.

This Sunday when Roger arrived, his cast was off and he was walking cautiously with a cane. Rob came out to greet him and they walked along the garden paths together in the morning sunshine.

"I'm the bearer of good news and bad news today," he said, "from Craig."

"Oh, I know that old joke," Rob said half seriously. "Give the bad news first."

"Okay. Bad news. Craig is coming half an hour early."

"That's bad news?"

"Now the good news. He's bringing your mother and his mother."

"Oh, great!" Rob enthused. "My dad, too?"

"Craig didn't say."

"Is that the bad news?"

"No, the bad news is that Donna can't come today. Her aunt and uncle are in town," he ended lamely.

Rob's face clouded. "This visiting system is the shits," he declared and walked on inattentively, staring into space. In a moment he took a deep breath and said, "Oh, well, there was some good news, too. Is that enough walking for you?" he asked as Roger stopped and rubbed his leg.

"No, I'm fine. It hurts but that's supposed to be good for all those muscles I haven't been using. No pain, no gain. That's what that sadist doctor tells me." They walked on. "I was wondering, Rob, about your printing. Is it good enough yet, that you could get started on wedding announcements and births and things like that? There's a big market for hand printed things—snob appeal or whatever, but it pays big bucks." He paused while Rob stopped walking and thought. "I'll tell you what. I'll bring you out some blanks and some samples and you give it a try and we'll go from there. Have you got enough pens and whatever else you need."

"Yeah, that's a great idea," he said with a big happy smile. "I'll tell you what the first one will be. It will say," waving his hand in the air: 'Robert Turner and Donna Penser wish to announce to all their friends and relatives that they were married on such and such a date in lots of time for the baby.. Only lavish gifts of exquisite taste with price tags attached can be accepted. A birth announcement will follow eminently.' How do you like that?" He was laughing with his fist raised shoulder high.

"I'd like it better with 'imminently," Roger said.

"Oh, is there a difference?"

"You can bet your baby's bootees there's a difference!"

"No sir! No sirree! This daddy's not going around betting his baby's bootees on anything. And you can bet your own bootees on that!"

By this time they had walked around a patch of lawn and garden that fringed the visitor's car park.

"Rog, can I ask a favour?"

"Shoot! Anything," Roger replied.

"Mind if I cut our visit short. I got so caught up on practising my engraving that I didn't have time to shave and shower and change, and I would really like to be looking spiffy when my mother arrives."

"So you're asking me to bugger off, are you?" And the smile said no offence was taken. The walk to the car continued.

"Thanks, Roger. Thanks for coming. It means a lot," Rob said as Roger opened the door.

"You'd be surprised how much it means to me," Roger answered and he put out his arms and held Rob for two long and shaky breaths.

"Couldn't Dad come?" Rob asked his mother after a long hug and some tears.

"Robbie, he wanted to, really he did. But the head office wanted him to make up the time he took off for your trial and he did. Then what with getting settled into a new house, there was a thousand things to do and he was getting desperately tired. Then last week they got a monstrous order from Montreal and everybody went on overtime until it's finished. It's all political stuff and there will probably be more. He's sorry, he really is. He sends his love."

Marion was watching Rob's face as Claudia talked. She couldn't decide whether he was trying to hide anger or disappointment. Whatever emotion it was, it disappeared when he turned to greet her, his face now alive with delight in seeing her. "U.U.! My love!" came the old familiar salute with arms outstretched that brought tears to her eyes. "I thought you had forsaken me."

"Oh, Robbie," was all she could manage for the moment as she held him tight and then tighter when he made a move to end the embrace.

Finally she released him. "There!" she said. "That makes up for some of it."

Craig was watching in total approval and over their shoulders he saw Bev and Richard standing in the parking lot looking lost. He left quickly and called to them. Bev rushed towards him and then saw Rob and her mother and plunged through the hedge that bordered the lot and flung herself at her brother without a word.

"Well, hello there, preggie!" he said as he held her close.

"Hello yourself!" she said as she reached out a free hand to Richard. "That's the first hug I've had from you since I stopped tucking you in."

"That's because you stopped paying me for hugging you," he teased.

"Where's Donna?" she asked, looking around. Rob explained her absence, and the family talk started. Bev and Richard had left their child sleeping in the care of the twelve year old next door so they talked first and fast and rushed their goodbyes. Craig and his mother left quietly to do her shopping, leaving Rob and his mother sitting on a bench under a tree, holding hands.

"Oh, Robbie," she said again. "You look so well! You're brown already."

"Hard work, hard play, good food and lots of sleep," he said. "But tell me, mother o' mine. How come you're grey all of a sudden."

"There's nothing sudden about it," she exclaimed. "I just stopped dyeing."

"You? Dyeing? Moth-er! How could you! Deceitful wench!"

"Oh, Robbie! You knew!" she said and watching his sly smile, started to weep. "Oh, Rob, I do miss your silliness! I don't think anybody laughs in Prince George."

They talked about the institution, about the other inmates, his dorm, his hobby, his workouts in the gym, his plans to go back to work for Roger, about Donna and the baby and about when he would be getting out.

"July 7th is the end of six months," he told her. "Maybe one month or even six weeks sooner if I've been good. June 7th if I've just been good, but May 24th if I've been really, really good."

"And have you been really, really good?" she asked, smiling.

"Cross my heart," he said and made that awful pretend raking-up-a-gob and spitting thing that she hated. Then he said, "Maybe except for one thing. Me and another guy were horsing around and one of the guards thought we were fighting. He told us to shake hands and apologize and I said, 'Why do I have to apologize for having some fun?'. He said, 'Watch you mouth or I'll put you in my book.' Maybe he did, I don't know. I won't know until I come up for review. But it might cost me those two weeks."

"Oh, that doesn't seem right," she protested. "Can't you...?" He sat shaking his head, saying nothing, his face sober.

The silence that followed was short. She accepted that he knew this system and that bucking it was not the answer. But, she thought, that's not like him and she hoped it would not change the Robbie she loved.

"What are you and Donna going to do about the baby?" she asked cautiously.

"What do you mean," he responded.

"Well, she didn't get an abortion, so...I just wondered."

"Of course she didn't. It's my baby, too." His tone was edging on sharpness but she persisted.

"So you're going to keep it, then—not give it up?"

"No way, Mom. It has never crossed my mind and I don't think Donna has ever thought of it either."

"Are you going to get married?" she asked in a voice mixed with caution and hope.

"Yes!" he said firmly. "We are. I asked her and she said 'Yes'. But we have to have parental permission so we decided to wait until I get out and we will both be of age."

"I would give you permission if you could tell me that that's what you really wanted," she said.

"Mom, I don't know how to say it. It's not that I want to get married, or married to Donna, it's that I need to. I need a woman to make me remember what I am. She will be—she is now—a rock or an anchor that will hold me and keep me from drifting. Just like Craig. He's always there, solid and true and trusting. And he keeps me from drifting. I sometimes think that without him I'd be lost—I'd be something else."

"I don't know what you mean, Rob," his mother said, her face drawn with concern.

He sighed and, after a moment of thought, decided it had to be said. "Look, Mom," he said, "you know I love Craig."

"Of course," she said.

"Perhaps more than any other person in the world? More than you or Dad or Bev or Donna?"

"I didn't know that," she said in a shaky, uncertain voice.

"I think that's true, but I'm not absolutely sure. That's how mixed up I am. And this is the hard part, Mom. Sometimes I feel drawn towards men."

He stopped and looked closely at her. Her face told him nothing so he plunged on.

"I'm saying that sometimes I want to love a man, and I don't want to at the same time, but the wanting scares me and that's why I have to get married to Donna and have a baby so I can't...drift."

She said nothing.

"Those feelings are different than loving Craig... totally and completely different. You see, I am Craig and Craig is me. And if Craig and I got sexy, (he paused for the briefest moment while years and times kaleidoscoped like I sometimes feel about some other men, then it would be no different than, well, masturbation."

"Oh, Robert! I don't know what you're saying. I don't think I even want to hear it." The confusion disappeared from her face and was replaced by hurt and tears.

"I know, Mom, and I'm sorry. You asked me if I loved Donna and I had to be honest with you and tell you why I need her and want to marry her—not only want to but have to. Craig understands," he added simply.

"Yes, of course," she said in a moment while wiping her tears. "Because Craig is you."

They saw Craig and his mother drive into the visitor's lot and dried their tears. Rob leaned over and said quietly, "I'm glad Dad didn't come. I couldn't have said what I just told you."

"Oh, God, Rob! He would never understand and I'm not too sure I do. I'm certainly not going to tell him. It would be torture."

They stood together, face to face, and holding hands. He suddenly let go of one of her hands, reached up and tickled her under the chin and said, "Ticky-ticky!"

She ducked her head down and laughed. "Oh, Rob!" she said.

"It looks like they had a happy time," Marion said to her son as they neared. "I'm glad we thought to leave them alone."

CHAPTER 77

On Wednesday, May the 26th, at 11:30 A.M., the telephone at Cranston's Carpets rang and Dorothy answered it. The male caller asked to speak to Craig Williams.

"He is out in the shipping room right now. Could I take a message or have him call you back?" Dorothy asked.

"It is very important," the caller replied. "Is there no way you can contact him now?"

Dorothy paused, hearing a note of urgency in the caller's voice. "Just hold on," she said. "I'll see if I can find him." she pressed the hold button but in less than ten seconds, she was back on the line. "Hello? He's just coming in to the office now. I'll put you through."

She held the phone with her hand casually over the mouthpiece. The caller heard her muffled voice say, "Craig, this call's for you. It sounds urgent," and then a familiar voice, "Thanks, Dorothy. I'll take it over here."

Craig picked up another phone. "Craig Williams."

"Come and get me," a voice said.

"Rob? Rob? You're free?"

"At twelve o'clock. Hurry up!"

"YAY!" shouted Craig before he put the phone down, making Rob wince, and three office women and his boss jump. "I've got to go!" he said to Dorothy as he headed for the door. "I mean, I've got to go."

"What was all that?" Carl called from his office.

"It sounds like his friend Rob is getting out," Dorothy said.

Carl smiled and went back to his work.

Craig, normally an inordinately cautious driver, rushed several yellow lights, jumped some reds and passed most of the dawdlers on the road. He arrived at the parking lot of the Administration Office at twelve o'clock exactly just as Rob came out the door carrying a cardboard box of possessions. Craig rushed to meet him, grabbed the box from him, tucked it under his left arm and threw his other arm over Rob's shoulders as they walked a few feet to his car, both smiling broadly. He opened the passenger door and put Rob in as if he were fragile, placed Rob's box on the back seat and got in behind the wheel where he sat, just smiling.

"C'mon, buddy! Let's get out of here," Rob said. "And when we get outside the gate, stop for a minute."

Craig drove away and stopped just outside the gate. Rob got out and stood looking back at the buildings.

"FUCK YOU! FUCKYOUFUCKYOUFUCKYOUFUCKYOU," he shouted and got back in the car. "There!" he said. "I thought I should say goodbye. Let's go."

They drove, more slowly this time, back toward the city. Rob's arm was draped over the driver's seat and he squeezed Craig's neck gently. After a couple of minutes of silent communication, Rob said, "Miss me?"

"You bet!" Then, "Where to?"

Rob took his arm off the back of Craig's seat and said, "Home, James!" He slouched down in the seat with his knees against the dashboard, his arms folded across his chest and stared straight ahead, immersed in private thoughts that Craig did not interrupt.

When they arrived at Rob and Donna's little basement suite, Rob said quietly, "Come in," without looking at Craig. Craig heard the unspoken 'please' and turned off the motor and went in with him, knowing that the empty room would be depressing for Rob. Inside Rob looked around and smiled approvingly at Donna's attempts to make the place homey with pictures and little ceramic pieces. Then he saw the new door cut into the wall close to their bed and cautiously opened it. Inside he found a tiny room, papered in nursery rhyme paper, with a small window letting in the early afternoon sunshine and lighting up a crib, a rocking chair and a padded board on top of an ancient chest of drawers.

"She didn't tell me," he said in a croaky voice to Craig who had followed him in, "Did you know?"

Craig shook his head. Rob took another step into the room and sat down in the rocking chair. He buried his face in his hands and wept. Craig watched silently until Rob said, more to himself than to him, "I think I'm going to make it, Craig. I'm going to make it."

"Sure you are, Rob!" Craig said, moving to him and putting a comforting hand on his shoulder without knowing the source of his friend's distress.

In a minute, Rob straightened up in the chair and Craig said, "I gotta go, buddy. You okay?"

"Sure! Thanks."

"I wouldn't except we've got a training session I started and it's the last one and I should be there to thank the guy," Craig tried to explain.

"That's okay. I know. I'm going to shower and change and catch Donna when she gets off." He went to the door with Craig and hugged him fiercely before the door closed.

When Craig stepped out, he glanced into the open door of the garage and saw Rob's bike. Examining it, he found a flat tire and a chain that had to be adjusted, so he tied it onto the roof of his car to take home to fix.

At the plant, the teaching session was in progress. Carl was sitting in at the back of the group and Craig went in and found a chair beside him.

"Did your friend get released?" Carl asked in a whisper.

Craig answered with a happy nod.

"I'll leave you to tidy up here," Carl said, touching him on the shoulder before leaving quietly.

"Did I see Craig come in?" Dorothy asked when Carl came back into the office.

"Yes, he's finishing up the training session," Carl replied.

"And?" Dorothy asked. "Come on, Carl. You know! Did his friend get released?"

"He didn't say so in so many words, but yes, I guess he did."

"Good," Dorothy said, approvingly as she turned back to her machine. "Then Craig's world will get back on its axis again."

Rob stood outside the Sweet Spot watching Donna work. Bruno came to the serving window with a plate, saw Rob and when Donna came to the window, he pointed to him. Donna screamed and rushed outside and their greeting was framed in the window of the small cafe, to the great pleasure of those within. When they came inside, Rob smiled and waved a hand to some shouted welcomes before escaping into the back with Donna. Bruno shook Rob's hand and said with a great smile, "So you be good boy now, eh?" And to Donna he said, "I phone Phyllis and she's a comin' toot da sweet, she's tell me. Den you go home." Donna couldn't say anything so she flung her arms around Bruno's neck and cried on his shoulder and then she realized she had a better shoulder nearby and turned again to Rob.

That's the way Phyllis found them and after her hugs and mothering she watched them leave and started cleaning up.

Rob and Donna walked home holding each other close. When they turned in the driveway to their door, Donna saw a curtain move. "Oh," she said quietly, "Mrs. Lasseret saw us. Let's go up and get it over with first."

Inside she went directly to the connecting door and called, "Mrs. Lasseret? Rob's home! Can we come up?"

The door at the top of the stairs opened. "Come up, come up!" Mrs. Lasseret called. "Oh, Rob. Welcome home."

They went up and the excited old lady hugged Rob hard with happy tears in her eyes. Wally left the TV and came out and shook Rob's hand and said, "What do you think of the baby's room? Your rent is going to go up, you know."

"Wally!" she scolded. "This is not the time to talk about increasing their rent. Besides, I'll be the one to say how much and it will be half as much as you would gouge them for. So be quiet!"

"Did you do all the carpentry yourself, Wally?" Rob asked to mollify the old man's hurt feeling from her scolding.

"The whole thing—walls, door, window, wallpaper, everything. Of course, the women picked out the wallpaper. I had no say in that and they kept their nose out of my carpentry," Wally said, returning to his usual assertiveness.

"We've got to go," Donna said. "We've got a lot to catch up on but we thought we'd better say hello."

"Oh, yes. Of course," Mrs. Lasseret said and blushed while Wally tried to hide a smirk.

"I think they've got dirty minds for old people," Donna whispered as she sat down beside him on the edge of the bed which was the only place they could sit together.

"Oh, I don't know," Rob said with a grin that was pure lechery. "I think I was thinking what they were thinking."

Their lovemaking was gentle but quick and, they agreed, worth repeating, which they did with more success. Another bonus for Rob, when it was finished, was that he realized his mind had not wandered to any other person.

They talked for a while but the small room began to close in on Rob. So they dressed and caught a bus down to English Bay where they walked the beach at low tide until the May sun lost its warmth. From the window of a coffee shop, warming their hands around an espresso and eating huge cookies, they watched the clouds cooperate with the sinking sun to create yet another incredible sunset.

When Craig came home and drove into the garage, his mother's car was gone so he did not bother going into the house. Taking the bike off the roof, he examined it and found the tube to be so patched and old that it was not worth repairing, so he checked the tires on his own bike and gave it a fast clean-up.

Then he tied it onto the roof of his car and drove to Rob's where, without disturbing anyone, he put it in Wally's garage for Rob to find.

Going home again, he found his mother's car in the garage. Out of the kitchen window, she saw him drive into the garage and close the doors, then hurry across the lawn and land on the top step with a thump. She looked up from the sink where she was peeling vegetables and saw her son's glowing face and shining eyes, and she knew the cause in a second.

"Guess what, Mom?" he said as he came to kiss her hello.

"I couldn't guess in a million years!" she said and smiled. "Unless it is that Rob is home."

"How did you know?" he demanded.

"Oh, Craig," she exclaimed. "One look at your face and I know it was something better that winning the 6/49. When did they let him out?"

"At noon today. I went out to pick him up."

"Break any speed limits?" she asked, smiling.

"Oh, Mom!" he said.

"Oh, Craig!" she mimicked. Then, touching his cheek gently, she said, "I'm so happy for you both," just as the phone rang.

She went to answer it and he went upstairs, two at a time, and flung himself on his bed with his hands behind his head, smiling at the ceiling.

CHAPTER 78

The date was set—June 6. The appointment was made—three o'clock in the afternoon at the office of a Marriage Commissioner at Broadway and Yukon. The wedding party would consist of Robert Turner, the groom; Donna Penser, the bride; Beverley Lewis, the matron of honour; Craig Williams, the best man; Marion Williams, representing the parents of the couple and witness; Roger Todd, escort for Marion Williams and second witness.

Donna and Bev, both more than half-way through their pregnancies, spent a happy Saturday afternoon at Preggie 2, a shop specializing in used maternity clothes. Both emerged with adjustable outfits to wear to the wedding and for the rest of their pregnancies. (Donna had firmly rejected Marion's tentatively made suggestion of white with veil and train and other paraphernalia.) She bought some shoe dye to match the peach outfit she had selected. Bev's wedding outfit was much the same as Donna's except it was a rosy beige. She said she thought she had a pair of shoes that would go with it. "But, what the hell," she said, "if they don't match it doesn't matter, I can't see my feet and who looks at the matron of honour, anyway."

Marion had flung an armful of dresses on her bed and spent two hours trying on most of them that were, first of all, too loose and secondly, she hated them. Some of them, stylish at one time and offensive now, looked like they had been designed out of bedspreads or kitchen table cloths and she threw them out into the hall to be picked up later. The best she could do was a dark, pearly-green one. The hemline was much longer that this year's demand, but she didn't care about that because she had never liked her legs anyway.

"What are you going to wear?" she asked Craig.

"I dunno, my jacket and slacks, I guess," he answered casually.

"How long since you've worn them?"

"Oh, at the Christmas party, probably."

"Well, bring them down and let me see if they need pressing." But he didn't, and at one o'clock on Saturday he was struggling with the steam iron and trying to eliminate creases he had ironed into his slacks that seemed to go north and south when he stood east and west. In the end, because of time constraints, interested observers were given a number of creases to choose from.

"What are you going to wear to your wedding?" Roger asked Rob as he saw him shrugging into the black leather jacket Donna had given him for Christmas.

"This, I guess," Rob answered, obviously never having given a moment of thought about such matters.

Roger restrained himself from laughing or shuddering and said, "Come with me!"

Downstairs, he opened his clothes closet and shoved around a half dozen sports jackets. "We're about the same size—try this on!" he ordered Rob, who obediently took off his leather jacket and put on the grey cashmere jacket Roger handed him. Rob was slightly taller than Roger and the sleeves were shorter than fashion would dictate but since the bride and groom would not be appearing on the social pages of the Vancouver Sun, nobody cared. "Wear your black slacks and a white shirt. Got a tie?"

"Yes, master," Rob said with a grin.

"Yeah, I bet," Roger said and fingered through a rack of ties hanging in the closet. "Here, wear this," handing him a wide Hawaiian tie with a naked girl and a palm tree.

"Jesus, Roger!" Rob protested.

"Okay! You only get one rejection—that was it!" Then he pulled out another tie and handed it to Rob who looked at it with a smile of relief.

CHAPTER 79

They arrived back late Sunday night. Rob could see a crack of light in the window and knew that Donna was still up. When he got out of the little car he stood for a minute looking at Roger, finally saying, "Thanks, Rog." He put out his hand but Roger deliberately missed it and they grasped arms instead.

"See you tomorrow, buddy." Roger said as the door closed.

"You bet," replied Rob, frowning a little at the buddy term.

In a quiet moment on the TV. Donna had heard the Porsche pull away and was looking out the window when Rob walked up the drive. She met him at the door with open arms. He held her close and they kissed each other again and again and he realized how much softer she was than the man he had held in his arms last night and two nights before that. Even softer than Craig, he thought, but that was so long ago—so long ago, way back to Lake Lovely Water.

"You look beat," she said as they disengaged from each other.

"Yeah, we came back a longer route. I had to do some thinking. It was a nice trip." He sat down on one of the kitchen chairs and took off his shoes.

"Hungry?" she asked. "I could make a grilled cheese." One of his favourites.

"Great!" and he smiled for the first time since the greeting and got up and flopped on the bed.

"How's your Dad?" she asked, busy in the little kitchen.

He told her of the accident and the damage and, with some difficulty, the prognosis as he had understood it from the doctor, saying nothing of his father's rejection of him.

"Oh, isn't that awful," she said, and added, "He'd be better off dead." She stopped, then said. "I'm sorry, Rob! I shouldn't have said that."

He nodded. "It's okay. You're probably right."

They were quiet for a moment while she brought him a sandwich and a glass of milk. "Want some coffee too?" He nodded over a full mouth. "I do, too. I'm not supposed to drink much and I miss it" From the kitchen, she continued. "We finally figured out that Roger drove you up."

"Haugh-ch? he said, trying to say 'How' with his mouth packed, and hearing himself, suddenly heard his father's disowning voice and saw the baleful eye.

"Oh, women have a network," she laughed. "You phoned Bev from Prince George and she called Craig's mother and she told Craig and when Craig went over to see Roger about golf times and saw a 'Closed for Vacation' sign and he came over and told me then your mother phoned Bev and Bev phoned me to say you and Roger were on your way. So I was expecting you around midnight or later. See? It's simple when women get on a case."

"You covered all the bases, didn't you?" he grinned, but wanted the subject closed. He gave a huge yawn.

"Tired?" she asked. He nodded. "Me, too."

He got up and undressed. While he was in the bathroom she slipped off her dressing gown and got into bed. When he came out he could see no signs of arousal. He turned out all the lights and crawled in beside her.

"Rob?" she said. "No funny stuff, eh?

He alerted, thinking 'Where did I hear that before? Has she been talking to Craig?' Then he relaxed and asked, "But cuddling's okay?" wrapping his long limbs carefully around her as she backed into his angular body.

"Sure is," she said wiggling in. "It's just that I'm getting close and I don't want to start things before it's ready."

He tossed and turned most of the night and awakened Donna with his nightmares. He was trying to put blankets on two horses in a stall: one horse glared at him with a wild eye and struck out with his front feet and screamed, the other kept nuzzling him and pulling the blanket off every time he got it on. Craig drove slowly back and forth in a red Porsche filled with golf clubs, calling, 'You were supposed to play with ME!' and Judge Ellen Harley Moore sat on a bench in her robes by the horse stalls with a comforting arm around his mother.

Rob went to work the next morning looking bedraggled and tired. He had been working on back orders for more than an hour and a half before Roger put in an appearance. "Hi!" Roger said coming over to Rob and laying an arm on his shoulder. "How's my buddy and travelling mate?"

Whether it was fatigue, the 'buddy' thing or the fondling hand on his neck, Rob tensed and drew away, saying only "Hi" as he continued working. Then, feeling that his greeting was unfriendly, he added, "Have a good sleep?"

"Yeah, sure. Not as good as the night before though," Roger said smiling as he put both hands on Rob's shoulders and massaged them gently. "Hey, you're full of tension!" he continued. "Come on into the bedroom and I'll give you the works. I'm the past grand master of massage. I can take kinks out you never knew you had."

Rob twisted his shoulders, partly to move away from Roger's hands and partly to test if he really did feel tense. "Oh, I don't know, Roger. I never thought massaging ever did much good—well, sometimes it did," he added, changing his mind. "Like when you get a bad bang-up playing football, I guess then a massage is okay, I used to do Craig and he would do me." He laughed reminiscently. "Then he read about Geisha girls walking on men's back in their bare feet and he thought we should try it. He's got bony feet. He nearly killed me." Roger took his hands away. Rob continued, "So we went back to the regular massage.

"We should try it some time," Roger said, and in the same breath, "Have you had breakfast?"

Rob nodded.

"I'll put the coffee on. Come on down when you're ready."

"Sure," Rob answered, "I won't be long."

Roger had only just disappeared down the stairs when Allen Singh knocked and came in. "Oh, so Roger is back from his vacation," he said in his soft voice. I came by on Friday with some orders and saw the sign on the door. I have many orders for you—mostly engagements and marriages. Very good, very good." He smiled and brought out his order book.

"Roger has just gone down to put the coffee on," Rob said, feeling a sense of relief that Allen had appeared. "Let's go down and show him and see what he says." He noticed Allen giving him a strange look and added. "It's time for a coffee break, is it not?" he asked, trying to mimic Allen's lilting voice.

"Did you have a good rest on your vacation?" Allen asked Roger when they went downstairs.

"Yes, but not long enough," Roger replied, giving Rob a sulky, frowning look that said, 'Why did you bring him down?'

They looked over Allen's orders, with Roger showing only the most casual interest.

"This one is required very soon," Allen said. "I didn't know you would be away and I thought I could work on it on the weekend if Rob could get it ready. Would it be agreeable if I took over whatever Rob was doing while he does the hand printing for this order and then we could get it out on time?"

"It makes no difference to me," Roger said in an offhand manner. He got up and rinsed out his cup and went upstairs. The other two followed.

Rob showed Allen what order he had been working on and then settled into the small work cubby hole where he kept his hand printing equipment. He did not know why he had been quietly relieved when Allen had appeared, but, now, working alone and concentrating on his project, another part of his mind kept flicking back to Roger's constant attentions and to a feeling of being manipulated. After a while, he straightened up from the desk and stretched. Roger caught his eye and smiled at him with a big wink, and Rob felt a surge of some emotion he could not explain as he returned the smile and turned back to his work. He remembered that tomorrow was Donna's last day at work and that some sort of party was planned for her at noon and he was expected to be there. He wondered if he should invite Roger to come, but quickly rejected that idea.

When Donna arrived for work the next morning, Angela was already there doing the morning routines and chatting with an old customer. Donna had made Rob put on a good sports shirt and dressy jeans and made him promise to be at the Sweet Spot at 11:30 and not a minute after. She had dressed up in the maternity outfit she was married in and she looked so rosy and healthy and pleased with her world that Rob left for work wondering what had possessed him to cheat on her—with a man, at that! "Don't get sweaty!" she called and he waved.

Bruno and Phyllis had made handwritten invitations for a Free D.L.L. (Donna's Last Lunch) and had handed them out to all their old regulars. All the tables had been reserved. Phyllis had thought that the regulars would come and go and that casuals could be accommodated at the counter. Instead the regulars came early with no intentions of eating and running as usual. The small cafe filled up and when Rob arrived, he was pressed into service as a quasi maitre d' explaining to casuals that a private party was in progress. Following that chore, he found himself back in the kitchen becoming acquainted with the dishwasher. He emerged when Phyllis rattled a spoon and announced that the total contributions to the baby pot amounted to $134.72.

"Pitall put in the two cents," someone shouted and everyone laughed.

"Pitall started it all," Donna said in his defence and leaned over and kissed Ptolemy on his bald spot to many cheers and cries of "Me next!"

Then Phyllis hushed everybody and said that Bruno had decided to match the baby pot and gave Donna a cheque for $134.70 cents. Donna cried and tried to thank everyone and Pitall got up and marched over to Bruno and gave him two cents, saying, "Don't be a piker, Bruno. If you gonna match, then match!" Then Donna stopped crying and laughed with everyone else and put her arms around Bruno who took his chef's hat off expecting a kiss on his bald spot, but got one full on the lips instead. He looked warily at Phyllis who smiled at him, so he said, "What da hell!", grabbed Donna and gave her a proper, sound Italian smooch to some rousing cheers before he escaped to his grill.

People started to leave to go back to work. They said goodbye and good luck to Donna. Some of the younger men shook hands and some older men gave her a hug and a paternal peck on the cheek. When the last of them had gone, Angela and Phyllis sat down with her and watched her cry and laugh happily alternately.

"Rob!" Donna cried, suddenly.

"He's out doing dishes," Angela said. "Leave him alone."

Donna rushed out to the kitchen and found Rob deep in dirty dishes and grinning as she flung herself at him and clung tightly.

"Oh, Rob! Wasn't it wonderful? I didn't know there could be such nice people."

"Thousands more out there where they came from," he told her, thinking as he said it, "But I'm not one of them. I'm a shit—a total goddam worthless cheating shit! I've got to talk to Rog!"

For the next ten days they worked together, neither of them making any move to discuss their earlier trip or their feelings. Then a parcel arrived in the mail addressed to Roger from the motel they had stayed at on the way home. It contained one of Roger's silk shirts.

"How did I forget that?" Roger asked to nobody in particular.

"You didn't forget it. I did. I was wearing it," Rob said. "You said I looked sexy in it."

"Oh, yeah," Roger said, but he flicked his eyes and jerked his head in the direction of Allen who appeared not to be listening.

When Allen left late in the afternoon, Rob stopped working and said, his face taut with strain, "Hey, Roger. Can we talk?"

Roger looked at him and knew that Rob was not wanting to talk about business and his face brightened. "Anytime, buddy. Let's lock up and go downstairs."

"I'll clean up this printer first," Rob said as Roger was locking the doors. "I'll be right down."

While he was cleaning the machine, he kept remembering how Roger's face had brightened and wondered what Roger had been thinking when he asked 'Can we talk?' and pondered about what he wanted to say.

"Want a beer?" Roger asked, already sitting on the sofa with his shoes off and his leg up on a stool and a beer in his hand, when Rob joined him downstairs.

"Sure," Rob said, getting a beer from the frig. "Leg bothering you?" He sat down on a lounge chair across from Roger.

"Sometimes. But not as much as you keeping your distance. Come on over here where we can talk," Roger said, patting the sofa seat beside him.

Rob crossed the room, smiling, and sat on the sofa with his back against the arm, one knee up on the seat with the other knee hooked over its foot.

"How's Craig doing?" Roger asked as if this were a social event, not a 'Let's talk' situation.

"Okay, I guess. He was pissed off with you for quitting golf but he found a threesome that he likes playing with—a father and son and another guy we knew from school." He paused. "I don't see much of him these days."

"Miss him?"

"Yep," honestly. "A lot."

Silence.

"What do you want to talk about, buddy?" Roger asked, reaching over and giving Rob's knee a shake.

Rob took a long pull on his bottle of beer, thinking, I wish to Christ he would stop calling me 'buddy' and stop touching me. It makes it hard. Then he asked, "Rog? Remember when we were talking serious stuff about sex and feelings and stuff? The last night that we....of our trip?"

"Sure," Roger said, smiling gently. "A good night!"

"Remember I told you that I could go either way and I still think I can but I'm not sure I want to, right now. I was thinking we should break it off, Rog."

Roger's face paled. "C'mon! Rob!" he said. "What do you mean—break it off? We've got something very, very special going for us."

"I know it's special and I don't want to lose it or do any-thing to ruin it, but I'm married and I'm going to be a father any day now and I have to check out that whole scene before I make up my mind one way or the other. Don't you see?" There were tears beginning to show in his eyes.

"You were willing, Rob," Roger said very softly,

"I know," in an equally soft voice.

"I don't think I forced you. And there was a lot of enticement, you know."

"What do you mean—enticement?"

"Look at yourself, right now, Rob!" Roger said. "There you are, sitting spraddled legged with your crotch available, inviting, and within easy reach of my hand or I could lean over and bite you." Rob twitched slightly as if Roger intended to. "And your smell! You don't know what it does to me. Remember my shirt that was mailed back—the one you wore? Well, I could smell you on it and it drove me nuts. I put it on my pillow and I had some really, really raunchy dreams in which you figured in a variety of ways. Dreams are okay but I'd rather have the real thing."

"Rog, I'm sorry. I didn't know. I thought...well, I don't know what I thought," he finished miserably.

There was another tight silence.

"Maybe I should quit and get another job," Rob said shakily.

"No! No! No! No!" Roger almost shouted. "Don't do that! We'll work it out.

"Okay, Rog," Rob said, standing up. "Let's try."

He put out his hand and Roger stood up and said, "Good friends hug, re-member?"

They stood in a tight, close embrace for a long minute, until Rob patted Roger on the back and said, huskily, as they released each other, "I gotta go."

He went up the stairs slowly. Just as he opened the door he heard Roger call. "Rob? Are you going to run all this past Craig?"

"I dunno yet," he answered and waited briefly for another word from Roger.

When there was no further word from downstairs, he closed the door softly and rode toward home, peddling hard, the wind in his face making his eyes stream.

CHAPTER 80

For the next few days Roger and Rob worked together without any mention of their earlier conversation. Roger had just left for an overnight trip to Seattle and Rob was alone when Craig phoned late in the afternoon. "Hi there! Friend, neighbour and stranger!" he said. "What's new?"

"Stranger!" Rob replied. "Look who's talking! Look who doesn't even know his best buddy is working his ass off. Look who doesn't even invite his best buddy over for supper when he works late into the wee small hours. Look who won't walk around the corner to say "hello, how are you or go to hell" to his very best buddy in the whole goddam world."

"Finished? Want to come over for supper tonight?"

"Sure. What are you having?"

"Up yours! See ya!"

He was over in less than two minutes, smothering his U.U. with sloppy smooches until, laughing heartily, with Craig looking on with an approving grin, she had to slap at him to get him to stop.

"Okay, you grinning ape! It's your turn...after I phone my ever lovin'."

"Who will that be today?" Craig asked.

"Smartass! Watch out!" Rob said as he dialled. "Hi, doll! How're you doing?" when she answered on the first ring.

They talked together with a lot of light banter and laughter and he told her he was supping grandly at the Williams and would give her a rundown of every course as soon as he got home.

"After work," he added. He continued, through her objections, "Sorry, Babe. Sorry. sweetie-pie. Sorry, love. Sorry—somebody help me out. I'm running out of love words."

"Sorry, sweetheart," Craig shouted.

"That was Craig. He says he's sorry, sweetheart."

He listened for a moment, then said, "I'll tell him. See you later." He turned to Craig. "She says to tell you she's sorry you're sorry and I can kiss you to make it better."

He stomped toward Craig with gorilla arms and they both raced down the stairs to the family room where Marion could hear them wrestling and laughing. She listened at the top of the stairs, smiling to herself. Not bad, Robbie, my love, she said to herself. You made three people happy in less than ten minutes. Might even be a record.

She returned to the kitchen to look after the cooking and discovered she hadn't put the oven on. Going to the top of the stairs again, she called, "Rob, are you in a hurry?"

"Never, as long as you are near me," he called back.

"Oh, Rob, listen. I forgot to turn the oven on. If you have to get back to work, I'll cook something different."

"U.U., my love, I've got all the time in the world. I haven't even started on my lover-boy yet."

"Knock it off, Rob, for God's sake," she heard Craig say as she returned to the kitchen.

Then they talked, filling out not quite all of the details of their lives since they last had talked at length. They talked of work and golf and Donna and marriage and pregnancy and fatherhood and on and on, covering the base of every relationship they could easily bring to mind. Suddenly, Rob realized with an awful clarity that never in the whole goddam fucking bastard wide world could he tell the person he loved most of all in that world that thing about himself that he desperately needed to tell him, and his eyes filled with tears and spilled over.

"What's wrong with you?" Craig asked.

"You stuck your finger in my eye," Rob said. "I'm going to tell your mother!" and he raced upstairs.

Craig followed behind and heard Rob say in a little sad voice, "He stuck his finger in my eye and he did it on purpose!"

"Oh, for goodness sake, you two!" Marion said in a casually scolding voice. "Shake hands and say you're sorry."

"Oh, we don't shake hands anymore—AIDS, you know! We hug instead," Rob said, turning away from Marion and putting his arms around Craig.

Craig could feel him taking small, shaking breaths so he held him close, wondering, but saying nothing.

Suddenly, Rob said, "I gotta go to the bathroom," and rushed away. In the bathroom, he washed his face and eyes with cold water and urgently grabbed for control. When he came out he announced, "Craig didn't flush the toilet. I know, because the toilet seat was up."

"I did so!" Craig said.

They did a fast sequence of did-not did-so's until they got it mixed up and laughed.

Marion said, "Are you two never going to grow up? Come to the table."

They ate together, feeling as close as they had ever been. Without hurrying, Rob asked to be excused, pleading more work before going home. Craig went with him to the door.

"Okay?" he asked, touching Rob's arm.

"Sure thing, buddy. Thanks," Rob said turning quickly away.

Craig could not see the strained face of his friend, no walking away toward the house he had grown up in—no longer home.

Donna phoned her doctor and spoke to his nurse. "I feel funny and I look funny," she said. "Everything seems to be out of place, like it all slipped. And he's not kicking as much."

The nurse laughed and said, "It's probably nothing to worry about, Donna. The baby probably just dropped into position. But we better have a look. How about this afternoon? Four o'clock?"

"Okay, thanks," Donna said. "If there's a cancellation, will you call me?"

"Alright, Donna. But don't worry! What's going on is very normal. The baby is just getting ready to be born. See you at four o'clock."

She phoned her aunt without waiting for the evening rates. "She said the baby probably just dropped," she wailed. "What does that mean?"

"It's just a term, dear. Don't get yourself upset. I don't know why they use that word anyway. The baby doesn't actually drop, like you drop a carton of milk, which I just did, by the way, and what a mess—I'm standing in it—it sorta moves lower with its head down and its arms tucked in by its sides and its little legs tucked up ready to shoot out—whoosh—when its ready. So it has just moved, you see, just moved into a position ready to be born. You must be getting close. Are you excited?"

"No, I'm getting scared!" Donna said. "No," she corrected herself quickly, "I'm not really scared, just a tiny bit, but I can't tell the difference between excited and scared. I wish I had taken that maternity course the nurse told me about, but I thought we had done it in school in socials. Nobody mentioned anything about dropping babies and 'whoosh', babies shooting out all over the place." Then she started to laugh and her aunt laughed with her until there were tears in her eyes.

"Oh, here comes your Uncle Steve and I'm standing in a puddle of milk with tears in my eyes. He'll make a thing out of that. Now you call me and tell me what the doctor says, will you?"

"Yes, I will, for sure. And Aunt Ella, I love you. Bye."

Then she phoned Rob and sounded very knowledgeable about babies dropping and 'whoosh' and all the rest.

"Do you want me to come with you this afternoon?" he asked.

"No, father's are not necessary yet. You just have to promise to be there when it goes 'whoosh'. Sounds like you should bring your baseball glove."

Rob told Allen what Donna had said and Allen's face darkened. "I have had five children," he said in his serious lilting voice, "and, believe me, there is no 'whoosh'."

Donna and the doctor were looking at the dark blob on the ultrasound screen. "He's not being very cooperative," the doctor said. "He's a little early, but that doesn't matter. Normally babies drop into position head first, but sometimes feet first, which isn't as good, or, like this little fellow they wriggle around and drop any old way and try to get out bottom first." He pointed to the blob on the screen and outlined the buttocks with his finger. "Called the breech position." He paused and considered. "So we have to see if we can get him to move around a bit and change his attitude about facing the world."

"You keep on saying 'he' and 'him'," Donna said. "Is it really a boy?"

"Oh, I just call the wriggly ones, like this one, he, and the quiet, docile ones, she. I just don't like calling them 'it'. And you don't want to know anyway, do you?"

She shook her head and smiled. "I like surprises," she said.

"Now then, it's not a big baby, but you're not a big girl. If the baby doesn't turn, or we can't turn it, we have to consider a Caesarian. I want you to take it easy and rest as much as you can and if there is any change at all, anything, phone the nurse. She'll call me if she thinks it necessary. She'll know what's going on. She's been in the baby business a long time, and so have the other two nurses who are on rotation." He stood up, felt her bulging stomach again, said, "Don't let your imagination run away with itself. I'll be there as soon as you need me. Okay?"

She nodded tearfully as he left the examining room.

When she got home she called Rob. "Please don't work late tonight," she said. "I need you."

"Okay," Rob answered quickly, hearing a note of panic in her voice. "Anything wrong?"

"I'll tell you when you get home," she said and hung up, leaving him anxious and wondering.

"That was Donna, Roger. I gotta go home right away."

"Don't tell me the baby's on its way!"

"I think its something else. She sounded scared. See you tomorrow." He gave Roger a wave and headed for the door. Roger always wanted to hug him when he said goodnight, and right at this minute he did not want to be touched.

Donna poured out her anxieties to him when he got home. Their pooled knowledge of childbirth was not enough to pacify Donna.

"I know what a Caesarian is," she fumed. "I don't want to be cut open. I don't want an anaesthetic. I want to see my baby born!"

"Like whoosh! Pop! Your baby, madam," Rob said, standing like a waiter, except for the smile, with a tray over his head.

"Oh, Rob! You're a nut," she said, wiping her eyes as though she were finished weeping.

He made a cone out of folded newspaper and put it over her stomach. "Now, listen up in there," he said in a loud voice. "This is your father speaking! You stop being a naughty girl right now and causing your mummy grief and pain. I want you to get right back up there, right side up or top side down or something. You know where you belong, now let's do this thing proper. Do you understand?"

He put his ear against her stomach and listened, then suddenly straightened up with a big smile. "She said something! Do you know what she said? She said 'Yes, Daddy'!"

They laughed and cuddled happily until Donna's upset was finished.

"I know something I could try," she said. "I could try standing on my head, but not really on my head, but sort of upside down, and maybe she'd slide back up where she's supposed to be."

"You be careful," he told her in a terrible mock-serious voice. "You might get her started and can't get her stopped and she'd go 'whoosh' right out your mouth like that Greek god."

"What Greek god?"

"I dunno! Jonah?"

"Jonah wasn't Greek. He got puked up by a whale."

"Yec-chh! He shoulda been Greek. Then I wouldn't have failed History and some other...."

Suddenly the goofiness reminded him of Craig, and he got a catch in his throat that stopped him from saying anything more. In a moment he managed a croaky, "I gotta pee!" and rushed to the bathroom. He stood in front of the mirror staring at his image. His wet eyes blurred and swirled the reflection until he saw the wavery face of Craig in front of him. "Shitface!" he told himself softly. "Haven't even got the guts to tell your best friend!"

Rob went to work in the morning with his face set in anger with himself, leaving Donna sleeping soundly making fluttery snores. When he opened the door, he found Roger up, dressed and working. "What are you doing up?" he asked.

"I couldn't sleep, so..."

"Oh, Rog!" Rob interrupted. "I'm in such a fucking, god-awful, son-of-a-bitching mess, I don't know if I'm punched or bored." He went over behind Roger's chair and laid his arms on Roger's shoulders with his chin on Roger's head. "What the hell am I going to do? I can feel my little girl kicking around in my wife's tummy and the three of us are there and I think that nothing could be better. Nothing! I WANT to be a father and a husband just like every other son-of-a bitch in the world. And then there's you! You can't fit into that picture and I can't make myself let go of you. I WANT to be with you, just you, just you and me. What the hell do I do?" He stood up, taking his arms off Roger's shoulders.

Roger remained seated and did not turn around. "Have you told Craig?" he asked softly.

"Hell, no! Roger, I can't tell Craig! It would rip him apart."

"But one of these days you might tell me that being a husband and father is all that you want. You don't think that will rip ME apart?"

"I'm caught. Aren't I? I'm going to hurt someone no matter what I do. You or Craig—and Donna and U.U. and my mother and sister and...oh, shit!" He turned quickly and went down the hall toward the bathroom.

"You're loading the dice, Rob!" Roger called quietly.

"I know—and I can't help it," came the shaky response.

When he came out of the bathroom, his upset was less obvious. Allen had arrived and greeted him.

"How is the little mother this morning?" he asked solicitously.

"Sleeping when I left, but she's getting close," Rob answered.

"You must be very careful now," came Allen's singsong advice. "This is a very special time."

At three o'clock, the phone rang and Rob, who was closest, answered it.

"Rob!" Donna shrieked, recognizing his voice. "My water broke! I'm sitting in a great big puddle! I need you!"

"Okay! Okay! Calm down. I'll be right there. Everything will be alright. Now don't panic!"

"I'm not in a panic—I'm in a puddle! Ye-e-cch! Hurry up!"

"Donna's water broke. I gotta go!" Rob shouted.

"Come! I will drive you!" Allen volunteered immediately. "I know the way. I have been there many times."

"Good luck!" Roger shouted as the other two raced out.

On the way, with Rob sitting tensely beside him, Allen chatted, trying to keep Rob's anxiety but sometimes choosing the wrong subject. "My wife was very lucky. Very easy births—all five! For some women it is a very difficult time. Many hours of pain, terrible, terrible pain."

They arrived sedately in Allen's big car. "I will wait here," he announced. "Perhaps you will bring a blanket with you, Robert. For the upholstery, you see," he explained primly.

Donna appeared very composed and calm when he arrived but when he held her, he could feel her shaking. She had changed into dry clothes and had her little bag ready. Rob introduced her to Allen.

"It was good of you to drive Rob," she said. "I thought he would come racing through traffic on his bike like a madman. Then I thought, surely he would take a taxi home and then to the hospital. But this is much better. Thank you, Mr. Singh."

"My pleasure," he said, with a little nod and approving smile.

"Rob, I was sitting on the edge of the bed when it happened but I jumped up and sat on the kitchen chair so it spilled on the linoleum, The top sheet got a little wet but that's all. I took it off, but you'll have to wash it when you get back. I didn't have time."

He was amazed at her control, and he wished Allen would speed up so she wouldn't have the baby in the back seat. "Can't we go faster, Allen?" he asked.

"If we drive the speed limit, we won't get stopped by a policeman," Allen explained patiently. "It would take very, very much time to explain to a policeman, so to go slower is to arrive sooner. You see?"

They arrived at Grace Hospital.

"This is a very good hospital," Allen assured her as he leaped out and opened the door for her. "All my children were born here. Five of them—two boys and three girls. And four grandchildren. Very, very fine hospital." He smiled broadly. "Maternity admissions next floor up. Elevator on your left. You see, I have been here many, many times."

Allen drove back to work and found Roger working at his desk with files piled high.

"Well, I delivered them on time," he said as soon as he came in. "She is a very strong girl. Very, very strong."

"I'm glad you were around to help. I would have let Rob have the Porsche but I don't think he was in any condition to drive and it's a hell of a car for a pregnant lady," Roger said.

"I was glad to do it, very glad." Allen nodded several times and the conversation seemed finished.

"Allen, pull up a chair. I'd like to talk to you," Roger said.

"Oh, yes, indeed," Allen said, reaching for a chair and seating himself somewhat primly. "I hope it is not that you are not satisfied with my work." Allen's face was long with anxiety.

"Oh, no! Nothing like that," Roger replied with such a hearty laugh that Allen relaxed. "You know the business and you are better at everything that goes on here than I am, or Rob or even Rob's father."

"Such a terrible thing that happened to his father. I am so sorry. I was told yesterday by an acquaintance. Terrible, terrible thing."

"Allen, I have a business proposition to make to you. I want to sell this business, everything. I want to sell it fast and I will accept any reasonable offer. I know you retired too soon and you are anxious to keep busy. I want you to think about it very seriously and remember that it must be done quickly."

"Roger, it is very kind of you to think of me, but I have very little money to invest. My pension is adequate, my house is paid for and I have some bonds and other small investments. But, I am really quite a poor man. Rich, in many ways, but not monetarily. What do you think would be a reasonable offer," Allen asked abruptly, forsaking, for the moment, a plea of poverty.

"I think it is up to you to make the offer. I have no set price in mind," Roger said gently. "And I am quite willing to hold the paper for you but not for every buyer."

"You will certify that the building is free and clear and that there are no liens against it or the equipment?"

"Certainly."

"I will be permitted access to your business accounts in order to estimate the value of the business?"

"Of course."

"I may bring an appraiser in?"

"Yes."

"And you will hold the mortgage...but, oh, my! The mortgage rates are very high right now, very, very high. I do not know. I do not know." He sighed. "I will tell you honestly, Roger, because you have been honest with me. My son has two taxi licences. Worth very much money. But driving taxi is very dangerous now in this city, very dangerous. I will talk to my family and other people, perhaps I can persuade my son to sell his taxi licences and come into business with me. He knows nothing about the printing business but Rob and I can teach him. Rob is a very talented young man, very talented. He will stay on, will he not?"

"I can't speak for another man, Allen."

"Of course not. No, of course not." He paused, deep in thought for a long time, his normally open and friendly face closed as he shut out everything in order to think. Then, he rose to his feet with a kind of dignity. "Roger," he said formally, "I will give you my hand to indicate that I will do my best to give you an offer soon. I am indeed interested. Now you must tell me the limit of time that is open to me."

"A week. At the very most, ten days."

Allen pursed his lips and shook his head. "You must know that the less time I have to evaluate, the lower the offer must be."

"I am aware of that, Allen."

"Would it be proper of me to ask if you have approached any other prospective buyers or have been approached by anyone?"

"You are the very first, Roger. I only made the decision to sell this morning."

"Very well, Roger," and he offered his hand and they shook. "I have much work to do, it seems. Goodnight." He gave a little salaam bow and hurried out the door.

Roger sat for a long time, staring at the ceiling.

***

After Allen had smilingly pointed the way for them, Rob and Donna thanked him warmly and took the elevator up to admissions, using the slow ride for a little cuddling.

"Things happened so fast, I didn't have time to call my doctor," Donna explained to the matronly receptionist.

"Well, wouldn't it be nice if everything else went fast and easy, too? We'll call him. Name?" with a friendly smile.

"My name? I'm Donna Turner. This is my husband Robert Turner. My doctor's name is Dr. Abbott."

"That's the way I like the information—short and snappy." She finished her typing. "The rest can wait until we get you out of those wet clothes and into bed."

"Oh, migod! Am I wet again? I didn't even feel it! And look at the floor. I'm sorry," Donna said looking terribly embarrassed.

"My dear, it has been baptised many times before," the receptionist said laughing. "Now then, we are going to get you into bed and properly admitted and prepped. I suggest you kiss this handsome young expectant father and tell him to come back after supper, because there's nothing for him to do until we're finished. The cafeteria is that way," she waved a hand. "The coffee's awful."

He kissed his wife tenderly and with some passion and felt himself getting an erection. She felt it too, so she slapped him gently, and said in a whisper, "This is not the time or place to get raunchy. Come after supper?"

He nodded and left.

***

Craig left the plant early, before the announcement that Dorothy was typing could be tacked up on the bulletin board. He landed with a thump on the top step and his mother knew something was right in his world, maybe he'd seen Rob again.

"Guess what, Mom?" He was beaming.

"I couldn't in a million years," she answered.

"Carl's going to start retiring and he wants Dorothy and Larry and me to take over and run the plant as a sort of management committee. How about that?" he finished proudly.

"Craig!" she exclaimed after a few seconds to catch her breath. "Really? That's wonderful!" She moved to him with her arms extended to congratulate him, but stopped halfway to take her apron off, and he laughed at what she was doing.

"Can't congratulate me with your apron on?" he teased.

"Oh, I don't know why I did that," she said, putting her arms around him. "Oh, I am so proud—really I am!"

"And raises, too. But guess what? The committee decided we wouldn't take a raise right now. We're going to wait and see how we do for six months and then ask Carl's advice. The guys I talked to all thought that was a neat idea."

Somehow the schoolboy phrase 'neat idea' coming out of her son on a 'management committee' caught her emotionally and she clung to him, saying again "I am so proud!" Then the schoolboy emerged. "Hey! What's for dinner?" he asked.

She released him, picked up her apron and used it to dab at her eyes. "Have you told Rob yet?"

"No, I thought I'd catch him after supper. He'll be surprised," he added, grinning.

Yes, she said to herself, smiling as she turned back to her cooking... surprised, pleased, happy, supportive, 100% behind his very best friend in the whole wide world.

Craig walked over to the Turner's after supper but there were no lights on and Roger's car was not in the garage. At home, he phoned Rob and Donna's but there was no answer. Upstairs, he flopped on his bed and wondered if they might have gone out to a show and then drifted off into a daydream about his future.

Rob walked without purpose in the late September evening, his mind in a turmoil, wishing he had dared to talk to Craig. He stopped for a hamburger that he forced down untasted and walked aimlessly again, with his eye on his watch, wondering what 'after supper' meant. Finally, he turned back in the direction of the hospital, He asked directions at the desk to find his wife, and when he found her, she was propped up in bed waiting for him.

"Where have you been?" she pretended to scold. "I had my supper two hours ago." She giggled after he kissed her. "Do you know what time they brought me supper? At four thirty. Four thirty! Can you imagine? And it was already cold."

He smiled at her, happy that she was not showing any fear.

"What did they do to you?" he asked, holding her hand tight in both his.

"You're cold," she said bringing her other hand over to rub his. "What did they do?" she repeated. "Take my advice—don't ever have a baby if you embarrass easy. First of all they shave you, wanna see?" She looked to see if any of the other patients were watching and lifted the covers while he peeked. "Isn't that weird?"

"Geez!" he exclaimed, chortling. "I hope that never gets to be the style."

A nurse stuck her head in the door, "Anything?" Donna shook her head. The nurse disappeared but came back in immediately. "Are you her labour coach?" she asked Rob.

"What's that?" Rob asked.

The nurse sniffed. "Well, he looks like a flopper anyway," she said to Donna and disappeared.

"What the hell was that all about?" Rob asked.

Donna told him the things she had learned only today. "Some of the husbands faint in the delivery room. They're called floppers." She stopped and gritted her teeth and closed her eyes. Then, a minute later she opened her eyes, looked at her watch and marked the time on a piece of paper by her bed.

"And what are you doing there?"

"Keeping track of the contractions," she said simply.

"Do they hurt?"

"I guess so," shrugging and looking away.

"I thought they hurt so bad that women screamed and cursed and passed out," he said.

"Look," she said in a blunt voice. "When you've been beaten by a drunken father or a drunken mother and sometimes both with a broomstick or whatever is handy, you learn to run and hide while they're catching their breath and you bite your knuckle 'til it hurts more than the broomstick or the buckle end of the old man's belt. That way, because you're doing it to yourself, you don't whimper or cry and get more of the same. Sure it hurts, so what!"

"Oh, migod!" cried the woman in the next bed.

Donna pulled the curtain back enough to look across. "Sorry, lady," she said. "I'm one of the lucky ones."

There was silence in the room for a long time. Finally Donna said, "Well, what about this coach thing?" She was smiling.

"Not me! Sorry!" he answered quickly. "I'd be a flopper."

"Yeah," she was able to say through gritted teeth.

The 'flopper' nurse came in with a nurse's aide. "Another one?" she asked casually. Donna nodded agreement, but the nurse was looking under the tent on Donna's knees and said, finally. "Well, you're bigger than a nickel but not quite a quarter. Time to call the doctor," and left the room.

The nurses aide waited, looking anxiously at the bedside record until Donna blew out a long breath.

"Well, they're not coming any faster," she said. "How's the pain?"

Donna blew out her cheeks and shrugged, "Okay, I guess. There's no way to measure."

"Well, let's see. On a scale of one to ten, one would be an infected hangnail and seven would be like having your tits caught in the wringer, and then we go eight, nine and ten." She waited. "So?"

"I think I'm coming up to seven," Donna said and Rob got whiter.

"I thought so, too, tough girl," the nurses aide said. "I better get you set for a little buggy ride down to surgery. Oh, there it is!" She cocked her head and listened. "They're paging Dr. Abbott now." She disappeared.

"What are they going to do?" Rob asked.

There were sudden tears in Donna's eyes, not tears of pain but the tears of a little girl who finds, unwrapped on a chair beside her bed, a flannel nightie and a colouring book, instead of the curly headed doll that could go to sleep and say "Mama" that she dreamed over on the Santa pages in Sears catalogue.

"I think they are going to do a Caesarean," she said. "Oh, I so wanted to see my baby born."

A nurse came in with a cart on wheels and said excuse me to Rob as she pulled the hanging sheets around the bed shutting him out, but he heard her say, "Dr. Abbott will be along in a minute. I'm going to take your temperature and blood pressure and measure the dilation, then we'll be ready for the doctor when he arrives. "Do I have to have a Caesarean?" Donna asked.

"You can't go on like this, Donna," the nurse said behind the hanging sheets. "The baby is not going to move and nothing will happen except damage to the baby and to you. The doctor could go in and try to turn the baby with forceps but he is very reluctant to do that—they all are. Believe me," she continued almost conversationally, "when you see your baby for the first time. it will be perfect—no bruises or cuts... I'll be right back."

There was silence for a long time, then Rob heard Donna give a groan and say "Jes—us!"

"That was a big one," the nurse aide said. "Hurt?"

"A little," Donna said.

"You mean, 'you're goddam right it hurt!'"

"You're goddam right it hurt!" Donna said with feeling and they both laughed.

The curtains were whipped back. Dr. Abbott's head appeared. "Hi, Donna," he said, as he stuck his head under the tent. "You about ready for a little visitor? Yeah, I think so," he said emerging smiling and answering his own question.

To the nurses aide he said, "Get somebody to help you wheel her up." And to Donna, with another smile and a pat on the hand, "See you there."

Rob stuck his head around the curtain, wide-eyed and white. "Hi!" he said, tentatively.

"Hi," she responded in a tired voice and closed her eyes. After a minute she continued, "Tell you what, Robbie, my love, if they're all going to be like this, I'll agree to you being a daddy one more time, then to hell with it. You can have a dog."

While she was talking, two nurses came in, unhooked things and started to wheel her out. "Don't I get to kiss my husband before I get dragged away?" Her voice was getting thick.

"Oh, he can come," one nurse said. "He can watch but he can't go in. Follow us," she said to Rob.

They seemed to race. Everything was speeded up. He watched people outside the operating theatre flop Donna onto a narrow stretcher and wheel her in and flop her on a platform under bright lights surrounded by machinery and dials. He was steered like an automaton over to a window where he could watch without getting in the way. Beings from outer space dressed in green gowns and floppy slippers with nightcaps on their heads and masks covering their mouths walked around, some with rubber hands held up in the air beside their heads while they leaned over and watched a grey blotchy screen. Donna was in the middle of everything—at least her swollen belly was. Her legs were up in the air draped in a tent and people kept popping into the tent to have a look. Then her legs were lowered lightly, people gathered around her on the table making swift movements as they handed strange instruments back and forth, their foreheads and eyes frowning in concentration. Suddenly, what Rob could see of their faces brightened. One of the people held up a bloody slimy wriggling object and flopped it on Donna's chest. Then someone snatched it away and heads were lowered over Donna's now flat belly. Someone, who had taken her mask off, was wiping off the thing that could now be recognized as a baby—a boy. She was smiling. Another nurse, also unmasked directed her attention to Rob watching, staring, open-mouthed through the observation window. They said something to each other and the first nurse picked up the baby boy and carried him on a towel three steps over to the window for the father to see. They were both smiling, The baby appeared to be howling. The second nurse took the baby by its ankles and lifted it and with her gloved finger pointed to a small, purple, perfectly shaped, butterfly birthmark on the baby's buttocks. She was smiling and then her mouth shaped the word "cute". Rob flopped.

Somebody was putting something strong and breath catching under his nose. He jerked away from it and looked numbly around. Three people were standing around him. He tried to struggle to his feet but a man in a gown put a restraining hand on him. "Give yourself a minute. You fainted. Feel alright? I'm Dr Abbott."

Rob nodded and tried to put out his hand but the effort made him dizzy. The doctor put something under Rob's nose and watched him jerk away again and come alert.

"Good, you're not the first father to take a tumble watching a Caesarean. Now, then, both your wife and baby are fine. Donna won't be out of the anaesthetic for at least 30 minutes. She'll be a week or ten days recovering from the surgery but she's young and healthy and it may be sooner. Your son is a beautiful child with a remarkable set of lungs. He looked mad enough to slug me for keeping him in there so long."

Rob struggled to his feet and the doctor, who had been squatting beside him, stood up also. Rob, towering over the very small doctor, asked, "Doctor, did you see a mark on his bottom or was that blood?"

"Yes, he has a butterfly shaped birthmark on his right, I think it was right, but I'm not sure, buttock. Very clearly outlined, almost like a tattoo. Birthmarks are not uncommon—seem to run in families—a genetic link. Do you have one?"

Rob shook his head.

"They sometimes skip a generation." He was about to shake Rob's hand and leave but Rob turned away and sat down on a chair against the wall with his head lowered onto his hands. The doctor handed a nurse the ampoule and said, "He might need another whiff," and left.

The nurse watched Rob for a minute and saw the tears spotting the linoleum in front of him. She said to another nurse, "He told me he wanted a girl. Do you suppose....?"

"Surely not!" the other one replied, and they left him alone.

When Rob raised his head five minutes later, nobody seemed to be concerned with his presence in the entry area to the operating room. His head was pounding and he felt as though a band of steel had tightened around his chest so that he could not get a deep breath, only shallow, almost whimper breaths that were not enough to help him stop the shakes and trembles that racked his body.

Shakily he got to his feet and walked past the cleaning staff, down the stairs and out into the night.

He started walking again, not easy long strides, but short, stumbling steps, like a drunk, his head down, his fists rammed deep into his pockets. He was not crying any more. His face was pale, his features set in a strange torturing emotion. After a dozen faltering blocks, his mind cleared and focused. He located himself and headed for a main street. On the corner of a 7\11 lot, he found a telephone box and closed the door, leaning into the corner of the box with the receiver held against his ear so that nobody would disturb him. Slowly, he dug a quarter out of his pocket and, after another hesitation with the coin held poised, let it drop into the slot and dialled Craig's number. Marion answered.

"U.U.," he said, his voice strangely dull and hoarse, "I want to speak to Craig."

"Robbie!" she exclaimed so loudly that Craig heard her over the TV, muted it and came to the telephone. "How's Donna?"

"Fine," Rob said. "Is Craig there?"

She handed the receiver to Craig. "It's Robbie. He sounds upset."

"Hi, buddy," Craig said. "What's up?"

"I'll tell you what's up, buddy! Meet me at Balaclava Park by the hut right now!"

Rob's voice was rasping and so unlike him that Craig said, "Rob!?"

"Just get there! NOW!" He slammed the receiver down, banged open the door of the booth and headed out with long, furious strides toward the park where they had often played ball.

"Something's wrong with Rob! I've gotta go see," Craig shouted to his mother as he grabbed his jacket and keys and ran.

There were no cars in the small parking lot when he arrived. He got out, looking around in the dim light that was left from the sunset.

"Rob?" he tried in a loud whisper.

"Over here."

He looked around in the dark towards the voice and saw a tall dark figure he knew to be Rob gesturing to him from the back corner of the caretaker's hut. "Over here!" he heard Rob say in a hoarse voice. He hurried to meet him. He stepped off the asphalt of the parking lot and around the back corner of the hut and was met with a blow on the side of his face that stunned him. Another blow to the other side of his head knocked him down and suddenly Rob was on his back pounding him with his fists, not hitting with knuckled fists, but swinging wildly with the side of his fists and pounding Craig's head, shoulders, back—anything, growling obscenities with every blow. Craig had tried momentarily to protect himself but now lay still with his arms wrapped protectively around his head.

"Rob! What are you doing? What's wrong? Cut it out! Get off me, you stupid fucker!"

Rob grabbed Craig's wrists and bent forward, his legs locked around Craig's so he could not struggle, their two heads together facing the ground. They were quiet for a moment. Rob raised his head and wiped his nose and tears on the collar of Craig's jacket. He put his head down again.

"You were my buddy! You were my very best friend. I loved you more than anyone in the world. More than my Mom or Donna or anybody." He stopped and used Craig's collar again, then put his head down and said bitterly "And what do I find out? You goddam, rotten, sneaky, shit-faced bastard, you son of a bitch! You come crawling around when I'm not there with your cock in your hand and you screw my wife anytime you want to and give her a baby and let me think it's mine!" He raised up and grabbed several parts of Craig and flung him over onto his back and then sat on him again, face to face.

"I...didn't...mean..." Craig tried to say.

"Shut up with your fucking excuses," Rob shouted and slapped at Craig's face hard several times while Craig tried to cover up. "You knew I wanted to be married and have a child so I wouldn't be a fucking gay, didn't you?" And he hit him again. "Then I thought I'd better try it, and I wanted to try it with you and I couldn't, I just couldn't so I did it with Roger. You didn't know that, did you? And I should have done it with you!" He put his face against Craig's neck and sobbed. "And then I decided to hell with it, I'd rather have my wife and my baby and my best friend and I take her to the hospital and my baby pops out only it isn't my baby, it's a cuddly little blond thing with a butterfly on its bum! YOUR BABY! YOUR SON!" Sobbing, he pounded Craig's face and head and shoulders hard with the side of his fists and his open hand. Craig was struggling to escape and avoid the blows but never struck back until the crack of a breaking nose bone stopped Rob. He looked at Craig, bleeding from a cut on his eyelid and from a split lip with blood streaming from his nose, and the blinding fury that had possessed him vanished. "Oh, Craig!" he cried. "Craig, I'm sorry! Oh, Jesus, Craig, I'm sorry!"

He leaned over and took Craig's face gently in his two hands and kissed him again and again and again, full on the lips, Craig's blood smearing his face and hands and clothes, their tears mingling.

After a few minutes, when his heart stopped most of its violent pounding, Rob helped Craig to his feet. He took the car keys out of Craig's pocket and helped him into the car. He got in and headed for the nearest emergency. On the way, he demanded, "Give me your wallet!" Taking only the money out of the wallet, he shoved it into the glove compartment and, opening the window wide, tossed the wallet over the car onto the sidewalk of a dark street.

At the emergency entrance, he got out and helped Craig out of the car. "Listen to what I tell them," he said to Craig. "Understand?" Inside the building, he shoved Craig into the nearest chair and went directly to the desk. "He's bleeding bad," he said to the first person who looked at him. "We got beaten up by a bunch of fag-bashers. I just gave them my wallet and ran but he stayed and tried to fight. I came back and got him but now I'm gonna collect some of my buddies and go after them. I know where the fuckers hang out."

He walked out the door without looking back and drove to where he and Donna lived. Quietly, he collected his clothes and shoes and his kit from the bathroom. Looking around to make sure he had collected everything he could call his, he shoved it all into a green trash bag leaving only the leather jacket hanging in the closet. Then he drove to Craig's, put the car in the garage and, leaving the keys in the ignition, he closed the doors and walked, like an automaton, the hundred or so yards to the house he had always called home.

Taking the key from where it had been hidden all his life, he opened the door and without turning on any lights, went directly to the master bedroom. He showered and shaved, put his bloody clothes in the washer, and, dressed only in his shorts, waited, in the quiet of the house, with a thousand memories flooding over him, for Roger's return from Seattle and the solace he would bring.

To a distraught, almost hysterical Donna, the nurse said as she gave her a pill. "He was here and he saw the baby, then he fainted and disappeared. Nobody saw him leave."

Craig took a taxi home. He raided his mother's purse without waking her and found taxi money. Then he turned out all the lights, locked the doors, looked at his cut, stitched, bloody and bruised face again and lowered himself onto his bed, flat on his back with the tears rolling off to soak the pillow. Late the next morning, knowing he would have to face her soon, he came downstairs and she screamed. When she calmed down he told her of how they had been mugged, leaving out the fag-bashing bit Rob had created, and how Rob had run away. "You mean Rob ran away and left you?" she said unbelievingly.

"Yes, he left me," he said morosely, and went back to his room.

Just as dawn was breaking, Roger parked the Porsche in the garage and locked it. The house was unlocked when he tried the door and he stopped for a moment, puzzled. He thought for a minute he could smell Rob as he went down stairs for a beer. When he came up and opened the bedroom door, he turned on the light and startled Rob out of a light doze. They both stared at each other for a moment until Rob said, "Hi, Roger! I'm back. This time I brought my clothes," and he waved to the trash bag on the chair where he had dumped it.

Roger walked slowly over to the bed. "Rob? Rob? he said, his voice so husky the words were scarcely discernible. He sank to his knees beside the bed and stretched out his arms. "Migod!" he breathed, his eyes muddied with emotion and his voice thick. "I thought you had gone forever! When you rushed out with not a thought in your mind except being a husband and a father I thought you had discarded me like—like—I don't know what!"

Then Rob, his head nestled in the crook of Roger's arm, told him the whole long agonizing soul-destroying betrayal by his wife and someone he had once called his very best friend in the whole world—for life! So, fuck it!

Late Monday morning, Allen let himself in. "Roger? Roger, are you here?"

Roger came quickly out of the bedroom, closing the door firmly behind him and tying up his bathrobe. "Sorry Allen, I should be up getting things organized, but I didn't get back from Seattle until dawn. Come downstairs and I'll put some coffee on."

"No, thank you, Roger. I will not stay. I came to tell you that my son is negotiating the sale of his taxi licenses and I have talked to my family and they are agreed that we can pool our resources and come up with an offer within two or three days. I also wanted to see Rob to ask him if he would stay and work for me. Have you seen him?"

"No, I haven't," Roger lied, hoping Rob would not make a noise to give him away.

"He will be very busy soon now with a first born child. If you see him tell him my family prays for him and his family." He smiled his gracious smile and said, "Well, I hope to see you very soon, yes, very soon and we will do business together."

Donna waited another two days in abject misery before she phoned her aunt. Not even the placid, blinking gaze of her son as he nursed comforted the hurt. Her aunt said she was coming down right away and she arrived at the hospital in the farm crew cab late the next day. She listened as Donna poured out her story. "He saw the baby and just left and I haven't seen him. Some-thing's wrong!" she wailed. She gave her aunt her house key and they made plans to call the police the next day to ask about accidents or arrests or anything that would give them a clue to his disappearance. Her aunt left and returned within an hour. The nurse protested that it was long past visiting hours. "I don't care. This is important," the aunt responded as she brushed past the desk to Donna's room. In the dim night light she could see Donna's eyes, wide, watching. She took her by the hand and said, without emotion, "No need to put out a search party, Donna. He seems to have disappeared—gone! Everything! Shoes, shirts, underwear, razor, everything! The only thing he left was a leather jacket."

Donna did not cry out or scream. Her face showed the terrible pain she was suffering. She was biting down hard on her thumb knuckle.

***

Allen said, presenting Roger with a paper, "This is the offer I am preparing to make to you. I think it is a fair offer. I have tried not to be influenced by your need for a speedy conclusion. However, I cannot meet your deadline. I need another five days to put my offer in order. I am sorry, very sorry. Instead of withdrawing my offer, I propose to you that, if you accept this offer, for every twenty four hours that I am late in finalizing our business, the sum of two thousand dollars will be added to the purchase price."

Roger looked at the offer and then at Allen who met his gaze. Both knew that the rules of the game necessitated some bargaining. "It is a good offer, Allen. I accept it—." Allen let go of the long breath he was holding. "—with one exception." Allen looked cautiously at him.

"The twenty four hour penalty must be three thousand."

Allen's face relaxed. "Twenty two fifty," he said.

"Twenty seven fifty."

"Twenty five hundred."

"Agreed," Roger said, putting out his hand. They both smiled, knowing that they had played the game.

Allen moved to the door. Roger followed. "I think we...I think I might go away while you're working things out. I'll call you at home with a number where I can be reached. The key will be in its usual place if you need to get in."

The door closed and a smiling Roger opened the bedroom door.

"Did you hear that?" he shouted. "Let's go!

***

"I don't care if you need me at home," Donna's aunt said to her husband on the phone. "Donna needs me more. Steve, she's just had surgery and her rotten husband just grabbed everything he owned and walked out on her. I'll bring her home in the truck when she and the baby are fit to travel. Phone Colin and tell him to get home and give you a hand. It's time he gave up this jockey nonsense anyway. Goodbye, dear. Another five or six days. You'll love Donna, Steve. Really you will."

***

Craig's bruises were fading and the swellings were going down. Doctor Strawburn said he would remove the stitches in a week or sooner, depending—he had said, pulling on his lower lip and forgetting to finish the sentence. "You'll probably have quite a scar on your eyelid and your lip," he had said. "And you certainly won't have a little button nose any more. It was a good nose," he had said with a smile.

Craig phoned Carl and said he would be back in a week.

***

A little red Porsche crossed the border that afternoon with two men and two suitcases in it. They registered at a downtown hotel in Seattle and went on a shopping spree for one of them, who vehemently resisted the other's insistence on adding a leather jacket to the growing wardrobe he was being given. Dressed in their new clothes they found a gay bar and grill and watched the dancers while they had dinner.

***

Two days after the agreed deadline, Allen phoned Roger and said he was prepared to close the deal. He asked Roger to note the date and time. Roger made a call to Vancouver, then called Allen back and they agreed to meet at ten o'clock the next morning in the office of the lawyer Roger had dealt with last year when he bought the business. He returned to Vancouver immediately and alone. Getting packing boxes from U-Haul he packed his personal effects, taped them securely and addressed them to himself at an address in Palm Springs. He ate alone at a nearby Italian restaurant, spent a boring evening in front of the television and went to bed where he stared wakefully at the ceiling until one thirty when he phoned Rob, who said, "I knew you'd call. I've been waiting." Then he slept.

***

When they met at the lawyer's office, Roger told Allen that he had left all the household appliances and furniture and hoped they would be of use to his family. Allen said that they could not possibly have concluded their business yesterday when he called so late and that he could not contest an extra day's penalty. Each having given something, they smiled, signed, shook hands and parted. The courier company came on time and picked up packing boxes. He phoned Rob and said only, "I'm on my way." He checked the house one more time, looked smilingly again at the marks on the doorframe of the kitchen noting the annual growth of two children, picked up his briefcase stuffed with personal papers, and a suit-case of clothes, locked the door and hung the key on the accustomed nail under the step. He stopped at the bank and then crossed the Canadian border for the last time.

On the same morning Donna and baby Turner were discharged from the hospital and driven carefully home by Aunt Ella. Wally and Mrs. Lasseret came down to approve of the baby with "Ooh's" and smiles. Somehow they sensed it was appropriate not to ask about Rob. During the evening, while Donna rested on the bed, her aunt packed cardboard boxes picked up from the Superstore with everything Donna claimed as hers, with the exception of the leather jacket that hung in the curtained off place known as the closet.

Early in the morning, the truck was packed, Donna and the baby were safely tucked into the crew seat and the truck headed north to Sheridan Lake. Six hours later, Donna greeted her Uncle Steve and her cousin Colin, eighteen years old and so much a miniature of Rob that she had to stifle a sort of whimpering sob when she saw him, dark, slim, handsome with a welcoming smile and a devil hiding behind sparkling brown eyes.

***

Craig went cautiously over to the Turner's old house and was greeted by Allen and with the news that he had bought the business from Roger, and that Roger was travelling in the States, he thought. He said the only thing Roger had forgotten was a bloody shirt in the washing machine. Craig asked, in as much of an offhand manner as he could muster, about Rob. "No, I haven't seen him. I hoped he would come and work for me. He was very talented, you know, very, very talented."

Marion asked Craig twice about Rob and on each occasion she received such a carefully chilled response that she did not ask again, but she agonized privately over her son's torment.

Craig knocked on Donna's door several times, until Mrs. Lasseret popped her head out the front door and told him that Donna's aunt had taken her and her baby, (Oh, such a dear, sweet baby boy! So blond—not a bit like Rob!) back with her to the Caribou someplace, Carlton Lake or something like that. No, she didn't know the aunt's name, didn't know that she had ever heard it. Did you, Wally? No, he says he doesn't know, either.

For no planned reason he drove over around Balaclava Park and stopped for a while to watch boys horsing around outside the hut and the small kids on the swings and teeter-totters. Then he drove down to Spanish Banks and watched some freighters jerking at their anchors and probably the last cruise ship of the summer moving out under the Lion's Gate Bridge, glistening in the late sun as it headed out for ports unknown to him. It was the last day of September, summer was gone. The north shore was dotted with the yellows and oranges of autumn. By four o'clock the few people who had been sunning on the beach had dressed and gone. He suddenly felt an awful loneliness and he wept. Then he gathered himself together and drove to the Lasserets and wrote them a cheque to cover the rent until the end of the year in case Rob came home and needed a place to stay and didn't want to stay with him.

On Monday he would go back to work.

EPILOGUE

A little red Porsche left Seattle and wandered south. It stopped casually at Las Vegas, stayed two weeks in San Francisco and another two weeks in Los Angeles. After San Diego, it crossed the border into Mexico through the madness of Tijuana, travelled the tourist route to Mazatlan where it visited several special import car dealers until it found an agreeable home.

In a partial exchange, the two young men in it, having practised the cultural art of polite bargaining, drove away in a Volks station wagon, of the kind that is easily repairable by any Mexican village mechanic. Their travels ended in Guadalajara where they bought, from a pair of disillusioned ex-VietNamers, a gallery specializing in Mexican paintings and carvings, but not pottery. When they were suitably settled into the cultural village of the city, they were able to buy for a penny and sell for a pound, as the saying goes, and thus to thrive on the naiveties of tourists. American tourists, in particular, delighted in dealing with a dark skinned, brown eyed, black haired, teasingly witted young man whose English was as good as, if not better than, in opinions of most buyers, his Spanish. The combined knowledge of local art charmingly exhibited by this young man, and his quieter partner, was less than accurate but rarely challenged. His partner, an adoring friend and companion, who claimed to have no ear for the Mexican language, was content to remain in the background.

Twelve years after their arrival, the older of the two men died agonizingly of AIDS, following a year of tender ministrations by his companion and by compassionate villagers. The other man, made thin and darkened by grief, was given comfort by a widow with two children whom he renamed Craig and Donna, with the permission of the widow and the approval of the village. His engravings and carvings are much admired and sell easily. He lives quietly with painful and sad memories, his dark skin and black hair permitting him to obscure an identity he wishes to forget.

Donna and her son, whom she had named Robin (much too fancy-Nancy-the-pillow-goes-under-the-head for her aunt,) found the warmth of a family she had never known. The abbreviated name, Rob, lent credence to the lingering memory of another Rob. Her cousin, Colin, gave up his love affair with horses and accepted the role of surrogate father with a passion that satisfied any paternal urges he may have harboured to the extent that he never married. In his horsey, rural way, he called the boy 'Budty', which was their private joke—a muffled sound between 'Buddy' and 'Butty'—a teasing allusion to butterflies. When the boy reached the age of seventeen he left the home in which he was raised and, following his Uncle Colin's earlier path, became well employed as a professional jockey known for his desperate struggles to maintain his weight. He rode under the name "Budty" Turner. His mother found casual employment in 100 Mile House clerking or waitressing while continuing to live and help out on the farm.

Marion withered when Robbie disappeared and Craig cooled to any mention of him. Edith, of course, told her that she had always seen something sinister in Rob's black eyes and she proclaimed that she had indeed, if you care to remember, prognosticated an unfortunate end for him. Harvey nodded, in solemn non-listening agreement. Dr. Strawburn had either neglected, or Marion had discarded, advice about Premarin or other medications for menopausal women. Now, fifteen or more years later, she still found pleasure in working daily, hunched and puffing, in her garden, proud of her flowers seen through smudged glasses.

Of Marion's long standing bridge group, Isabel, now a widow, was always the first to arrive and the last to leave the Thursday meetings. Cora's lacquered nails remained unchipped, and Dot maintained the local gossip. As for the others, their ages, approximately, could be judged by the inches of slip showing beneath decorously long skirts, only casually hidden behind the two-wheeled carts they pulled to and from the supermarket. The same eight old friends still play regularly on Thursdays and, by unspoken agreement, avoid any discussion of replacements in the event of....

After fifteen years as a non-communicating, partially paralysed invalid, Glen Turner died, suddenly and mercifully from Claudia's perspective. On her most recent annual trip to Vancouver to visit with her daughter and the family while she stayed with Marion, they talked about Glen's cold, unremitting rejection of his son.

"I have never understood it," Marion said. "Robbie was such a loving, spontaneous boy! How could he not respond? And Robbie seemed to try so hard to win something from him—anything!"

After a long silence, Claudia said, "Maybe I should have told you, Marion. You, of all people, deserved to know, because you loved him so. Glen was not Robbie's father."

Marion could find no response. The silence between them demanded an explanation from Claudia. "No," she said. "Sometimes I have regretted it and sometimes I feel warmed by the passion of his conception. He was a tall, dark, beautiful—if you can call a man beautiful—Italian who worked in a hotel where Glen and I went for a convention—I forget the cause this time, we were always off chasing one great cause or another. But Glen seemed to be on every committee that met all day every day, and the sun and the beaches and the wine and the loneliness got to me. And then," she said, her voice almost a private murmur in the remembrance of it all, "this beautiful man got to me with his soft eyes and his soft voice. And Marion, I didn't care! I didn't give a shit, as the kids say! And all my life, every time I looked at Robbie, I have never regretted it. Not once!" She paused, looking back at the distant past. "We stayed together, as you know, Glen and me. He forgave me, he said, but deep down, he could never forgive Rob."

She sat weeping, with Marion looking at her wide-eyed and stunned. "Now I need a drink!" Claudia said. "A bloody great stiff one, because I've said to you something that I didn't think I would ever say to anybody. You're the only person in the whole goddam wide world, besides me, that knows what I have just told you."

They talked long into a night when sleep was of little importance.

At Cranston's Cartons, Larry retired, which left only Dorothy and Craig as a management committee. Then Dorothy begged off on legitimate reasons of health and age, leaving Craig as a committee of one with Carl's constantly required assistance in spite of his determined effort to retire. Carl offered the business for sale to any employee or group of employees with the sale price reduced from its appraised market value on a formula based on years of service. No one employee, or group of employees, in spite of Carl's willingness to wait and to advise, could make an offer. The business was eventually sold and became Leung's Packaging Company Limited. Carl and Craig had a somewhat emotional leave-taking of each other. Craig visits the Cranstons routinely.

Craig's scars from his last rendezvous with Rob are now more psychological than physical. His bruises had healed quickly and easily. The cut on his eyelid had been stitched by an interne and he was left with an eyelid that would not quite close when he blinked. His nose healed crooked, as the late Dr. Stawburn had predicted, and the scar across his upper lip now lent a somewhat ground-less sinister look to what had been an open warming smile. But it was what lay behind the eyes that kept people aloof from him—something that spoke of hurt and protective distance, not fear or coldness as much as it was doubt of any other person's intent.

Craig continued with his night courses and finally achieved a bachelor's degree in Economics based mainly on his computer expertise. Because of some relationships in recent living experiences, he concluded that, for him, proscribed personal contact with others could serve as an adequate substitute for the closer human relationships ordinarily sought by others. To satisfy the social demand for some degree of interpersonal exchange, he obtained a second degree in Education.

When Cranston's Carton's became Leung's Packaging, his services were no longer required. The following year, he found employment as a substitute teacher and after two years as a substitute, he found a permanent position in a high school in Surrey. He teaches Math and Computer Science and coaches the Senior Boys basketball. As Coach, he is required to accompany the team on out-of-town trips and chaperon their behavior. He frequently finds their ani-mal charisma disturbing and not only recommends, but insists upon, as coach, cold showers before lights out. He still lives with his mother who privately despairs of him ever finding some nice girl to share his life with. Occasionally, when strangers press, he will create a broken romance out of his first love affair, a romance crushed by the racial prejudice of the girl's father.

In February, Craig received a letter mailed from a small town in Mexico that he could not locate on any map. The letter was from a Luis Cuevas who stated that he was a lawyer representing Robert Turner. In stilted English, Sr Cuevas said that an attached notarized statement 'could please be presented to Mrs. Robert Turner or maiden Donna Penser for the purpose of initiating divorce action should she so wish whose address is not known'. In a postscript to the letter, he stated that a small parcel from Mr. Turner was being carried person-ally to Canada by a colleague attending a conference and would be mailed from Toronto to avoid customs.

The attachment, written in a flowing hand on crisp paper, certified in for-mal terms that Mr. Robert Turner was living in a state of marriage with Frida Juarez, a widow with two children and that they were recognized publicly as be-ing man and wife. The notarizing seal covered a quarter of the page. Sr Cuevas's signature was a work of art.

Craig told nobody of the letter and responded immediately to Sr Cuevas, telling him that he did not know the whereabouts of Donna (Penser) Turner and asked that his best wishes be extended to Robert Turner. He said that he would appreciate hearing from Robert Turner first hand.

In April a small parcel arrived from Toronto with no return address. It contained a man's silver ring on which was engraved the initials RT+CW enclosed in a squared-off heart. Craig put the ring on his finger and closed the door to his bedroom for two days, rejecting any food or drink his mother offered. It appeared to her that he had come down with a sudden case of flu so she phoned the school on his behalf and said he would be absent for the rest of the week. In May, his letter to Sr Cuevas was returned stamped in Mexican with something he interpreted to be 'No Such Address'.

Midweek, in the last week of June, to avoid the weekend crowds, he put on his big backpack with the small tent and foamy and drove to the trail that marked the way to Lake Lovely Water. There was a crushed down area for parking now, but there were no cars on it. Two old and leaky rowboats were tied casually off the shoreline. He took one and rowed across to what he remembered as the proper landing spot. Tying the old boat on the other side for his return he set out on the trail, now so well marked by hikers boots there was little need for the pie plate markers on the trees. In some hard spots, the trail had been hacked out into steps to assist the less vigorous hikers but if the climb, hands, knees and feet, to the very top, was still demanding and the view was the reward. He stood again at the beginning of the trail down to the lake, remembering with a terrible yearning the first time he had looked down, and the incapability of either of them to give adequate expression of what lay beneath them. The tranquil lake, an unbelievable aquamarine colour he had seen before, unbelieving, only in paintings, was rippled occasionally by breaths of infant winds and dotted with the rings of trout capturing the unwary fly. The reflection of two lonely clouds on the surface seemed to deny perfection by not belonging. The smell of resin and growth and naturally composting vegetation was overwhelming as was the silence when he stepped off the top of the ridge out of the wind and started his descent to the valley. He passed the cabin on the point and listened for a welcoming bass voice that did not come. At the end of the lake where tent sites marked places where people wanted to catch the morning sun, he chose one that brought back a shiver of memory. Setting up this tent and spreading his foamy and sleeping bag, he kept a wary sense alert for anything that would keep open the floodgates of his memory. He caught two small trout without effort, lighted the fire and cooked his dinner as the sun went down. In the morning, he thought, I will find the RT+CW tree. The sun set, some early stars emerged into the first darkness and were followed by the millions more until the sky was blanketed. Occasionally, a shooting star or a flashing satellite seemed caught in the web of stars or, more mundane, a plane, flicking its warning lights minutes in advance of its noise, offered a puny challenge to the shimmering sky. In time, his little fire died to embers. He stretched and retreated to his tent where he lay on his back, arms behind his head, and listened to the sounds of the night: the waves softly licking the shoreline, the rustle of a small animal in the under-brush, the yelping of a distant coyote and, on the far shore the melancholy call of a loon.

For an hour he listened to the loon, trying to decipher out of its garbled lonely cries a word like "Rob" or Robbie", but nothing emerged. In the cold, quiet of the night, the memory of other times obscured the dying night sounds and consciousness faded eventually into restless sleep.

ISBN 141202129-4